MERIDA'S ISEKAI ADVENTURE

Age of Dragons

By
DAVID KELLY

MERIDA'S ISEKAI ADVENTURE

Copyright © 2024 by David Kelly

All Rights Reserved. No part of this publication may be reproduced, stored in a retrieval system, or transmitted, in any form or by any means, electronic, mechanical, photocopying, recording, or otherwise, without the written permission of the author.

Printed In United States Of America
Published by : ACH Publishing

TABLE OF CONTENTS

CHAPTER 1:	1
CHAPTER 2: THE SECOND ORIGIN	8
CHAPTER 3: CHANGING SOCIETY	18
CHAPTER 4: THE VOTE	33
CHAPTER 5: A ROYAL VISIT	46
CHAPTER 6: MEETING OF REVELATIONS	58
CHAPTER 7: THE PERSONAL TOUCH	72
CHAPTER 8: THE ELF AND THE STONE	81
CHAPTER 9: FROM DAUGHTER TO FATHER	103
CHAPTER 10: FORWARD MOMENTUM	130
CHAPTER 11: ON TO ORLIMAR	136

CHAPTER 12: THE MEETING OF SIX	148
CHAPTER 13: CONFLICTING IDEOLOGIES	164
CHAPTER 14: DIVINE INTERVENTION	175
CHAPTER 15: WELCOME REINFORCEMENTS	189
CHAPTER 16: THE BATTLE OF ORLIMAR	198
CHAPTER 17: REQUIEM	220
CHAPTER 18: DINNER WITH THE DEVIL	232
CHAPTER 19: GIFT GIVING	247
CHAPTER 20: THE DESCENT	266
CHAPTER 21: AWAKENING	281
CHAPTER 22: CLAIMING ARONTHOK	295
CHAPTER 23: EXEMPLAR KORABIN	310
CHAPTER 24: RETURN TO ORLIMAR	319
CHAPTER 25: CATCHING UP	329
CHAPTER 26: SERENA'S PROPOSAL	339
CHAPTER 27:	351

AND THEN THERE WERE TWO

CHAPTER 28:   359
FAMILY MEETING

CHAPTER 29:   382
A HERO RISES

CHAPTER 30:   405
CONSOLIDATION AND INVESTIGATION

CHAPTER 31:   414
CONVICTION

CHAPTER 32:   426
DISILLUSIONMENT

CHAPTER 33:   447
UNWORTHY OF QUEENSHIP

CHAPTER 34:   463
A GREAT DECEPTION

CHAPTER 35:   471
WHERE I AM BLIND

CHAPTER 36:   481
THE PRINCESS CALLS

CHAPTER 37:   490
THE TRUTH OF VAR KORAN

CHAPTER 38:   508
REWARDING LOYALTY

CHAPTER 39:   516
THE PANTHEON REUNITED

CHAPTER 40:   531
DAY OF RECKONING

CHAPTER 41:   562
IN ALL THE YEARS TO COME

CHAPTER 1:

That first day seemed so long. Though, to be fair, most days did when you were as old as I was. Thanks to amazing breakthroughs in modern medicine I was one hundred twenty-six years old. It was November 3rd, 2109. I looked at the empty side of my bed where I still looked for my wife after she'd passed away two years ago. I sat up out of bed, dressed myself, and made myself some breakfast. I fed the chickens, dogs, and cats. I then tended to my garden, and did just a little smithing in the forge I'd made in my backyard. These old bones couldn't handle much, but I still managed to put a little hammer to steel. Then I made my way to the tv and turned on my old gaming console.

I was going to celebrate the 100th anniversary of my favorite game, Age of Dragons, with a fresh playthrough. Fresh is relative, of course. I'd played the game so many times that there wasn't any kind of playthrough I hadn't experienced, but that never really stopped me from enjoying the game. I'd fallen in love with it back when it had originally released and I'd played it so many times since then that it was essentially a comfort experience for me.

The Ancient Dragon swirled and screamed onto the screen. The title screen popped up and the rising tones of the theme music greeted me. New game. It was time to create a character. I decided that for this run I was going to play a female dwarf noble. I always wished there was a way to mod the console version to play as a mage this way, but that was the limitation of the console version. I was alright with that.

My mind was ready to start the game, but my body had other plans. Even as I was preparing to press start, my eyelids grew heavy. I wasn't in any hurry. I didn't really have anything else to do, after all. So I allowed myself to drift off for a little nap to the sound of the game's music.

Imagine my surprise when I woke up to a very different view. My tv, pictures, and old dvd's were replaced with a high stone ceiling, muffled excitement, and strange clarity of vision that I hadn't had for nearly seventy years. I tried to move but my arms would barely respond properly to my commands, my head was heavier than it had been since I could remember. I could barely move without some form of over exaggeration, as if my body wasn't used to receiving commands at all.

That's when someone came over and looked down at me. Maybe that was it? Had I somehow, fallen off the couch and hit my head? Was I in a hospital? That would explain a few things. That theory went out the window when the person stopped being a blur and my eyes managed to focus in on him. No doctor in the world would have a beard that long, that thick, or that adorned with rings.

He reached down and scooped me up as easily as one would scoop up a... baby? He hugged me to his chest and smiled down at me. He turned and I was able to move my head enough to find a crowd of other people staring up at me. Were they... dwarves?!? Short, stout, bearded. Stone floors, walls, ceilings. Why did this all seem so familiar?

"My people!" the one who was carrying me called out. "It is with great pleasure that I present to you your new princess! Raise your voices and your cups in celebration! I present to you, Merida Nordrucan, born in this tenth year of the ninth era!"

The people below let out a loud series of joyous cheers. The sound was almost painful, but everything suddenly clicked! I was being held by Triston Nordrucan, the father of the noble dwarf protagonist in Age of Dragons! The realization nearly overwhelmed me when two others stepped up to join Triston's... I mean, my father's side. A younger looking dwarf with a stern demeanor, and a female dwarf around my father's age both stood to either side of my father.

"She's so well behaved. Look at her, not even a chirp of protest," the female said with a tired smile. That had to be Olga! That's actually Olga, Triston's wife and my mother! I finally got to see her. She was never in the games so this was a real treat!

"Indeed, mother!" the stern looking male dwarf replied. "She truly has the countenance of a Nordrucan."

"Trenton!" a sharp, high pitched voice called out. Was that… my voice?

It took a moment to realize that the cheering had stopped. Father, mother, and Trenton were all staring down at me in shock and confusion. I blinked up at them, then with great effort turned my head to see the crowd frozen in place, gawking up at us. I turned back to look at my family. I was just as confused as they were.

"Did she just say my name?" Trenton asked with shock in his voice.

"She did," Father confirmed.

"She really did!" Mother replied and laughed.

That's when I remembered what Trenton was like in the game. He was principled, stern, pragmatic, and taciturn. If you read his codex and journal entries you'd understand that it was never meant out of anger or spite. He only ever wanted what was truly best for Cragmorrar, and possibly to secure his own power. For the most part, he was a good person, if you measured good by being willing to grind everything in your way down so that others could be lifted up. Still, he could come off as arrogant and aggressive towards the player character. I decided I'd try to change that starting right now.

With a surge of effort I raised my hands up to reach toward my brother, hands outstretched, and tried to smile as best as I could, "Trenton! Trenton!"

Trenton looked taken aback but Father only chuckled as he offered me over to my brother, "It seems she wants you to hold her, Trenton."

"Days old and already speaking!" Mother chimed in. "And she learned your name first, Trenton! She must truly love you! Go on and hold her."

Trenton looked flustered as he begrudgingly took me into his arms, "I've barely even seen her since she was born."

"That doesn't seem to matter," Mother cooed.

"Indeed," Father added. "It seems you've made quite the impression on her. And look, she seems so secure with you holding her."

It was tough just to say Trenton's name, or anything for that matter. This body simply wasn't used to speaking yet. Still, I was determined to ingratiate myself with him no matter what. I took as deep a breath as I could manage and huffed out, "Brother. Safe."

Now, that might not seem like a lot, but it was a great deal of effort. The body of a baby isn't all that strong. All that effort took its toll and I started to drift back off to sleep, but not before feeling Trenton's hold on me grow firmer and hearing him say 'Indeed, sister. You are safe with me.'

That first year was largely uneventful. I learned to walk quickly enough. After all, I'd been doing it for over a century by now. Talking came quickly too once I got used to it. I never realized that being so young allowed you to burn through so much energy so quickly. I finally understood naps as a child. I had so much energy that I could do so much in just a few hours but would need to nap to regain that energy. It was amazing.

Trenton had taken me under his wing, defying Mother and Father when they suggested I be given tutors. He taught me to read and write the Dwarven language. He brought me to the Memorium, the palace where all of our history and records were kept, daily to instruct me on the history of the dwarves. There was so much lore to discover that I began borrowing stacks of books to read while I wasn't there. The Memorialist, the dwarf in charge of the Memorium, was none too pleased about that, but he wasn't about to argue with Trenton.

Along with my history lessons, Trenton ensured that I learned the names, sigils, and history of every noble house in Cragmorrar. Great or small, I'd know them all (as Trenton was fond of saying). By the time I was ready to turn one, Trenton and I were an inseparable pair. He made sure I went with him wherever he needed to go, so that I could learn and observe. Father and Mother barely got to see me, though when they did they would dote on me. Trenton insisted that I be treated as if I were his age, but our parents seemed to want to cherish what little time they had with me.

Things were going well that first year until the night before my birthday. That evening, something had happened to me that hadn't happened in over a year. It was something that I had assumed would never happen to me again. When it happened, I was amazed. That night I dreamed. I stood in the haze of the Dimvolmn, mist gathered at my feet as I looked out at the twisted reimagining of the throne room. Upon the throne sat my Father. He leaned in and beckoned me forward.

"Who are you?" I asked. My cherubic voice was more stern than this spirit might have expected.

It looked surprised, then smiled, "What do you mean? I'm your father. Don't you recognize me?"

I knew better than to fall for this. I was in the Dimvolmn, but dwarves aren't supposed to be able to access the Dimvolmn. The Dimvolmn is the realm of spirits and dreams, and dwarves didn't dream so they couldn't access it. Maybe I was able to because I wasn't originally a dwarf? Regardless, there was no way I was going to be swayed by some demon.

I crossed my arms and stood up straight, giving off the most commanding presence as I could manage for a one year old, "Don't toy with me, demon. I know what you are and what you're trying to do. You'll get nothing from me."

'Father' stood from the throne and placed its hands behind its back, "It seems not. But you are so curious. I've never seen something like you before. You shouldn't be here. How did you manage to enter the Dimvolmn?"

"That's my secret," I said flatly. I wasn't about to tell it that I didn't know. "Now leave me alone. This is my realm and you aren't welcome."

"You're realm?" the spirit asked incredulously. "You're realm? This is the Dimvolmn, child of Stone! This is the realm where I live and you have no claim to it!"

"Wrong!" I responded, my confidence in the world's lore coming back to me. "This area of the Dimvolmn might be where you reside, but it is shaped by the dreamer; namely me! You didn't choose the throne room, my mind did! You only chose a form I might trust to ingratiate yourself to me."

"So young, yet so knowledgeable," the spirit chuckled. "I admit, I underestimated you. Can you ever forgive me?"

Its tone suggested mock humility, but I was willing to play the game. After all, I knew of several interesting circumstances concerning spirits and mPetrals. I considered my options for a few moments before replying.

"What do you offer for my forgiveness?" I asked with as authoritarian and noble a tone as I could muster.

The spirit paused. I couldn't tell if it was confused or surprised by my question. "What?" it finally asked.

"You heard me," I snapped back. "You have offended my intelligence and mocked the image of my father; King Triston Nordrucan, with your charade. You asked for my forgiveness. What do you offer for it?"

Spirits in the Dimvolmn wanted nothing more than to enter the physical world. They would make pacts and deals in the hopes of tricking mortals into allowing them to possess their bodies. But that was when a mortal wanted something from the spirit. This time, the spirit had asked for something, even if it didn't mean it. Spirits were influenced by the minds and imaginations of mortalls. So in my mind, I took the offer as genuine. The spirit, in turn, was influenced to believe it was.

"I have nothing to offer for your forgiveness," it said as it tried to process what was happening.

"Wrong," I said as I smiled confidently. "You have your service and your knowledge of the Dimvolmn. Swear your service to me, and me alone, and I will forgive you for your rudeness. You will be free to do what you will while I'm awake. However, when I come to the Dimvolmn, you will help me do whatever it is I need help doing. Do you agree?"

It took the spirit several moments to consider the offer before it kneeled in front me, transforming from the image of my father and into a spirit of Purpose, "I agree. To gain your forgiveness, I will serve and aid you, child of the Stone."

"Princess Merida Nordrucan," I corrected the spirit as I reached up to place a hand on its shoulder. Even kneeling it was still considerably taller than I was. "You may call me Princess Merida."

"As you wish, Princess Merida," Purpose said as it looked at me. It almost seemed pleased to have a reason to interact with me. "Is there anything I can help you with before you wake?"

I grinned and nodded, "As a matter of fact, there is."

CHAPTER 2:

THE SECOND ORIGIN

On the morning of my first birthday, I woke up to an uncomfortable feeling. There were rocks and pebbles in my bed. I sat up and looked around. There weren't any rocks or anything else around the bed or anywhere in the room, apart from the standard gems and geodes set out as decorations. I couldn't help but laugh. It had worked! I'd worked all night with Purpose to learn my very first spell!

Dwarves couldn't enter the Dimvolmn, and because they didn't have that connection, they couldn't cast magic. But for whatever reason, I could access the Dimvolmn. I assumed it was because I had originally been a human in my first life. So when I finally found myself in the Dimvolmn, I worked with Purpose to learn a single spell. Dream time was relatively slower than time in the real world, and I had spent it all practicing the Stone Armor spell.

Evidently, I had managed to cast it in the real world while I was sleeping. I stood up and steadied myself before calling the magic forth. The spell was simple enough, and maybe it was my dwarven connection to the stone that made it easier, but as soon as I pulled the mana from my reserves, a thin layer of rock and stone formed over my small frame. It was like a carapace that allowed me to move freely, but kept me safe. I would need to test the strength of the armor, but for now, it was better than nothing.

"Trenton!" I called out. Trenton had basically become my nanny in almost every way. He helped me get dressed and would carry me to breakfast (the only time he didn't make me walk).

The door to my bedroom opened and in came Trenton, awake and followed by a few other dwarves who were likely still trying to finish a meeting. My room was essentially his closet, though that isn't saying it wasn't spacious. It was large enough for a one year old dwarf. Trenton's eyes widened as he neared by bed and spotted the rubble among the bedding. He sprinted the rest of the distance to get to me, scooping me up quickly and looking around for a possible crack in the ceiling or other signs of a cave-in.

"Merida? What happened here? Are you alright?" His tone was pragmatic and direct to anyone else, but I heard the worry and concern in his voice. I was more than just an intelligent child in his mind now. I was his beloved sister and a precious jewel who held great promise for the Nordrucan family.

"I'm fine, Trenton," I reassured him.

"Where did all this rubble come from?" he asked quickly.

I sheepishly bowed my head, "We should discuss this in private."

Trenton turned and waved for his courtiers who had rushed in with him to leave the room. In my first year I had revealed some of the knowledge I had about the world to Trenton. Not much, but enough so that whenever I told him I needed to speak in private, he took me seriously. He knew I was more intelligent than I let others believe, even if he didn't say it. He waited for the door to be closed, then carried me over to a tuffet where he would normally place me while we picked out what I would wear each day. When he was satisfied that I was steady on my feet, he moved to the closet.

"Mother has, no doubt, had a new outfit created for you since it's your birthday," he said patiently as he pulled out a box from one of the shelves that contained my jewelry. "Whatever it is you need to speak to me about, do so quickly. She and Father will likely be here soon."

I nodded and stood on my tip-toes to look into the box, pointing out suggestions for the pieces I would wear for my birthday, "I have learned that I can cast magic, Trenton. Just one spell so far. But that's what made the mess."

"Don't speak such nonsense," Trenton snapped. He cared a great deal for me but he didn't brook foolish, pointless talk. "Dwarves can't cast magic. So don't lie to me."

I popped the edge of the box to grab Trenton's attention, "I'm not lying! I can cast the Stone Armor spell. I've been practicing all night and I can prove it."

Trenton's expression grew stern, the way it would when he was on the verge of yelling at a servant, "Can you now?" He placed the box down with a hard thump, his frustration clear with the motion. "Very well, then. Prove it. But the moment you can't-"

I didn't give him the chance to finish the thought. I called the mana to me and the rocks and stones returned to me, covering me up to my neck in a carapace of stone once more. Trenton froze in shock as he stared at me. I stood there defiantly, proud in my thin layer of rock and stone.

"Well?" I asked. "Do you believe me now?"

Trenton snapped his head back to the door, paranoid that anyone might have come in since I cast the spell. He looked back at me and waved his hand sharply, "Be rid of that this instant! We cannot let anyone know about this until we speak with the Memorium of Memories. People may try to abduct you or kill you for your unique abilities."

"What about Mother and Father?" I replied. "Should we not tell them?"

"Not yet," Trenton lowered his voice. "Father would be too proud and would announce your abilities right away. We need to ensure that you are capable enough with them to defend yourself before we tell anyone else."

The concern in Trenton's voice actually surprised me. Even as I stumbled and fell while I was getting used to walking, Trenton had never sounded genuinely concerned for my health. With such concern coming from him, I nodded in agreement.

"As you wish, Trenton," I said meekly. I sometimes forget that I was still just a child. Not even a child; I was a toddler, physically at least. "I won't tell anyone else, and I won't show anyone else what I can do until you think I'm capable of defending myself."

"Good," he said flatly. He stood and made his way to the door, "I'll get a servant to clean up the rubble. You pick out your jewelry."

Later that day I sat at the head of one of the long tables in the throne room. Mother had indeed commissioned a new dress for me. It was made of padded garnet fabric with golden thread designs, brass corner clips and silver studs. Father had commissioned a thin, golden tiara that was studded with precious jewels and silver clan designs. I looked quite royal.

Trenton insisted on sitting to my left, with Father and Mother to my right. Among the guests at the dinner were more family members, friendly nobles, and a few select nobles that were of little note, and some members of the Warrior caste. Family and friends ate, drank, sang, played games and wished me well. Most seemed to think my early intelligence and quick progression to walking and talking were a sign of great things to come. Trenton thought that most of the people who attended were only here to garner favor. He was likely right. I had no intention of anyone making me a part of their plans. I had plans of my own.

As the celebrations reached their peak and I had accepted gifts from all in attendance, Father stood and called for everyone's attention, "I wish to thank you all for coming here today to celebrate the birthday of my daughter, Princess Merida."

Fists and mugs hammered the tables in good spirits to signal approval of the speech thus far.

"While my daughter has thanked each one of you personally for your gifts, I wish to convey my thanks as well," Father continued. "Traditionally, my wife and I would now give our gifts to the princess, but as you can no doubt see, she is already wearing them. My wife gifted her the beautiful dress she is wearing, each piece meticulously crafted by the talented Ferrous family!"

More thumping fists and mugs, this time as the head of the Ferrous family stood and took a bow for his family's efforts.

"I was happy to gift our daughter with the tiara she now wears. It was crafted with all care by the craftsmen of the Silrea family!"

More applause as the head of the Silrea family stood and waved.

"There is one among us, however, who has not given the Princess a gift yet," Father said as he turned and looked to Trenton. "Prince Trenton! My son. Are you prepared to give your gift to your sister?"

Trenton stood and nodded firmly, "I am, Father."

"Very well," Father replied and waved to Trenton as he took his seat. "Present your gift."

Trenton placed his hands behind his back and stood tall, looking out over the gathered guests, "As you all will no doubt have noticed over the past year, I have taken it upon myself to look after Princess Merida's well being. I have seen to her education and etiquette lessons. However, I have mounting responsibilities, and I understand that her view of our world cannot be shaped by my perception and opinions alone."

He smiled down at me then moved across the throne room to a door that was reserved for the staff to come in and out as they brought food and drink, and cleared out empty dishes, "As such, I have searched high and low for someone who would be as dedicated in her upbringing as I would be. Someone who would dedicate their very life and the lives of their family to ensuring my sister's safety and education. I am happy to say that I have found that someone."

He opened the door to reveal a female dwarf who might have been called beautiful if not for a severe burn scar covering her right cheek. Standing next to her were a five year old girl and a three year old boy. Murmurs of confusion, shock, and abhorrence spread throughout the guests.

"Silence!" Trenton barked. To his credit, the guests stopped their murmuring. He let the silence settle for several moments before continuing. "This is Kara Bromnin, and her two children Rita, and Faren. I met Kara in the market and watched as she and her children ran a small stall. Even at their young ages, Rita and Faren were quick to organize their merchandise, keep the stall clean, and bark for their mother's wares. If she could raise two such young, industrious children like that, I could only imagine what she would do for my sister."

Trenton began escorting the family to the table where I was seated. He was putting on a good show. I knew this wasn't something he wanted to do, but I had convinced him that this would be to his advantage.

"I will be taking new quarters in the palace soon, and my sister will be taking over my current rooms," Trenton continued. "Kara has dedicated herself to the well being of my sister, and has dedicated her children to befriending and caring for the Princess as well."

Silence gripped the room as Kara, Rita, and Faren took their places behind me. I smiled at Faren, who smiled back.

Trenton stood beside me and placed a hand on my shoulder as he continued to address those gathered, "No doubt you've noticed that Kara was casteless from the burn mark on her cheek where her brand was removed. She did this to herself when she swore her life, and the lives of her children to Princess Merida. To reward such dedication, I have worked with the Memorialists to elevate her and her children to the Servant Caste. If I hear even a whisper of dissent, or of someone speaking to them as if they were casteless, I will personally see that person's throat opened. So… what say you all to my gift?"

The room was as silent as the Stone for several moments until Veron Bastol, a lesser noble of no real notoriety stood, "I commend the Prince in his efforts to find someone who would dedicate themselves so much to our Princess."

Before anyone else could say anything, Trental Harbon, another lesser noble stood, "I agree! Our Prince shows his considerable judgment and immense generosity in this gift. Two generations of caretakers for the Princess who he has elevated from the dregs of the Casteless. A toast to Prince Trenton! A toast to Princess Merida! Cragmorrar's future is truly bright with such admirable successors to the Nordrucan line!"

Not wanting the intense moment to continue, every guest in the room, as well as Father and Mother, raised their cups to the toast. A cry of 'To Prince and Princess Nordrucan' was called out over and over for several minutes. By the time it died down, no one bothered to even look at the caretaker's way.

Trenton took his seat beside me once again and looked at me, "There. You have your promised servants. Are you sure this will be worth it?"

I smiled at my brother and nodded, "Lord Bastol and Lord Harbon will be in your debt till the end of their days."

"I still don't know why you wanted them, of all people, to be here," he replied curtly.

"Because," I said with a little smirk, "Lord Bastol is the father of Rita, and Lord Harbon is Faren's father."

Trenton tried to hide his surprise as he looked at me, "What? How do you know?"

"When you were speaking to Kara in the market, I was speaking to Rita and Faren," I explained. "You thought we were playing, but Faren is more important than you know. When I heard Kara's name, and Faren introduced himself, I knew who I was dealing with. The only thing I didn't know was the name of their fathers until I spoke with Kara. I asked you to make them my caregivers for my birthday because I knew Faren would become a great warrior, and I knew the political currency they held with their fathers."

"So you waited to have me reveal them as your caretakers until now so that Vernon and Trental would recognize Kara, and quickly silence any questions by agreeing with what people would think was my decision?" Trenton asked in amazement. This was the first time I felt that he was truly inspired by my actions.

I nodded happily, "That's right. And they no doubt believe you already knew they were the fathers of Kara's children. While Lord Harbon might not be seen in too negative of a light for having sired a son with Kara, Lord Bastal would be dishonored for having sired a daughter and not raising Kara and Rita up."

"And Bastal would still see some dishonor for knowingly bedding someone who should rightfully be a member of another noble family," Trenton finished. "One day, sister, you'll tell me how you knew about all of this. I'll wait because it's your birthday but you still gifted the Nordrucan family with the compliance of two noble families."

"You're welcome, Trenton," I giggled.

Once the ceremony was over and the guests had gone, Trenton carried me back to my room with Kara, Rita, and Faren in tow. At the door to the room, he gave me a hug then handed me over to Kara.

"She is your responsibility now," Trenton said in all seriousness. "Care for her like your life, and the lives of your children, depend on it. Because they do."

Kara curtsied with a quiet, "As you command, my Prince."

I looked up at Trenton and clicked my tongue at him, "This is no time for threats. She's my caretaker now. So treat her with kindness."

Trenton let out a doubtful hum before taking his leave, "Be sure to keep to her schedule. I expect you to have her at her lessons on time."

Kara bowed her head as Trenton walked away, "As you command, my Prince."

Rita opened the door and we entered my room which had been renovated to be a small living quarters for the family. Kara carried me over to the changing area while Rita and Faren looked around the room.

"This room is bigger than our home," Rita said in amazement.

"I told you it would be," Faren said as he placed his things on one of the new beds, claiming it as his own. "Get the Princess' nightgown."

"You're not my boss!" Rita argued.

"Rita!" Kara said as she carefully undid the clasps on my outfit, "Do as your brother says. He's helped us get this far, you can take a little more direction from him."

Rita huffed and went to fetch one of my gowns as Faren sat down next to me, "So you actually pulled it off. I'm pretty impressed."

"I told you I'd get you and your family here, and I meant it," I replied.

"And we're eternally grateful to your Majesty for your effort," Kara said as she took great pains to handle the new outfit with care. "I'd all but given up when I was left to waste away in the lower wards for a second time. Faren has been so remarkable in helping us thrive… but when you took an interest in us that day…"

Kara started to cry but Faren pat her arm, "It's alright, Mother. Princess Merida is like me. She has knowledge of this world from before she was born. She'll help keep us safe, and together we can build a new Cragmorrar."

I leaned forward and hugged Kara's neck, "I promise you that your faith in me will be rewarded, and that Rita and Faren will become nobles one day."

"We'll be nobles?" Rita squealed with delight. "Do you promise?"

"Her Majesty said she promised so that's a promise," Faren answered for me.

I smiled at them. Trenton would always look out for me however he could, but Kara, Rita, and Faren were the keys to my plans for the future. What I never told Trenton was that Faren had been reincarnated just like I had been. He was two years older than I was and had spent his time bartering with merchants using certain items he knew he could sell for more than he would buy them to make a profit. While I wasn't expecting to meet their family so soon, it was thanks to Faren that Trenton and I had happened upon them while we were walking through the market district one day.

Faren was smart enough to ensure that their stall had their family name on it. He'd done this so that if another person happened to be in his same circumstances in Cragmorrar, they might recognize it and speak to them. It was an idea that paid off. I had wailed and swatted at Trenton, insisting on stopping at that stall. They were only selling used goods, which Trenton would never stoop to even spitting on, but he stopped all the same for my sake.

As soon as Trenton started speaking to Kara, I went to her children and introduced myself. When Faren gave me his name, I was overjoyed. Faren

Bromnin was the default name of the dwarf commoner origin. Being careful not to be too obvious with my knowledge, I asked why his mother was selling used goods when she looked like she might be better at cleaning chimneys, which was her profession in the game. Faren caught on quickly and asked if my 'friend' Bilfern would be along any time soon. Bilfern was the name of the youngest son of the dwarven royal family in the game. When we realized we were from the same world originally, I told him we would come back, and that I would have a plan to bring him and his family into the palace.

I convinced Trenton to bring them in as my caretakers. It took a few weeks of convincing. Faren convinced his mother to allow Trenton to burn off the casteless tattoo, and to agree to care for me. The burning took him more time to convince her of than becoming a servant in the palace. After all, anything was better than the lower wards.

I made sure that they were provided with clothes that were appropriate for the personal servants of the Princess. I also made Trenton promise to have Faren study under our best warriors, while Rita was educated in the mercantile arts. All in all, the plan had gone perfectly. I had three new caretakers, two noble families to call upon if I ever needed scales tipped in my favor, and one person who was from the same world I was from who was also one of the other game's default character options.

If all went according to plan, they would be nobles in the next few years.

CHAPTER 3:

CHANGING SOCIETY

Four years had passed in the blink of an eye since Faren joined me. In that time, I had worked with Purpose every night in my dreams to study magic. Now I was capable of casting Stone Armor, Dream Shield, Heal, Living Bomb, Winter's Grip, and Lightning. Purpose would help me hunt wisps and lesser spirits in the Dimvolmn so that I could gain experience with my magic. Eventually, however, I would need a staff and a very particular gemstone.

Rita had become a capable merchant in her own right even at ten years old. She learned from only the best from the merchant class. My father had taken a hit in popularity and influence when Beltia was named an Exemplar, an ideal dwarf who achieved a unique accomplishment in and encompassed the highest virtues a dwarf could aspire to, in the same year that I was born. However, I was able to help him regain some of what he'd lost by allowing Rita to sell what Beltia had come up with; a smokeless coal that could be burned without ventilation. It only took me a few moments to realize she had simply made coke, which was essentially just charcoal that had been cooked till all that was left was the carbon. This made Rita a popular contact in the merchant Mage Towers, and made House Nordrucan a more enviable House. Beltia's legend took a significant hit after her discovery was repeated so soon, and Rita's reputation soared for being the only one selling the product en masse.

As a result of Beltia's reputation not being as revered as it had been in the games, she and her husband Durdren didn't grow so distant as they had in the game. To balance this out, and to help Faren become the warrior I knew he could be, I had Father issue an invitation to Durdren; he would serve as my bodyguard until he thought Faren was good enough to take up the position. You meet Durdren as a drunken sod in the game, but that was because he and Beltia had fallen out with each other, and she had left him for his cousin before taking their entire House into the Under Roads in search of the Soul Smith; a magical item that allowed dwarves to create golems.

Durdren's reputation prior to his trouble with Beltia was that of Cragmorrar's rising star. He was considered among the most elite warriors in the entire city. Because Beltia wasn't as admired as she would have been in the game, he had kept that reputation. He took the position as the Princess' bodyguard so that he and Beltia would hold more equal positions.

Faren took to the lessons with the vigor of youth. Now he was eight years old and many whispered that he was Exemplar Nordrucan reborn. He was scraped and bruised almost every day, but Durdren could only sing his praises. It wouldn't be too long before Durdren wouldn't be needed and Faren could take up his place as my personal guard.

For her part, Kara was true to her word. She cared for me as if I were her own child. She kept close to me at all times, ensured I was never late to my lessons, and kept my family well informed on my progress and about when I needed things like new clothes. She was very kind and never mentioned elevating her position, or my promise to raise them up to the rank of noble. One of the best things she did was promote meetings that I desired. Whenever I wanted to meet with a member of another noble House, she was like a tick; latching on to the request and draining the patience of the noble with requests until they gave in.

Not everything was lessons and meetings, though. I was also trained as a warrior by Trenton, and as a smith by Beltia. Trenton wanted to make sure that I was capable of defending myself in combat, as was proper for a Nordrucan, whose House was raised to nobility by the acts of the greatest warrior in Dwarven history. He took those training sessions to question me about my magic and to test how well I was coming along with it. We still hadn't told anyone that I was a mage.

Beltia had agreed to teach me smithing when I approached her one day when she had come to the palace with Durdren. There really wasn't much she could really teach me since I had been forging in my first life longer than

Beltia had been alive in this one. However, I revealed my skills as her lessons progressed, making her feel like an excellent teacher and that she was creating a prodigy in me. Trenton didn't think I should lower myself to the forging, but I convinced him that anything made by an actual Nordrucan would sell for a king's ransom and would likely become an heirloom to other Dwarven families.

I was also able to make new friends. Among them were Petra of the Warrior caste, and Darina and Rick of the Smith caste. I looked for them specifically because of their quests in the game.

Petra was a sweet girl who was turning into a fine warrior, but her parents insisted that they came from House Petran, whose founding exemplar was Korabin Petran; the dwarf who created the Soul Smith and used it to create golems. Eventually, we would prove her and her parents right by reclaiming Petran Hold.

Darina was a dwarf obsessed with magic and learning about it. I always adored her in the game and decided that when I was able to reveal that I was a mage, she would not only become super devoted to me, but together we could research magic in the hopes of making more dwarves capable of becoming mages.

Rick's story was always so tragic that I wanted to keep him safe. I asked Beltia if she would bring him with her during my 'lessons' so I could have someone closer to my age to learn with. Eventually, I would ask him to remain with House Nordrucan to be one of our smiths.

For my fifth birthday, I asked Father and Mother to bid the guests bring no gifts. Instead, I wished to speak to the Assembly on my birthday about a matter that I believed could enrich the lives of everyone in Cragmorrar. Apparently, those who normally attended my birthday parties were disappointed, and insisted on at least celebrating with a dinner after I spoke with the Callers of the Assembly. Father agreed. I wasn't so sure things would be as celebratory once they'd all heard what I had said to the Assembly.

My birthday came, but not without presents. Rita and Faren had used some of the funds Rita had raised selling coke and some of my early blacksmithing works to pay Beltia for a suit of armor. Beltia and Durdren had arrived just as I woke up to bring the armor to me. It was amazing; as black as night and polished to a mirror shine. It was meant to be worn over a garnet and gold gambeson that served as a battle coat that went down to my ankles. It was a style I fell in love with and would work diligently to reproduce in the future.

Trenton gifted me with a 'walking staff' that held a blade in it. He assured me that it was for more than just swinging and tossed me a wink when he said it. Apparently he had it commissioned from 'some expert craftsman' that lived on Lake Kaleshin. I was so happy that I embarrassed him by jumping up and giving him a hug while I was adorned in my new armor.

Mother had heard about the armor Beltia was making for me and had been the one to commission the garnet and gold gambeson. She wanted me to have something to wear that looked respectable, even when not worn with the armor.

Father's gift was, of course, pulling enough strings so that I could speak to the Assembly. It was no secret that some of the Callers thought it ridiculous that a child, no matter how intelligent or talented, would be able to address them on any subject worthy of their time. But I was still granted the time and I was going to use it to make Cragmorrar the most prosperous it had been since the fall of the Dwarven empire.

In the afternoon I was escorted to the Chamber of the Assembly. I was escorted by Trenton, Durdren, and Faren. I could hear the arguments and shouting of the Callers from behind the stone doors that led to the Assembly Chamber. For the first time in a long time, I felt nervous. What I had done for a living did require that I speak to groups regularly, but never one so large or about something so controversial. I found myself hesitating when the Assembly doors opened and Steward Brandon called for us to enter.

Faren gave me a reassuring expression, Trenton clapped my shoulder, and Durdren just grinned and said 'Knock 'em dead, Princess! We're right beside you!'

I swallowed my nervousness away, put on an air of dignity and confidence, and marched into the Chamber of the Assembly. Making my way down the stairs to the center of the chamber, I was reminded how small I still was. The center of the chamber was the lowest point in the circular room. Rows of seats were placed at multiple levels of the chamber, with the most prominent members being seated at the bottom, and the least influential at the top. Father, of course, was seated directly across from the stairs I descended from, smiling confidently at me.

All was quiet as I stopped.

Steward Brandon smiled and bowed to me, "Lady Nordrucan, it is with no doubt in my mind that I, on behalf of all the Callers assembled today, gladly welcome you to the Assembly Chamber."

He was sincere in his welcome, but I knew that he was lying when he included everyone else in the Assembly. Still, I smiled back at, "Thank you for allowing me to speak."

"Of course, Princess," the Steward said. "Whenever you wish to begin, you may."

I nodded and motioned to Faren who was holding a large stack of parchments, "Before I begin, I would like to hand one of these pamphlets to everyone present. In fact, they are labeled for which Caller should receive which pamphlet."

"Guards!" Father called out. "See those passed out quickly."

The chamber guards obeyed and took the pamphlets from Faren.

"I ask that no one open the pamphlets until after I say so," I spoke to the Assembly. "What I have come to speak on today will be explained in finer detail as it pertains to your House in your personalized pamphlet."

"I would have this request enforced," Steward Brandon said. "If our Princess has gone to the trouble to create so many personalized items, we should honor that effort by hearing her out first. Do I have a second?"

I knew that Father couldn't vote on the request, but I didn't need him to.

"Aye, I will second that motion," Beltia called out from only a few seats down from my father. "Who will join me?"

More and more agreement came from the chamber, quickly following Beltia's lead. After all, who didn't wish to curry favor with the first living Exemplar in four generations?

"So be it," Steward Brandon said. "All Callers will place their pamphlets on the Stone at your feet until the Princess bids you read them."

There was a loud murmur and the shuffling of papers as the pamphlets were placed down.

Steward Brandon bowed his head to me, "It is done as you wished, Princess. If you are ready, you may begin."

I nodded and took a breath, trying my best not to let my nervousness show, "Lords and Ladies of the Assembly, I am Princess Merida Nordrucan. I have come to you today to speak of the so-called Surface Caste."

I was cut off by a hail of derisive shouts and a few slurs. Trenton and Durdren both drew their blades shouting for anyone who would slander me again to speak. I'd never seen either of them so infuriated. Those threats quickly silenced the Assembly. I waited for a few moments before continuing.

"The Dwarven Empire was once a continent-spanning series of roads and Holds, larger than any surface kingdom or empire, or all of them combined!" I put some passion into my voice to stir the pride of the nobles. "Since the first Scourge and the efforts of my ancestor, the Exemplar Nordrucan, we have slowly lost our empire and our Holds to the scourgespawn menace. With the loss of our territory came the loss of great swaths of minerals and material goods, including farmable land and underground rivers we used for fishing, drinking, and smithing. Now, only two cities remain, with only a limited number of routes which are barely safe enough to travel connecting them."

I turned, trying to make eye contact with each Caller as I spoke. There were eighty of them, so I had enough time in my speech to give each one ample time with my gaze.

"Since then, we have seen more and more Dwarves leaving for the surface, becoming Cragmorrar's lifeline for materials and food, while also being stripped of their castes and heritage."

"As well they should be!" Someone shouted and others began to shout in agreement.

"Be silent!" I shouted right back, allowing just a hint of mana into myself to magnify my voice to a surprising degree. It overwhelmed the Callers and they were cowed back into silence. Trenton would likely understand what I did and scold me later, but it rocked the Assembly to have a child literally shout them down.

"The surface dwarves have somewhat kept to our traditions, creating minor castes where they adhere to the hierarchical traditions of the dwarves," I continued. "In doing so, they have accrued vast amounts of wealth and prosperity that would make most of you in the Assembly here today blush with envy! They profit from the surface races as well as their own people who actively scorn them. What do we do? Argue back and forth on whether they should keep their caste or not for financial or personal gain, never considering how Cragmorrar could benefit from them, never considering how the Dwarven Empire could benefit from them!"

I pointed an accusatory finger up at the Assembly and turned, to make sure they were all included in the blame, "You only think about yourselves and your Houses. You've forgotten where we came from, what our people used to be. You've forgotten our combined ancestry in favor of your personal ancestry! You've put your Houses before Cragmorrar! You've put personal gain over the gain of your people!"

Now I lowered my voice so that everyone would have to lean in to hear me. It was a bit theatrical, but it would get their attention, "I am a child, and even I can see how small we are compared to what we used to be." And now I shouted, juxtaposing the lament with exaltation, "Every Caller in this room represents a House in this city which once ruled a Hold of its own, answering to none but the Royal House itself! And still, you would eschew the resources for regaining our lost Holds so that you can scheme among yourselves in the Noble District!"

I stepped forward, locking my gaze with my father, "Answer me, all of you! Do you lament the loss of our Empire?"

A unifying cry of 'YES!' followed the question.

"Do you wish to regain as many of the lost Holds as we can by the end of your days?"

Another unifying cry of 'YES!'

"Then I tell you now that the Surface Caste is the key! But not in ways that have been proposed before…" I stepped back to the center and placed my hands behind my back, moving to a professional parade rest. "Lords and Ladies of the Assembly, I propose we create an official Surface Caste, one whose sole purpose is to bring in the materials we need to retake the Under Roads and the lost Holds. However, because some will see this as a way to gain personally, I propose we institute the following requirements for Dwarves to become part of the officially recognized Surface Caste."

I held up a hand and raised a finger for each requirement as I proposed them, "The official recognition of all Surface Caste members will be held two years hence. This will give any who wish to become Surface Caste time to prepare. First, in order to be recognized as Surface Caste, a Dwarf must open a business dedicated to bringing in materials, goods, or wares that Cragmorrar requires not only for daily life, but also those needed for the aggressive push of retaking the lost Holds."

"Second, each business must have a stone building carved into the side of the mountain path that leads up to Cragmorrar's gates. This will ensure that each business is dedicated and prepared to function in perpetuity for the good of Cragmorrar and the return of the Dwarven Empire."

"Third, prospective Surface Caste members must show a reliable, and constant ability to provide the materials, goods, or wares which they have dedicated themselves to procuring over a period of at least ten months from the establishment of the Surface Caste. This will show the business' ability to reliably provide what it has dedicated to providing."

"Fourth, each business must provide a list of twenty other prospective businesses that they would recommend for admission into the Surface Caste, even if they themselves are not admitted. This will require the businesses to work together and create ties within the Surface Caste community, promoting an air of cooperation and promotion."

"Finally, the Fifth requirement. Every head of each business will agree to renounce any familial ties they have to any noble House, or lesser family they have in Cragmorrar, and agree to have the Assembly choose another dwarf from another business to be married to. Also, anyone working for that business will be integrated into the family that is created this way. This will allow the Assembly to create larger businesses from the ones already established and help integrate the new Surface Caste families together, condensing their influence, and dwindling the population of the lower wards, which will open room for more prosperous dwarves of lower castes to expand their shops and workhouses."

I looked around the Chamber and found, to my surprise, most of the Callers with looks of genuine consideration. I waited for the conditions to sink in before taking a deep breath and continuing, "I think this proposal will remove any thoughts of inherited debts, financial gain, or creating a new Caste that is too large to control. Now, I will ask that you each open your pamphlets."

A rush of parchments was all that could be heard for several moments, "Inside you will find that I have listed every member of your Houses or branching family, servants, or associated families from other Castes that have gone to the surface. I have ensured the reliability of this list through conversations with you or someone from your family, as well as by cross checking that information from records in the Memorium."

"I have also included all possible debts owed to you, or by you, through those on the surface should you wish to take this proposal in a different route. Also included are what you will gain if you agree to go through with this proposal. Each House will be required to help retake the lost Holds, and to do so their Warriors and other support personnel will need the best materials the surface can provide. This means that your houses will receive a percentage of all materials the Surface Caste provides, as well as a percentage of the taxes brought in by the Surface Caste in order to pay your Smiths, Artisans, Servants, Warriors, and some to keep to bolster your own coffers."

I looked around the chamber and saw a mixture of emotions, but none so often as awe. They were surprised at the thoroughness of the proposal and the information in their pamphlets.

I finished in a thankful tone, to suggest that it was the Assembly that did me the favor of proposing something that would bring them riches and entire cities to rule over, "With that, my Lords and Ladies, I conclude my proposal. It is my hope that you will consider what I have said, and vote to agree to the implementation of the Surface Caste."

It took Steward Brandon several moments to come to his senses as he was still in the middle of looking over his own pamphlet. He cleared his throat, "Lords and Ladies of the Assembly, our Princess has finished her proposal and awaits your decision. This is a matter of monumental effort and importance, so I ask you all; does anyone wish to question the Princess for details?"

Deafening silence followed the question. The Steward was about to ask for a vote before one of the Callers asked, "How do we know that House Nordrucan doesn't plan to gain more than anyone else from this?"

"You swine!" Durdren growled and drew his blade once more. "How dare you suggest that-"

I held my hand out to stop the warrior from trying to cut the Caller down. I recognized the speaker, "Lady Credash, my Father can read our pamphlet to you if you wish. House Nordrucan will receive a smaller share of goods and taxes than any other House."

"Why would you do that?" Lady Credash asked quickly. "How does House Nordrucan gain from taking a smaller share?"

It was my turn to growl, "Have you not heard a word I've said? My concern is not for House Nordrucan, it's for regaining our lost empire! But to answer your question, my Lady, House Nordrucan will take a smaller share because the ruling family already gains more in taxes and tithe from the surface than any other House. We need less, so we get less. And if you doubt my sincerity then I will have Steward Brandon read our pamphlet out loud to you."

With the threat of an angry Durdren, and no other voices joining in to voice doubt or concern, Lady Credash sat back down in silence.

"If there are no other questions for Princess Nordrucan," Steward Brandon called out, "then I ask the Assembly to ready their voices. "The question that stands before us is as follows; should the Assembly agree to creation of a new Surface Caste two years from now under the conditions set forth by Princess Nordrucan. All those in favor of this proposal, say 'aye'."

A resounding cry of 'Aye!' echoed through the halls of the Assembly.

"And all those opposed?" the Steward asked.

"Nay!" shouted Lady Credash.

No sooner had the word left her mouth than several of the Callers around her set upon her with their weapons. They cut her down and left her lying at her seat in a pool of her own blood. I was shocked by the sudden explosion of violence, but didn't dare protest the behavior.

Steward Brandon cleared his throat and ignored the occurrence entirely, "There are no dissenting votes. Princess Nordrucan's proposal passes. The announcement will be made in the morning in each quarter, and we will-"

"Wait!" my father called out and stood, approaching the Steward.

Steward Brandon knelt before him, "My King. We will gladly hear what you have to say."

Father stepped toward me and looked at me as if seeing me in a new light, "Lords and Ladies of the Assembly. I ask that we charge my daughter with the responsibility of making this announcement to every quarter, as well as to those gathered in their stalls outside the city gates. If she wishes to see this done, then the first step of this journey should be hers to take. What say you all?"

This suggestion came as much of a surprise to me as it did to the Assembly. This would mean putting me in harm's way by going to the lower wards, and possibly making me Casteless if the creation of the Surface Caste didn't actually happen by sending me to the surface. To me, this suggested that he had faith that the proposal would succeed, and give me even more reason to help push the efforts forward.

The Assembly mumbled in shock but ultimately agreed to my father's suggestion.

"You should have seen her!" Father bellowed with laughter as the dinner guests, some of whom had been in the Assembly, listened intently. "As fierce as an ogre's roar she barked them all down with a 'Be silent!'" He laughed uproariously, "And they did! No one made so much of a peep until the Steward gave them permission! The whole of the Assembly was brought to heel by a five year old girl!"

"She showed the true fierceness that the Nordrucans are known for," Trenton said with no small amount of pride.

Mother was busy fussing over me, telling me how proud she was of me and how she hoped my venture would be a success. As soft spoken as she was, she truly was the heart of our family. Trenton strove to maintain order and the good name of the Nordrucans, Father's rules upheld the traditions of our family, and I was reshaping Dwarven society with every step. Mother, however, was the glue that held such powerful and influential personalities together.

The evening dragged on, and for the first time in almost a year, I started to nod off in exhaustion. As funny as it is to say, it was well past my bedtime. I excused myself and was escorted to my room by Kara, Faren, and Durdren. My armor and matching gambeson were placed on a form nearby and would be cleaned before I wore them again the next day.

I spoke with Faren for a few minutes, discussing how everything he'd helped me plan for the proposal had gone. Together we had gone over all of the possible things that the Callers might rail against and found solutions for them. Appealing to their national pride was paramount, but appealing to their personal greed with promises of more revenue and goods was also needed. In the end, we had been successful, and the next day would be crucial in rallying the support of all the other castes, especially the casteless.

As I slept, I spoke with Purpose in the Dimvolmn. It was pleased that all my planning had come to success and assured me that it would be there for me through this next venture. Purpose was always there for me, helping me learn magic and giving me encouragement and reassurance as I worked toward each of my goals. For the next two years, Purpose would be doing me a world of good.

The next day I put my gambeson coat and armor back on. I took my staff and left the palace with Trenton, Durdren, Jaren, Kara, Rita, and Beltia in tow. With us were one hundred of House Nordrucan's finest warriors. The first stop was the Memorium where all the nobles had been instructed to be gathered. I announced my plan but it was likely no surprise to any of them seeing as their House Caller or a friend of the family had already told them what was happening. There were mixed reviews, but I expected as much. The nobles had the least to gain in the short term from this, after all.

Next came the market level where the majority of Cragmorrar's population lived. I gave a similar speech that I had given to the Callers. This time, however, I not only appealed to the dwarve's national pride, but also to the opportunities the smiths, artisans, and merchants would have with so many extra materials and goods that would come flowing into the city. That's what really appealed to them. Some questioned where this new caste would rank among the others, and I told them that the Assembly would be considering that over the next two years, but in all likelihood the Surface Caste would rank equally with the Merchant Class (which meant they weren't nobles, servants, or castless so they were basically equal to everyone else).

Then came the most dangerous part of the day; the lower wards. I have to say, seeing the reality of the lower wards and the people assembled there was so stark compared to the game. The people were gaunt and sickly, with more fear in their eyes than anything else. I catered the speech to emphasize the opportunity that the Surface Caste would represent. Even Casteless could become Surface Caste members regardless if they couldn't start a business; all they had to do was work for a business and they would become members of the family that the business is turned into. I left the lower wards seeing teary eyed faces full of hope. In fact, many of those gathered simply walked with us to the gates of Cragmorrar; eager to offer their labor for the chance at a better life.

As we reached the gates to the surface, I felt a great sense of trepidation. It had been five years since I'd seen the sky and for some reason I felt nervous about stepping through the gates into the wider world. Still, the gates were opened and I couldn't show any hesitation. I shielded my eyes as the first rays of sunlight that I'd seen in five years nearly blinded me. The brightness surprised me, but what surprised me more was the cold. I knew the gates to Cragmorrar were high in the Dragonspire Mountains, but I had been living in the mountain that was heated by lava flows and well maintained fires.

I'd hated the cold in my former life and it wasn't any more welcome now than it had been back then. Luckily, my gambeson kept me warm enough to stop my teeth from chattering.

The guards suggested I make my proclamation from the stairs in front of the gate, but there were too many Nordrucan guards and citizens from the lower wards vying for room for that to be practical. Also, I wanted to be able to say that I was out on the surface, and not just on the gate steps, which is what allowed the gate guards to keep their caste. So I moved to the large dais that was in the center of the ring of merchant stalls in front of the gate. The family guards surrounded it to keep me safe and I announced the plans for the Surface Caste, and explained how I was putting my caste and position on the line just standing there telling them the news.

The joy that this news brought to most of the dwarves gathered around me was palpable. They were even in awe that I would risk my position as their Princess to make this happen for them. There were chants of 'all hail Princess Nordrucan!' and 'Princess Nordrucan is an Exemplar!' I admit that it was rather overwhelming. I stayed there for nearly an hour, answering questions, offering reassurances, and reiterating all the conditions for anyone to be named Surface Caste.

By the time Trenton insisted that we leave, the area was abuzz with plans for businesses and a good number of merchants were organizing casteless dwarves into creating camps and preparing to dig into the mountainside.

The day was nothing less than a triumph. However, we left one of our numbers behind. Rita had planned to stay on the surface to begin importing lumber and making coke on a massive scale. We had designed an entire building where she could produce tons of it weekly with the right source to bring the lumber. We'd even found a few families from the Smith, Artisan, and Warrior Castes to help her set up her business. Those families did this in the hopes of joining a prominent Surface Caste family with close ties to the Nordrucans. Even as I was giving my speech in the Noble District earlier that morning, those families had already set up a large camp just outside of Cragmorrar's entrance and had begun digging into the mountainside.

Father and Mother both expressed how proud they were of me and their hopes for the future. We had a good dinner and everyone was discussing the next steps to ensure the success of the venture. Faren and I celebrated back in my quarters by talking about how we could support Rita over the next two years. As I slept, Purpose took great pleasure in my success with the announcements.

It had been a busy day all in all. And for the next two years, this was going to be my everything.

CHAPTER 4:

THE VOTE

The next two years, seemed to drag by. Every day was filled with my lessons at the Memorium, my standard lessons with Beltia, but fewer and fewer lessons with Trenton. According to Trenton, I'd learned almost all I could from him, so he began allowing me to train with Faren and Durdren. I also had multiple meetings with a large variety of people every day. From nobles to casteless, I met with them all; answering questions, offering suggestions, and trying to ease fears or concerns. While the majority of Cragmorrar's citizens were excited for the establishment of the Surface Caste, there were still some hold-outs. I also had daily reports coming in detailing new surface contracts, amounts of materials and goods that were imported, how much gold was exchanging hands, and how much in taxes were being collected.

At least once a month I would leave Cragmorrar to go see the progress of the businesses being set up along the mountainside which the people had started calling Merida's Steps. With every visit there was more and more progress. Vendors would insist on giving examples of their goods, reports on how they're shipments are doing, or offering me tours of their houses/businesses (because they were one in the same in these cases). Each time I visited, Father insisted I bring one hundred Nordrucan guards, and had the same ones on standby. Each time, they had their hands full of goods and samples by the time we left.

Rita was doing wonderfully in her efforts. The Dwarven smithing fuel factory she'd set up was easily the most productive business set up so far. She'd gained a fair number of contracts with human lumber providers and received trees almost daily. She used them to provide Cragmorrar with more of the clean burning fuel than ever before, while still being able to sell half of what she made to Dwarven smith families, or human merchants who paid top price for such a marvelous product. It became so popular that the product was named after Beltia, and the secret to its production was limited to House Beltia and Rita's business by decree of the Assembly. That edict had essentially given Rita a highly lucrative exclusive contract.

Faren's training was coming along excellently. Now that I trained alongside him sometimes I could see the gap in our skills. Trenton likely made a mistake when he insisted on training me for as long as he did instead of allowing Durdren to take over when he was brought in to train Faren. While he wasn't as physically strong as Durdren yet, Faren was nearly just as skilled. In a few more years, he would be a match for most of the warriors in the city. He'd decided on specializing in wielding the sword and shield so he could protect me better, while I opted for the greatsword. The 'staff' Trenton had given me was still tall enough that the blade hidden inside could serve as a greatsword, but that would be changing soon enough. I was still growing, after all.

As far as my time in the Dimvolmn went, Purpose had helped me with learning new spells. I added Stoneshot, Icet Weapons, Rejuvenate, Cone of Cold, Aura of Heroism, and Blizzard to my list of spells. With all the new spells I had access to, Trenton insisted we tell Father and Mother. They could help figure out how best to reveal this to the rest of the world. They said they would think about it, but Mother said she had a good idea. What I didn't tell Trenton was that I actively used Aura of Heroism whenever I would go out into the city or visit the surface. Unlike in the game, there was no visual cue that the spell was active, but it did require a dedicated amount of my mana to maintain. I tested it with Trenton, and it did serve to reduce the impact of incoming projectiles, but it also seemed to have a morale boosting effect on those within a thirty yard radius around me.

To say that I didn't have much downtime was an understatement. In fact, the most levity I had during those two years was with Kara, who seemed to have adopted me as a surrogate daughter once Rita had left for the surface. So she made sure that when I woke up, and as I was getting ready for bed were times where I could relax and take a breather. She helped me prepare for the day, and helped me unwind by allowing me to vent my frustrations. She also ensured that my meals were as stress free as possible. Though since most meals were also meetings, that wasn't always possible. Overall, she was a wonderful attendant and cherished friend.

Trenton also had mounting responsibilities and concerns and wasn't able to help me with as many lessons. We didn't spend as much time together as we used to, but I did see and speak with him every day. He had concerns about the Surface Caste but as I showed him the reports, he couldn't argue with the results. Morale in the city seemed high and the revenue was excellent, and Trenton could see how that would benefit the throne and the family. Regardless of what most believed about him, he wasn't emotionless. He didn't necessarily agree that someone should pay the price for crimes their ancestors from ten generations ago committed.

I made another new friend in those two years as well. Ninta Hermis. She was a few years older than I was, but we met when she was brought along by her brother Drerin Hermis for one of our meetings. Drerin was the Caller representative of House Hermis, and was a very forward-thinking dwarf, much to his mother's chagrin. Ninta and I would have little chats here and there, and she would sometimes come for dinner whenever I had a night where dinner wasn't another meeting. We got along very well, and I fostered the friendship because I knew that Trenton would eventually have eyes for her. If the Dwarven Noble character was a male, Ninta would be a love interest that couldn't happen, but if the Dwarven Noble character was female, and I was, Ninta would become Trenton's fiance. So I get a good friend, and Trenton gets a wonderful fiance. It was a win-win for everyone.

But the day of the vote was coming up and those last few days were hectic with preparation. Meetings on top of meetings. Stacks of reports kept flowing in. It was everything we could do to keep all the information as up to date as possible. Not that it really mattered. There were more materials and more gold in Cragmorrar than there had been in generations, and that was just with the efforts of setting the businesses up. I couldn't imagine a single Caller voting against the Surface Caste's official establishment, especially considering the social ramifications it would have. Riots would be the very least of the Caller's worries should they vote the establishment proposal down.

The day of my seventh birthday had come and I was again gifted with a suit of armor, this time made by Rick and Beltia, but enchanted by Darina who had taken an obsessive interest in enchantments. I may have whispered in her ear that I could use magic… The armor was black as night and as intricate as you could want. In fact, they had smelted down my armor from two years ago and incorporated the metal into the new set.

Trenton had a cape commissioned with Nordrucan symbol clasps. It was beautiful and apparently made from the toughest bronco hide he could find. He chuckled and said that it would make a fine aramis cloak one day, but for now it was a fine cape.

Mother had once again commissioned a garnet and gold gambeson cloak to wear beneath my armor, this time with silvered thread and jeweled studs in the padding corners. It sparkled with every movement and I couldn't help but marvel at it.

Father was surprisingly absent from the breakfast festivities. He'd never missed my birthday before. In fact, he would always make sure to have the entire day to spend taking me through the city, presenting me to the people and doting on me as if I were Cragmorrar's greatest national treasure. His absence was peculiar and I asked Mother about it. All Mother would say is that Father was dealing with something important and that it would be something we would never forget. She seemed to get teary-eyed when she answered me, and that only served to increase my curiosity.

Once again I was escorted to the Chamber of the Assembly by Trenton, Durdren, and Faren. But I was also escorted by the one hundred Nordrucan warriors who would escort me to the surface. Apparently Father had insisted before he'd left for the Assembly. The path to the Assembly was packed with nobles, their retainers, and merchants who had received permission to set up stalls in the Noble District. Today was a big day. I received shouts of 'Happy Birthday!', 'All hail Princess Nordrucan!', 'We're rooting for you, Princess!' and the like. Today was a celebration and a day of hope for the entire city. I couldn't help but feel sorry for any Caller who voted against the creation of the Surface Caste.

When we reached the Assembly, I was happy to see Rita waiting for us. I ran forward and gave her a hug. She was easily the best example of what our people could achieve if given the opportunity. She wished me luck and said she'd be cheering me on.

We entered the Assembly building with cheers at our backs.

When the doors closed, Steward Brandon was there to greet me. He offered me a bow, "Lady Nordrucan. First, allow me to wish you many happy returns on your birthday."

I returned his bow with a curtsy of my own, "Thank you, Steward Brandon. I hope I'm not late for the Assembly."

"My Lady," the Steward replied, "I'm afraid the Assembly has already taken the matter to vote."

"What?!" I shouted in genuine panic. I stared up at the Steward in disbelief. "They couldn't have! It was my proposal, and I am allowed my time to speak on it! Why would they hold the vote without giving me my allotted time?"

Steward Brandon smiled and bowed his head, "Forgive me, Lady Nordrucan, but they saw no need to hear you on the matter."

"And why is that?" I asked angrily. "I've worked for two years to prepare for this day. There are literally thousands of people outside hoping that I get to speak for them, their hopes, and their futures! What am I going to tell them when they find out the Assembly voted without allowing me to speak?!"

"Princess," Brandon said in a calm, soothing tone, "you may tell them that there was no need for you to say anything. Over the past few months the Callers have come to recognize the full benefits of the Surface Caste, as well as admiring your concerted effort and earnest strides in the matter. King Triston called an early start to today's proceedings because he believed in the decision the Callers would come to."

"And?" I asked with trepidation. I found that I'd taken a small, anxious step forward. "What was the result of the vote?"

"Eighty to zero," the Steward replied. "All in favor. The Surface Caste is now officially a caste within Dwarven society. And it's all thanks to you, Princess."

I nearly broke down on the spot. Two years worth of effort were a success, but I wasn't able to be there when it happened. I was certainly teary-eyed and doing my best to keep my composure.

"The Callers have decided to allow you to make the announcement, Princess," Brandon added as I let the relief sweep over me.

"I suppose I'll do that now, then," I said, wiping my eyes.

"Actually, Princess…" Brandon said as he cleared his throat, "There is another matter put before the Assembly that they're voting on today that they would like for you to be in attendance for."

I looked up at the Steward in veritable confusion, "If this has anything to do with the Surface Caste, I brought all the financial numbers with me, along with-"

The Steward chuckled and shook his head, "No, Princess. While the matter came up because of the Surface Caste vote, it is something entirely separate. Would you honor the Assembly with your presence?"

I looked up to Trenton, clearly confused. He smiled and nodded, "Hear what they have to say, Merida. You've come all this way as it is. You may as well hear them out."

I nodded and looked back at the Steward, "Very well. I'm happy to be of service to the Assembly."

"Excellent, Princess. Please, follow me," he motioned to the Assembly Chamber doors which were opened by the Chamber guards.

This time all one hundred of my guards filed in behind me. The center of the Chamber was quite packed with us all.

Steward Brandon waited for everyone to settle in before addressing the Callers, "Lords and Ladies of the Assembly, today we have made history. Because of the efforts of Princess Merida Nordrucan, Cragmorrar is more prosperous and is seeing higher spirits since before the loss of the great Holds. We expect that this prosperity will only continue to grow and grant us the chance at regaining ground we've lost to the scourgespawn menace. I believe the first way to show our appreciation is with a round of applause."

There was a cry of 'Here here!' before a round of applause echoed through the Chamber that didn't settle down for a few minutes. When the applause finally relented, it was Father who stood to speak.

"My Lords and Ladies," Father began while smiling down at me, "what our Steward said is true. My daughter has brought about a time of excitement, prosperity, and positive change for our great city."

Many Callers slapped the stone in front of them, stamped their feet, or banged the hilt of their weapons and staves on the floor in approval.

"It is extremely rare that a single dwarf contributes so much to our society," Father continued. Was he… was he starting to tear up? His eyes were glassy… "Indeed, the last two years of effort on her part will have a permanent effect on Dwarves everywhere, and will be the reason we have hope for the future!"

More slapping, stomping, and banging in approval.

"It is with great joy, pride, and no small amount of fatherly regret…" Father almost seemed to falter as he looked down at me. He *was* crying! "That I ask you all to consider naming my daughter, Princess Merida Nordrucan…" his voice cracked when he said our family name… "an Exemplar."

If my eyes could pop out of my head, they would have. I stared up at him in shock and disbelief. The moment between us seemed to last an eternity until the first 'Aye!' came from the side. I forced my gaze away from Father to see Beltia standing and smiling. Another 'Aye!' from further up, this time from Drerin Hermis. Two more came from the top of the Assembly, from Caller representatives of House Bastol and House Harbon. Soon the Chamber was ringing with approval to the motion.

There wasn't a single dissenting vote.

Steward Brandon looked to Father and said, "The motion passes, Your Majesty. Not a single Nay."

Father nodded and looked back at me, teary eyed but proud. He looked up at the Callers, "Lords and Ladies of the Assembly, today history has been made twice. First, the creation of the new Surface Caste. And now, the individual who helped bring the Surface Caste into being has been named an Exemplar without a single dissenter. There is but one thing left to do, and that is to ask our new Exemplar, Lady Merida, what the name of her new House will be."

Father met my eyes once again and I subconsciously touched the Nordrucan Caste clasps of my cloak. I looked up at Trenton and even his eyes were swelling up with tears. He had known even before we came here. I looked to Durdren and Faren, and the expressions they gave me told me that they had known as well. I was an Exemplar now, and I would no longer be thought of as a Nordrucan. I would be starting my own House, my own family.

"Well, my Lady?" Father asked with some sorrow in his tone. "The Assembly awaits the name of the newest Exemplar. What shall we call you?"

I stepped in and gave Father a hug. He knelt down and wrapped me in his arms.

"I want to be a Nordrucan," I whispered to him, realizing that I truly meant what I said.

"You will always be a Nordrucan," he whispered back. "And you will always be a part of our family. You are welcome home whenever you please, my girl."

"But I still have to choose," I whispered, choking on the words.

"You still have to choose," he whispered in reply, squeezing me tighter.

I nodded into his shoulder and savored a few more moments in his embrace before stepping back. I looked around at the assembly, tears in my eyes but with the conviction of the duty I had to perform in my expression, "I am Lady Merida Orodum, Exemplar and Princess of Cragmorrar!"

Everyone in attendance fell to one knee, Father included, and in unison shouted, "All hail Exemplar Orodum!"

Orodum was a Dwarven word meaning hope, obligation, fate, or something unavoidable. I thought of it as an obligation, though others might see it as fate or something that was unavoidable.

Father, Trenton and the rest of the Callers stood up and Father motioned behind me, "As a gift to you on this the day of your naming and the day of your birth, Exemplar Orodum, I present to you one hundred of House Nordrucan's finest warriors, to keep you and your House safe from harm. These men and women have guarded you for the past two years and have each voluntarily offered their services ahead of time. They are now yours to command as you see fit."

I turned to look at the warriors who were still kneeling. I had taken the time to at least learn their names, but it still seemed surprising that they would all wish to stay with me. I had to give a good impression, though. I understood that much at least.

I squared back my shoulders and looked over the warriors, "Who among you will command my House Guard?"

"My Exemplar," Durdren said, still kneeling. "If it pleases you, I will command your guard until Faren is capable of doing so. Each warrior here has agreed that this would be best."

"Durdren, of House Beltia," I replied, trying to retain my air of professionalism, "You are already sworn to your wife's House. No doubt you have responsibilities there that would prevent you from overseeing my guard?"

"If I may speak, Exemplar Orodum?" Beltia called from behind me.

I turned and looked at her. In all respects, Beltia was now my only peer in the room. We technically outranked my father. "Exemplar Beltia?"

"My husband has trained our guards well enough that he can take the time to assist your House with establishing itself," Beltia said with a smile. "In fact, it was my suggestion. You are my student and I consider you a dear friend. And in this, I cannot think of anyone better to protect you and yours until young Faren grows into the role. We've worked out the details already and are happy to work with you if you agree."

I couldn't help but smile at Beltia, "If you insist, my friend, then I am happy to agree."

"Then it would seem there's only one thing left to do," Father said.

"What's that?" I asked as I looked up at him.

"You have an announcement to make, and there are thousands of people outside waiting to hear the news."

I sighed and nodded my head. It was all starting to really settle in now. There were two announcements to be made, but I was only making one of them. Who was going to make the other? I felt a hand on my shoulder and turned to find that Beltia had come over.

She smiled down at me, "Let's go tell them, shall we?"

I nodded and turned, preparing to go when Trenton stepped in front of me. He looked down at me before kneeling and bringing me in for a firm hug.

"Thank you for everything, Trenton," I said to him with genuine affection.

"No, sister," he replied. "Thank you. You've shown me that there are other ways to work toward the benefit of our people and our family. You're an example to us all. I mean it. You've made your family proud. I am honored to call you my sister and my Exemplar."

I smiled at him. This was the first time Trenton had ever spoken to me in such a way. It was humbling.

"Please make time to visit?" I pleaded.

He nodded firmly, "As often as I can. Now go. Do your family, and your new House, proud."

I nodded and released my hold on him. I gave him and Father one last smile, then started toward the Chamber doors. Beltia kept pace with me while Durdren and Faren fell in behind us, and the new warriors of House Orodum stood and fell into formation behind them.

"Exemplar Orodum!" Trenton called after us.

I turned to look back at him, wondering what he was going to say.

He smiled confidently and shot me a knowing look, "You should tell them now. Show them all what you can really do!"

It took me a moment to think of what he meant, but when it finally clicked I couldn't help but grin at him. I nodded and moved to exit the building accompanied by my new House.

Beltia and I stopped at the steps leading up to the Assembly building, flanked by Durdren and Faren. The crowd was dead silent, all eyes were on me. A sea of dwarves were waiting with baited breath to hear the results of the only vote they were aware of.

I looked out over the crowd and found Rita nearby, just as hopeful, nervous, and expectant as all the others.

"People of Cragmorrar," I called out so that my voice could carry over the massive crowd, "for the past two years I have worked tirelessly for each and every one of you. My every waking moment has been dedicated to seeing each of you benefit in some way with the creation of the Surface Caste. Whether it's to bring you more materials with your craft, to elevate your position within our society, or to put more coins in your coffers, I have tried my very best to see that the whole of Dwarven society benefits from a historic change to our caste system."

I scanned the crowd and let the words hang over them for just a moment before continuing, "I genuinely hope for the best for each and every one of you, and because of that, because of the love I have for each and every one of Cragmorrar's citizens, I have spent a good portion of my young life dedicated to making this happen for all of you."

I paused again. I wanted this to be a moment they would never forget, so building the anticipation was key. You could almost see them trembling to hear the results at this point. Some eyes were even tearing up after I said how much I cared about them. It was mostly showmanship but not totally untrue. I did want what was best for everyone, and I did care for them as a noble and one of their potential future rulers.

"So, it is with a full and happy heart then I am pleased to announce…" one more pause, but I could see the ripple of excitement rolling through the crowd with the positive preface, "that the vote to establish the Surface Caste has passed with a unanimous vote of eighty to zero!!!" I cheered the last part, but my cheer was almost immediately drowned out by the crowd.

The crowd surged up and forward, roaring in excitement and celebration. Individual dwarves became a single roiling mass of joy.

As a teenager I'd gone to a college football game once in my past life. The excitement of the game with each touchdown hurt my ears back then. That is the only thing I had in my experience that could possibly compare to the roar I was hearing now, and every single bit of it was directed at me. It took a few minutes for the crowd to calm down, and even when it did there were still cries of hope and support.

It took Beltia to hold up her hands and wait a full two minutes to recapture the attention of the masses.

"There is one more announcement to be made!" Beltia began before I could start. She looked down at me with a grin.

I looked up at her and nodded. The news would come best from another Exemplar.

"For her efforts in this historic moment in our history, and the effect her work will have on all Dwarves in Cragmorrar from now and into perpetuity, the Assembly has declared that the Lady Merida Nordrucan…" now she paused for dramatic effect. "Shall be known henceforth as Exemplar Merida Orodum!"

If the first roar from the crowd had hurt my ears, this second reaction nearly made me deaf. I admit, the joy of the crowd forced a wide smile on my face. I raised a hand to acknowledge their cheers, but chants of 'all hail Exemplar Orodum!' and 'long live Exemplar Orodum!' went on for some time.

I started holding up my hands to try and regain the crowd's attention.

Beltia had to help and it still took us a few minutes for the crowd to regain its composure. They had learned about the new Surface Caste, that there was a new Living Exemplar among them, what else could they possibly expect to hear?

"There is one more thing I must tell you all, something just as monumental and unique as the declaration of the Surface Caste," I started, nervous and excited to finally reveal my true nature to them.

I stepped forward, the tips of my toes just at the edge of the top step to the building, "For the first time in Dwarven history, a dwarf has been born with the power to wield magic! And I, Exemplar Merida Orodum, am that dwarf! Witness now the power of dwarven sorcery!"

I raised my hand above my head and summoned freezing winds and snow, creating a blizzard over the entire crowd. Not a single dwarf moved or cheered. Every one of them were frozen, not from the cold, but in sheer awe of what they were seeing. I let the blizzard rage and swirl for a minute before releasing the magic and allowing the air to settle down once more.

Every dwarf stared at me in amazement. From the lowest merchant to Beltia, Faren, and Durdren, and all one hundred of my new House Guard. Then it happened. A roar of excitement so loud I had to turn my head and brace myself to endure the sheer force of the magnitude made the sound genuinely painful.

I used some of my mana to enhance the volume of my voice to shout over the cheering crowd, "I am Princess Merida Orodum! I am your Exemplar! And my House will be looking for those of you with the most potential and strongest will! We will not sit on our laurels and be content with the contributions of the past! Our eyes turn to the Under Roads, and to retaking the lost Holds of our people! Who's with me!?"

The Memorium will tell you that the response to my speech shook the very foundations of Cragmorrar. You will never hear me argue otherwise.

CHAPTER 5:

A ROYAL VISIT

Three years had passed and I was now ten years old. House Orodum now ranked as the largest noble House in Cragmorrar. It took me a year to meet with every family that wished to swear their services and bloodlines to my House. Servants, Merchants, Artisans, Warriors, Surfacers, and what few casteless there were left all made requests to join. I even had families already dedicated to other noble Houses seek to join House Orodum.

I respectfully declined anyone who was already sworn to another House. This was met with disappointment from the applicants but respect and thanks from the Houses they were from. For everyone else, I had to think of a way to discern who I would accept and who I wouldn't. In the end, I asked the applicants to create the exact same thing. Smiths would design a set of armor for the warriors of my House, Artisans would craft something with the symbol of House Orodum on it depending on what their crafting specialty was, while Servants were given the same room to clean and the same meal and guests to serve. The ten best applicants were accepted into the House, those who were not accepted were given my assurances that something special would be happening in the next few years where they would get an extra opportunity. This left them with some hope.

Warriors were a different matter altogether. House Nordrucan boasted the strongest warriors in Cragmorrar and I was given one hundred of them already. These one hundred warriors belonged to a total of seven families. A laughably small martial force for a medium sized noble House. It wouldn't be nearly enough for House Orodum. So over the next two years I went to every Testament Bout tournament that was held. Faren and I wrote down statistics on the warriors who participated, the families they belonged to, and their win/loss records. We obviously couldn't claim the veterans, since they would belong to other Houses already. But the youngbloods? The up-and-comers? Those were who we kept our eyes on.

By the time I turned ten, House Orodum boasted the one hundred most skilled young warriors in Cragmorrar and had the loyalty of their families. All told, House Orodum had nearly one thousand warriors. Luckily for us, Rita had managed to convince several farming focused Surface families to join House Orodum so we weren't hurting on food or supplies.

Rita was the first family I accepted into House Orodum. The Assembly, with a recommendation from me, had arranged a marriage between Rita and a surface business owner named Veron Barask. Veron's business focused on importing specialty goods and had a wide network of surface merchant contacts that could find just about anything. He was also formerly castless just like Rita, and they were close to the same age. He was young, but he was talented when you gave him a chance to schmooze someone into a deal. They were going to be married when they both came of age.

Veron was so grateful for the marriage recommendation, and to be part of House Orodum because of it, that he swore that if there was anything he could ever do for me, I simply had to name it. So I gave him something to look for and two names he might look for to start. If he could find what I wanted, it would create a massive opportunity for bringing more hope to the Dwarves and retaking the lost Holds.

Faren was thirteen now, and growing into his strength. He was pushing Durdren to his limits in some of their sparring matches. It wouldn't be too long now before Faren took command of the House Guard. Granted, Durdren was in his thirties and was losing a step or two, but you'd never hear me tell him that.

Not that it mattered, really. Durdren and Beltia were expecting a baby soon. Thanks to diminishing Beltia's reputation slightly by figuring out what she had created, and then endearing myself to her by becoming her student in smithing, she never became obsessed with the Soul Smith. Without this obsession, she and Durdren continued to grow closer. I was genuinely excited for them and insisted that I be named an aunt. They agreed, of course. Why wouldn't they?

Darina had become one of the best enchanters in all of Cragmorrar. Her obsession with the craft only grew when I was able to show her all of my magic. We used a great deal of funds to acquire fresh dimvyum, an ore-like material that held magical power, so that Darina could ensure that every warrior in House Orodum was granted an enchanted weapon. Darina was also able to indirectly peruse the library of Falladrin's Mage Tower. This was made possible when representatives from the Tower started visiting Cragmorrar after they heard of a dwarf that could use magic. I agreed to speak with them and run tests for them, but only if they came to Cragmorrar, and only if they brought ten books every two weeks.

Darina had gone through so many books on magic now that she was able to help me refine and perfect my spells. I wondered what good the Tower was when someone with no magic could teach someone with magic how to cast spells in a more efficient and precise manner. I remember that in the third game, Darina had become a master enchanter, and I wanted her with me every step of the way.

Kara was now my personal attendant and the head of my Household. All the servants reported directly to her. She ensured that the actual house was immaculate and that I never looked out of sorts. My clothes were always immaculate and whenever the artisans who made them presented them to her, she ensured that their level of quality and design were up to her standards; which is to say, well beyond what my Mother would have expected. This had an additional benefit in that any clothing or crafts sold from House Orodum's craftsmen were highly sought after.

Rick had continued to study under Beltia and was now nearly as respected a smith as the Exemplar. He also had the opportunity to study under some of the other great smiths I'd accepted into House Orodum. To his credit, he was getting used to modifying some of the outfits that were made for me with bits of tactically placed armor. If I'm being honest, I was starting to enjoy the mixture of regal wear with armored pieces and polished metal accessories. As thanks for his dedication, I invited his family to join House Orodum. His father was ill, so giving him comfort and giving his mother reliable quarters seemed the least I could do.

One dark cloud among all the silver linings was that I was no longer the youngest Nordrucan. While he'd come along a little later than expected, my mother gave birth to Bilfern not long after I'd been named an Exemplar.

Faren and I had discussed that this might not mean much of anything at this point.

Normally in the noble dwarf character's story, Bilfern would have had Trenton murdered and the noble dwarf character, in this case, me, blamed for it, forced them to be an outcast, and took over House Nordrucan. Now, though, he'd be about five years younger than normal, and I made sure to dote on him even more than Trenton did with me.

Trenton was, of course, curious about why I would devote so much of my free time, which was extremely rare, on Bilfern. I explained to him that I wanted to be just as good of a big sister to Bilfern, as Trenton had been a big brother to me. It also didn't hurt that I was hoping I could change Bilfern from being the wicked little schemer that he ended up being, into a more noble and admirable person. So while I couldn't spend much one-on-one time with Bilfern, I had insisted to Mother that he be brought to me every day once he could walk so that I could be an example of how productive a member of House Nordrucan could be, and how much good we could do for our fellow dwarves.

I took an additional step by befriending Franklin Irono, the eldest son of House Irono. Franklin was considered to be an honorable and trustworthy dwarf who you could fight in a Testament Bout in the game. You could even send him the helmet won from the Testament Bout as a symbol of how much you respected him. It's never revealed why, but Franklin lies about what happens to Trenton and your character is blamed. It's believed that Bilfern has some sort of leverage against him, which would explain why he did something so obviously against his character.

I 'happened' to be seated next to Franklin at a Testament Bout two years ago and struck up a conversation. We'd become fast friends as we discussed the Testament Bout combatants and how we believed the results of the Testament Bout would be. Over the next two years I fostered the friendship by inviting him and his family to dinner dozens of times, asking them to help me choose through some of the applicants for House Orodum. If I'm honest, I'd always shipped the female dwarf noble and Franklin, so it was my way of seeing what he was like and if my ideas of what he was like were anywhere close to the reality of him. I'm happy to say that they didn't do him justice.

Since we had met, we had spent a considerable amount of time together. He'd even begun escorting me around the city along with Faren and Durdren. Whenever he came to the House, he would always bring some sort of trinket or present. His devotion was apparent and I couldn't help but find it flattering. It got to the point where seeing us apart was more uncommon than seeing us together. I started to feel like things weren't quite right on the days he wasn't with me, and grew more comfortable on the days he was. He became a reason for me to smile.

The big event was that everyone was preparing for was a royal visit. King Marshal Thirston of Falladrin had sent an envoy requesting permission for he and his retainers to visit Cragmorrar as a diplomatic visit. He wanted to strengthen the ties between Falladrin and Cragmorrar. The entire city was abuzz with activity in preparation for the visit. The surge of commerce from the Surface Dwarves, and a smithing renaissance that had been occurring in Falladrin thanks to the Beltian fuel had made King Marshal wish for the visit.

I was extremely excited because King Marshal knew the way to Petran Hold, and that meant that I could help Petra find the papers which proved she and her family were nobles. Beyond that, it meant that I could actually meet King Marshal, Prince Clifford, and Logan McTosh! These people were legends in the lore and I was not going to miss an opportunity to meet and speak with them.

I had House Orodum working overtime to prepare the quarters for guests. I might not get to house any of the guests but I wasn't going to take any chances. Veron had found some of the finest wines and ales from everywhere except Fransway for me. I specified that absolutely nothing was to come from Fransway.

Father had swore to me that I would be given the chance to host the guests for dinner at my home at least once for the two weeks they would be here. He also mentioned that he thought that my reaction to their visit was the first time he'd ever truly seen me act like a child. I suppose I was especially giddy over the chance of meeting them. I actually found myself giggling over the idea.

Rick and Beltia worked overtime to fashion a set of armor for me to wear for the occasion, and the artisans of House Orodum worked tirelessly to craft jewelry and a new gambeson coat as well. I instructed them to craft rings with the symbols of Thirston, McTosh, and Orodum; one for King Marshal, one for Prince Clifford, and one for Duke Logan. Darina even set to work enchanting the rings with resistance to cold.

One thing I had insisted on was that House Orodum have outfits crafted for Father, Mother, Trenton, and Bilfern. I was not going to outshine my family. I wanted us all to look as grand as possible.

On the day of their arrival, Father insisted that the royal family be at the gates, ready to welcome them. We stood together at the top of the steps that led to the gates of Cragmorrar. Father and Mother in the center, with Trenton on their right, and me on the left with Bilfern in front of me. On one side of the large market area were two hundred warriors from House Nordrucan, and on the other side were two hundred warriors from House Orodum. Along the mountainside, surface dwarves stood to watch as the human royal procession climbed the path to Cragmorrar.

We could hear them before we saw them thanks to the echo off the mountain and sting from the sunlight. When the first banner crested the hill, I squealed with delight, and as the King came into view I actually jumped for joy and pointed.

"Calm yourself, Exemplar," Trenton chided. Yes, he still chided me. Though, not nearly as often as he used to. Only when he knew it was particularly needed. "Show some decorum."

I stopped jumping but couldn't really stop grinning or squealing, "I'm sorry, Trenton. I'm just so excited!"

Father cut in with a chuckle, "Come now, Trenton. Allow her some levity. This is the first time she's met another royal family."

Trenton sighed and shook his head.

Mother laughed, "You may act taciturn, Trenton, but I know you're just as happy as your father and I am to see her acting her age for once."

Trenton let out a huff, but he didn't argue. Did he really regret me not ever acting like a child?

I knelt down and leaned over Bilfern to point out the people approaching, "Look Bilfern! That's Marshal Thirston, the king of Falladrin! And that's his son, Prince Clifford Thirston! Oh oh oh! Look! Look there! That has to be Logan McTosh, Duke of Yivreon, the king's best friend, and one of the greatest warriors and strategists alive today!"

Bilfern looked at me, "Are they friends?"

"Absolutely! They're going to be great friends!"

"How do you know so much about them?" Trenton asked.

I paused, realizing I was basically fangirling right now but I quickly smiled at Trenton, "I ask the mages all I can when they come to visit. I've learned all about them."

Trenton grumbled again, but that seemed to satisfy him.

The procession stopped as soon as King Marshal stopped in front of the steps. Along with Clifford and Logan, Marshal had brought five hundred soldiers along with a retinue of retainers and support personnel. Marshal dismounted, followed by Clifford and Logan.

Approaching the steps, Marshal bowed, "King Nordrucan, it is my greatest pleasure to see you once again."

"The pleasure is all ours, King Marshal," Father responded. Can this be Prince Clifford with you?"

Marshal nodded and clapped Clifford's back, "Indeed it is! Clifford, say hello, lad!"

Clifford fumbled from the clapping and gave an awkward bow, "Greetings, King Triston. My father has told me a great deal about you."

"Has he?" Father chuckled. "All good things, I'm sure."

Clifford seemed to flinch, not expecting the response, "Ah! Yes, of course! I've never heard him say anything poorly about you."

Logan laughed and moved forward, offering a bow, "Don't prod the boy, Triston. He'll faint from nervousness."

I could feel Trenton bristling from where I stood and I didn't even have to look at him. Logan had called Father by his name, without his title. I was surprised Trenton hadn't set upon the man to throttle him or simply died from an aneurysm on the spot.

Father simply laughed, "Logan! I'm surprised Marshal still puts up with you."

Marshal smiled and stepped closer, "I wouldn't be where I am now if not for Logan. I'll always find a way to deal with him."

The three of them enjoyed a laugh before King Marshal looked at Trenton, "Prince Trenton? Is it really you?"

Trenton offered a bow of his head, "It is indeed, Your Grace. It is an honor to welcome you back to Cragmorrar."

Marshal took a few of the steps so that he could take Mother's hand and kiss it, "Queen Olga, you're as lovely as ever. It's wonderful to see you again."

Mother offered a small curtsy, "Thank you, Marshal. It's been too long. We're so happy to have you in Cragmorrar again."

"It's a pleasure to be here," Marshal replied. "Will you introduce me to your two youngest children?"

"Of course!" Mother chirped. She tapped Bilfern on the shoulder, "This is our youngest, Prince Bilfern Nordrucan."

"Prince Bilfern," Marshal said and bowed to Bilfern.

I gave Bilfern a gentle nudge and he returned the bow, "The pleasure is all mine." It was a bit of a rocky introduction, but he managed it and he was only two, after all.

Marshal then turned his attention to me, "And who is this lovely young woman?"

I admit, it was everything I could do not to squeal. I was definitely grinning like an idiot, though and blushing like mad, no doubt.

"This is our daughter, Princess Merida Orodum."

Marshal paused and looked at my mother, "Orodum? Is she adopted?"

"Not at all," Father interjected. "Merida was named a Exemplar by the Assembly three years ago after she organized the establishment of the Surface Caste. Tradition dictates that a Exemplar gains a House of their own, and takes a name of their own if they are already a noble. House Nordrucan was founded by Exemplar Nordrucan, so tradition dictated she choose another name."

Marshal locked eyes with me, "Is that so? You seem to be someone worth keeping an eye on." He offered me a deep bow.

"I'm flattered that you think so, Your Grace," I responded, lowering myself into a respectful curtsey. "I'm truly honored to meet you and to welcome you and yours to Cragmorrar. I hope I'm lucky enough to spend some time speaking to you while you're here."

"I would like that very much," Marshal replied as he turned to Father. "Now, with the formalities out of the way, shall we head inside?"

Father nodded and turned, signaling for the rest of us to do the same. We allowed Father and King Marshal to walk ahead while Mother took Bilfern and followed behind them, then Logan and Trenton went together, and Clifford joined me by hooking his arm around mine. The human retinue filed in behind us, then the Nordrucan warriors, and finally the warriors of House Orodum. The entire procession received cheers from the Market District and all through the Noble District.

That evening he had a large feast with a number of the more important human guests and nobles from Cragmorrar. Everyone ate, drank, sang, and celebrated well into the night. I took Bilfern to his room and sat with him until he fell asleep. After that, Clifford insisted on a dance which was sweet but awkward. A ten year old female dwarf is considerably shorter than a fifteen year old human male. Either way, the effort was sweet and appreciated. After a few gangled attempts at dances, I insisted he allow me to lead so that I could do most of the dancing while he mostly guided me around; this was I could do most of the moving and he could stand tall and regain some of his pride.

If I'm being honest, Clifford worked very hard to treat me like a princess. After the dance I insisted on showing him the Noble District, and we were escorted by Durdren, Faren, another House Orodum warrior, and two of the soldiers from the human retinue. We walked to the very end of the district, all the way to House Orodum. I explained to him that the district had to be expanded to accommodate the house and its grounds. I gave him a tour of the home and by the time we were finished speaking it was late into the evening.

The human guards insisted on returning the Prince to the palace, but I argued that it was too late for Clifford to be walking the streets. I offered them all rooms for the night and sent a messenger to the palace explaining the situation, claiming all fault for keeping the Prince too late. Clifford and his guards ended up staying the night.

Kara woke me up early the next morning, insisting I get dressed quickly. She had me dressed and sorted in a few minutes and then brought me to the dining room where Father, Mother, Trenton, Bilfern, King Marshal, and Duke Logan were all sitting and talking.

I could feel the blood draining from my face as the embarrassment of not greeting them flooded through my mind.

Logan was the first to notice me. He stood and approached me, offering me a bow, "Princess Orodum. Please, forgive our presumptuousness but your lady-in-waiting… Kara, I believe her name is? She insisted we come in and help ourselves to some breakfast. I hope we didn't disturb you."

I couldn't help but notice that Logan had placed himself between me and the rest of my family and guests to allow me a chance to regain my composure. It took me several moments but I finally put a smile on and came to my senses.

"Of course!" I exclaimed while giving Logan an expression of thanks. "My family and such distinguished guests are always welcome in House Orodum."

Logan gave me a reassuring smile then escorted me to the head of the table like a gentleman, pulling out my chair for me, pushing it in, the whole nine yards.

"When we received your messenger last night saying that my son would be staying for the evening, I suggested we come for breakfast this morning," King Marshal explained, shooting my father a wily expression.

"And I concurred," Father said. "I thought we'd make it a family affair. By the way, where is Prince Clifford?"

"I'm here, Your Grace," Clifford replied as Kara escorted him into the dining room. "Apologies. Your daughter was such a gracious host last night, allowing me to bombard her with questions about her life and your fine city. She was kind enough to entertain my queries and put up with me well into the evening."

"Goodness," Mother chuckled and grinned. "You should consider how you phrase such things, Prince. One could easily misinterpret your meaning."

"Mother!" Trenton and I both protested.

That, and Clifford's verbal tumbling in response to Mother's needling elicited a thunderous bout of laughter from Father, King Marshal, and Logan.

"Exemplar Orodum wouldn't risk such a scandal," Trenton insisted. "And she's far too young for such talk."

Marshal laughed and shook his head, "Ah, Trenton, even as a boy you were never much for levity."

"Levity is all well and good, Your Grace," Trenton rebutted, "but not at the expense of my sister's reputation."

"Calm yourself, Trenton," Father laughed. "No one here would believe such a thing, and everyone in the house knows no such thing happened. Allow yourself some room to laugh."

And so went breakfast; with my parents, Marshal, and Logan digging into the evening Clifford and I shared while taking every opportunity to make a suggestive joke.

Ironically, it was left to me to entertain Clifford during most of the visit. So I escorted him around Cragmorrar, showing him the Market District, the recovering lower wards, the surface market and the businesses along the mountainside. I took him to a Glory Testament Bout and eventually to the Memorium, which was my favorite place in all of Cragmorrar. All of this was over the course of days. Unlike in the game, Cragmorrar was massive and it took a great deal of time to walk anywhere. We became great friends over the course of the visit and I admit, I could see what Anna, the woman who he would be engaged to, would eventually see in him; sweet and placating, but not the sharpest knife in the kitchen. He also ended up staying at House Orodum for the entirety of the visit.

It was the second week when I got my personal meetings with King Marshal and Duke Logan. What they told me during that meeting, however, was not something I expected to hear.

CHAPTER 6:

MEETING OF REVELATIONS

It was the first day of the second week when Clifford, and just Clifford, had been invited by Trenton to dinner. I had asked if I could join them but Trenton insisted that I could not. It was strange. Trenton took every opportunity to spend time with me that he could, but this rebuttal was so blunt and decisive that it took me by surprise. I almost wondered if he was going to chastise Clifford for spending so much time with Cragmorrar's Princess and putting me in a compromising position by staying at my home for the duration of the visit.

I have to admit that it hurt that Trenton didn't want me at dinner, but the reason quickly became clear. Not long after Clifford had left, a human messenger came by the house asking if King Marshal and Duke Logan could come to supper this evening. I, of course, agreed to have them over and the messenger let me know that they would be there around six that evening.

Needless to say, the house was a whirlwind of activity. Kara made sure that the house was kept spotless, but you would think that it was a trash heap from the way she was barking at the servants to get everything in order. Dinner was going to be a simple shepherd's pie, but now Kara was ordering whole chickens, lamb, and pigs to be readied. Thankfully I was able to convince her down to some chickens and vegetables. It was only three people, after all.

As for me, I spent the next few hours with Faren trying to figure out what I should try to talk to Marshal and Logan about. I was going to insist that Faren be in the room with us as my guard so that he could listen in and maybe remind me about things I'd forgotten to ask. There were so many things we could tell them, try to influence events in the future, or just completely avoid certain events altogether.

We couldn't avoid the Scourge. Marshal and Logan had already been to Forster Hold as they had done in some of the game's supplementary material and unintentionally set those events in motion. Now, all we could do was prepare for the Scourge, and take advantage of the thinning number of scourgespawn in the Under Roads when it happened. I'd been thinking about the Scourge since I came to the world of Thoros and what the dwarves could do during the Scourge. We had two options, technically three, but which one we would take would be up to more than just me.

Time seemed to fly by when Marshal and Logan arrived. I might have hurt one of the servant's feelings by yelling at them as they went to open the door. I wanted to be the one to greet them. Yes, I was still very much fangirling over the fact that I got to meet with these legendary lore characters. I apologized to the servant, then composed myself, put on that very stupid smile I was sure I'd been wearing every time I got to speak with them, then opened the door.

"King Marshal, Duke Logan," I said with as welcoming and cheerful a tone as I could muster, "Welcome back to…"

I stopped when I was staring at a teenage human girl with long, blonde hair who sported a House Coreland brooch on her blouse. Behind the girl was standing King Marshal, Duke Logan, and an awkward looking boy around my age with short hair and looking like he wanted to laugh. My confusion was palpable before something clicked.

Looking up at the girl, I offered a little smirk, "Elissa?" Elissa was the default name for the human noble character from the game for the female human noble.

"Serena, actually," she corrected. "Serena Coreland." She gave me a polite curtsy, "I didn't default."

I was right! I should have known, though! I'd completely ignored all the banners and symbology in the retinue on the day of King Marshal's arrival. I was too excited at the prospect of meeting Marshal, Logan, and Clifford. Did that mean that the boy with them was…

I returned the curtsy, "Lady Coreland, it is an absolute pleasure to finally meet you. I am Exemplar Merida Orodum, daughter of King and Queen Nordrucan of Cragmorrar. Please, won't you all come in. I'll have some extra food prepared. We only expected two guests."

King Marshal entered first and the others filed in behind him, "Don't go to too much trouble. We're not here to eat you out of house and home."

"I told you we should have been forthright with who we would be bringing to begin with, Marshal," Logan chastised his king. "Exemplar Orodum has been treating your son, and us, with all due care since we've arrived. The least we could have done is tell her how many people were coming to dinner."

"I'll make it up to her tonight, I'm sure," Marshal reassured Logan as I led them to the dining room.

I nearly cried out in thanks when we entered the dining room and Kara smiled at me. The table was set with everything she'd wanted to have cooked earlier. That woman looked out for me in so many different ways that I'm not sure what I would have done without her. I mouthed a silent 'Thank you!' to her, to which she simply bowed her head in response.

The boy laughed when he saw all the food, "You must not have much experience with humans, Exemplar Orodum. This is enough food for a banquet. I've seen Logan eat, and I'll admit that even he wouldn't be able to gobble all of this down."

"Alford may jest, but it does seem like you over prepared for us," Marshal said with a laugh. "Or you somehow caught wind of how many people we were bringing and were simply being polite at the door."

I knew it! It was Alford! Alford was a fan favorite character who appeared in every game in some form or another. He wasn't the most intelligent character, but he had a good heart and a charming, numbskull personality.

"Well…" I said and I motioned for everyone to take their seats. "We wanted to make sure no one went without something they might like."

I took my place at the head of the table. King Marshal sat to my right, Logan to my left. Alford sat beside Marshal while Serena sat beside Logan.

"It would seem introductions aren't exactly needed," King Marshal began, "but formalities are formalities. This is my son, Alford."

Alford nodded to me, "A pleasure, my Lady."

I smiled and bowed my head, "The pleasure is all mine, Alford."

Marshal was claiming Alford? Yet he didn't present Alford to my family when they first arrived. This had to mean that Marshal didn't claim him as a legitimate heir yet? Was he protecting Clifford and Anna's succession? Or perhaps he was waiting to announce Alford's legitimacy later on?

"And this is Lady Serena Coreland, who is currently Duke Logan's ward," Marshal continued.

I looked to Serena who bowed her head, "Exemplar Orodum. A pleasure."

I responded in kind, "Lady Coreland. You have no idea how happy I am to have you here."

"And why is that, exactly?" Logan asked with a hint of suspicion in his voice. "As far as I know, the two of you haven't met until just now."

The question wasn't one I was prepared to answer, but luckily for me Serena was.

"She's one of the six, Duke Logan," Serena stated matter-of-factly. "Exemplar Orodum is like me. We were each born with knowledge of the world beyond what we should know. We're… Fated."

The description Serena gave hit me hard.

"And how do you know that?" Logan asked. "You've only just met."

"Because Orodum is a Dwarven word meaning obligation, *fate*, or something unavoidable," I responded. "I took the name when becoming a Exemplar because I felt an obligation to use my prior knowledge to help my people. I saw it as my fate."

"Is that so?" King Marshal asked between bites of his chicken. "Then perhaps you can tell us what might happen in the next ten years?"

"The fifth Scourge," I said bluntly, seriously, with no hint of hesitation. "And it will happen because you and Duke Logan went into the Petran Hold and accidentally led the scourgespawn to the imprisoned old god Fariastren."

"That's not exactly how it went," Marshal responded as he looked at Logan, the memory of the events seeming to flood back to him.

"But it's a close enough synopsis," I said, reading the tone correctly. "The Scourge will happen in ten years. We can't stop it because we don't know where Fariastren is right now. But we can lure the scourgespawn to where we want them."

"And how would you propose we do that?" Logan asked.

"I know how," I said, smirking to try to ease the tension in the room. "It's rather easy, if I'm being honest with you. But for that information, I'd like something in return."

"You would withhold such information from the king?" Alford asked in shock.

"Begging your pardon, Alford," I said with a smile, "but he's not my king."

"How dare you?" Logan snapped and slammed a fist on the table.

"Now now, Logan," Marshal said as he held up a hand to calm his friend down. "She's right, after all. I'm not her king and hold no authority here. I'm simply a house guest who happens to be a king in another kingdom."

"Forgive me, Your Grace," I said softly, "but I am a Exemplar. By all rights, I outrank my father, and even as one of the Fated, my concern is for my people first. We are constantly dealing with scourgespawn. We don't have the luxury of waiting for a Scourge. So asking for something in return for the information on how to lure them to where you need them seems like I'm getting the short end of the stick."

"She's not wrong, Your Grace," Serena said. "If it weren't for the scourgespawn, the Dwarves would be much stronger allies. If we can help them in any way before the Scourge to ensure we have their aid when the time comes, it would be a worthwhile investment."

"And how is it that she has this key bit of information and you do not?" Logan asked, a sharp hint of irritation in his voice. "If you are both Fated, then shouldn't you know what she knows?"

"Not necessarily," Serena said calmly, unfazed by Logan's tone. She'd clearly gotten used to him. "We were all born with knowledge beyond what we should know, but that doesn't mean we all have the same knowledge. We know about the Scourge, the events that should be surrounding it, and about things that will happen after it. But what we know about the rest of the world or past events will be different. Whether that's because of where we were born, or who we were born to, who's to say?"

Serena conveniently left out that what we would know would be dependent on how much of the lore we knew about the franchise before we were reborn here. It suddenly occurred to me that Faren and I hadn't actually had a good lore dump since we met each other. We really hadn't even discussed our lives prior to coming to Thoros. The only time we did was when we were comparing notes on my plans. I really needed to correct that.

"She's right, Logan," Marshal sighed. "And it's not like we haven't already made concessions in this matter."

"That explains that," I chuckled.

"What's that?" Marshal asked. His tone suggested that he wasn't just curious, but he was testing me somehow.

"The concessions you mentioned," I replied, sitting up a bit taller. "You have Alford with you, and Lady Coreland is Duke Logan's ward. If I were to guess, Lady Coreland has convinced her Father to let her travel with you and

Duke Logan to collect, or meet with, the other Fated. In return, Logan has promised to safeguard Lady Coreland during the journey, and you have promised Alford's hand in marriage to Lady Coreland."

The table sat silent for several moments.

"Was I right?" I asked with a bright smile.

"It's as if you were there when it all happened," Marshal said, clearly impressed. "How did you know?"

I couldn't help but laugh, "It's what I would have done. Duke Logan is a trusted and loyal man, who puts the safety of Falladrin above all else. He would gladly take on the responsibility of someone who has the knowledge to save the country. And Alford has Thirston blood, and will make a fine husband for the second most powerful family in your country. A small price to pay to get Lady Coreland's help, and secure an alliance with the Corelands."

Taking a few moments to consider everything else, I looked to Serena, "Did you take the Earling as well?"

"I'm working on that," Serena said with a smirk. "Earl Strowe is a snake and I won't allow him to become a threat to my family."

"When there's proof," Logan said, clearly not wanting that subject to go any further if his tone had anything to say about it.

"Indeed," Marshal agreed. "And I think that's proof enough that she is indeed one of the Fated. So the question becomes; what do you want in return for the information on how to lure the scourgespawn?"

I sat back in my chair in as dignified and professional manner as possible, "I want assistance with the scourgespawn for myself and my people after the Scourge has been dealt with, and I want detailed directions to Petran Hold."

Marshal and Logan exchanged looks with each other.

"Why do you want to know how to get there? Because that's where this all began?" Logan asked.

I shook my head, "Not at all. We can't change what's already happened. But my goal is to help my people retake as many of the lost Holds as possible once the scourgespawn are dealt with. But before we help you, I want to retake Petran Hold. It has great value to my people."

Serena looked almost horrified, "You don't plan to use the Soul Smith, do you?"

"The Soul Smith was made for a good purpose, but the unprincipled nobles at the time corrupted its purpose," I said with a calm explanation. "It was supposed to be used by volunteers."

"But it wasn't!" Serena protested. "They even used it on Korabin!"

"I know," I responded calmly. "But I also know that the golems should have been able to keep their minds. Korabin and Gniess are both examples of dwarves who remained sentient after the process. I imagine this was the intention all along. My plan is to find Korabin, and ask him for his help."

"By subjecting more of your people into becoming golems?" Serena nearly screamed.

"By helping the dwarves rid Thoros of the scourgespawn and hunting down the remaining old gods," I said firmly. I turned my gaze to Marshal, "Your Grace, I know how to lure the scourgespawn to where you need them to be. And I know how to hunt down every remaining old god and kill it before it can become an archdemon which will each start a Scourge of their own."

The room went dead silent. Even Serena couldn't believe what I was saying.

"This effort will require the sacrifice of more dwarves than I care to imagine. It will be the work of decades. We will have to dedicate the whole of our society to doing this, and each step will require that we clear out the Under Roads throughout the process. But I know the numbers, and I know we can do it. All I'm asking from you and yours is to help us with the first few steps after we've helped you lure the scourgespawn and stop the

Scourge."

There. My aspirations were out for this group to know. I planned to stop the scourgespawn and handle the rising of the old gods.

"So… the golems…" Serena almost whispered.

"Will be a last resort," I nodded. "Dwarves who are fatally wounded will have the option to become golems only if we can figure out how to let them keep their minds. We will give them the opportunity to continue fighting for their families, their Houses… for all of Thoros."

"So you want the help of our armies after the Scourge," Marshal asked. "To do what? You mentioned the first few steps."

"By all accounts there are anywhere between twenty to thirty thousand scourgespawn at any given time," I began. "They're scattered all throughout the Under Roads. During a Scourge, about seventy-five percent of them will be a part of the Horde, give or take. Twenty percent are left to harass my people here and in Kal-Sharok. The other five percent are spread out through the Under Roads or raiding on the surface."

"What I want from you is to bring your forces to Cragmorrar after we've dealt with the Scourge and bolster our numbers for two years as we not only retake the closest lost Holds, but secure the connecting Under Roads to them as well."

"You're asking for two years worth of commitment for a few moments worth of advice?" Marshal asked. "Now that is a bit much, regardless of how helpful the advice is."

"To say the very least," Logan added. "It's too much."

"I'm not asking you to do anything more or less than what I'm willing to do," I replied confidently. "In return for you giving two years of your life to my people, House Orodum will dedicate two years to helping your people before the Scourge."

"How so?" Serena asked. She seemed genuinely intrigued now.

I gave her a smile, "House Orodum boasts the most skilled and dedicated craftsmen and artisans in all of Cragmorrar. And I am deeply loved by my people. So in just under eight years, I will bring the entirety of my House to Orlimar. I'll likely come with a great deal more dwarves as well. We will bring materials and all of our skills to reinforce the fort in preparation against the scourgespawn and lend our warriors to the fight."

"That is certainly a worthy contribution to these efforts," Marshal said as he looked at Logan, his brow rising as if to ask if his friend agreed.

"I should say so," Logan conceded.

"Years and manpower for years and manpower," Alford chimed in. "Looks like we're in for a fun decade in the next few years."

"There's also one more thing I'd like," I added. "But it's a deal I need to make with Serena."

"Is she able to give you something I can't?" Marshal asked with no small amount of doubt.

"She can't give this to me, but you can," I replied diplomatically. "However, I would like her to make an agreement with me since I won't be able to leave Cragmorrar for the next few years."

"So?" Serena asked. "What do you want?"

"Kallian. Or Darrian, if their name were defaulted," I smirked.

"The City Elf?"

"Indeed," I nodded. "Have them sent to me, and you can grab the mage and the Paddish elf. We'll keep the six of us in two different groups to ensure our safety. Three here in Cragmorrar, three with you, King Marshal and Duke Logan."

"Wait, does this mean you already knew there were others like us?" Serena gasped.

I couldn't help but laugh and then looked to my right, waving for Faren to join us.

"Meet Faren Orodum," I said with a smile. "Faren is the dwarf commoner. I met him when I was two, and he had already started improving the life of his family. He's now one of my personal guards. Faren, please introduce yourself."

Faren, dressed to the nines in the fine plate armor of House Orodum bowed to the guests and removed his helmet, "Your Grace, Duke Logan, Lady Serena, Alford."

"Hey…" Alford protested at being left last in the greeting.

"I am Faren Orodum, of House Orodum," Faren continued without a pause. "It would seem that I am one of the Fated, as you call them. Lady Merida has spoken truthfully with you. She wants nothing more than to work together to stop the Scourge, retake our lost Holds, and end the threat of the scourgespawn for good. We've worked together for the past seven years to get our people to where we are now. If there is anyone in this world that you can rely on to combat the Scourge, it's her."

"…How old are you, Lady Merida?" Marshal asked.

"I'm ten," I replied with a smile. "Faren is twelve."

"Ten years old?" Logan repeated. "And you've burdened yourself with such responsibilities since you were… three?"

"Earlier," I said. "Since before I was one. But I could only start to act on my plans when I was three. I had to grow a bit first, learn to read and write our language, and walk of course."

"How sad," Alford sighed. "You've never allowed yourself a childhood?"

"My childhood is a small price to pay to save my people, and the people of Thoros," I responded. Though their pity for me did sink in a bit. I'd had a chance to live life from the beginning again, to enjoy my youth. I looked up at my guests and smiled, unsure if I had completely hidden any regret I might have felt, "You know what they say; youth is wasted on the young. I did not intend for this to be true of myself."

"Nor did I," Faren added.

"Nor did any of us," Serena added. "We were all born at this time to help save Falladrin from the Scourge. And now I know that we were also born to help end the Scourges once and for all. Lady Merida has the right of it."

Marshal and Logan shared an expression of concession and respect between them before Marshal smiled at me, "Very well, Lady Merida. In seven years, we'll meet you and yours at Orlimar. And once we've dealt with the Scourge, we'll help your people secure your lost Holds."

"And the Elf?" I asked.

"I will not force this elf to come here," Marshal hesitated. "But I will have Lady Serena explain things to her. If this elf agrees, they'll arrive within the next few months after our visit is over."

"Thank you, Your Grace," I bowed my head to Marshal. Looking back at Serena I arched a brow, "Have you already collected the mage or the Paddish Elf?"

She shook her head, "Not yet. Duke Logan believed it was prudent to get the dwarves on board to help against the Scourge before the mages since the mages are obligated to help one way or another."

"And it would seem like I was correct in my insistence," Logan crossed his arms, rather proud of his intuition.

"As you always are," Marshal chuckled.

"Would you do me a favor after you've stopped at the Mage Tower to collect the mage?" I asked Serena.

"What's that?"

"Send word back to me if the mage is an elf or a human," I said thoughtfully.

"Well… on that note, I was wondering if you remembered the default names," Serena replied with a bit of embarrassment.

I smiled and nodded, "I'm willing to bet that the mage will be a human, a member of the Lemlal family. Either Daylen Lemlal or Solona Lemlal. If it's an elf, their default name will be either Alim or Neria. And in case you need the Paddish name, it will be Theron or Lyna."

"Thank you," Serena bowed her head. "I couldn't remember. But I knew the middle child of the Nordrucan family would be one of us. It was another reason I agreed to come to Cragmorrar first."

"I am always happy to be of service," I said with a bright smile.

We spent the next few hours speaking about plans for the Scourge and how we could use the six Fated to our best advantage. We went over how we could prepare over the next few years. I managed to finagle a few sparring and training sessions with King Marshal and Duke Logan, because how amazing would it be for Faren and I to be able to learn from two of the greatest warriors of the Age? At the end of the night, I presented King Marshal and Duke Logan with the rings I'd had House Orodum craft for them.

The rest of the week went as planned and was largely uneventful. Trenton had come by the day after my dinner meeting and apologized for the way he snubbed me. Well, he apologized and brought me a literal cart load of gifts. He also asked if Ninta was expected to stop by today. Was love in the air? True, Ninta was a few years away from being named an adult, but noble plans were always long term. Trenton always insisted on keeping ties between House Nordrucan and House Hermis close in his journal entries.

Faren and I were able to spar and learn from both King Marshal and Duke Logan. They were so far beyond our current abilities that it was almost disheartening for me. Faren seemed to take it as a challenge. I wish I had his enthusiasm, but I think my mindset towards physical combat had changed a bit with everything that I was learning. It still amazed me how skilled your average warrior was compared to the people who studied medieval combat in my original life. They were so lost compared to what the reality was.

The rest of the week was filled with meetings, planning, and consolidating it all into a solid timeline. We informed Father of my intent to aid the humans with rebuilding Orlimar, but we didn't share the reason why quite yet. I was going to handle that announcement myself. When King Marshal took his leave, the Dwarves of Cragmorrar had done a great amount of trade and were out in droves to wish them all well.

As for myself and House Orodum, we had some work ahead of us.

CHAPTER 7:

THE PERSONAL TOUCH

It was a few weeks after the delegation from Falladrin left, on the anniversary of the third Surface Caste, which was also my birthday. Kara was scurrying about getting me ready for my day. She was especially excited because today was a Testament Bout, and that meant that Franklin would be coming by to bring me to the Testament Bout Arena. Kara had noticed how well Franklin and I got along, and how punctual he was on Testament Bout days. She dressed me in a red gambeson with a gold necklace and bracelets. She also insisted I wore polished brass hair rings in my braids.

Breakfast was served a little earlier than usual since Faren was working on gathering our Testament Bout statistics. We always went over them before leaving for a Testament Bout, so we needed to eat earlier than normal. This was going to be one of the last Testament Bouts we needed to go to before I would make my final offers to warrior families.

We also had to eat early because Franklin had sent word that he wanted to go to the Market District before the Testament Bout. After breakfast, Faren welcomed Durdren and they both selected the guards who would be escorting me out for the day. Typically, ten guards were chosen for escort duty while the rest stayed behind to train. Since most of my warriors had been chosen through Testament Bouts, I insisted that they train daily and that only the winners over the past few days of mock battles would get the honor of escorting me. That meant that any time I was being escorted through the city, it was by the ten strongest warriors in House Orodum.

As we stepped out of the house, Franklin and his men were waiting for us. Franklin stepped forward and took my hand, placing a kiss on it, "Lady Orodum, it's a pleasure to see you again."

I couldn't help but smile and blush lightly. Franklin always treated me like a princess, a fairy-tale princess, not an actual princess.

"Thank you for joining me today, Lord Irono," I bowed my head as Franklin released my hand gently.

"No, Lady Merida," Franklin smiled and motioned for me to lead the way, "I should be thanking you. There's no one who will envy you for being with me. I'm the one who's going to be the envy of all of Cragmorrar for being by your side."

I couldn't help but smile wider in response to the flattery. I started to head toward the Market District. Franklin moved to walk beside me. As we reached the doors that led from the Noble District to the Market district, Franklin moved to my side and hooked his arm with mine. The motion took me by surprise and I looked at him with surprise. I couldn't bring myself to pull away, though.

I could hear Faren's hum of disapproval behind me. I looked back at him with an expression that warned him to keep those thoughts to himself, but I don't think he saw it since Durdren had smacked the back of his head for his slip in protocol and etiquette. I decided that Durdren's chastisement was enough so I faced forward again, flashing Franklin a smile.

We entered the Market District and the citizenry immediately noticed. To be fair, they noticed whenever the door to the Noble District opened, but whenever it was me walking through the door, things tended to get a bit wild. There were wishes for a happy birthday and offers of gifts which the guards took for me as we were swarmed with happy citizens as well-wishers. There were also a number of people who mentioned how cute of a couple Franklin and I made.

I did what I did best by schmoozing and meeting with individual citizens, listening to how I'd helped them and their families with the creation of the Surface Caste. I asked about what more I could do, taking an interest in their family's wares and goods, and promising to stop by later to see if I could use their services.

This went on for nearly an hour and Franklin simply allowed me to engage with the people. He hummed softly after a bit, "It's amazing how you can connect with people so easily, Merida. The people seem to truly love you."

"I think it's more appropriate to say that they appreciate what I've done to improve their lives and the prospects for their families," I shrugged.

Franklin shook his head in denial, "No, My Lady. That may have something to do with their reactions, but they do genuinely love you. Appreciation is one thing, but the way the streets essentially turn into a celebration when you arrive is something else entirely."

I decided not to argue the point and just offered a thankful expression, "If you say so."

"I do," he chuckled and led me to a store that was closer to one of the larger mines. The store was carved into the stone, which meant it belonged to one of the more prominent mining families and had likely been open for generations.

As we entered, I couldn't help but allow a quiet 'Oh…' as the sight of precious minerals, stones, and geodes filled my gaze.

An elderly dwarf greeted us from behind the back counter, "Greetings! Greetings! Welcome to Tegran Minerals, how may I- Oh! Oh my!"

The dwarf took a few moments longer than most to recognize us, but once he did he moved around the counter and approached us with a deep bow, "My Exemplar! Lord Irono! Your visit to our humble shop will be recorded and celebrated as a blessed day by my family!"

I quickly dipped into a curtsy in response, "You honor us with your words. Did you say your family name is Tegran?"

His smile brightened, as if me simply remembering the name of his shop was a blessing, "I did, My Exemplar!"

"Is your family descended from Exemplar Filras' line?" I asked with no small amount of curiosity and excitement.

His old eyes seem to sparkle with the question, "We are, My Lady! Our ancestors were cousins to the King of Cragmorrar at the time, whose son was Exemplar Filras. I'm surprised you would recognize the name."

"Our Lady is an ardent study of familial lines and history," Franklin bragged. "I'd wager she could recite Cragmorrar's history if we gave her the time."

"Please, My Lady, allow me to offer you a gift for visiting our shop and taking it upon yourself to remember our family in your studies," the dwarf bowed deeply.

I let out a soft laugh, "I think you might want to introduce yourself first. I want to know who I should thank for any gift."

The dwarf looked horrified that he'd forgotten his manners, "Oh, please forgive me, My Lady! The excitement of seeing you and hearing your knowledge of my family overwhelmed me, and I forgot my manners. I am Kroff Tegran. My son, Trent, leads the family now, but I now manage the business on a day to day basis."

"Well, mister Kroff, I suppose it's your son's loss and your gain that he gave up the day to day management of the business," I joked with him.

Kroff laughed, "Oh, he won't believe me. He decided to go to the Testament Bout today, so I have no way of actually proving that you were here."

I couldn't help but grin mischievously, "I think I can figure something out. You mentioned a gift?"

"Oh! Oh yes!" Kroff gasped. "Please, My Lady, follow me."

"Actually, Princess," Franklin interrupted with a polite tone, "I would like to speak to mister Tegran before we continue, if I may?"

"Hm?" I hummed curiously. "Of course, if you wish." I smiled at Kroff and nodded to let him know that he should speak with Franklin.

Franklin took Kroff to the side for a few moments. While they spoke I looked back at Fraren and Durdren, "How are we doing on time? I don't want to miss the first match of the Testament Bout."

"We have plenty of time, Princess," Durdren responded. "Another half hour or so before we need to head to the Arena."

I hummed and looked at Faren, "Faren, I have a task for you."

"I'm at your command, My Exemplar," Faren bowed his head.

I explained what I needed Faren to do just before Franklin called for my attention, "Princess? Mister Tegran is ready to give you your gift. Don't keep him waiting."

I returned my attention to Kroff and Franklin and joined them after a moment.

"Here, My Lady," Kroff reached out and offered me a mithril collar. It gleamed like moonlight and was clearly designed for nobility with its dwarven styled links and plates. It was far too big for me as small as I was now, but it would likely fit me well when I grew up.

My eyes widened and I looked at Kroff, shaking my head as I gasped, "Mister Tegran! This is too rich of an item to be given away simply as a gift!"

"No, My Lady!" Kroff insisted. "This collar has been passed down in my family for generations. It would honor us if you would wear it one day and think of us."

I took the collar and marveled at it. It was true that the make of it was older, but the intricacies of the sharp designs was masterful even by modern standards. I bowed my head humbly, "Thank you, Kroff. Your generosity is peerless and I will ensure that you will be among the first to see me wearing it."

Kroff bowed in return, "I have no doubt that the day you wear the collar will be a day celebrated by all of Cragmorrar, My Lady."

Franklin had one of the Irono guards take the collar back to House Orodum.

"Now, I actually brought you here to get an idea of metals and gems that you like," Franklin brought us back to purpose. "I was hoping we could look through their examples to see what piques your interest."

"Oh? May I ask why?" I smirked in a playful manner.

"I expect there will be a number of your birthdays we'll celebrate together," he explained casually. "I want to be able to offer you presents that I know you'll like."

"A man who looks to the future," Kroff approved. "Truly a young gentleman."

We walked through the shop and I pointed out some beautiful rose gold, silverite, and emeralds. All the while, Kroff made notes and different suggestions on the subtle differences between the items I chose. By the time we left, Franklin had a decisive list of my preferences.

When we arrived at the Testament Bout Arena, there was a large crowd getting prepared for the opening matches. People made room for us as Franklin and I entered the arena. Nobles would always sit in the higher portion of the stands, but I had always wanted the bottom row, right in front so I could see every movement and the subtleties of the combat. Franklin had given in to my preferences. It was always something special for the commoners whenever I would sit with them.

Eventually, the Testament Bout Master appeared on the balcony and called for attention. Once everyone quieted down, he bellowed, "Lords and Ladies, ladies and gentlemen, welcome to this Glory Testament Bout! Today's Testament Bout is in celebration of the birth of the Surface Caste and to celebrate the birth of Exemplar Merida Orodum!"

The crowd cheered in excitement.

"I am honored to announce that Exemplar Orodum has joined us today and is seated in the first row!" The Testament Bout Master continued.

The crowd's excitement grew louder. I stood and waved at everyone, the cheers of 'happy birthday', 'we love you', and 'our future Queen' came from the people.

"I'm sure we would all be grateful to hear a word from our beloved Exemplar," the Testament Bout Master looked down at me. "Would you do us the honor, My Lady?"

I waited for the crowd to die down, keeping my smile genuine and patient. I turned and called out, "It honors and humbles me that all of you have come today to celebrate what I believe is one of our greatest achievements in the Surface Caste."

The crowd roared and it took a minute before I could continue.

"This is a day that we celebrate honor and the dwarven devotion to duty," I folded my hands into my lap as I gazed at the crowd. "Everyone credits me with the success of the Surface Caste's creation, but in truth I was only its advocate. The real success behind the Surface Caste are all of you who worked tirelessly over the two years between its proposal and its implementation. You dedicated your every waking moment to its success by giving it your maximum effort, by rededicating yourselves to your crafts with a vigor that has brought dwarven society into this new age."

The crowd was silent, eyes wide and smiles that seemed happy and humbled.

"I know of someone who is here today…" I continued, then raised my voice. "Trent Tegran! Would you please come here?"

A murmur rushed through the crowd as everyone looked around, settling in a particular direction where Trent stood from his seat, "Me, My Lady?"

"Are you Trent Tegran, of Tegran Minerals?"

"I- I am, Princess," he responded.

I motioned to my side, "Then, please, come here."

He began to rush down the rows of stands, being pushed along by other dwarves eager to see what I wanted with him.

Trent bowed low when he finally managed to stand before me, "My Exemplar, how may I serve you?"

I moved my hand to Trent while looking at the crowd, "On a day we dedicate to the hard work of our people, this man left his business to his aging father so that he could attend a Testament Bout. This is the antithesis of this celebration."

Trent's eyes widened, horrified at my accusations. Before he could protest or offer an apology, I pressed on, "Had he been dedicated to his duty, he would have been the one to greet me when my dear friend, Lord Irono, took me to his family's shop to show him what metals and gemstones I prefer."

I turned back to look at Trent, smiling, "While choosing a Testament Bout over his duties was a mistake, it gave me the opportunity to meet his father, Kroff, who treated me like a treasure in the most personable and polite manner. I can only imagine that he passed these traits on to his son, and that they were passed to him from generations before him. These traits are some of the greatest we can expect from a dwarf."

I placed my hand on Trent's shoulder, directing my gaze at him while my words were for everyone, "It is my hope that, in the future, we can remember why we celebrate this day and how we should celebrate it; with hard work and finding ways to rededicate ourselves to our craft and our goals."

Trent nodded silently, firmly, before I turned and opened my arms toward the arena, "Now let us enjoy the hard work and dedication of some of Cragmorrar's greatest warriors in today's Glory Testament Bout!"

The crowd leapt from their seats with a roar.

The Testament Bout was one of the fiercest in memory. Franklin had surprised me by having each contestant give me a flower before each match. By the end of the Testament Bout, I had a whole bouquet.

Franklin walked me home afterwards and stayed for dinner. We talked well into the night about the contestants and poured over the information Faren and I wrote down through the matches. We joked and laughed well into the night, enjoying one of the few free evenings I had. When he finally took his leave, Franklin promised me that he would be going back to Tegran Minerals to have some jewelry commissioned for me.

CHAPTER 8:

THE ELF AND THE STONE

Serena and I kept in relatively regular contact. Logan had insisted that human messengers make regular runs between Cragmorrar and their group that was looking for the Fated. I was pleased to learn that the mage origin was found, and that it was human; Allen Lemlal. Serena's report suggested that he was well on his way to mastering almost every elemental and healing spell.

The next letter I received said that they wouldn't be heading for Demirren as she expected. They received information about a group of Paddish Elves in the southeast, so they were going to see if the Paddish origin was among them. That would be one of the trickiest Origins to find since the Paddish were nomadic and it wasn't a guarantee that any clan they met would be the right one. She sounded hopeful, though, and that was something I was pleased to see. Apparently their visit to Cragmorrar was more productive than they expected when they met Faren and myself, so that gave Serena's story some merit and lifted the morale of King Marshal and Logan.

It had been four months since King Marshal's visit and in that time one of Veron's sources had found the item I had challenged him to look for. He was rather proud of himself that he was able to pull off that particular task. I was so happy that I assured him that when he and Rita were finally wed, I would offer a wedding gift that would make even the wealthiest of nobles blush with envy. I meant it, as well. I had an idea in mind that would surprise everyone.

I took the next month to make preparations to leave for the surface with a large contingent of my household Guard. I had to take advantage of the next seven years and this was going to be an important step. The servants busied themselves by stocking up on provisions, while I made sure to get my riding lessons in. I was quite a proficient equestrian at this point, if equestrian was even the correct term for someone who rode a rhoarno instead of a horse. Rhoarno were a large breed creature that looked like a pale combination of stegosaurus and rhinoceros. While they couldn't exactly jump a hurdle, they could most certainly plow through one, and my stable master assured me that there wasn't much of anything on the surface a rhoarno couldn't smash its way through if the need called for it.

It was actually during one of those riding lessons when a group of Nordrucan guards approached the practice yard with an elf in tow. Franklin was watching me practice from the fence that enclosed the area I used to practice my riding. He let out a loud whistle and called my name to get my attention.

I guided the rhoarno over to the yard fence and waved a greeting to the guards, "Ser Darev, Ser Kirfto! It's good to see you!"

The dwarven guards bowed, with Darev responding, "Exemplar Orodum, it is a great pleasure to see you once again. You've become an excellent rider since last we watched you on the field in your younger days."

I snickered and winked, "I thought that I was still in my younger days."

Darev floundered for a response but Franklin just chuckled and elbowed the guard, "She got you there, Darev."

We shared a laugh before I nodded my head to the elf who seemed to be a few years older than I was; if I was any decent judge on the age of an Elf, "Who's your friend?"

"My Exemplar," Darev shifted to move out of the elf's way, "This is Trianna of clan Saber, a Paddish elf who was sent to your care by Lady Coreland."

She sent me the Paddish elf? I was hoping for the City Elf, but I supposed it didn't matter so long as we were all safe and separated so that nothing could happen to all of us at once. This did, however, mean that

Serena's lead had paid off and that they'd found the Saber clan.

I climbed down from the rhoarno, took its reins, and squeezed through the fence. I tied off the reins quickly then approached the Elf, offering a curtsy, "I'm so pleased to meet you, Trianna. I am Exemplar-"

Trianna cut me off, much to the chagrin of Franklin, Darev, and Krifto, "Exemplar Merida Orodum." Her tone suggested some irritation. "Yes, yes. A pleasure."

I paused and looked up at her in confusion. I'll admit, I was rarely spoken to rudely in my first life and never spoken to rudely since I was reborn, so this was like a slap to the face.

Still, I regained my composure before Darev or Krifto could say anything, "I see Lady Coreland has already informed you of who I am and of our situation."

"She did," Trianna said. "And she said you insisted on having one of us with you as insurance."

I had to wonder if maybe our plans had been lost in translation somehow when Serena had explained things to her. "Just so that we could be safe and not caught or attacked together," I explained. "Honestly, I suggested that the city elf be sent here. I figured you would prefer to stay above ground, and that the city elf would be more comfortable in another city."

"Don't get me wrong," Trianna replied, "I get the idea behind it all, but I was close to activating the illusavin network with the mirror that was in the Berrustian Forest ruins."

"You actually found it?" I asked with a mixture of surprise and envy.

"I was there for the past twelve years," she replied curtly. "I was the Elder's First and when I showed signs of magic and advanced knowledge, I was able to convince them to go to the area that had the ruins."

"Wait," I paused, "You're a mage?"

Trianna arched a thin, black brow, "Well, yes. A First and the Elder have to be mages. How else do you think I was able to safely activate the illusavin?"

My face hurt with how wide I was smiling. I looked at Darev and Krifto, "Thank you both for bringing Lady Trianna to me. I'll see to her care from here on."

Darev and Krifto both bowed before taking their leave.

I motioned for one of the stablehands to put my rhoarno up, thanking her as she took the reins, then took Trianna's hand to walk back to the house proper with Franklin in tow.

"The Paddish Elf doesn't normally have the option to be a mage," I said excitedly.

"I was playing with a mod," Trianna answered. "I think that's what influenced it."

"Really?" I asked. "I suppose that tracks."

"What do you mean?" she asked.

"I'm also a mage," I said with a smile. "I wasn't playing a modded version, but I was wishing I could play a dwarven mage."

"Dwarves can't use magic, though," Trianna observed.

"I wasn't a dwarf," I suggested. "So I think our minds from before still follow the same rules they did from before."

"I guess that would make sense," Trianna said thoughtfully. It was the first time she'd said anything that didn't sound barbed with irritation. "How many spells have you learned?"

"About a dozen," I admitted.

"What? How'd you learn so many? You're younger than I am!"

"I've had help in the Dimvolmn," I grinned. "I met a spirit who helps me hunt other spirits every night while I dream."

"Wait…" Trianna said, stopping dead in her tracks. "You mean to tell me that you don't even rest in your sleep? You just… keep working on things?"

"Well, just on magic," I said sheepishly. "But it gives me plenty of time to practice and learn. And Purpose, that's the spirit who helps me, has made sure that I'm never in over my head."

"Still, though," she said exasperated, "that would mean that you have… how many years of active magic use?"

"Nine and a half. I started on the night of my first birthday."

"That's just as much as I have, and I'm three years older than you are!" Trianna exclaimed.

"It's not a competition," I laughed.

Trianna sighed, shaking her head, "Seeing what all you've accomplished makes me feel like I've been wasting the past thirteen years."

"I disagree," I said, looking up at her. "We know that the illusavins are a network of traveling portals. And since you're close to unlocking their method of travel, we can use that knowledge to our advantage."

"How?" Trianna asked. "Do you happen to have one we can wield?"

I shook my head, "No. But the lost Holds have a few since a number of them were built under, or around ancient elven cities. They're also in the Dimvolmn."

"It takes a lot of magical power to redirect a mirror to the Dimvolmn," Trianna added. "Do you know of any Holds that have an illusavin in them?"

I grinned up at her, "I do, actually. And your timing couldn't be better. We're about to take the first step to getting there."

"I don't know why Serena wanted to send me here, but I think we both lucked out that she did," Trianna said, smirking. It was the first time I'd seen her with any sort of positive emotion since she'd arrived.

"I concur," I laughed. "I don't suppose you've learned to ride yet, have you?"

"What? Why?"

A few days later we left Cragmorrar. I brought Faren, Trianna, Franklin, and Darina with me along with the original one hundred guards gifted to me when I became a Exemplar. Those hundred warriors were fiercely devoted to me and I knew I would be safe with them at my side. Each member of the expedition was mounted on a rhoarno, but Trianna was… less than competent on the mount. I had a few of the guards keep close to her just in case she started to fall.

We were going to be gone for at least a month, possibly two, so I had Rita represent me in the Assembly. We had to be quick about our business, because one additional stipulation for the Surface Caste was that Surface Caste dwarves would be required to spend fifty-two percent of their time underground. This was added because dwarves who spent too much time above ground lost their stone sense, and there was no convincing enough of the assembly that a dwarf who lost one of the key things that dwarves were known for could still be considered respectable. It was a fair enough rule, and one that most Surface Caste worked with. They had taken to designing storefronts that were above ground, while their storehouses, factories, smithies, etc that were far enough below ground to keep their stone senses honed.

This new rule meant that once we returned from the trip, I would need to spend the next four months underground. No problem there. I was planning on staying underground for the next six to seven years anyway.

We were on our way to the village of Honneleth, far to the south. I did want to stop by Cliffside on the way to meet Earl Edward and Duke Tristain, but I decided to wait until the trip back. I had time, after all, and they weren't going anywhere. Cliffside, and by extension Lake Kaleshin, were one of Cragmorrar's best trade partners. The dwarves primarily brought ore and dimvyum to trade for other goods from Falladrin and Fransway. With the establishment of the Surface Caste, the dwarves were starting to expand on the goods they imported and the goods they exported. I was curious to see how this affected the area.

It took nearly two weeks to get to Honneleth. I'm glad we brought the rhoarnos. Walking would have taken twice as long. When the town came up on the horizon, I had a guard ride ahead to announce our arrival. I didn't want to frighten the townsfolk with over one hundred dwarves riding rhoarnos just showing up on their doorstep. Not that I had planned for all of us to enter the town. Still, I didn't want it to come as a surprise.

Just outside of the town I had the majority of the guards stop and wait for my return. When the rider I'd sent ahead returned and said the village would admit us, I brought Faren, Trianna, Franklin, Darina, and ten guards with me. In order to present myself properly to the people in charge, I was dressed in my finest gambeson and armor, with a silver and gold tiara. We dismounted and entered the village with the guard surrounding me, Trianna, and Darina. Faren and Franklin walked ahead of us.

Upon reaching the village square I set my eyes on Gniess for the first time. She stood there, frozen in her stone glory as a silent reminder to the power and violent potential of golems thanks to one person.

A small entourage of humans approached, intercepting us before we could approach the frozen golem. Among them was a tall, rail thin woman with haughty, sharp features. She looked over our group, trying to figure out who to address. She settled on addressing the group as a whole, "My name is Petricia Sulentruv. We welcome you all to the town of Honneleth. But I must ask what business brings such a large contingent of armored dwarves to our small town."

I stepped forward and offered the woman a curtsy, something I couldn't help but notice she went without offering us, "Greetings, Lady Sulentruv. I am Exemplar Merida Orodum, Princess of Cragmorrar, daughter of King Triston Nordrucan. It's a pleasure to meet you."

If Petricia had panicked in the slightest at her lack of propriety, it never once showed. She bowed and offered a smile, "My Lady, if we had known we were to expect such distinguished guests, we would have prepared a proper welcome worthy of someone of your station."

I shook my head, smiling, "Please, think nothing of it. As to our purpose here, we have come to do you two favors."

"I wasn't aware we were in need of favors, My Lady," Petricia said. Her ability to maintain her composer to the unexpected was impressive to say the least. "Whatever do you mean?"

"I have come to rid your village of a demon and a golem," I stated as cheerily as I could.

"Gniess?" she asked. "What do you mean you've come to rid us of that thing? And what demon?"

"We've found out that there is a demon in the deepest level of your husband's cellar," I said, moving from a cheery tone to one more suited to business. "It is bound there with a magical barrier but it still has enough influence to attempt to lure others to it."

"I know nothing of any such demon," Petricia said haughtily. "Why would my husband do such a thing?"

"Because he was a mage outside of the Mage Tower and conducting experiments that, should the Church learn of them, would have your lands taken from you by King Marsgal," I said directly. "You may have thought him eccentric, but your husband was experimenting with powers well beyond his control."

"How could you possibly know that?" Petricia hissed. Now she was losing that calm demeanor.

"It's what killed him," I said, motioning to the frozen figure of the golem behind her. "His experiments only led to his death. In his passing he left you with a village to run and a demon beneath your feet with the shroud weakened. I'm here to solve the demon and shroud problem, and in return, I will take Gniess off of your hands."

"The golem is of no use to you without its control rod," she seemed to snort.

"Leave that detail to me," I said. "Would you please direct me to the entrance to your husband's cellar? The sooner we get this over with, the sooner your village can be safe and we can be on our way."

"You must be joking," Petricia sneered. "Do you think I would let you into my husband's cellar just because you claimed there was a demon there?"

"You're more than welcome to come with us," I offered. "You can see the creature for yourself. If I'm lying, I will give you my tiara. It's made of silver and gold, and made by the finest of Cragmorrar's craftsmen."

"And if you're not lying?"

"We'll have rid the village of a demon and the golem," Franklin said as he stepped to my side to support me.

"Since we're getting into negotiating the safety of your village," I added after giving Franklin an expression of support, "I will also ask for all the books and gems in your husband's cellar."

"I can understand the gems," Petricia said, obviously playing on Dwarven stereotypes, "but why the books?"

"I like to read, and my arcanist would like to start a library for magical research," I admitted.

Petricia took a moment to consider the offer she had dug herself into, "And if I refuse?"

"At this point? I'll simply take Gniess and leave you with the demon," I said bluntly. "I came to offer our help freely, but you met my offer with paranoia and offense. I could understand some emotional reaction since it was Gniess who killed your husband. But the emotion I would expect would be gratitude. So, I ask you, do we have a deal?"

Patricia seemed like she wanted to snipe back at me, but reconsidered when she assessed the situation. There were twelve well armed dwarves a few steps away from us. I'd wager they were glowering at her for the way she was speaking to me.

"Very well," she relented with a huff. "If it is as you say I will give you whatever you like from my husband's cellar. But I will be coming with you to make sure that this is not some scheme to rob me of my husband's goods."

"You impertinent wench!" Faren said, marching forward and drawing his sword. This caused the other dwarves to draw their weapons, and the one human among Petricia's retinue who had a weapon to draw his.

"Exemplar Orodum has spent two weeks riding straight to your little spot in the road village to do nothing but aid you, and you treat her like some thief?" Faren barked. "I should run you through!"

"Faren!" I called out. I allowed him his speech, but I didn't think he'd actually threaten the woman. "Stand down. I'm sure Lady Sulentruv did not mean that I am a thief, only that she did not want me to act like one. A sentiment I'm sure we all share, yes?"

Faren glared up at the woman before sheathing his sword and stepping back into the formation, "Indeed, My Lady. Please, forgive my outburst."

Looking up at Petricia, I smiled, "I apologize for his attitude. My guards hold me in high regard and are rather sensitive to possible slights against me."

"Not at all," Petricia responded, clearly shaken by the threat. "The fault is mine for not having spoken in as clear a manner as I might have."

I offered a bow of my head to accept her apology, then offered my hand up to her, "We have a deal, then?"

Patricia shook my hand daintily, "It would seem so, Princess. Come this way. I'll show you to the cellar."

Petricia and her retinue led us up a small hill and to the right, coming to a wooden door on the side of the largest house in the village. She took a few moments to unlock the door then led us inside.

The smell of books and parchment greeted us along with the sight of dozens of shelves of books. I could feel Darina's excitement behind me and heard her mumbling about what she could see. The information in those books would be worth a fortune to the right buyer, but they were going to become part of my library instead. I hadn't intended on things going this way, but Petricia's attitude rubbed me the wrong way, so I figured I may as well take advantage of the situation.

We passed through the hall with a small resting room, a room with large casks, then up some stairs into what I always called the 'study room' which held a few more bookshelves, scrolls, and gems. Moving through this largest room, we came to another door that Patricia had to unlock for us.

"This is where things will get dangerous, Lady Sulentruv," I said as Faren and a few guards passed through the doorway. Please, stay near me while we continue further on. My guards and I will protect you."

"How could you possibly know it's going to get dangerous?" Patricia asked.

"Because the shroud is thin here," Trianna answered for me. "Spirits could have easily passed through and started wandering the place."

"I see..." was all Patricia said in response.

I had to wonder why she would take Trianna's word for it when she did nothing but question me. I chalked it up to being more of a child and much smaller than Trianna. It might also have something to do with me just showing up and talking about demons and taking Gniess. Still, she could at least show some deference for my status as a princess. I had to wonder if she would still be alive if Trenton had been there to hear what she said. I didn't let that thought linger.

We continued the slow trek down into the cellar, with Faren taking the lead and Franklin close by my side. I couldn't help but notice how much more comfortable it felt being underground again. However, the comfort of being underground was muddled with the unease I felt at the thin nature of the shroud in the area. It was like feeling a silk curtain billowing across my senses.

There was the smell of rotting hay mingled with the staleness of the air as we entered a room that looked like a strange, small stable. As if on cue, a series of high pitched screams erupted from nowhere in particular before three ghost-like phantoms erupted from the dust in the room. They were thin and gray of color, wrapped in tattered cloth and pallid flesh stretched across a macabre skeleton. Another creature appeared as well, twisting into a spiral. Its body was an open carcass with exposed ribs and an ethereal orange glow coming from its insides.

"Spirits!" Darina shouted.

"And a Cinder Wraith!" Trianna added as Faren and the other warriors formed a perimeter around us.

As Faren began to command the warriors to keep me safe, I was quick to call upon my mana and cast the Frozen Weapons spell, "Your blades will bite more fiercely now that they're enchanted with cold! Show them no mercy!"

Trianna let loose with a blast of flame, aimed at the Ash Wraith to keep it at bay.

The warriors set upon the spirits, three warriors to each spirit while Faren and Franklin held the Cinder Wraith at bay. Darina had enchanted the weapon of every Orodum warrior, allowing them to cut into the spectral essence of the foes. The fight was over fairly quickly. The guards dispatched the spirits with ruthless efficiency, crying out 'For the Exemplar!' and ' For House Orodum!' When the spirits were finished, all ten warriors set upon the Cinder Wraith in brutal fashion, hacking away at it while bolstering Faren's bulwark and Franklin's offensive. It was rather spectacular to watch, even if the battle only lasted about a minute.

"My word…" Patricia gasped and looked at me. "You were right. There are spirits here."

"I don't trade in lies, Lady Sulentruv," I said as I scanned the area for any more threats. "Let us move on. We don't want to linger any longer than we have to while the demon is keeping the shroud open. Faren, let's move."

"As you command, my Exemplar," Faren replied, then commanded the warriors to get back into formation.

An alcove at the back of the room opened into a massive chasm, large enough to swallow a house. I wasn't able to tell how deep the hole went even with my stone sense. A small wooden bridge was built into the wall of the chasm, leading down to another alcove. The bridge was plenty wide for dwarves, but Patricia had to watch her step. Passing through the alcove, we entered a carved hallway, at the end of which was a soft glowing magical barrier.

"Prepare yourselves," I said to everyone cautiously. "When we pass through the barrier, the demon will be waiting. It will try to sway us from our purpose here, or manipulate our minds. Do not listen to it. As soon as I give the word, cut her down. She may summon reinforcements, so I want at least four of you to stay close to Lady Sulentruv and Lady Darina. Keep them safe."

"Your safety is paramount, My Lady," Faren said.

"I have given my command, Faren," I replied. "Trianna and I can handle ourselves if push comes to shove. I want the non-combatants to be kept safe."

"As you wish, my Exemplar," Faren said. He turned to the other warriors and pointed to four of them, "I want you four keeping Lady Darina and Lady Sulentruv safe. Nothing gets close to them. The rest of you, keep the formation tight and be ready to bring swift, decisive violence down on this wretched creature."

"Aye, Ser!" the warriors responded in unison.

Franklin moved beside me and gave Faren a reassuring look, "I'll keep the Princes safe."

I continued to reserve my mana for the Frozen Weapons spell, but reserved some more of my reserves to cast Rocke Armor to give myself some additional protection. More of my mana was held for Aura of Heroism. Once my spell preparation was ready, I motioned for Faren to continue leading us forward.

We passed through the barrier and entered a large, round area built from stone bricks with several pillars supporting the weight. I had to wonder if all of the other dwarves were offended by what passed for acceptable construction of such a space as I was. The disappointment about the area's construction quickly dissolved as the demon stood up from where it had been sitting in the middle of the room. It walked over a series of puzzled tiles which would remove the barrier, but was unable to be interacted with by anything from the Dimvolmn.

The creature's face curled up in a sultry smile, its heavy voice calling out to us, "What do we have here? The wretched widow, a contingent of dwarves, and a lost little elf. Have you come to set me free?"

"I can't believe it…" Patricia gasped, "He really did summon a demon…"

"Don't act so surprised," the demon purred back. "You knew how much he lusted for power. Did you really think it was beyond him?"

"Now!" I shouted. I held my staff out and summoned a Blizzard centered at the back of the room. This would allow the effect of the spell to encompass all but the edge of the room we were in, but enough to catch the demon in it.

As the demon moved to leave the spell's effect, Trianna followed up by casting Field of Repulsion. The pulse from the spell slammed into the demon and shoved it back into the blizzard's effect.

At the same time Faren surged forward with six of the warriors joining him. I had ensured that Darina had enchanted the warrior's armor in House Orodum resisted frost magic so that they could wade through my blizzards without taking any frost damage. The warriors took full advantage of this fact as Faren rushed the demon with his shield, shoving it further into the blizzard, by flanking the demon and attacking it with coordinated strikes from high and low. The demon did what it could to ignore the blows as it worked to cast a spell of its own. Faren's shield clapped its jaw and broke its concentration, however.

Between the combination work of Faren's shield, the warrior's coordinated attacks, and Trianna and I casting spells like Rock Fist and Blast of Flame, the demon had no time to do much of anything. Still, even with the barrage of attacks and spells we threw at it, the demon held on for a full minute before we were finally able to bring it down.

"Get back!" I shouted as the demon crumpled to the floor. I canceled all the spells I had active at the moment as the dwarves quickly backed away, just in time to be out of range as the remains of the demon erupted in a ball of flame.

"By the Creator," Patricia said in stunned shock. "I had no idea…"

As soon as the fireball from the demon's death had subsided, Darina was already where it had been, scooping the remaining pile of ash into vials for testing and rambling about the possibilities it could do for her research. Faren and the other warriors fanned out to check the area while the dwarves ordered to protect Darina and Lady Patricia just sighed as Darina had bolted from their care. There really was no controlling her excitement.

I turned to check on Patricia, smiling up at her, "Are you alright, Lady Sulentruv?"

She looked down at me, fear and shock readily apparent on her face, "He really did bind a demon. I never thought…"

I pat the air to dismiss the guilt she was feeling for doubting me, "It's alright. We're happy to have been able to help. Luckily, there weren't as many spirits in the area as I thought there might be. I guess it's because we got here before things got any worse. Kind of lucky!"

Patricia was still trying to come to terms with everything that had happened in the span of just a few minutes, "Lucky? I suppose that's a matter of relativity in cases like this. Still, we owe you our thanks."

I shook my head, "I was happy to help. And I do believe we already agreed on terms for the matter. I don't suppose you wouldn't have known if the stuff down here just up and disappeared, would you?"

From what I could tell, Patricia seemed to be fighting back a scowl, "No. I don't suppose I would."

I smiled innocently. It still worked at ten years old, "And if nothing else, you can rest assured that anything down here won't continue to give you any more problems."

That seemed to seal the deal, because her expression seemed to tell me that she hadn't exactly considered that as a possibility, "How can we help get the items to you?"

"My Lady," Faren called as he made his way back to me, bowing his head before continuing, "The area's clear of any other threats. Shall we begin making our way back out?"

Turning to Faren I gave him a nod, "Yes. Send one of the men to the rest of the guards that are waiting outside of town. Let them know we're going to be packing their saddlebags full, so they need to get ready to be quick and efficient."

"As you command, My Lady," Faren responded, then turned and quickly sent one of the other dwarves to execute my instructions.

Patricia looked between Faren and myself, "Exactly how many men did you bring with you, Lady Orodum? Did you expect to walk away with all of my husband's things?"

It was Trianna's turn to speak up, "Lady Orodum had only intended to come with the dwarves you see here. The people under her command and in the city hold her in such high regard that they insisted that she bring one hundred guards. And each one you see eagerly volunteered for the chance to escort her."

"And the only thing she came for was that golem," Darina added, smiling wide as she rejoined the group, carefully packing away the vials of demon dust remains into a pouch. "She never mentioned we'd be helping to rid the place of a demon. That was just a bonus."

"A bonus that some ungrateful woman was less than pleased about fulfilling," Franklin scowled up at Petricia.

As happy as I was to have my friends come to my rescue, I still answered for myself, "I offered to do this because I wanted to keep you and your people safe. If you'll recall, I offered you my tiara if you found out that I was lying, and it was you who asked for terms if I was not lying. We dwarves are rather insistent when it comes to our contracts. My original offer was to do everything for free, then you asked what I would want if I wasn't lying."

Patricia stared at me as if she were trying to figure out just what, or who, I was, "You genuinely came here just to help us and take Gniess?"

Another innocent child's smile and nod, "I did."

She seemed to regain her composure. Her demeanor softened even as she brought herself to stand up straight once more, "Then I believe that my husband's work is a small price to pay for the good you did here today. And I have no doubt that he would find it rather exceptional that dwarves, of all people, had taken an interest in his work."

Faren and the warriors escorted us back to the surface. The rest of my warriors arrived a few minutes later and spent the next hour carefully emptying the cellar of every book, crystal, parchment, box, and object used for magical study and experimentation that they could find. Darina coordinated the effort, buzzing round the warriors like a mayfly in her excitement. She would be reading books for the next two weeks while we rode back, and would likely devour the rest of them before my birthday. Hopefully something beneficial would come from it.

While the packing effort was underway Patricia, Faren, Trianna, Franklin, and I made our way up to Gniess.

"I still don't understand how you're going to activate it without the control rod," Patricia mused.

"I wasn't planning to activate her without the control rod," I said as I pulled my sword from my staff. The control rod rested snugly in the bottom of the blade's fuller. It was just small enough to fit between the blade's fuller and the sheath. I plucked the rod from the sheath, then allowed the blade to slide back down into the staff with a crisp snap.

"You had the rod this entire time?" Patricia asked incredulously. "Why didn't you say so?"

"Did you think I would come all this way without it?" I laughed.

"Why didn't you just activate Gniess when you arrived?"

"I'm not a rude guest," I answered immediately. "And my primary concern was the demon."

"I feel like I've misjudged you, Princess Orodum," Patricia said with some regret. "I misjudged you from the very start. Can you ever forgive me?"

I chuckled and dismissed her concern, "I'm used to it, Lady Sulentruv. Forgiven, forgotten. Now, I'll have to kindly ask you to leave."

The sudden demand for her to leave seemed to fluster Patricia, "Excuse me? May I ask why?"

"Oh, because Gniess hates you," I said with a bright smile. "I mean, she *really* hates you since you were the one to convince your husband to chisel her down in size. So I'd rather not activate her only to have her try and stomp you to death."

"How did you-" Patricia began to ask, then simply shook her head and offered a curtsy. "It doesn't matter. Thank you again for your help, Princess. If there's any way we can help you in the future, you have but to ask." With that, she took her leave.

I waited until Patricia was well out of sight before approaching Gniess and held the control rod up, "Dulen harn."

It took a few moments before Gniess's form began to creak and scrape, and she was able to move freely. Her stone arms dropped to her side as she looked down... then further down until her glowing white eyes rested on me. She groaned, "Just my luck. Another mage."

I loved Gniess so much. I grabbed the flowing skirt of my gambseon and dipped into a very low curtsy, "Lady Gniess Cragmor, it is a very great pleasure to meet you."

"What?" Gniess asked in confusion. "What did it call me?"

"I called you Lady Gniess Cragmor," I answered. "That is who you are."

"My name is Gniess," she responded with hesitation, "but I don't know anything about a Cragmor. Why does it call me that?"

"It's your name, my Lady," I smiled, remaining polite. "And I am Exemplar Merida Orodum, daughter of King Triston Nordrucan, Princess of Cragmorrar."

Gniess hummed as she assessed me, "It looks like a dwarf and it has a dwarf name, but dwarves cannot be mages. Is this some sort of trick?"

"It isn't," I promised. "I am one of a few individuals who are able to… break the rules of the world. This is Faren Orodum, the head of my House Guard, Trianna of Clan Saber. We are three of the known six Origins, some people call us the Fated. We were born with vast amounts of knowledge about the world of Thoros, including its past, present, and specific events in the future."

"And it believes the knowledge it has of me is correct," Gniess asked with some scrutiny.

"I know it, my Lady," I responded confidently, still all smiles. "In fact, I went to great pains to retrieve your control rod, and traveled from Cragmorrar to free you."

"Why would it do this?" The golem continued to prod for information.

"Because, my Lady, it is our goal to stop a Scourge that will occur ten years from now," I explained carefully. "We also intend to hunt down and kill the rest of the old gods before they can be used to start more Scourges in the future."

Gniess gave a low hum of consideration. "And it believes I am an important part of its plans to be successful?"

I bowed my head. "I do, Lady Cragmor. I believe you and Exemplar Korabin will both help us succeed where we might not be able to. Only golems are resilient and strong enough to be relied upon to see us through to the end. We creatures of flesh are so easily struck down, so I look to you and yours for your aid. You and Korabin are unique amongst the golems, as only you two have kept your minds, though your memory has been lost."

"It proposes that golems fight with the dwarves and the elf? It… has the control rod, does it not? I am awake, so it must," Gniess said with no small amount of paranoia. "It can simply command me, and I must obey."

I smiled up at her and presented the control rod. "I do have it. But it will not work on you anymore. It was only useful in waking you."

"It does not work? How can I know that?" Gniess mused. "Well, go on then, out with it. Give me a command."

I shrugged and stepped forward, then pointed the control rod at Gniess. "Crush me to death."

Gniess stood in place, staring down at me. Her face was impossible to read, "And... I feel no compulsion to obey. What it says must be true. But why would it give me such a command? What if the control rod had worked? It would be dead now."

"I told you," I snickered. "I knew it wouldn't work. And what better way to show you how much faith I have in you than literally putting my life in your hands?"

"It is certainly not what I expected from a mage," Gniess responded, seeming somewhat surprised.

"Perhaps you could simply think of me as a dwarf who can use magic," I offered. "After all, anyone who can show up the mages at their own game must be better than a standard mage, yes?"

"Hey..." Trianna protested.

I looked back at her with a grin and winked.

Gniess considered that for a few moments before nodding. "I suppose I could at that. At least it isn't one of the filthy human mages. Ugh! The last one who had the control rod was a wretched creature."

"I hope you will tell me all about it," I laughed.

"I suppose I have two options, do I not?" the golem pondered. "Go with it or... go elsewhere? I... do not even know what lies beyond this village."

"May I make an attempt to sweeten the offer, My Lady?" Faren asked me, stepping up to my side.

I nodded to him encouragingly.

Faren looked up at Gniess and grinned, "Lady Cragmor, if you choose to join My Lady Orodum, she will be bringing you back to Cragmorrar. There are no birds in Cragmorrar, except ones that are dead and cooked."

"It makes the situation sound better and better!" Gniess bellowed, then looked at me. "I will follow it about, then... for now."

"Excellent!" I exclaimed, with Faren, Franklin, and Trianna giving a small cheer as well. "You have no idea how happy and honored I am to hear that, Lady Cragmor! You've made this trip well worth it!"

"This should be interesting," Gniess mused. "Will we be off, then? Or is there business yet to attend to in this dreary little mudhole?"

"My men are currently emptying your former master's cellar of all its storage," I explained lightly. "It won't take them more than an hour. If you'd like to leave the village now, we can wait for them some ways out."

"Yes," she agreed quickly. "I would very much like to put this place behind me."

We left the village of Honneleth behind with Gniess in tow. We didn't wait long for the guards to finish emptying the cellar before they returned to us, packs filled with arcane lore and items that would keep Darina busy for the next year. Or so I hoped.

Gniess was able to keep pace with the rhoarnos, so we didn't lose any time as far as that was concerned. We did stop in Cliffside for two days. I really wanted to see it! We met and had dinner with Earl Edward and Duke Tristain. That was a real treat! They were pleased to meet me as well. Apparently, they had wanted to meet the person who was responsible for increasing the trade between Falladrin and Cragmorrar.

I found out that the Surface Caste had started calling long-term contracts made with humans a Meridian Pact; named in honor of me. Apparently, things had gotten so lucrative that a Meridian Pact was the preferred method of doing business now. Guaranteed long-term gains were becoming preferential over single shipments or as-needed orders. It was rather flattering to have my people think so highly of me that they would name things that would last a long time after me.

When we returned to Cragmorrar, there was a great amount of fanfare. Apparently, people had been worrying for me ever since I left. When one of my guards rode ahead to announce our return to the gate guards, word spread throughout the outside and inside of the city like wildfire. The streets were packed with cheering dwarves who offered their well wishes, others offered goods, food, and their services. I understood that my actions had helped the dwarves considerably, but I hadn't honestly thought I was so well regarded in their minds to warrant such fanfare. It would have been a slight to refuse anything offered, so I had my guards collect the things given and make note of those who offered their services, so I could at least commission something from them.

Gniess was an inspiring sight to the dwarves, though she loathed the amount of activity as we entered the city. Still, once we'd gotten home, things were much quieter. The servants, Kara especially, fawned over me for some time and tried to figure out how to handle Gniess. In the end, Gniess would stick close to me whenever she wasn't exploring the House grounds and figuring out the lay of the land.

I had commanded our miners and smiths to have Darina's library and laboratory significantly expanded. She would need it to accommodate all of the items we'd procured for her during our trip. I also invested into a much larger stable and put out the word that House Orodum needed more warriors, more servants, and potential applicants. The trip had confirmed the practicality of some ideas I'd had and gave me a few more ideas for new efforts moving forward.

When the time to confront the scourgespawn at Orlimar and retake the lost Holds came along, I was determined that House Orodum would have a force unlike any other.

CHAPTER 9:

FROM DAUGHTER TO FATHER

Over the next few months, after returning to Cragmorrar, I busied myself with a few things. First, I met with several warrior houses and noble Houses, the ones I had the best relations with and who Faren believed had the most steadfast and talented men and women at arms. Second, I scheduled several meetings with every Caller in the Assembly to gain their help and their discretion. Third, I began visiting the market and the surface districts much more. All of this was in preparation for the upcoming year.

Father was coming up on his silver anniversary of being King of Cragmorrar. It will have been twenty-five years since Father took the throne of Cragmorrar. He was well-loved by the people and easily the most respected ruler in generations. He had sired three children, all of whom were either respected, honored, or loved. Trenton was highly respected, primarily with the nobles but also with the warrior caste. I was honored, obviously, since I was named a Exemplar and respected by all of Cragmorrar. Bilfern, while young, was well-loved by the people since I had him in my care as often as Trenton had me in his. People were wondering how amazing he would turn out to be if Trenton and I had been such promising royals.

With such an amazing track record and reputation, I believed that all of Cragmorrar owed him a great debt. I intended to see that debt paid in full with a gift unlike any other; one that would bring great honor to the name of Nordrucan, and start to fulfill my promise to the people of Cragmorrar.

Trenton and I spent more time together while preparing the gift that it almost seemed like old times when he would take me everywhere he went. It was nice, and I admit that I felt secure with him nearby. He was still a taciturn man with a stern demeanor, but the harshness of his attitude was blunted somewhat from our time together. He was no longer so quick to anger or harsh in his judgments. He had some wiggle room in his mindset now. Not much, but some. I put Trenton in charge of the planning, while I was in charge of rallying support. I had to admit his superiority in logistics, while he admitted my higher regard with the people.

My birthday came and went, with some fanfare and a bit of a surprise. Durdren and Beltia's child was born on the same day! Everyone saw it as a good sign, and I was delighted to have a 'nephew' I could share my birthday with. The baby was named Aedun, in honor of the Exemplar Nordrucan; the greatest warrior in Dwarven history.

A month before the anniversary, everything started to move into full throttle. Trenton told Father that I was going to take him to scout a few possible trade routes leading down the mountain that might be worth carving out tunnels to. He let Father know that he expected the trip to take a few weeks, perhaps a month. The Callers in the Assembly started requesting so many meetings with Father that they would keep him extremely busy for the duration of our trip. Slowly, over the last four weeks, supplies were gathered and prepared while scouts were sent out ahead.

The funny thing about being the ruler of a people is that you don't actually interact with them very much. You mostly interact with those who help you govern. In fact, you rarely even get to see your people or get out of the palace or even a few general areas. Father so rarely stepped outside of the Noble District that it was more of an event than anything else. So when the day came to leave Cragmorrar, Father was none the wiser that Trenton was leading us into the Under Roads, not the surface. He was also none the wiser that ninety percent of Cragmorrar's warriors, young nobles, scouts, smiths, servants, and Memorialists were going with us. He was also unaware of the speech that Trenton gave to everyone assembled in front of the gate that led to the Under Roads.

Trenton sat upon his rhoarno that he was borrowing from House Orodum, gazing out upon the largest force of dwarves set for battle that had been seen in Cragmorrar since the loss of the great Holds. "People of Cragmorrar. You have all answered my sister's call to collaborate in this great effort. You have answered the call of your Exemplar to honor my father, your

King, on his twenty-fifth year as ruler of Cragmorrar."

A cheer rang out across the crowd! The people loved their king, and they loved his children.

"I am honored to command this great undertaking," he continued. "As your Prince, my priority is seeing the city and its people thrive. Sadly, I cannot claim to have been as successful in my efforts as my sister. For that, I apologize. By way of apology, I have volunteered to command this great effort to ensure as many of you come back home as possible. I thank you, as your Prince and in the name of my father, for your dedication to our King. Now, my sister would like to say a few words."

I doubt many people even heard much of anything after Trenton said 'my sister' as a roar from the crowd erupted to drown them out. I actually felt bad for Trenton. He had worked so diligently his entire life to be seen as a good and dedicated prince, then he raised the person who overshadowed him in only a few short years. He wouldn't let anyone see it, but I think it hurt his pride. I offered him a thankful expression as I pulled my rhoarno up beside his and waved to the crowd.

The cheering went on for some time before I was able to speak. "People of Cragmorrar... Lords and Ladies, warriors, smiths, servants, and all. I cannot tell you how much it warms my heart to see how many of you were willing to answer our call."

Another deafening series of cheers blasted us.

"I dare say that if King Triston could see you all now, he would be truly humbled by how many of you are willing to undertake this with us," I called back. "Six years ago, I promised you that with the establishment of the Surface Caste, we would begin to take back our lost Holds. I want you to take a moment and look around you. Memorize the faces that you can see and make note of this moment. I want you to remember it, etch it into your memories."

"This will be the moment you can tell your children about," I continued, trying to add an air of importance and gravitas to my tone. "You can tell your grandchildren about how you, your friends, your people, your Prince, and your Exemplar took the very first step of the journey to make good on my promise. Your names will go into the Memorium as heroes who dedicated the first step of reclaiming the Dwarven Empire to King Triston Nordrucan! Your names will be written alongside those of nobles, royalty, and Exemplars! You! The people of Cragmorrar, will be remembered for this day as long as dwarves live, as long as etchings remain within the stone! Follow your Prince! Head his commands! Today, we leave Cragmorrar, and when we return, we will have reclaimed Nordrucan Hold!!!"

I was told that the cheers in response to my speech were so loud that Father asked what all the Rickus was about. Luckily, those left in the city were able to convince him that a truly amazing spectacle was happening at the Testament Bout Grounds.

Logan had sent me instructions on how to get to Korabin's Cross, once the largest crossroads in the Under Roads. It was southeast of Cragmorrar and connected the city with many of the lost Holds. From there, signs and directions were readily available. The Under Roads may have been mostly lost to the scourgespawn, but the scourgespawn didn't really care to ruin infrastructure. They were mostly focused on killing things.

The Under Roads were wide enough for eight rhoarnos with carts to ride side by side. Even as wide as they were, Cragmorrar's forces stretched back for a mile, and we weren't stealthy. Thousands of dwarves, most in armor, hundreds of rhoarnos, carts, and equipment caused a thunderous echo through the Under Roads. The scourgespawn knew we were here. It was true, the majority of the scourgespawn were spread throughout the Under Roads, and many more seemed to have begun the journey south, but even if this were just twenty percent of the total number of scourgespawn that were around, we had our work cut out for us.

The journey to Korabin's Cross was a little over three days from Cragmorrar if you weren't being harassed by scourgespawn. It turns out that it takes about five days if you have thousands of warriors ready and willing to cut down the scourgespawn when they harassed the convoy. scourgespawn are brave when they're in groups with superior numbers than their opponents, but hesitate to attack when outnumbered. Still, that didn't mean that we didn't attract attention.

The convoy was led by House Orodum's cavalry, nearly three hundred armored rhoarnos in tight formation. Trenton and I were kept at the center of the formation, with Faren to my left. Franklin Irono had insisted that he also accompany me as a guard; we'd spent a great deal of time together now so I assumed it was this familiarity that warranted the insistence. That, or he simply wanted to be seen with me to increase his prestige. Gniess walked along to my right, occasionally complaining about how the dwarves were crowding her, or lamenting that the rhoarnos were the better company since they at least kept quiet. I found this amusing because, by and large, no one really said anything while we traveled unless it was to relay orders for a rest, for an attack, or to announce that we were either setting up, or breaking camp.

One interesting thing about the Under Roads that I noticed was that there were the occasional series of buildings dotted along the way. Trenton explained that they used to be smaller towns; places people could rest off of the road for an evening. The towns survived by doing business with passing caravans and providing them with supplies like food, water, and shelter. Others were large inns and taverns. I admit, I had never considered that they would actually be there while playing the game, but it made sense. The distance between Holds was massive. It could be a week to walk normally between Cragmorrar and the Nordrucan Hold, which would mean that rest stops and smaller towns would be a necessity.

Following the Orodum rhoarnos were our warriors, then a thinner line of warriors on either side of the road flanking carts of materials, food, and supplies for the mission. Dwarven archers rode the carts, giving them an excellent angle to attack any scourgespawn from. This middle part of the convoy was the largest and was attacked most often. The warriors in charge of guarding it rotated between marching and riding on the carts to keep up their strength. At most, the groups of scourgespawn numbered in the dozen or so and were quickly put down. I had issued one command that all dwarves had to obey without hesitation: if a dwarf looked like they were about to be captured and pulled into the tunnel the scourgespawn had come from, all efforts were to be made to either rescue or kill the dwarf.

Scourgespawn did not reproduce exactly. They were created by female dwarves, humans, elves, and atoshi who had been infected with the blight and turned into broodmothers. These broodmothers cold spawn thousands of scourgespawn throughout their lives. So allowing any dwarf to be taken alive was not something we could afford. Pikes and shields were the weapons called for withstanding the skirmishes; keeping the scourgespawn at bay and minimizing the chance of blight infection was key.

The back of the convoy was made up of about two hundred rhoarno riders mixed with heavy infantry in case any scourgespawn got the bright idea to try and attack the cavalry from behind. This kept the front and back of the convoy as solid as possible, protecting our supplies and our more vulnerable members.

Mixed into the convoy were three regiments of the Fallen Legion: Cragmorrar's most intimidating and devastating branch of the dwarven army. Technically, the Fallen Legion answered only to the monarch, specifically my father. However, when Trenton met with their Commanders and informed them what we were planning, the Commanders argued among themselves which regiments would join us and which would stay to protect Cragmorrar. In the end, we received thirty percent of the Legion's troops to augment the small armies offered by the nobles and other castes.

When we reached Korabin's Cross on the fifth day, most every warrior had seen some action, including myself. I knew Korabin's Cross would have more significant resistance than anything we'd seen thus far. That morning, Trenton, the representatives of the noble Houses, the Legion Commanders, Gniess, Trianna, Faren, and I all met to discuss the battle plan. The Legion Commanders recommended shock and awe, charging in with the cavalry to disrupt what little organization the scourgespawn might have, then follow through with Legionnaires so that the noble forces could retain their strength. The loss of a Legionnaire might be a harder loss than the loss of a member of the warrior caste, but fighting scourgespawn is what the Fallen Legion specialized in. With a rhoarno charge disrupting the scourgespawn, the Legion Commanders believed that they would be easily cut down.

No one was about to argue with the Legion Commanders, but Trenton suggested that I help to lead the charge with my magic. The suggestion put most everyone in the meeting on edge. No one wanted me to be at risk. I did my best to assure them that I would keep my distance from any direct combat and use my magic to best assist where I could. I also explained to them that, as with the warriors of House Orodum, I'd had Darina enchant the armor of the rhoarnos with frost resistance. My warriors and rhoarnos would be able to wade through the blizzard I would cast, and the Legionnaires could charge in as the storm dissipated.

The rest of the convoy would be on high alert, ready to strike at any forces that might try to flank or flee through tunnels we hadn't noticed, or reinforce the assault as needed if Trenton gave the command.

We did our best to approach the crossroads stealthily, coming into formation a little over three hundred yards from Korabin's Cross. I was placed at the back of the rhoarno charge. I wanted to be a part of the initial assault, but Faren and the rest of my warriors insisted I be at the back so that they could take the brunt of the assault. I sat there, looking around at all of the determined faces. Franklin was on my right, Faren on my left, both of whom had insisted they stay by my side in case something happened.

Then came Trenton's call, "For Cragmorrar! For King Triston! Charge!!!"

Short, sweet, to the point. We dug our spurs into the sides of our broncos and surged forward. The warriors of House Orodum roared with ferocity, and I wish I could say that my war cry was something worthy of joining them. But at eleven years old… I doubt it did anything more than be drowned out by those around me.

The closest warriors drew their bows, launching a volley at the entrance to the crossroads, in an attempt to take out the scourgespawn manning a pair of ballistae on either side of the entrance. One of the monsters caught a few arrows and fell, but the other managed to pull the release and sent a bolt flying. The bolt miraculously sailed over the first several lines of cavalry before slamming him into the side of a rhoarno on the right side of the formation. The rhoarno and its rider fell to the wayside.

We continued forward, war cries growing louder and stronger. Once it looked like we were ready to burst through into Korabin's Cross, I stood in my saddle and lifted my staff high, calling upon my mana and summoning a blizzard at the center of the area. Wind, snow, and ice swirled in a freezing flurry, and the formation drove into it.

I could hear the sound of combat all around me, though the blizzard did have the drawback of obscuring everyone's vision outside of a few yards. The rhoarnos were putting in heavy work, mowing down scourgespawn in droves. The plan was to charge around the Cross' center pillar and move forward, crushing any scourgespawn underhoof as we left the blizzard to let the Legionnaires to mop things up. It should have only taken a minute or so to cross the distance, but that minute was interrupted by the shout of 'Ogre!' coming from somewhere to my right.

Before I could react, something slammed into my shoulder and I was sent flying from my rhoarno. I hit the ground hard, my small body bouncing and rolling across the stone. There was a loud ringing in my ears that mixed with the raging of the blizzard's winds. I was on the ground, which meant I wasn't at all safe.

I forced myself to focus, summoning my mana to call up my Stone Armor just in time as a scourgespawn sword caught me in the shoulder. The sword rang off my rock-covered pauldron and the force of the blow sent me spinning. Crying out, I planted my feet and focused my vision on the creature. It laughed and lunged at me. I quickly launched a Stone Fist spell, catching the creature in the chest and knocking it back on its heels. Before it could recover, I pulled the greatsword from my staff and charged, swinging through with all my might and lopping one of its legs off at the thigh.

The scourgespawn dropped to the stone and I quickly buried my blade into its throat. No sooner had I killed the thing than a few members of the Fallen Legion began to surround me.

"My Exemplar," a female dwarf said as she looked me over and the others formed a protective Mage Tower around me, "are you alright?"

I looked up at her and nodded, "I'll be fine. I just need to get back to my rhoarno and I'll join them for a second run."

"I don't think that will be necessary, My Lady," the dwarf explained as she looked around. "House Orodum's rhoarno charge seemed to do a great deal of damage. The Legion is mopping up the rest."

"That's good," I nodded and looked across the crossroads at what was going on. The Fallen Legion was moving across the area, killing any scourgespawn that remained somewhat alive. A few dozen cavalry chased down some fleeing monsters, but otherwise things had gone well.

Turning, I began to make my way back to the convoy, "One of my men's rhoarno was hit by a ballista bolt. I need to check on him."

"Forgive me, Exemplar, but our priority is getting you to a healer," the Legionnaire stated.

I arched a brow as I looked back at her, "What? I'm fine. Just a little shaken up is all."

"My Lady, you're bleeding, your face is covered in blood," the Legionnaire explained, holding me in place. "Please, My Lady. Sit and wait for someone to come check on you. Battle can cloud the body to the extent of its injuries, but as the fervor Dimvolmns, you'll start feeling your wounds."

I stared at the dwarf for several moments. She seemed so familiar to me. Reaching up, I wiped my brow and then looked at my hand. My gauntlet was covered in blood. She was right, my adrenaline was still telling my body to pump endorphins through me. A head injury had the potential to be much worse than what anyone could see on the surface.

I nodded in agreement, taking a seat out in the open with the Legionnaires continuing to surround me, "What's your name, Legionnaire?"

"Sidra, My Lady," she replied, bowing her head.

"Sidra?" I asked, looking up at her with a smile and chuckled. "Really? I don't suppose you'd stick close to me for the rest of this venture?"

"If that is your wish, My Lady, I would be honored," she smiled down at me.

I returned the smile and nodded.

Just then Faren and Franklin returned on their rhoarnos. Both of them quickly dismounted and ran to me.

"By the stone," Franklin gasped as he dropped to his knees before me. "When I saw that boulder hit you, I thought you were dead!"

"What?!" I shouted.

"We had to continue through the blizzard," Franklin explained. "Forgive us, but we didn't want to take the chance that our rhoarnos might crush you or the Legionnaires in the confusion."

The endorphins were slowly starting to die down and the pain from my head was beginning to creep in. I pat the air to calm their concerns, "It's fine. I'm fine. We got through it. Could someone, please, get Trianna. She has more healing spells than I do. Have her see to any of the other injured first."

"Begging your pardon, My Lady," Faren interrupted, "but if anyone heard that she prioritized anyone over you, they might just kill her. There are only a few injuries, but you take priority. You are our Exemplar. You must accept that while we are your priority, you are ours."

I sighed, giving in to the logic, "Very well."

The convoy entered Korabin's Cross, filling the old crossroads and spreading out evenly along the roads that connected it in order to spread out the defenses. Trenton was in a fury when he found out what had happened to me, but I did what I could to calm him down. It wasn't something that could be avoided, after all. Trianna healed my injuries, then moved on to the few others that had been hurt.

We made camp for the evening, and Gniess made it known that it was foolish of me to pick a fight with any kind of rock, let alone a flying one. Faren and Franklin fussed over me as I dealt with the remaining pain from my injuries. Sidra had helped me clean up after the injuries were mended.

I attended dinner with Trenton, the representatives of the noble Houses, and the Legion Commanders. We discussed the success of the assault, and I was told many times how brave I had been and how impressive it was that I had killed the scourgespawn in singular combat. I suppose it was an impressive feat for an eleven-year-old, but if any more had joined the fight, I would have been done for.

We also went over the plans for retaking Nordrucan Hold. We had the layout of the area from old maps, but what we didn't know was where the scourgespawn had dug tunnels. It was decided that the rear guard of the rhoarno cavalry would guard the entrance to the Hold, while the Fallen Legion would support the main army by stationing themselves at every tunnel we came across. With three regiments, I didn't think we'd lose too many Legionnaires to tunnel duty. Once scourgespawn had a path to a place, they rarely made another one.

The next task was clearing streets. scourgespawn never seemed to take advantage of buildings to hide or take shelter in, so urban combat wasn't going to be as bad as it could be. Still, tight quarters meant the charging in the rhoarnos wasn't going to be our best bet. We decided that the best decision was going to be checking individual streets. If the streets were clear, we'd send a rhoarno charge down it in case there were any concealed scourgespawn waiting to ambush patrols we might set up later. If we found scourgespawn, then the plan was to shower them with arrows while they charged at us because they would… then cut down the ones who managed to make it to the main force.

Trianna and I were being reserved for scourgespawn spellcasters. No one would even listen to my protests about being separated from my cavalry unit. The moment that ogre hit me with that boulder, I was no longer going to be part of an actual fight. I was a bit disappointed that I was being relegated to support, though. I hadn't been training with Trenton, Durdren, and Faren for all these years just to be told to watch and wait. I admit it was a close thing between me and that singular scourgespawn, but it would have been much more in my favor if I hadn't just been stick by a boulder and fallen nearly six feet off my rhoarno.

Still, caution was going to be the word of the day. Slow, steady, purposeful. The evening before the push into Nordrucan Hold was filled with last-minute plans and checking scout reports. Trenton had asked to speak with me once things were settled, so that had to wait till just before I went to bed.

Faren, Franklin, and Gniess escorted me to Trenton's tent.

As I arrived at Trenton's tent, one of the guards bowed, "Exemplar Orodum, it is a pleasure to see you again, and to see you in such good health after Korabin's Cross."

I bowed my head and smiled, "Your concern is touching. I'm happier that we've had so few injuries throughout the endeavor so far. Is Prince Trenton in?"

"He is, My Lady," the guard replied. "However, he requests the audience be a private one between the two of you, and asks that your entourage remain outside for the duration."

That caught me by surprise, but I wasn't going to let it show. I simply gave a polite smile and nod, "Of course. If it pleases my brother, then I'm happy to acquiesce to his request."

I turned and looked at my friends, "It seems this will be a family meeting. I hope you don't mind waiting?"

"I see no reason to listen to this little prince," Gniess protested. "But if you wish to see him alone, you only need to call if you need help."

"I doubt she will be in any danger while alone with her brother, Lady Cragmor," Franklin said, as if to remind her that we were family.

"Lord Franklin speaks the truth, my Lady," Faren added. "Lord Trenton has taken care of Lady Orodum since she was only a few days old. If she is safe with anyone, it's her brother."

"Very well, very well," Gniess grumbled. "But… if…" She looked down at me, the insinuation of her aid left hanging in the air.

I chuckled and bowed my head in thanks to the golem, "I appreciate your concern, Lady Cragmor. I truly do. I don't think I'll be too long."

I excused myself and turned, walking into the tent as the guards pulled back the flaps. As the tent closed behind me, I saw Trenton sitting at a small fire. He had a couple of chairs set out for us, as well as some cheese, meat, and nuts. I stood there watching him quietly, reminiscing on all the times he'd sat like this with me going over lessons, teaching me the ins and outs of dwarven politics, filling my head with the history of House Nordrucan and stories of our ancestors. I had come to love my brother dearly and realized just how much I missed spending time with him.

He must have known I was standing there because he reached over and patted the chair beside him, "It's rude to enter someone's room without announcing yourself. I would have thought that was one of the first lessons I taught you."

A giggle escaped me as I made my way to Trenton. I offered him a curtsy before moving to the chair and slipping into it. I grabbed a small piece of cold nug meat and ate it, "What did you want to speak about, Trenton?"

"Before I begin," Trenton mused as he stared at the fire, "I want you to know that what I'm about to tell you is not, in any way, a slight against you. Nor does it reflect any animosity on my part towards you. Do you understand?"

I didn't know why, but my insides tightened up and my spirits dropped when I heard what he said. I grew worried, and the tremor in my voice likely gave that away, "Trenton? Is… something wrong?"

He turned to me, and his smile was a mixture of pride and sorrow, "Do you know that every time I look at you, I cannot imagine having someone I could be more proud of? Even after the first few weeks that I began taking care of you, I knew that one day you would change everything. I could see it."

The fire snapped and cracked beside us. Its heat was the only thing keeping me warm at this point because I could have sworn all the blood was running from my face as my imagination ran wild, wondering where Trenton was going with all of this.

I could barely manage anything above a whisper, "I… I've only done my best to live up to your expectations, Trenton. I wanted to make you proud."

He chuckled quietly, his shoulders bouncing with amusement, "Oh, I can't imagine being more proud of anyone. You are everything I imagined you would be, and more. You have done so much for our people that I honestly believe that they should think of a higher tier of title to grant you. There is no one in this world that I hold in higher esteem than you."

"Trenton…" I whimpered, "you're scaring me. What's this about?"

"Our future," Trenton said directly.

"What?" I cried. "Trenton, please, tell me what you're talking about. You're starting to frighten me."

I must have looked terrified because he stood up and moved to my chair. He grunted as he lifted me up and hugged me. At eleven years old, I wasn't exactly scoopable anymore, but Trenton was plenty strong enough to lift me. He turned and sat down in my chair, placing me on his lap. It was actually reassuring to me to have him holding me like this again after so many years.

He leaned in and kissed my forehead where the scar from Korabin's Cross still remained. "Merida, once we have taken Nordrucan Hold, I'm going to be staying with a contingent of the Nordrucan forces that came with me."

"What?!" I yelled so loudly that one of the guards poked his head into the tent.

"My Exemplar, My Lord," the guard queried. "Is everything alright?"

"Everything's fine," Trenton barked. "Leave us."

The guard bowed his head and slipped out of the tent. When Trenton focused back on me, my eyes were beginning to well up with tears. He dabbed them away.

I tried to control myself and my volume, but the emotions were beginning to overwhelm me. "Trenton, why? Why would you stay here? You're too important to Cragmorrar to stay here!"

He smiled softly and shook his head. "I'm flattered that you still believe so, Merida, but you're smarter than that. The preparation for this venture had me at more meetings with more nobles than had bothered to speak with me for the past two years."

I stared at him, not saying a thing, curiosity plastered over my face.

"If anyone wishes to speak to a Nordrucan, they speak with Father," Trenton explained. "If they want to speak to someone influential, they speak with you. I've been regulated to the person people see if the two of you are busy or won't see them. My future is not in Cragmorrar."

I shook my head in defiance of his words. "No! You're the future king of Cragmorrar! You're the heir of House Nordrucan!"

Trenton's gentle smile never wavered, his head shook softly. "Cragmorrar isn't destined to have a king when Father finally leaves the throne. It will have a Queen. You... are undoubtedly going to be the Assembly's one and only choice for the throne. Your intelligence, your powers, your way with the people, and the way you established the Surface Caste are all reasons they'll pick you over me. And do you know what?"

"What?" I whispered, hanging on his every word.

"I hope they choose you," he leaned back. "I wish they had placed the crown on your head the day you announced the success of the Surface Caste proposal. I don't think anyone, Father and myself included, has more love and concern for our people than you do. When you decided to take this first step, I agreed to help so that I could begin securing the Hold for you. I understand you're doing this for Father, and that's what I expect you to tell him. But I'm doing this for you. So that when you are crowned Queen of Cragmorrar, the Nordrucan Hold will be ready to serve you. We'll be ready to help our Queen retake the lost Holds and reestablish the Dwarven Empire in your name."

I stared up at Trenton in wonder. I honestly had not seen this coming. Trenton had always been so stoic, so set in his path. He had the North Star in his eyes where his goals were concerned. I could always tell when he was hiding his emotions behind his sense of duty and practical nature, but this came as a surprise to even me. The idea that he thought of me so highly, that he was doing all of this with the idea that he thought of me as his Queen and was preparing to help me achieve my goals, stunned me.

"Trenton..." I muttered, my mind racing, "I... I don't know what to say to that..."

"You don't have to say anything," he patted my back gently, trying to calm me down.

I smiled sadly but leaned in to rest against him, curling up into him as best I could with my head against his chest. I closed my eyes and hugged him close, "Brother. Safe."

"Indeed, sister," he comforted me with a firm hug. "You are safe with me."

I found out that all of the exertion over the past few days, and the effort of preparing for the next day's push into Nordrucan Hold, had taken a larger toll on me than I thought. I had passed out in Trenton's arms. Faren told me that Trenton had held me for a while before he carried me back to my tent. He'd insisted on dressing me for bed since it would be the last time he could. He tucked me in and stayed with me for about an hour before returning to his tent.

I woke up to the sound of the convoy preparing for this assault of Nordrucan Hold. Sidra was sitting in my tent, waiting for me to get out of bed. She'd taken to helping me get my armor on in the mornings and eating breakfast with me, Faren, Franklin, and Trenton.

Sitting up from my bed, I looked over at the Legionnaire and smiled, "Good morning, Sidra."

She looked over at me and stood, "Exemplar, good morning. Are you ready for today?"

I shrugged as I slipped out of bed, "Ready or not, we're committed at this point."

Sidra helped me get dressed and armed. After that, we had breakfast and there was a final meeting between the leaders of the convoy. Within an hour of waking up, I was on my Rhoarno and forming up with my men.

The Holds of the Dwarven Empire were typically filled with scourgespawn since dwarves regularly tried hunting through them for relics, historical documents, or remaining treasure. We went in expecting the absolute worst. The Fallen Legion moved to the front of the formation, leading us into the Hold. A few scourgespawn met them within the first few hundred feet, but they were nothing that the Legion couldn't handle. They scouted the general area out, then opened their ranks to let Nordrucan warriors march through, followed up by House Ordum warriors and Rhoarnos (I was still placed at the back of the rhoarno formation).

We pushed into the city for three hours with small skirmishes here and there. We hadn't found many tunnels, but the Legion did as planned and stationed a squad of Legionnaires at each of them. It was surprisingly light work until we came to the old noble quarter. This section of the city was separated from the rest by a bridge that ran over a flowing river of lava. As the recognition of where I was dawned on me, someone shouted 'horde!'

My Rhoarno was several yards past the bridge when a veritable wave of scourgespawn surged toward us. Nordrucan warriors formed a shield wall ready to brace for impact as House Orodum warriors began to pepper the charging spawn with arrows from behind the defensive lines. I looked around and found that Trenton was still on the other side of the bridge. To my shock, there were scourgespawn coming from that side as well.

I was the one in charge on this side. Trenton would have to keep things handled over there.

I willed mana to flow through me so that my voice could carry over the men, "Warriors of Cragmorrar! Hold fast! On my signal, let the Rhoarnos through!"

Faren looked at me, "My Lady, you cannot charge into the horde!"

"We have to break through their ranks and give our men the chance to push further forward," I barked. "We have our backs to a bridge that's full of warriors, and a river that will cook us if we're pushed back. We don't have a choice!"

"She's right," Franklin said, backing up my decision. "We'll just have to do our best to keep her and Trianna safe."

My personal wards and buffs had been up since that morning, but now was the time for some offensive magic. I weaved a few instances of Walking Bomb on scourgespawn a few ranks behind those actively engaged with our frontline. Since those were the monsters still being hit with arrows, I just had to wait for one to drop.

The first scourgespawn finally fell to my spells, and it set off a chain reaction. Walking Bomb's primary effect triggered upon its death and the scourgespawn exploded, causing magical energy to burst from it. The explosion killed several scourgespawn around it, including another which had Walking Bomb affecting it. The domino effect happened in the span of two seconds, but in those two seconds, dozens of scourgespawn exploded and died, causing a few moments of confusion and hesitation from the ranks of monsters that were close to it.

"Make a hole!!!" I cried out. "Bronto's, charge!!!"

"For the Exemplar!" came the cry of hundreds of House Orodum cavalrymen.

We surged forward, thunderous hooves beating into the stone. We flew past the dwarven ranks and into the waiting sea of scourgespawn. By the time my rhoarno broke through the dwarven line, the stone was covered in the blood and broken bodies of the monsters. This time, I put myself behind my men, adhering to their wishes. Standing up in my seat, I cast a Blizzard as far out as I could, while Trianna, who rode by my side, summoned a Tempest.

The foot soldiers charged forward after the rhoarnos pushed past them, cutting down the shocked and confused scourgespawn that were left after the explosions, gaining ground that we made for them. They moved up a solid twenty yards before they began to reform their lines. As the lines were reforming, the cavalry turned in a wide arc to return back behind the warriors.

Trianna and I busied ourselves hurling spells to keep the horde from reforming too easily against our rear flanks. Normally, this would be a job for a dozen mages, but the streets of the Nordrucan noble district helped to funnel the scourgespawn in such a way that we were able to handle the job ourselves. Between my Blizzard and Trianna's Tempest spells, a solid portion of the open street was covered in dangerous magic.

Franklin, Faren, Trianna, Sidra, and I regrouped with the other rhoarno cavalry. Gniess was busy at the front lines, literally crushing the scourgespawn underfoot.

"Get back in formation!" I commanded, looking around quickly to assess the situation.

We'd gained twenty yards, and forces from the other noble houses were pushing through, including House Orodum's scout forces led by Petra.

Some of the Fallen Legion were beginning to push over the bridge as well.

As the cavalry reformed, I turned my rhoarno so that I could move toward the dwarves joining us. The leaders that made it over looked to me for my orders.

"Scouts and archers, move to the sides and take cover where you can," I shouted. "I want long arcs, weaken them as they try to get to us! Heavy infantry will join the line and reinforce the front. Give your brothers some time to breathe!"

One of the Legion Commanders waved at me, "Do you want us to push through, Exemplar?"

I shook my head and pointed to a series of alleys we had managed to push past, "No, Commander. I need you and your men to work through the alleys; make sure there aren't any shrieks or cloaked scourgespawn waiting to ambush us. If you can, use the alleys to flank the enemy and use hit-and-run tactics. Make them fear being too close to the buildings. I want them funneled into our magic and rhoarnos."

The Commander understood the gravity of what I was asking him to do. The alleys would be dangerous. The combat would be in tight quarters, and they would likely take heavy losses if groups of scourgespawn were there waiting to ambush anyone. But that was what the Fallen Legion was for… they served Cragmorrar as they did because each one of them had already had a funeral and considered themselves dead already.

"It will be done, my Exemplar," he bowed his head before turning and barking orders at his soldiers.

I pulled the reins on my rhoarno to guide it back to the cavalry formation, looking to my friends for support. "Prepare for another charge!"

The order was passed forward to the front line with a series of relaying shouts.

Sidra's face was set and determined, seeing that I was trying to keep my mind off of having sent stone knew how many dwarves to their death with the order I'd given the Legion Commander. "Don't second-guess yourself,

My Lady. The strategy is sound, and someone needed to do it. It's good that you sent the Legion. They'll know how to handle it."

"I hope so," I growled at myself. On my signal, Trianna summoned another Tempest as I brought forth a Blizzard.

Another series of Walking Bomb incantations went off, and we charged forward once again.

The battle in the noble district lasted seven bloody hours. The rest of the day was spent clearing the rest of the city with the occasional skirmish here or there. The day was long and arduous, and no one ended it without some kind of injury.

The surviving leaders, and the replacement leaders for those who died, met after camp was set. It was a somber meeting. We'd lost half a regiment of Legionnaires, and a little over two hundred warriors. Close to a thousand dead; around five percent of our total number.

That was the bad news.

The good news was that we'd cleared Nordrucan Hold. The losses we suffered were nothing compared to the scourgespawn dead. Rough estimates put the total at around seven thousand dead scourgespawn, with a good number of ogres among them.

The new Legion Commander who was field promoted after the battle in the noble district said that we should be proud of the work done that day. I would have been more proud if I could have heard that praise from his predecessor.

The next few days were all about cleaning up the bodies of the scourgespawn, basically all of which were thrown into the lava rivers. While the men cleared the scourgespawn dead, the Fallen Legion scouted the tunnels. Trianna focused on using her magic to heal who she could, while I helped seal the tunnels the Fallen Legion had found with my magic to mold the stone, but making sure the walls were more reinforced this time around with cross-sectioned wrought iron bars.

On the third day, Legion scouts reported finding a broodmother down one of the tunnels that hadn't been sealed yet. Apparently, it was trying to flee the area, albeit slowly. Trianna and I were asked to help kill it since we could use magic. I suggested the overkill option by bringing every remaining warrior of House Orodum, as well as a full regiment of Legionnaires.

Apparently, two thousand soldiers were more overkill than they preferred, but the number of scourgespawn guarding the broodmother proved me right. We only lost a handful of Legionnaires to the creature, but that was worth the price of killing a broodmother that could spawn thousands of her ilk if left alone.

On the fourth day, I took the morning to retrieve the Shield of Nordrucan as the forces who weren't going to be staying in the Hold prepared to leave. True to his word, Trenton stayed, along with his men and a few dozen nobles, along with their forces, retainers, and households. Those who would remain would clean up Nordrucan Hold and get it up and running to become a functioning city once again. One of the Legion regiments decided to stay as well; to protect Trenton and those who remained, and to create a new base that was well outside of Cragmorrar that they could operate out of.

The way back to Cragmorrar took a few days less than the trip to Nordrucan Hold. That was mostly because we weren't being attacked by scourgespawn. We could have made better time, but we stopped at every tunnel entrance that wasn't dwarven made and sealed it the same way we did the ones in Nordrucan Hold. The remaining full regiment of Fallen Legion were split along the interspersed inns and towns that we passed so that they could help clean them up, prepare them for merchant caste and warrior caste families so that the route to Nordrucan Hold could be secured. The last regiment, which had taken the most casualties, escorted us the rest of the way home.

We arrived back three days before Father's Silver Anniversary. Cragmorrar was abuzz with our return, but the Callers and nobles knew better than to say anything about what we'd accomplished. Instead, those who needed to prepared for the anniversary celebration. I had already done what I needed to do on the way home, so I took those three days to sleep, rest, and stood for a fitting for my artisans who were preparing a new outfit for me to wear for the celebration.

On the day of the Silver Anniversary, I arrived at the palace at the time Trenton typically would. I wore a black gambeson coat tailored to resemble a courtier's dress, with a brass symbol of House Nordrucan clasped to the right sleeve cuff, and a brass symbol of House Orodum clasped to the left sleeve cuff. The rest of the gambeson sported polished steel studs with the symbols of House Nordrucan and House Orodum. In my hair, I wore golden thread weaved into my braids.

I greeted Father and Mother as they left their bedroom.

Father stopped in his tracks and gave a clap. "Merida! Oh, I'm so glad you were able to make it back in time for the anniversary!" He moved in to wrap me up in a firm hug, which I happily returned.

"Where's your brother, Trenton?" he asked, glowing with fatherly pride. "This is a day the whole family should be together."

I smiled, stepping back. "He's at home right now. We've been working on your anniversary present."

"Oh!" Father chuckled. "You shouldn't have bothered with all that. Having all of my children with me would be present enough."

"Nonsense," Mother chimed in. "If they've gone to the effort, you should be grateful. Now, weren't you going to grab Bilfern so we could have breakfast?"

"Ah, I did promise to bring him to breakfast this morning," Father remembered. "Forgive me, Merida, but I'll see you at breakfast, yes?"

I bowed my head. "Of course, Father. Tell Bilfern I got him a present that I'll give him tomorrow after the celebration has died down. That might put some pep in his step."

Father laughed as he went to fetch Bilfern.

I looked at Mother, who smiled at me. "I take it you were successful?"

I nodded and joined her as we walked to the dining room. "We were. Not without losses, of course. But it's done, and the Legion is securing the route to and from even as we speak."

"You weren't injured, I hope," Mother asked.

"Nothing too bad," I bent the truth a bit with that one. "Nothing permanent, anyway. I'm here, though, and that's all that matters."

"What about Trenton? Why isn't he here?" she asked, a bit of concern growing in her voice.

"He decided to stay in Nordrucan Hold," I reassured her. "He… wanted to get it up and running."

"He wanted to get out of your way, you mean," Mother observed.

I paused during our walk and looked up at her, surprised that she had seen through my explanation and Trenton's motivations. "……Yes…"

She stepped up to me and gently rested a hand on my cheek. "Oh, Merida. I hope you know he wasn't angry with you. Trenton wants what's best for Cragmorrar and her people. He was sure he was what was best for the city for a while, and he acted accordingly. But I could see it in him when he realized that was no longer the case. He changed, but it might have taken his mother to notice it."

She moved her hand to the small of my back to guide me softly and encourage me to keep walking. "He understood that you were Cragmorrar's future early on, and instead of working to be the best Prince he could be, he worked to make you the best Princess you could be. Him staying in Nordrucan Hold is his way of saying that you're ready to take on the role of Cragmorrar's next leader, and that you no longer need him. If I know Trenton, he's likely preparing the city to serve you."

I couldn't believe how accurate she was in her estimation of the situation. Her insight and understanding into her children was astounding. She had always been insightful, but I hadn't ever considered how well she knew us. As a queen, Mother wasn't able to spend as much time with us as a normal mother would. Meetings, diplomacy, and other responsibilities kept her away from us a majority of the time. Still, she had somehow managed to get to know us so well over the years.

I chuckled quietly. "It's like you were there…"

We entered the dining room and sat down, continuing our discussion for a few minutes until Father arrived. Bilfern sat next to me, and we talked throughout breakfast. Father tried dragging the meal on in an attempt to delay the festivities. He knew this would be the quietest, most relaxing part of his day. I didn't let him, though. With Trenton gone, I was responsible for keeping on schedule.

I had him, Mother, and Bilfern prepared to leave the palace by eight that morning. Father mentioned how strange it was that he hadn't received any well-wishers or guests so far. I tried assuring him that everyone was probably preparing their gifts for such a large anniversary. Nordrucan warriors formed behind us as we exited the palace to a completely empty Noble District.

Father looked around, paranoid. He knew something was up at this point, "Merida? What's going on?"

I smirked up at him. "I told you, Father, everyone's preparing your gifts. I'm going to give you mine first, though."

"What are you up to?" he asked.

"Just follow me," I said as I led them toward the entrance to the Noble District. Instead of leaving the district, I guided my family to the stairs that went up to an overlook where you could see most of Cragmorrar from.

I approached the guardrail of the overlook and waved my arm for my family to approach. When Father stepped forward, his gasp of surprise was drowned out by all of Cragmorrar cheering for him. Every single citizen of Cragmorrar, apart from my family and the guards who escorted us, crowded into the market district to present themselves to their king.

I allowed the cheers to go on for a few minutes before raising a hand, calling for silence.

The cheers died down and I stepped forward, "People of Cragmorrar! You have all worked together to celebrate the twenty-fifth anniversary of

King Nordrucan's rule!"

More cheers rose from below.

I turned and looked at Father, still keeping my volume high enough for those below to hear me, "Not only have we all come together to cheer for you, My King, we have also worked together in the last few months to give you a gift from each and every one of us. Every merchant, every smith, every warrior, artisan, and servant, every member of the Surface Caste contributed to this gift in one way or another. On behalf of every dwarf in Cragmorrar, on this, your Silver Anniversary, I grant you the gift of Nordrucan Hold! Ready and reclaimed by your subjects!"

The roar of the dwarven citizenry was unlike anything I had ever heard. The look on Father's face was something I'll never forget.

Before he responded, I continued, "And what would Nordrucan Hold be without a Nordrucan to rule it? In your name, Prince Trenton Nordrucan has taken his rightful place in Nordrucan Hold, and has begun leading the effort to reestablish the Hold's industry and commerce. The road to the Hold has been secured by the Fallen Legion, and all of Cragmorrar contributed to its reclamation. All in your name! In the name of King Triston Nordrucan!"

The roars echoed throughout the city.

"And as proof of this great undertaking…" I motioned for one of the guards to approach with an item wrapped in cloth. I took it and unwrapped it, holding it up for the people, and Father, to see. "I present to you the Shield of Nordrucan! Wielded by Exemplar Nordrucan himself, kept in Nordrucan Hold, and only obtainable by one who wears a Nordrucan signet ring!"

The roar was at a fever pitch. Father took the shield and seemed lost for words. For the rest of the day, I escorted him through the festivities. We went through raucous market celebrations, games, and attended one of the fiercest Testament Bout tournaments I'd ever seen. We stopped at several impromptu feasts and spoke with dozens and dozens of Cragmorrar's citizens.

People begged Father to accept gifts that their families had bought or made for them. Father accepted every gift, with the guards taking them and holding onto them. Father enjoyed the appreciation of his subjects through the late afternoon. The guards watched over him the entire time, while I was asked to speak with people as well. I tried my best to speak with whomever I could while still making the day about Father. In fact, to make sure my time speaking with others didn't take too long, I volunteered to take care of Bilfern so I could always use the excuse that I had to keep him with Father and Mother.

When we finally returned to the palace, there was a massive dinner waiting for us with family, friends, the Callers, and other nobles waiting for us. We feasted and made merry for a few hours before everyone finally left. By that time, I had already put Bilfern to bed, and I was ready to go home myself.

However, Father had asked to see me. Tired as I was, I wouldn't refuse his request. I came to Father and Mother's quarters and knocked on the door.

Mother opened it and welcomed me in, "Merida. Thank you for coming. Your father was hoping you'd join us."

"I can't refuse when Father asks for me on his anniversary," I smiled as I entered their chambers.

"So dutiful," Father said from the sofa. He'd made himself comfortable.

I approached him and lowered myself into a curtsy, "Father? You wished to speak with me?"

"I did," he replied as Mother sat next to him. "Or rather, we did, I should say."

I looked between my parents curiously, "May I ask what for?"

Father nodded and leaned forward, "Merida, your mother and I have been speaking about Trenton's decision to stay in Nordrucan Hold."

"His decision seems to have been more of a surprise to me than it was to Mother," I offered.

"Your relationship with Trenton made it a surprise," Father chuckled. "Frankly, the decision surprised me as well. Thankfully, your mother is more astute than either of us when it comes to the hearts and minds of our family. However, that isn't the point. The point is, I concur with your mother's intuition and your brother's decision."

Father stood and moved over to me, placing a hand on my shoulder. His expression was a mixture of affection and resignation. "In light of Trenton's decision, I have decided to name you my heir."

My eyes widened in shock. "Father…"

He interrupted me. "Understand that this doesn't guarantee you the throne and does not grant you rule over Nordrucan Hold. What it does do is make you the head of House Nordrucan until Bilfern comes of age if I should pass before then. It also signals to the assembly that I would name you as the next ruler of Cragmorrar."

"As you know," Mother added, "the Assembly chooses the ruler of Cragmorrar after the current ruler's passing to the stone. For the past few generations, a Nordrucan has been chosen. In light of your accomplishments and with the love our people have for you, we have no doubt that you will be chosen to rule after your father."

"Naming you as my heir shows how much faith I have in your future leadership," Father smiled. "My daughter, I am so proud of you. And I'm so very thankful. You've brought our people together in a way I never could to make good on your promise to retake the lost Holds… and you rallied them all to dedicate that first step to me. I cannot thank you enough."

We talked for a while longer until I started to nod off. Father asked some of the guards to escort me home. When I finally got to bed, I slept hard. The social and emotional drain on top of my physical exhaustion from the mission to Nordrucan Hold, which I still hadn't recovered from, knocked me right out the moment my head hit the pillow. We had all achieved our goal. We had surprised Father and recovered Nordrucan Hold.

That first step had been a doozy.

CHAPTER 10:

FORWARD MOMENTUM

The next six years were intense. After Father's announcement that I would be his heir, there were a number of things to be done. I had to be acknowledged by the Assembly as a formality. I had to undergo a number of practical lessons about how to conduct myself as the heir, not that they taught me anything I hadn't already learned from Trenton. I also had to attend more meetings that were pertinent to Cragmorrar's governance so that I could be aware of everything going on with the overall politics in case something happened to Father. I had to be able to at least be the interim leader until the Assembly could vote on the next ruler.

Truth be told, almost everyone had been treating me as the heir even before the announcement. Trenton's move to Nordrucan Hold had created a shift in political power. It allowed the unspoken assumption of me overtaking my brother in the eyes of the nobles to be spoken aloud. It surprised me how quickly the change came. Even on the trip back from Nordrucan Hold, the nobles had begun trying to curry more favor with me. I was used to the obsequious behavior because I was a Exemplar, but now that I was named the heir, that treatment rose to a ridiculous level. Now, whenever I met with a noble for the practical purposes of securing materials, manpower, or assistance in acquiring something they specialized in, they were overly eager to acquiesce and offer more than I needed. While it was helpful, it was also rather irritating. The blatant brown-nosing was…off-putting.

Two years after the reclamation of Nordrucan Hold, I convinced Father to let me lead another expedition to retake Petran Hold. The goals for this expedition were threefold: retake the Hold so that it could become another thriving city, it could help me prove that Petra's family were nobles, and it would get us closer to Cragmor Hold. This expedition went smoother than the effort to retake Nordrucan Hold. There were fewer scourgespawn, and we'd made sure to scout every step of the Hold itself carefully instead of just marching in with confidence. To be fair, though, the whole marching in with confidence thing was done on Trenton's insistence.

While we were there, we found the papers which proved that Petra and her family were actually nobles. Since I knew this would happen, I had been sure to insist on bringing lesser noble Houses who would be keen to help her reestablish her noble House as a favor to me, of course. In the end, Petra ended up as the Caller representative of House Petran in Cragmorrar while the rest of her family remained in Petran Hold to focus on rebuilding it and getting it back into a productive state.

Because they weren't an established House in Cragmorrar, I allowed Petra to continue staying in House Orodum. I also used the research I'd done on all of Cragmorrar's families back when I was trying to convince them to establish the Surface Caste to find all of the debts that the families owed to House Petran. The debts owed could never be defaulted on since they'd been recorded in the Memorium memories. The amount owed was enough to start work on getting a new house worked on in Cragmorrar, with a little left over to send to Petran Hold. The establishment of the Hold would be slower going than Nordrucan Hold, but over the next few years, it would start to flourish. Petran Hold had a strong river flowing through it, which meant it was a valuable source of fresh water filled with delicious, healthy minerals and fish. Proximity to the river also meant that they would have excellent soil to grow crops.

As thanks for my aid in retaking the Hold and raising her family back into nobility, Petra agreed to take Faren as her husband when they were both of age. Faren agreed to the match as long as he could remain in Cragmorrar and remain my personal guard. Normally a Warrior Caste member wouldn't be able to marry into a noble family without a great deal of payoffs, but when I was named a Exemplar and established House Orodum, I chose who would become part of my family. Faren, Rita, and Kara were all chosen. This made them nobles in the eyes of the Memories, and so they were able to marry up if given the chance.

Not long after we retook Petran Hold, Mother began to grow ill. Father began to spend less time in the Assembly and more time with Mother. Trianna tried every healing spell she could muster, but to no avail. We even brought in some mages from the Mage Tower, but they couldn't help either. The Surface Caste came through for us in the end. The contacts and networks of the Surface Caste managed to find a physician who was able to find a treatment for her. Unfortunately, all the physician could do was treat the disease's symptoms. He was unable to cure her. She was able to hold on for just a few more months than she normally would have been able to, and I took full advantage of the time, visiting her every day. The visits took up time I should have been using to prepare for things, but I didn't care. I wanted to have as many memories of her as possible.

Mother died in her sleep three months before my fifteenth birthday. The city mourned her death. She was beloved by the people for her kindness and fair treatment of others. Father, Brehlen, and I traveled with a large following of mourners to Nordrucan Hold where she was entombed; a tradition we could practice again now that the Hold had been recovered. Her loss hit father hard, and I took over some of his duties for a few months.

Following Mother's loss, I also took Bilfern into my permanent care. Father simply wasn't up to it after Mother passed. I took a different approach with Bilfern than Trenton had with me. Instead of just taking him to lessons, I would take Bilfern with me to all of my meetings and everywhere else I went. I taught him his lessons in between meetings as we walked and in the evenings after dinner. I also had Darina begin teaching him about enchantments. Bilfern would need something to set him apart from myself and Trenton, and I thought that if he could learn enchanting, he would bring House Nordrucan a unique talent. In truth, I wanted a second enchanter to call upon.

In the end, Bilfern would begin seeing me more like a mother than a sister. He was only four years old when Mother died, and those memories of her would quickly fade. To avoid them from disappearing completely, I had several dozen portraits of her commissioned before her death. The portraits were of various sizes, some small enough to fit into lockets, others large enough to hang on the walls.

I took advantage of the time that I filled in for Father to prepare for another expedition. This time we would be focused on retaking Cragmor

Hold. This was something I wanted to do for Gniess. It would also put us much closer to the Soul Smith. There were some who questioned who would take control of the Hold once it was retaken, but I had no illusions that it would be Gniess.

Each time we marched to retake a Hold, the city would bustle with excitement and wish us well. Our tactics were refined with each outing. With the way things were going, Cragmorrar's warriors were getting better and better at fighting the scourgespawn. This time, however, we took back Gniess's home. There were more scourgespawn in Cragmor Hold than there had been in Petran Hold, likely because it was further south, which is the direction most of the scourgespawn were headed as the time of the Scourge closed in. We encountered another small horde similar to the one we'd fought in Nordrucan Hold, but this time losses were a mere fraction of what they had been that first time. We had learned from our mistakes, adapted our strategies, and improved our combat skills against the scourgespawn.

Once we'd taken the Hold, the nobles who had joined us in the effort began to petition me to name them as the new rulers of Cragmor Hold. I called a meeting of the nobles who were present and informed them that Gniess was actually Gniess Cragmor of House Cragmor and was the rightful heir to Cragmor Hold. Since she was the only remaining member of her House, Gniess was granted special dispensation to choose members of her House as if she were a Exemplar.

At first, Gniess couldn't care less about the matter until I showed her the monument to the dwarves who had volunteered to become golems for the sake of all dwarves. When she saw her name on the monument, something inside her struck home. Her investment in seeing the place brought back to its prime solidified, and she worked diligently with me to pick members for her House from the nobles present. We also discussed the golem monument together for some time. I tried to convey to her that the creation of a golem was a precious and noble gift, and that every volunteer who became a golem gave their life to ensure the preservation of dwarven society. They were the physical manifestation of dwarven honor and duty. Without the golems, there might not even be a dwarven society left.

Gniess remained in Cragmor Hold after it was retaken, intent on turning the place into a living monument to the sacrifice of the dwarves. The nobles and other families from the various castes who stayed with her had to swear their loyalty to Gniess before the remaining Houses who hadn't been chosen, as well as myself. If they ever tried to betray Gniess, they knew that House Orodum and the others would march on Cragmor for a far more sinister reason. In the end, Cragmor Hold had a healthy starting population with the right people to get things up and running.

I considered trying to push through to Korabin and the Soul Smith, but I figured that trying to convince Korabin not to destroy the anvil wouldn't be as effective as it would be after the Scourge. Korabin just wanted the anvil destroyed and to have the chance to finally die himself. I needed him alive and the anvil functioning, at least for the foreseeable future. My thought process was that I could convince him to help us if we proved we could handle the Scourge. After all, if we could do that, we would obviously be capable enough to hunt down the remaining old gods and kill them before they were able to be used to start more Scourges.

I believed that using that reasoning, I could convince Korabin to help us… at least until after the old gods were handled. It was true that there were other threats out there other than the old gods, but the dwarves were particularly suited for dealing with this problem.

When I returned to Cragmorrar after helping Gniess settle in, I made it my purpose to prepare to leave for Orlimar. I sent scouts to Orlimar to get its actual layout, building plans, and detailed maps of the topography in a thirty-mile radius of the fort, with an emphasis on cave systems. I began to bring in engineers and military strategists. I needed to get an idea of how we could fortify the fort and strike at the scourgespawn. I remembered that the fort had underground tunnels, so we would need to secure those against scourgespawn tunnelers. We'd also need a way to quickly flank the monsters so that they couldn't retreat. Last but not least, we needed a way to bring the Archdemon to the ground so that the Scourge Sentinels would be able to kill it.

It's true that the archdemon didn't show itself at Orlimar in the game, but I had a theory about why that was.

Stone, metal, wood and more were needed. I wanted to have basically everything we would need for the plans we were making by the time we left Cragmorrar. House Orodum would bring everything we could to aid against the Scourge, and everything we needed to do the work we had planned. I insisted that the engineers work out how efficiently they could get the work done. This meant that they needed to have work schedules set out for round-the-clock building, places to set materials with efficient routes to get them to where the work was being done. We planned on which places to reinforce, which places to build new fortifications, and where to dig to allow our forces to pop up behind the scourgespawn lines.

The military leaders helped me plan how to defend the fort and flank the scourgespawn. I insisted we make the plans with the assumption that we would not receive any assistance other than a handful of Scourge Sentinels. This way we could be sure of our success when we were joined by the human forces. Every plan we made was with the assumption that there would be sixty thousand scourgespawn on the field as well as the Archdemon. We ran military exercises with these numbers in mind. We refined the plans over and over and tested them again and again.

By the time my seventeenth birthday was coming up, we could have waged the battle in our sleep.

Franklin and I spent more time together during this period than we ever had before. We were together almost daily. He volunteered to do a lot of the running around between different meetings for me so that I didn't have to be bothered with refreshing information, confirming troop numbers, or ensuring supply shipments. More often than not, he slept in House Orodum, and it wasn't uncommon for us to spend the days together from breakfast to dinner. Over those years, he became more than a friend in my eyes, and I found myself falling in love with him. His steadfast loyalty and determination to support my efforts were flattering. I couldn't help but open my heart to him.

CHAPTER 11:

ON TO ORLIMAR

The day of my seventeenth birthday was rather surreal. I woke up knowing that the very next day I would be leaving Cragmorrar for at least three years, and I might not come back alive. It was strange to think that this new home of mine had grown on me so much after everything that had happened.

Still, I was now a fully grown dwarf. I was a bit taller than Kara at this point and was slightly tall for a female at four foot six inches. Faren was four inches taller than I was, a mountain of a dwarf if you'll excuse the pun. Trianna was a foot taller than I was. I had to wonder how much taller Serena was now after these last few years apart.

It's strange what you think about when you know that things are about to drastically change for the foreseeable future.

Kara had made sure that I was treated to my favorite breakfast foods and had surprised me by inviting Father, Bilfern, Rita, Veron, Durdren, Beltia, Aedun, and Petra to join Faren, Trianna, and I in the meal. Franklin wasn't there, which disappointed me, but otherwise, it was like a small, private birthday celebration. The day had also become known as The Medarius, a new dwarven holiday celebrating the birth of the Surface Caste.

Rick and Beltia had worked together tirelessly to craft me a new suit of armor: black as the knight with crushed ruby powder on the chest in the symbol of House Orodum, an anvil with six stars surrounding it. They worked with Darina to have her enchant the armor against cold, fire, and poison.

Father had continued Mother's tradition of having a new garnet gambeson created for me. This one had silver thread and golden studs with the symbol of House Orodum stamped into them. The collar was raised and came up to my jawline. If I wore it without my armor, it was designed to look like a professional gown and helped to cut an impressive figure.

Trenton and Ninta had married the year before, and Ninta had moved to Nordrucan Hold. They had sent their regards with a messenger who'd brought a present. Trenton had another staff made for me, tall enough for my adult height. He'd learned from the last design and ensured that the 'staff's' handle was thin enough for me to grip properly and had a bit of a crossguard where the two pieces met. The staff itself was made from stained hazel wood, and the mages at the Mage Tower had ensured it would increase my mana reserves and enhance elemental damage that I cast. He had the blade made of white-blue silverite and had Darina enchant it with cold, fire, and lightning damage.

Rita and Veron probably did the best by far. The box they gave me was no larger than a simple ring box, but inside it was a gem-like phylactery. They warned me that something spoke to those who touched it. Veron had remembered me mentioning it one day when I was speaking with Darina. He had hired dozens of adventurers to search for the thing. As soon as I touched it, flashes of memories and a voice cried out to me. I assured the spirit trapped within that I would help it if it would teach me its skills. While it would take some time, I would ensure that it was set free. It seemed content with the exchange.

Petra gave me a journal to write about my time in Orlimar. The binding was beautifully red stained leather, with black inlaid pictures of House Orodum and House Nordrucan symbols. There was also an ornate inkwell and feather pen that went along with it. The journal was thicker than my arm. Petra was sure the Memorium, and Cragmorrar's citizens, would want an exhausting record of the events. I promised that I would write in it every day.

Faren and Trianna had commissioned an artisan to craft a set of jewelry for me. In all, it was a tiara, earrings, a necklace, and a ring. Each bore the symbol of House Orodum. The ring had an inscription on the inside of it which said 'Fate brought you to us'.

Franklin arrived with a messenger from Cragmor Hold just as we were finishing our private celebration.

The messenger explained that Gniess hadn't even considered sending a gift until the nobles who had joined her House convinced her to. Once they convinced her, she had ordered some of her craftsmen to forge a smithing hammer for me, though she had apparently insisted that if it could be used to shape metal, it could be used to crush heads as well. So she had a belt with a loop on it to carry the hammer fashioned for me as well. I thanked the messenger and asked that he tell Lady Cragmor that I would keep it at my side always. As proof, I put the belt on right then, and slipped the hammer into its loop.

As the messenger took his leave, I rushed over to Franklin and slipped my arms about his neck to hug him close, "I was wondering why you weren't here."

He hugged me in return, his embrace warm, comforting, and secure. He smiled down at me with the most doting expression.

"Merida," he called me by my first name with no 'Lady' or 'Exemplar' title attached. This wasn't uncommon since we were friends, but it was the first time he'd done so around others. He would always keep to etiquette in the company of other people.

"We have been good friends for years now," he began. "House Irono has been a friend and ally to House Nordrucan for generations, and I have done my best to foster that friendship through to House Orodum after you were named an Exemplar. I believe that we have grown close over the years, and that more than friendship has blossomed between us; though events have kept us too busy to properly explore that connection."

He risked a glance at everyone else in the room before pulling a beautifully carved wooden box from his pocket. He moved to one knee and opened the box. Inside was a pear-cut emerald that had been shaped and polished in a way that reflected light and color in a dazzling display. The ring it was attached to was some of the warmest color rose gold I had ever laid eyes on. It was inlaid with silverite depictions of various flowers, the petals of which were colored with fine dust from precious stones.

A hand subconsciously rose to my mouth in disbelief. The ring was beautiful beyond measure, but Franklin's intent astounded me.

"I freely admit that I have fallen in love with you," Franklin continued. "I understood it for certain six years ago when you fell onto the ogre's boulder and my heart sank for the fear of losing you. Since that day, I have wrestled with my feelings and did my best not to pressure you into reciprocating them while you were busy with your plans. I believe you hold strong feelings for me, just as I do for you."

He took my hand gently and slid the ring onto my finger. The fit was perfect.

"But now, the planning is done and tomorrow we set out to see those plans come to fruition," Franklin said with a growing, but managed, desperation in his voice. "So, I ask you now: will you take my hand in marriage?"

I can safely say I wasn't the only one in the room who was surprised by the proposal. Usually, this would have been done through offers from family members, with dowries and negotiations that could go on for months. Franklin was the head of a now-prominent noble family, and I was the head of a new and highly-regarded noble family. A proposal between two such families could easily take a year or more to iron out.

This, though? As far as I was aware, something like this between two people of such high stations was unprecedented.

I was at a loss for words and stared down at him, unaware that my cheeks had flushed red, tears had begun to well up in my eyes, and a smile had crept up onto my features. I didn't know how to answer, and apparently, I had been keeping everyone in suspense for longer than they could handle.

"Merida?" Father called gently from behind me.

I turned my head to look back at him.

"Answer the man," he encouraged me softly.

I looked down at Franklin, whose hopeful eyes gazed up at me. I sniffled a bit before quietly nodding, "Yes, Franklin. Yes, I will marry you."

My friends and family cheered and clapped excitedly as Franklin leapt up and took me into an excited, warm embrace. He easily hoisted me off my feet and spun me about in a joyous hug.

"You don't have to worry," he reassured me as he set me back on the floor. "My brother is ready to become the head of House Irono. I am happy to be a part of your House."

Father chuckled as he approached us and placed a hand on Franklin's shoulder. "I hope you've planned out an impressive dowry, my boy. There are those in Cragmorrar who would give all they had, and more, to ensure a match with my daughter."

It turned out that Franklin had indeed thought of a dowry to offer. Unlike in other cultures, it wasn't necessarily the woman's family who paid the dowry. Dwarven culture dictated that it was the lesser family that paid dowries to the higher-ranked family. In this case, it was House Irono that would have to pay. Franklin had ensured that House Irono would become a vassal House to House Orodum. It essentially guaranteed that all of House Irono was subject to House Orodum; its materials, gold, and manpower was mine to call on as I saw fit. He had also made arrangements so that ten percent of all revenue collected by House Irono would be sent to House Orodum over the next ten years. As if those two things weren't enough, he had a few of the other Houses that members of House Irono had married into would also send between one and five percent of their earnings to House Orodum over the next five years.

I understood why they would agree to this, of course. By sending the gold, they hoped that I would look to them when it came time for me to contract out work for House Orodum. Doing the work would help them recoup some of the lost revenue while also increasing the prestige of their craftsmen, which would, in turn, bring in more work and thus more gold. It was a capital investment, and one they considered worthwhile enough to dedicate themselves to.

The rest of the day was spent walking the city and surface with my friends and guards, with Franklin by my side. The guards had to rotate out because I was given so many gifts by the people that they couldn't carry them all. Most of the gifts were in the form of provisions and materials we could use at Orlimar. Some gifts were tokens, crafted weapons, clothes, or other goods people wished for me to have.

In turn, I had my guards hand out one gold sovereign to people at random. It was my way of giving back to the people who loved me so much.

When we got to the surface, I announced my engagement to Franklin. The crowd's reaction was rapturous. The Surface Dwarves lavished us with gifts as congratulations. The day became a massive celebration. It was nice to spend the day before leaving surrounded by such happiness.

By the time the evening came around, I was mentally exhausted. Truthfully, I didn't even want to sit down to dinner, but Father insisted we celebrate my engagement. It was going to be my last time seeing him for three years, so I agreed.

I admit that I wasn't the most engaging guest of honor. I smiled, nodded, and engaged in some small talk, but otherwise, I was simply there. I could tell that Franklin's mother was rather insulted that I wasn't very engaged, but she hadn't had the day I did. Still, she wasn't one to hold that against me. We had known each other for years now. I was sure she understood why I wasn't as outgoing as I normally was at dinners. Franklin's brother, Woryek, seemed especially pleased with our pairing since he had made regular comments throughout the years about how we seemed made for each other.

Franklin, along with my guards, escorted me home after the dinner. Franklin and I shared a kiss at the door before I wished him a good night.

After I fell asleep, I met with Purpose who was speaking with someone I didn't recognize. It was an elf who seemed like he was suffering through some great trauma. When I approached them, the elf looked up at me and seemed to panic.

It ended up that the elf was the spirit trapped inside the phylactery. He hadn't been able to speak to anyone directly in Ages. We did our best to console and calm him. We spent the entire night doing so. Before I woke, we at least managed to get him to accept that we weren't there to hurt him. I managed to figure out that wherever the phylactery went, he was pulled along through the Dimvolmn. Using this information allowed me to convince Purpose to follow him so that it could stick with me over the next few years.

The next day, House Orodum, several other noble Houses, as well as many other dwarven warriors, smiths, and artisans gathered outside Cragmorrar, ready to leave for Orlimar. Kara wanted to go with me, but I insisted she stay and take care of Bilfern. Father and the Callers, as well as a great many citizens, saw us off. We were going to be gone for the next few years, so it was the last time we would all see each other for some time.

We left with great fanfare, with people still trying to give us gifts and provisions for the trip. The journey to Orlimar would take a month even with the rhoarnos. Orlimar was located in a small mountainous area at the edge of the Karaoke WIldlands, which were a large swath of swampy woodland.

The trip took a bit longer than it normally would have because I insisted that we stop by Cliffside to meet with the Earl and Duke. While we were there, I went through the market to see how it had been coming along. To my surprise, the size of Redcliff had doubled in the years since I'd last been there because of the market and increased trade coming in thanks to the creation of the Surface Caste. Earl Edward escorted me through the area himself but made mention that there was a Syndicate presence in the market and asked if there was any way we could help handle it.

I honestly hadn't thought about the Syndicate since I was reborn into Thoros. The Syndicate was essentially the underground criminal element in Cragmorrar and throughout the Under Roads. They were smugglers, assassins, and all-around thugs. I assumed their presence would have been wiped clean with the implementation of the Surface Caste since Syndicate members were all casteless who turned to crime to survive.

I assured the Earl that I would send word to Cragmorrar, requesting that they make hunting the Syndicate among their top priorities. Luckily, I had close friends in the Assembly who would keep me apprised of everything that was going on.

When we left Cliffside, Earl Edward added twenty carts to our caravan, hitched to rhoarnos that weren't already hauling goods. The carts had food, building materials, and one was packed with wine. He wanted to be able to help in the rebuilding effort somehow.

I might have let it slip to him that he would want to look in on his son because I thought I sensed magic coming from him. Now, you can't actually sense magic from a person, but Edward didn't know that. And I just knew that if left alone, his wife Gertrude would hide the fact that her son was a mage. That would lead to a horrific series of events. Better the boy be looked after properly than by anyone untoward.

We had left Cragmorrar in the last week of winter, and by the time we arrived in Orlimar, spring was in full bloom. The place was more of a ruin than a fort, but it was large enough to be a solid defensible position against a force like the scourgespawn who would simply charge in with no real tactics in mind. The reports from our scouts were extremely detailed, and my engineers assured me that they believed we could get everything done according to our schedule; sooner if the humans showed up to help.

Our first priority was securing the tunnels below the Tower of Mythral, which was on the western side of the fort. This would allow us to prevent the scourgespawn from using the tunnels to take the tower and would give us a place to remain underground for the purposes of keeping our castes. There was some dispensation for the people who came with me because we couldn't guarantee that half the time we were there would be underground, but we were going to do our best to rotate the work so that three shifts could work on the fort for eight hours every day while we went back to the tunnels for the rest of the day.

Within the first two months of around-the-clock work, the tunnels were fortified, expanded, and secured. The Tunnels became a large town in its own right, with room enough for the rhoarnos to wander and for the smiths and artisans to set up their crafting stations so they had more than enough room to work. There was an armory, a few different galleys, and sleeping quarters for each House's warriors, servants, and artisans. The nobles received small houses of their own where they could stay and take meetings. We converted some of the larger spaces that were already in the tunnels into training grounds, and one area we had to dig out into a meeting room where larger meetings of the nobles, warrior commanders, and engineers could take place. Each space was designed with the idea of making it a defensible position to fall back to in case the scourgespawn tunneled in during the attack.

In the third month, King Marshal's forces had arrived. By then, we were working at the base of the fort, securing some of the failing stonework and reinforcing the gates. When the scouts reported that King Marshal was close, I hurried to the tunnels to wash and change into something presentable. I was helping with the smithing work and molding the stone with magic when needed so I was an absolute mess.

By the time King Marshal arrived, there were one hundred House Orodum warriors arrayed on either side of the road, with warriors from the other noble Houses positioned there as well. I stood at the entrance to Orlimar, flanked by Franklin, Faren, and Trianna. Behind me were a handful of nobles who weren't currently on their shift, who joined me to make as respectable a welcome as we could.

King Marshal brought his horse to a stop a few yards from us and dismounted. I could see Duke Logan behind him, dismounting as well. I recognized Serena, Clifford, and Alford. They had two other individuals with them as well: a male elf and a male human. I assumed those were the city elf and human mage origins.

I lowered myself into a graceful curtsy as Marshal approached. "King Marshal, it's an honor to have you join us. I hope our early arrival didn't force you to hurry any plans you might have had."

Marshal smiled and bowed. "Exemplar Orodum, it is a great pleasure to see you again. I must say you've grown into a beautiful young woman."

"And to answer your question," Logan interjected, "we did not rush any of our plans. We assumed, and rightly so if the state of the fort has anything to say about it, that the industrious Princess of Cragmorrar would not sit idly by while she waited on our arrival."

I smiled and bowed my head. "You give me too much credit, Duke Logan."

"I don't think that's possible," Marshal doubled down on the sentiment. "It seems you've put your people to work. The place is already cleared of debris."

A chuckled slipped from me as I turned and motioned for the pair to follow me. "If I may?"

Marshal signaled for his people to dismount and begin setting up their tents, then he and Logan fell in step behind me.

"As you can see," I began, with just a small amount of pride in my people's work, "we have cleared the area of debris and leveled the best places for your people to set up tents. We have already fortified and expanded the Tower of Mythral and the tunnels beneath it. I hope you don't mind, but we've taken the tunnels as our living quarters for the duration of the time we'll be here."

"You should make yourselves comfortable, of course," Marshal nodded.

"Thank you, Your Majesty," I continued, leading them to the bridge that spanned the gap of the chasm between the eastern and western towers of the fort. "We're currently working on the lower part of the fort: repairing and reinforcing the stonework there. We'll work our way up over the next few months before we begin work on the bridge. We've brought enough materials with us to get the fort back into prime condition."

"Did you consider that we might want a say in how things are done, Princess?" Logan asked, ever the realist.

I stopped and turned on my heels, pure positivity directed at the more taciturn of the pair. "I did, indeed, my Lord. Which is why I'm bringing you to the engineering headquarters we've set up. I would like you and your engineers to look over our plans. We were only able to make them from scout reports. We believe they're accurate, but we want your input on any changes or alterations you would like to make."

"Earl Edward sent several cartloads of materials and supplies as well," I added, making sure to give the man the credit he deserved. "We can use those to help with anything further that you might want done. I assume you brought your own materials, supplies, and ideas as well. So I'm eager to see how our plans can work together."

"You were right, Logan," Marshal laughed and clapped his friend on the back. "It's not possible to overestimate this young lady. She has an answer for everything."

"So it would seem, Marshal. The same seems to be able to be said for all of the Fated," Logan mused. He looked down at me with an arched brow. "Tell me, Princess. We received reports of dwarves riding large creatures south from Cragmorrar. Where are these beasts?"

"You must mean the rhoarnos," I assumed. "They're in their pasture below the Tower of Mythral."

"I was unaware that dwarves used beasts for more than pulling carts," Logan mused. "Do you ride them into battle as well?"

I looked up at the man with a proud expression. "We do! House Orodum sports the largest cavalry in all of Cragmorrar, and we've brought all of our rhoarnos with us. Two hundred rhoarnos. Some of the other Houses have brought some of theirs as well, but House Orodum makes up the bulk of our cavalry."

"And do you intend to utilize them during the battle?" Logan pursued the topic with interest.

"We do," I confirmed. "We have already used them in three large battles against the scourgespawn since last we met. So you don't have to worry about inexperience being an issue."

We continued to speak for some time as I escorted them around the fort, showing them work we were doing, and the work we had accomplished. I also showed Logan the rhoarno pasture, which seemed to impress him. They went over the plans we had laid out for the fort's repairs and fortifications, and let us know what differences they had planned for.

When I asked if they would join me for dinner tonight, King Marshal informed me that a dinner together would have to wait. The other Fated wished to meet with Faren, Trianna, and myself this evening. Marshal had not only assured them this would happen, he prioritized a large tent to be set up so that we could all meet in private.

It seemed I was about to meet the last two origins at long last.

CHAPTER 12:

THE MEETING OF SIX

Once we had finished bringing King Marshal and Duke Logan up to speed, Faren, Trianna, and I spent the rest of the day preparing to meet the other origins. Franklin had ensured that our armor was polished to a mirror shine and had the servants prepare my best garnet and gold gambeson. This gambeson had gold studs with raised House Orodum's sigils. Franklin also made sure that the jewelry Faren and Trianna had given to me was laid out for me to wear. I also decided to wear the old cape that Trenton had given me as an aramis cloak over my left shoulder.

Faren would wear his armor as he always did, while Trianna decided to wear a set of black and green armor made from beautiful rhoarno leather. The floral designs stitched into it were elegant and made from silver thread.

The three of us discussed what we would go over with the others once we'd met them. Faren and I had only met Serena those few years ago when she visited with Marshal and Logan. Serena and I had kept in touch through letters, but we mostly shared important news or how we were doing. She didn't share anything about the other origins apart from the fact that she had found them, their names, and that they were safe. This was intentional, though. We didn't want to give away too much in case the correspondence was intercepted somehow.

I had asked if we needed to bring food for the dinner but was given reassurances that King Marshal was having the meeting catered by his own chefs.

At the appointed hour, we were escorted to the tent that had been set up for us. Outside of the tent, there were Falladrin royal guards, guards from House Coreland and House Lemlal, and now I was adding House Orodum guards to the mix.

One of the guards pulled back the opening to the tent and announced us, "Exemplar Merida Orodum, Princess of Cragmorrar, and her escorts Lord Faren Orodum, and Lady Trianna of Clan Saber."

As we passed through the entrance, the guard closed it behind us. Inside was a large, round table set with ornate chairs and several dozen candles. The aroma of the food had my mouth watering as I caught the scent of food I hadn't eaten since before I was reincarnated. Around the table sat Serena, a human male, and a male elf.

The human let out a long whistle, "That's an impressive series of titles."

"Allen," Serena scolded the young man, "act accordingly." Serena stood from her chair and curtsied, "Exemplar Orodum, it's been far too long. I'm glad to see you doing so well."

I dipped into a curtsy, "Lady Coreland, you've grown since the last time we met."

That got a laugh from Serena, "I could say the same for you. You've certainly sprouted since we last met."

We laughed together before I looked at the two people I didn't know, "Proper introductions are in order. I am Princess Merida Orodum of Cragmorrar."

Faren stepped forward, bowing his head, "I'm Faren Orodum, Lady Orodum's personal guard."

"Trianna of Clan Saber, First of Clan Saber," Trianna offered.

"As you all know, I am Serena Coreland, Earl of Coralstine," Serena joined in.

The human stood and offered a sweeping bow, "I am Allen Lemlal, head of House Lemlal."

The elf stood and bowed his head, "Aelfric, Duke of the Demirren Elvienage."

"Now that we've all introduced ourselves, I have a question," Allen said as he pointed at Faren. "We all have unique names, Faren. But your name is a default name. Why is that?"

Faren chuckled, "I thought you would have figured it out by now. I chose the default name before I was brought here. I always preferred to jump right in. No real need to choose a unique name."

"See? I told you so," Serena chuckled.

Allen snapped his fingers and sighed, "Well, I suppose my theory on how high the origins were in the social order has been debunked."

"Excuse me, but…" I looked around at the tables of food that were sitting nearby, "do I smell cornbread?"

Everyone looked at me in confusion for a few moments before they each erupted into laughter.

"I suppose we should eat and talk or the Exemplar will waste away to nothing," Aelfric said.

"Not that there's much of her to waste away as it is," Allen quipped.

I huffed and lifted my chin haughtily, as I made my way to the food, "I may be short but I outrank everyone in this room. So I get first dibs."

That got a laugh from everyone. Even Faren started to loosen up a bit around others from the same world as us. We all fixed our plates and sat down around the table. Faren and Trianna sat to either side of me while Serena, Allen, and Aelfric sat opposite us.

I was so excited! Apparently, Aelfric had made a name for himself as a cook in Demirren, making food from our world which helped to draw the attention from the nobles. He had taught the recipes to others for a hefty price, and used that gold to improve the Elvienage and over time, turn the Elvienage into an area where people would go for specialty cuisine.

I said a silent prayer to the stone as I looked at my plates: cornbread, cranberry sauce, Cajun-seasoned pork chops, mashed potatoes, buttermilk fried chicken, pork belly burnt ends, biscuits, pumpkin pie, and fruit cobbler!

"Someone was Southern," Aelfric said as he watched me dig into my meal.

I had tears in my eyes. I hadn't had these foods in almost two decades. It was a taste of home that brought back a thousand memories. I actually started to cry.

"My Lady," Faren gasped as he reached over to place a hand on my back. "Are you alright?"

I nodded and sniffled, continuing to eat and broke all etiquette as I spoke through a mouthful of food. "Yes, I'm sorry. It's just… These were some of my favorite foods from before. I haven't tasted them since then. I'm just… remembering so much that I haven't had the will to think about in so long."

Trianna's hand joined Faren's and rubbed my back.

Aelfric smiled. "I'm glad I could make something you loved. I tried to have the chefs make as many types of dishes that I remembered in the hopes that something would be from a general region we might have come from."

We ate in silence for several minutes as everyone enjoyed a little taste of home.

When everyone other than Faren and myself seemed content with how much they'd had (dwarves can really pack away the food), Serena began to outline what all we needed to discuss.

"So, now that we've… mostly all had our fill…" Serena chuckled. "I think we need to outline what we need to discuss, then go over everything in detail. First, I think we should each go over what we've done to build up our resources and avoid some of the worst things that could happen."

"I figure you can start, then, Serena," Allen said as he leaned back in his chair. "It seems to be your show at the moment."

Serena looked over at me and chuckled as I smiled up at her with a mouth full of food, "I suppose I could go first. As you all know, I'm the human noble origin. House Coreland didn't have many issues to handle other than Earl Strowe. Princess Merida gave me the idea I needed to deal with him."

Everyone looked at me for an explanation, but I was currently stuffing my face with fried chicken and waved a drumstick at Serena for her to continue.

Serena laughed and explained, "She had a dwarf from the Surface Caste approach Earl Strowe with false plans about the ground beneath Castle Coreland. The plans detailed false gas pockets that would kill the inhabitants of the castle if the gases somehow leaked to the surface. Strowe was stupid enough to sign a contract detailing the plan for the dwarves to dig tunnels up to the castle to funnel the gases through them, and he was even more foolish to pay with heirlooms of his House."

"Mm hm mm hm," I agreed with a mouthful of pumpkin pie.

"The dwarf then brought the contract with Strowe's signature and the heirlooms as proof to King Marshal," Serena finished explaining. "Once the king saw this, he confronted Strowe and stripped him of the Earling, which he turned over to me as a dowry for my marriage to Alford."

I wiped my mouth and smiled, "I'm looking forward to attending the wedding. When will that be?"

"After the Scourge is handled," Serena said. "But with the Earling now in my possession, we've fortified Watcher's Keep and worked to help bolster Coralstine's port presence with help from the dwarven Surface Caste's surge in commerce."

"Wait," Aelfric interrupted, "if you have control of the Earling, why aren't you an Earl?"

"She isn't married yet," Trianna guessed. "She gets the title when she marries Alford."

"Correct," Serena confirmed with a nod. "At the moment, I'm a caretaker until the title is officially passed on after the marriage. Now, who's next?"

"I guess I'll go next," Allen volunteered. "It took me some time, but I managed to rise up in the Mage Tower to the point where I could pass my challenges early. When Serena and King Marshal came to the Mage Tower and took me with them, I focused my efforts on reorganizing my House."

"Isn't that seated in Fetral? In the Independent Marshes?" Faren asked.

Allen nodded in confirmation, "Yes. King Marshal escorted me there. My Great aunt and uncles were still alive, though they were dealing with a bout of cholera. We managed to save them just in time, and I proved to Uncle Aristide that I could lead the House to future greatness. He forgave his daughter, but I was named Head of the House after I proved to my uncle that Garlen was simply spending the family's funds on gambling."

"Wait," I pounded a fist to my chest to help quickly swallow some of the Cajun pork, "does that mean we have access to Hank, Carter, and Bellany?"

Allen smirked, "Garret Lemlal, yes. We also have their father, Matthew, as well. You see, I had started to focus on elemental spells, but once I thought about what the main issues of the Lemlal family were, I specialized in healing magic."

I leaned forward, eyes wide, "But that means we can deal with Varrimus before he becomes an issue, right? Since Matthew was the one who sealed him away…"

Allen nodded, "I've spoken to him about it already. Varrimus is similar to an arch demon, in that he can transfer his essence to anything tainted by the Scourge within a certain distance. Unfortunately… we don't know what that distance is."

"A problem for later, then," Trianna mused.

"It would seem so," Allen admitted. "It's almost a non-issue since he can't be released without someone from my bloodline performing the ritual to let him loose."

"Let's put that on the back burner, then," Serena said. "Aelfric, why don't you go next?"

Aelfric chuckled and motioned to me. "Well, as you can see, I focused primarily on food to get to where I am. I admit, I started as a thief and developed my skills there for a few years until a guard in Demirren sneered at me, saying that knife-ears like me should at least be able to contribute something worthwhile to society."

"For some reason, that really struck home and I had to think about what it was that I could do that no one else could," Aelfric continued. "So I remembered that I could cook, and that the food here is lacking in overall flavor. I was a chef before, so I figured I could be one again. I opened a small stall in the market district. The humans wrecked it a few times, but eventually, enough people tried my food that no one would attack the stall anymore. Eventually, I was able to open a small restaurant, the first of its kind in Demirren."

"I can see why! I'm going to eat as much of this as I can before we leave!" I said, still very much enraptured by the taste of the food.

Aelfric laughed. "And that's the very reason I got to where I am today. My food became so popular that nobles began taking up every seat for every meal. My reputation reached Serena and King Marshal. When they came to see me, Serena discussed who we were. The king hired me to teach his cooks how to make the foods. I bargained for more, though. I insisted that he invest in the Elvienage so we could turn it into a space for culinary cuisine. The elves really dove into becoming chefs. It was relatively easy, and after a few months of lessons, they were beginning to create their own culinary goods."

I looked at Faren with wide, excited eyes. "We're going to Demirren after all this is over with!"

That elicited a chuckle from everyone.

Aelfric continued, "With the culinary renaissance I brought to the city, I was named the Elder of the Elvienage, and King Marshal named me a Duke and granted the Elvienage to me so that I could continue to help it prosper. Though, I have to say, the dwarven Surface Caste really helped with procuring the spices and goods needed to make some of the confections we created. So I'm rather grateful for your efforts, Lady Merida."

"Just send one of your chefs to Cragmorrar to cook for me from now on, and we'll call it even," I squeaked as I gazed at the slice of pumpkin pie I was about to eat.

Serena laughed. "Who's next? Faren?"

Faren shrugged. "There's not much to tell. I had convinced my mother to start a small stall to earn money. It accomplished my primary goal, which was to grab the attention of the dwarf noble origin. Since then, Lady Merida has worked diligently to elevate my family and care for us. So I've done whatever I could to support her. She has the power and influence to get things done for our people."

"Wait…" Allen said, leaning forward. "So you've basically done nothing but guard Princess Merida? You didn't change things or make plans?"

"Why should I?" Faren asked. "Princess Merida's plans were the same plans I would have had, but she already had the power to influence things. I would have had to work this long just to be able to talk to a noble to start the process. Dedicating myself to protecting the person who could get things done faster just made sense. If nothing else, my plan was to keep her alive so that she could do just that."

I smiled at Faren. "And I thank you so much for that, Faren. I couldn't have asked for a more dedicated partner."

"Trianna?" Serena asked. "I know I took you away from what you were doing when we met and sent you to Cragmorrar. Have you been able to do much while there?"

Trianna looked at me and I gave a reaffirming nod. "Tell them."

"Very well," Trianna began. "I was, and still am, the First of Clan Saber.

I have kept in close contact with my clan through messages over the years. Before I left, I had nearly figured out the secret to activating the Illusavin Network."

"And you stopped her from doing something so useful?" Allen asked Serena incredulously.

"It was necessary to keep us all safe," Serena defended herself.

"What's done is done," Trianna interrupted the squabble before it could really take off. "I admit, I was angry at first. But there were benefits in going to Cragmorrar. Princess Merida and I were able to work on our magic, research the scourgespawn, and work with my clan to direct them on which steps to take to prepare for the Scourge."

"Such as?" Allen prodded.

"To hunt down the Alerion clan and bring them together," Trianna explained. "We also directed them to call the Bronheran, Rillfraen, and Gahlian clans to a clan meeting. Lady Merida and I were able to attend the meeting since it was held near Cragmorrar. We were able to convince the elves of the truth about some of our traditions and convince them to join together into a singular elven clan. They'll be ready to join us soon."

"That's actually really impressive," Serena said as she thought about it. "I can't imagine all of that went over smoothly. There had to be some blowback."

Trianna nodded, "There was. It took months to convince them, and I still need King Marshal's help to finalize some of the promises I made."

"As a fellow elf, I have to ask," Aelfric cut in. "What promises would need King Marshal's help?"

"You're talking about the Paddish elf epilogue, aren't you?" Serena gasped.

"Wait, what?" Aelfric nearly jumped out of his seat. "You mean you're actually going to ask him for-"

"I won't be asking for anything," Trianna quickly corrected Aelfric. "It is the price for the aid of the Paddish. And I have Lady Merida's assurance that she will stand by me in my request. I've seen how she's worked to improve the lives and treatment of her people, and I will be doing the same for the elves. We won't be second-class citizens anymore."

Everyone went silent for several moments before Serena cleared her throat, "Well, Merida? Care to let everyone know what you've been up to?"

I choked down a mouthful of fruit cobbler and dabbed my mouth with a napkin, "Delicious! Oh, and yes! I'd be happy to."

I sat up straight and smiled, "So far, I've managed to establish the Surface Caste, which has helped to create more upward momentum among the dwarves and brought more wealth to Cragmorrar in generations. It also seems to have helped a few of you in the process. We also managed to retake Nordrucan Hold, Petran Hold, and Cragmor Hold, reestablishing them as functioning cities as the first steps toward recreating the Dwarven Empire."

"You already took back the Holds!?" Serena asked in shock. "I thought you were going to wait till King Marshal could bring his men to reinforce your people! And how did you even find Petran Hold? You needed directions when we last met."

"I got them from Duke Logan," I explained. "He sent me the directions after we exchanged a few letters. I was going to wait for the humans, but the resources that the Surface Caste brought in was beyond what even my most favorable estimations could have predicted. So, I figured we should start right away. We took Nordrucan Hold the year after we met. Then we took the Petran and Cragmor Holds as well."

Serena, Allen, and Aelfric stared at me in stunned silence.

"Faren and Trianna have been by my side this entire time," I continued, "helping me every step of the way. We've fought against thousands of scourgespawn and managed to kill about a dozen broodmothers."

"So you've already been fighting the scourgespawn all this time?" Allen asked.

"What did you expect?" Faren asked. "We're dwarves, and the scourgespawn are a constant threat."

"Still, it's one thing to go up against a few roaming bands," Aelfric said. "It's something entirely different to go through the Under Roads and retake the lost Holds."

Allen laughed, "What are you trying to do, become Queen of the dwarves?"

"No," I shook my head. "I'm just trying to do what I can for my people."

"Well, I suppose that covers what we've all been up to," Serena said. "So what's next on the agenda?"

"Shouldn't we discuss our plans for the Scourge?" Trianna suggested.

"You all arrived before we did and have been working pretty diligently for a few months now," Aelfric said. "Why don't you tell us what you have planned so far?"

"Very well," I called from the food tables. I had begun filling up a third plate. "We brought enough supplies to basically rebuild the fort, but we're focused on repairing it and reinforcing it for now. By the time we're done with it, it'll be as good as new."

"We've also brought supplies to build barracks and other proper facilities for long-term use," Trianna added. "Once the fort itself is ready, we'll be building permanent housing and other structures."

"And as far as tactics go," Faren joined in on the explanation, "we've brought a thousand of House Orodum's warriors, as well as warriors from other noble Houses. We have two hundred rhoarno for our cavalry units, all with their own armor that are already used to charging through scourgespawn ranks."

"What about the Paddish elves?" Aelfric asked Trianna. "Didn't you mention they were planning to help?"

"They'll be here for the battle, don't you worry," Trianna reassured him.

"What about the rest of you?" I asked after I sat back down, balancing a few plates on my arms and setting them in front of me. "I saw a lot of soldiers arrive with you and noticed the materials as well. King Marshal said you were planning on doing repairs to the fort and then scouting the wilds?"

Serena nodded, "I figured that since we had a few years to make things work, we could repair the fort then get the lay of the land so we could prepare traps to cut down the scourgespawn's numbers before they made it to the fort."

"If it weren't for Logan pulling out of the fight, Clifford could have won the Battle of Orlimar in the game. They had the numbers and the strategy," Allen reminded everyone. "So we figured if we could prepare for the battle ahead of time, the fight would become even easier."

"Oh…" Faren, Trianna, and I said in unison.

The disappointment in our voices must have been obvious because Serena's face flushed red, "What do you mean, 'Oh'? Why change what works?"

"Because we still need a piece of the puzzle that Logan didn't approve of in the game," I said. "We still need the Scourge Sentinels, and we do all remember how Logan acted when Clifford depended on the Sentinels, right?"

"He won't argue against King Marshal," Serena insisted. "The Sentinels have already been welcomed back into Falladrin by the King."

"They were welcomed back by King Marshal in the game as well," I countered. "And Logan didn't agree with the invitation then, either. Some caution is warranted."

"I'd say that's fair," Aelfric chimed in. "The man is still a curmudgeon and while he may be loyal to the King, we don't know how strained that loyalty might be when we have to depend on the Sentinels to finish off the Archdemon."

Serena and Allen shared a look that said they didn't like it but they'd accept it.

"Anyway," I quickly added, "Having more options on top of what we know works is only a good thing."

"Let's move on to our future plans after Orlimar," Serena suggested.

"Well, now that I've heard what Trianna has in store, my plans might be changing," Aelfric laughed.

"What!?" Serena gasped. "But we had planned on you working to expand the Elvienage and working on human/elf relations in Demirren."

"That's true," Aelfric apologized, "but if Trianna is essentially setting up a new elven territory, I can bring my people here to help establish the place as a new culinary center. That could help with relations by bringing visitors to us, where we could share more of our culture."

That news seemed to irritate Serena, but she shrugged it off.

"As far as I'm concerned," Serena offered, "I plan on turning Everrup into the largest port city in Falladrin and making the market in Cliffside seem puny by comparison. The Earling will thrive with all of the extra trade."

"As for me, I want the Mage Towers abolished in favor of magical colleges," Allen said. "I intend on changing the Mage Tower in Fetral first using my family's influence. The Church has no right to oversee the private lives of others."

"I tend to agree," I nodded. "The Church has taken their duty to guard the people against possessed mages too far. It's become an institution of prison slaves who are only let out if their families are rich enough to bribe the Church or the kingdoms they're in have need of their mage's power."

"That's right…" Allen said thoughtfully. "You're a mage, aren't you? I remember hearing the mages in the Tower speaking excitedly about a dwarven princess who could cast spells. How did that work?"

"The same way I'm a mage," Trianna lied for me. "Starting the game with mods."

"So it was our character class choices that determined what we are," Aelfric hummed.

"I think that freeing the Mage Towers is something we can all agree on," Faren said. "The question is, how to go about it. The Church won't release their hold on the mages without a fight, and the Templar's addiction to Dimvyum is another reason they won't want to let the mages go."

"Well, we can do something about the Dimvyum supply," I smirked. "Dwarves are the only ones who can mine it safely."

"Cutting off the supply would only upset the Church and the Mage Towers at the same time," Allen shook his head. "It's not a good solution."

"We don't need to cut off the supply," I said through a mouthful of pie. "We can increase the price, making it so that the Church is forced to use the supply in a more effective manner. Kingdoms will insist on their Mage Towers using the Dimvyum to enchant weapons and armor, and creating other magical items. The Church will say they need the Dimvyum for their Templars. They'll solve that problem themselves. In the meantime, we'll offer Allen's college the Dimvyum at a premium rate as a way for the dwarves to endorse more… life-assuring methods of mage training."

"That could actually work," Allen mused. "It doesn't deny the supply, but it would increase the demand. That could be an excellent first step, Merida."

"I'd ask what Faren's plans are," Aelfric said, "but I'm pretty sure he would just say 'whatever Lady Merida has planned'."

"That's not true," Faren growled. "I am going to help Lady Orodum every step of the way, but while I do that I also plan on rising to become the High Commander of Cragmorrar. I will reorganize Cragmorrar's forces into specialized branches, which will give even the casteless the chance to rise up into the Warrior Class."

"That will take a lot of effort and pulling a lot of strings," Serena finally spoke again.

"I'll need to prove myself in battle," Faren agreed, "But I won't need to pull a single string. Exemplar Orodum has already assured me that she would use her influence to make the reorganization happen."

"It's one more way for us to improve the lives of our people," I smiled at Faren with cheeks packed with pork bites.

"And what about you?" Serena asked me. "Are you still determined to achieve the same goals you told me about when we spoke in Cragmorrar?"

I nodded firmly, "I am. After this Scourge, there will still be two more old gods left: Raziel, the Dragon of Mystery, and Luscan, the Dragon of Night. There might be a third that the Church wiped from the records… but I can't remember if that was ever confirmed or not. I'm still determined to hunt them down while they're sleeping and kill them before they can be used to start their own Scourges."

"You certainly don't lack ambition," Aelfric hummed. "How do you propose to find their prisons? It's not like that information is readily available."

"True," I admitted. "But I know who does know how to find out where the prisons are. So once this business in Orlimar is done, I'll work with my people for some time to secure the Under Roads around the Holds, then make my way to get that information."

The meeting went on for another few hours, discussing plans for Orlimar, scouting the wilds, and other things of a more casual nature. With Alford as her betrothed and Durdren and Gniess in Orzamar and Cragmor Hold, we had nearly everyone we could get our hands on. By the time we were finished, Faren and I had nearly emptied the table of food, and I took a pumpkin pie back to my quarters for myself.

Over the next two weeks, we all met a few more times, and I explained the changes we would be making to the fort to help make the original strategy more sound.

Trianna and I also met with King Marshal to make the offer of giving the Orlimar and the surrounding giant forests to the Paddish after the Scourge. I informed the king that Cragmorrar would support this proposition, as it would give the elves a place to call their own within the realm and would help to ease relations between elves and humans. It might also serve as a cultural buffer between Falladrins and the shamanic tribes of the wilds. In the end, Marshal said he would agree to the proposition as long as I could guarantee that dwarves would serve as intermediaries in the case of any problems between the humans and elves.

Those first two weeks with everyone there were busy, with everyone trying to fit into the overall business of restoring the fort, scouting the area, and training the troops. It was refreshing to have so many extra people there.

CHAPTER 13:

CONFLICTING IDEOLOGIES

M"y Exemplar!" a servant shouted as she threw open the door to my bedroom.

I was startled out of my sleep and shot straight up, "What?! What's wrong?"

"A large force of humans have gathered outside the tower," she said as she scurried about the room, grabbing some clothes for me. "They're demanding to see you and have threatened to come in and take you if you don't meet with them!"

"They're armed?" I asked as she helped me get dressed.

"They are, My Lady," she confirmed, still taking the time to ensure that everything fit correctly. "Ser Faren is outside with several warriors guarding the entrance to the tower, but they won't be able to hold for long if the humans decide to force their way in."

"Who are they? Have they identified themselves?" I probed as my mind began to wander.

"No, my lady," the servant said as she led me over to my vanity and set me down so she could begin braiding my hair. "They've refused to say who they are until you come out to meet with them."

"Where is King Marshal? Has he not ordered them to disperse or to pull back and treat with us peacefully?" I inquired.

"Forgive me, Princess," she replied, shaking her head, "but I do not know. I was only told as much as I've told you now, and to bring you to the entrance to the tower when you're presentable."

It had been almost two months since King Marshal and the other origins had arrived. There hadn't been any quarrels that I was aware of, and the worst thing that I could think of happening was when my engineers and Marshal's engineers wanted to do repairs in different ways. To have a force of humans acting so aggressively outside our quarters and demanding my presence this way didn't make any sense. It took several more minutes to get my hair braided, my makeup done, my armor equipped… and an additional number of minutes just to make them wait. Faren would forgive me.

When I was finally prepared, I took my staff and left my room. Several warriors were already in the hall and fell into formation around me. Dwarves all throughout the tunnels were moving into their battle positions, and I stopped to give them some particular orders of my own. If King Marshal wasn't able to stop this force… or didn't want to stop them for some reason… I wanted to be prepared for a fight.

One of the guards around me ran ahead to let Faren know I was about to arrive.

As I approached the doors to the tower, two guards opened them for me, and Faren announced me.

"Here she is," he yelled over the crowd. "Exemplar Merida Orodum, Princess of Cragmorrar!"

Faren and the other warriors outside of the tower all bowed. I stopped at the edge of the top step, looking down at the gathered humans. There were hundreds of them, most heavily armored. Those who weren't armored wore robes with stylized sun symbology on them. Templars and members of the Church. What did they want with me?

I glared imperiously down at them, not allowing an ounce of concern or fear to show through. "I am Lady Merida Orodum, Princess of Cragmorrar. By what right does the Church and its Templar knights have with me that they would demand my presence by threatening force against me and my people, and risking a war with the dwarves of Cragmorrar?"

An elderly human woman with white hair and golden robes stepped forward. "Greetings, Miss Merida."

The lack of any title other than 'Miss' rankled me. I can only imagine what the reaction of the dwarves around me was.

"I am Grand Cleric Elemena," the woman continued. "I have brought the Templars because word over the years has reached my ears that you are a mage, and a powerful one at that."

"What business is it of yours if I am, Grand Cleric?" I asked, not letting the imperious air I was putting on falter, and intentionally using her title.

"As I'm sure you're aware," Elemena responded, "part of the Church's duties is to protect the people from unchecked mages. We have come to escort you to Falladrin's Mage Tower where you can live safely and in comfort, Miss."

I narrowed my eyes and took a few moments to collect myself. "To be clear, Grand Cleric, you heard that I was away from Cragmorrar and thought I was finally vulnerable. So, you decided you were brave enough to take on an isolated force of dwarves, and you gathered as many men as possible and came here to drag me back to the Mage Tower, whether I agreed to go peacefully or not."

"If you wish to put it that way, Miss," the Cleric said with a soft chuckle. "We would prefer that you come with us peacefully, but we are willing to bring you with us by force."

"And what does King Marshal have to say about all of this?" I asked. "I doubt he would approve of the Church risking a war with Cragmorrar by abducting a dwarven Princess and Exemplar, and killing her people in the process."

"My authority comes from beyond the king," Elemena said softly. "Now, if you would please come with us, Miss, we can avoid any unpleasantries."

"Do you think our Exemplar would go without a fight?" Franklin growled as he stepped forward by my side.

I looked at Franklin and placed a hand on his chest to calm him. "Give me a few more moments with her. If things should turn for the worst, you know what to do."

Franklin bowed his head. "As you wish, beloved. But know that we will not let them take you."

I gave Franklin a smile, showing him my appreciation. "I know."

My demeanor turned to ice as I turned away from Franklin and back to the elderly woman. "Grand Cleric Elemena, you have come here uninvited. You have threatened me, but more importantly, you have threatened my people. You have purposefully disrespected me by not once acknowledging my titles as a noble, royalty, and a Exemplar. Your old age must be affecting your judgment and your eyesight because we are neither helpless nor human. We do not subscribe to your religion, and we are not bound by its dogmatic tenets of slavery for the greater good."

"The Church does not endorse sla–" the old woman tried to protest.

"Silence!" I barked. "Since your arrival, you have done nothing but provoke us, disrespect me, and have tried to enforce your dogma on those who don't belong to it. However, since it seems you want to force a cultural exchange, I will oblige you."

I turned and motioned to the Tower of Mythral. "This tower and its surrounding walls were little more than a ruin a few months ago. Now it is a fortress all on its own. The tunnels beneath the tower have been fortified by Cragmorrar's finest engineers, artisans, and military minds. We have been able to do this because we are connected to The Stone, and it shows us how best to mold it to suit our needs. Do you know what that means, Grand Cleric?"

"Please, enlighten me," Elemena replied, seeming amused.

"It means that the moment you approached this tower, you were outnumbered and surrounded," I stated matter-of-factly. "You've been so concentrated on where we leave the tower that you didn't consider that we would have created other exits. Take a moment and look around."

Elemena arched a brow curiously, then began to take a look at her surroundings. Her expression changed from that of a patronizing old woman to one of surprise and concern. The ramparts were suddenly packed with dwarven archers, as was every window of the tower and the top of the tower. Behind them were a few hundred rhoarno cavalry who had left from the tunnels we'd made that led to the battlefield and Mage Towers around to flank the Church forces.

"What you don't see is inside the tower," I explained. "There are thousands of dwarves armed and ready to die to protect me. They will swarm through these doors in a fanatical frenzy if you dare lay a hand on me. While it's true your templars will be able to prevent me from casting spells, you're outnumbered twenty to one. If you take one step toward me, my betrothed will order my men to attack and every one of you will die in the next few moments."

"You wouldn't dare!" an armored man who looked to be in his fifties shouted as he stepped up to join Elemena. "If you kill the Grand Cleric then the Church would respond with an Exalted March against you and your people."

"And why should I care?" I asked as I grew more and more angry. "It would seem the Church is only brave enough to challenge the dwarves when we come out of our mountain. Did you come here hoping that threat would cow me into submission? That the threat of war would scare me into agreeing to your demands? Dwarves live in a state of constant war! We are battle-hardened from birth to fight and die for our people!"

I slammed the foot of my staff into the stone steps, summoning my mana to me. "I have come here with my people to help save your country from a Scourge, and you repay my generosity by demanding I become one of your enslaved mages? I will show you how magnanimous I am. I'll give you this one chance: command your men to lay their weapons down at my feet, or I will have my people slaughter you here and now! Make your decision."

The stalemate lasted for what seemed like ages. The Grand Cleric wrestled with her resolve while I dug deeper into my defiance. You could taste the tension in the air. It was the cleric's resolve that cracked first.

"Very well," Elemena conceded. "Templars, lay down your weapons before the Princess."

"Grand Cleric!" the older man protested. "We cannot do this!"

"Knight-Commander," Elemena silenced him, "I have made my decision. I will not sacrifice hundreds of lives in a hopeless effort. Now lay down your arms, all of you!"

One by one the Templars and warriors brought by the Church set their weapons down at the bottom of the tower's stairs.

"Now, we have done as you asked," Elemena grumbled. "May we leave in peace?"

"No," I snarled, marching down the steps and over the pile of weapons, flanked by Faren, Franklin, and my other personal guards. "You will surrender to me. My men will bind you, and we will keep you here until the Church makes amends for your threats and arrogance."

I stopped a foot away from the cleric and stared up at her, my expression daring her to refuse or strike me. "Now kneel, and command your men to do the same."

Elemena took several moments before moving to her knees. She was slowly joined by the others she'd brought with her.

"Faren," I called.

"Yes, Princess?" Faren stepped forward, bowing his head.

"Command the men to bind every human here. They're now our prisoners."

"As you command, My Lady," he turned and relayed the order. My guards and other warriors who were waiting for orders inside the tower got to work taking custody of the humans.

"Lord Irono," I called again.

"Command me, My Exemplar," Franklin stepped forward.

"I want cells dug into the tunnels by the end of the day," I stated firmly. "Bars, doors, and all. Don't bother with individual cells. Make three large enough to accommodate our guests for the long term."

"It will be done," Franklin obeyed. He marched back into the tower to make sure the cells were prepared.

I glared down at Elemena now that she was on her knees, "I hope you'll find your accommodations comfortable, Grand Cleric. You'll be here for some time as recompense for your arrogance. Now, if you'll excuse me, I need to speak with King Marshal about what I'm going to do with you."

Faren remained at the tower, overseeing the capture of the Melindrians while a retinue of guards and nobles escorted me to King Marshal's quarters. We didn't make it halfway across the bridge spanning the fort's chasm before Marshal, Logan, and several dozen knights approached us on horseback.

Marshal looked down at me in confusion, "Lady Orodum? Where is Grand Cleric Elemena? We were told she had arrived with a large number of Templars and marched straight to the Tower of Mythral."

I glared up at the King, "King Marshal, would you do me the pleasure of bringing me to the meeting hall? We have something we need to discuss. And could you call for the Fated also? I'd like their opinion on this as well."

Marshal considered my tone and body language and nodded, "Of course, Princess." He dismounted and helped me up onto his horse and commanded Logan to gather the other Fated before turning and bringing me to the meeting hall.

It took some time for Logan to round everyone up, but we were eventually all together and seated in the meeting hall.

"Now that we're all here," King Marshal began, "would you like to tell us what's going on?"

The table we were at was set up so that Marshal, Trianna, and I could sit at the head of it as the primary representatives of our respective peoples. Logan, the other Fated, and a few select dwarven nobles sat along the longer ends of the table.

I stood with a stern expression, "Today, Grand Cleric Elemena marched through the fort without so much as asking for anyone's permission and set themselves outside of the Tower of Mythral. They demanded I speak with them or they would set upon my people and drag me out of the tower. They demanded that I submit to the Church and allow myself to be brought to the Mage Tower to be held for the safety of Falladrin's citizens."

"What?" King Meric gasped. Logan and the other Fated seemed shocked as well. "Why would she do such a thing without consulting me first?"

One of the dwarven nobles slammed his fist onto the table. "She said that her authority came from beyond you, King Marshal. She said it as if you weren't part of her concerns!"

"Why would she do something so foolish?" Logan asked.

"Because she's a mage," Allen guessed correctly. "I'd wager they thought she was vulnerable enough on the surface to try to come for her. They took the chance."

"That's exactly what happened," I confirmed. "The Grand Cleric all but admitted it."

"There's another question that needs to be asked," Marshal hesitated. "Why were you coming to see me without the Grand Cleric? Why is she not here?"

"Because I took her and her people prisoner," I stated with authority.

"You did what!?" Marshal nearly shouted in horror. "You cannot take the Grand Cleric prisoner!"

I turned on the king, glaring at him. "And why not? What would you have done, King Marshal, if an enemy force marched up to your front door and threatened to kill your people and take you prisoner? She should be thankful she isn't dead."

Marshal stared at me. I could see how he was wrestling with the logic. Eventually he nodded in agreement. "You make a fair point. How long do you intend to keep them prisoner?"

"Until Pope Tressina herself comes to sue for their release," I responded, crossing my arms.

"Are you mad?" Serena balked. "You can't demand that the Pope come here just to negotiate the release of prisoners!"

"I can and I will!" I shouted. My patience had worn thin. "I was accosted in my home by a Grand Cleric; the Pope's primary representative in Falladrin! Grand Clerics answer to no one but the Pope herself. So it will be the Pope I speak with, and no one else. That is my right as the victor."

"In this, you are correct. Only the Pope can answer for a Grand Cleric," Marshal conceded. "But by doing this, you risk an Exalted March. Would you like us to send a messenger to explain things?"

"Would the news coming from a human messenger not send with it certain connotations?" Aelfric asked.

"What do you mean?" Logan arched his brow suspiciously.

"A human running to the Pope to tell her that a dwarven princess has captured one of her Grand Clerics and a number of Templars might seem like asking for aid in rescuing them, regardless of the actual reason the Grand Cleric is being held," Aelfric explained. "I think it would be better to send a human and a dwarf. That way, it looks more like a plea for diplomacy instead of a plea for aid."

"A fine point," Marshal agreed. "And to drive home the importance of the need for the Pope's diplomatic intervention, I'll have Duke Logan be the human messenger."

Logan glared at Marshal. "You're sending me to Fransway? After we spent years throwing those bastards out of our country?"

"Who else should I send that would be able to drive home the need for urgency?"

Marshal growled back. "You will go, and you will ensure that whoever the princess sends is heard in the proper manner. Do you understand me? Only someone who has defeated Fransway will be able to command the attention this matter deserves."

Logan remained silent for a few moments before sighing in resignation. "As usual, you are right, Marshal. I apologize for my outburst."

"I'll have Lord Irono go with the Duke to represent me," I decided.

"Your betrothed?" Marshal clarified. "Are you certain? Wouldn't you prefer to have him with you?"

"I would prefer not to have to have had to do any of this at all," I scolded the king. "But no one will represent my interests with more purpose than Franklin. Additionally, he was with me when the Grand Cleric was making her demands; he is a witness to what all took place. So he can give a firsthand account of what happened."

Marshal nodded in agreement. "Very well. Until then, I insist that the Grand Cleric and her retinue be treated with all care."

"I'm not a monster," I huffed. "I'm having large cells carved out for them even now. We'll bring in cots and tables for them to sleep and eat in comfort. But they will not leave the cells until after I've spoken with the Pope."

"Surely, My Lady," Logan said reticently, "they won't be forced to stay underground for that entire time?"

"They will," I replied with no room for negotiation. "We're spending a great deal of time above ground because we came here to help against the Scourge. They can spend a few months in our tunnels. After all, it's better than being buried in the ground."

"That's a fair point," Logan conceded.

"Take some men and prepare to ride to Fransway, Logan," King Marshal commanded. "Be prepared to leave when Lord Irono is ready."

Logan stood and bowed to Marshal. "As you command, Your Grace." He left the hall and prepared for his journey.

We decided to end the meeting there. King Marshal accompanied me back to the Tower of Mythral to speak with the Grand Cleric. I informed Franklin of his impending journey. He was rather eager to give the Pope a piece of his mind, but I hammered home the need for professionalism. He was representing me in this matter, so I expected him to act with all tact and care.

Franklin and Logan left within the hour. However, the capture of the Grand Cleric began to create a divide within the fort. Humans began to look at the dwarves with scorn. Their animosity was restrained by King Marshal, who decreed that the Grand Cleric was considered a renegade, and those who had joined her in the attempt to capture me were criminals as well. If any humans attempted to start a fight over it, they would be severely punished.

That evening, I met with Purpose and the elven spirit of the phylactery. I was determined to double down on my magical training. If the Church thought I was a powerful mage now, I would eclipse their expectations of me a thousandfold.

CHAPTER 14:

DIVINE INTERVENTION

It took nearly six months for Franklin and Logan to return from their trip to the Pope. It had been just over a year since we'd come to Orlimar. The repairs for the fort had been completed, and we were well on our way to finishing up the additions to make the battle go more smoothly and give us a better tactical advantage. Machicolations and balistraria were added to each wall. The gates were fixed to a weight system so that they could be opened and shut within moments.

There were two main projects going on right now. The first was a pair of massive ramps that went from the top of the fort and down deep into the forest by way of a large, curved path. The ramps would be fully enclosed in the next few months, and gates would be added with a similar weight system to open and close them.

The second project was completing all of the permanent buildings that we'd offered to help build for the humans. There were a few buildings like the meeting hall, and a few storehouses that were done already. Now we were primarily focused on housing, better stables, and creating better stations for the artisans. My smiths insisted that the humans get some decent forges as well (which meant the human forges were horribly inadequate and the dwarves couldn't stand watching them use such substandard equipment).

As far as the prisoners were concerned, they were comfortable. The three hundred prisoners were kept in three large cells that we had dug out. Over time, we had smoothed out the cells, added furnishings like beds, benches, and tables, and offered them things to do like small games and books to read. They were well-behaved and never tried to attack the dwarves who came in to do work on the cells. Not that it would do any good. Dwarves made terrible hostages, and if they had taken any dwarves hostage, the dwarves would prefer to fight and die… and a few thousand other dwarves would have a problem with the death of their fellow dwarves.

The Grand Cleric was given her own cell. It was comfortable enough for someone who had been so brazenly rude to me, and willing to put me in a cage after snatching me from my people. Her men were following her commands, so they were housed and fed well. The Grand Cleric was housed and fed well enough to keep her healthy and comfortable. She did not get anything else to pass her time with beyond her own thoughts, and her cell was well away from anything else in the tunnels. She was left to silence, and the only company she was given was the dwarf who fed her three times a day.

Franklin and Logan returned with a Franswanian rider to announce that Pope Tressina would be arriving in three days along with several dozen high-ranking Church members and one hundred Franswanian chevaliers.

We had a long meeting to discuss how things had been going and what had occurred in Fransway. Once that was finished, King Marshal and I escorted Franklin and Logan through the fort to show them our progress. Logan insisted on seeing the prisoners so that he could ensure they weren't being mistreated. I suppose he thought we would treat them the way humans treated their prisoners because he had thought they'd all be withered and thin by now. Logan expressed his surprise when he found the prisoners to be healthy and thriving.

I held a special feast in the tunnels for Franklin's return.

The next few days were business as usual for us. The humans were scurrying around like ants, preparing for the Pope's arrival. It wasn't like there was much they could do. We did help by expanding the stables, but I didn't think it was worth wasting all that lumber for a single visit. The horses could double up. The one thing we did do was construct a large bench in the meeting hall from which the Pope, King Marshal, and I could sit for the Grand Cleric's hearing.

The Pope's arrival was met with formality and fanfare on the part of the humans. All six Fated joined King Marshal and Duke Logan at the gate to welcome her to Orlimar. Tressina was old, easily in her late sixties or early seventies, and was tired when she arrived. She kept to her duties, however, and met with us in the meeting hall.

We sat at the table surrounded by dwarven warriors, King's guards, and Franswanian chevaliers.

King Marshal got things started, "Pope Tressina, we thank you for making the journey to Falladrin to see to this matter personally."

"Duke Logan and Lord Irono made it seem like I didn't have much choice in the matter," Tressina said quietly. "Not if I wanted the prisoners to be freed at all. I take it this is Exemplar Orodum, who Lord Irono has boasted about so much?"

I bowed my head to the Pope, "I am, my Lady. Princess Merida Orodum of Cragmorrar. At your service."

The old woman stared at me, appraising me carefully, "You do not seem to hold much malice for the Church, child. I understand the reason for the steps you have taken, but you must understand that many in the Church demanded I call for an Exalted March when they heard the news. Your actions have created quite the stir."

"It's a shame that the Grand Cleric's actions didn't create just as much of a stir for their audacity and shamefulness," I quickly retorted. "You understand that she was willing to start a war over capturing me, yes?"

"Don't misunderstand," Tressina replied in a patient manner, "the Church is rather split in their opinions. Some have called for an Exalted March, while others are surprised we aren't mourning the death of the Grand Cleric and her men."

"Where do you stand on the matter?" I asked directly.

"I believe the Grand Cleric was only doing what she believed to be right," she dodged the question diplomatically. "However, yours is a unique case and she should have recognized that the Church has no sway over the dwarves. She should have also used much better judgment when attempting to abscond with a princess of any kingdom. Being as old as you are, she should have understood that you were no danger as a mage unless provoked."

"How should she think that when mages die of old age in your Mage Towers without ever being a threat to anyone?" I couldn't help but snipe.

"Princess, this might not be the time to discuss Church practices," King Marshal inserted carefully.

"No," Tressina patted the air. "She has a point, but this is something we should discuss over time. For now, we should focus on diplomacy. What is it you desire for the release of the Grand Cleric and her men, Princess?"

I sat up a bit straighter now that we were getting down to business, "What Grand Cleric Elemena did was not only wrong, but nearly set off a war. She attempted to kidnap me, was willing to kill my men, and was willing to start a war between the dwarves and the Church while putting Falladrin in the middle of the fighting. Her actions would have cost the lives of thousands, if not tens of thousands, of people."

"You ask what I desire for their release? First, I ask that she be stripped of her position and be demoted to the level of Lay Sister without the possibility of being raised above a Lay Sister. Someone with such poor judgment should not be given the level of responsibility and influence of anything more than that. If she truly wishes to serve the Creator, she can do so in that capacity."

Tressina simply hummed in response, "And next?"

"Second, the Templars who simply obeyed her command without protesting or seeking a way to avoid the situation should be demoted to a position commensurate with the poor judgment they showed," I continued. "Soldiers are not mindless creatures, and they should have the mindset to question an order if they can foresee that it would be detrimental to the overall good. They did not show the wisdom that should come with their rank."

"In this, I agree," Tressina nodded. "But who will take their place? I understand you have many Templars in your tunnels."

"If I may make a suggestion?" Logan queried.

"Please," Tressina replied simply.

"The failure of the Templars is clearly with their command structure," Logan explained. "I would ask the Knight-Commander to name officers that he meets with. Replace the Knight-Commander and the men he names. Have them demoted and transferred. Promote the Templars still in place, and bring in Templars from outside Falladrin to shore up the numbers."

"Would this be satisfactory, Princess?" the Pope looked at me.

I gave a polite bow, "As always, Duke Logan provides an elegant and practical solution to the issue. I would agree to this solution as long as the Duke is willing to oversee the change in command. I trust him to make sure everything goes smoothly for the sake of good relations between Falladrin and Cragmorrar."

"I would be happy to be of service," Logan offered.

"Very well," Tressina conceded. "Is there anything else?"

"Yes," I replied, then looked to King Marshal, who gave me a firm nod. Then I looked to the other end of the table at Allen, who smiled at me.

"There are two other things," I said with as serious a tone as I could muster. "Cragmorrar has demanded that Elemena be put on trial for attempting to kidnap me."

"A trial?" Tressina gasped. "You are already having her stripped of her position, what more could you want from her?"

"Your Grace," Marshal interjected, "Elemena tried to kidnap the princess of one of our allies. That is tantamount to the declaration of war. By all rights, they should demand her execution, but Princess Orodum has worked tirelessly to convince them not to press for a death sentence. King Triston would be well within his rights to execute her. You must admit that this was a possibility you considered would happen."

The Pope sighed and nodded hesitantly, "I admit, it was something I was surprised had not happened yet. I assumed you hadn't done so because you feared the threat of an Exalted March, but now I see you waited to hold the trial so that I could be among those who would sit in judgment."

"The judgments would not be considered true and valid without your consent," I stated. "Any punishment we decided on without your consent could have been rescinded if you disagreed with it."

"And any judgment we come to while I'm here will go unquestioned," Tressina finished the thought. "You are indeed wise for your age, Princess. I can see why Duke Logan and Lord Franklin spoke so highly of you. Very well. I will agree to assist in the trial. What is the other thing you desire?"

"I would like to disband the Mage Tower in Falladrin," I announced, then pressed on before she could outright refuse. "In its place, I would like to help establish a mage's college. Anyone showing magical ability in Falladrin would be required to attend up to a certain age in order to train them to control their magic and defend their minds against demonic influence. They will be able to leave the college to visit their families during small breaks throughout the year and will be allowed to live freely once they've reached a certain point in their training."

"You would have apostates roaming the country without Church supervision?" Tressina asked.

"I would have people live freely without the yoke of dogma around their necks," I retorted with a snap. "These free mages would be allowed to use their magic however they see fit as long as it wasn't against others or by practicing forbidden magic such as blood magic or by summoning demons or undead."

"Falladrin is also willing to allow the mages to join the army where they will help see to the defense of the country," Marshal offered. "We are also considering a position for mages to become the local protectors for any village or town that they reside in and gain a stipend from the crown for their service."

"And to ensure that no illegal research or spellcasting is being performed," Marric quickly added, "we would have Templars perform inspections on a regular basis. This would allow Falladrin Templars to continue watching over the mages, just in a different method which would allow the mages their freedom."

"You believe freedom will stop mages from becoming maleficarum? What happens if a mage decides to give into a demon's temptations while there are no Templars around?" Tressina asked pointedly.

"The same thing that happens already when a mage runs away or dabbles in blood magic within the Mage Tower walls out of desperation to be free," I countered. "I am a mage and have been so all my life. I have never needed anyone to tell me not to give in to the promises of a demon. But I've also never been locked inside a tower and unable to leave. I've never been desperate to be free from being watched day in and day out by people willing to kill me if I step out of line. Neither have you. I would think that level of desperation would drive anyone to do what it takes to be free."

Pope Tressina remained silent for several moments. "I'll concede that you have some points, Princess. If King Marshal is willing to oversee the process, then I am willing to give this a try. I assume that you would like the senior mages to become the instructors at this college?"

"I would like it," I confirmed with a nod. "However, if the senior mages do not wish to stay, I would like for them to become town protectors."

"The details can be worked out with the mages when the time comes," Marshal said.

"If that is all," Tressina began, but I had to cut her off.

"Unfortunately, it won't be," I sighed.

"I believe those were the last two things you said you wanted," Tressina observed.

I nodded and sighed again. "Those were the last two things that I wanted."

"But Elemena did not simply transgress against the Princess and Cragmorrar," King Marshal put forward. "She mounted what constitutes an attack against Falladrin's allies. Allies who are actively helping us prepare for a Scourge. She marched through our camp and declared their intent to attack those allies. This was an act of aggression against Falladrin and myself because I would have had no choice but to join in the fight in order to aid my allies."

Tressina gave a moan of concession. "You are right, King Thirston. You could not have known her intentions, and the attack would have required a response. How can I compensate you for her lack of judgment?"

"Falladrin will soon be facing a Scourge," Marshal explained calmly. "We could use more men, and we will certainly need Scourge Sentinels. If you can promise us reinforcements and send for a force of Sentinels to aid us, I would consider the debt paid."

"That will be simple enough," Tressina agreed. "When I leave, I will command one hundred of the chevaliers I brought with me to remain here until after the Scourge has been defeated. As for the Sentinels, I will dispatch a messenger this very day to their headquarters and have every available Scourge Sentinel here immediately."

"I thank you, Pope," Marshal bowed his head.

"Is there anything else anyone wants as a concession?" the Pope asked, clearly losing her patience.

Silence met her question.

"Then may I see those you have captured and ensure their good health?" she asked.

I bowed my head and smiled, "Of course. Please, follow me."

I led the Pope to the Tower of Mythral, then down into the tunnels where we had made our home and kept the prisoners. As we walked, Tressina questioned me on the work we'd been doing so far and how the tunnels seemed like excellent examples of dwarven craftsmanship. I had to admit, she had a way of trying to worm her way onto one's good side. However, I was experienced enough to know when someone was trying to placate me.

Pope Tressina noted that the prisoners were in far better health and spirits than she had imagined. She had to admit that they were treated better than she expected. Elemena was a different story, though. Her desperation for socialization had worn her ego and she began to weep in the presence of the Pope. Her tears only flowed more freely when Tressina explained that she would now only ever be a Lay Sister and that she would be put on trial in the next few days.

We held a dinner that evening for the Pope, and the conversation was more cordial. Pope Tressina was interested in getting to know me and how I was able to become a proficient mage without training or succumbing to demons. I left out anything about Purpose and simply marked it down to hard work. I also told her that I wasn't sure how I was born with magic, only that I learned I could use it and trained diligently to master it. I also explained how we had retaken the three Holds and were slowly securing the Under Roads between them.

The next few days were spent in meetings, and with the Pope touring the fort. The meetings were mostly to discuss steps on changing the Mage Tower into a Mage College and how mages would be established as village protectors. We also discussed the details of the trial and how things would go. The Pope insisted that Elemena not be chained during the trial, to at least allow her to save some face. I agreed so long as she wore the robes of a Lay Sister and not the golden robes of a Grand Cleric, and that she be referred to as Lay Sister as well.

The day of the trial arrived, and the paths from the Tower of Mythral to the meeting hall were packed with dwarves and humans alike. Elemena was escorted to the meeting hall surrounded by dwarven warriors. The crowd had mixed words for her as she passed by. When she arrived at the meeting hall, Elemena was placed on a podium where she would stand for the duration.

Around the meeting hall sat dwarven and human nobles, some of the Church representatives that Tressina had brought with her, and the other Fated. They were all there to witness the trial. We didn't want anyone to say things didn't go properly. The demotion and trial of a Grand Cleric was an extremely rare thing, after all. Sitting in judgment was Pope Tressina, King Marshal, Trianna, and myself. Trianna was allowed a seat because Elemena's actions would have brought the elves into the war as well since the elves were invested in keeping the efforts of Orlimar in full swing and thus were allied with the dwarves who they saw as the reason for getting to inherit the fort once things were done.

"Lay Sister Elemena," Pope Tressina began, "you are charged with starting an insurrection, marching an armed force through the camp of King Thirston, declaring martial intent against the Princess of Cragmorrar, and the attempted kidnapping and imprisonment of the Princess of Cragmorrar. How do you plead?"

"Pope Tressina," Elemena pleaded, "I only sought to adhere to the Church's tenets. Magic is made to serve man, never to rule over him."

"If ever there was a misinterpreted and abused tenet of any faith," I barked, "it is that one! Why is it whenever the Church needs to justify enslavement, the kidnapping of children, or any kind of power grab, they drag that phrase out and shove it in everyone's face?"

I pointed an accusatory finger down at Elemena, "For a thousand years, you and people like you have justified your actions under the guise of faith. Ironic, as it was Saint Mellina who used that phrase while she was referring to those who were abusing their power to enslave others."

"Princess Orodum, please," King Marshal said diplomatically, "It isn't the Church who's on trial here."

I bowed my head, "Apologies. But this has hurt me personally, and it has hurt untold people over a thousand years."

"I believe we can understand and forgive the Princess' distress," Pope Tressina reassured everyone. "After all, who would not bear a grudge against a policy which they are not subject to? A policy, Lay Sister, that I am sure you are aware of, does not extend to the dwarves who do not share our beliefs in the Creator or Saint Mellina."

"There has never been such a precedent, my Pope," Elemena cried. "Dwarves have never been able to cast magic, so we have never had to enforce the tenet with them."

"And why is it you believe humans have the right to subject their beliefs onto any other race?" Trianna asked. "We Paddish do not believe in the

Creator either, yet your Templars have hunted us over the years to take our mage children."

"And you have allowed human mages to live freely in some circumstances," King Marshal added. "Why is it that elves and Princess Merida must be brought to the Mage Tower, yet some humans can live freely?"

Elemena hesitated to answer. Everyone, including Pope Tressina, knew what the answer was, but it had to be spoken out loud or it couldn't be dealt with.

"Those humans..." Elemena floundered.

"Those mages who have been allowed to live outside the Mage Tower without oversight have all been nobles whose families have paid the Church for their family member to be free," Tressina admitted.

"Have we come to the heart of it?" I asked with a thoughtful tone. "Were you planning on taking me to the Mage Tower until my father, King Triston, paid the Church to allow me my freedom?"

"What?" Elemena gasped as the crowd began to mutter and discuss the spoken truth behind the practice. "No! I was only adhering to the tenets of my faith!"

"If that's true, then why did you wait until I was away from Cragmorrar?" I accused her. "At any time, you could have marched your forces up to Cragmorrar to demand I be handed over. If your faith is so important, then why wait until I was more vulnerable?"

Elemena lowered her head in silence.

"I think we have our answer," Pope Tressina looked to the rest of us. "The Lay Sister lacked the faith of her convictions. You knew what would happen if you marched on Cragmorrar, didn't you, Sister?"

"...I did," Elemena admitted.

"You made the decision to come for the Princess here because you believed you could avoid the consequences of marching on Cragmorrar, correct?" Marshal pressed.

"Yes, Your Grace," she whispered.

"Did you stop to consider the ramifications of marching an armed force into the King's camp and threatening an ally of Falladrin and the Paddish?" Trianna slapped the bench.

"I did not know she was an ally of the Paddish," Elemena shook her head.

"Which is to say you did know that she was an ally of Falladrin," Pope Tressina said with disappointment. "And Falladrin is the country which you are supposed to care for and offer advice to. Falladrin, whose king has trusted you to see to the affairs of his country while he prepares to put his life on the line against a Scourge!"

Elemena bowed her head. "I have failed you and my King."

The questioning continued for nearly three hours. We had Elemena explain everything from the time she first heard about me, all the way to the time she arrived in Orlimar. She gave us the names of the Templars who helped to convince her that it was finally time to try and bring me to the Mage Tower. Not once did she mention considering that I was clearly in control of my power and thus was no threat to Falladrin.

"Have you anything to say in your defense before we pass judgment?" King Marshal asked.

"No, Your Grace," Elemena said defeated. "Except to say that I did what I did for what I thought was in the best interest of the Church."

"Then we shall deliberate," Pope Tressina said. "Take the accused to a room where she will be alone, and clear this hall until we are ready to give our verdict."

It took us three hours to go over all of the information Elemena had given us. There was no small amount of disagreement on what the Church could and couldn't do, how far the Church's power extended and to whom, and other ancillary topics. This trial would have massive ramifications for the entire Melindrian world, no matter what the decision became. In the end, we decided that life in prison would be the appropriate punishment. We all agreed to allow Pope Tressina to pass down the sentence.

Everyone was recalled to the meeting hall and Elemena awaited her fate.

"Lay Sister Elemena," Pope Tressina called, "it has come to me to pass on the judgment of this council. Before I pass down the judgment, you should know that your actions have caused great strife not only between nations, but also members of the Melindrian faith. There is now a rift and cracks in the foundations of the beliefs shared by millions. What you have done, and the questions that are already beginning to rise in response to it, will shake the world."

"I understand, and I apologize," Elemena bowed.

"You should also know that even though Princess Orodum is the offended party here, she has worked in your interest with her people so that they did not call for your death," Tressina stood and stared down at Elemena.

"I thank you for your generosity," Elemena managed to smile fearfully up at me.

"Because you are my subordinate, I have been given the responsibility of handing down the judgment," Tressina intoned. "Lay Sister Elemena, for the crimes of treason against your king, treason against your faith, the attempted kidnapping of a member of the royal family of Cragmorrar, inciting war between the Church and the kingdoms of Falladrin and Cragmorrar, as well as the Paddish elves; I, Pope Tressina the Third, sentence you to death by hanging."

That drew a roar of surprise from all the witnesses, as well as surprised expressions from King Marshal and Trianna. I couldn't help but see the reason behind the decision, and it wasn't because of what she said next.

Tressina waited for the shock to subside before continuing, "As magnanimous of a gesture as Princess Orodum offered by working with her people to calm their rage, she cannot calm the rage that you have raised in the Church. And treason, especially treason against your king, cannot call for any less of a sentence. Therefore, as your Pope, I have sentenced you to die."

Elemena lowered her head in sorrow. "Yes, Your Grace. I have heard your judgment and am prepared to meet the Creator."

"Guards!" Tressina called. "Have her taken back to her cell. She will be executed tomorrow morning."

Elemena was brought back to her cell in the tunnels. Tressina's judgment caught us all off guard, and it was the only thing discussed at dinner. King Marshal set some of his men to construct a gallows.

The execution was a morbid affair. All executions are. Pope Tressina gave a simple prayer for Elemena before she was hung. She was allowed to hang there for two hours before she was brought down, and the gallows were turned into a funeral pyre for her. It took a few weeks for things to completely go back to normal.

Pope Tressina left Orlimar a few days after the execution. True to her word, she left the chevaliers she promised. The humans and dwarves began to get back to work on the fort. King Marshal, Allen, and I had decided to take a trip to the Mage Tower to announce the dissolution of the Mage Tower and start the establishment of the Lemlalian Mage College.

CHAPTER 15:

WELCOME REINFORCEMENTS

King Marshal, Allen, and I remained at the Mage Tower for three weeks, discussing the details of converting the Mage Tower into a college and allowing the mages freedom to live life normally. We also went over the plans to allow mages to become village protectors with a stipend from the crown. This encouraged a focus on battle magic, but it didn't exclude the study of other magic. Marshal also offered preferential posts to any mage who volunteered to help with the Scourge. Allen offered positions as professors to the mages who helped with the Scourge and wished to stay at the Mage Tower to train younger mages.

With the option to be able to visit family or leave when they chose to, a surprising number of mages decided to stay at the Mage Tower. It seemed like they developed a more familial social system in the tower since they didn't have anyone else they could really interact with. The news about the change from a Church-controlled Mage Tower to a state-funded college went over well. It would take some time for them to figure out when students would be able to leave and see their families, but it was agreed that until that time came around, students' families would be able to come and visit them.

By the time we were done, letters had already been sent out to families with the news. I saw Veron at the tower's shore with a crew of dwarves setting up a new pier. While King Marshal was focused on the state policies of the college and its mages, Allen and I focused on the ancillary aspects like transportation, supplies, and infrastructure. Allen signed an exclusive contract with Veron to build and manage the new dock and harbor, as well as to deliver dimvyum to the college. This meant that Veron and Rita would have a ridiculous amount of gold coming in, and as their patron House, I would get a solid percentage of that coin.

We returned to Orlimar with nearly two dozen mages ready and willing to unleash their full potential against the scourgespawn. I wasn't sure how much good two dozen mages would do, but I could think of ways they could be put to good use if we managed them tactically. The mages could deal a lot of damage if given the room to really let loose. I had a pretty good idea.

Over the next few months, I had some extra materials delivered from Cragmorrar. To my very welcome surprise, Petra had come along with the materials, bringing with her four hundred warriors of House Petran. I made sure to ensure that she hadn't brought too many warriors so that the Hold was left undefended, but she assured me that things were handled. She also hinted that these were not the only reinforcements coming from Cragmorrar.

That intrigued me.

We feasted that evening, bringing together all the dwarves in a massive hall that had been prepared as a command station for the dwarven forces. I expected Faren to have a happier reaction to Petra's arrival than he did, but he seemed rather neutral about it all. Still, his reaction didn't seem to affect the mood of any other dwarves, and Petra seemed to have expected that sort of reaction.

House Petran was added to the battle plans. They would assist the cavalry in the flanking maneuvers so that the dwarves could stick together. However, this would require Petran soldiers to be first out of the ramp gates. They wouldn't be able to keep up with the rhoarno charge down the ramps. The drawback was that House Petran would be facing the scourgespawn alone for about a minute before the cavalry arrived to break the flanks up into more manageable pockets of resistance. It was dangerous, but they were willing to accept the risks since it would also give the cavalry time to be as effective as possible.

Two months after House Petran arrived, we received the Franswanian Scourge Sentinels. Nearly fifty Sentinels arrived on horseback. They were an impressive lot, and there were also two dwarves sprinkled among them. It was heartening to see my own kind with them.

The arrival of the Sentinels lifted everyone's spirits. We feasted on their arrival and met with them afterwards.

Sentinel Clarel looked around the large table in the meeting hall, seeming to appraise us, "Your Graces, Lords and Ladies, as you know I have been sent here by Pope Tressina to assist you in preparing for an upcoming Scourge. However, we have seen no signs of a Scourge on our journey here from Fransway, nor have we seen any signs of a Scourge since our arrival. What I do see, however, is a large set of armies that have gathered together in a large fort preparing for something that we Sentinels should know is coming."

She paused before asking, "May I ask how you know there is a Scourge coming when the Scourge Sentinels have seen no sign of one."

King Marshal leaned forward, "I believe Princess Merida will best be able to answer that question, Sentinel Clarel." He looked at me and gave me a nod to explain.

I returned the nod then smiled and bowed my head to Clarel, "Falladrin has had six Fated individuals born roughly twenty years ago. These Fated were gifted with vast knowledge of Thoros' past and limited information on events that will happen in the future. In the next year or so, a Scourge will begin forming in the Wilds."

"'Fated' individuals?" Clarel almost scoffed. She'd held back the mockery in her tone likely because her time in Fransway had driven home how you could, and should, speak to royalty and nobles. "How do you know that these individuals are even speaking the truth and aren't spinning some fanciful tale in order to curry favor and seem more important than they are?"

"Because I don't lie," I replied with a cool voice, but shot a glare at the Sentinel that could melt stone.

Clarel looked like she was trying to process what I just said. "Forgive me, Princess, but are you saying that you are one of the six Fated individuals?"

Marshal answered for me, "Princess Merida is indeed one of the Fated. I can attest to her knowledge. When we first met, she told me about a journey that Duke Logan and I had gone on years before she was even born. We've never spoken of the journey to anyone. Yet somehow she knew."

"Each of the Fated have the same general knowledge of the world," I added. "But each Fated also has knowledge that others do not. That is how each of us has managed to improve the lives of our people and work to improve things in Falladrin in general."

The Sentinel considered the information for some time. "If what you say is true, can you tell me what I did before joining the Sentinels?"

I smirked, "You were a mage in the Franswanian Mage Tower; more specifically, you were an Enchanter. As I understand it, it was your talent as an enchanter that the Sentinels recruited you for."

Clarel stared at me as if she couldn't believe what she'd heard. She took a deep breath then sighed in resignation, "You're correct. I don't know how you know, but you're correct."

"Is that proof enough?" King Marshal asked. "I doubt anyone here other than some of your fellow Sentinels knew the answer to that question, let alone a young dwarf."

"It's proof enough," Clarel conceded. "So if you believe there is a Scourge coming, the Sentinels will aid you. How long do we have until the scourgespawn arrive?"

"Approximately one year," Serena answered. "We're not sure of the exact day, but we have seen the start of some scourgespawn activity deep in the Cariok Wilds. They're just small raiding bands right now, but as the year progresses, we expect to see more and more."

"And we know we'll need the Sentinels to kill the Archdemon," Trianna added.

"Bringing down the archdemon will be no easy task," Clarel mused. "We have to get it to land if it shows itself. And wherever it lands, it's going to cause a massive amount of destruction."

"Over the next year, we're going to be setting up trebuchets around the fort," Logan offered. "Dozens of them. As many as we can manage."

"They'll fire flechette ammunition," I clarified. "Our engineers have designed them to slice through anything they hit, and they'll fly in a group so that each shot will cover a wide area in the air."

"I've seen the human and dwarven forces, but what about the Paddish?" Clarel asked, looking at Trianna specifically since she was the only elf in the hall and the Paddish representative.

"The Paddish will arrive for the battle," Trianna responded with confidence. "I can at least tell you that the Paddish will be blocking the scourgespawn's retreat. We'll be behind them, harassing them forward into your formation."

"What if the back line decides to turn and fight you instead of continuing forward?" Logan asked.

"Then we'll fight them," Trianna said decisively. "If nothing else, it will separate their forces and make things easier on everyone."

"I would think that would be the best possibility," I suggested eagerly. "That would mean the cavalry would be able to harass the back lines of the split forces with more impunity."

Ser Michel de Chevin, the leader of the Franswanian chevaliers that Pope Tressina left with us nodded, "Princess Orodum makes a fine point. The cavalry will do its duty no matter what, but we will be more effective the more disorganized the enemy is."

"There are ways to disrupt the enemy's position without troops," Marshal mused. "We could use the trebuchets on the horde with standard stone ammunition until the archdemon makes itself known."

"Continuous fire into the battlefield could endanger the cavalry and infantry we have out there," Clarel countered. "We don't want to fire onto our troops."

"Perhaps we could practice our timing so that one volley from all of the trebuchets cuts through the middle of the horde just before the cavalry and infantry exit the gates," Faren tapped the table. "A volley like that would likely cut a large swathe through the horde that the cavalry could take advantage of. We can force one half towards the fort, and the other half back towards the elves."

Ser Michel de Chevin nodded in approval, "The terrain will be pockmarked after the volley, so the cavalry will need to take care, but that would be an effective tactic."

"And there will be multiple mages with the elves," Trianna built on the strategy being put together. "Princess Orodum will be with the cavalry. So there will be magic front, back, and center. Splitting the horde will crush both sides between blades and magic on one side, and cavalry and magic on the other."

"House Nordrucan will gladly join House Petran to back up the cavalry," Trenton said as the door opened suddenly.

"Trenton?" I gasped. "Trenton!!!" I shoved myself back in my chair and ran down the length of the meeting hall to the shock and surprise of everyone, leaping up and hugging my brother's neck, laughing excitedly. "You didn't send a messenger! Why didn't you tell us you were coming?"

"Sister…" Trenton cleared his throat, giving me a gentle hug in return. "You've forgotten your decorum."

I looked up at Trenton with confusion before his words clicked. I looked behind me, and everyone was staring at me, smiling warmly and others chuckling softly. I turned back to Trenton and just hugged him tighter. "I don't care! I haven't seen you in years, and you just showed up out of the blue! How can I not be excited?"

Trenton sighed, giving in to me once again. "Yes, well… It's wonderful to see you as well, Sister. We can speak personally after the meeting. For now, we have plans to make."

"You're sitting with me," I demanded as I took his hand and pulled him along to my seat at the head of the table. One of the dwarven nobles quickly brought his chair over so that Trenton could use it.

Sentinel Clarel chuckled at the commotion. "It's always nice to see family reunited. You're the Princess' brother?"

Trenton bowed his head. "I am Prince Trenton Nordrucan, eldest son of King Triston Nordrucan. I govern Nordrucan Hold and have the great honor to be Exemplar Orodum's elder brother as well."

"It's good to have the reinforcements, my Lord," Clarel bowed. "May I ask how many men you've brought?"

"I came with five hundred Nordrucan warriors," Trenton explained, "as well as four hundred warriors from House Cragmor, and two regiments of the Fallen Legion."

"Nearly three thousand?" King Marshal asked with an approving tone. "Impressive. You've essentially doubled the dwarven presence in the fort. I hope those tunnels have enough room for all of you."

"We'll make room in no time, won't we?" I asked, looking at some of the other dwarven nobles who quickly excused themselves to relay the need for the construction to begin.

"I should also mention that we brought Lady Cragmor with us as well," Trenton added.

The other Fated gasped with excitement. They had been wanting to meet her for a while now.

"House Beltia has also arrived," Trenton continued. "Beltia and Durdren decided to head to the tower to begin setting up camp. They came with another five hundred warriors."

The other Fated squealed with excitement once again at the prospect of meeting Beltia and Durdren.

The meeting continued well into the evening, with dinner and other food being served as needed. We discussed tactics and the expansion of the underground tunnel systems. With the amount of additional forces, we also had to start plans on the expansion of the fort at the top level, as well as planning on what we would do to expand the base level below the chasm to accommodate the elves when they made their appearance.

Tactics were laid out for several scenarios on how the battle could go and for where the archdemon would land. Typically, the archdemon would just fly around the battlefield as it augmented the scourgespawn by attacking us with its flame weapons. It wouldn't engage directly unless it was forced to the ground. We decided that by spreading out the mages, a specific arcane bolt would be sent into the air to signal where the archdemon went down.

Next was the establishment of the chain of command. We decided to divide the forces up into three sections: the main infantry, the cavalry, and the Paddish. The main infantry would be under the command of King Marshal, with Serena, Clifford, and Logan as his primary officers. They would control the ballista, trebuchets, and the main defensive force.

Trianna would command the Paddish. Her officers would be Aelfric, Allen, and one of the Paddish Elders. They would command the Paddish and work to break the backline of the scourgespawn. Trianna assured us that she had some additional surprises in store for the enemy. That made me curious, and no matter how much I asked about it over the coming months, Trianna would only ever smirk and say 'you'll see'.

I was in command of the cavalry unit. The cavalry would be backed up by House Nordrucan, House Petran, House Beltia, and Fallen Legion warriors. Because we were going to have the Franswanian chevaliers augmenting our rhoarno cavalry, I named Ser Michel de Chevin one of my officers. Trenton and Beltia would command supporting infantry. House Nordrucan and House Beltia would focus on pressing the scourgespawn back into the Paddish assault, while House Petran and House Orodum would press against the scourgespawn still capable of marching on Orlimar. The cavalry would harass the backlines and keep those ranks broken and incapable of forming a proper defense.

The Scourge Sentinels would be spread out in pairs around the battlefield with the main three forces so that they could respond quickly to the archdemon's vulnerability when it went down. They would also be able to help suggest strategies wherever they were in response to their connection with the scourgespawn. We would depend on them to direct more precise, impromptu troop movements.

It was close to midnight by the time the meeting concluded, with other smaller meetings being scheduled over the course of the next few months. The next day, I escorted Trenton, Beltia, Durdren, and Gniess around the fort. The other Fated tagged along so that they could meet them. We caught up on everything that had happened over the past few years and just enjoyed the day.

The next few months were filled with expanding the tunnels, practicing different battle scenarios, and building more accommodations for everyone. We also began to see more and more signs of scourgespawn, which put everyone on edge. It wouldn't be too long until we would be facing the horde and the archdemon along with it.

CHAPTER 16:

THE BATTLE OF ORLIMAR

Scourgespawn were spotted more and more often over the following months, always to the south in the wilds. Scout forces regularly came back with reports of encountering multiple roaming bands of scourgespawn: some organized and raiding local settlements, some simply exploring, and others setting up small camps. Slowly but surely, they were drawing closer to Orlimar. It would only be a matter of time before the horde made itself known.

Eventually, the day came. Every scout party returned within only a few hours of leaving the fort with the same news; the horde was amassing for an attack. There was no going back now. No more time to plan or prepare. All we could do now was stand and face it. Last-minute preparations were in full swing: ballista and trebuchet ammunition was available, the mages were scrying and preparing larger spells, and everyone was double and triple-checking their weapons and armor.

There was a tension in the air that couldn't be denied. We could all feel it. There were small, quick meetings to make sure everyone was where they needed to be, had what they needed to have, and knew every plan and contingency. Nearly twelve thousand united humans and dwarves rushed around, preparing for the battle. Another three to five thousand elves were somewhere waiting to strike. We had nearly twenty thousand warriors of all kinds, and we were still outnumbered nearly three to one in the best scenarios.

I sat in the dining room of my home beneath the Tower of Mythral and looked at those sitting at the table with me. Trenton, Darina, Faren, Franklin, Durdren, Beltia, Petra, Gniess, and Sidra were all there. We were meeting to discuss last-minute changes to any of the battle plans.

"We're certain the ramps are still secure?" Trenton asked Sidra, who had become my personal Legion representative.

"They are, my Prince," Sidra confirmed. "The Legion has been keeping scouts and archers along the length of the ramps all day. No scourgespawn have come anywhere close to the treeline. We don't expect any of the fiends to approach until the battle begins."

"Scourgespawn typically just charge anything they see," Durdren augmented Sidra's answer. "But hordes are a bit different. They'll wait until the full mass is ready to push forward."

"And since Exemplar Orodum understands that there's an archdemon guiding them, it will likely wait until after dark," Sidra finished. "The sunlight weakens them, and they're stronger and see better in the dark."

"I think we can safely say we're as prepared as we're going to be," I tried to say with as confident and chipper a tone as I could muster. "I'd like to move on to a different topic, something that doesn't have anything to do with the Scourge."

Trenton looked at me and raised a brow. "Oh? And what's that, Sister?"

I smiled and looked over at everyone. "I'd like to discuss wedding plans. Specifically, I'd like to discuss the three weddings that we'll be having when we return to Cragmorrar: Faren and Petra's, Rita and Veron's, and then mine and Franklin's."

Everyone seemed to find my suggestion amusing.

"I should think the marriage of Cragmorrar's Princess and Exemplar would be first and foremost in the subject," Trenton suggested.

I shook my head. "Any wedding I have will overshadow anyone else's. I'm not so ignorant of my standing with the people that I would think otherwise. I want you all to enjoy proper wedding festivities before Franklin and I are wed."

Petra smiled at me. "You're very considerate, My Lady. My parents and I have been sending letters back and forth, discussing the dates and plans for the wedding. We were planning to wed only a few weeks after we returned home."

"Is that so?" Darina asked with excitement. "Will you be wed in Petran Hold or Cragmorrar?"

"Cragmorrar," Faren said with a determined tone, just as Petra replied, "Petran Hold."

The two looked at each other, but Petra just chuckled. "We're still figuring things out. Cragmorrar is Faren's home, Petran Hold is mine. I think it would be best to hold the first wedding of House Petra's family in the Hold."

"And I simply wish to be wed somewhere that would not inconvenience Lady Orodum who made the wedding possible in more ways than one," Faren clarified.

"Oh, Faren," I sighed. "There's no inconvenience on my part to go to Petran Hold to witness your wedding. So long as you're both happy, so am I."

"And you're certain you'd rather wait until after Rita and Veron are married?" Franklin leaned over to gently place a hand on my wrist.

I nodded. "I am. Rita is as much of a sister to me as Trenton and Bilfern are my brothers. She and Veron deserve the attention for a while before our wedding."

Franklin smiled and patted my hand. "Your consideration is commendable, my love."

I blushed softly. "Not at all. I simply want my friends to have the celebrations they deserve."

"It will be sad to go our separate ways after all is said and done," Sidra sighed. "It's been nice to make such amazing friends."

"I would think that you'd stay on with Exemplar Orodum as the Legion's liaison, Sidra," Petra suggested.

"I am a Legionnaire, my Lady," Sidra bowed her head. "My duty is to protect Cragmorrar from the scourgespawn. I can't do that if I'm always with the Exemplar."

"Nonsense," Beltia chimed in. "After this battle, the Fallen Legion won't be needed near as much. With the force we have assembled here, I doubt there will be hardly any scourgespawn left."

"I suppose we'll see," Sidra mused.

The discussion went on like that for another hour or so before a messenger arrived to let us know that the sun was about to set. It was time to get ready, but everyone was already prepared. There wasn't anyone in the fort who wasn't armed and armored. I commanded everyone to get to their stations and to prepare for the assault, while Faren escorted me across the bridge to meet with King Marshal, Logan, and the other Fated.

They seemed to have had the same idea as we met halfway across the bridge.

I offered everyone a curtsey, "One last meeting?"

Marshal bowed, "I suppose so. We wanted to wish you luck in the coming battle."

"We won't need luck," I smiled grimly. "We have plans on top of plans and contingencies for our contingencies. We may be outnumbered, but we have strategy and actual teamwork on our side."

"You keep yourself safe," Allen stepped forward and bowed his head. "I can't have the vice dean of the Lemlalian Mage College dying so soon after its establishment. It would look bad."

I smirked up at him, "I don't know, it might benefit you to finally be the most powerful mage there."

Allen laughed, "Oh? You think you're the most powerful mage among us, do you?"

"This will be a fine night to find out," I challenged him with a grin.

Allen nodded, "Hmmm, sounds good. I'll give you my count after it's all said and done."

"You both just be safe," Aelfric chuckled. "Don't go putting yourselves in danger just to get a higher score."

"You stay safe as well," Faren pointed at Aelfric. "You have an important role here after this is over with. Between you and Trianna, Orlimar has a bright future."

"You humble me, Faren," Aelfric dipped into a low bow.

"None of us should be worried more than these two," Serena scolded everyone. "Most of us will be far enough away from the fighting to stay relatively safe. Faren and Merida are charging right into the middle of the horde. You two be safe and don't extend yourselves too much. There's no reason for you to take any additional risks."

I looked up at Serena, trying to discern her for a few moments. She always seemed to hold something back. Still, I smiled and nodded, sighing, "This has been the plan since day one. We knew what we were getting ourselves into."

Marshal cleared his throat, "Alright, kids. Let's get to our positions."

The other Fated bowed and turned to head back across the bridge.

Marshal looked down at me, "Merida. Please come back to us. Among the Fated, you're unique. You've done more than the rest of them combined to bring everyone together. Thoros will be a lesser place without you."

I stared up at him. A thank you seemed like it would fall short, so I simply dipped into a curtsy, "We'll be ready for our signal."

We went our separate ways. Marshal would be on the front lines with the Falladrin army. I only hoped it wouldn't be his last battle. He was in his early fifties now and while he was still a capable warrior, the energy and endurance of youth had left him.

I returned to the tunnels and joined the rest of the cavalry. I mounted my rhoarno and moved it to the head of the formation. I turned to look out over my warriors, silently wondering how many of them would be coming back from all of this. With all eyes on me now, I did what I expected the others were doing at the moment. I said what I could to encourage them.

"Warriors of House Orodum…" I called out over the crowd of mounted warriors. "This moment has been years in the making. My entire life has been dedicated to this precise moment. Thankfully, I have gathered the strongest warriors in all of Cragmorrar to my side. Every one of you was hand chosen to be here, to stand with me, to fight alongside me to end this threat before it truly begins."

The warriors turned their mounts to face me properly, listening intently.

"I won't lie to you," I continued, "In this moment, I find that my spirit is trembling. With anticipation. With fear. With hesitation. But I have the strength of will to face it because I have you by my side! Every one of you is a brick in the wall we'll be placing before the scourgespawn! Dwarves have always been the bulwark against the fiends and today, we will show them why! We will show the humans and the elves why the scourgespawn fear the dwarves! We will show them the ferocity and stubbornness of our people!"

The warriors began to cheer.

"We are the Stone!" I shouted. "We are born from it! We embody it! The scourgespawn tide will break upon it! And some of us might return to it today, but in the end, our names will be carved into it and we will be remembered until the stone itself is no more!"

More cheers, more excitement.

"When we ride down those ramps, we are not cavalry!" I cried. "We are the stone! We are boulders rushing down the mountain, and anything in our path will be crushed beneath our fury! Will you ride with me?"

A loud affirmative cheer rang out.

"Will you fight with me?"

Another, louder cheer.

"Then ride down with me!" I yelled with fervor. "Follow me down into the scourgespawn pit and crush them beneath our fury!"

The cheering came at a fever pitch now.

Suddenly a horn came from the tunnel entrance. It was the signal. The horde had begun its charge.

I turned my rhoarno to the ramp's entrance, "The signal horn! Falladrin calls for the aid of the dwarves! Now ride! Ride! Ride to answer the call!"

The stone shook with the thunderous hooves of the rhoarnos charging forward and the fever-pitched roar of the dwarves. We rode down into the ramp's darkness, speeding through the path the same way we'd practiced a thousand times now. We had changed one part of our plan, which was to have the dwarven infantry wait along the inside walls of the ramps so that the cavalry could charge through. Then, they could quickly file into the field afterwards. The dwarven foot soldiers who would enter the battlefield after us cheered us from the side of the tunnel as we passed them. It took nearly a minute to reach the end of the ramp. Its gate opened at the last second, just as we practiced.

I rode through first, and the sight that welcomed me nearly took my breath away. We had expected there to be a large amount of devastation after the trebuchets fired onto the field, but the reality of the barrage left me stunned. A massive swath of the ground was obliterated. There was a massive crater, and dozens of smaller craters and long gouges cut into the field. And the scourgespawn caught in the area had been crushed and shredded. Their inky blood was all over the place. True to the plan, the scourgespawn horde had been split in two. I pulled the reins of my rhoarno to veer toward the scourgespawn closer to the fort.

"There they are!" I pointed my staff at the scourgespawn. "Crush them down! Don't let them get back into formation!"

There were spells swirling all over the horde, with arrows raining down in angry, stinging swarms. I added a blizzard of my own several yards into the horde as we took our first pass along the back lines, letting our rhoarnos do most of the work. In the distance, on the opposite side of the field, I could see the Franswanian chevaliers leading the other dwarven cavalry into the ranks of the scourgespawn caught on the opposite side of the craters.

Once we finished our first pass, I turned and prepared for another go. The first pass was the easiest since we rode into a shell shocked and disoriented mass. This time, the scourgespawn were regrouping. I was lucky enough to be able to ward them off with spells and clear a small window for Faren and Franklin, but we took our first casualties on that second run. House Petran and House Orodum warriors had begun spilling out of the ramp gates as we returned and were already engaging with the scourgespawn. House Nordrucan and the other families were coming out of the opposite ramp to pinch the scourgespawn between our forces. The Legion of Dead had split themselves between both ramps and would charge past the others to cover the middle.

The closest ogres were now making us their primary targets and began to lumber their way towards us. I summoned another blizzard to slow them down. Now came the time where I had to put faith in the training of my people.

"Cavalry with me!" I cried as I turned my rhoarno into a straight charge into the horde. "We have to stop those ogres!"

Without a moment's hesitation they followed me as I drove my rhoarno into the scourgespawn ranks and crushed them to the ground, plowing through them to reach the first of the ogres. The brutish monstrosity roared, grabbed one of its smaller kin, and hurled it at us with ease. The scourgespawn bounced off of my rhoarno's armored side and shook me heavily, but I had learned over time to brace myself against those sorts of attacks.

I returned fire with a blast of chain lightning to keep the ogre and the surrounding scourgespawn stunned for a few moments. While we closed in,

I weaved a few instances of virulent walking bomb into the smaller spawn. Tugging hard on the reins, I brought my rhoarno in close behind the ogre so I could knock the back of its knee in with my staff. This caused it to stumble, then Franklin, Faren, and the others followed along, cutting it and the other scourgespawn down.

As the other scourgespawn died, virulent walking bomb was triggered and the scourgespawn exploded, causing massive damage to those around them and infecting others with the spell.

We rounded back and pushed towards the dwarven lines. The rhoarnos were excellent for devastating cavalry charges, but they didn't have the stamina of horses. It had only been a few minutes but we needed to give the mounts some time to rest. There were retainers who would be bringing fresh mounts down the gates in a minute. All we had to do was get through our friendly lines.

"Lord Irono!" Faren shouted.

I turned to see that Franklin had been knocked off his rhoarno and quickly brought my rhoarno about to help him. The cavalry behind us pushed on, blocking the scourgespawn from swarming Franklin from one side, while Faren and I moved around to grab him. I cleared the area around Franklin with quick casts of Stone Fist and put my rhoarno between him and the scourgespawn. Faren moved in and helped Franklin up onto his mount. Just as we were moving to head back to the dwarven lines, an ogre crashed through the formation and sent us all flying.

I was heavily dazed by the time I came to, but I couldn't have blacked out for too long. Franklin and Faren were already up and fighting.

"Get her up, Faren!" Franklin shouted as he parried a scourgespawn's axe and quickly drove a dagger into the creature's eye. "Hurry and get her up! We need to get her back to the lines!"

Faren was dealing with scourgespawn of his own as he tried to slowly back up towards me, "I'm trying, my Lord!" He bashed his shield into one scourgespawn, putting it on its heels before stabbing another creature's leg to keep it at bay. "My Lady! My Lady, can you hear me? My Lady, please! We need you!"

I stood on shaky legs. I looked around then scampered over a few feet to pick up my staff. "I'm up. How are the rest of the cavalry?"

"Reforming as we speak," Franklin called back. "We have to hold out until they can get back to us."

"Then we will hold out until then," I growled and summoned forth my mana and set up Aura of Might, Shimmering Shield, Dimvolmn Shroud, and Stone Armor to bolster myself with combat magic. I placed Lifewards on Franklin and Faren to give them bursts of healing magic if they took too much damage.

Without my magic, I was a respectable enough warrior in my own right. However, once all of my combat magic was active, I could surpass King Marshal and Duke Logan in their prime. The magic helped me move faster and in ways mortals typically couldn't. It allowed some blows to slip straight through me or cause them to miss entirely. It enhanced my strength and durability so that I could rival Gniess.

"Get together!" Franklin called out to us. "Backs together and keep it tight! We only need a minute or so. I can see them forming up for the charge!"

The ground around us became a killing field. Three of Cragmorrar's finest combatants, working together in unison, practiced over years against the mindless charging swarm. We'd fought so often against the scourgespawn together that the three of us could naturally respond to each other's movements. Stepping in, swinging, blocking, and shifting as a well-practiced trio. By the time the cavalry got to us, there was a small wall of scourgespawn starting to build up around us.

"My Exemplar!" Sidra shouted from a rhoarno as they neared our location. "We'll cover your retreat!"

"Faren, Franklin!" I shouted. "Let's move!"

Faren shifted, moving in front of me to guard my path as always, shoving his shield and sword through spawn after spawn. Franklin covered our flank, the ringing of steel and death cries of scourgespawn following us.

I swatted back any of the creatures that tried to come at our sides. We pushed our way forward, trying to close the gap between us and the rhoarnos.

As Sidra pulled her rhoarno close, Faren moved to the side. "Go, My Lady! Get on!"

"I'm not leaving you two!" I refused.

"Forgive me, my love," Franklin said as he grabbed me by the waist and hoisted me up for Sidra to grab my hand, "but we don't have time to - ARH!!!"

I nearly fell back to the ground as Franklin's grip on me disappeared. Luckily, Sidra had a firm grip on me and kept me aloft. I spun to look back, horrified at the sight of Franklin staring up at me; pain and panic in his eyes as a spear erupted through his chest, followed by two more as the scourgespawn on the other end of the weapons cried out with wicked delight.

"Franklin!" I screamed as I reached back for him.

He gave me a grim smile. "Go… Be right behind you…" He turned hard, forcing the spears from the grips of the scourgespawn and swung his sword to cleave one of their heads in two. He let out a roar as he stepped forward to cut the other one open at the belly. "For Cragmorrar! For Exemplar Orodum!"

He charged the third creature and buried his sword into its chest, then waded back into the sea of scourgespawn.

I screamed, begging for him to come back, but Faren had already blocked the way, keeping my escape safe. Sidra pulled me up onto the rhoarno and took me back to safety.

We got back behind the dwarven lines, and I was forced to regain my composure — to take the pain of losing Franklin and shove it away, at least until everything was over. Sidra brought me to the Command line, where the Legion Commander for our side of the field was posted.

I slid off of the rhoarno and marched up to the Commander.

"My Exemplar, thank the stone you're safe," he bowed.

"Do not thank the stone," I replied. "Thank Lord Irono. He gave his life so Faren and I could escape."

"We will honor him after the battle," the Commander stood and moved back to overlook the battle. "For now, we can honor his sacrifice by ending this."

"What's the situation?" I asked quickly. "Where can I be most useful?"

"We can't allow you to put yourself in any more…" the Commander began to protest until I shot him a look that would melt steel. He quickly reassessed his answer. "Fighting is thickest on the sides of the field near the ramp walls and against the human army at the front, My Lady. The scourgespawn are moving as far from the center as possible since most of the magic and arrows are covering that area."

"I'll prove to them that they're not safe from magic anywhere," I growled. "Do we have any fresh mounts?"

Sidra stepped forward, "Forgive me, My Lady, but we took the fresh mounts to stage your rescue. They're already making a second pass."

"Where is your regiment in all of this?" I asked as I looked over the field. Dwarves have excellent vision in the dark. Everything is in blacks, whites, and grays, but we can always see even in the bleakest darkness.

"Augmenting House Petran and House… Irono… My Lady," the Commander responded, trying not to inflate the pain of my recent loss.

"How many can you spare?"

The Commander paused and looked at me curiously, "What are you thinking, My Lady?"

"We gather the remaining rhoarnos and let them rest while you pull your regiment back," I pointed to the ever thinning middle of the battlefield. "We form up and drive through the center. The rhoarnos can reinforce the front, and the Legion can press the scourgespawn from the sides. We pin them between us and the wall."

"Allowing the mages and archers to concentrate their fire," the Commander considered the suggestion. "This would allow us to cut them down quickly, but it would also leave Houses Petran and Irono unsupported for the few minutes it would take."

"House Petran and House Irono have some of the greatest warriors in Cragmorrar," I said as I turned and signaled to Sidra to let the cavalry know the plan. "They'll hold the line once the orders are relayed to them because that's what warriors do. Now see it done! We're ending this!"

The Commander bowed and barked out the orders. In the end, he also had the same orders related to the eastern side of the field. Both Legion regiments would charge in behind the rhoarnos and crush the scourgespawn between their respective walls.

I was offered a fresh rhoarno, but refused. I would charge in at the back line of the Legion, that way I could help reinforce House Petran and House Irono. Trenton and Gniess were on the eastern field, along with their houses. I had more faith in them to hold the line than I did Petra and the others if I'm being honest.

Several minutes later, Faren and Sidra stuck by my side as the formation prepared the charge. The rhoarnos advanced rapidly in a wedge formation now that the center was mostly free of enemies. They plunged through the back ranks of the scourgespawn fighting against King Marshal's army, and sowed havoc as the appearance surprised the beasts. The Legion followed closely behind, turning in to press the attack on the scourgespawn that were trying to stick close to the walls.

Sure enough, the archers and mages clued in quickly, and volleys of spells and arrows pelted the dark mass of monsters.

Faren, Sidra, and I arrived with my one hundred personal guards to bolster the warriors of House Irono. We pressed in, fresher than the other warriors who we pressed past so that they could rest a few moments. I heard a familiar battle roar.

"Woryek!" I called as we cut our way through to join him. Woryek

Irono was Franklin's elder brother and a peerless warrior. He was famed for never using the same weapon twice in Testament Bout tournaments.

Woryek crushed a scourgespawn beneath his warhammer and quickly used the momentum from the swing to bring the hilt of the hammer around to open another spawn's throat. He turned as a few of his warriors moved to engage more dawkspawn so he could have time to speak with me.

I could feel his expression behind his helmet; his voice was an abyss of sorrow, "My Exemplar... Where is Franklin?"

Woryek and I actually got along very well. He reminded me very much of Trenton in his younger days. I had to steel my expression, though no doubt some of my sadness broke through as I quietly shook my head.

He marched over to me, grabbing a scourgespawn by the throat after it broke through his men's defensive line and simply ripped its throat out without missing a beat. His brutal efficiency was inspiring. He moved his hammer to the bloody hand and wrapped an arm around me, "He died fighting by your side, Merida. He would have wanted nothing more. Let's finish this for him."

I hugged the man tight and nodded into his armor, "For Franklin, then."

We separated, and he motioned closer to the wall, "We have this section, My Lady. House Petran might need your aid closer to the wall. The beasts seem to be in a panicked fever now."

"Can your men let us through?" I asked.

"We'll happily get out of your way, My Lady," he said, turning. "House Irono! Your Lord and my brother, Lord Franklin Irono, has been cut down by the scourgespawn while defending your Exemplar! Show them the fury of House Irono! Show them the price they must pay for taking our Lord away!"

If a single warrior of House Irono was saddened by the news, they masked it so well in their fury that I couldn't tell. The entire lot of them lunged forward in such fury that we had a clear path to the wall in mere moments.

"Thank you," I said to Woryek.

"Kill them all," he responded and turned to wade back into the fight.

We hurried forward, running past the line of House Irono's berserking warriors. I could see where House Petran was beginning to falter. Their line had been pressed back, and they seemed to be struggling to contain the scourgespawn. I shouted out to let them know we were coming, and we were able to slip past the pressed warriors into the fray. As we engaged the scourgespawn, I noticed that they were surrounding a pocket of dwarves who were cut off from the main line.

"We have to rescue them!" I commanded as I slammed the hilt of my sword into a scourgespawn's face, stunning it so that someone behind me could finish it off.

We put ourselves between the exhausted Petran line and the scourgespawn attempting to flee. It was a hectic series of moments as we forced our way to join the cut-off dwarves. As we reached them, I realized they had formed a circle and were fighting fiercely just to survive.

The first dwarf that caught sight of me smiled through his exhaustion, "My Exemplar! Thank the stone you've come! My Lady! Exemplar Orodum is here!"

Petra, who was among the group, turned and smiled, "Lady Merida! Oh, thank the St–" Her words were cut short as the dwarf next to her fell to a scourgespawn blade, then a sword pierced her throat from the side.

Her eyes snapped wide with shock. Petra had been my dear friend early in my childhood, and we had worked together for years to retake her family home and reestablish her family within the nobility. We had worked so hard to fulfill her dreams, and now this. The expression of disbelief and confusion on her face is something I'll never forget.

I only remember screaming. Screaming and running forward, nothing more. It was Faren who told me that as I moved, the ground itself jolted up into stone spikes, impaling every scourgespawn for dozens of yards.

The next thing I remember was holding Petra in my lap as Orodum and

Petran warriors raged forward, thanks to the momentum the stone spikes had given them. They didn't ask questions or hesitate, they simply allowed me my time with Petra while they pressed the attack.

Petra looked up at me, gasping for air as her own blood slowly drowned her. Her tears spilled over her cheeks, and she somehow managed a weak smile. I could only try to match it, but I was certain I failed. She died right there in my arms. I hugged her body close, kissed her forehead, then gently set her down to get back into the fight.

The rage of losing two of my best friends in such a short time welled up within me, and I could feel power flowing through me. My rage and magic flowed like an angry river, and I charged forward ready to make every single scourgespawn pay for what they'd taken from me. The next hour or so was a blur. Eventually, we overwhelmed the scourgespawn and finally joined our lines with King Marshal's men who had held the fort.

The elves were emerging from the forest alongside the chevaliers who survived the battle. Trianna and I had brought two very special things with us from Cragmorrar: illusavin mirrors that we had found in Cragmor Hold. While the humans and dwarves were practicing their plans, Trianna was searching the illusavin network for the mirror that she'd left behind all those years ago. Once she'd found it, we had set the mirrors inside the hollowed trunks of trees. She had waited in the limbs of one of the trees for the horde to pass before activating the mirrors so that the elves could pass through and charge the back lines.

Faren, Sidra, and I had linked up with King Marshal, Duke Logan, Trenton and Gniess, as well as the other Fated. Trenton held me close when he heard about Franklin and Petra, comforting me since he knew how much I'd cared for both of them. Faren informed Marshal and Logan of everything that had happened. The other Fated discussed how they'd done and what had happened with them. By and large, things had gone relatively well. Losses were slightly less than expected thanks to my decision to pierce the center.

We were all exhausted and taking a moment to observe the battle's end when it happened: a deafening roar that rolled out from the woods, and entire trees bowed beneath the winds caused by the beating wings of the archdemon as it appeared over the treeline. It was as if we had a spark of hope that was kindled by the battle's end, and the archdemon sensed it enough to snuff it out.

The creature was black as ink and slid through the night sky like a thunderbolt. The call went out for the ballistas and trebuchets to ready their shots. Warriors began to scramble to get back in formation, spreading the line around the field to ensure we wouldn't all be caught together when it was brought down.

This battle was limited to archers, mages, and the ballistas. The ballistas fired a dozen volleys. Fire, lightning, and ice flew into the sky to break upon the wyrm. It almost looked like fireworks if not for the situation. Several agonizing minutes passed before the archdemon began to falter, its wings in tatters thanks primarily to the ballistas. It fell through the sky in a manic spiral as it clawed the air beneath its now-tattered wings, slamming down to the ground in an explosion of dirt and dust, blessedly in the middle of the field.

There was a hushed moment before King Marshal looked to myself and the other Fated. "Now's our chance!"

"Have the warriors support the elves," I shouted as I prepared my sword. "It can still summon reinforcements! We can handle the archdemon with the help of the Scourge Sentinels!"

Marshal, Logan and Faren sent the orders out. There seemed to be some hesitation on the part of the armies, but eventually thousands of warriors began to run towards the trees where the elves were waiting.

While the soldiers moved to obey their commands, we began to move toward the archdemon before it could recover from its fall. King Marshal, Duke Logan, Gniess, Durdren, Beltia, Allen, Serena, Aelfric, Faren, and I spread out.

"Lady Orodum, Allen, Aelfric, Lady Serena," Marshal commanded as we rushed the creature, "I want you all to keep your distance! Use your magic and bows from an effective, safe distance. The rest of you, spread out and don't clump together. I don't want a single attack able to hit more than one of us at a time. If you can manage it, take out its legs. If not, keep it flinching and keep it reeling. Try not to let it focus!"

Everyone shouted their acknowledgement of the plan. To ensure that the archdemon's senses wouldn't come back as quickly as they might, I pumped mana into a Stone Fist spell and launched it ahead of us. The spell slammed into the side of the demon's head and caused it to stumble. Those few moments gave the others time to close the distance.

Marshal and Logan reached the archdemon first, with Marshal weaving his sword through the air expertly to keep the snapping jaws of the monster at bay. Logan augmented the effort of controlling the demon's head by ducking beneath its neck and restricting its movements by slamming his shield up against the demon's jaws and neck.

Gniess charged in and slammed a stone fist into one of the demon's forelegs while Trenton continued forward, ducking under the useless wing and raked his sword across the demon's hind leg. Durdren, Faren, and Beltia went for the legs on its other side. I moved to the left of the dragon's head, keeping my distance. Serena was to the right, trying to land her shots in the demon's neck while Aelfric was closer to the monster's right wing aiming for its sides and belly. Allen wasn't too far from me, thankfully. While my magic was focused on the offensive, his efforts were focused on healing the frontline members of our party.

When the warriors had joined the elves to prevent any additional scourgespawn from joining the fray, someone had told Trianna what was happening. She'd run back to join us and placed herself just to the left of the tail.

It might have had its wings clipped, but the archdemon was still formidable. Try as they might, the frontline members of the party couldn't hold it still. Unlike in the games, the archdemon was still mobile, and it easily bodied the others out of the way. We had to constantly maneuver around and adjust our placements to keep ourselves safe.

Unfortunately for Serena and Aelfric, they quickly ran out of arrows and became all but useless. To make matters worse, everyone was running on fumes. If we were all fresh, the story might have gone differently, but eventually, everyone started to slip. Trenton was knocked unconscious by a kick that sent him flying. Beltia, Faren, and Durdren suffered similar fates when the archdemon shifted quickly away from an attack and the demon either trampled them or swatted them with its tail. I couldn't quite tell from where I was.

Logan easily got the worst of it when the demon jumped backwards suddenly and snapped him up in its jaws, then flung him dozens of yards away. The archdemon charged forward, flinging Allen away when he couldn't dodge one of the limp wings.

"You are waking."

Time seemed to slow to a crawl. I watched as Trianna's lightning slowly clawed its way through the air. I could see the Scourge Sentinels swarming in from every direction, running at what seemed to be a snail's pace.

"Open your eyes. Wake and join the whole."

The dirt that the archdemon was throwing into the air with every stride slowed more and more until everything stopped.

"Awaken!"

I wasn't me anymore. I was tall. I felt like the size of a mountain. I could feel my panic for the Princess running through my head as I chased after the demon. I was fighting the scourgespawn alongside the elves, keeping the monsters at bay so the Scourge Sentinels could finish the archdemon off. I hurt to my core at the loss of my brother, his potential, and the love of a Exemplar who was to be my sister-in-law. I was sitting on my throne worrying for my daughter and all those who'd gone with her. I was sitting at the gate in the tunnels, looking out as the battle raged on, hoping everything would be ok and wondering about what new magical knowledge I could gain from it. I sat in my studies, fiddling with a locket and staring at the portraits of my mother and sister, whom I missed deeply.

A thousand, ten thousand, hundreds of thousands of thoughts raced through my head in an instant. I knew everything, was every one of my people all at the same time. I wasn't me, I was the whole. I could feel the memories back before the Memorium began to record them, I knew the souls of all those who had been returned to the Stone.

Just there? Parts of the whole, my children, were in danger, fighting a small swarm of the infection and a slightly larger growth of the Scourge. It needed to be dealt with, and this particular child was determined to see this through. Yes, I could work through it. All that was needed was to bathe the child in the light of my blood to purify it. This would reconnect it fully to the Stone and allow the child to properly shape it. Give it the natural ability and instincts it had lost.

I was me again, larger in spirit somehow and bathed in a blue light. The archdemon was bearing down on me, its maw open wide.

"No!" I said calmly and raised a hand. At the same time, a massive spear of stone erupted from the ground and slammed into the demon's side, sending it toppling to the side. I watched it fall and reached out with a grasping motion, and the ground swelled up to grab the forelegs of the archdemon and held them tight, denying the creature the ability to move.

I marched forward, the blue light still swirling around me as I glared at the monster. "I have thought about nothing but you since the day I was born into this world. My every second has been building to this very moment. Not once while I was awake, or even while I slept, did I ever do anything more than prepare for this day."

I waved my arm out sharply to the side, and a stone block reached up and pinned the archdemon's head to the ground. I moved in close, placing my face near one of its eyes, glaring into it.

"I united the Dwarven people," I lowered my voice to a growl. "I worked with my friend to unite the Paddish clans in Falladrin, joined with the human armies, and worked for three years in this very spot to repair this fort, improve its defenses, and practice strategies just for this exact moment."

I leaned in, staring at the demon's eye and the reflection of myself in it with the strange blue energy swirling around me. "And we still almost lost to you. Two of my closest friends, my fiance… are dead to your scourgespawn. I don't yet know how many more of my people will never walk from this battlefield. And if it wasn't for this new intervention, I might have joined them."

"But I'm alive. I beat you. In a few moments, a Scourge Sentinel will come here to finish you off. And after you die, I'm going to hunt down Raziel and Luscan before they can be infected with the Scourge. I'm going to kill them. I'm going to end this vicious cycle. And only after you and your kin are nothing but memories, will I rest."

I turned and walked away, raising my hand up into a claw. The Stone responded to my will, and several stone spikes jutted up from the ground and impaled the archdemon.

The Sentinels had stopped in their tracks and were staring at me. Faren, Serena, Aelfric, Trianna, and Marshal watched me, slack-jawed.

"Hurry up and kill it," I said as I passed Sentinel Clarel, with tears beginning to run down my cheeks. "It will bleed out if you don't, then we'll have to do this all over again."

Faren was the first to get to me, grabbing me by the shoulders to look me over wide-eyed. "My Lady? My Lady, are you alright? What happened to you? How did you do that?"

I could only stare at him and shake my head. "I... don't know. I have an idea but... We're not done. The scourgespawn..."

A massive burst of bright energy exploded from behind me, followed by a huge concussive burst that nearly knocked us off our feet. One of the Sentinels had killed the Archdemon. The burst was the demon's death throes, the light was its soul trying to escape and find a new host, but was dragged back into the Sentinel who had killed it, taking the life of the Sentinel at the same time.

"That will send them fleeing back into the Under Roads," Trianna said as the others approached. "It looks like we're giving chase but I'm sure some of them will still... By the ancients... your eyes!"

"What?" I asked, trying not to let everything that I'd gone through in the battle and with whatever power I'd just been infused with overwhelm me. "What's wrong with them?"

"They're blue..." Serena gasped. "Like dimvyum."

I looked at everyone before simply crumpling into Faren's arms, submitting myself to the exhaustion of the day.

CHAPTER 17:

REQUIEM

I woke up late the next morning with cuts and bruises from the battle, causing me to ache and wince. I didn't call for a servant; I simply sat in my bed, trying to push the memories of Franklin and Petra's deaths from my mind. I was in shock, still numb to the realization of it all being real, even though I had been there when it happened. I stayed in my bed for so long that it took one of the servants coming in to check on me to find out that I was awake.

"My Lady…" the servant asked tenderly, "Is there anything I can do for you? Is there anything you want?"

I remained silent and simply stared at the blankets.

"People will want to know that you're awake," she pressed just enough to do her duty. "Shall I tell them you're too tired to meet with anyone today?"

To her credit, she waited a few minutes for me to reply before she began to slip back out of the room. "I'll tell them you're in no condition to see anyone today."

"Wait…" I choked out quietly.

My voice alone seemed to give her some hope. "Yes, My Lady? What may I do for you?"

"My diary," I looked over at my desk. "Could you bring it to me, please?

I didn't write in it last night, and I need to write down the day's events."

The servant bowed her head. "Of course, My Lady." She fetched the diary and placed it on a meal tray I would sometimes use to take my meals in bed, along with my ink and quill. She set the items before me. "Forgive me, My Lady, but are you sure you wish to recall the battle in detail so soon?"

I looked up at her, tears in my eyes. "This diary was a gift from Lady Petran. I promised her that I would write in it every day I was here. She'll never get to read it… but I'll keep my promise…"

She sat next to me and hugged me. "Then I will bear this pain with you."

We sat there for the next hour as I wrote down everything. The experience was painful but cathartic. Once I was finished with the journal entry, the servant helped me get dressed. She braided my hair and made me as presentable as if I were holding a feast for my father. She had to redo my makeup a few times when I started to cry in the middle of the process. Eventually, she settled on a less-is-more approach.

It was nearly noon by the time I left my room. Faren was standing just outside the door and fumbled over me when I made myself available.

"My Lady," he gasped gently, "everyone's been so worried about you. Are you alright?"

I stared at him with a forlorn expression, the cuts and bruises on my face only just hidden by my makeup. "We need to help with clearing the battlefield."

"But, My Lady," Faren protested in shock, "you're in no state to-"

I didn't let him finish. I simply began marching to the tunnel exit that led to the battlefield. "I wasn't asking permission."

Faren and the other guards double-timed it to keep up with me, "My Lady, they've been clearing the bodies since early this morning."

"Have they found Franklin and Petra?" I snapped.

Faren was silent for a moment, trying to figure out how to answer the question. "Not that I'm aware."

"I want someone to run ahead," I commanded. "Tell everyone, no one touches them but me."

"What about Lord Woryek, My-" Faren tried asking. He had to stop immediately and try not to bowl me over as I halted in my steps and whirled on him.

If I could have given the archdemon the look I gave Faren in that moment, I would have cowed the creature into submission. "I said 'no one'! Not Woryek, not King Marshal, not the Creator himself if he thinks now is a good time to come back and help out! If their bodies are found, NO ONE touches them! They send word to me and then they wait! Am I understood?"

The blood drained from Faren's face and he nodded silently. "Y-yes, My Lady. Of course. Please, forgive me."

I turned and marched back to the exit. "No one's running yet!"

Faren commanded one of the guards to run ahead and relay my command to everyone in the field.

No one had started clearing the field until after sunrise. The Paddish had been kind enough to set guards along the forest line so that predators wouldn't begin prowling the area and feeding on the dead. Now that the sun was up, archers were watching the skies for birds that might try to do the same. The Paddish were primarily focused on clearing out their dead from the forest, while humans and dwarves were clearing the main field. My command had slowed the process because now every human had to be paired with a dwarf just in case they found Franklin or Petra.

With my command going ahead of me, it signaled for most everyone to gather at the exit. When the doors were opened, King Marshal, Trenton, and the other Fated were standing there waiting for me. I had been rather hoping I could avoid them all but knew deep down that I couldn't.

I offered them all as bright a smile as I could muster and a curtsy, "Good morning to you all."

Trenton walked right up to me and hugged me close and tight, "You shouldn't be out here, Merida. You need to rest."

I returned the hug, "I have to find them and I have to take care of them."

"We can do that for you," he said quietly. "Don't put yourself through all of this."

I looked up at him and shook my head, my eyes puffing with tears, "Let me do this. Let me find Franklin and Petra. Then…I'll just supervise if you like."

Trenton seemed hesitant but nodded and released me, "I'll accompany you."

The others bowed their heads, touched my shoulder, or quietly offered me their support. They filed in behind me as I started to make my way across the field. I've always been good with directions. Even in my past life, once I'd been somewhere, I could always get back there even if I weren't going the same way. It's like maps and directions just formed in my head, and I could simply follow them. Things hadn't changed since then.

I could estimate the path the cavalry took out of the gate and back through its second pass. I approximated where we had intercepted the ogres and started there. I found the area where we had held off the scourgespawn for a time. I stood in the center of the circle we'd made, "Just here… Franklin, Faren, and I were knocked off our rhoarnos after an ogre charged through the cavalry line. We stood right here… back to back… keeping each other safe…"

I walked south several yards to the point where Sidra had rescued me. I tried to ignore the shiver that ran through me as the memory flashed back. I pointed to the spot. "Faren ran in front of me, Franklin guarded our backs as we moved to get to the rhoarnos. Franklin… he saved me by forcing me to get onto Sidra's rhoarno. Three scourgespawn…"

I turned back to the fort, adjusted my direction slightly and continued on, slower, and more carefully. It took me longer than I expected to find him. He hadn't simply walked away and died. Franklin had continued through the scourgespawn ranks for another minute or so before finally falling. I nearly lost my composure when I finally found him. His body rested on top of a dead scourgespawn, his hand still resting on his sword's pommel where he'd pierced the creature's throat, the three spears he'd been pierced with still impaling him.

I almost broke right there. My knees were about to buckle but I braced myself on one of the spears and forced myself to pull it from his body.

"Merida," Serena gasped. "Please, let us help."

"Don't you touch him! Don't any of you touch him!" I screamed up at her as I shoved the spear at Faren. "Hold on to these. Don't clean them."

Faren took the spear and stared at it in confusion. "As you wish, my Lady…"

I removed the other two spears and gave them both to Faren. Then I sat down and pulled Farin's body over to lay in my lap, cradling him for a few minutes and went over everything we'd been through, then talked about the plans we'd been making for the future. He'd been so looking forward to starting a family with me. He'd wanted at least four kids, to establish yearly family traditions, to work with the Memorium to have more of Cragmorrar's history available to the public, and to establish a new annual tournament to honor the Exemplars (he wanted to be the first to fight in the name of Exemplar Orodum).

While I was taking my time with Franklin, one of the nearby carts stopped and waited for me. When I was ready, I called upon my mana to enhance my strength, then lifted Franklin with all care and placed him carefully on the cart. I instructed the men hauling the cart to take him directly to the tunnels and to have him cleaned and preserved for the trip home. When the cart left, I began to make my way quietly to the ramp wall.

It was easy to find Petra. All I had to do was look for the stone spikes with impaled scourgespawn on them. I stood above my dear friend trying not to cry. She still had that forced smile on her face, the one she'd given me as if to try and let me know everything would be alright. I moved to my knees and scooped her carefully into my lap, holding her close. Now, I did cry.

"This was my fault," I sobbed.

"You can't believe that," Trianna said as she dropped down beside me and hugged me close.

"It is, though," I kissed Petra's forehead. "She dropped her guard when I arrived. She looked to me for relief, as someone who'd come to save her. And the moment she looked to me…"

"Don't," Trianna interrupted. "You can't blame yourself for that."

"She's right, My Lady," Faren agreed quietly. "She was a warrior. She knew better than to drop her guard in the face of an enemy, but she forgot herself. I understand you blame yourself for her decision… but it was a failure in judgment that led to her death."

I wanted to hate Faren for saying what he said. I wanted to snap at him, scream at him, tell him to be quiet. He was betrothed to her, after all, so he could have shown a little more compassion. All I could do was hug Petra and apologize to her again.

We waited for a few minutes for another cart to come by, and I placed Petra on it, giving the carriers the same instructions I had with Franklin. Dwarves wouldn't be left here. We were going to preserve them and bring them home to Cragmorrar.

"Faren…" I said as Petra's body was carted away.

"Yes, My Lady?" he stepped forward hopefully.

"Send a rider to Cragmorrar with haste," I instructed him. "Tell them I want a mausoleum built for everyone who fell in the battle. It needs to be ready before we arrive. Every dwarf who died here today will have their own special placement. Their names, their deeds… everything will be recorded on plaques. I want the mausoleum placed in the Halls of the Exemplars, beside the city doors."

"As you command, My Exemplar," Faren bowed deeply, then hustled off to see it done.

I took a deep breath and turned to the others. "I suppose we should plan our ceremonies and speeches."

Marshal knelt in front of me and placed a hand on my shoulder. His expression told me that he understood what I was going through completely. "Why don't we work on that together, my dear?"

I smiled sadly at Marshal and nodded.

It took two days to completely clear the field of the dead. Another few days were spent building a massive funeral pyre for the humans and elves. After a week, the scourgespawn were all but gone, burned in one of the craters made by the trebuchets.

A week and a day after the Battle of Orlimar, everyone was gathered in the western part of the fort. The dead had been wrapped and laid on the funeral pyre. The dwarven convoy was prepared to leave with caskets for the dwarven dead, frozen with magical ice so we could transport them back to Cragmorrar for their funerals. Marshal, Trianna, and I stood on a stage built for the occasion.

Marshal stood at the front of the stage, looking over the crowd. "We've gathered here today to mourn the loss of those who fell in the battle against the Scourge. For the first time in centuries, humans, elves, and dwarves stood together, lived together, worked together, and fought together for the common good of the realm."

"For the past three years, we have learned to work together," he continued. "We have become more than friends. Many of us have become family. We've worked so closely together for so long that we mourn the loss of every fallen comrade on the field. Things have happened to strain that relationship, but our common goal kept us together."

He turned and pointed to me. "But the person who brought us together, the person who made this a common goal, is still here with us. I give you Exemplar Merida Orodum, Princess of Cragmorrar."

There was a long applause as I stepped forward, then turned and motioned to the massive funeral pyre. "This is the price of victory. Friends, family, comrades. Men and women we came to know personally. Warriors all. They fought and died for every one of us. Their names will always be remembered. Their sacrifice will be etched into the stone itself."

I went quiet for a few moments before raising my head and looking out over the crowd. "I lost two of my dearest friends in the battle. One of them was my betrothed. They followed me here because they believed in this cause, they believed in my ability to see this through, and they believed that dwarves, elves, and humans could work together to make this world a better place for everyone."

"They died for that dream," I squared my shoulders and raised a fist up to my chest. "It is up to us to live for that dream! Every one of us here was a part of something horrible but special. We have shown the world something it hasn't seen in over four hundred years! We have shown the world that together, dwarves, elves, and humans are an alliance that no force can stand against! We have shown the world that we can happily live together and work together!"

I summoned my mana and activated Heroic Aura. "It is my hope that every one of you will go out and become a witness to the hardiness and loyalty of the dwarves, the reliability and focus of the elves, and the adaptability and generosity of the humans! I hope that you will let the embers of sorrow grow into flames of passion for the unification of Cragmorrar, Orlimar, and Falladrin."

I spread out my arms to encompass the crowd, "From this day to our last day, whenever we're presented with a challenge, I hope that every one of us can say 'if we could achieve victory at Orlimar, we can achieve this.' If we see another person being degraded for being a dwarf, a human, or an elf, I hope we can defend that person by saying 'we came together at Orlimar, and they stood with me against the scourgespawn'."

Finally, I folded my hands into my lap and spoke mournfully, "I hope that each of you will remember this. I hope you'll all remember those who weren't able to stand here with you. I hope for the best for all of you. I hope… and I hope you all will as well. Remember what we sacrificed here. Remember what we sacrificed it for. Remember who stood beside you when those sacrifices were made."

Trianna stood beside me and placed a hand on my shoulder, "We have all lived together for three years. We know how well we've worked together. We know how strong we are together. We defeated a Scourge and an archdemon in one night! We have a chance to take the sacrifice of these men and women and turn it into something amazing! The Paddish are ready to integrate ourselves with Falladrin and share our culture with you. The dwarves of Cragmorrar have begun uniting us all through trade. The humans of Falladrin have offered the Paddish a home and land to hunt and tame."

Marshal stood on my other side, placing his hand on my shoulder, "We have a chance to become something greater than the sum of our parts. Do not let the sacrifice of these brave men and women be wasted. Remember these years. Remember the friends you made. Remember the relationships you fostered. For the rest of your days, Orlimar should be a rallying cry for unification. When you return home, I hope you will find the need to pass on what you have learned here and work with us to keep Falladrin, Orlimar, and Cragmorrar united and growing stronger together. Now, if you would all bow your heads and say a quiet prayer before we light the pyre."

Thousands of heads bowed, humans, dwarves, and elves together in mourning. As they prayed, Marshal took a torch while Trianna and I simply conjured fire into our hands. We moved together and put the flames to the pyre. The flames caught quickly and spread easily.

I waited for the pyre to burn down about halfway before I took my leave. I said a tearful goodbye to Trianna, who I'd been with for ten years now. She and Aelfric would work to lead the Paddish into establishing Orlimar into a fine Paddish settlement. Allen and I agreed to meet once a year at the college to discuss educational reform of the lessons and working with King Marshal to establish the village protector and army mage positions. Serena ensured I would be sent an invitation to her wedding to Alford.

We left Orlimar less than a half hour after our goodbyes. The journey back to Cragmorrar was somber, and I confess that I didn't say much. It took me some time to mentally prepare myself for the welcome we would be receiving. In fact, I knew it wouldn't be a celebration right away. I had riders go ahead and let everyone know we had dead to put to rest, and that was our priority.

On the day of our arrival, I wore a long, black gown. An actual gown, not a gambeson. I ordered everyone in the convoy to wear black or darker clothes as well. The homecoming could wait. I wanted the burial service to be the priority. I also had everyone dismount from their rhoarnos. We would walk them in quietly.

There were no cheers or smiles as we approached the city. Dwarves were out in droves and bowed their heads as the procession made its way through the expanded surface market and up to the city gates. Father and Bilfern, as well as Petra's parents and Franklin's mother and sister, were waiting for us at the top of the steps. I could see Rita and Veron off to the side; they seemed relieved to see that Faren and I were safe.

We stopped at the steps, and I dipped into a deep curtsy before Father. He looked almost ancient now. "Father, your people have returned victorious from Orlimar. We would like your permission to lay to rest our fallen friends and loved ones."

"Exemplar Orodum," Father said somberly, "we welcome you all back to Cragmorrar. Please, bring the fallen in. We will place them in the memorial mausoleum with honor."

I led the procession into the Hall of the Exemplars, stopping momentarily to hug Franklin's mother before moving on. At the other end of the hall were a set of ornate doors on the right, just before the entrance to the city. If the doors were ornate, I couldn't properly describe the beauty inside the mausoleum.

Father had outdone himself with the construction and presentation. The place was massive, with lanes wide enough for two rhoarnos to walk side by side comfortably. We'd lost just over five hundred dwarves to the scourgespawn, and each of them had a dais and stone caskets carved out of the stone in a massive semicircle. Dimvyum ornamentation decorated every dais, and the name of every dwarf was etched into the caskets with dimvyum as well. Franklin and Petra's caskets were at the center of the semicircle. There was a large wall behind the caskets that told the story of Orlimar and, to my surprise, had the speech I'd given at the ceremony. No doubt Faren or Trenton had something to do with that.

Because there were stone caskets with names already carved into them, each body that was brought in had to be announced. Luckily, the mausoleum already had a very dedicated crew of caretakers who had memorized the location of each casket. We made a ceremony of it, though. A name would be called, their family would be allowed to approach and help carry their loved one in, and help inter them. I made sure that Petra and Franklin were saved for last. I did that so that I could help carry them in personally.

As we finished entombing Franklin, I approached his mother, curtsying before her, eyes filled with tears. "Lady Irono…"

"Morcha, please," she insisted as she leaned in and lifted me from my curtsy. "Thank you for bringing my son home, My Exemplar."

I shook my head. "I'm so sorry. It's my fault. He died saving me."

"No, Merida," she broke all protocol by leaving out every title and simply calling me by my first name. She pulled me in for a hug and squeezed tight. "Don't you think that it's your fault. Don't you dare. He loved you and he believed in you and your vision for the future."

She eased me back and smiled at me, tears in her eyes as well. "After some time, please come calling. I will show you the letters he sent me. He raved about your ability to bring everyone together, to keep up morale, and how you kept everyone happy. He admired you so much."

Her words brought back all the hurt I'd felt from Franklin's loss, and if it weren't for her holding me, I would have fallen to the floor and broken down then and there.

Woryek stepped in and embraced me, holding me firmly. "Your hurt for his loss honors him and our family, Princess. No matter what happens, we will always consider you family. If you ever have need of us, even if it's simply to talk and remember him, you need only ask."

"Thank you, Woryek," I choked, hugging him tight.

Faren stepped up beside me and cleared his throat. "My Lady, let's get you home."

"Thank you, Faren," Woryek said as he carefully passed me over to Faren. "She should rest. She's gone through a lot today."

Faren escorted me outside of the mausoleum, and I had to take a few minutes for Father to say a few words about the mausoleum and how we wished for everyone to take the day to reflect on the sacrifice those interred had made. Once that was done, Father, Bilfern, Trenton, and Faren took me home.

Kara was an absolute mess when I arrived, fussing over how distraught I looked and how much she missed me. I took the next few days to mourn over my lost friends properly; days I didn't have to give speeches, hold meetings, or be looked at to lead a convoy. I took the time to simply cry, talk with Kara, Rita, and Faren, and reflect on how everything I'd worked for over the past twenty years had finally come to a head.

On my last day of mourning, I went to the Memorium and gave them the diary Petra had given me before I left for Cragmorrar. True to my word, I had written in it every day, detailing the events of each and every day, including the day I turned the diary over to the Memorium. All in all, there were over twelve hundred pages of entries. Because I would mention who I spoke to each day, and the fact that I spoke to every dwarf, including the dead, the Memorium insisted that the pages be inscribed into the mausoleum. The caskets were even moved so that each casket was in order of the dwarves being mentioned. I refused to let them move Petra and Franklin, though. I wanted them in the center, and they were mentioned almost every day once Petra arrived in Orlimar.

I had new goals to work toward, and mourning the dead wouldn't help me achieve them. Life had to go on. Cragmorrar was ready for more change, and I was ready to help make it happen.

CHAPTER 18:

DINNER WITH THE DEVIL

The first few months after returning to Cragmorrar were primarily for resting and recovering from the daily stress of preparing for battle. I brought Bilfern back into my home so I could catch up with him and check on his studies. He was so happy to have me back, and we made sure to spend as much time as possible together. Father had grown thin and sick with worry for Trenton and me, so I also made sure that I was at the palace for at least two meals a day to encourage him to eat and relieve him of his worry. He regained much of his vigor over time.

There were a few things that had to be handled, however. There were three years' worth of dowry payments from House Irono and their smaller allied Houses to deal with. I met with Woryek a few times to discuss the matter since he had become the head of House Irono after Franklin's death. Morcha had asked, only once, if Woryek and I would consider marrying, but Woryek wouldn't consider the option because he saw it as dishonoring Franklin's memory, and I considered Woryek to be more like a brother. In the end, we had decided to arrange a marriage between Bilfern and Woryek's young cousin Bheret.

The dowry they had paid already would be more than appropriate, and the remainder was divided evenly as gifts of thanks to the families of those who died at Orlimar. Woryek and I accompanied Bilfern and Bheret as they delivered each portion to the families as thanks for their loved ones' sacrifice. This went over very well, as it showed that there was a young generation of nobility coming along that understood and were grateful for the efforts of the lower castes. It also helped that they got a visit from one of their Exemplars in the process.

I had taken some time to go to the Memorium to champion one of Franklin's causes; which was to have much of Cragmorrar's history available to the public outside of the Memorium. Mind you, I wasn't interested in all of the boring detailing or monies owed, or who was removed from which House. I wanted the history of Cragmorrar and its people readily available. I worked with the Memorium to discuss what should and shouldn't qualify as pertinent history, then worked with the Callers to get each noble family to contribute money to the project.

The Callers also declared the victory of Orlimar a dwarven holiday and announced that day would be used to commemorate those who died by holding a tournament where the descendents of the Exemplars would battle in the name of their House's founding Exemplar. That might have been my suggestion since it was one of Franklin's desires.

The Fallen Legion gained a new purpose now that scourgespawn weren't as much of a threat. A small contingent of Legionnaires were dedicated to guarding the Orlimar Mausoleum. There was one Legionnaire to each casket as well as guards at the entrance. Over time, the Legionnaires would establish the tradition of memorizing the deeds and the journal entries I'd made concerning the interred dwarf they were guarding. This way you could have a detailed history spoken to you in the mausoleum. However, there was also a practical reason for the guards; the mausoleum was filled with refined dimvyum as part of the plaques and decorations and it made a tempting situation for thieves.

One pleasant surprise for me was that Aelfric had sent a few of his best chefs to House Orodum while we were in Cragmorrar. They had taught my servants all the recipes I loved. I was now able to enjoy all of my favorite foods from my first life while in Cragmorrar. I spent a lot of time trying to figure out how I could possibly thank him for that.

There was a problem I needed to solve, however. The Syndicate was still a nuisance in many markets outside of Cragmorrar. While the dwarves were making massive inroads with the other races with the Surface Caste, the criminal organization that was the Syndicate was diminishing that reputation with its activities. So I did what any pragmatist would do to solve this problem; I put out word that I invited their leaders to dinner (it's not like it was a secret who they were, just where they could be found). I promised that no one would be captured or arrested. I simply wanted to talk.

I had my servants prepare all of my favorite foods as well as many dwarven staples. I instructed the servants to treat them like any guest ought to be treated in my home, and ensured that no guards in the city would harass them for the evening so long as they didn't do anything illegal. I half expected to dine alone. To my surprise, however, a knock came to my door at the appointed hour.

Brevaht and Jennia arrived at the exact time I'd asked. Half the nobles couldn't manage that small feat. My servants led them into the dining hall where I was waiting. To their credit, they'd dressed formally and groomed themselves appropriately.

"Mister and misses Formon, My Lady," the servant announced.

I offered them both a curtsy, "Thank you both for accepting my invitation. It is a pleasure to have you in my home."

Brevaht stepped forward and offered a bow, "My Lady, how could we refuse such a request?"

Jennia offered her best curtsy, "It's an honor to have been invited."

"Won't you both please have a seat?" I offered.

"Before we sit," Brevaht said, "we would like to present you with a gift."

"There was no need for gifts," I smiled.

Jennia looked back and nodded, then one of my servants approached with a wooden crate, "My Lady, we were surprised and curious as to why you would want to meet with us. The fact that you used your influence to ensure our safety as we moved through the city inspired us. We only wish to thank you for the favor and the honor of meeting with you."

The servant placed the crate down and I looked at it curiously, then looked back at the Syndicate leaders.

"Please," Brevaht insisted, "open it. We hope you will like it."

The crate wasn't sealed. It had a hinged lid which I lifted to peek inside. What I saw elicited an adoring squeal from me. I reached inside and pulled out a mavrosk puppy. I hugged the little creature close and smiled brightly at the pair, "A mavrosk war hound? I've wanted one since I was little."

Brevaht and Jennia both chuckled.

"We thought it appropriate," Jennia insisted. "Only a mavrosk could hope to match the diligence and fierce loyalty you've shown the dwarven people."

Faren, who was off to the side as my guard, hummed in disagreement. I knew for a fact he would love this puppy, though.

However, Jennia's choice of words caught me and I looked at the pair, "Curious, then, that the Syndicate should still be in business the way it is if the dwarves have someone like me looking out for them."

Brevaht just grinned and nodded, waggling a finger at me, "I knew you had business with us somehow. It's what I've always admired about you, Princess."

I grinned right back and took a seat, keeping the puppy snuggled in my arms. "Well, then, let's make ourselves comfortable because we do, indeed, have business together. But before that, please enjoy some of the dinner my servants prepared for you. Some of these have become my favorite foods since my time in Orlimar."

"I'd heard there were new delicacies being created by the elves," Jennia said as she took her seat. "Did you bring some of them along to cook for you, My Lady?"

I chuckled and shook my head. "Not at all. Duke Aelfric actually sent some of his best chefs here to teach my cooks the recipes."

"Your dinners are sure to become the envy of Cragmorrar, then," Brevaht mused as he looked over the offerings. "It is an honor to be among the first to experience them."

We enjoyed a fine dinner, making small talk for about an hour. Brevaht and Jennia marveled over the different foods and flavors that were on offer. They seemed to love it almost as much as I did. Before long, I set the puppy down on a cushion I'd had a servant bring in for it. It curled up and began to sleep.

Satisfied that the puppy wouldn't be moving any time soon, I motioned for Faren to join us at the table.

"Now, I'm sure you're familiar with Ser Faren, my personal bodyguard," I began politely.

"We are," Brevaht bowed his head to Faren. "His prowess is spoken of in high regard.

Trained by Ser Durdren Beltia and considered to be among the elite warriors in all of Cragmorrar and the Holds."

"You didn't invite us here so you could have him kill us, did you?" Jennia smirked.

"I think you know if I wanted you both dead I could just whip the entire city into a frenzy till they found you," I laughed as I shook my head. "No. Faren has given me an idea, and I've taken some time to consider it. I think you should as well."

The two Syndicate members shared a look with each other, then back to me.

"We're listening," Jennia encouraged me to continue.

"I want the Syndicate to go legitimate," I said and noticed the sharply cut-off laughter from my guests. "I could understand the need for the Syndicate in a world without the Surface Cast, in a world without the possibility of upward momentum. But we don't live in that world anymore."

"Thanks to you, Princess," Brevaht bowed his head. "However, upward momentum isn't the only thing the Syndicate strives for."

"It was never the reason it existed in the first place," I retorted in a tone that told them I wasn't stupid enough to ever think that. "We're not here to blow smoke. We're here to discuss terms. I know the Syndicate takes its business very seriously, and so do I."

"By all means," Brevaht grinned. He seemed to appreciate me more when I showed my business side. "We'll at least hear your terms even if we won't agree to them."

Faren huffed, "I would agree no matter the terms. Exemplar Orodum could kill you from her seat without standing, but she'd likely just have the guards in the city do it for her."

"Kill us, and someone will just take our place," Jennia countered.

"Now, now," I interrupted chipperly. "I would hate to think you would believe that I would invite you here for something like this without an offer that would make it worth it."

Brevaht gave Jennia a look that told her to hold her tongue, then smiled back at me, "Princess, if I believed anyone could have come up with an idea to convince us to make the Syndicate go legitimate, it would be you. Now, please, let's hear what you have to say."

I sat up straight and snapped my fingers. A servant came in quickly and cleared my plates while Kara entered with several thick tomes and placed them before me. I thanked them both as they took their leave.

I opened up one of the tomes and began flipping through it, mostly for show, "I'm sure you understand that I have a reputation for bookkeeping. It's primarily how I was able to accomplish my goal of creating the Surface Caste. I went through all the memories in the Memorium and found everyone's debts. And do you know what else I found?"

"Enlighten us," Brevaht responded, an expression of intrigue written on his features.

"I found discrepancies," I replied chipperly, offering up my most positive and innocent expression. "I never pointed them out in my reports, though. It wouldn't do to antagonize the people I needed votes from, after all. But... they were there." I tapped the page I was on for emphasis.

"Discrepancies that, what, pointed to Syndicate activities?" Jennia asked, almost amused.

"Oh, not directly," I set the book aside and opened another one, turning to a marked page. "But when a family suddenly loses money on a deal, or the Syndicate steals some property, then a member of that family is whisked away from the city before a trial, or they happen to get a shipment of dimvyum that wasn't supposed to arrive for a few months... Well, it's not difficult to connect the dots, but it is enough to cast aspersions on your benefactors."

"I doubt that old dealings with the Syndicate would be of note after so long," Jennia countered.

"No," Brevaht disagreed. "They gave up on centuries-old debts because the Surface Caste would bring back a great deal more money. They'd be more than happy to use that information as leverage against other Houses."

"And what lengths do you think those Houses would go to in order to get rid of that leverage?" I asked, my expression turning sharp, letting the implication hover in the air.

"Death threats aren't exactly an offer to stop our business, Princess," Brevaht said coldly.

"I'm offering the opposite, actually," I smiled again. "I'd like to ask you a question before we continue if you don't mind."

"Please do," Jennia responded after looking at Brevaht for a moment.

"Who do you think the Assembly will vote to become the next ruler of Cragmorrar?"

The two looked at each other. The question seemed to take them off their guard. I could see the wheels turning in their heads as they tried to figure out if I were trying to play some kind of game with them or if there was some kind of trick to the patently obvious answer.

After a minute, Brevaht cleared his throat. "I don't think there's a dwarf alive that believes it will be anyone other than you, Princess."

I gave a small bow of my head, "I'm humbled you think so. I tend to agree with you, and if I'm being honest… I'm a bit nervous. While I doubt there's anyone in Cragmorrar willing to plot against me, I've had experiences outside of Cragmorrar that show that there are others who will."

"When the news about what the Church attempted reached Cragmorrar, your father nearly gathered every able body and marched to Orlimar," Jennia grinned. "Would have been interesting."

"I tend to agree," I chuckled. "I'm glad he didn't, though. I had everything handled."

"Oh, we heard," Jennia smirked.

"I'm sure you did," I quickly moved to my next point, "but I also had to hear from folks like Earl Edward and King Marshal, who mentioned that the Surface Caste was an excellent addition to their markets but that the Syndicate's presence that inevitably followed it was not. I'm sure you can understand that I don't particularly appreciate one of my greatest successes being associated with one of Cragmorrar's worst aspects."

"I can appreciate that, Princess," Brevaht nodded, "but we go where we can do business. It's just logical."

"It's insulting to the Exemplar's efforts, is what it is," Faren growled.

I leaned over and placed a hand on Faren's shoulder to calm him down. "You being where business is going on is the entire point. But you're focusing on the wrong business."

That seemed to pique their interest.

"Here is my proposal," I said as I closed the book and stacked them all neatly, pushing them slightly to the side. "I would like to reorganize the Syndicate into an arm of Cragmorrar's military. Direct conflict would not be what we want from you. Instead, the Syndicate would become our spies; the eyes and ears of Cragmorrar. You would keep a lookout for threats from within and without Cragmorrar."

"Spies?" Brevaht asked, a hint of intrigue in his voice.

I nodded as I continued, "The Syndicate would, of course, have to cease all illegal activity and would be pardoned for past indiscretions. You would report on any other organizations trying to fill the void the Syndicate leaves behind, have members in the courts of other kingdoms to listen out for any threats or opportunities that affect Cragmorrar, and if the need arises, you'll be asked to eliminate threats."

The pair stared at me as if they were trying to discern my true motives.

"I'm trying to figure out if you're being serious or not, Princess…" Jennia hummed.

"Indeed," Brevaht agreed with her. "You have a reputation for carefully thought-out plans, a positive outlook on life, and an extreme preference for peaceful and beneficial resolutions. This proposal seems to be… unlike you."

I smiled softly, "I think the two of you can appreciate that people are more than their public persona. When the public sees me, they see a symbol of hope, of positivity, prosperity, and forward momentum. They see Exemplar Orodum, a historical figure living among them and offering them hope for a better world."

"What they don't see is the detail-oriented pragmatist who weighs every decision carefully and makes that decision decisively," Faren added. "Princess Merida genuinely wishes the best for her people, but where they see her as a kindly benefactor, she is actually a mother bear. She will do whatever it takes to see the dwarves safe and thriving. She would burn the world down if it meant the dwarves thrived in the act."

Brevaht looked at me and shook his head, chuckling, "I knew it was impossible for someone to be that good."

"I am that good," I said decisively. "But being good doesn't mean I'm incapable of doing terrible things to uphold that good. Dwarves have not needed an official group for espionage because we haven't been as active on the surface as we have till now. It also means we will be experiencing new, more subtle threats to our way of life and commerce. We don't have time to train warriors in the art of spycraft. We need experienced individuals ready and in place before these threats make themselves known."

"People will grow suspicious if the Syndicate just suddenly vanishes," Brevaht doubted.

"It won't," I explained. "I'm about to start cracking down on the Syndicate. They've become a nuisance to too many people in too many markets now, and the pressure is going to start coming from various leaders for something to be done."

"So you'll use the campaign of fighting the Syndicate to establish your spy network?" Jennia guessed with a grin.

I gave a nod, "Precisely. When I announce that I'm going to be hunting the Syndicate, I'll also announce an amnesty period. Any members willing to submit themselves to justice will be given lighter sentences. I want the two of you to suggest that there is more to gain by submitting to me than there is continuing to run the Syndicate. Anyone who stays loyal to you will be considered for the network."

"What about those who continue performing Syndicate work?" Brevaht asked.

"We'll hunt them down and kill them," Faren said without hesitation. "Or rather, you will hunt them down and bring them to us for execution. That will be your first mission under the Exemplar's command."

Brevaht sat back, looking both shocked and impressed, "You'll use us to hunt down our own by using our knowledge of the resources, hideouts, and contacts."

"And after they have been brought back to Cragmorrar for justice…" Jennia began to put all the pieces together. "You'll have us use those same resources, hideouts, and contacts to begin our new duties… if we agree."

"Using former Syndicate members to get rid of the Syndicate holdouts and setting us up to be able to take down other criminal organizations because they won't know that we're no longer Syndicate members," Brevaht chuckled, shook his head, and clapped. "Absolutely brilliant."

Brevaht shook his shoulders and shivered, saying soberly, "Honestly… It's frightening how you've decided to go about this. I can see why you invited us first. But I have to ask; since we do what we do for the money, why do you think we would give it up?"

"Because you can't spend money if you're dead," I replied, the promise quite clear in my tone and expression. "Understand, if you say no, you won't leave the city alive. If you say yes, then you will be helping me secure our people from more subtle threats."

"When you put it like that," Jennia said carefully, "it doesn't sound like you're giving us much of a choice."

"Not all choices come with a benefit," Faren smirked.

"But luckily for you, this one does," I smiled brightly. "You see, once the disloyal members are dead, and you take up the guise of the 'Syndicate' once again, you can continue conducting your business as usual. There would be a few differences, though."

"Such as?" they asked in unison.

"I would have thought they'd be obvious to such astute and cunning individuals such as yourselves," I motioned for Kara to come to me. When she approached, I instructed her to have dessert brought in. I turned my attention back to the Syndicate pair. "First, no killing anyone unless sanctioned by the King, the Assembly, or myself."

"I noticed you included yourself as equal to the King and the Assembly," Brevaht mused.

"I'm an Exemplar," I responded with a smile. "By all rights, I outrank them both, at least as far as my opinions are concerned. But I was referring to myself in the sense that I'll likely be named Queen."

"Fair enough. What are the other stipulations?"

"All criminal activities which result in a profit will have those profits reported to the Assembly so that we can return them to their respective rulers at the end of each year," I continued. "This will help us keep up the guise that we are constantly cracking down on Syndicate and Syndicate-like activity."

"We don't even get to keep a percentage?" Jennia frowned.

"The percentage will come at the end of each year," I clarified. "We'll be using some of what you manage to get from other criminals to add to your funding."

"Incentivizing us to do a better job in finding more criminals every year," Brevaht nodded in appreciation.

"Precisely!" I chirped. "The other kingdoms won't know how much we took in, and I'm sure they would thank us by letting us keep some of the gold."

"Lastly, there will be no more smuggling of dimvyum," I stated firmly. "Our primary export cannot be allowed to be sold by anyone other than through the contracts made by the Assembly. You can promise dimvyum, but you cannot deliver it. Is that clear?"

"That will be a hard sell," Brevaht said. "I can see the wisdom in it, but a lot of members make a lot of gold off the stuff."

"Then those members will be hunted down and killed," Faren said for me. "Occasionally, when the King, the Assembly, or the Exemplar believes it is necessary, you might be given some to help an operation along, but otherwise none will be smuggled."

"To discourage the smuggling of dimvyum, I will be pushing for the Assembly to increase the punishment of smuggling it to a death sentence," I explained carefully. "No matter the amount. No matter the reason. Dimvyum is a treasure that dwarves alone can safely mine. We alone control it as a resource. Those that would steal that resource from their people deserve nothing less, as the act spits in the faces of our ancestors, our Exemplars, and those living."

"The more we talk, the more I think you would make for a formidable enemy," Brevaht smirked. "I'm glad we're speaking now and not after your announcement to crack down on the Syndicate."

"I prefer to foster talent into a positive direction," I bowed my head. "Now, there's one more stipulation I'll have to add before I let you decide on what you want to do."

"What is that?" Jennia asked, clearly interested.

"You don't tell a single Syndicate member about what's coming, what's going to happen, and how they'll benefit from shutting down the Syndicate," I sat back, putting on an ominous air. "I want those willing to stop their criminal activity to be rewarded, and those who don't want to stop dead. No warnings, no heads up, nothing. Just a simple announcement that you're done and that anyone who wants to continue working together can do so with your legitimate Surface Caste family."

Jennia's eyes went wide, "You know about our Surface Caste family?"

I couldn't help but laugh and tapped the books, "I told you, I'm meticulous."

"Beyond measure," Brevaht sighed. "If you know about our caste family, then that means you likely have enough evidence to have us all taken in."

I squealed with delight as the servants brought in a fruit cobbler, setting a plate before each of us. I thanked them before taking a bite and savoring it. "Oh, this is delicious. Please, try some! You'll love it!"

There was no reason to affirm Brevaht's assumptions. I simply let him understand what it would mean for those in his family if he refused my offer. I was a mother bear, after all, and his family and business threatened those in my care if left to their own devices.

"However, I don't want you to think that there's no upside to this beyond simply being allowed to live," I smiled between bites of cobbler. "If things go how I've asked, I have a special perk for you."

Brevaht, who had taken one bite of the cobbler then gobbled it down with enthusiasm, raised a brow. "What might that be?"

"I will have House Orodum become your family's patron."

"That's…" Brevaht gasped as he looked to Jennia.

"My Lady, that's far too magnanimous and not worth us simply quitting the Syndicate," Jennia said in surprise.

"Then you'll both agree that My Lady is being more than generous," Faren said as he ignored the fact that I was stealing his plate of cobbler since he hadn't touched it yet. "I recommend that you agree to her proposal. As generous as she's trying to be, she'll be equally as ruthless if you refuse."

"Faren," I scolded him as I began to eat his share of the cobbler, "you don't need to threaten them. I'm trying to encourage good decision-making, not discourage poor decisions."

"Apologies, My Lady," Faren bowed his head. "I would insist you have my dessert to make amends, but you already seem to be enjoying it."

I smiled at him and hummed happily as I took another big bite. I looked at Brevaht and Jennia. "So, now that all of our cards are on the table, I have to ask: what is your decision?"

In the end, Brevaht and Jennia agreed to my terms. We talked details for the next hour or so before they left. My command to allow them to leave the city freely was still in effect, so they weren't harassed.

"You didn't offer them the weapon," Faren observed as we went to the study to read our books.

"I don't want to introduce firearms to Thoros if I can help it," I responded.

"The atoshi have cannons, though," he retorted as he took a seat. At the end of every evening, we sat and read books together as a way to unwind.

"Using an unstable alchemical solution, and only on their ships as far as I recall," I shook my head.

"But aren't others slowly developing ways to make bombs?" he asked as he thumbed through his book.

"The key word is slowly," I emphasized. "Eventually, someone will think to condense it and turn it into a more portable weapon, but I would rather that not be because of me. I have considered it, though."

"You've done more than consider it, My Lady," Faren reminded me pointedly. "How many designs did it take Darina to perfect the model you settled on?"

"We went through several dozen designs, but in the end, we settled on a few different designs."

"And you're sure you don't want to give them to the dwarves? We'd be a power to be feared," Faren suggested.

I shook my head, "Not unless it's absolutely necessary. Advancing too quickly would have some extremely negative consequences. Now, no more talk about them. Let's just enjoy the rest of the evening."

"As you wish, My Lady," Faren yielded.

A month after that evening, I met with the Assembly and made my announcement that we should be cracking down on the Syndicate, and that we should be treating dimvyum as a natural treasure. I suggested the death penalty for anyone who would steal that treasure from the dwarves. I also insisted on the death penalty for all Syndicate members who were still operating after the amnesty period. Anyone who would jeopardize the Surface Caste and relations with our allies by continuing in such activities put their livelihood over that of the dwarves and thus did not deserve a livelihood.

Both topics were controversial. No one wanted the Syndicate around... officially, but some noble families worked very closely with them. The Callers of those families were the primary hold-outs. In the end, both motions passed the Assembly vote. The world would change with the dwarves treating dimvyum as a cultural treasure, but I was determined to see that change work for the better in the long run.

CHAPTER 19:

GIFT GIVING

Since I'd returned to Orlimar, Bilfern and I had reconnected and caught up on the past few years. We had, of course, sent letters about everything that had been happening over that time, but nothing beat speaking in person. Bilfern had become an excellent enchanter, and his other studies were coming along wonderfully. Darina insisted that if he kept it up, he would likely become Cragmorrar's premier enchanter.

He'd done a great deal to help me recover from my losses at Orlimar by being there for me. I don't discount Faren or Kara's efforts, but Bilfern was my younger brother, and his efforts to bolster the spirits of his elder sister were more appreciated somehow. His studies had come along so well that he really needed more hands-on experience when it came to politics and diplomacy. I had retaken my place on the Assembly now that I'd returned home, and Rita was able to return to her and Veron's business.

Bilfern would accompany me to every meeting of the Assembly, and while Callers and petitioners were giving speeches or arguments, I would quietly test him. I would ask him who the person was, why they would be arguing for or against the issue they were speaking on, and what their motivations might be. I ensured he looked beyond the obvious reasons that were given and searched for the intricacies: who did the speaker owe, which House or caste would benefit, how did the speaker benefit if the issue passed or failed? All these things were important to understand when deciding how to vote on any given issue.

We'd been expanding in the Under Roads by securing more of the areas around the reclaimed Holds. I wasn't personally present for these particular efforts, but I made sure House Orodum had a presence in each expansion. The roads beneath northern Falladrin were respectably secure. Scourgespawn encounters were very low, and tunnels were sealed in a similar method as we'd used to seal them when we retook the Holds.

Before I could continue my work on hunting down the old gods before they could become archdemons, I sent word to Verrloft Fortress using the fledgling spy network that Brevaht and Jennia had started creating. I was very specific about what information I needed and who I wanted to speak with about it. I knew it would take time to get an answer and longer still to meet with who I wanted to meet with, but it wasn't exactly a time-sensitive issue.

Rita and Veron were married a few weeks after I'd taken my place back in the Assembly. I paid for the whole thing myself and refused to let Veron's family spend a copper on it. I just wanted them to enjoy the occasion. I even convinced Father to let them use the throne room for the ceremony and festivities. The whole affair was wonderful, and a great many friends and family attended. Trenton even surprised everyone by sending a small herd of rhoarnos as a wedding gift to help them haul trees up the mountain, and haul the brankite they produced back down the mountains to human and elven vendors. I gifted them an expansion to their home, specifically an outside expansion by creating a larger storefront, upper levels with a balcony for them to enjoy the view from, and a small pasture inside the mountain to hold the new rhoarnos in.

Shortly after my twenty-first birthday, a messenger arrived with an invitation from Serena and Alford to attend their wedding. It would be held in Watcher's Keep, the seat of power in the Earling of Coralstine. The wedding would be held in two months' time, so that gave me plenty of time to prepare and make my way there. One thing I'd set House Orodum and some other smaller families under my patronage to was to explore the Under Roads and secure a route to Watcher's Keep, which had a connection to the Under Roads.

In the Roused Sleeper expansion, you would have to seal this connection up or else the scourgespawn could use it to invade the Keep. When Serena announced that she had finally gained the Earling back in that first year we were in Orlimar, I'd sent word back to House Orodum in Cragmorrar that I wanted the route found. We had the route figured out two years later and had used it as a relatively safe route to transport goods to Coralstine's port.

I say relatively safe because there were still scourgespawn in the Under Roads, but nowhere near as many as there used to be. After Orlimar, the scourgespawn presence was especially low. We wouldn't really have to see the surface until we got to the Keep.

I'd decided that my wedding present to Serena and Alford would be doing what had been done in the expansion; I would have the Keep's walls rebuilt to dwarven standards. It sounds silly, but the difference between dwarven stonework and anyone else's is like night and day. There's simply no comparison, and it would ensure the wall's integrity for hundreds of generations. It would also likely be more expensive than all of their other gifts combined, except for the Earling itself.

I'd spoken with a number of dwarven caravans who'd come and gone from Watcher's Keep in order to get an estimate of the materials that would be needed to rebuild the walls. The convoy that would be coming with me to the wedding would bring the supplies with us.

The trip to Watcher's Keep would take three weeks. When I left, Faren, Bilfern, and Capone (my quickly growing mavrosk pup) accompanied me, along with one hundred of my House Orodum warriors and all of the masons and engineers that would be needed to rebuild the walls. The trip itself was relatively uneventful, but I had some scouts head through some unmapped roads that led north, specifying that I wanted them to search for exits along the Lightning Coast, west of Wyrm Island.

Serena and Alford, as well as a gaggle of human nobles I didn't recognize, welcomed us when we arrived. I had insisted that the masons and engineers stay further back and not make themselves known so I could surprise the happy couple with their present.

Trianna, Aelfric, and Allen all arrived the next day. I was so excited to see Trianna that I knocked her to the ground with the enthusiasm I put into the hug I gave her. That evening, all the fated sat in private to discuss what had been happening and to compare notes.

"You got rid of the Syndicate?" Serena sipped a hot cup of tea.

"We're in the initial stages of it," I clarified. "We've only been at it for a few months, but it's a concerted effort."

"That's certainly going to keep your people busy," Aelfric said over a small stack of notes. "It's not like they're going to just roll over and die. And since they're so spread out over the Surface Caste markets, it will take a lot of intel to find each pocket and weed them out."

I just smiled with cheeks full of cornbread. Somehow, Aelfric just made it better than anyone else. "I think we have all the information we need at this point. It's just a matter of time."

Allen chuckled and leaned forward in his seat, looking at everyone and waggling a finger at me. "There's something she's not telling us. She knows something."

I just laughed and winked.

"All right, then," Trianna smirked, "keep your secrets. We have some news as well."

"Oh?" Serena perked up. "So, then, tell us how things are in Orlimar."

"Well... We have good news and bad news," Trianna hesitated.

"Let's get the bad news out of the way first," Allen sighed as he sat back, preparing himself for the news.

"Serevas has made an appearance," Aelfric said with a warning tone.

Serevas was an elf from the third game in the series who was actually known as Trith'Emel; the Hungering Hound. Modern elven mythology said he betrayed the elven gods and imprisoned them. In the lore of the series, it was Serevas who separated the physical world from the spiritual world by creating the shroud. The physical world became known as Thoros, while the spiritual world became known as the Dimvolmn.

He made a mistake by giving a powerful elven artifact to an ancient Vintari magister named Varrimus, who used the artifact in an attempt to destroy an anchor which prevented anyone from gaining control over the Dimvolmn.

"Already?" Faren grumbled. "It's not nearly time."

"The elves already have a stronghold and there are larger changes coming than there would have been by now thanks to us," I suggested. "He sees a base power structure he can attach himself to and manipulate to bring about the original world through."

"Why would he bother, though?" Serena asked, setting her tea down and crossing her legs. "Isn't he strong enough to do that on his own?"

"Thankfully no," Trianna shook her head. "Or, at least, he's not strong enough yet. He only woke from his slumber about a year ago."

"He shouldn't have woken up for about another ten years…" I rubbed my chin in thought. "Perhaps there was something else that caused him to wake. I don't suppose you could ask him?"

"We could," Aelfric shrugged, "but who even knows if the answer he gives would be the truth. I'm guessing we all know that he's a liar."

"And that he doesn't consider the elves of this era to be true elves," Trianna added with a scowl. "But that doesn't stop his charisma or his appeal to the elves in Orlimar."

"He's actually staying there?" I asked in surprise.

Trianna nodded, "He's saying he's just a wanderer who has researched the history and traditions of our people. But he's growing a following slowly but surely. We need to find a way to contain his influence."

"Can't just send him away either, can you?" Faren mused after taking a draught from his mug of mead.

Aelfric shook his head, "No. He's already too well known, and it would go against our policies of welcoming all elves to Orlimar."

"But it does bring us to one solution we've decided on," Trianna smiled.

"What's that?" I asked as I noted the change in her demeanor.

Trianna and Aelfric shared a smile before Aelfric nodded to her, "Go on. But prepare for the reaction…"

That phrasing surprised everyone.

Trianna just chuckled and nodded as if in acceptance of the inevitable. "Aelfric and I have decided to get married."

Everyone's reaction to the news was drowned out by my shout of excitement as I jumped from my seat, cleared the space between Trianna and me, and sent the loveseat she was sitting on toppling backwards as I jumped up and hugged her in excitement. The commotion from the toppled furniture, along with my shout, alerted the guards, who jumped through the door to check if everything was alright.

Serena assured the guards that everything was fine.

"I honestly thought she'd be louder," Allen laughed.

"She really held back the enthusiasm, too," Aelfric snickered.

"I expected her to just know at this point and announce it herself," Faren shrugged and sipped his mead.

Trianna and I laughed and hugged for a few minutes as I asked her a thousand questions about when the wedding would be, where it would be, if we would be invited, and so on.

"Merida! Merida!" Trianna laughed. "Let's get the seat back up, and I'll tell you everything."

"I'm so excited!" I cheered as I leapt up and simply righted the loveseat back up with Trianna in it. "Tell us everything!"

I grabbed my chair and hauled it over to sit beside Trianna, gazing up at her excitedly.

"Nothing much to tell," Aelfric laughed. "We grew closer together over the years at Orlimar, then as we helped each other throughout the past year with running the place and organizing everything, we fell in love. A week ago, I asked her to marry me."

The expression I gave Aelfric was full of disappointment. "You could not have told that story with less enthusiasm if you tried."

"I didn't know I was expected to make a grandiose tale of it," he shrugged in apology.

"You really do need to spice it up," Serena said, agreeing with me. "It's a story you'll tell your children, and your people will tell about their leaders."

"But that's all there was to it," Aelfric sighed defensively.

"I'll work on the embellishment," Trianna chuckled.

"I'm surprised that particular tale hasn't already been told among us," Allen mused thoughtfully.

"What do you mean?" I asked, looking at him as if he had some sort of idea.

"He's just being foolish," Faren growled. "Pay him no mind."

Allen cleared his throat and sat back from Faren's snarl, "Indeed so…"

"Anyway…" Trianna tried to diffuse the situation, "We plan on marrying in the spring. We want you all there."

"Of course we'll be there," I shouted as if that was the obvious answer.

Serena clapped, "Indeed! We'll all be sure to make it."

Trianna looked at me, "And, Merida?"

"Yes?" I asked, all smiles and excitement.

"Since maids of honor aren't a thing in Thoros," she began but had to increase the volume of her voice over my lengthy, exuberant squealing, "we would like you to preside over the ceremony."

I screamed with excitement and toppled Trianna and the loveseat with another hug, "Yes!!! I would love to!!!"

"Huh… no guard," Allen chuckled. "She restrained herself that time."

"Or they're starting to expect it," Aelfric sighed in amusement.

"You make another joke and they'll have one less guest," Faren eyed Allen.

Allen just raised his hands up as if in surrender.

"As joyous as this news is, there's something else we need to discuss," Allen cleared his throat.

That brought the mood down instantly.

"After going through everything in the college, I managed to convince Marylen to help teach some of the more…" he paused as he considered his next words carefully, "esoteric magic that she knows."

"That's good, right?" Trianna asked.

"That's not at all like her. Did you give her the grimoire?" I demanded.

Allen's expression tightened. "That's what I wanted to talk to you all about. She agreed to teach at the college for five years if she could have the grimoire."

"And you gave it to her?" Aelfric balked.

The grimoire in question was a book of secrets and spells that Marylen had searched high and low for in the games. If you managed to find it and gift it to her, she would become even more powerful over the course of the games. The grimoire also held secret rituals and rights you could perform in the game that would alter the game's ending in profound ways.

"I needed someone like her to help with different studies at the college," Allen defended himself. "And she's a genius when it comes to researching older magic. We could use her knowledge to our advantage."

"For five years, maybe," Serena chided. "If she doesn't bother disappearing before then. This is going to have her sending people after Franeth!"

"I doubt that part will matter," I hummed. "Franeth was never in any danger to begin with. You could kill one of her bodies, but she'd just find another one to inhabit. Besides, if Serevas has made himself known, we'll probably need help from Marylen and Mythriel to defeat him."

"Mythriel?" Faren asked.

"Franeth's true name," Trianna clarified. "I'm surprised you didn't know that."

"A lot of the lore confused me, if I'm being honest," Faren finished his mead. "I'm surprised Merida can remember as much of it as she does."

"Merida?" Allen teased. "Don't you mean Exemplar Orodum?"

"If he kills you in a fit you riled him into, no one here will call for any punishment," Serena warned.

"Is there a reason you're needling Faren tonight, Allen?" I asked with an exasperated expression. I was trying to be excited for my friend's engagement.

"I just hate to see an opportunity go to waste," Allen huffed. "Neither do you, Merida. Everything you've accomplished proves that."

"And what opportunity is being missed that has you goading Faren into a fight?" I crossed my arms in irritation.

"Are you joking?" Allen barked a laugh. "Trianna and Aelfric get together, but you and Faren haven't even considered it?"

"I'm going to pretend you didn't just suggest that," I hissed as tears welled in the corners of my eyes.

"What? Why?" Allen asked incredulously.

"Because she just got over losing her fiancé!" Serena moved over to rest a supportive hand on my shoulder. "They were friends for over ten years! Don't you have any scruples?"

"I'm sorry, I thought that was more of a political thing," Allen admitted. "I honestly didn't think that the feelings were genuine. Or, at least not yours, Merida."

"Why would you think that?" Faren growled, standing now and absolutely fuming.

"Because she's a dwarf," Allen explained. "You may not remember it, but dwarves typically have one spouse but multiple partners to ensure they have plenty of heirs and warriors. The entire caste system is built so that people can marry up through noble hunters and the like. So I figured Merida was marrying Franklin for political leverage, and that the two of you would just have your own thing going on the side."

I glared at Allen for several moments then just lowered my head and fondled the ring that Franklin had given me with his proposal, "That's not what it was."

"Again, I'm sorry," Allen apologized. "It's just, you and Faren are always together, and he gets so defensive over you even when someone says anything."

"I'm her personal guard," Faren insisted. "It's my duty to get defensive whenever someone threatens her person or her reputation."

"Clearly," Allen sighed.

The rest of the evening was more sober. The argument had left feelings raw but we muddled through, sharing news, discussing plans, and getting things squared away for the ceremony.

The ceremony itself went off without a hitch. It was a lovely white affair with flowers everywhere.

Trianna and Aelfric gave Serena a sacred tree seed, which Trianna used some magic to encourage it to sprout. It was meant as a symbol of the connection between Serena and Trianna. Alford saw it as an excellent future tree for their grandchildren to climb on.

I surprised Serena with my gift of the Keep's walls being rebuilt and had the dwarves get to work that same day.

I also made a pig of myself by enjoying as much of the delicious food as possible.

Allen presented the couple with rings that would shine whenever one of them was facing the other, no matter the distance.

I insisted that Faren and Allen make up later that day. I knew Faren would hold onto that grudge for some time, likely forever in some small way, but I didn't need bad blood between the Fated. There were still threats to deal with in Thoros, and I needed us to be able to work together to defeat them.

We stayed for another two days before taking our leave. I took a great deal of time speaking with the human nobles who'd arrived for the wedding and introduced Bilfern to them as well. King Marshal and I had a conversation about Logan's death, as well as trade prospects and how he could help with hunting down Syndicate members. Allen and I took some time to go over the college expenses and a few possible expansions to the tower, which I could work on having done as long as he passed the coin for the materials and labor my way. I promised Trianna that I would write and that I would arrive early to help in any way I could to prepare for the wedding.

We left the masons and engineers behind. It would take them three months to finish the walls properly. The trip home to Cragmorrar was interrupted one evening as Faren and I were reading in our tent about a week into the journey.

A loud sound outside caught our attention. Another sound, similar to the first, had us looking at each other in confusion. Faren stood and grabbed his sword, then moved slowly to the tent's entrance.

We both gasped when a tall, elderly woman with white-styled hair and elegant leather armor entered the room. Her yellow eyes grinned down at us, "Ah haha! I see I've interrupted your reading. Do forgive me."

I stood in shock and stared up at the woman, whispering in terrified awe, "Mythriel…"

She cackled and smiled, "My my, someone does know more than they should, don't they? But, do please, call me Franeth. Everyone does." She looked at Faren and chuckled, "You may put the weapon down, master dwarf. I'm no threat to your Lady. In fact, I'm here to give her some gifts."

The way she said it didn't exactly put Faren at ease, or me for that matter. Faren looked back at me and I simply nodded for him to stand down.

"Please, let us sit and talk," Franeth's voice wormed its way through the room. "May I?"

I bowed my head and motioned for her to take one of the chairs for herself, "By all means, My Lady. It's a true honor to have you here. I trust my guards are alright?"

"Oh, they're just sleeping," she laughed as Faren moved to stand beside my chair. "They'll wake right as rain after I depart. But I must say, the honor is mine, Princess. Exemplar Orodum is a name that I've heard often enough as of late. And seeing you handle that archdemon? A sight to behold. Like the ancient dwarves of old."

"You saw that?" I asked in confusion. "Were you scrying the battle?"

The crone just tilted her head back and laughed, "No, Princess. I was there."

Faren and I looked at each other, then back to Franeth, "I think we would have noticed you, of all people. You tend to stick out."

She laughed again, "Do I? I'm not so sure. I can blend in when I wish. After all, I ran right past you and you didn't notice."

"What? When?"

Her laughter was bathed in pure amusement, "Oh, my dear, I wouldn't worry about it too much. You were going through quite the metamorphosis at the time."

"I wasn't," Faren protested. "And I didn't see you."

"No, you weren't," Franeth sneered. "You were trying so desperately to get to your beloved… Princess."

"You had to be in disguise," I shook my head. "It wouldn't matter what I was going through, I would still have noticed you."

Franeth hummed in consideration, placing a finger on her chin in mock thoughtfulness, "Yes. I suppose you would have. You tend to have an eye for detail, don't you? No matter. I will admit that I was in disguise, as one of the Scourge Sentinels, in fact."

"As one of the… By the Stone…" I gasped quietly.

"Now you understand," she chuckled. "But there's no need to fret. Fariastren's soul is safe with me for now. I have no desire to see it used to create another archdemon."

"You can't keep it with you," I exclaimed.

"Oh? And why not?" Franeth canted her head in amusement.

"Because Trith'Emel has awoken," I explained with a small amount of fear creeping into my voice. "He's going to try to unmake the world by removing the shroud. He'll kill you to gain your soul and Fariastren's to do it. Then he'll hunt down Raziel and Luscan and take their souls for himself as well."

Franeth's eyes narrowed, and her jovial demeanor disappeared. "Trith'Emel is awake? How do you know this?"

"We're Fated," I motioned between Faren and myself. "Us and four others. We were born with knowledge about Thoros' past and future. We're trying to work together to end the largest dangers we know of and improve the world in ways we know we can."

"Indeed? I suppose this is why the elves now have a home in Orlimar," Franeth surmised. "And why the dwarves have gained the Surface Caste in such a short span of time. Let us suppose that what you say is true, that the Hungering Hound has returned to Thoros. What is it you plan to do to stop him, Princess? I can't help but believe you have some plan."

I nodded firmly. "I do have a plan. It wasn't to stop Trith'Emel; it was to keep Thoros safe. But it will help to stop Trith'Emel."

"Indulge me, then," she grinned, her amusement returning. "Tell me your plans."

"I had planned to hunt down the remaining old gods and kill them," I admitted. "I know the people who are aware of their prison's locations. I'm going to bring my people to the prisons, clear the paths to them, and then I'm going to kill them myself."

"I sense that those plans have changed slightly," Franeth hummed. "Does this have something to do with what you did at Orlimar?"

I nodded slowly. "Yes. I need to get answers. I need to learn how best to use these powers."

"You're seeking answers from your parents? Do you think they'll even speak to you?"

I nodded again, desperate. "From the Titans, yes. They spoke to me to endow me with this power. They trusted me to see these things done."

Franeth hummed in consideration. "So… The pillars of the earth have begun to wake again, and they're working through you?"

"And you killed some of them…" I let the information hang in the air. "But I don't care about that. I care about keeping Thoros as it is now. Trith'Emel isn't strong enough to do anything just yet. So I need to learn to master this power before he regains all of his."

"Do you think your power could rival one of the Gospinia?" Franeth chuckled.

"It took all of the Gospinia and your people to put the Titans to sleep," I confirmed. "I'm a powerful mage in my own right. I'm likely one of the most powerful mages in Thoros now as I have been training since I was one year old every single night and most days. And now I'm beginning to wield the power of the Titans. I'd say I'd be able to at least challenge him if I can master these powers."

Franeth sat forward and cackled. "Oh, my dear Princess, you are exactly the person I'd hoped you would be. After everything I've heard, and having spoken to you now, I believe you'll take special care of the gifts I brought you. Please, come in."

An older dwarf poked his head into the tent. "Everything alright in here?"

"Of course," Franeth replied with a smile. "Both of you come in now. I would like to introduce you to the Princess."

The dwarf waved to someone. "Come along now, my boy. We're going to meet someone very special."

I recognized the voice, but when I saw a young dwarf around my age with no beard and pale skin, smiling absently at me as he trotted in, I gasped. "Samy!"

"Dimvyum?" Samy asked.

Franeth laughed. "I suppose I shouldn't be surprised you would know these two."

Brifford, the older dwarf, bowed low. "It is an honor to be in your presence, Exemplar Orodum. I don't believe we've met, but you seem to know my boy."

I moved from my seat and approached the pair. "I know you, as well. Brifford Devrik and your adopted son, Samy. It is my pleasure to meet you both."

Brifford tried to get Samy to bow to no avail. "Forgive him, My Lady. He's a bit touched."

I chuckled and shook my head. "I understand. I want the two of you to make yourselves comfortable. You will become a part of my House, and I will keep you under my protection."

"You are most generous, My Lady," Brifford bowed once again.

"Not at all," I motioned to Faren. "Faren here will make sure you're comfortable during the rest of the trip back to Cragmorrar. When we get there, I'll have quarters set up for you and your boy."

Faren approached Brifford and nodded. "Come with me. I'll get you set up in camp."

"As you say, Ser," Brifford complied with a smile. He placed a hand on Samy's back to guide him along. "Come along, my boy. This nice man is going to bring us to our beds for the night."

"Dimvyum?" Samy replied curiously.

"A very comfortable bed," I assured them.

"Dimvyum!" Samy cheered as they left the tent.

I turned back to Franeth, taking my seat across from her once again. "So… He does have the soul of Kaneya inside him, then?"

Franeth hummed in dismay. "Known to the elves as Kaneya. Even I don't know how her soul bound itself to the boy. But it is there. And I knew that if anyone could keep him safe, it would be you, Princess."

"No harm will come to Samy or Brifford so long as I live," I promised.

"I don't doubt that at all," Franeth grinned. "But there is another gift I must give you if you truly believe Trith'Emel is awake and regaining his strength."

"What's that?" I raised my brow in curiously.

Franeth stood and approached me, taking my hands in hers and helped me to my feet. Her expression was serious with a deep sorrow. "Understand, I would have kept this burden to myself if I did not believe it safer to have it hidden away from the Hungering Hound."

"I thought you said it was a gift," I replied hesitantly, a growing fear crept into me.

"It is..." Franeth's tone was almost apologetic. "It will give you a great deal more knowledge than you already have. But knowledge is, in itself, a burden. The source of this magic is also a burden. Will you accept it? Will you keep it safe?"

My mind raced as I tried to conceive of what Franeth, of all people, could possibly wish to give me that could cause her to act this way. Melancholy was not in her wheelhouse, and it was rare that she ever broke out of her snarky, flippant demeanor. In fact, I could only recollect two times it ever happened. My eyes widened with a mixture of realization and shock.

"But if I take it..." I whispered with no small amount of fear, "that would mean that..."

Franeth nodded, "It is true. You will become like me. Ageless, like the stone you venerate. But you must agree to accept it. A soul is not forced upon the unwilling, Merida. If you agree to take it, listen to the whispers. You will learn much, and you will grow in power."

"Won't this kill you?" I asked shakily.

"Kill me?" Franeth broke into a laugh. "My dear child, I'm not giving you my soul. I'm giving you Fariastren's... or should I say Jeron's? At least, what is left of it after its transformation."

"The elven master of crafts," I mumbled as my recollection caught up with what was happening.

"Just so," Franeth smiled. "I am certain you will be able to put his knowledge to good use. And her power will aid you in what is to come."

I stared up at the ancient creature before me and tried to process or comprehend what all this could possibly mean. In the end, I simply took a deep breath and nodded firmly, "I'm ready."

No sooner had I said the words than a magical blue orb of light slipped out from Franeth's chest, trailing wisps of smoky energy. It hovered between us for a few moments before it slipped inside me. I braced myself for something to happen. My eyes were shut tight for several moments before Franeth burst out with laughter.

I dared to peek at the old woman, "I don't... feel any different."

"Give it some time, my girl," Franeth chuckled. "You will feel the power swell within you over the next week or so."

"Then what?"

"Just do whatever it is that you were planning to do to begin with," she chuckled. "You will grow attached to the memory of Jeron, and you will gain an affinity for his powers and skills. But in the end, you will still be you. Continue to serve your people as admirably as you have already, and I'm sure you will use this gift well."

"What about you?" I couldn't help but ask.

"Me?" she scoffed. "Well, I, for one, am not meant for the Under Roads. I made an exception to come meet with you. I will take my leave. When next we meet, I hope that it will be as allies to save this world from its Creator."

"If you need anything from me, if there's any way I can help, please let me know," I offered.

"Just keep yourself, and the boy, safe," Franeth patted my hand. "If you must engage with Trith'Emel, do so with caution. He will not be able to sense the spirit within you, but he may be able to recognize other things about you that could clue him in. And he is a wily one."

"I'll be careful," I promised.

With that, Franeth took her leave. The rest of the trip back to Cragmorrar seemed to take forever to me. The power from Fariastren's spirit had begun to infuse itself with my own and the process took its toll on me. I felt drained of energy for the remainder of the trip and even had to take another week to recover once we were back in Cragmorrar.

I had Darina work with Samy while I recovered. Bilfern was a dear and looked after me almost as much as Kara fretted over me. Faren was tasked with preparing a sizable convoy after some of my scouts returned with good news.

These next few steps were going to be big ones. Thanks to Franeth, I would be more capable of seeing them to completion.

CHAPTER 20:

THE DESCENT

It had been a few months since Franeth had left Samy in my care. In that time, I had managed to connect with him in the Dimvolmn. His spiritual self was astounding, and he was more cognizant of himself and his thoughts. I theorized that this was because his mind had been overwhelmed by Kaneya's spirit when he was far too young, and he simply never recovered from it. His spirit, however, was a different story. It was able to converse relatively effectively, though he still spoke in half-meanings and riddles.

Purpose was glad to have Samy, as it gave it a renewed goal to work at. Each evening, I would speak to Samy in my dreams, then go hunt demons while Purpose worked with Samy to bring more of the person out from the torrent that was Kaneya's influence.

Bilfern had taken a shine to Samy, and the two were often found in Darina's enchanting chambers, working with her on refining the process and innovating the craft. House Orodum was becoming known for its exceptional and unique enchantments.

My scouts had returned with news. They'd found a section of the Under Roads along the Lightning Coast that seemed to lead into a forgotten Hold. They had left some guards there and had mapped a course. They also mentioned that it seemed like the area was much lower than the standard depths of the Under Roads and that they had to construct a lift in order to get up and down between the initial cavern entrance to the Hold.

This was exactly what I'd hoped to hear.

I quickly gathered a few hundred warriors, had Rita informed that she would need to attend the Assembly in my place, told Father I would be back in a month or two, and asked Bilfern to look after the House for me. I left within a few days of receiving the news. The scouts had marked the path through the Under Roads, but it was still slow going. We had to take detours around certain sections that had crumbled or caved in due to a lack of maintenance, clear debris from the paths to allow the rhoarnos and carts through, but in the end, we made it to the destination.

I could hear the angry waves of the Lightning Coast echoing down through the caverns above us. It was surreal to think of all that water being nearly over our heads, but I suppose it isn't all that much different if you consider we typically had an entire mountain range over them.

As we arrived at the lift, the scouts were searching for the few they'd left behind to guard the area.

One of the scouts approached me as I dismounted my rhoarno and looked around at the abandoned camp. "My Exemplar, I'm not sure what's going on. Once we found the place we set up patrols and guards so that the camp would have someone in it at all times."

"Could it have been scourgespawn?" I asked as I walked around, looking for any signs of the spawn.

"Unclear, My Lady," she responded. "I've seen no signs that would point to scourgespawn, but I don't think we can discount the possibility. But I'm doubtful."

"Why's that?" Faren asked, his eyes darting around the cavern as he searched for threats.

"We haven't seen many scourgespawn around Cragmorrar or further north since the Scourge ended," was the reply. "Even if it was scourgespawn, there's no blood or anything to say that this was an attack. None of theirs or ours. No signs of struggle or battle. The camp simply looks abandoned, as if the scouts simply walked away."

"Did you contact the Legion about the place?" I asked as I checked a tent and noted nothing out of turn.

"We did, My Lady," she confirmed with a nod. "They should only be a day or so behind us. I'd recommend we wait for them before venturing further down."

"I tend to agree, My Lady," Faren added. "If it is scourgespawn, I'd prefer to have the Fallen Legion with us."

"Very well," I granted. "Inform everyone to make camp. I want overlapping guard shifts. Whatever happened here will not happen again. I'll work on making the path down easier for us."

"It will be as you command," Faren bowed. He turned and began to relay my orders to the rest of the convoy.

While everyone else set up camp, I wielded my new powers to create a series of stone ramps wide enough for a rhoarno to walk on along the side of the crevice, down to where the lift would take us. This was a slow process because while the lift would take a minute or two to go from the top to the bottom, a walkable path took several more minutes as it would need to weave back and forth. The entire project took me about two hours, but it went faster as time went on.

I was still getting used to purposefully molding the stone through my will. I had been practicing with the ability daily and had learned that basic shapes were simple and could be done with almost no thought; I just had to will a spike or a sphere and know where I wanted it, and it would appear. Complex or precise constructions took focus. A smooth, flat surface extending for dozens of yards in a precise angle was surprisingly complex. If I lost focus, or if my mind wandered for even a moment, the resulting imperfections would be noticeable.

Once the task was complete, I wanted to move deeper into the cavern, but Faren and my other guards refused to allow me that curiosity. It wasn't safe, and they insisted that we wait until the Fallen Legion arrived to reinforce us. I understood their intentions and agreed with their council. As much as I wanted to delve deeper, it wasn't like anything was going to go anywhere. I was, however, worried about the missing scouts and believed that waiting only wasted time in finding them.

Faren had to point out that they could have gone missing a few hours after they were left them alone and would be a month dead by now if that was the case. I couldn't help but agree with him, as much as I hated the thought.

We actually didn't have to wait a day for the Legion to arrive. They arrived the very next morning. Apparently, after hearing that I had gathered my men and supplies and set off quickly, the Legion had done the same and were only a few days behind us. They gained ground because we had to spend time clearing the way and ended up only about a half a day behind us by the time we set up camp.

It was a pleasure to see Sidra leading the company of Legionnaires. She smiled as she bowed before me, "Exemplar Orodum. Captain Sidra, at your service."

I stepped forward and hugged Sidra, "I'd heard of your promotion after Orlimar. Congratulations, Captain."

"Please, My Lady," she returned the hug, "Call me Sidra. We've been through too much to stand on titles."

"Then you must call me Merida," I insisted.

Sidra laughed and shook her head, "I'm afraid you have too many titles to ignore, My Lady. But if it will make things seem more personable, I can call you Princess instead of Exemplar."

"Whatever you prefer, Sidra," I chuckled.

"Thank you, Princess," she laughed and motioned to the camp. "Should we discuss what's been found?"

"Indeed," I turned and led her and her officers to the command tent.

When we were all seated, I began the meeting, "We arrived just yesterday to find the camp deserted. No signs of struggle, attack, or accident. It seems like the scouts who were stationed here simply abandoned the place."

"Unlikely," Sidra contemplated. "Not scourgespawn either. There would certainly be signs of scourgespawn."

I concurred, "Just as we thought. This cavern leads to the Ruins of Hardrin Hold. And it is guarded by dwarves calling themselves the Hal-Ifden."

"I've never heard of them," Sidra said curiously. "And the Legion has visited the Hold a few times and never reported encountering them."

"The Legion never went deep enough to find them," I responded. "And it's good that they didn't. Any of the Hal-Ifden we might encounter are their most dedicated warriors who drink dimvyum to enhance themselves physically and wear dimvyum-laced armor grafted to their flesh. They're fanatics and are not to be taken lightly."

"Fanatics?" Sidra questioned skeptically. "Just what is there to be so fanatical about down here, Princess?"

I stared directly at Sidra, and my expression was dead serious. "They're guarding our birthright, our origins. They're guarding one of the few remaining ancient beings in all of Thoros; a creature that existed before the creation of this world. They're guarding a Titan."

"A Titan?" Sidra gasped, reeling back at the suggestion. Titans were supposed to be myth to the few people who'd even heard about them. Some Legion members would have seen rumors or suggestions of their existence in the older Holds, but they were always considered to be mythology; stories to explain the dwarves' connection to the stone.

"Are you certain?"

I nodded with all the certainty I could muster. "I am."

"How can you know? Is this some of the knowledge you gained being one of the Fated?" she pressed.

"Partly, yes," I admitted. "I knew they were here from the start, but we haven't been in a position to get to this point until now. However, I can also feel it. Ever since Orlimar, I've been able to feel the connection to the Titans. I believe my ability to manipulate the stone is a bounty from that connection."

Sidra stared down at the table, reevaluating everything she knew with the confirmation that the Titans, and their role in the creation of the dwarves, were all true.

"I'm hoping that they'll see my connection with the Titans and leave us be," I continued. "But if they don't... we'll be hopelessly outnumbered if they call in all their people instead of just the current number of guards along the path."

That snapped Sidra back into her soldier mindset. "How many could we expect if they call for reinforcements?"

"Supposedly?" I assumed. "An entire city's worth. The information anyone has on them is vague at best, but what we do know is that the ones that are here are simply the most fanatical soldiers dedicated to the Titan's protection, or simply the ones currently chosen to serve as its defenders. Think of them as our equivalent of the Fallen Legion, except that they consider it the highest honor to serve in that respect. They train all their lives for the honor."

"So they're more like zealots," Faren grumbled. "And what do we do if they acknowledge you, but not the rest of us? We can't just let you go alone."

"I'll try to convince them," I could only shrug. "They speak ancient Dwarven. I have a fairly... basic grasp of it thanks to the memories I was granted by the Titans. I've been practicing it in what little spare time I have. If nothing else, I might be able to convince them to allow a small group through. In fact, it might be better to go with a small party and not the entirety of our force."

"That would put us at a severe disadvantage right away," Sidra sighed.

"If it puts us in a better position to continue unscathed, it would be worth it," Faren countered. "And we can't forget about the missing scouts. We need to hope that they're still safe."

"Assuming it was the Hal-Ifden who took them," Sidra suggested.

"We can only hope that it was, and that they haven't hurt the scouts yet," I sighed. "We'll continue with a small party of ten. Faren, I want you to choose three warriors from House Orodum. Sidra, choose four Legionnaires. They need to be patient and level-headed; I don't want anyone who will fly off the handle or be provoked easily into a fight."

"What about reinforcements?" Faren asked.

"We have to assume we won't get any," I conceded. "Once we enter those tunnels, we're on our own. Everyone else will only be able to wait for us here."

"They won't accept that," Sidra suggested. "They'll want to avenge you if something happens."

"Then let's pray nothing happens," I could only hope.

The next day, Faren, Sidra, and I, along with seven other warriors, set off for the deeper tunnels leading to Hardrin Hold. I honestly expected to find scourgespawn in the initial areas once we entered the Hold. Strangely, there was no resistance; not from scourgespawn or the Hal-Ifden. We made our way slowly through the Hold, noting the older-style construction and decor. Still, the lack of resistance disturbed me. These areas should have been swarming with powerful scourgespawn. In the game, you would find ogres, warlocks… every kind of scourgespawn, alphas included.

We made our way through the crumbling and failing infrastructure of the ancient Hold as carefully as possible. I helped us navigate the place to the best of my ability using my memory of the path that was laid out in the game. However, there was considerably more to the Hold than was presented in the game, and the process took hours. One thing was for certain, though… the closer we got, the more we could all hear the song of dimvyum, and I could sense the connection to the Titan growing stronger.

Unfortunately, we also began to see more and more signs of scourgespawn. Tracks in the dust, and their telltale scent was unmistakable. Imagine our horror when we passed through a doorway into a large, open area filled with scourgespawn. The spawn lined the walls, five or six figures deep, and glared at us hungrily. Strangely, they didn't so much as move to attack.

The blood from my face drained when I realized why. At the opposite side of the area, sitting on a throne of dead dwarves, sat a massive alpha… and behind him stood the Crafter. The alpha was grinning wickedly, seeming pleased that we had arrived. He waved his fingers at us to approach.

"Come, dwarves," he chuckled menacingly. "Do not fret. I will not allow my underlings to harm you. Not yet. Not at least until we speak."

"My Lady, we need to retreat," Faren whispered.

"We can't," Sidra said shakily. "There are more behind us… and we wouldn't be able to outrun this many. Not with how far we'd have to run."

I glared at the scourgespawn. It was able to talk. It could command the others. Was it somehow controlling the Crafter as well? Was it awakened?

"I want you all to remain silent," I said quietly. "Act as if this is normal, but be on your guard. Do not act unless I command it."

"As you command," the others said in unison.

I straightened my posture and approached the scourgespawn leader with a professional air, offering it a curtsy as I stopped a couple of yards away from it. "Greetings. I am Exemplar Merida Orodum, Princess of Cragmorrar. May I ask who I have the pleasure of speaking with?"

The leader chuckled and leaned forward. "Exemplar Orodum? There was never a Exemplar named in this era other than Beltia. Who are you, really?"

It refused to answer me. I needed to consider a new way of addressing it but decided to remain civil for now. "I didn't lie. I'm precisely who I introduced myself to be."

"So an Exemplar and a Princess, then?" it hummed in consideration. "Was it you who manipulated the events at Orlimar? I remember seeing you atop your rhoarno, and how you handled the archdemon."

That took me aback. This creature had been watching me at Orlimar?

"I was there," I admitted. "I'm not sure how I managed to defeat the archdemon. Up until that moment, I wasn't able to do any of those things."

"You're trying to tell me it was a fluke?" it laughed. "Or divine intervention?"

"I think you already know the answer if you're here," I countered. "Now, before we continue our conversation, might I ask for a chair? We've been walking for some time, and I would appreciate a respite."

The scourgespawn leader glared at me for several moments before cackling madly, "A chair? Really? Of all things, that's what you want at this moment?"

"I would appreciate it," I smiled.

The leader looked back at the Crafter. "Can you believe her? I'm sitting on a pile of dead dwarves, they're surrounded by a thousand scourgespawn, and she wants a chair."

The Crafter stared down at me calmly, coldly, indifferent. "She has been walking for some time. They have not stopped for a rest. It is understandable."

"Well," the leader said with a mocking sigh, "I'm afraid we are out of chairs. Unless you'd like to borrow one of mine?" It slapped the face of one of the dead dwarves it was sitting on.

I ignored the disrespect to the dead dwarf and shook my head. "That's alright. I'll get my own."

I moved to sit down and willed the stone beneath me to form into a simple block that I could rest on.

That seemed to get the leader's attention. Its eyes considered the display with interest.

"Now, I believe you were about to introduce yourself?" I said with a chipper tone and subtle insistence.

The leader considered the demand for a moment before it leaned back. "Scourgespawn are not given names. But if you must call me something, you may call me Seven."

I tried to hide my surprise, but I doubted that I was successful. "Seven? As in the seventh origin?"

Now it was Seven's turn to look surprised. Its surprise turned to wicked amusement as it leaned forward quickly. "I knew it! You're like me! You know everything that should be going on right now! And you're the reason things haven't gone the way they should!"

I bowed my head, conceding his point. "Myself and five others."

"So... all seven of the origins are here in Thoros?" it grinned. "No wonder... I thought we could have slaughtered the forces at Orlimar and gone on to tear through Falladrin. But all of you... you stopped that from happening."

I stared at Seven, almost horrified. "What are you saying? Are you saying that you wanted to kill those people? That you wanted to spread the Scourge? Why? Why wouldn't you want to bring peace to this world? You could end everything on your own by reigning the scourgespawn in!"

"And why would I want to do that?" Seven burst out with a wicked laugh. "Wait, let me guess; you're one of those people who always chose the best options every time because you didn't like the bad things that happened when you didn't make the optimal choices. How boring can you be? Stories are so much more enjoyable when things don't go according to plan."

"For instance, like right now," he motioned around us. "Here, the heroes are surrounded by overwhelming odds. They stare certain death in the face, and the protagonist is speaking with the villain in the hopes that she can somehow convince him to spare the lives of her people. Isn't that interesting? Doesn't that raise the stakes? The tension? Isn't that more interesting than everyone simply getting along?"

"Is that why you're doing this?" I asked incredulously. "You're not going to do what's best because you enjoy things going wrong?"

"How is what I'm doing wrong?" Seven barked, standing and glaring down at me. "I am a scourgespawn! There is nowhere in this world where we belong, nowhere we can go where we won't be attacked on sight! We war against ourselves when not being controlled by an archdemon. We're enslaved by the archdemon whenever one appears. We cannot reproduce, we cannot build a society, we cannot gain free will except by the awakening process, but even that has its limits."

He leaned in so close that his exposed teeth nearly bit at my nose as he spoke, "What would you have me do? Would you prefer if I gathered all the scourgespawn together and set them on fire? Perhaps have us hunt down all the broodmothers and kill them so we all die out of starvation, in battle, or old age? Simply tuck ourselves away, out of sight, out of mind, so the rest of Thoros can live peacefully?"

"You could rebuild the Under Roads," I countered as I tried to buy some time to think. "You could live in any of the lost Holds and create a place for your people to be productive."

"And how would we sustain ourselves? Hm?" Seven growled. "Tell me that, Exemplar. Would we be allowed to hunt rhoarno or perhaps hunt game on the surface? Would anyone trade with us? Would anyone risk the taint by allowing us to peacefully enter their towns or cities?"

"I never said it would be easy," I countered.

"You may as well have said nothing," Seven waved a dismissive hand. "No, Princess, I will lead the scourgespawn to do what we are meant to do. I will hunt down the old gods, and I will kill them, claiming their power as my own. And once I have done that, I will come for the dwarves, the humans, the elves, and the atoshi. All will fall before the scourgespawn tide, or be tainted and brought into our fold."

I scowled, hearing his plans. "You'll be long dead before you ever find another archdemon."

He glared at me and grinned, "Oh, I don't think so. You see, I know who knows the location of the remaining prisons. And I already have swarms of scourgespawn hunting them down for the information."

This concerned me, so I decided to call his bluff. "You may know who has the information, but do you know where they are? It's not like you could just walk up to them and ask politely."

His grin became a sneer, "Verrloft Fortress, in the southern Felback Mountains. I will find the First Sentinel, and I will flay them alive, inch by inch, until I get the information I need."

I took a long, slow, calming breath. If he knew where Verrloft was, then it was only a matter of time before the scourgespawn would reach the fortress. I could only hope my spies got there first. Otherwise, we would be doomed.

"You're going to send scourgespawn to attack a fortress with hundreds of Scourge Sentinels in it?" I asked, keeping my tone calm and even. "Scourge Sentinels, the one force in all of Thoros trained to specifically track and battle scourgespawn? That's like sending a mouse into a house full of cats."

"Hundreds of Scourge Sentinels are a force to be reckoned with, it's true," the Crafter acknowledged. "However, they cannot hope to match the thousands of scourgespawn we've sent to find them."

"I'm afraid you'll find that we have taken that into consideration when assaulting our natural enemies, Princess," Seven chuckled as he sat back down. "Now, I'm sure you're wondering if there's some way you can get out of this current situation alive."

I arched my brow and canted my head to the side curiously, "Now why would I be wondering that?"

"It would seem she has accepted defeat with some dignity," the Crafter offered. "That is commendable."

"That's boring," Seven snorted. "We saw how she handled the archdemon. I doubt someone like the Princess would give up without a fight. Do you have a plan yet, Princess?"

"I do," I nodded in affirmation. "I don't think I could kill all of you quickly enough to save my party. But I could kill most of you quickly enough to give us all a chance. But they are my friends, so I'm willing to negotiate an end to this confrontation until we meet again."

Seven roared with laughter, "Your arrogance astounds me, Princess! You honestly believe you could kill most of us on your own?"

A shriek echoed from the side. When Seven and the other scourgespawn looked to the source, a spawn was suspended in the air, impaled on a spike.

Seven looked back at me, seething with rage, "You dare? Against these odds?"

I remained calm, but my expression was dangerous, and my tone shifted to dead serious, "I defeated the archdemon in a matter of moments when I was first gifted these powers. Do you think a small horde of scourgespawn would take me much longer? As I said, I believe I could kill you all... but I don't think I could do it fast enough so that all of my friends remain safe... So I'm willing to negotiate for now."

"Don't worry about us, My Lady!" Sidra called out. "Our duty is to keep you safe. We're all willing to die to see such a threat ended."

"But I'm not willing to let you die when I can work to allow you to live," I responded without letting my gaze move from Seven's.

The expression Seven gave me could melt steel. I could feel the rage coming from him. He wanted nothing more than to kill me at that moment. He thought he'd trapped us, but he didn't realize that my control over the stone had come as far as it did... and there was nothing but stone surrounding us in the Under Roads.

"I suppose we'll allow you to leave for now," Seven spit. "Go, and we will not follow."

I shook my head, "No. You and the Crafter will leave. You will not harm a single dwarf back in the camp. And if I ever see you again, or if a single scourgespawn attacks Cragmorrar or any of the Holds, I will make it my life's mission to hunt you down and turn your existence into nothing but pain."

"And what of the scourgespawn who are with us?" the Crafter pressed, understanding that I only meant to allow the two of them to leave.

"I will be magnanimous," I responded, raising my chin to show authority. "How many dwarves are you sitting on, Seven?"

Seven considered the question for a moment, "A handful. No more than twenty."

"Very well," I looked to one side of the room, and then the other. Stone spikes leapt from the walls and floors, impaling dozens and dozens of scourgespawn in an instant. "There. I believe we can all agree that two scourgespawn dead for every dwarf is fair."

"I'll kill you for that!" Seven roared in fury.

I stood and stared at Seven, raising my voice now, "I would slaughter the lot of you here and now if it weren't for my friends' safety! Two dead scourgespawn for one dead dwarf isn't remotely fair. A thousand dead scourgespawn aren't equal to a single dwarf's life! Your kind is a plague, and one day I will wipe you out like the useless vermin you aspire to be! Now leave, before I let my friends convince me to risk their lives."

Seven hummed in thought, "We will leave for now. But now that I've met you, now that I know that you have been the thorn in my side for all these years, I know who I'm preparing to face. And now, I understand the power I have to overcome. The next time we meet, I will slaughter your beloved friends and feed them to you while I torture you and turn you into a broodmother."

"You will try," I said defiantly.

Seven growled and stormed off through the way we'd come.

The Crafter stared at me calmly, "I understand why you view us the way you do. We do not produce anything. We do not contribute to the world as a whole. But if everyone was joined by the taint, we could work together for the common good of all."

I craned my neck to look up at the Crafter, "Forcing everyone to become tainted is a simple violation of their existence. You cannot bring about peace by forcing others to conform to your way of life."

"You can if those who do not conform do not survive," the Crafter responded passively. It wasn't a threat or even said with any sort of passion. It was a pure, factual statement.

"What sort of world would it be if you killed everyone who disagreed with you just so that you could rule over those who comply with you?"

"Peaceful," the Crafter said succinctly.

"Experience and history has taught me otherwise," I sighed. "Seven doesn't want peace. Not truly. I think you know that. What you have to decide is if it's worth helping them burn the world down out of spite... or allowing the scourgespawn to fade into history to allow the world to go on in peace."

"I admire your spirit, Princess," the Crafter bowed his head. "I will consider your words. But understand that I must also do what I consider best for my people."

"As will I," I matched his point.

The Crafter followed after Seven, with the other scourgespawn swarming out of the area and giving Faren, Sidra, and the others a wide berth.

I watched them leave with trepidation. Someone had been resurrected as one of the scourgespawn... And it wanted nothing more than to simply wipe the world clean simply for the sake of having nothing else to do. I didn't know which threat was worse; Serevas or Seven. For now, I could only forge ahead and hope that the Titans could give me the edge I needed.

CHAPTER 21:

AWAKENING

The encounter with Seven had left everyone on edge. The elevator that would lead us to the tunnels inhabited by the Hal-Ifden was only a few yards away, but we decided to take some time to catch our collective breath.

"A Fated scourgespawn..." Sidra cringed. "That's not something I would have ever wished to imagine."

"We should be grateful that we're still alive to talk about it," Faren replied as he continued to look around the area, paranoid that more scourgespawn would come swooping from the shadows.

"True enough," Sidra agreed, then bowed her head to me. "Thank you for keeping us safe, Princess. I would have preferred that you had killed that monster here and now. Our lives would be a small price to pay to see it dead, but I am grateful to be alive all the same."

"If I were more confident in my abilities, I would have done just that," I admitted. "I blame myself for not dedicating more time to mastering my stone manipulation. If I had, this wouldn't have been an issue, and Seven would not be free to hunt down the power of the old gods."

"Don't say such things, My Lady," Faren said as he placed his hands on my shoulders in a comforting gesture. "You already do more for your people than anyone else. You cannot be blamed for being diligent enough. Who could have imagined the fates would allow a scourgespawn of all things to have the knowledge of the Fated?"

I smiled softly at Faren's encouraging words. "Thank you, Faren. Your support is always a comfort."

"I will always be here to support you, Princess," he assured me.

With his confidence, I turned to look at the elevator. "This is where we need to go. This will take us further below than any dwarf has gone in ages. At the bottom, we'll find the Hal-Ifden. Beyond them, we'll find the Titan."

"We're ready when you are, Princess," Sidra affirmed.

We stepped onto the elevator to make our way down to the lower tunnels. The trip to the bottom took several minutes. It was a marvel to think that anything so thin and rigid could extend far without snapping, but this was the wonder of ancient dwarven stonework. Thousands of feet below Under Roads, the darkness seemed to creep in. I could feel it enveloping me like an ominous blanket.

"I never thought I'd say this," Faren gasped, "but I'm having trouble seeing very far ahead."

Sidra and the others nodded in agreement.

"It's like a new depth of darkness," Sidra said with surprise.

I looked around, trying to figure out what they were talking about. "Are you certain? I don't see any difference between this and the Under Roads."

"Merida…" Faren gasped, using my first name without a title in his shock, "your eyes are glowing."

"Are they?" I asked curiously. I looked to the others for confirmation.

Sidra stepped forward, gawking at me. "The blue is so vibrant now. It's like looking at raw dimvyum glowing in the mines."

"I suppose that explains why I can see just as well here as I can anywhere else," I surmised. "You can all see me, though, right?"

Everyone nodded.

"Alright. How far out can you see past me?"

"About ten yards," Faren answered.

I nodded, "That's not too bad. Just follow me, then."

Sidra chuckled, "So just do what we always do."

I grinned back at her, a bit of mirth in my response, "Isn't it nice having a plan that works in multiple situations?"

That got a chuckle from the group as we pushed forward. It wasn't long before we began to find our way into areas that were lined with dimvyum. I stopped immediately when I noticed a row of Hal-Ifden aiming mechanized crossbows at us. I held a hand out to signal for the others to halt.

I stared at the Hal-Ifden for several intense moments before one of them seemed to consider me closer, then spoke to one of the others. The other turned and called out behind them. A few moments later, a Hal-Ifden in armor that seemed more imposing than the others stepped forward. The crossbowmen stepped aside to allow him to pass.

The leader approached me slowly, as if he was trying to figure me out.

I took the initiative and spoke to him in ancient Dwarven, "I am Exemplar Merida Orodum, Princess of the Dwarven city of Cragmorrar. We do not mean you or the titan you protect any harm. I simply wish to speak with the titan."

The leader froze in what I could only assume was surprise. The helmet that was fused to its skin didn't allow for me to see its face. It leaned in and pointed at me, "You speak our language? How did you learn it?"

I motioned to my eyes, "The Titans have touched me. I wield their powers and have seen the memories of our people. Those memories came with this language, but I've yet to speak with anyone else using it. I hope I'm not offending your ears with my first conversation."

"You speak it well," the leader said, his tone honest. "As if you were born to it. You say you were touched by the Titans, and you have eyes similar to ours. But how can we know what you say is true? You may have simply learned of our traditions and practiced them in order to gain our confidence."

"Would a demonstration of the titan's power be proof enough?" I asked diplomatically.

"Show me," the leader insisted.

I looked around the space we were in. Part of it had been dwarven-hewn, while other parts were still natural cave formations. I waved my arms out in either direction, and the natural stone molded itself to match the lines of the dwarven stonework.

The leader's body language showed that he was shocked. He took a step away from me, then dropped down to kneel. The other Hal-Ifden followed suit.

"You are truly touched by the titans," he said, head bowed. "It has been untold generations since the titans have shared their gifts through any dwarf. As you are titan-touched, we are obligated to assist you however we can."

That lifted a weight off of my mind. I didn't want to have to fight my way through the Hal-Ifden just to commune with the titan.

"Will you escort my people and me to the titan's heart?" I tried to keep my tone as respectful as possible. "I wish to speak with it and understand its purpose by working through me."

The leader raised his head and seemed to look past me at Faren, Sidra, and the others. "Our duty requires that we keep all those not touched by the titans, or a part of the Hal-Ifden, away from the titan. You may go, Princess, but the others may not."

That disappointed me, but I wanted to remain on good terms with these dwarves. They were far more dangerous than the group I'd brought with me. Faren and Sidra might be their equal, but I doubt the others might be.

"Perhaps just my personal bodyguard?" I suggested. "I will not allow him to do anything to disrupt the titan. He will simply stand by and ensure my safety. The others can wait at a point you deem close enough."

The leader took some time to consider the proposal. "None are supposed to be allowed to pass… But I will grant your request as a titan-touched. Your word that your bodyguard will not step out of line is enough assurance for me. I trust you will not make me regret my choice."

I offered the leader a curtsy. "I swear to you upon the stone itself, no harm will come to the titan. I want it to remain safe just as much as you do, for reasons you would not believe."

That seemed to grab the leader's attention, but he simply stood and motioned for us to follow. "Very well, Princess."

As the leader gathered up his men, I turned back to the others with a smile. "That went well."

They all seemed to be holding their collective breath and released it in relief.

"What did they say?" Faren pressed.

"They'll lead us to the titan," I explained. "However, only Faren and I will be allowed to go to the titan. The rest of you will have to wait at a point they determine. They will not harm you."

"Why will we need to wait while the two of you go on?" Sidra asked skeptically.

"They don't let anyone who isn't Hal-Ifden or titan-touched see or interact with the titan," I condensed the conversation I'd just had. "They see me as titan-touched and have allowed one person to accompany me as a favor according to that status."

"If it keeps you safe and prevents us from having to contend with the Hal-Ifden, I see this as a good scenario," Faren approved.

"Better than having to fight them just to get to the titan," Sidra said. "I don't particularly like being contained in an area with enemies around us, but if you're sure they won't attack us, I guess it's the best we can hope for."

"They're not our enemies," I quickly corrected her. "The Hal-Ifden are still dwarves. They're also far more closely linked to our origins than we are. We can only take them at their word for now. They have no reason to betray us."

"Princess?" the leader called to us. "Shall we be off?"

I turned and nodded, "Yes. I apologize, but I was translating your instructions to my guards."

He simply nodded, then turned and started to lead us toward the titan.

Granted, I knew for a fact that we were already inside the Titan. The moment we stepped off the elevator, we were inside the Titan. However, I didn't know where the Hal-Ifden would consider too far for the others to venture. The leader didn't know I had this knowledge, so I was guessing that he was willing to allow the others to go far enough before reaching the open air.

Sure enough, after some time, the leader stopped and pointed at the rest of the group, "Here is where your people must stop, Princess. They can go no further. Collect your bodyguard, and we will continue."

I turned and was about to translate his words, but Sidra was already signaling to her men to rest.

"I'm willing to guess that's our cue to stay," Sidra sighed as she prepped to rest.

"I'll try to return as soon as possible," I said apologetically.

"Return when you're ready, Princess," Sidra responded. "Get all of the information you need from the titan. The information you can get from a titan is worth us waiting however long you need."

"Thank you for your patience, Sidra," I bowed my head. "Faren, let's go."

Faren stepped forward, "As you command, Princess."

Faren and I continued with the leader for a few more minutes, curving through the gradually widening tunnel before I could start to see light slipping in. We rounded a bend, and the cavern opened up into an entire world.

The large cavern stopped, and in its place was a stone bridge that led to pillars so large that they held small villages worth of buildings around them and so tall that there was cloud cover several hundred feet below us. They reached so high we couldn't see the top. Entire mountain ranges pierced the cloud cover and rose above us. Light as bright as the surface day illuminated the world space. There were birds in the sky above us, suggesting this was home to an entirely unique ecosystem.

Faren and I both stopped along the bridge to simply admire the sight.

"That's amazing..." Faren said with awe.

"The game never did it justice," I whispered in amazement. "A titan really is its own world."

"Wait, we're inside the titan already? I don't remember this in the game," Faren said in surprise.

I shook my head with a bright smile, "This wasn't in Origins. It was in Inquest. It was a DLC, one of my favorites in the entire series, really. I never thought I'd be able to get here safely... I'm so happy to be here right now."

I was marveling at the sight when I felt something on my hand. I looked down and found that it was Faren's hand slipping into mine, his fingers intertwining with my own. I looked at him in surprise, but he simply stared out at the view. I didn't say anything. I simply smiled and enjoyed a few moments with him as we took in the sight.

The leader cleared his throat after a bit to get our attention, "Shall we continue?"

We pushed ourselves away from the side of the bridge, and I bowed my head. "Apologies. The view simply took us off guard."

The leader grunted. "I understand. It is something to behold. But our destination is down there." He pointed to a large platform below us that held a massive blue crystal.

I'd been so captured by the view that I hadn't even noticed or looked for it.

"That's the heart!" I said with excitement.

"It is," the leader confirmed. "If you are to commune with the titan, that is where you will likely have your best chance."

We continued our way for some time, going over different bridges and down several levels until we neared the platform where the titan's heart rested. I could feel the energy coming off of the massive crystal, like the thrumming hum of the world in my soul.

The leader stopped halfway across the bridge to the platform. "I shall remain here. I do not want to risk intervening in your communion. When you are ready to return to your friends, I will be here."

I bowed my head. "Thank you... Wait. You haven't given me your name."

"It's Croft," he said simply.

"Thank you for showing us the way, Croft," I bowed my head once more.

"I am happy to be of service to a titan-touched," Croft bowed in response.

Faren and I continued across the bridge, and I felt something calling to me. My mind was being pulled toward the crystal, and I could tell I was going to lose my balance.

"Faren," I called out dizzily. "Faren... catch me..."

Sure enough, Faren was already there and guiding me down to hold me in his arms. "Merida? Merida, what's wrong?"

I blinked hard through the dizziness. "Nothing… My mind is… being pulled to the titan. Just… hold me for now."

Whatever Faren's response was, I wasn't privy to it. My eyes closed and my mind was whisked into the embrace of the titan. I could feel the memories and thoughts of all the dwarves at the back of my mind, but this time they were held at bay. In their place was a presence so incomprehensibly large that I could not fathom it made itself known.

"Merida," its voice made my psyche reel back defensively in response to its power and magnitude. "You have come. So quickly. So dutifully."

"It's been almost two years," I tried to explain. "I should have come sooner."

I felt the presence's mirth at my response. "Our children measure time in increments so short we cannot truly understand them. We called, and you answered. That is enough to know."

"As you say," I could only accept its explanation. "I have come to answer your call."

"You have need of us, child," it responded. "A need that is true and genuine. It is not simply a wanted connection like the Hal-Ifden. We have called you to explain this need."

"I would first like to thank you for helping me against the archdemon," I tried to supplicate myself before the presence, but I could only assume that my intent was enough since I wasn't currently using my body.

"You led our children against the taint, against the infection," it responded. "You needed to prevail to keep our children safe. You were worthy of our blessing. You are worthy of the effort to communicate with."

"Still, I thank you. And I thank you more for the honor," I responded. "I seek your aid in the coming future. Trith'Emel has returned. He seeks to destroy the world as it stands now. I would ask for your aid against him."

The presence was silent for what seemed like centuries. "Trith'Emel. The Gospinia. They waged war against us when we molded the world. Too attached to their temporary crafts, were they. Too beholden to their sedentary existence. They slew some of our kind."

"Mythriel did, right?" I asked curiously.

"Not alone. Never alone. Gospinia are potent together, never apart," it clarified. "Mythriel's plans, Mythriel's designs."

I had to assume that it was speaking from its own perspective. A single Gospinia was a dominating force if Franeth and Serevas were anything to go by. They had power enough to sunder the shroud or destroy the world with their magic. If the titan considered them a threat only when they combined their powers, then the depths of the titan's abilities were astronomical.

"Mythriel remains alive," I explained. "But she no longer wishes harm to the world or to the titans. She wishes to work with me to stop Trith'Emel."

"Cunning is Mythriel," was the response. "Assurances will be needed. And you, child, will need to grow in strength."

"Mythriel has given me the soul of one of the Gospinia, and has returned a dwarf to me that also has the soul of one of the Gospinia bound to it."

"You speak of Samy," the presence knew. "He was to be our vessel. Our avatar. The Gospinia bound itself to him too early. Too young. Before we could work through him."

The thought that Samy had been destined to become the avatar of the titans astounded me. There had always been theories about who, or what, Samy might be but nothing like this had ever been considered. At least, not as far as I knew.

"If I required more strength, and you required an avatar," I began hesitantly, unsure of how this proposal might turn out, "then, may I suggest that you use me as your avatar? Grant me access to your power so that I can stand against the Gospinia in your stead."

The presence went silent for some time again. "You drove the infection away from us just now."

I was going to say that it was a few hours ago, but I quickly remembered that it was speaking from a much different perspective of time.

"I did," I agreed. "It is another threat I must contend with. It has gained sentience and wishes to envelop the world using the souls of the Gospinia. They will become a threat if they succeed."

"You did not eradicate them," the presence seemed disappointed with the fact that I had let Seven and the Crafter go.

"I wanted to save my friends from harm," I explained. "I understand a handful of dwarves do not seem like much, but it was worth it in my mind to keep them safe."

"This is the response of a mother," the presence said without any real judgment in its tone. "You must pick your battles. You must guard the children. In this aspect, you have been acting in our stead. Your desire to protect our children is palpable. Your desire to see us saved from the Gospinia is paramount. Your suggestion to become our avatar is wise. Will you accept this burden?"

"Yes!" I confirmed emphatically. There was no joy in the answer, but there was a willing acceptance of whatever may come with the role. "Whatever is needed, I will endure it to keep the dwarves and all of Thoros safe."

"Then wake now," the presence commanded. "You are now our avatar and the mother of dwarves. Wake and see to the preservation of your children."

My eyes snapped open, and I shot straight up. It took me several moments to realize where I was. I found myself in a nightgown, resting comfortably in my bed. Suddenly, Faren jumped up from a chair he was sitting in and hugged me tight. "Merida! Bless the Stone, you're alright!"

He turned his head from me and shouted toward the door to my chambers, "Mother! Gather everyone! She's awake!!!"

There was a rush of excitement and shouting for several moments before Kara, Bilfern, Trenton, Father, and Rita rushed into my chambers and surrounded my bed.

I looked at everyone's grateful expressions in confusion. They were crying and saying how happy they were to see me awake and well.

"Wait…" I looked at Faren, pure confusion written over my features, "How did we get home? We were with the titan only a few moments ago."

"That was weeks ago, My Lady," Faren answered. He was clearly exhausted. The bags around his eyes were deep and his expression was labored with worry that was slowly beginning to fade. But his eyes… his eyes looked like mine. They were the same dimvyum blue that mine had turned when the titans originally blessed me.

"When you collapsed, you began to scream," Faren slowly explained. "I thought you were dying. Croft wasn't even sure what was happening. We didn't know what to do until the titan spoke to us. It told us you would be growing in power, but that it would take time. So, I thought it best to bring you home."

The memory seemed to haunt Faren as he recalled it. "You screamed the entire way home."

"You've been screaming almost nonstop for weeks," Kara cried as she held my hand and stroked it, trying to comfort me from a pain I didn't recall. "We had no idea how you could continue so long without losing your voice."

"The screaming stopped last night," Father smiled and patted my leg. "Oh, my girl, we were so afraid when the screaming stopped."

"We thought you died," Bilfern sniffed, trying to hold back his tears. "But Trenton said you were just resting now."

"I was on watch," Trenton clarified. "We've been taking shifts to sit with you since you returned. Well, all of us except Faren, who hasn't left your side for a moment."

I looked at everyone and felt guilty for everything I'd put them through, unintentionally or not. "I'm so sorry to have worried all of you. In truth, I didn't realize that was happening. When Faren caught me after I collapsed, I started speaking with the titan. We had a short conversation, then it told me to wake up. So I did."

"A short conversation?" Trenton scoffed, remaining taciturn if not for his eyes glazing over with tears he was holding back. "It's been weeks."

"Titans work at their own pace, it would seem…" I could only say. I suddenly realized that I was ravenous. I'm guessing I'd only had water or some other drink since I'd been out, and my stomach ached terribly.

"I'm sorry," I apologized, "but I'm starving right now. Can we continue this over some food?"

That request got a laugh from Trenton. "Only you, Sister, would ever go screaming for weeks on end before asking for food. Come everyone, let's let her get dressed, and we can share a meal together."

Kara agreed and began to shoo everyone out of the room.

Once they'd all filed out, she shut the door and smiled wearily at me. "Oh, Merida. You have no idea how happy we all are to see you recovered from your ordeal."

"I never meant to make everyone worried," I said bashfully as she helped me from my bed and began to choose an outfit for me.

I wasn't going to tell everyone just yet, but I was seeing everything differently now. I could see the stone move even as it stood implacably still. I could see the imperfections in the stonework that no one else would ever notice. I could feel the footsteps in the floor, echoes of everyone's movements within hundreds of yards, and could track them accordingly. The stone around me was now an extension of myself, separate but entirely able to give me information I needed from it.

I was beginning to understand what the titan had meant. I was its avatar now. Even as Kara fussed over my outfit, I was actively molding the stone to correct the imperfections in the stonework. I was altering the room in subtle ways to make it even more stable. I extended my will and did the same for the rest of my home… and further out into the Noble District. Even as I was experimenting with this new level of control, I somehow understood that this was merely my eyes fluttering open to the world around me. In terms of potential, I was still waking up to this new power. I had yet to lift my head or even extend a finger.

These were simply the first groggy motions of a sleeper finally waking.

CHAPTER 22:

CLAIMING ARONTHOK

My twenty-second birthday came and went. I spent more and more time in the Assembly with Bilfern at my side. Rumors had spread throughout the city after my return from Hardrin Hold. It was no secret that I had been screaming the entire time; there was no way to hide it or mask it. I worked a great deal to reassure everyone that I was fine and promised to explain everything eventually. Surprisingly, there was so much concern for my health and safety that the citizens petitioned the Assembly to have me surrounded by guards nearly every waking moment.

I was used to having guards around me, but it was getting to the point where I couldn't even stray from my path to check in on a shop, or say hello to anyone. I had to remind the guards several times that I was always happy to speak to any of Cragmorrar's citizens if I had the time. They were zealous in their duty, which I appreciated, but the frustration it could cause me occasionally was genuine.

On the bright side, such was my reputation now that anything that might seem like a political power grab was reported to me by my budding spy network. It was how I'd discovered that House Dacken had finally figured out the location of Aronthok, a dwarven Hold which was more of a research center whose location was never really revealed. This prompted me to pay House Dacken a visit before they sent anyone out to claim the area.

Guards had run ahead to announce my arrival, even though I hadn't actually bothered to make an appointment. I found that I no longer needed to; most everyone was happy to receive me at any moment. By the time I arrived at House Dacken, its ruling family stood outside to greet me. Ronus, the House patron, and his sons Mandar, Brogan, and Jerrik were grouped together in traditional fashion at the front door of their home.

I dismounted from my rhoarno a few yards away from the men, then approached and offered them a polite curtsy. I was the visitor, and etiquette dictated that I be the first to greet them. "Lord Dacken, it is a pleasure to see you once again. Your sons seem as fit and capable as ever."

Ronus bowed low, followed by his sons. "Exemplar Orodum, you honor House Dacken with your visit. To what do we owe such a visit? I don't suppose you've come to court one of my lads?"

We shared a laugh, though I noticed at least two of his sons seemed surprised by the suggestion. It was no secret that nobles had been trying to find a way to put their sons in front of me in the hope that I might fall for them ever since Franklin's death two years prior. Honestly, I was surprised they had waited so long to start the attempts.

"Handsome as they might be," I replied tactfully, "I'm here on business. However, it's business your sons are familiar with. So I was hoping we could all sit down to some lunch and go over some things."

"My Lady, nothing would please me more," Ronus replied and bade me come into his home. He turned and walked through the door, while his eldest son, Jerrik, hooked his arm around mine congenially to escort me inside.

I was led to a respectably lavish dining hall where Ronus insisted I sit at the head of his table. I politely refused but accepted the seat to his right, where Jerrik would normally sit. Jerrik pulled my chair out for me, then slid it back in as I took my seat. He was playing the devoted gentleman to perfection.

As everyone was getting seated, I smiled at Ronus. "How is your father, Anwer?"

Ronus sighed, "On the decline, I'm afraid, My Lady. Like your father, he's getting on in his years and he cannot always see to his remaining duties."

"Is he not here today?" I queried.

"No, My Lady," Jerrik answered in his father's stead. "Grandfather is visiting House Hermis to speak on trade matters."

"I'll have to find a way to make up for not seeing him," I added, a bit of disappointment in my tone. "He was always so kind to me when I was growing up, and he never failed to teach me an interesting fact whenever we would speak."

Ronus chuckled. "My father has always been one to appreciate good trivia."

We continued idle chit-chat until after the meal. As we sipped our wine, I turned to Jerrik and smiled, broaching the reason for my visit. "I understand you've rediscovered Aronthok Hold, Jerrik."

This seemed to take all of the men by surprise, but Jerrik just nodded his confirmation. "We have, My Lady. It was an exciting and lucky discovery. Rumors of what the Hold held are rather fantastic in nature."

I beamed. "The golems, you mean?"

"Yes!" Jerrik said excitedly. "Supposedly, it is the site where Exemplar Korabin's research was brought to in order to reproduce the secret for creating golems."

I nodded, as that was as much as what I expected him to know. "It's true, his research was brought there. But you don't need to go to Aronthok to discover how golems were made. I can tell you how it was done."

They all looked at each other, stunned by the revelation.

"My Lady," Ronus fumbled, "If this is true, then why have you not given this knowledge back to our people? The golems could turn the tide against the scourgespawn."

I sighed and sipped my wine as I wondered how best to answer that question. "Because the creation of golems requires the life of a dwarf. For every golem that was ever created, a dwarf's soul was used to animate it."

Mandar nearly choked. "Wait, so that means Lady Cragmor really was a dwarf at some point?"

I nodded sadly. "It's true. She and many others volunteered their lives to become golems and help save the dwarves. However, many more were murdered and forced to become golems. It's because of this that control rods were created. Control rods rob the golems of their sentience and make them no more than slaves to those wielding the rods."

"There's no such information recorded in the Memorium concerning this," Jerrik mumbled.

"No," I looked at him. "There wouldn't be, would there? If our people knew that the noble caste murdered thousands of dwarves, turned them into golems, and enslaved them, do you think they would have let that stand?"

"A fair point..." Jerrik conceded. "If you already know how the golems were created, and you know Aronthok holds those secrets, why come to us? Was it to stop us from revealing this information?"

"Not at all," I confessed. "The researchers at Aronthok failed to duplicate Korabin's research. In fact, they tried to use spirits from the Dimvolmn and only succeeded in creating monstrosities. No, I'm here today to offer your family a deal."

This seemed to set Ronus into a less favorable mood. "Princess? Are you going to bribe us not to go to Aronthok?"

I tittered with laughter and shook my head. "Not at all. No. What I'm offering to do is to pay you to lead me and my people to Aronthok so that I can remove the dangers from the area and make it safe to repopulate. You will allow me and mine to secure the Hold, and I will petition the Assembly to name House Dacken as the ruling family of Aronthok as thanks."

Jonus' sons seemed elated at the proposal, but Jonus himself was skeptical. "So, you wish to pay us to lead you to Aronthok, allow you clear the place out for us, then name us as its head family? Forgive me for my cynicism, My Lady, but how does any of that benefit you?"

Before I could answer, my reputation spoke for me through Mandar.

"Father, don't you see? Exemplar Orodum is doing what she has always done. When one of the lost Holds has been found, she's mounted an expedition to clear it of scourgespawn and promoted those who aided in its reclamation to govern it. She's only doing what's best for our people, as she has always done."

"I'm offering to pay you because your family already invested in a small expedition to find the Hold," I built upon Mandar's answer. "I want to compensate you for the time you've already put in as a way to thank you for your diligent effort. I ask that my people be given the role of ridding the Hold of any threats because the threats there are magical in nature, and I'm afraid of what might happen if warriors not used to combating such things should run afoul of them."

Jonus considered the explanations carefully. He'd always been a sly one. "And once the Hold is safe, you will petition the Assembly to grant House Dacken governorship over it?"

"In fact, I will insist that you have a force of dwarves ready to move in as soon as we're finished so that I can inform the Assembly that House Dacken is going above and beyond their duty by securing the Hold for whoever is chosen to govern it."

A chuckle escaped Jonus. "And since the Assembly will wish to avoid any scrambling and grasping for power, they will take your petition and the desire to see the matter settled quickly and declare that since House Dacken is already holding the Hold, we should go ahead and govern it. Brilliant, Princess."

I bowed my head. "Kind of you to say so, but I'm sure it's no more than anything you wouldn't have thought of."

"I think you overestimate most everyone," Jonus laughed. "So, if I understand you correctly, you prefer that any members of House Dacken we send to aid you simply wait until you've cleared out the Hold? You don't wish for their aid?"

I shook my head. "No. Not because I don't have faith in House Dacken's warriors. There are simply dangers in Aronthok that need to be dealt with in a specific way. I would prefer to keep your people safe while we deal with the dangers. I trust you don't object to this."

"Not at all," Jonus assured me. "However, if word got back that House Dacken did not aid in the reclamation, it would cause a scandal."

"I can assure you that none of my people will see it that way," I smiled. "We've been fighting monsters for the past twelve years now. In the end, we've grown rather accustomed to it, and my warriors would prefer to keep things simple. I admit that I do tend to indulge their wishes when I can."

"This deal seems too good to be true, if you don't mind me saying so," Brogan replied. His tone was skeptical, but he was coming around.

"I'm not sure what else I can say to convince you," I shrugged. "I don't have anything to gain beyond a new Hold for our people to reclaim. That's my only concern. House Dacken stands to gain governorship over the Hold."

"Brogan, Exemplar Orodum is offering us more than our family could have hoped for, even if we had managed to scrape some information from the Hold," Ronus reeled in his son. When Brogan sat back and signaled that he'd cease voicing any more skepticism, Ronus smiled at me. "House Dacken will be happy to show you the way, Princess. If you prefer we wait for your people to handle things, then that's exactly what we'll do."

I bowed my head thankfully. "Excellent. I will add that there will be some dangerous materials in the Hold that we'll be placing in containers and transporting out so that we can properly dispose of them. They won't leave any residual effects, but if we didn't remove them, they would prove deadly. I hope you won't mind that we take our time to do this as well?"

Uranus shook his head. "Not at all. In fact, it simply tells me that you have everyone's best interest in mind if you're willing to take on that additional risk to make the Hold safe."

I nodded, "Thank you, Lord Dacken. Now, may I ask when the soonest your people will be able to leave?"

The question seemed to catch Ronus off a bit. Expeditions typically took some time to plan. "Well, if your people will be providing the bulk of transportation and guards, and we're simply providing directions, I'd say we could be ready by tomorrow."

"Why don't you take a week to prepare?" I suggested. "Discuss things with your family and the details with the families under your patronage. Some will need to remain in Cragmorrar to represent House Dacken, both for business and in the Assembly. The rest can pack up and join us while on the trip so that you can immediately begin moving into the Hold and preparing it for larger occupation by those who choose to join you there."

Ronus considered the advice before nodding in agreement, "As always, Princess, you offer excellent advice. Very well, then, we will prepare to leave one week from today.

I stood and offered Ronus a curtsy, "Then I look forward to traveling with you."

Ronus and his sons stood with me and bowed. I left House Dacken to their preparations while House Orodum busied ourselves with our own special preparations. What I had told Ronus was true; the research into Korabin's method of creating golems had failed in Aronthok. They had succeeded in creating monstrosities which even now swarmed the ruins of the old Hold. Those monstrosities weren't why I wanted to go to Aronthok, but they were excellent cover to spirit away the true treasure of the Hold.

A week later, House Dacken and House Orodum met at the entrance to the Under Roads. Jerrik had been chosen to remain behind in Cragmorrar as House Dacken's representative; a choice I had manipulated slightly by making a house call to his grandfather since he hadn't been home during the initial meeting. Jerrik had the most information about the Hold, it's true, but that information could have possibly given him enough information to cause issues with my plans. So I had suggested to Anwer that Jerrik's intelligence and cunning mind would be best put to use in representing House Dacken in the Assembly. With the decision made, it would be years before Jerrik could even visit the Hold, and by then, I would already have covered up anything that would go missing.

The trip to Amgarrok went smoothly. There wasn't a scourgespawn in sight. Apparently my threat had been taken to heart, and Seven was making sure that the scourgespawn kept a wide berth from the dwarven-controlled portions of the Under Roads; either that, or he was planning something devious. The trip took us through Cragmor Hold, and I convinced Gniess to join us in the effort to help us with the golems that we would have to deal with.

We had House Dacken hold their position when we were about a mile out from Aronthok. Once they were set, we continued on and pushed into the abandoned research Hold.

"I still do not understand why it needs me to deal with golems," Gniess complained. "Surely it is capable of managing something on its own."

I tossed Gniess a sly smirk. "Are you saying that you're no match for a fleshy princess?"

"Not if the princess in question is it," Gniess admitted. "I have seen what it can do to stone with but a wave of it's hand. As a creature of stone, I must admit that the possibility is rather terrifying."

"Well, I think we're good enough friends that you should have no fear of me," I chuckled. "And hopefully, we will be able to get you some like-minded company while we're here."

"Now it has made me curious," Gniess mused.

We moved through Aronthok slowly, careful of scourgespawn, but I wasn't sensing any. What I was sensing, however, were hundreds of small creatures. It had to be the fleshwroughts. However, they were no threat to us thanks to my newly acquired Titan powers. I reached out through the stone and ensnared them one by one. It was like picking flowers in a spring meadow. They didn't know I was coming and couldn't stop me if they wanted to. I pushed them through the stone and into small cages that Orodum soldiers had set up before we entered. We'd brought all of our cavalry and just as many carts to stack the cages on. The fleshwroughts were an excellent bonus to this trip, but they weren't the objective.

It took some time to find what I was looking for, but when we did find it, everyone gasped. The dimvyum well. A sphere of stone wrapped with thick metal bands which were infused with dimvyum crystals and runes.

"What is it?" Gniess asked, clearly awestruck.

"It's a dimvyum well," I explained as I approached the well's containment area. I reached out and let my fingers glide along its surface. "A brilliant device which can shift certain areas, or partial areas within its influence, into different dimensions of the Dimvolmn. You can lock areas off, or even allow entrance, based on which dimension they attune themselves to by using pedestals in the area. It's an ingenious method of defense."

Faren approached it and hummed in thought. "Defense is one thing, but its ability to facilitate offensive maneuvers shouldn't be underestimated."

I looked back at Faren and smirked. "Getting ideas, are you?"

"Only thanks to your foresight to come here and learn about these things," Faren bowed his head.

I chuckled and reached out to tap a finger under his chin so he would lift his head, "Take credit when you deserve to, Faren."

Faren almost seemed to blush. "As you say, My Lady."

I nodded and turned to look back at the dimvyum well. "I'm going to need to study this for a bit to make sure that everything won't come down on top of us if we turn them off."

"Why would they?" Faren asked.

"It's a dwarven creation," I laughed. "We always build things so that we can collapse the ceiling down on top of it just in case we need to stop an enemy from taking it."

"Fair enough…" he sighed and turned to the group of guards who'd accompanied us. "Set up a perimeter. We'll give our Lady all the time she needs to decipher Aronthok's secrets."

The soldiers spread out close to the entrance, though there was no need. I couldn't sense anything around us for miles, save for House Dacken's people, and some wild spiders, nugs, rhoarnos, and crawlers. I didn't tell them that, though. It's not my place to tell them not to perform their duty.

I studied the well for nearly two hours. In that time I tapped into Jeron's spirit, using it to help me discern the method that went into its crafting. I could see each piece and how they fit together. I read the magic and how it was infused into the dimvyum to create the effects of accessing partial dimensions of the Dimvolmn. It astounded me that the well could transport others partially into the Dimvolmn while still keeping them safe from spirits and demons. It was true that the occasional spirit or demon might find its way in, but one or two wasn't a concern.

"I've got it," I announced, exhausted.

Faren approached me and gave me a concerned expression. "Are you alright, My Lady? Why don't you take a few minutes to rest."

I gave Faren a reassuring smile. "It's just mental fatigue. Once we finish a few more things, I promise to take a nice nap as we head home."

"I'll hold you to that," he huffed.

I reached out my hand and deactivated the dimvyum well. Luckily, there was a safe method to deactivate it that wouldn't trigger a destruction sequence. Another act of will had the well swallowed up by the stone and moved swiftly to the men outside of Aronthok, where they would crate it up. I did the same for the other wells and pedestals. With those taken care of and deactivated, the whole of Aronthok was open to us without having to step through dimensions.

"Now we need to see what we can do about the golems," I sighed. The Titan's powers weren't exactly strenuous to wield, but I was still getting used to the nuances. And it didn't help that whenever I tapped into Jeron's spirit, I was overwhelmed with ideas and information.

"Yes, the golems," Gniess almost spat. "Do they not have names of their own?"

"If they did," I responded quickly, "I would have called them by their names. But for now, we'll need to simply call them golems until we can manage to figure out their names. Sort of like how you still call me 'it'."

Gniess paused and gave a low rumble, "I do know its name."

"Then perhaps you would kindly begin to call me by my name, Lady Cragmor," I added a bit of snark to my voice.

"I… will try," she replied hesitantly.

I couldn't blame Gniess for her habits. She understood that she had been a dwarf, but she'd been a golem for centuries, and for a good amount of that time she'd been under the influence of a control rod. She thought of herself more as a golem than a dwarf and considered dwarves and other creatures of flesh to be things more so than people.

"That will have to do," I smiled and led everyone out.

We took our time searching the Hold until we found a room full of golems standing along the length of its walls. I remembered that there were triggers in the floor that would activate the golems to attack, so I insisted everyone wait at the entrance.

I moved to the closest golem and stared up at it, "Now… who are you?"

Golems were essentially just stone statues with crafted joints and the soul of a dwarf fused into them to give them the ability to move on their own. These were runic golems; upgraded with dimvyum runes to give them elemental defenses. If this were the case, then perhaps…

I partially shifted into the Dimvolmn using my combat magic and could see the soul of the dwarf melded into the golem. I took a moment to consider how it appeared, then looked back at Gniess. Gniess's soul seemed more intact, where the other golems seemed to flicker and twist. I had to imagine this had something to do with the connections to the control rods.

Jeron's whispers directed my thoughts and senses to find the connection the golems had to Aronthok's systems. I summoned my mana to me and cast a directed counterspell.

With the golem's control connection to Aronthok severed, each golem lurched forward. Some caught themselves from falling, others fell flat, while some simply dropped to their knees. I had to dodge back as the one in front of me fell to one knee.

Faren and the others nearly sprinted in, but I held a hand out to stop them. I wanted the golems to have a few moments to collect themselves.

I reached out and cupped the golem's cheek. "Are you alright? Can you think clearly now?"

"Where… where am I?" the golem rumbled.

"You're in Aronthok Hold," I answered softly. "You're safe now."

The golem stood to look around and assess the situation.

"When you're all ready, please come to me," I called out to the others. "I will answer any questions you might have."

It took a few minutes for all of the golems to orient themselves and gather around.

They all had questions, but I raised my hands to quiet them down. "First, allow me to introduce myself. I am Exemplar Merida Orodum, Princess of Cragmorrar. I came here to free you and other golems from the control magic that has kept you all from being able to be free. Is anyone feeling overly disoriented?"

No one answered, but one of them spoke. "You call yourself a Exemplar and a princess of Cragmorrar. Since when did Cragmorrar have a princess?"

My expression was one of pity and understanding. "You've had your minds taken from you for so long. Suffice it to say, you've been under the control of magic for hundreds of years now. When the thigh fell, only two remained: Cragmorrar and Kal-Sharok. Cragmorrar is now the capital of the remaining dwarven Holds, and its rulers are the royal family. My family is Nordrucan, but I was named a Exemplar some years ago."

The golems gasped and spoke among themselves, wondering how it could have been hundreds of years.

"I understand that you might have trouble believing me," I conceded. "However, I have someone here who can vouch for my words. Lady Gniess

Cragmor, would you please come here?"

Gniess moved from the entrance to approach the golems, "The Exemplar speaks the truth. We have been controlled for hundreds of years. The Exemplar is seeking to break that control and give us back our minds."

"Why?" one of the golems asked. "What do you gain from this?"

"Nothing," I responded but motioned to Gniess. "I simply want to do what's right by my people. In fact, I would only ask that you take up residence in Cragmor Hold so that you can assist Lady Cragmor in its management."

To her credit, Gniess actually managed a bow, "Cragmor Hold is where golems were dwarves volunteered to become golems. We have a monument to their courage. If you join me there, we shall make the Hold a place where golems can thrive."

There was a commotion among the golems about how they all used to be dwarves and the prospect of going to Cragmor Hold.

"I understand that this is a lot to consider so soon after being freed from the control magic," I assured them. "What I propose is this: you follow us as we free the other golems in the Hold. You can help us as we assist them with reorienting themselves. Once we're finished, you can decide what you would like to do. There are members from House Dacken who will be coming in to occupy Aronthok Hold once we're done. You can choose to stay here, join Lady Cragmor in Cragmor Hold, or choose any of the other retaken Holds to live in. There's also Cragmorrar. I'd be happy to host you in House Orodum until you're prepared to make a decision."

That seemed to placate the golems. It took us a few more hours to locate and free the rest of the golems. Like everything else in this world, it was much larger than the games showed. In the end, most of the golems decided to go with Gniess to Cragmor Hold while some of them chose to go with me to Cragmorrar. As we exited the Hold, the House Orodum soldiers had all of the fleshwroughts in boxes stacked onto the carts and strapped down tight. We left the Hold and met up with House Dacken. I stopped and dismounted to speak with Ronus.

"My Exemplar," he addressed me, "I trust the Hold is now safe to occupy?"

I gave a firm nod, "It is! We've boxed up the creatures that were inside, and we'll dispose of them safely before we return to Cragmorrar."

Ronus gazed over the carts and then looked over the golems, "You did not have any golems when you left us here, My Lady. Have you taken them from Aronthok? Should we not be able to keep them?"

"Do you remember how I told you golems were made, Lord Dacken?" I asked pointedly.

"I do, My Lady."

"Those golems were being controlled by defensive magic systems," I explained carefully. "If you had gone in and begun exploring the Hold, they would have activated and begun slaughtering anyone in the area. There were no control rods. So I broke the control magic keeping them in place. They have their minds again, like they were supposed to have had for centuries now. They have chosen to leave."

"And where will they go?" Ronus asked, a hint of suspicion in his voice.

"You're asking if I convinced them to join me," I stated bluntly.

"I did not mean to imply…" he floundered.

"I understand," I reassured him. "I gave them the choice to choose where they would go. Most have chosen to accompany Lady Cragmor, while a few have chosen to stay with me in Cragmorrar until they decide where to finally settle down."

"I suppose it makes sense for them not to wish to stay in a place where they were enslaved," Ronus conceded. "And I would imagine they would prefer to be with someone of their own kind or the person who freed them. However, if they wish to return to Aronthok, please let them know that they will be welcomed with a respected position. Their sacrifice should be honored."

"Indeed so," I agreed. "I will pass along your invitation. I should also let you know that whatever magic was powering the forge in Aronthok has been spent or gone missing. I assume the mages that helped create it somehow managed to take it back. I think I understand what powered it to work the way it did, so I'll be trying to replicate it. Once it's finished, I will have it brought here so that you can take full advantage of the Hold's systems."

Ronus bowed deeply, "I would be grateful, Princess. As always, your consideration and generosity is to be commended.

I simply smiled and bowed my head in thanks. I obviously wasn't going to tell him that I was the one who took the dimvyum well and its pedestals. If I believed he wouldn't try to exploit them for an advantage over myself or the other Holds, I might have left them in place while I studied them. However, the Dacken's had a reputation for hardline negotiations, and I didn't want to bother with that. Better for him to believe I had recreated the system and give it to him so he would be grateful, than to have him withhold the pieces for personal gain.

"Not at all, Lord Dacken," I insisted. "I'm simply happy to help my fellow dwarves. And if figuring out how the forge was properly powered will aid in Aronthok's production, then I will see it done."

"I look forward to it," he said as he bowed. "Now, I suppose I should coordinate my House to begin occupying the Hold. I'm sure there's quite a bit of work to be done."

"Good luck, Lord Dacken," I replied with a smile. "If you need anything, let House Orodum know. We will do what we can to help."

We said our goodbyes and went our separate ways. We traveled back to Cragmor Hold and remained there for a few days. Gniess assisted the newly freed golems to acclimating to their new home. After nearly a week, I made an announcement that seemed to make everyone happy. Since we were already on the road, we'd be stopping by Petran Hold and pushing further into the Under Roads from there. It was time we brought Korabin back into the dwarven fold.

CHAPTER 23:

EXEMPLAR KORABIN

Franklin's mother, Morcha, had insisted that we stay in her home when we arrived in Petran Hold. Woryek gave me his room even though I was only going to be spending a day or two in the Hold while we gathered our supplies. The first evening we spent dinner catching up since the last time we'd met. We had a nice, cathartic conversation about Franklin and about how House Irono was preparing to create a program in Petran Hold to allow Casteless to become Warriors so long as they served at least ten years in the city guard.

Apparently Franklin had marveled at how the Surface Caste had promoted more work and prosperity in Cragmorrar and wanted to present the proposal to me as a wedding present. Morcha said that she was using the money they'd collected for the dowry and was using it to fund the program. It melted my heart to think that Franklin, who was a staunch traditionalist by most standards, saw how the Surface Caste had worked out and was inspired by it enough to find more ways to make our people productive and useful.

Thinking of how Franklin had been working on this behind my back as a surprise made the memory of him hurt just a bit more.

During the time with House Irono, Faren was in more of a passive mood. He kept to himself and didn't speak much. His interactions were limited to following any commands I might have. I wasn't sure what was going on with him, and any time I asked if he was alright, he'd simply nod and say he was just having difficulty working over some plans in his head. I knew Faren better than to believe such a shoddy excuse, but I didn't press him. He clearly wasn't ready to talk about whatever it was.

We left two days after our arrival, pushing west into the Under Roads. Travel through the area was quiet. I used my new Titan powers to sense things through the stone for any possible threats. So long as we were below ground, we were nearly untouchable. While I was constantly looking for threats, I would tell the guards that I could only sense a smaller distance away. I didn't want them to grow complacent. My powers were becoming finely tuned, but I didn't want to take the chance that Seven had learned something that was able to get around them and ambush us.

We traveled through the Fallen Trenches and I couldn't help but marvel at the sheer scale of the Under Roads as the caverns opened up. Normally, the shattered series of bridges would have hindered our progress and forced us to take a much more winding path through the tombs of the Fallen Legion. However, this was no longer a problem. I dismounted from my rhoarno and took a position up the edge of the broken bridge. I used my will to command the stone to extend itself out and repair the bridges. I took a few minutes to ensure that the stone was molded to the same style and had to sort of guess at what sort of engravings would be on the bridge's barriers, but after a few minutes, you'd have never known they were broken to begin with.

"Brilliant work, My Lady," Faren said in awe.

I smiled at him, "You'll get there."

"Doubtful," he shook his head. "The Titans may have touched me when I was needed to take you home, but I doubt I'll ever attain the level of skill that you have with stone molding."

"I don't doubt you can attain anything you set your heart on," I tried to encourage him. The response he gave confused me.

Faren cleared his throat and looked away, "There are some things in this life that I can never gain, My Lady. Try as I might."

I stepped in close and gave him a curious expression, "Oh? Name one thing in this world that someone like you couldn't get if you worked for it."

He stared at me for a few moments and the look he gave me unlocked something in me. The expression was a mixture of defeat, sadness, and longing.

"We need to keep moving, Princess," Faren said as he moved to my rhoarno to help me up. "This detour is keeping us from Cragmorrar longer than you had intended."

I hesitated in my response as I considered the expression Faren had given me. Still, I nodded and joined him at my rhoarno, "You're right. I don't want to leave Father alone for too long."

We continued on through to the Soul Smith. There were still no scourgespawn in the vicinity, unlike in the game when there was a small horde of creatures to get through. When we approached the room that contained a series of point traps, I reached through the stone to throw the proper switches so that we could pass through safely. There were golems in the area that I could free, but for now, I left them as silent sentinels. My goal wasn't far away.

I stopped for a few minutes to examine the soul siphon. In the game, it acted as a sort of puzzle or miniature boss fight, but the purpose of the room was actually meant to siphon the soul of a dwarf and process it so that it could be placed into a golem. Jeron's spirit was speaking in excited whispers about the construction of the siphon, but I didn't really want to take the time to figure out how it worked. It was a mechanism that was used to murder and enslave thousands of dwarves. I didn't want it to be used for something like that again.

Something inspired me in that moment and I looked at Faren. "Faren, have you figured out the minutiae of your defense idea yet?"

Faren shook his head. "Not yet, My Lady. There are a couple of details I need to iron out. Why?"

"I think there may be a way to make it an offensive strategy as well," I grinned.

Faren seemed to mirror my expression, "Don't tease me like that,

Princess. Please elaborate."

I smirked at him, "Oh, you know you like it when I tease you with my ideas."

Faren almost seemed to blush and his response was more of a blusterous huff than anything else.

"Come on, we're getting close," I shrugged.

We continued through the opposite doorway which led to the final path. We followed it through to Korabin's… I suppose the best term would be home. It was an open chasm with pillars of stone wrapped in thick veins of dimvyum. Dozens of inert golems lined the opening and beyond them stood Korabin. He was still a massive metal golem, far more armored and stylized in his design than even the runic golems.

The massive golem's head moved slightly as I passed through the entrance to the cavern. When Faren, Gniess, and the guards followed through, Korabin stood and moved forward to close the distance between us.

"Who are you that comes here after so long?" his metallic voice rang out.

I dipped down into a curtsy, "I am Exemplar Merida Orodum, Princess of Cragmorrar." I turned and motioned to the others, "This is Faren Orodum and Lady Gniess Cragmor."

"Gniess?" Korabin gasped. "Ah! There is a name I recognize. Step forward."

Gniess took a few steps close, gazing up at the massive metallic golem, "You know my name? Is it you who forged me, then?"

"You have forgotten, then?" Korabin sighed. "It has been so long. I made you into the golem you are now, Gniess. But before that you were a dwarf, just as I was. The finest warrior to serve King Valtor, and the only woman to volunteer."

"Yes, so my friend Merida has told me," Gniess responded. "I had my doubts, but your words have laid them to rest."

"Your friend told you, you say?" Korabin asked as he looked back at me. "You said you were an Exemplar and a Princess?"

I curtsied once again, craning my neck up at him, "Merida Orodum, at your service."

Korabin hummed curiously, "Well, Exemplar, what brings you here? Are you hoping to find the Soul Smith and discover its secrets?"

I shook my head, "Not at all. I'd rather see that wretched thing destroyed. I mean no offense, of course. It is a brilliant creation, but it was used to horrible ends. However, I can't deny that its use saved the dwarven race."

Korabin hummed as he considered my answer, "How did you know Gniess was a dwarf? Or how the Soul Smith was used?"

"Faren and I are two of seven Fated," I explained. "We were born with knowledge of Thoros' past and some of its future. We've used that knowledge to affect the world and stop a Scourge."

"You've stopped a Scourge?" Korabin echoed. "Then tell me, Exemplar Orodum, if you haven't come here to destroy the Anvil, why have you come here?"

"I've come to bring you back to dwarven society," I said matter-of-factly. "I understand you have a great deal of regret about what happened to you and how the Anvil was used beyond your intentions, but we need you now. New enemies have surfaced that will require every resource we can gather."

"You think you understand how I feel?" Korabin's tone was extremely doubtful.

"I don't pretend to understand all of the nuances of your feelings," I clarified, "but I do know how you feel when it comes to losing people while they helped to execute a plan you came up with. But I don't wish to engage in a game of who understands what more. I simply wish to convince you to come back with us, more specifically, to go back with Gniess."

"Tell me of these enemies and why I should return to the dwarves," Korabin demanded.

"The first is one of the Gospinia," I replied. "One of the elven gods who has returned and is likely preparing to recombine the physical world with the Dimvolmn. The other is one of the Fated who was born as a scourgespawn. He is hunting the remaining old gods to steal their power for himself so he can burn the world down."

"I am unfamiliar with the Gospinia, but if it is as you say, a god will be difficult to defeat," Korabin mused. "Do you think you could manage to find a way to defeat such an opponent?"

"I am the way," I responded with an air of confidence in my tone. "I have been blessed by the Titans themselves and am growing in strength and power."

To emphasize my point, I willed the stone around us to grow and form into an intricate arch and series of twisting fences.

Korabin watched the display and gasped, "The Titans? Truly? If this is true, why would you need the help of the other dwarves?"

"I don't know if I will," I replied honestly. "But I know I can defeat him with everyone's help. We've gathered many resources, but your abilities as a smith will be crucial to keeping Cragmorrar and the retaken Holds safe. There are things that need to be built and perfected, and I don't know if I can do it without you."

"I exiled myself because even after the dwarves defeated the scourgespawn, the nobles took the power of my creation to create an army of slaves," Korabin revealed. "Why would I want to go back with the idea that the nobles might repeat the same horrible actions?"

"I can tell you why," Gniess interrupted. "Merida worked to create the Surface Caste which allowed even the Casteless to move up in station and has brought wealth and commerce back to the dwarves. She has also retaken four of the lost Holds and helped to set them up in such a way that those lower in station could make a name for themselves by moving to the Holds."

Gniess looked at me and almost smiled, "Merida has changed the culture of dwarves in her time. Very few dwarves, nobles included, will ever openly decry the work she's done or the changes she's brought to our people. Her brother has taken over Nordrucan Hold so that she has a better chance of being voted to become Queen when her father is no longer fit to rule."

"Our people love her," Faren added. "She's adored beyond reproach. The people even demanded she be given a constant guard. She cannot walk the streets without being cheered and given presents by the citizens. She is changing the mentality of everyone from the Castless to the Nobles. She has presented them with a brighter future through a change in our culture. If there is anyone you can trust to keep the ne'er-do-wells in line, it is Exemplar Orodum."

I couldn't speak. Gniess called me 'Merida'. She didn't call me 'it'. That made me so happy that I was speechless.

Korabin was silent for some time as he processed what the others said, "What of this Fated scourgespawn? How do you plan on defeating it?"

I shook myself from my stupor and focused on Korabin again, "I'll use the resources I've gathered for the Gospinia, and alliances I've made over the years. We'll need to work together to defeat it if it manages to get the power of the old gods."

"You would be wise to try and stop it before it could manage to gain that power," Korabin pointed out.

"I'm working on that," I tried to reassure him. "I have people hunting for the information I need to get to the old gods before the Seventh does."

"Why do you call it the Seventh?" Korabin asked.

"It's the Seventh one we knew of," I bent the truth. "And it named itself Seven. Out of the rest of us, I'm the youngest, so I would be considered the sixth."

Korabin hummed, "What is it you expect me to do if I join Gniess?"

"Gniess has reestablished Cragmor Hold," I motioned to Gniess. "She is turning the Hold into a place where golems can live and try to live a life they should have been allowed to live after the sacrifice they endured for the dwarven race. I would like you to help her do that, and help the dwarves with your genius. We're trying to make the lives of all dwarves better, no matter what form they're in."

"Two golems does not seem like it will be much of a population," Korabin countered.

"I agree," I nodded and motioned to the other golems who stood frozen in place. "But I have the ability to break the control magic that binds the minds of golems. I hope to free all of them that I can. The more we find, the more the golem population can grow."

"If you can free these golems, then why haven't you?" Korabin pressed me.

"When they're broken free from they're confused and dazed," I replied. "They need help and someone to guide them. So I thought I would speak with you first before releasing them. It was my thought that they would appreciate having you and Gniess to guide them."

Korabin looked at Gniess, who gave him a firm nod. When he looked back at me, he bowed his head. "If you can free those who were bound in service because of my mistake, I will take responsibility for them."

"Then I'm happy to have you back," I smiled and reached out to find the magic that bound the golems in the chasm, then countered the magic.

The golems stumbled from their control. Korabin and Gniess both moved to help them regain their senses. We all left together after a while, and I freed more golems on our return trip.

Korabin agreed to come to Cragmorrar after he'd helped settle all of the golems from Aronthok and the Fallen Trenches. I would need his help on a few different projects, and his return would be a big deal. If he stayed with House Orodum and gave me credit for convincing him to come back, my reputation would only grow.

When we returned to Cragmorrar, the golems who had chosen to come with me offered to become Orodum guards. They didn't need to sleep, so they were perfect for the position.

Bilfern and Darina were set to work on inspecting the dimvyum wells and figuring out how to best replicate them. I would help as well, but I knew I was going to be busy. I'd make Korabin's coming a surprise for them. I had a feeling Darina would freak out, and I was looking forward to her reaction.

I continued to sit in on Assembly meetings alongside Father. Rita would sit in my place. Father needed my help with focusing on things sometimes, but he also wanted my advice. Things had changed drastically since I was born, and he was having trouble keeping up. There was more than just Cragmorrar to worry about now. The other Holds had issues that needed to be addressed as well, and they couldn't simply wait until the Assembly had time for them.

However, as spring rolled around, I started to notice that I wasn't receiving my weekly letters from Trianna. I started to grow concerned because it wasn't like Trianna to simply go silent. There were ways to check on her from Cragmorrar, but I thought it might be best to do so in person. At best, it would be a two-month trip. So I began to gather supplies and guards. If something had happened to Trianna and Aelfric, I didn't know what I would do. Something wasn't right, and I was bound and determined to find out what was going on.

CHAPTER 24:

RETURN TO ORLIMAR

The trip to Orlimar was as uneventful as you could hope for. We made our standard stop in Cliffside to see how the market and city had grown. It was also a chance to look for the new spies that I'd had infiltrate the Surface caste merchants so I could get an idea of the day-to-day operations and how they were keeping an eye on illegal activity. The contacts in the Cliffside market made sure to take some time to meet with me and help me understand what they were working on.

As it happened, Earl Edward's son Connor was visiting the city at the same time. I asked him about how his studies were going now that the Mage Tower had converted fully into the Lemlalian College. I wanted to get an idea of how things were while I wasn't visiting the college and I wasn't around any of the professors or Allen. There was a thought that I might not get a proper evaluation if any of them were present.

I had written to Allen before my departure from Cragmorrar to schedule our annual meeting. He would be attending Trianna and Aelfric's wedding, of course, but that was no place to hold our meeting about the state of the college. That, and I didn't want Allen and Faren around each other for any longer than was necessary. No one wanted a repeat of the last time we'd all been together at Serena and Alford's wedding. Still, even with the written request, I asked Connor to relay the request once he'd returned to the college.

We left Cliffside after only a day. I didn't want to waste too much time getting to Orlimar.

When we arrived at Orlimar, I couldn't help but notice that a number of the elves had shaved their heads and were espousing the ideology of Serevas. There was no small amount of arguing over a recent series of arrests. Trianna and Aelfric's names were whispered with concern.

One thing that was refreshing was that my arrival brought a good many well-wishers. Many elves lined the road to watch the procession of my guards and myself. The dwarves that had remained were all in attendance, cheering us as we rode past. It almost became an impromptu parade if it weren't for the concerning conversations I was hearing about Trianna, Aelfric, and Serevas.

I stopped at the Council Building and dismounted. My guards filed around the stairs that led up into the building, and Faren escorted me to the door where a pair of elven guards bowed low.

"Andarn Atish'an, Princess Orodum," one of the guards said.

"Aneth ara," I replied with a bright smile and a curtsy. My reply was more sociable and typically only used among the Paddish themselves, and not with or by an outsider. I had learned to speak the language from Trianna but didn't flaunt the fact more than needed. I was named an elf friend, though, so the greeting was still appropriate.

"Is the Council in?" I asked. "I have come to speak with them about a matter dear to me."

The elves exchanged looks before one answered, "Word of your arrival has spread quickly, Princess. Someone is inside waiting to speak with you."

I arched my brows, "Someone? Not the entire Council?"

"There have been complications as of late, my Lady," the other guard chimed in. "You've come in a turbulent time."

"Well, no one better to handle a rocky situation than a dwarf," I jested but steeled my mind for a problematic conversation. "May I go in?"

"Of course, Princess," the guard bowed his head. "However, we were asked that the conversation be a private one. We would appreciate it if your man would remain outside for now."

"Her man?" Faren growled.

I patted Faren's shoulder and snickered, "You know he didn't mean it like that. Stay here for now. I'm sure I'll be fine."

Faren hummed in disapproval but simply bowed, "As you command, Princess. If you have need of me…"

"I'll call," I assured him. I turned and stepped through the large doors.

As I made my way in, I looked around the meeting hall of the council building, noting that all but one of the seats were empty. Sitting at the head of the table was Serevas. His placid smile irritated me immediately, but I wasn't going to let that distract me from my purpose for coming here. If he was who I needed to speak to, then he was who I would speak to. I gathered up my resolve and approached.

"Serevas," I said pleasantly as I dipped into a curtsy.

He rested his hands on the table, knitting his fingers together, "Princess Merida. To what do we owe the honor of your visit?"

He was pretending not to know. I wasn't foolish enough to believe for a moment that he wasn't aware.

"I'm not sure if you know this or not," I began politely, "but Trianna and I exchange letters weekly. It's been over a month since she's written to me now. She announced that she and Aelfric would be married in the spring, so with the timing, I decided to come check on my friends and help with setting up the wedding."

"You fear something untoward has happened to her and you were uninformed?" Serevas reiterated.

"I do," I confirmed.

"Ah, I see now why you came to me," Serevas sighed. "You see, Princess, this situation puts everyone in quite a predicament. Will you please sit and allow me to explain?"

I hesitated a moment before taking a seat. Once I was comfortable, I set my gaze directly on Serevas. "I have a reputation for solving predicaments. Please, tell me everything."

"I will be blunt with what you will consider to be the most important detail," Serevas kept his tone neutral. "Trianna and Aelfric, as well as several council members and their Firsts, have been brought into custody."

"Under what charge?" I kept my tone more curious. I didn't let a hint of suspicion make its way into my voice.

"Insurrection," Serevas confirmed bluntly.

"Insurrection?" I asked dubiously. "How could Trianna be brought into custody for insurrection when she is the leader of the elves? Did she plan on usurping herself?"

Serevas let out that soft chuckle that I had at one time taken comfort in when I used to play Inquest. "No, Princess. Insurrection against her people. Lady Trianna and Duke Aelfric were gathering people to actively hinder the progress of our people."

"Lady Trianna successfully united the clans of Falladrin," I countered. "She worked to ensure your people were able to have Orlimar and its surrounding lands as their own and was working with the clans to integrate traditions and rights to ensure that every path your people have followed for generations was recognized and became a part of this fledgling nation-state. How could that be construed as actively hindering the progress of the elves?"

"You do not understand, Princess," Serevas responded with that subtle hint of impatience he could get when trying to explain things to people when he was in an impassioned mood. "My people were not destined to settle in some human-made fort at the south end of a backwater, human-ruled nation. We were destined for greater things."

"What you mean to say is that you used to be immortal beings who enslaved your own people and any others you saw as lesser in a land where the physical realm and the Dimvolmn were each part of the same world, and you want to bring your people back to that state no matter how many lives of other races it might cost," I stated boldly, with no subtlety to my expression.

"If that is how you see things, Princess, I cannot blame you," he said, still keeping that neutral edge to his voice. "But you cannot understand the world I have come from. You cannot understand how far removed this world is from that one, and how things must go back to the way they were so that all can be right again."

"That is where you are wrong," I shook my head. "You are not simply speaking to a dwarf, Trith'Emel."

Serevas' expression changed when I called him by his true name, but I wasn't going to let him recover from that. It was time we put our cards on the table.

"You are speaking to a Titan," I allowed the light of the Titans to shine through my eyes so that they glowed a brilliant dimvyum blue. "My creators have gifted me their powers, and now your ancient enemies are here to safeguard the world that you yourself rent asunder. I will not allow you to kill millions of innocent lives, lives that have worked so hard to live the way they wish to live, simply to make up for your own rash actions in the past."

"If you know who I am," Serevas replied with a warning edge to his tone, "then you know what I am capable of. Do you think your newly lent power can contend with one of the Gospinia? Do you think yourself capable of defeating the person who imprisoned the other Gospinia?"

"Do you think I would have come here to save my friends if I didn't believe that I could?" I asked pointedly.

He considered me carefully for several moments before responding, "No. I do not. Tales of your exploits and meticulous planning are well known, Princess. May I ask why you bothered with any pretense at all?"

I slipped back into my conversational demeanor, "My mother used to tell me that you can always start nice then move to angry, but you can't start angry and move to nice. I prefer to do things the nice way if possible. That, and I believe we will need each other before too long, so being antagonistic with each other isn't going to help."

"I'm curious," Serevas admitted. "We are clearly at cross purposes. How do you believe we will need one another?"

"There is another Fated that the others have not met yet," I explained. "He is an omega hurlock. He has other sentient scourgespawn with him, and they are actively searching for the location of the last two old god prisons. He hopes to reap the power of the old gods from them and eventually wage war on all of Thoros."

Serevas stared at me intensely, as if considering the consequences of what I had just told him. "Scourgespawn do not typically wish to kill the old gods. If what you say is true, and this particular Fated does wish to gain the power of the old gods, then we must join our forces to stop them. I suppose the question now becomes, how do we ally our forces, knowing that we will be enemies after this common threat is dealt with?"

"You cannot do what you wish to do without those souls and the power they command," I began carefully. "However, if he gets them, he will become a force to reckon with. If allying with you means we can stop him, then I will do so. I won't move against you until Seven has been dealt with."

"Seven?" Serevas asked.

"The scourgespawn in question calls himself Seven," I clarified.

"A curious moniker," Serevas hummed.

"That's not exactly the point we should be concerned about," I sighed.

"No, you are right," Serevas agreed. "I assume for this alliance to work, you wish for me to release your friends."

I smiled snarkily, "You assume correctly. If you wish to lead the elves who believe in you, you should also take them elsewhere. Orlimar was given to the united clans. Taking control over it will eventually bring down the ire of King Marshal, and I will be obligated to aid him in any liberation effort he may attempt."

"Are you saying this to give up my hold on this budding city or because you are concerned that such actions would destroy what you and your friends have built?" he asked with what seemed to be genuine curiosity.

"Both," I replied bluntly. "Your occupation of the city threatens to undo all the work the elves have done to make it a place where they can set down roots as a people while sharing borders with genuine allies. You are putting thousands of lives in danger simply by trying to take control here."

"And where would you suggest I go?"

"I don't particularly care," I admitted. "But I'm sure you could lead those who follow you to Frosthold. It's nice and remote, and out of the way enough to not bother the powers that be."

"So long as they are the powers that be," Serevas snipped.

"Assuming I'm one of them, I intend to keep them as they are. This alliance is only temporary, after all."

Serevas considered the proposition for some time. "What incentive do I have, other than hostile actions by Cragmorrar and Falladrin, to move my people to Frosthold? It is a ruin, after all."

"I will provide food and some supplies for your people," I suggested diplomatically. "You'll have what you need to establish yourselves, as well as repairs to the fort's foundations as an added gesture of generosity, but nothing more."

"A generous offer, regardless," Serevas bowed his head. "Very well, Princess. I will agree to take my people to Frosthold. They will bring what supplies they can with the assurances that your people will deliver what you have promised in a timely manner."

"And you will release my friends and those loyal to them this instant," I insisted.

"Very well. Please wait here and I will bring them to you," Serevas stood up and made his way out of the council hall.

I was left alone for some time, but in that time a knock came from the hall's doorway. When I turned to see who it was, a smile spread across my face. A clean-shaven dwarf with light brown hair, wearing a thick, brown leather jacket with silver clasps sauntered into the room. He wore a cocky, confident expression and exuded a swagger that spoke to his roguish nature.

The dwarf stopped a few feet from me and dipped into a sweeping bow. "Exemplar Orodum."

"Varren Threshar!" I was grinning from ear to ear. Varren was an absolute fan favorite character and was extremely handsome for a dwarf. "Did Brevaht and Jennia recruit you?"

He seemed surprised that I knew who he was, but being ever the professional, he didn't let it faze him. He simply nodded. "They did. And as you may suspect, they sent me to deliver some news to you."

"It may have to wait until we have some more time," I hummed. "What does it concern?"

"The state of the Scourge Sentinels, My Lady," he answered with a tone that suggested the news wasn't good.

"I see…" I thought about the situation for a moment. "My allies will be returning in a few minutes. I'll take some time to get them situated and oversee the exodus of Serevas and his followers. We can speak this evening in my quarters."

Varren nodded, "As you say, Princess."

I heard the door to the building open but leaned into Varren, "I'll also need you to do one more thing for me."

"What's that, Princess?" Varren asked curiously.

"I want you to think of a nickname for me. I hear you have a reputation for great nicknames," I smirked.

Varren chuckled and looked at me slyly, "I'll get right on that."

At that moment, Serevas entered the chamber followed by Trianna, Aelfric, and several other elves. Trianna's eyes lit up when she saw me, and she rushed past Serevas to wrap me in an embrace. I hugged her back tight enough for her back to pop.

"I was so worried about you," I said softly.

"I was hoping you would be able to help," she responded with relief in her voice. "I guess you came because I stopped sending letters?"

I nodded, "And because I said I would help with the wedding."

"We're grateful for your aid, Merida," Aelfric added. "We're in your debt."

Serevas approached calmly, "As promised, your friends have been released, and they are unharmed."

"And you'll be leaving as soon as possible, yes?" I looked up at him.

"It shouldn't take more than a few hours," Serevas nodded. "I trust you'll keep your word on the supplies and repairs?"

I gave a nod and motioned to Varren, "Indeed. I was just telling one of my men to relay the order. The supplies will be coming directly from Cliffside, and the masons will be coming from Cragmorrar, so they might take some extra time to arrive, but you'll get what I promised."

"Very well," Serevas conceded. "I will take my leave and gather those who wish to join me. We will be gone before the end of the day."

"It was a pleasure speaking with you, Serevas," I curtsied.

"And you, Princess," Serevas bowed. "You live up to your reputation. It is rather a pleasant surprise."

"Wait, what's happening?" Trianna asked with a mixture of surprise and suspicion.

"Serevas is leaving and he's taking his followers with him," I started to explain. "I'm going to send them some supplies and have some masons help shore up their new home."

"Where are they going?" Aelfric asked.

"Frosthold," I responded with a wink. "Don't worry. He's seen the wisdom in taking his leave."

"Frosthold is a formidable fortress," Aelfric said in thought. "It will be difficult to take if it ever comes to that."

"Let me worry about that," I grinned. "For now, let's just focus on bringing the elves back together and on your wedding."

Trianna chuckled and shook her head. "At least your priorities haven't changed. Also… is that Varren?"

"That is Varren!" Aelfric exclaimed.

"How do all of you know who I am?" Varren wondered.

Serevas gathered his people and left within the day. All told, he took the equivalent of two clans' worth of elves with him. It wasn't a significant number, but it was enough to concern some of the Elders on the Council. Rumors spread that I had come threatening military action against Serevas, but that wasn't exactly true. Still, it dampened my reputation with some of the elves in Orlimar who believed it was possible.

With the Serevas situation on pause, we were able to focus on Trianna and Aelfric's wedding.

CHAPTER 25:

CATCHING UP

Over the next few weeks, Trianna, Aelfric, and I began preparing for their wedding. Swift riders went out to invite key nobles in Falladrin, including King Marshal, Earl Edward, Allen, and of course, Serena and Alford. Interestingly enough, there was some controversy on which version of the elven ceremony should be used. Elves from the Elvienages wanted to see a ceremony in line with their customs, while the Paddish wished to honor their traditions. Since Aelfric grew up in an Elvienage, and Trianna was Paddish, there was equal merit to which should be honored.

However, Trianna insisted that they meld the practices just as the two cultures had been doing with different holidays and traditions already. They would have the leader of their faith speak, then have a family or friend who knew the couple speak. Afterwards, the couple would swear their vows to each other, and then the day would be spent in celebration.

The belief in the elven pantheon held sway in Orlimar, with Melindrianism being frowned upon after the incident with the Church trying to kidnap me, so a Paddish Elder was selected to speak for the religious part of the ceremony. I was given the honor of speaking as the trusted friend since both Trianna and Aelfric's parents had passed away already. I couldn't help but be pleased that I would get to speak in the ceremony, but I also realized that having the dwarven princess of Cragmorrar, and heir apparent, helped to bolster the prestige of the occasion.

Serena and Allen arrived on the same day. Serena had left earlier and went to the Lemlalian College where Allen and his retinue joined her on the way to Orlimar. Alford and a decent contingent of guards and other nobles traveled with Serena. Marylen, Garrett, Bethany, and a number of templars had joined Allen for the trip. Their arrival was a day ahead of King Marshal, who was joined by Clifford, Anna, and several Earls from around Falladrin.

Trianna's wedding was just as much of a who's who of Falladrin nobility and influential people as Trianna's had been. You might argue that it was more so when you considered that Serena and Alford were now an Earl and Earlessa, which meant there were technically more elevated nobles in Orlimar than there had been in Watcher's Keep. I had to wonder if that little detail rubbed Serena just a bit raw or not.

The night before the wedding, all of the Fated gathered for a private dinner. We met in the Council Hall, which was decorated for the festivities. Food was set out over three tables so we could pick and choose what we liked. Each of us was dressed as if we were going to a ball because when the Fated gathered, everyone seemed to expect the occasion to be important.

"It's been too long since we've all been together," Trianna smiled as Aelfric squeezed her hand.

"Over three years," Allen agreed. "Time flies when you're-"

"Managing the everyday minutiae of a region or college?" Serena tittered.

"To say the least," I agreed with a mouthful of steak.

"At least we have a chance to finally catch up," Aelfric spooned at his soup. "Apart from the issue we had with Serevas, Trianna and I have mostly been trying to codify the traditions that all of the different clans and Elvienages had into a single series of cultural events."

"That sounds like it could become a bit convoluted," Serena tapped her chin. "How do you avoid making it seem like you're favoring one clan's traditions over another?"

Trianna leaned in, "We actually have a whole process where the Elders from each clan come together and find the similar aspects of each tradition, keep those aspects, then filter through the different aspects and find the ones which hit the key points of the traditions the most."

"It's not a perfect process," Aelfric admitted, "and there is some arguing, which is to be expected when people are defending their traditions and are being asked to only pick and choose different parts of them to keep. But in the end, we've come up with results that seem to please everyone."

"Have you had a year when all of the newly amalgamated traditions have been used?" Faren asked after a long draught of ale.

"This will be the first year, actually," Aelfric replied with a cocky smile. "The wedding of people from different clans or Elvienages, or between Paddish and Elvienage, is different than ceremonies between people who are in the same community. We've had those before. But this is a wedding between elven leaders, so it's setting a precedent for weddings that come after it."

"Seems like you're both breaking new ground every day," Allen hummed. "It's a fascinating thing to watch as a new culture begins to define itself. Have you been documenting things?"

Trianna nodded, "There are a number of Elders and scholars who are keeping daily documentation on various aspects of the way Orlimar is developing. Some record the daily things that happen, others record the minutes of each Council meeting, and others still record moments of historical importance."

"I'd be interested in reading any of those," Allen rested his chin between his thumb and index finger. "Do you think annual copies of those recordings could be made and sent to the college? We have plans on building a library that isn't focused on magic, and books on local history would be a boon to add to the collection."

"I'm sure we can work something out," Aelfric looked at Trianna, who nodded in agreement.

"If you like," I chimed in after swallowing a large mouthful of baked potato, "I can have the Memorialists begin making copies of Cragmorrar's general history as well. We have new Memorialists who are dying to put some ink to parchment for an actual purpose beyond mundane record keeping."

"That would be amazing, Merida," Allen perked up. "We'd be in your debt."

I waved a hand dismissively. "They'll be excited to be contributing dwarven history to a true library instead of to a noble's personal stock."

"Anything special going on in Coralstine?" Aelfric asked Serena.

Serena grinned wide. "Lots, actually! We're looking to expand the city so that it fully encompasses the inlet and make it the largest port city in Thoros."

Aelfric whistled to show he was impressed with the thought. "That's an aspirational goal. I imagine you have people scrambling to line up for the work."

"It's been a challenge to contract it all out," Serena admitted. "We've had some help with the Surface Caste, who are willing to come down on prices with the promise of future tax exemptions and more relaxed shipping regulations."

"She means that the Surface Caste wants to keep more of their money and keep harbor inspectors' noses out of their business," Faren chuckled. "And she's willing to do that so long as the work gets done."

"Exactly what are they transporting that they don't want the port masters to inspect?" Allen smirked wily.

"Nothing illegal," I said with assurance. I'd stopped eating for that question. "The Surface Caste loathes overly invasive searches of their goods, which they take precision and care to store in specific ways for stability and sometimes shelf life. Certain inspectors like to look through everything and take valuable time away from the vendor. We prefer to avoid that when necessary."

"Are you certain they're not trying to smuggle dimvyum?" he pressed with a slight glint in his eye.

"Considering My Lady worked to make the smuggling of any amount of dimvyum an executable offense," Faren rumbled, "I doubt they'd be stupid enough to try."

"Wait," Serena gasped, "you fought to make smuggling dimvyum worthy of the death penalty? How many have been put to death for that?"

"Three since the law went into effect," I stated calmly. "The last one was about a year ago. Since then, no dimvyum has been smuggled or sold from Cragmorrar or the Thigh."

"That you know of," Allen chuckled.

"Oh, I'd know," I glared at him. "I have more sources than you realize, and they are constantly watching the dimvyum supply lines from the initial mining to the shipment and delivery of orders."

"You're rather serious about this," Serena steepled her fingers together in thought. "Is there some reason for it beyond dimvyum being a valuable resource that only the dwarves can relatively mine safely?"

I sat up straight and gave a firm nod, "There is, actually. Dimvyum is literally the blood of the Titans, who are the creators and parents of the dwarves. This makes dimvyum a cultural treasure for the dwarves, and we have decided to begin treating it as such. Now, anyone who would smuggle and sell it to benefit themselves is considered to have stolen from our entire people; a crime that warrants death."

"That's rather cruel, don't you think?" Aelfric asked as he sat back, thinking over my rationale.

"Not at all," I shook my head, keeping my tone conversational. "All proceeds from the sale of dimvyum now go to public works, which fund the maintenance of the capital, the Holds, and the Under Roads. What isn't spent on public works is put into two accounts: an emergency account and an annual account. The emergency account is saved in case something happens and we need to pay for emergency supplies, food, or assistance. The annual account is emptied at the end of each year and divided among every adult dwarf."

"Are you saying that every dwarf gets a share of the annual account passed out to them as their fair share, even if they didn't contribute to the dimvyum process?" Allen asked for clarification.

I nodded, "They do contribute to the process. Every dwarf works to make life function properly for those above them and below them in the caste system. One way or another, the miners, refiners, caravan crews, and merchants are supported by their castes. So every dwarf enjoys the fruits of that labor at the end of the year."

"Surely those directly involved with the process must profit more than those who aren't," Allen argued. "Otherwise, what would be the point of being in the business of dimvyum for them?"

"They gain priority on dimvyum requests so that they can use it to create goods," I explained. "They also get substantial tax breaks for their family's other businesses, which end up saving them more money than they would have made normally."

"So they're working for the benefit of everyone while gaining bonuses for their family at the same time," Allen mused. "Incentivizing the continuation of your largest product by incentivizing free labor through tax incentives? An interesting tactic."

"I suppose that answers what you've been up to, then," Trianna chuckled.

"I trust you're feeling better after whatever happened?" Serena asked. The question grabbed everyone's attention, and everyone's head turned to look at me. "I had heard you were injured and had to be carried back to your home."

I nodded and sighed, "It's true I had to be carried back, but I wasn't injured. I was recovering from an encounter."

"An encounter that didn't injure you but had you screaming as you were carried through Cragmorrar?" Serena pushed a bit.

"I suppose now is as good a time to tell you all as any," I sighed and stared at my food in disappointment. I wasn't going to get another bite for some time.

"Would you prefer that I tell them?" Faren asked with concern for what I was going to have to relive in the explanation.

I smiled at him with appreciation, "No, it's alright. I can manage it." I directed my attention to the others. "To begin with, there is another Fated. This person was born as a scourgespawn; an omega hurlock to be specific."

"What?!?" the others shouted in surprise.

"You have to be joking," Allen insisted. "A Fated scourgespawn? What did it want?"

"It was waiting for us in Hardrin Hold, at the great elevator that led down into the depths," I began to explain. "It called itself Seven since there were already six of us. It had wanted to meet me because my actions with the lost Holds and our actions at Orlimar had set his plans back over and over again."

"His plans?" Trianna asked.

"It wishes to hunt down the remaining old gods to claim their power as its own," I answered with some hesitancy. "If it's successful, it will have astounding power."

"You didn't try to stop it? Or did you try, and that's what caused your screaming episode?" Serena pressed.

"I probably could have killed it," I lowered my eyes in shame, "but we were surrounded by so many other scourgespawn, as well as the Crafter. I didn't want Faren and the others to get hurt or possibly killed…"

"You had the chance to end such a threat, and you threw it away out of sentiment?" Serena almost screeched.

"What would you have done if Alford and your friends were surrounded, and you had the chance to save them?" I snapped back with tears welling in my eyes. "I wanted to kill them all! I probably could have too, but I wasn't willing to risk the lives of the others just then."

"And when was it ok?" Allen sniped. "You were alright with risking their lives at Orlimar. Why not then?"

"Orlimar had to happen, and you know it!" Faren stood and pointed at Allen. "We have been fighting the scourgespawn since we were children, and Merida has never once run from that responsibility! She has already been searching for the old gods, and we know the Under Roads better than the blighted filth! We'll find them before it does!"

"Everyone calm down!" Trianna slammed a fist onto the table. "It's easy to think that we would have done things differently, but we also know that Merida weighs her decisions carefully. If she didn't attack then, she had a good reason. Let her finish what she was saying, and then we can ask questions and figure out what we need to do to help her deal with Seven."

Serena was about to argue before Aelfric interrupted, "Don't. Let's hear what else Merida has to say."

Serena and Allen settled back and stared at me with irritation and impatience.

"I warned Seven not to allow a single scourgespawn to come near the dwarven Holds, or I would use my abilities to hunt him down," I continued more subdued. "I allowed them to leave after killing a number of them in retaliation for the deaths of a dwarven scouting party they were responsible for. After they left, we went down the elevator."

"We met with the Hal-Ifden, and they escorted Faren and me to the titan…" I almost whispered. "Their leader brought us to the heart of the titan where I was able to communicate with the titan. According to Faren, I blacked out as soon as I made contact with it. While I was unconscious, it spoke to me and acknowledged my desire to stop the scourgespawn and to do what was best for my people. So it blessed me with its power."

"It kept her unconscious for weeks as it infused her with power," Faren interrupted. "We brought her back to the city, and she screamed the entire time. Even when she was home and in her bed, she screamed day in and day out. When she finally stopped, we thought she might be dead. But then… she woke up the next morning… like nothing had ever-"

I was shocked to see Faren break down in tears. It seemed the others were as well, but I was the only one who moved to comfort him. I moved from my chair and wrapped my arms around him, easing his head to my bosom and stroked his hair gently. I looked at the others and allowed the titan power to come forth, causing my eyes to glow the brilliant dimvyum blue.

"I am as much a titan now as I am a dwarf," I said with some authority. "With the power at my command, I can command the stone at will. I can feel every vibration that runs through it. If I wished to, I could topple Orlimar with a thought and rebuild it again within moments. I allowed Seven to leave because I believed the Titan would aid us in defeating it. It has given me the means to do so."

"You're a titan?" Trianna whispered in awe.

"The titans were the enemy of the Gospinia," Serena said, all anger lost from her voice. "It took Mythriel to bring one of them down. You could be a match for Serevas."

"It took more than Mythriel, according to the titan," I clarified. "However, Serevas knows what I am and will be preparing for it. But we can still defeat Seven if we find the two remaining old god prisons before he does. Luckily for us, I was able to contact the Scourge Sentinels in Verrloft and will get the location of the prisons before long."

"This is good news, then," Allen offered a laugh. "Why didn't you just skip to that part?"

"Because she thinks everyone should know the dangers first and then offer solutions to consider," Faren said as he raised his head from my chest, his eyes still red with tears. "If you weren't so impatient to hurl your protests at her, you would have come to this conclusion without the need to upset her."

"I'm sorry, Merida," Serena bowed her head. "It was unkind of us to doubt your decisions. You've never given us a reason to doubt you. We should have known better. Can you forgive us?"

I nodded my head and gave Faren's shoulder a squeeze. I knew he would bark them both down if I didn't reign him in quickly.

"Perhaps we should all retire for the evening?" Trianna offered diplomatically. "We have a wedding tomorrow, after all, and we should all be fresh and ready for it."

"Agreed," Allen chimed in quickly.

"You all go ahead," Serena responded. "I need to speak with Merida about something privately for a few minutes."

I arched my brow at Serena but simply nodded, "Very well. Faren, will you wait outside for me? And don't hit Allen…"

Faren stood and bowed. "As you wish, Princess. If you need me, just call."

Everyone filed out after a minute, leaving only Serena and myself sitting at the table. I stared across at her. "What is it you wish to speak to me about?"

Serena's smile grew slowly into a grin. "I have a proposal for you."

CHAPTER 26:

SERENA'S PROPOSAL

Serena kept her seat as Faren and the others left. She remained silent as I prepared myself another plate of food. The conversation we'd just had caused my food to go cold, and some of those delectable dishes were best when they were nice and hot. Once I'd taken my seat, and managed to get in a few swallows from my plate, Serena offered me a smile. It wasn't a smile she'd ever given me before. It was fake, disingenuous, and clearly self-motivated. I knew Serena well enough by now that I could tell when she was being genuine with me and when she wanted something. This was clearly the latter.

"How's your father, Merida?" Serena asked. The way she said it was almost genuine, but her tone was off and it hinted that she knew the answer already.

"He's as well as one can hope to be at his age," I responded with a smile. "Much better than any human could hope to be at his age."

Serena nodded and tittered, "That's fair. He's getting on in his years, though. I was surprised Bilfern came along when he did. Your mother and father must have been surprised by his arrival."

I only shrugged, "Bilfern was a blessing. He's growing into a very accomplished enchanter. Darina believes he'll soon rival her in his prowess with dimvyum."

"And he's not as adept at politics as he would have been thanks to you,"

Serena winked. She was referring to how Bilfern manipulated the Assembly and certain events in the game to cause the dwarf noble, me in this case, to be banished from Cragmorrar.

"Oh, he's just as adept a politician as I am," I explained. "I made sure of that. He's been learning since he was little and he accompanies me when I meet with nobles and attend meetings with the Assembly. I want him to be as capable as possible."

"You're not afraid he might try to bring about a similar situation as he did in your origin story?" Serena asked, a hint of confusion in her otherwise nonplussed tone.

I shook my head. "Not at all. I love Bilfern, and he thinks of me as his dear sister and as the closest thing to a mother that he has. I've given him all the attention and care that he could want. He has no plans to hurt me physically or politically, I'm quite sure. In any case, even if he did want to, who among the dwarves would believe anything anyone tried to frame me for at this point? I have too much favor with every dwarf on Thoros for them to believe I would do anything so duplicitous."

"You've certainly endeared yourself to your people," Serena mused. She looked at me with a subtle quizzical expression. "I suppose you've resigned yourself to the inevitability of becoming Queen, then?"

I paused and took a deep breath, releasing it slowly before responding, "I honestly never considered becoming Queen until after we retook Nordrucan Hold."

Serena laughed. "Are you serious? What were you, ten at the time? You were already a Exemplar, and you'd rearranged Dwarven society by creating the Surface Caste. You honestly didn't think you'd be Queen after all of that?"

"I was nearly eleven, and no, I hadn't," I admitted. "I had lived my life with the idea that Trenton would be King, and I simply wanted Trenton to like me and consider me good counsel. It wasn't until the day before we retook Nordrucan Hold that Trenton revealed that he was going to remain there and step aside from consideration so that I would have an easier path to becoming Queen. I honestly would have preferred if things had stayed the way I was hoping they would."

"You don't want to be Queen?" Serena asked. For the first time in our conversation, the surprise and confusion in her voice were genuine. "Why not?"

I balked at her. "What do you mean? Look at everything I have to deal with now just as a princess. I've reclaimed the Holds, helped manage the battle at Orlimar, I oversee much of the dealings concerning the Surface Caste, and I can't even walk the streets of my home without fanfare."

"Yes," Serena said, her voice dripping with sarcasm, "I can see how horrible that could be."

"I mean it!" I insisted. "I don't get any time to myself. My entire day is spent in service to my people and others from the moment I wake up to the moment I go to sleep. And even then I don't sit idly by. I practice my magic and powers in the Dimvolmn. Out of all the Fated, I've never stopped working or training since I was a year old. But I keep my smile up, I keep pushing forward, I give everyone that beacon to light their way day in and day out."

"Why?" Serena asked curiously.

My expression changed to one of almost heartbreak, "Because if I don't, who will? This is a dark and dangerous world. People need someone to give them hope; someone who will point to a better way of life and lead them to it. They deserve that chance."

Serena remained quiet for some time before she let a dry huff of laughter escape her, "And here I was always thinking that you were just one big ball of positive energy, when in reality you were just as tired and exhausted as the rest of us."

"I wish I was the person people think I am," I sighed. "I wish I could live up to the idea they have of me. But it seems like every time I achieve a goal, every time I hit some marker that I think will make things easier, something happens that forces me to make more plans, more contingencies, and to work harder. First it was Trenton, then the Holds, then Orlimar, and now Serevas and Seven. I just want to know when I'll finally be able to relax for a few years."

"Well, if you ask me, I think you're already acting like a real queen," Serena offered in an encouraging and surprisingly sincere tone. "You set the bar for every one of us, Merida. And we all end up falling short, but end up further than where we would have if we hadn't been trying to keep up with you. Me most of all."

I looked at her in confusion, "What do you mean?"

Serena sighed, "I see you as a rival. Every accomplishment you make, I try to replicate. I want to keep up with you. So far, you're ahead. You were born as royalty, I had to marry into it. You became a leader of your people, I had to work to gain respect with mine. You'll no doubt be named Queen when your father passes or abdicates, so I'm trying to become Queen as well."

"You're trying to be Queen?" I asked in shock. "Didn't Alford relinquish his right to the throne as part of the deal that allowed you to marry him?"

Serena nodded, "Yes, he did. I, however, did not. I am still a Coreland; the second most powerful family in Falladrin. Alford has been acknowledged by his father as a legitimate son so that the marriage could happen. I now control Coralstine and I'm building it into the world's largest port city. I've been meeting with nobles to garner their favor, and I have met with King Marshal to be able to make you an offer out of… friendship."

Everything Serena said had added up in my head. When she mentioned friendship, the equation fell apart. It wasn't friendship she was about to make this offer out of. I narrowed my eyes conspiratorially, "Friendship? Or aspiration?"

"Both," Serena admitted bluntly. "It's my hope that you will accept this offer, and in return back myself and Alford as Marshal's chosen heirs."

"This sounds less like a gift and more like a bribe," I couldn't help but state.

"I hope you'll see it more as a gift," Serena shrugged. "It's something I think you'll be able to work with and it will open some interesting avenues for you in the future once things settle down. And before I tell you what it is, understand that I am only able to offer it because King Marshal himself has given his permission to make this offer. On his behalf, of course."

"Of course," I said with a mixture of curiosity and hesitancy. "What is it you're offering, then?"

Serena's smile turned wicked and predatory, "The Dutchy of Yivreon."

I stared at her for some time as I processed the idea, "I'm going to ask my questions that I'm certain you have answers for. But I will ask them all the same to cover my bases."

"Please do," Serena bowed her head.

"How can I be given the Dutchy of Yivreon?" I began, not really letting a moment slip as I continued asking questions. "Doesn't the Dutchy belong to Anna now that her father is dead? And can a dwarf rule over a human Dutchy? Where would that put me in Falladrin Hierarchy? I can't imagine many humans being happy about a dwarf suddenly outranking all but the royal family. And when you say that the Dutchy is mine, does that mean it's mine until I pass, or that it's mine and is passed along to my successors?"

"All excellent questions," Serena nodded. "As far as the how is concerned, I met with King Marshal and Anna. I pointed out that Anna doesn't want to bother with running the city, and that she shouldn't have to worry about it once she becomes Queen. So offering it to one of Falladrin's greatest allies and a future Queen would solidify relations between our two peoples. It took a bit of nuance and convincing, but they eventually agreed and said that I should make the offer while I was here for Trianna's wedding."

"King Marshal has admitted that naming a dwarf as a Duke would be a first, and it would set a unique precedent among the nobility; but his advisors have said that it shouldn't be too difficult to establish since Falladrin already boasts dwarven citizens, and the king may ennoble any citizen he pleases."

"I'm not a citizen of Falladrin," I couldn't help but point out.

"I think that's more of a matter of semantics," Serena waved the detail off. "As far as how long it would be yours, the title would act as any noble title does and would be passed down through your bloodline. So it would be yours in perpetuity."

"And in return for the Dutchy, you would want me to do what?" I asked, not certain how I felt about her ignoring the point that I wasn't a Falladrin citizen and thus couldn't rightfully hold a title.

"You back my position when I push for Alford and I to be named as King Marshal's heirs," Serena stated.

I stared at her doubtfully for several moments. "You are offering me the Dutchy of Yivreon, a noble title which currently belongs to Anna who is only agreeing to this proposal because she believes she won't need the Dutchy since she is becoming Queen. At the same time, you want me to accept the offer with the caveat that I back you as the choice for Marshal's successor, which would then leave Clifford and Anna with the Dutchy of Yivreon to fall back on."

Serena made an attempt to interrupt me, but I held up a hand to stop her as I continued, "Furthermore, you dismiss my concern that I am not a citizen of Falladrin and may not even be able to hold that title if Anna contests it. It seems that you're offering me gold from someone else's purse and expecting them to be alright with it. There has to be a detail you're leaving out, or some contingency that you haven't shared to make this work."

She shook her head as she smiled wearily at me, "I suppose I deserve that. It would seem like I'm handing you a poison apple, but I assure you that isn't the case. Once Anna realizes that she's lost the crown and the Dutchy, I will be ready to offer her the Earlet of Coralstine which will have been built into much more than it used to be."

"And you think she'll be content with going from a Duchess and prospective queen to an Earless?" I asked skeptically.

"Better an Earless than a corpse," was Serena's bold reply. "We both know that Anna is not one to sit idly by and be snubbed like this. But if she has a thriving Earling to soothe her wounded ego, I would like to think that she would take it and be content."

"You honestly don't believe she would be plotting your downfall from Coralstine?" I asked.

"She can plot all she likes," Serena snapped. "If I can get a whiff of it, then I'll have no other recourse than to have her executed. Otherwise, I'll be happy to show her favor."

"I think it's unwise to put someone who will be antagonistic toward you in charge of your largest port city," I suggested. "She'll use that income and influence to work against you."

Serena smirked, "Then I suppose the kingdom will simply have to find another city to build up as its primary port. I hear of a fine port city in the southeast that has potential."

She was referring to Yivreon. I had to give Serena credit; she had thought this through. However, there was the lingering detail of my citizenship. I sat back and considered everything for a time while I ate my food. The prolonged silence seemed to please Serena since it meant that I was thinking things over. Fortunately for me, I was thinking over the world's lore, and Yivreon had some special lore concerning dwarves.

I dabbed my mouth with a napkin and corrected my posture, "The biggest problem is the fact that I am not a citizen of Falladrin. I'm an ally at best. If there came a time of doubt, Anna could easily point out the fact that I cannot control a Dutchy since a non-citizen cannot hold a title. However, there is a method by which I can control the city without any chance of reprisal on Anna's part."

"And what might that be?" Serena smiled, eager to see that I was looking for a way to make it work.

"Will you trust me enough to back my idea?" I asked, not giving anything away just yet.

"I haven't heard your idea yet," Serena said with confusion.

"But do you trust me enough to agree to my idea even without hearing it?" I pressed. "If you wish to be the future Queen of Falladrin, this would be an excellent first step in proving that you trust the person who will be your closest, and most powerful, ally."

Serena seemed hesitant for only a moment before she nodded, "I trust you, Merida."

"Call for the King," I said. "I'll tell him what we've agreed to, and you only have to worry about supporting my idea."

Again Serena was hesitant, but she eventually nodded. She stood and left the room to instruct a guard to bid King Marshal join us in the meeting. It took some time for Marshal to arrive, but he did eventually come. Between Serena's initial message and Marshal's arrival, Serena tried pressing me to divulge some details about my idea, but I only ever responded with 'Just trust me'. The prospect of trusting me to ensure her plans came to fruition made her nervous and proved that her trust in me was surface level at best. She was taking this chance because she was desperate and had no other real choice.

We both stood as a servant came in and announced Marshal's arrival, "King Marshal of Falladrin!"

The two of us curtsied as Marshal entered the room and cast a curious glance at us. "I was told that I was needed for an important decision. Princess Orodum, can I assume this has something to do with the gift my daughter-in-law has offered you on my behalf?"

"It is, Your Grace," I responded with a bow of my head. "Would you like to sit and discuss the matter with me?"

Marshal kept a stern expression for a moment before letting it melt away into the kind demeanor I was more familiar with. "It would be a pleasure to discuss matters of state with you again, Princess. You always surprise me."

Serena and I sat back down as he took a seat across from us.

"I hope I can continue to do so in this conversation," I replied with a playful smile.

Marshal chuckled. "Oh, I have no doubt you will. So, what is it that we need to discuss? Did Serena give you all of the details?"

I nodded. "She did, Your Grace. However, there is a problem with the offer that I cannot see any way around."

"And what might that be?" Marshal asked, seeming intrigued.

"Merida isn't a citizen of Falladrin," Serena cut in with a tone that suggested she hadn't considered the idea. "You might allow her to rule Yivreon, but by our laws, she wouldn't be able to hold the title of Duke. Should any of the nobles protest, they would be within their rights to call for her being ousted from the city."

"I think that is a problem easily solved with a Landsmeet," Marshal offered. "Princess Orodum has curried a great deal of favor with her Surface Caste and standing beside us at Orlimar, the majority of nobles would have little issue with her being named Duke of Yivreon."

"It's not the majority I would worry about, Your Grace," I said carefully. "It's the minority that I would concern myself with. I wouldn't want to cause any hard feelings by being promoted above most of the nobles in the land out of nowhere."

"Then I take it you have a suggestion or a solution?" Marshal pinched his chin and arched his brows with anticipation.

I nodded, "In fact, I do. Are you aware that Yivreon was originally a dwarven outpost?"

Marric nodded. "As I recall, it became the city it is because a former Duke of Yivreon asked the dwarves to build the city and port so that the dwarves would have access to the sea lanes on that side of Falladrin."

"Correct," I nodded in affirmation. "However, the Duke never actually paid the dwarves for that work. The Duke took control of the city, but the dwarves were not fairly compensated for the work."

"It's a bit late to ask for payment for work done almost four hundred years ago," Marshal chuckled.

"I agree," I tittered. "If we kept that up, the debts would pile up on both sides and it would end in bad feelings and conflict. I'm not asking for compensation for Yivreon's construction."

"Then what are you asking for, Merida?" Marshal used my first name. He was making this more personable. That was good. He would call me 'Princess' if he wanted things to remain formal, but by calling me by my name, I knew that he was willing to hear out my proposal with an honest mind to considering what I said.

"In order to avoid any ill feelings by ennobling me above your own people, I would like to purchase Yivreon for my people," I smiled brightly.

Marshal stared at me in silence for a few tense moments, "You wish to purchase the Dutchy of Yivreon?"

"Not the title," I clarified. "Just the city and its lands. It was a dwarven outpost to begin with, then became a city built by dwarves. Now it will be a city run by dwarves and considered a dwarven Hold."

"It avoids any hard feelings on the part of the nobles, puts a large mercantile city in the southeast, and secures the dwarves as steady trade allies and a buffer against any threats from the southeast," Serena quickly added, catching on to the idea. "It also means that the dwarves will have supply lines we can use stretching across the whole of Falladrin."

"It would also mean that I will have given up two pieces of the country to foreign powers," Marshal retorted. "I've given Orlimar and its surrounding lands to the elves. Would you have me give up Yivreon as well?"

"You wouldn't be giving it away, you would be selling it back to its original owners," I clarified. "And I believe you could spin the loss in a positive way. You will be remembered as the king who gave the elves a homeland, and who bolstered the dwarves by giving them an outlet for trade. The king who united Falladrin and her allies for all time. It also wouldn't hurt that the price for Yivreon would be in the millions of gold. That could do a great deal of good for Falladrin's citizens."

"Fair points all," Marshal mused and nodded slowly. "I doubt you would like to pay all of the gold up front, however. How would you suggest paying for the city and what would we do with its current population?"

"Allow the current population to remain where they are," Serena said quickly. "The dwarves mostly wish to remain underground. Since the city would mostly be run by the Surface Caste, they would hire the humans to do business for them during the time they are underground."

I nodded in agreement, "That's how it would most likely work. If the humans wish to leave, we will pay for the homes they leave behind so they can have some coin to travel wherever they wish to relocate to."

"And the payment method?" Marshal asked, his tone still considering the idea.

"Made in four ways," I offered. "First, we would give you ten percent of the total cost up front. The city and its lands would be given over after the ten percent is paid. After that, we pay another forty percent over the next thirty years in annual installments. The remaining fifty percent would be paid in general labor. My people would dedicate themselves to creating better roads across Falladrin which would link each of Falladrin's cities and towns together. Better roads mean faster, more reliable transportation which will increase Falladrin's economy, and her emergency and military response readiness."

"You'll offer millions for the city and only pay half of what you offer?" Marshal asked, noting that half of what I would offer would come in the form of labor.

"Your Grace," Serena quickly interjected, "trust me when I say that the roads alone would be worth the city. No other country on Thoros has paved roads linking their cities together. This would put Falladrin ahead of the others by leaps and bounds. The money itself is really what you're getting on top of the infrastructure."

"Is that so?" Marshal asked as he looked between us. He nodded as he considered the prospect. "I suppose I can see how you would be right. Would you mind if I added a caveat to the proposal?"

"I'm always happy to entertain alternatives," I smiled. "What did you have in mind?"

"I will agree to the proposal in full as you've stated," Marshal said. "However, to incentivize the work on the roads, the remaining gold that you owe for the territory once the installments have begun to be paid will be forgiven after work on the roads has been completed."

My eyes widened in disbelief, "Meaning we would not have to pay whatever still remained once we've finished the roads?"

Marshal nodded, "Indeed. However, I don't want this to affect the quality of the roads just so you don't owe as much."

"You should know better than that, Your Grace," Serena chided the King playfully. "When has Merida ever done anything but to completion and satisfaction?"

Marshal chuckled, "That's true enough. Very well, Merida. I will agree to your offer. I'm glad Serena was able to propose the idea in such a way that allowed you both to come to this outcome. I think that this will benefit both of our peoples in the long run."

"Your generosity in offering the territory to begin with, as well as giving us a way to mitigate the cost was a welcome surprise, Your Grace," I bowed my head. "I'm certain my father and the Assembly will be overjoyed with the opportunity."

"And if they're not, I'm certain you'll convince them to be," Marshal laughed. "Now, before we put pen to parchment, I have one last stipulation."

Serena and I both looked at him curiously, "What's that?"

"You will let me escort you through the festivities tomorrow," Marshal told me. "We can enjoy the ceremony, look at how Orlimar has been coming along, and discuss things in detail."

I gave him a resigned smile, amused that he would want to bother spending so much time with me on a day like that, "Of course, Your Grace. I would be honored."

And Serena would have her plan in place. I had to wonder if Marshal suspected anything. He was a cunning man, and he could put a number of situations together to come to a conclusion. After all was said and done, I might have to ask if he'd known then what was going on.

CHAPTER 27:

AND THEN THERE WERE TWO

After our meeting with King Marshal, I insisted Serena help me with a few details before we retired for the night. I returned to the tunnels beneath the Tower of Mythral, where my quarters were made ready for me. Before going to my room, I informed Faren and a few of the local dwarven leaders, as well as some of my riders, about the plans for Yivreon and the deal I made to build the roads. I let them know that I wanted the first few yards of the road built before the end of the celebrations the next day as proof of our willingness to get the process started. There were dwarves heading to the surface to get started before I made it to my quarters.

Faren opened the door to my chambers, and I entered with a sigh as I noticed the gown that had been prepared for me. I stepped towards it and stared at it. The gown was admirable, with particular care taken so that the cut would accent my upper half with my preference for armored decorations.

"You'll look lovely in it, My Lady," Faren said as he began to prepare my nightclothes and a tea that would help me sleep.

"I'm certain I will," I said wistfully as I stared at the outfit.

Faren stopped what he was doing to look at me. "Princess? Is everything alright?" He'd clearly sensed something was off about my tone.

I shook my head lightly. "I'm fine." I turned and offered him a smile. "Just… thinking about how many of these I'll wear before someone will wear one for me."

"You're wondering when you'll be the one wearing a wedding dress?" Faren asked as he came to my side.

I took a deep breath and thought about the question. There were so many answers to that question. I had been married. I had been so happily married in my first life, and I doubted that I could ever feel that way about anyone ever again. However, I was also no longer back on Earth, and my spouse had died two years before I had. I still loved her, and the thought of marrying someone else still felt like a betrayal. However, I knew that she would have wanted me to be happy. She would want me to find someone who cared for me and supported me just as she had, and she'd want that person to make me happy and work to make my goals a reality.

In the end, I could only feel tears come to my eyes as I kept my smile. "I don't know. I know who I want, but she died before I did. I had someone I thought might be able to make me happy, but he died at Orlimar. I'm not built to be on my own…"

I sniffled as I realized how true that statement was. "I've been doing all of this since I was reborn with the idea that I'd probably have to be alone for the rest of my life. I convinced myself that as long as I could make everyone else's life better, I could stand the loneliness. I could deal with it. But as I'm watching everyone I know get married and knowing that every time I see them, I'll be the one person who's still alone…"

Faren's hands embraced one of mine, and he smiled. The next few moments drew on for what seemed like centuries. He spoke my name—my first name from my first life. He gave me time to register it before speaking my name again. "I'm right here. I've always been right here."

I stared at him wide-eyed. I could feel my tears running freely. "What? How do you…? I never told you what my name was."

Faren chuckled and gave a little shrug. "I figured it out before we left for Orlimar that night we spoke about our past. I even gave you a hint later on with the inscription in your ring that we gave you for your birthday."

It took me a few moments to register what he meant. When the realization hit me, the quote came out in a whisper of disbelief. "I have crossed oceans of time to find you… From Dracula…"

He nodded and sniffled. He was beginning to grow just as emotional as I was. "I didn't think you'd want me again. I thought that… maybe you and Franklin would be good for each other. I just wanted you to be happy."

Caution gripped me for a few moments. Faren knew my name, but that could have been a lucky guess. The way he felt about me and Franklin sounded like how my spouse would respond to the situation as well. I didn't think he would try to deceive me, but for some reason, I needed to be sure.

"Wait…" I said desperately. "What was your first tattoo and where did you get it?"

Faren stared at me, perplexed, for a minute before realization kicked in. "It was soot sprites gathering star candies. I got it at a convention in St. Augustine. You paid for it and stood there patiently the entire time."

I clapped a hand to my mouth in shock. "By the Stone… it is you, isn't it? Oh, you should have said something the moment you realized it!" I leapt forward and hugged him tight.

He wrapped his arms around me and squeezed me close. "I didn't want to make you choose."

I pulled away just enough to look at him. "It never would have been a decision. I have missed you since the day you died. I just went through the motions without you. I've done everything I've done in this life because I knew it's what you would have wanted and to make the world better."

"You're doing amazing," he replied, placing a hand on my cheek. "I'm so proud of how you've worked to make things better. Ever since I realized who you were, I've looked back on everything in a new light, and it's only served to make me happy to have met you all over again."

I gave an embarrassed huff of laughter and wiped my eyes. "Well, I hope you know you're marrying me again, right?"

Faren barked out a laugh. "I don't think many people would approve of a commoner-turned-warrior marrying their Exemplar princess."

"They'll approve because I approve," I responded confidently. "At this point, no one would be good enough. So better the person who's dedicated two lifetimes to me than someone who would be a simple political match."

"At this point, I'm not going to doubt you," he chuckled.

We spent most of the night talking and reminiscing about both our former lives and our current life. In fact, we spent so much time talking that when we realized what time it was, we only got about an hour's worth of sleep. Trianna and the others didn't notice my exhaustion. In fact, Trianna and King Marshal both mentioned that I seemed more exuberant and chipper than I'd ever been.

Marshal and I took the day moving from one celebration to another. Throughout the festivities, we discussed the details of Yivreon's purchase. There were other details that needed to be considered, such as whether the humans would remain Falladrin citizens or if they would be incorporated into the dwarven kingdom. I was also able to show him the first few yards of the road, which had been prepared by the dwarves at Orlimar's main entrance. I explained how there would be gutters to drain the rainwater down to underground rivers and streams that would need to be cleaned regularly.

All the while, Faren followed behind me quietly. He would occasionally offer additional insight about my plans that I didn't think were particularly important at the moment, but that Marshal seemed to appreciate. It was nice to realize that Faren had been continuing his role in our relationship the same way he had in our previous life this entire time. Now that I understood who he was, so many things made sense. Just knowing who he was made life brighter somehow, and I felt a renewed sense of self and strength— like a part of me that had been taken away was suddenly back again, and I was whole once more.

Finally, the time for the actual ceremony came, and we made our way back to the center of the budding city-fort. The large square had been prepared with a raised stage so that more people could witness the union. I changed into my gown and joined Trianna and Aelfric on the stage with Faren as my escort. A few other elves were up on the stage as well— elders mostly, who would bless the union.

One of the elders brought everyone to order and spoke at length about the merging of the different Paddish cultures with the cultures of the city elves, and how the joining of Trianna and Aelfric was more than just the joining of two people in matrimony, but that they represented the merging of elven cultures for the future. When he was finished speaking, he invited me to speak as a friend and loved one of the bride and groom.

I stepped forward and smiled at Trianna and Aelfric. The two seemed to be blushing with joy. I took my place between them and inhaled deeply. "I cannot speak of the merging of cultures as the Elder just has. I am a friend and ally of the elves, but I have not shared their history or their struggles. But I can speak to the union of Trianna and Aelfric, and to the hope and strength that love binds within us once we have found our life's partner."

I looked between the two before continuing, "Trianna was brought to Cragmorrar ten years ago in order to help keep her safe. She wasn't at all pleased about the decision, and we didn't exactly hit it off right away. But our shared love for the magic of Thoros and the good we could do for our people made us quick friends. I have fought beside her more times than I can count, and we have gone on many adventures together. I can say, without a shadow of a doubt, that she is my closest and dearest friend."

I reached out and took her hand, squeezing it gently. "Her friendship helped bolster me through dark and trying times as we worked to retake lost dwarven Holds and prepared ourselves to stop a Scourge. I assisted her in the effort to unite the Paddish clans and ensure that the elves had a place to call their own. Through all of this, we remained friends."

"Friends help each other. We support one another. We do what is best for one another. However, as much as we'd like to do more, we cannot take the special place in someone's heart that a wife or husband can."

I looked up at Aelfric with a playful smirk. "I liked Aelfric right away when we met him in Orlimar. Well, I loved his food, and that helped me like him."

There was a rumbling of laughter through the crowd. It was no secret that I gorged myself on Aelfric's cooking whenever I could.

"However, over the three years we spent preparing for the Scourge, I watched as my best friend began spending more time with someone of her own kind. It was a strange sensation, both happy and sad, to see her drift away from me and toward him. I wouldn't get to spend as much time with her as I would have liked, but I knew what she was doing was making her happy."

"After Orlimar, we all went our separate ways. I had to return home while Trianna and Aelfric had to stay here. I admit that leaving felt like I had left a piece of my heart here with me. But I was leaving it in good hands. And how could I not think that? Look at what they've accomplished together!"

I spread my arms wide to encompass the fort and everyone in attendance. "They worked together and supported each other as they built what was a newly refurbished fort into a budding and thriving city full of elven culture. The bond they share has brought them through scourgespawn, prejudice, and even betrayal and incarceration. Throughout it all, they leaned on each other to get through."

I took each of their hands and placed Trianna's hand in Aelfric's. "With the rest of their lives ahead of them together, I can only imagine what they'll manage to accomplish together."

I looked at them both in turn. "I wish you both all the happiness in the world. Durin an'ur varag, an'ur varag n'arazh vPetrar 'ur khazad khuzdul."

The last bit were a couple of dwarvish phrases which meant that I wished they had a long and prosperous life together. The literal translation was a couple of Irish phrases combined that I had remembered, which said, 'may your chimney always have smoke coming from it, and may a mouse never leave your chimney with a tear in its eye.' Fun little phrases that I liked to drop every so often.

The rest of the ceremony was taken up by another Elder who spoke more to the religious nature and traditions of the elves. When all was said and done, those in attendance cheered for the pair and released a large number of birds with small seed bags attached to their legs. The seeds would fall to the ground and germinate over time, creating a field of flowers. The bags were made of plant fibers so the birds could easily remove them.

I surprised Trianna and Aelfric with a new home that I'd molded with my powers while everyone's attention was on the ceremony. I'd chosen an area near the center of the fort that was typically used as an open-air market. I also promised to have the dwarves craft a new market closer to the entrance so that visitors would be more inclined to visit it and spend their coin there.

We stayed for another few days to help the new couple move into the house and spend some time together. By the time we were ready to go, Trianna and Aelfric were settled into their new home, and I was looking forward to going back home. As we were all saying our goodbyes, Allen flagged me down.

"Merida!" Allen called as he jogged over to me.

"Allen?" I curtsied to him with a smile. "Was there something you needed?"

Allen gave a quick bow to reciprocate the courtesy. "Yes, actually. My uncle seems to have taken an interest in you. I was wondering if you would do me the favor of entering into a correspondence with him. I have a letter he's already written to you if you agree."

"Your uncle?" I asked with some interest.

"Matthew Lemlal," Allen clarified.

"Oh!" I realized that he was talking about Lemlal's father from Age of Dragons 2. "He's interested in me? That's interesting to know. I'd be more than happy to correspond with him. As I recall, he's a rather accomplished mage."

"He is indeed," Allen nodded as he fished the letter from one of the pockets inside his robe and handed it to me. "When he heard about a dwarven mage, he became rather starstruck with the idea. I should expect to be asked some strangely personal, off-the-wall questions."

"I'm sure it will be fine," I chuckled as I took the letter. "I have some scouts with me. I'll read the letter today and pen a response this evening."

"Thank you, Merida," Allen smiled. "I appreciate you taking the time to engage with him."

"Don't mention it," I chuckled. "He isn't the first mage to be interested in me." I tossed Allen a playful wink before turning to climb onto my rhoarno.

He blushed furiously and cleared his throat. "Ah... Yes. Well, thank you again, Merida. Also, I thought for the next annual meeting I could come to Cragmorrar with some students so they could better understand the dimvyum refinement process by seeing it firsthand."

Once I'd finished mounting my rhoarno and took the reins, I looked down at Allen. "That sounds like a fine idea. I'll have some safety equipment prepped for them so they won't be affected by the fumes or any stray raw dimvyum."

"Sounds like an excellent plan," Allen bowed his head.

We left soon after, and I was genuinely happy to be returning home. My guards would note that we did a good deal of singing as we rode, where we would typically ride in moderate silence. My mood was elevated, and I was happier than I had been since I had been reborn, knowing that Faren was my spouse from my former life. My next goal was clear: announcing our engagement and planning the wedding. I wasn't going to let anything stand in my way.

CHAPTER 28:

FAMILY MEETING

Upon my return to Cragmorrar, I had a great deal of work to get done. My first order of business was to send a letter to Trenton, requesting that he come to Cragmorrar to join me in a meeting with Father and Bilfern. I received word from Trenton that he would be joining us soon. Once I received the response, I got to work making sure that everything I wanted to present to them was in order.

The day I received the response, I had Kara dress me in one of my working outfits; mostly thick cloth and leather designed to resist heat and burns. I always preferred to dress myself, but when I was home Kara insisted on helping me do everything.

"I'd do it for a thousand years and more to repay you for everything you've done for my children, My Lady," Kara chided me as I protested. "This is the role you gave me, and I will see it done properly."

I smiled and sighed, "You know, I need to have children soon so you can focus on them instead."

Kara chuckled and adjusted the straps to my leather apron, which had been designed to be a bit thicker than normal, as well as more form-fitting. "You'll need to marry someone first, My Lady."

"Good news on that front, at least," I smiled wryly back at her. "I think I know just the man."

Kara gasped and moved her head over my shoulder to stare at me, "Is that so? May I ask who the lucky man is?"

I hummed playfully, "I don't think I should say just yet. It's an unconventional choice. But I can say you most assuredly know his name."

She popped my shoulder in a playful manner, "My Lady, you shouldn't tease me like that. Now I'll be left wondering who it is until you announce your intentions."

I shook my head and placed a small kiss on the older woman's cheek, "I promise that you'll be among the first to know, well before the announcement. After all, we can't have it said that House Orodum's matron was unaware of her Lady's intentions."

Kara laughed as she fetched my smithing gloves, "I appreciate your concern for my reputation, My Lady. Will you be home for lunch?"

"I don't think so," I replied as I tucked the gloves into my belt and made small comfort adjustments to the outfit as I looked myself over in the mirror. "Would you be so kind as to have lunch sent to Darina's laboratory for everyone? We'll likely be there most of the day."

"Of course, My Lady," Kara curtsied before leaving to relay the request.

I stepped outside of my chambers in time to see Kara giving her morning greeting to Faren. I couldn't help but smile. She had no idea.

"It will blow her mind, you know," I quipped after Kara had taken her leave.

"It will be the same for everyone," Faren chuckled as he fell in just behind me.

We made some small talk as we wove our way through the estate and down into Darina's laboratory. This area was made with multiple levels to allow Darina to assign different projects to different spaces. The project we would be checking on today was one that would imprint all of us on the pages of history. As I made my way down the stairs to the lowest section of the laboratory, Darina and Bilfern were both there to greet me.

"Sister," Bilfern bowed his head. "We're excited you've come to see how the work has been going. I trust you were able to settle things in Orlimar and the wedding went well?"

I smiled and pulled Bilfern into a hug, squeezing him tight, "I've missed you, Bilfern. Everything went wonderfully. I have some amazing news to share once Trenton gets here."

Bilfern gave a stressed huff as I squeezed him, but still hugged me back, "I'm excited to hear the news."

Darina dipped into a curtsy, "It's wonderful to see you again, Princess."

I released Bilfern and turned to face Darina. I took one of her hands between mine and smiled, "How are you, Darina? The laboratory seems abuzz with activity."

Darina grinned wide. There was no hiding her enthusiasm for her craft, "Wonderful as always, Princess! Thanks to the items you procured, we've been able to make massive strides in enchanting and phase augmentation."

"Excellent!" I exclaimed. "Let's see what you've come up with."

There was no mistaking the excitement in the pair as they led us into the lab. I could see multiple dimvyum wells of various sizes as well as what looked like different versions of the activation units. Different parts of the lab seemed to hum into different frequencies, and I could see the aura of different animals in various magical colors moving about in confined spaces.

"We started with experiments on the dimvyum well," Darina said as she motioned to the original well I had brought back from Aronthok. "It took us some time to figure out how it worked and what it did specifically. It can be used to establish a frequency area where living creatures can be shifted into different dimensions of the Dimvolmn. Once we figured out how it did that, we had to figure out how to relay dials connected to it. The relays serve as remote adjusters to the frequency of the dimvyum well, allowing someone to key in which dimension the well should shift things into without direct manipulation of the well's settings."

"After that, we started working on the premise that multiple wells could be linked to the same relay, allowing anyone who interacted with one well to be in one dimension, while others would remain in the pre-established dimension," Bilfern added. "We also discovered that the relays do not need to remain in one place to keep their connection to their well; they simply need to remain in the well's area of influence, which appears to be an approximate area of ten miles."

"Ten miles?" I repeated with surprise. "That's an enormous range…"

Darina and Bilfern grinned at each other. Bilfern moved over to a nearby table and picked up a pair of gauntlets. He brought them over and handed them to me. "These are the smaller, portable versions of the relays. Each dial is linked to one of the five different wells we've created so far. Once a dial is activated, the wearer is synced to the proper relay. To sync to a new relay, you reset the first dial and activate another of your choice."

"So you could slip into the different dimensions on a whim or alter each well's specified dimensional sync on the fly," I speculated.

"Precisely," Darina nodded proudly. "The process for making the gauntlets is extremely time-consuming, and protecting the dials is paramount. But we made that pair especially for you, Princess. The dials attached to that gauntlet are stone and dimvyum instead of metal and dimvyum. It should allow you to use your Titan abilities to manipulate the dials with your will instead of manually turning them."

"Is that so?" I asked as I slipped each gauntlet on. One thing had to be said: the craftsmen of House Orodum knew my measurements perfectly. The gauntlets felt like a second skin as I flexed my fingers to gauge their dexterity. Once satisfied with the fit, I reached out with my Titan sense and felt out the intricacies of the dials. Though made of stone, they were masterfully crafted and woven with the finest thread of dimvyum to help conduct the magic. My senses also seemed to be able to detect which dial was aligned with each well.

I willed one dial to move, then reset it, then moved another. I shifted from one dimension of the Dimvolmn to another until I'd gone through all of the options. Faren seemed smugly excited, likely due to the fact that he had hoped for something just like this and had been training a number of

House Orodum's soldiers in mock exercises.

As I shifted into the last option, I was shocked to see Purpose standing beside me alongside the Paddish spirit who had been trapped inside the crystal phylactery. Faren, Bilfern, and Danga had disappeared, and now only the two spirits were with me.

"What...? What's going on?" I asked.

"Princess," Purpose bowed. "It is unlike you to join us for training so early."

"Purpose? Are you saying I'm currently in the Dimvolmn?" I posited as I looked around. This wasn't the Dimvolmn as I knew it. It looked like the laboratory in every way, only the people around me had changed.

The Paddish spirit put a finger to his chin. "Curious. You do seem to be able to see us. But we see you as in the Dimvolmn. What do you see, Princess?"

"I'm in Darina's lab as far as I can tell," I replied, looking around in surprise.

"Curious," Purpose replied. "Could you be in the shroud? Directly between the physical world and the Dimvolmn? Able to see what is here, but unable to be seen by those in the physical world?"

"If so... Darina and my brother have outdone themselves," I chuckled. "If you'll both excuse me, I will explain later when I return for my training."

"Of course, Princess," they both bowed. "We await your return."

I willed the dial to reset. Purpose and the spirit snapped out of view while Faren and the rest snapped back into sight. I was back in the physical realm.

Darina was almost dancing with excitement. "I think it worked! I think it really worked!"

"Are you alright, Princess?" Faren asked as he looked me over with concern. "You completely disappeared. No aura or anything remained to show us which dimension you were attuned to."

"Was it the Dimvolmn? Were you in the Dimvolmn?" Darina chirped with barely contained excitement.

"No…" I said with genuine amazement. "I was in the shroud. I was in between the physical world and the Dimvolmn. Everything remained the same as it was, but I could see the spirits in the Dimvolmn and speak with them."

"Oh my gosh!" Darina exclaimed. "That was a totally unexpected result!"

Bilfern sighed as Darina was too excited to explain. "We believed that since you were a mage, we could set a dimvyum well to send you to the Dimvolmn in case you needed to be there. If, instead, we sent you to the shroud, it means that the wells do have some limit."

"And that she can turn invisible!" Darina shouted.

"Within the confines of that particular well," Bilfern agreed. "Still, it's an impressive side effect. We'll see what we can do to make it more reliable."

"I trust you to do what is best," I smiled at Bilfern. "And you said that the gauntlets can be used by anyone, right?"

"So long as they're trained in the use of the proper dial settings and protocols, yes," he smiled and nodded. "What did you have in mind?"

I turned to Faren and motioned for him to make his proposal. He'd been planning it for some time. We spent the rest of the day going over the finer points of the dimvyum wells and how they operated, what they were capable of influencing, and how we could best utilize them for our people. It was nearly midnight by the time Faren and I returned home. The day had been busy, and now we had the means to help elevate Faren in the eyes of my family as well as the Assembly. In the next few weeks, House Orodum's craftsmen would be extremely busy.

Two weeks went by, and Trenton had finally arrived in Cragmorrar.

He'd taken a week to get Nordrucan Hold's affairs in order before leaving. Bilfern and I greeted Trenton and Ninta when they passed through the gates from the Under Roads. To my surprise, Trenton actually eschewed his normal craggy demeanor and rushed up to us, wrapping his arms around us and hugging us close.

"I've missed you both dearly," he smiled. "We should not be so long apart."

"You're the one who decided to stay in the Hold," I reminded him playfully as I hugged him back.

"The sacrifice I had to make as a Nordrucan," Trenton responded. He looked at Bilfern, "By the Stone, lad, you've grown! I see Merida hasn't skimped on the food."

Bilfern snorted and laughed, "She doesn't skimp on the workload either. I may become a rhoarno just to escape the burden."

Trenton barked out a laugh and slapped Bilfern across the back in good humor, "I guarantee you she isn't giving you any more work than I gave her. If anything, she's probably skimped on your martial training."

"I'll have you know he trains with Faren daily," I huffed. "And he spars with me once a week."

"Won a match yet?" Trenton chuckled at Bilfern.

"She uses magic!" Bilfern protested.

"You're confusing skill for magic, Bilfern," I teased him. "I haven't used a single ounce of magic on you yet."

"You're young yet," Trenton reassured him. "You'll be physically stronger than her soon enough. A bit more skill and you might be able to take her if she doesn't use her magic."

Faren gave a doubtful huff, to which Trenton tossed him a wink.

"You're in an exceptionally good mood, Trenton," I said with some small amount of paranoia. "What's going on with you?"

"We have good news," Ninta said as she approached with an obviously pregnant belly.

I looked at her, then squealed in delight. I pushed Trenton out of the way and ran to Ninta, giving her a hug. "Why didn't anyone send a letter? We could have had a celebration ready! I could have started having so many gifts made! I would have visited!"

"Why answer your own question?" Trenton asked.

I turned on him and gasped, "Are you saying that you didn't want me to visit?"

"Visit us, yes. The unborn child, no," he replied flatly.

"Oh, I am going to make you regret that," I said, putting my hands on my hips.

"Forgive him, Merida," Ninta laughed. "He was dying to tell you but I convinced him to let it be a surprise. We were planning on coming to Cragmorrar soon, anyway. Trenton wanted the baby to be born in the capital."

"Your letter was serendipitous," Trenton shrugged. "It gave us an excuse to leave earlier. Now what's all this about a family meeting? What's so important you needed to summon us from Nordrucan Hold that couldn't be relayed by letter?"

"I'll tell everyone once we're all together," I insisted. "I have a few things I want to talk to everyone about before bringing them to the Assembly."

"They're so important that you feel like you need to seek our opinions first?" Trenton asked suspiciously.

"Monumentally so," I assured him. "One is at least as important as the creation of the Surface Caste. The other is more personal, and I hope you will support my decision."

"The Assembly has no say in your personal matters," Trenton was almost offended that I would suggest such a thing.

"This is true, but in this decision, I think they will have a loud opinion which could trickle down to the rest of the people," I sighed. I stepped up to Trenton and took his hands in mine, gazing up at him pleadingly, "Please… Just try to keep an open mind when I tell you, alright?"

"Merida," Trenton said firmly but reassuringly, "ever since you were a little girl, I have only ever doubted your decisions once, and that decision proved to be a good one. I have no doubt that whatever you have decided for yourself will be the right thing for you and our people. I will support your decision no matter what."

I smiled up at Trenton, then jumped up and hugged his neck, "Thank you!"

While I invited them to stay with me in my home, Trenton and Ninta insisted on staying in the palace. Trenton wanted to be able to spend more time with Father, and I honestly couldn't blame him. I had a suspicion that he missed the comforts of palace living, which crept into my mind, but I didn't say anything. Trenton was in an exceptionally good mood, and I didn't want to spoil it.

A few days went by before we all agreed to meet in Father's estate in the palace. Father was obviously the first to be there and had gone to a great deal of trouble and preparation for the meeting. He had many different dishes prepared and had the palace cleaned top to bottom. He was a dear and was so excited to have all of his children together again in one place after a good many years.

Trenton and Ninta arrived next. Living in the castle for the moment allowed them to simply be ready. They sat and talked for some time, with Trenton catching Father up on everything that was going on in Nordrucan Hold. Ninta spoke about what they were hoping to achieve with the Hold in the future. The pair entertained Father with talk and stories for about a half hour until Bilfern arrived.

Bilfern smiled as the door was closed behind him, "Father, Trenton, Ninta. I hope you haven't been waiting for me very long."

Trenton arched a brow, "Where's our sister? I thought she would accompany you here."

"I am not Merida's keeper, Trenton," Bilfern chuckled. "She is mine. She said she had affairs to tend to and that she would meet us soon enough."

Father laughed, "I should think you would expect her to get busy by now, Trenton."

"It's not outside the scope of possibility," Trenton sighed, "but she is the one who called for this meeting. She set the date, the time, and the location."

"And she has been here the entire time, brother," I laughed as I appeared from the shroud.

Father, Trenton, and Ninta all jumped and gasped in shock.

"Where did you come from?" Trenton demanded.

"The shroud," I smiled and raised one of my gauntlets that Bilfern and Darina had made for me. "This was the first issue I wanted to speak to all of you about. House Orodum has created a magical defense system that will keep our people safe from any kind of attack and allow our soldiers to move throughout the entire city unfettered and unable to be attacked until they choose to engage the enemy."

Everyone but Bilfern seemed confused. Father leaned forward, "Could you elaborate, Merida?"

"Oh, I'm here merely as the demonstrator," I tittered. "Our young Bilfern will be the one to explain it all. Bilfern? Please explain everything."

Bilfern, at twelve years old, wore a rather proud smile as he stood and all eyes moved to him. "Darina and I have worked for some time recreating and modifying ancient dimvyum well magic. These dimvyum wells were lost knowledge until Merida found them again. What they do is allow individuals to key into certain dimensions of the Dimvolmn. If a person tunes into the well, they will be transported to that dimension. People in that dimension cannot interact with people outside of it, and vice versa. Currently, the dimvyum wells have four dimensions they can be attuned to, plus one additional one unique to Merida because she is a mage and can naturally pass through them."

As Bilfern spoke, I shifted between the different dimensions by using my gauntlets to tune into the different wells, my form seeming to shift into a blue, pink, red, and yellow ghostlike appearance.

"We have worked on creating pedestals which can be used in an emergency to allow Cragmorrar's citizens to use so that they can be safe from harm," Bilfern continued. "However, we have also created gauntlets that we can equip Cragmorrar's guards and warriors with so that they can traverse these dimensions and only shift back into the physical world when they're ready to attack."

"Fascinating!" Father gasped as he listened to Bilfern and watched me shift from dimension to dimension. "And it can cover everyone in the city?"

"So long as we station pedestals in enough places around the city, the citizens should all be able to use them in case of an emergency while guards respond to the incident," Bilfern nodded.

"Can they be misused?" Trenton asked, ever skeptical and ever practical.

"While anyone can activate a pedestal at any time, you will still be able to see them in one of the different colored auras," I responded. Bilfern expressed before the meeting that he wasn't prepared to answer any logistical or lawful questions about the system yet.

I shifted into the blue spectrum then back to the physical world once again. "As you can see, anyone utilizing the pedestals is still obvious to those who aren't using them. They simply cannot interact with anyone else. It should also be noted that doors and specific items can also be attuned to the different dimensions so that only someone in the dimension it's attuned to can interact with it. So, for matters of security as far as the palace and Assembly chambers are concerned, there is no need to worry about anyone using the system to sneak around the city or access places they shouldn't have access to."

"How do we know no one else will be able to turn invisible like Merida can?" Father asked, the detailed mind of a king coming into play.

"Merida is a mage, and with all the testing we've done, we believe a mage is needed to access the shroud's particular setting," Bilfern was quick to clarify. "We've used House Orodum's warriors to test the settings for months now, and not one of them has been able to access that particular dimension."

"And if someone gives this to a mage that isn't a dwarf?" Ninta asked. Her tone was more quizzical than demanding or skeptical. Unlike Father or Trenton, she wasn't trying to put Bilfern on his heels with her inquiry.

"The technology will be treated the same way as dimvyum," I answered. "Sharing it will be punishable by death as this technology has been created for the safety and security of the dwarves and our territory."

"That's rather harsh, don't you think, daughter?" Father asked me as he considered my suggestion.

I shook my head and kept my tone respectful. "Not at all, Father. This system is intricate, requires dimvyum to work, and will be critical to the safety and security of our people and our kingdom. I would not consider any punishment less than death appropriate for a dwarf that would put that system in jeopardy."

"She speaks true, Father," Trenton sighed grimly. "We have already made the smuggling and illegal sale of dimvyum punishable by death. This has stopped the illegal sale of dimvyum and has also all but eliminated the Syndicate. I think this is an acceptable thing to propose considering the expense of the project and how crucial it will be for Cragmorrar's defense."

"I see…" Father said as he nodded and considered Trenton's words. "So you would both consider it to be equal to treason, then? And what about you, Bilfern? Do you agree with your brother and sister?"

Bilfern looked from Father to me. I gave him a reassuring nod. He looked back at Father and seemed to stand a bit taller. "I do, Father. However, I would add that there is another reason beyond safety and expense to require such a punishment."

Father's expression probably seemed stern and cold to Bilfern, but I knew Father much better. I could see the pride and curiosity in his eyes. He was eager to see what Bilfern had to say and was proud that he was taking his own stance, separate from mine or Trenton's.

"And what might that be?" Father asked.

"I believe that this system represents the first of dwarven arcane engineering," Bilfern said proudly. "If I may say so, I believe that it's also groundbreaking in the world of magical research and application. With House Orodum's leading research and Merida's encouragement for dwarven scholars in the Lemlalian College, of which she sits as one of the heads, we are going to start seeing a large boom of new dwarven innovations in this field. While most might be practical in nature, we want to ensure the scholars and craftsmen of every caste that their creations and contributions to dwarven society will be respected and encouraged."

"If we want dwarves to not only push forward in new forms of study and crafting, we must show them that we take such efforts seriously and that we are willing to protect that effort fiercely, especially when it contributes so much to our dwarven way of life," Bilfern ended.

I couldn't help but look at him with pride and a raised sense of respect. He spoke wonderfully and definitively. It was bringing a tear to my eye.

Father, Trenton, and Ninta all seemed to look at Bilfern with surprise and approval. They were finally seeing him as I had been seeing him; as an intelligent and well-spoken young man worthy of the Nordrucan name.

"You make an interesting point, Bilfern," Father smiled. "And very well-spoken, as well. I admit I hadn't considered how Merida's seat at the college would affect our people, but now that you mention it, along with this new system as an example of what dwarves are capable of when we dedicate ourselves to a field of study... I can see why you would be so passionate about protecting this new system."

"Thank you, Father," Bilfern bowed his head.

Father sat back and looked at Bilfern and me. "I will consider what you have said. Of course, the ultimate decision is the Assembly's, but I will give my recommendation when it is brought before the Callers."

"That is all we can ask," I bowed my head to Father. "Thank you for the consideration. No matter what happens, we will still be offering this system to the entire kingdom. Cragmorrar and every Hold will be able to have such a system set up. House Orodum is prepared to share this knowledge freely."

"Let it be known, then, that Nordrucan Hold will want this system as soon as possible," Trenton said proudly.

"The Nordrucan Hold will also want to consider the next proposal," I grinned at Trenton. "In addition to the dimvyum well system, Faren has been training a special group of warriors in the tactics and use of the wells. If the system is approved, I would like to promote this group of warriors into a new fighting force for Cragmorrar akin to the Fallen Legion, except that it would be dedicated to protecting Cragmorrar, and the other Holds if it's established properly, directly. The Fallen Legion would continue protecting the Under Roads as it always has, while this new force would act as the standing army of the dwarven kingdom utilizing the dimvyum well technology to give it the advantage against foreign invaders, as well as the scourgespawn should they manage to get past the Legion."

"You have enough warriors ready to establish such a force?" Father asked with surprise and concern.

"Faren has enough warrior families who are ready to dedicate some of their members to the force, and those members have been trained in the use of dimvyum well tactics," I responded, rather proud of myself. "There will be no conflict of interest between these members and the Houses their families are dedicated to because the members will swear oaths to the crown and kingdom."

"Is this Faren's suggestion," Trenton asked, "Or is it yours that you are crediting to Faren?"

I turned to Trenton and looked at him with hurt in my expression. "I should think you know me better than to ask something like that."

"When we were discussing the possibilities of the dimvyum well system, Faren was the one to propose a fighting force that utilized it in an offensive manner," Bilfern came to my defense. "In fact, he was the one who suggested we try to condense the technology to fit them into the gauntlets so that individual soldiers could shift dimensions on the fly to more quickly respond to changes in a battle."

"Ah… well, if that is the case, then I apologize for my presumption," Trenton looked at me. "Faren is an intelligent and capable warrior. I was wrong to assume you were crediting him with your idea."

"He's always been dedicated to our people and looked for ways to help them," I smiled.

"I cannot disagree with you in that respect," Trenton nodded. "I think the idea is a good one, though it will mean more funds will need to be raised to fund a third standing force beyond the city's guards and the Fallen Legion."

"He makes a fine point, Merida," Father motioned to Trenton. "A standing army costs a considerable amount of money. Where would you propose these funds come from?"

"The dimvyum shares," I smiled. "By my estimates, we only need approximately ten percent of the shares to fund the system, setup and maintenance, as well as the standing force. We ask the people to agree to an annual payment that is ten percent less than what they receive now. It will sound bad at first, but if we tell them that we will prioritize setting up emergency pedestals in the sections of the city where the most agreements come from, I believe you'll see many families scrambling to get their names on the list of those who agree."

"Interesting," Father smiled and stroked his beard. "The kingdom would essentially pay nothing, and people would only stand to gain by choosing to receive slightly less at the end of each year than they normally would. A clever idea, my dear."

"What about the Holds? Would they also benefit from the same force?" Ninta asked. "You mentioned Faren had been speaking with and training warrior families on the tactics needed to best use these systems. Has he been working with families from the Holds also?"

I shook my head. "We have not had the luxury of reaching out to the Holds yet," I admitted. "However, Faren has made a list of currently trained warriors who he would trust to establish and train the forces for each Hold. They have agreed to go to the Holds to help with that training for however long they're needed as soon as the force is established and a Hold requests assistance."

"If the Callers do not approve this force, they're fools," Ninta told Trenton. "And if they prove themselves fools, we should at least ask for Faren to have some warriors train our warriors. House Orodum and House Nordrucan will have warriors with an extreme advantage over the other houses if the Assembly votes against the measure."

"I seriously doubt the Assembly will be that stupid, especially when a standing force will be funded naturally, without the need to further tax the people," Trenton replied, crossing his arms. "But if they are that stupid, I trust my sister to ensure that both our Houses have that advantage."

"Of course, Trenton," I bowed my head to reassure him.

Father hummed and gave a nod. "I think this is an excellent idea, Merida. I wish I could have spoken with Faren about some of the details, but I trust you'll pass on my appreciation for his efforts."

"I will, Father," I smiled.

"Was there anything else we needed to speak about?" Father asked.

I gave a firm nod. "I have two other things I wanted to speak about."

"What's next, then?" Father asked.

"I have agreed to purchase the Teynir of Yivreon from Falladrin," I smiled wide.

"You what?" Trenton barked. Everyone else in the room had similar reactions.

I placed my hands behind my back and took an educational tone. "Yivreon was originally a dwarven outpost. A human noble paid the dwarves to create a port town for him, and it has been in Falladrin's hands since then. I was offered the land and its port city as a gift, but decided to buy it instead."

"Why would you not accept it as a gift?" Father asked, the news seeming to take his breath away. "That is a kingly gift!"

"The reason behind the offer was not altruistic," I replied with a sigh. "It would have been used to gain a favor from me to back one of King Marshal's daughters in a political game. So I instead offered to buy it. However, I will only be paying approximately fifteen percent of the promised price."

"How?" Trenton demanded, quickly growing taciturn.

"I agreed to pay ten percent of the price upfront," I explained calmly. "I also agreed to build roads connecting all of the towns and cities in Falladrin. While this is happening, King Marshal has agreed that I will make a single payment each year while the roads are being built. Once the roads are finished, the difference between what has been paid and what is still owed will be forgiven."

"Do you know what you have promised?" Trenton stood in shock. "Do you truly understand what sort of undertaking this will cost in materials and manpower?"

I smirked. "Considerably less than you think when I travel to Demirren each year and use my Titan abilities to mold the roads as I go. We already have Surface Caste members helping to start on the roads. They're using materials sourced locally from the areas they're in. Whenever I travel, I will augment their efforts with my abilities. The Surface Caste representatives I've spoken with have already volunteered their manpower because the roads will help them move their goods faster and more securely."

"That is a relief to hear, my dear, but you still have promised funds to buy this land without asking the Assembly if they will release the funds," Father said, exasperated.

"I think you might be misunderstanding me," I looked at Father and Trenton. "I said that I have agreed to purchase the land. Me. As an individual. I never said the funds would be coming from the kingdom."

"Merida…" Ninta gasped and cupped her hand to her mouth.

"You're using your own coin?" Trenton whispered.

"That will bankrupt you," Father stared at me in shock.

I tittered and smiled at them. "I think you've all underestimated how much money I've managed to make through our enchantments, contracts through the Surface Caste, Rita's income with Brankite production, and other ventures I've entered into outside of Cragmorrar. Being as frugal as possible with that sort of income has allowed me to collect a considerable amount of funds."

Trenton blanched. "Merida… just how rich are you?"

"Rich enough to donate a brand new port city and Hold to the dwarven kingdom," I smiled sweetly.

"What?" Father asked. "What do you mean you're going to donate a new Hold?"

I laughed. "Our people are more productive and enterprising than ever. We have products and services that need more markets than are available in Falladrin and Fransway. We need to be able to reliably ship our goods to the Independent Marshes and other countries by boat. There is a city and a port there already, and we know the Under Roads connect to it because it was once a dwarven outpost. It's only right that we expand it into a new Hold."

"You would need someone to rule this new Hold, along with nobles to help with its logistics, warriors for its protection, craftsmen, and tradesmen…" Trenton went over the logistics.

"As it happens, I believe it can be more than a trade hub for us," I replied with a tone that suggested I had an idea. "I see the chance to establish a city and Hold that becomes the home of the most advances in arcane technology integrated into its daily life and infrastructure. We can make it the envy of the world and a place for people from all over Thoros to come to in order to learn from our smiths and enchanters."

"You seem to have a specific vision for it already," Father mused. "That is, of course, your right if you are the one purchasing the land. But if you donate it to the kingdom, that vision will likely never see fruition."

"I disagree," I chuckled. "That will only be the case if the wrong person is chosen to rule the Hold and city. Which is why I propose we place Bilfern as the lord of the Hold."

"What?!" Bilfern shouted in unison with Trenton.

"Me? But I have no desire to rule," Bilfern protested. "I want to study and work on the technological advances we've begun to discover."

This protest gained Trenton's ire, and he turned to growl at Bilfern, "You are a Nordrucan. Your life is already dedicated to service to your people by fate and right of your blood."

I turned and looked at Bilfern, smiling softly. "I think this is a perfect role for you, Bilfern. You can direct, encourage, and implement advances that your people come up with without having to move through the Assembly. The Hold will be a place for you to show the world what wonders the dwarves are truly capable of."

"But... No one's going to listen to me," Bilfern argued. "Here I am a prince and your sister. There are repercussions for ignoring me in Cragmorrar. Out there I'll be on my own."

"You should have faith in the authority the title will give you," I reassured him. "We will find nobles who will want to support you and the vision of the Hold. And I assure you, you will not be alone."

"The gift of a port, a city, and a new Hold will be looked upon favorably," Father stroked his beard. "In that light, I doubt the Assembly will have much issue with you promoting Bilfern to rule over it. If it works how you hope it will, then you are setting Bilfern up to become the lord of a Hold that will become more influential in the kingdom and on the surface than any other place in the dwarven kingdom."

"That is my hope," I smiled at Father, then looked at Bilfern. "I hope he will show us just what he's capable of by creating wonders that we can't even fathom yet and create a city and Hold unlike any other."

Bilfern looked extremely nervous but tried to show a look of confidence. "I'll do my best, Sister."

"We know you will, Bilfern," I said with no small amount of pride. "You always have, and you've never let us down. We all have faith in you."

"Here, here," Ninta cheered.

"Aye, she's right," Trenton sighed and sat back down. "You're smart and talented. You'll do well."

Father chuckled. "Your mother would be so proud of you, Bilfern. Your interest and talent with enchanting would have pleased her to no end."

"Thank you, all," Bilfern smiled.

"Now, Merida, you said there was one more thing you wanted to speak to us about?" Father shifted to the next subject.

"I'm not sure anything else will top the last few subjects," Trenton chuckled.

"Please don't doubt her in that respect, dear," Ninta laughed and rested her hand on Trenton's.

I rolled my eyes and shook my head. "I'm not trying to top anything. These were just things I needed to talk to all of you about before bringing them to the Assembly. Well, all except this last subject."

"This is the one you said would be personal, yes?" Trenton asked.

I nodded and looked over them all in turn. "I have decided that I want to marry Faren."

"Faren?" Father asked. "Your bodyguard?"

"He's a commoner," Trenton scoffed.

"A commoner who has saved my life multiple times," I pointed out.

"A commoner we'll be asking to train either our city's forces or our House's personal forces," Ninta reminded Trenton.

"Outside of this room, Faren is considered a hero," I explained. "There is no one more dedicated to me than Faren is. And it's not out of honor or his position; it's because he genuinely believes in me and believes that I'm the best force for good for our people. I believe he harbors feelings for me, and I have come to love him. I would like your support to be able to express that love publicly."

There was a long silence before Father spoke up, "Merida… You are a Princess of Cragmorrar. What's more, you are an Exemplar. The Assembly, and I daresay the people as a whole, expect you to marry someone who is at least your equal in station."

"Name the man who is equal to me in station," I sighed. "I will marry him. The only princes are my brothers. There is no male Exemplar. I have no real relationships with the other nobles, and too many of them around my age see me only as an Exemplar, or as a means to raise their House's prestige."

"But the world will see it as you marrying someone beneath you," Trenton tried to clarify.

"They'll see that no matter who I marry," I retorted. "By all rights, I outrank Father and everyone else. There isn't anyone who wouldn't be considered beneath me. I'm also the hero who defeated the archdemon at Orlimar. I'm credited with the retaking of the lost Holds. You also forgot that I'm the only dwarven mage. That status also would have set me above most if I were born a commoner. And are we forgetting that I'm technically a Titan now as well? I can mold the stone itself using only my will! Who would possibly be worthy of me with all that taken into consideration?"

"She has a point," Bilfern shrugged. "When you think about it, Merida is far and away above the aspirations of anyone we could think of. No matter who we chose, the people would think him unworthy. Why not let her choose who she thinks is right?"

Father rested back and crossed his arms, "I admit that the time after

Franklin's death was uncharacteristically respectful. The noble families didn't make any offers for your hand for some time, allowing you time to mourn. But as of late, we have been inundated with proposals and requests from every House in Cragmorrar and the Holds. If we do not believe any of the offers are worthy of Merida, then we will need to tell them that she is betrothed to someone."

"I mean no offense, Merida," Trenton sighed. His old taciturn self, mired in tradition, was showing, "Faren is intelligent. He is a capable warrior. He is dedicated and loyal. I have no doubts about any of that. Are you sure you wish to endure the blowback that might come from this decision? Because regardless of his merit, regardless of his status as a war hero, there will be nobles who will feel the harsh sting of rejection when we announce your betrothal to a commoner."

"Do you honestly believe any family would publicly voice dissent to the choice simply because Faren isn't a noble?" I asked, growing increasingly frustrated. "What more could the man do to prove himself worthy in everyone's eyes?"

"It's not everyone you have to worry about, my dear," Father tried to console me. "It's the nobles. You know that every citizen who isn't noble will be ecstatic to see you take a commoner as a husband. With your constant effort to promote the people above their stations, they will see it as further proof of your goodwill and belief in the potential of our people. Some noble Houses will see it as a slight against their family's standing and history."

"What could they do, though?" Bilfern asked. "If they tried to impede her in the Assembly, there would be too much political resistance for them to achieve anything. And if it was made public, they might face resistance and boycotts from their servants and warriors, as well as the other castes outside of the House. The love our people have for Merida is palpable... I shudder to think what would happen to anyone should they move against her in any meaningful way: politically or aggressively."

"They won't dare, of course," Father agreed. "But they don't have to. All they have to do is start voting against her measures. While they may still go through, the lower vote counts will begin to influence how large she can try to make her proposals, or even affect the people's opinion of her over time."

"This is supposition at most, Father," I said reluctantly. "It's just as likely that they'll approve of him as a fine choice because of his reputation."

Father stood and approached me, taking my hands in his and smiled wearily at me. "That may be so, my dear. And I truly hope that is the case if you do announce your intentions. But you must understand that the nobles are a fickle breed, and navigating their egos can be just as daunting a task as navigating the will and whim of the Assembly. I will support you if Faren is your choice, both as your father and as your King. He's a good man. Just know that you may encounter a great deal of resistance."

"I promised I would support you in this choice," Trenton said. "I will defend your choice, no matter what. I just worry that you may not be prepared for the resistance you'll meet. That's what I'm worried about."

"We'll all support you, Merida," Ninta smiled. "You deserve to be with the person who makes you happy. And we'll all defend your choice to anyone who may question it. Your family is here for you."

Bilfern walked over and hugged me. "I think Faren is the best choice. I'm with you."

I hugged Bilfern and looked at everyone else, my mind working on how I could make everyone else believe that Faren was the only choice for me. "Thank you, all. Your support is all I need to be able to make the choice I need to make."

We spent the rest of the time talking about other matters like Trenton and Ninta's child, and the plans everyone was making for the future. While we took the time to catch up and enjoy each other's company as a family, I was busy going through the options in my head.

CHAPTER 29:

A HERO RISES

The week after the family meeting was when I decided to announce everything I had presented to my family to the Assembly. I was diligent in my efforts to give the Callers time to prepare for a lengthy session, as I had a great many things to present to them, and they would need to consider and discuss the nuances behind each topic. I also assured them that every Caller needed to be present for this monumental meeting; no substitutes or stand-ins would be accepted.

Such was the seriousness of my demand that I had royal guards deliver notes that the Callers would need to sign, swearing they would be there. Typically, this was something only the ruler of Cragmorrar could do. I took the liberty anyway. Not a single complaint was made, however, as they were curious what could be so important that I would take such measures. I even received several letters inquiring about my health or offering aid if I needed any for whatever it was I was going to present to the Assembly. I took special note of those who sent such messages.

I spent a great deal of time practicing my presentation and working alongside House Orodum to outfit all of my warriors with the dimvyum well gauntlets. Faren drilled the warriors constantly on the formations and sequences they would be using in the Assembly. Darina and Bilfern worked tirelessly on a new set of armor for Faren. All the while, Trenton and Father assured the nobles that they knew what it was I intended to speak with them about, and that it would be historical in nature.

Rumors and curiosity abounded in the city as everyone tried to guess what I was going to announce. On the few occasions I took a break and went walking around the city to see what the market or craftsmen were working on, I was inundated with questions and speculation. There was also a fair amount of well wishes and encouragement from the populace, who had no doubt that whatever it was I was planning, it would be in their best interest. It made me smile to see how much faith they had in me and helped to reaffirm my convictions.

The day of the Assembly arrived with a great deal of anticipation. What I was going to do was going to change Cragmorrar and the lives of dwarves forever. Kara picked out a brilliant teal dress with gold trim and robin's egg blue sleeves. She wanted my outfit to compliment my eyes.

"Will you at least tell me if you're announcing the name of the man who has caught your eye?" Kara laughed as she braided my hair, intertwining gold ribbon in with the braid.

"I doubt that is something worthy of calling a special meeting of the Assembly," I smirked up at her. "People might be curious, but they're not that invested in my choice of a husband."

"I think you underestimate the interest the people have in you, My Lady," Kara shook her head. "Do you know that Faren won't even give me a single hint about the topic for today? I know he knows."

I could only chuckle, "He's as loyal as they come when it concerns my wishes."

Kara sighed, "Frustratingly so, My Lady. Oh, how I wish we were nobles. If you don't mind my saying so, the two of you would make a lovely couple. You interact so well together."

"Do you really think him not being a noble is a reason not to marry him?" I asked, her comment causing my curiosity to rise.

"That's not my place to say," Kara responded tactfully. "But I would think you would prefer to have someone closer to your own status. A noble, as an example."

"Well, when I accepted you into House Orodum, you were granted status," I replied in a diplomatic tone. "That status, while not nobility, at least allows you and your children to marry nobles as a matter of principle."

"A matter of principle, perhaps," Kara said hesitantly. "But as a matter of practicality… it has limitations."

"Well, I suppose that's just one more issue we need to address at some point, isn't it?" I smiled at her in the mirror.

I stepped out of the estate and found Faren standing at attention in formation with the House Orodum warriors. I smiled at him as he was wearing the new set of armor I'd had fashioned for him.

He offered me a bow, and the rest of my warriors did the same. "Princess, your warriors are assembled and are prepared to demonstrate the effectiveness of your technology. We're prepared to show the Assembly its effectiveness and bring House Orodum further glory in its debut."

My smile widened as the warriors roared in expectation. I stepped forward and cupped a hand to Faren's cheek. "I thank you all for your diligent work and practice. Today, we will demonstrate how strong the dwarves can become by utilizing our gift to wield and manipulate dimvyum in ways the other races of Thoros can only dream of!"

Another resounding roar came from the warriors.

My rhoarno was brought forward, and Faren helped me up onto it. "Are you ready?"

Faren smirked and nodded firmly, "I am, My Lady. We'll show them how much safer you can make our people."

"Then let's make some history," I smiled and directed my rhoarno forward. Faren fell in behind me, and the warriors marched in formation behind him.

We arrived at the doors to the Assembly Hall soon after. The guards stood at attention as I dismounted. One of them bowed, "Princess Merida, the Assembly is gathered and ready for you. Shall we announce you?"

"Yes, please do," I smiled as Faren moved up to my side. "Also, inform them that my House's warriors will be taking up some of the space for part of the time. There will be a demonstration that needs to be made."

"As you please, Princess," the guard bowed again and moved inside to announce our arrival.

Faren turned and barked out, "First company, fall in behind the Princess. Those remaining will await our return and assist the city guard in protecting the Assembly."

The warriors acknowledged their orders and set about positioning themselves around the building.

We entered the Assembly building and marched straight into the Assembly Hall, where my arrival was being announced. The Callers were all standing as I made my way down the stairs to the center of the room. I smiled wide as my eyes caught Father, Trenton, and Beltia sitting together. Beltia gave me a wave, and I bowed my head to her. My warriors fanned out around the Assembly, at least four to a tier.

Steward Brandon took my hands as I approached and gave each one a small kiss in turn, "Princess Merida. You look lovelier each time I see you. Are you prepared to address the Assembly?"

I tittered and placed a kiss on the old man's cheek, "Steward, it's so good to see you again. I am ready to address the Assembly."

"Very well," he replied and stepped back. He raised his arms and looked around the Assembly, "Lords and Ladies of the Assembly, Callers all, here now is Princess Merida Orodum come to speak to you this day. Listen close and hear what she has to say."

He looked back to me and bowed low, "Princess, the floor is yours."

I offered him a bow of my head in thanks, and then looked to the Assembly, "I wish to begin by thanking all of you for attending. I have a few matters to speak to you about, and then I have an announcement to make. I would appreciate your patience until I have finished making my announcement."

There was a general nod of agreement throughout the gathered Callers.

"First, I would like to announce that House Orodum has developed a special defense system for Cragmorrar," I began. "This system is called the dimvyum Well system. Dimvyum wells are a mixture of dimvyum and magic that can shift people and objects into different dimensions of the Dimvolmn. They can also be used to secure items or lock doors so that they can only be interacted with in the dimension they're tied to."

I held a hand up as a murmur began to rise through the Assembly. "This system requires very little maintenance and cannot be exploited since anyone in the different dimensions can be easily seen, as you can see by my warriors switching into those dimensions."

The warriors I brought used their gauntlets to shift between dimensions, leaving them to look like different colored specters of themselves. The Callers ogled at the spectacle and spoke in excited murmurs.

"The dimvyum wells are already set up for the city and are active," I continued. "We can create pedestals for citizens to use in the case of an emergency so that everyone can be safe during an emergency or an attack. We will be able to set the pedestals up over time."

I moved closer to Faren and motioned to him, ready to use the dial on his gauntlet. "Now, you may have noticed that my warriors are accessing the system using their gauntlets. Faren, who I know needs no introduction, convinced my scholars and craftsmen to create portable units built into gauntlets so that warriors can use this system to move around the area unfettered and unable to be harmed until they choose to shift back to the physical world."

I rested my hands behind my back and smiled. "In fact, he has also proposed a new standing military force outfitted with specialized gauntlets so that they can protect the city around the clock. He has also proposed that the funding for this force, as well as for the defense system, come from the annual dimvyum shares. If dwarves agree to receive ten percent less in their share from the sale of dimvyum each year, we can maintain the system and pay the warriors without any increase in our budget."

"Further still," I continued as the Assembly began to chat amongst themselves, "Faren has chosen some of our warriors to train warriors from the Holds in order to create similar forces in each dwarven bastion so that all dwarves can be protected by these warriors. House Orodum is also willing to create dimvyum well systems for the Holds if they request systems of their own. We would only ask for each Hold to provide the materials for the wells, as well as payment for the services of our craftsmen, who I believe we can all agree, deserve fair compensation for their work."

There was a small clamor at the idea of having to pay for the system's creation for the Holds, but I pushed forward to give them more to think about. "House Orodum will also gladly delay payment for our services until the annual dimvyum shares are distributed and collected from that. This way, no Hold loses out on its revenue or is forced to dip into their reserves to have the system set up."

That seemed to settle down the protests since the crown and the Assembly kept a fair portion of the dimvyum shares as reserve currency for emergencies or public works. I allowed the Callers to take a few moments to discuss things among themselves before moving on to the next topic.

"House Orodum would normally offer these systems free of charge," I sighed as a way to show some regret and remorse before I looked up with a smile. "However, we need the compensation, as I have personally negotiated with King Marshal of Falladrin to purchase the city of Yivreon. Some of you may know that Yivreon was formerly a dwarven outpost that was turned into a human port city. The city and its lands are now mine. And, as a show of my love for our people, I am donating it to the dwarven kingdom. It is a well-established port city with access to the Under Roads. This new Hold will give our people access to our own port so that we can expand the reach of our merchants to the Independent Marshes, Vintari, and more!"

The Assembly was abuzz with excitement over the news; the possibility of a port city sent the Callers into a frenzy of discussions. It took a minute for them all to calm down so that I could speak again.

I chuckled once they were focused on me once more. "I can appreciate your excitement. However, the port is simply a fringe benefit. I see Yivreon as a place where we can establish a place for dwarves to show how talented we are when it comes to the use of dimvyum and technology. A place where things like the dimvyum well system will become everyday items and seem mundane by comparison. To that effect, I would ask that we name my younger brother, Bilfern Nordrucan, as the lord of this new Hold. Bilfern has studied under the most experienced and knowledgeable arcanists in Cragmorrar and is one of the dwarves responsible for helping create the dimvyum wells, as well as the technology for the gauntlets. I ask that this be considered."

There was a rumbling amongst the Callers in response to this request, and I took a few moments to consider what the general consensus was. As the Callers discussed the possibility of appointing someone as young as Bilfern as the lord of Yivreon, I was allowing my stone senses to reach out into the depth of the mountain where I kept the fleshwroughts. I had been keeping them alive and imprisoned so that I could use them against Serevas or Seven. However, I was now going to release them onto Cragmorrar to give Faren the chance to use House Orodum's warriors to stop them and prove himself a hero.

No one would know I had set them loose. There would just be a sudden attack of monsters, and Faren would lead the only warriors who could safely traverse the city to put a stop to them. He would prove himself worthy, and then I would be able to announce our engagement. Just as I was willing the stone to open itself to allow the fleshwroughts their freedom, a thought occurred to me. Faren simply needed to prove himself. He was one of the most capable warriors in all of Cragmorrar. I chastised myself for the horror I was about to commit just to convince the Assembly and other nobles that he was a worthy choice. I would beat myself up about it for the rest of my life.

I shook the very idea of it and brought my senses back to the Assembly. I plastered a brave smile on my face and raised my hands. "As I always do, I will provide all the information needed for these proposals so that you can look them over, discuss them, and vote on them in the coming weeks. However, before I end my time and allow you to debate the merits of my proposals, I have an announcement to make. I would like your undivided attention for this."

Silence slowly tightened its grip on the room as I waited patiently for every voice to stop and for every eye to be focused on me. I drew a deep breath and spoke with a humble tone. "As you all know, I will be celebrating my twenty-fourth birthday soon. I should be long married by now, and the loss of my betrothed struck me deeply. Your families honored Franklin's sacrifice by allowing me a generous amount of time to grieve and settle into my life once again."

"Your patience and understanding during that time is more than anyone could ask for," I continued softly. "I don't pretend to be ignorant of the value I hold as a daughter-in-law to your families, or how desirous some are to make the best offer for my hand. I have discussed this matter at length with my family, and we have come to a conclusion: there is no man who could be offered up to me as an equal in station or deed."

I held a hand up as some protestations were presented. "Understand that I mean no disrespect to anyone. I am the Princess of Cragmorrar. I am a Exemplar. I am a mage, a hero, and the founder of the Surface Caste. There is no prince in the world to match my achievements, be they dwarf or otherwise. So I have decided how my husband will be chosen."

Now the Assembly was silent. Every Caller was present, but you would be forgiven for thinking that the hall was empty with how deathly silent it was as every dwarf in attendance listened for my decision. I could see Father and Trenton staring at me wide-eyed, wondering what I had come up with.

"I am asking for a Testament Bout to be held in one month's time," I looked up with an excited grin. "Anyone who wishes to seek my hand in marriage, be they commoner or noble, may enter for the chance to become my husband."

A clamor rose immediately, but I summoned my mana to enhance my voice. "This is my decision! There is no dowry that could now meet my demand, and no individual who matches me in deeds or station. I have lived my life trying to show that every dwarf, regardless of their station, can become greater if given the chance. I will continue to live my life this way in every aspect. If you have an issue with my decision, then you may voice them with a champion in the Testament Bout. I will take no husband who has not proven himself himself before our people and the ancestors that he is worthy and capable of protecting me."

As the cacophony of surprise rose, I smiled at Father and Trenton, who had both burst into laughter. They understood my plan to pit anyone who would try for my hand against Faren, a dwarf trained by Durdren, King Marshal, and Logan. I was a highly respected fighter in my own right, but Faren's martial combat put mine to shame. I turned on my heels and made my way out of the Assembly Hall, followed closely by Faren and the warriors of House Orodum.

The news spread like wildfire. By the end of the day, the entire city was buzzing with my announcement. Messengers were sent to the Holds and to the surface. Word spread from Cragmorrar quick as lightning, and within the next two weeks, the dwarven capital was bursting with renewed activity. Dwarves from all over Falladrin, Fransway, Var Koran, the Independent Marshes, and even Vintari arrived in the city. There were tens of thousands of merchants who came to sell their wares during the Testament Bout, to watch the spectacle, or to participate in the event itself. Every noble House had multiple representatives preparing to fight for my hand, as well as proxies who would be paid to offer my hand to another should they succeed.

The event had gotten the attention of foreign nobility. The other Fated, along with King Marshal, Cailain, and Anna, as well as a gaggle of other nobles, arrived to watch the event. There was even a small group of Franswayean nobility who arrived hoping to watch what would happen.

Because this Testament Bout would have an unprecedented number of participants, there were alterations made to the arena. The first round would take three days to get through all of the initial participants, so the arena was divided into twenty different even spaces for two fighters each. This way, there could be twenty fights going at once. While this required some minor alteration to the ceremony, it meant that more fights could be gone through faster. If the matches were done one at a time, the first round would have taken nearly a month. The second round would go much like the first, making it a two-day affair. The final rounds would take place over the next two days after that. Overall, this one Testament Bout would take a week or longer.

The first day of the event arrived, and Kara had a magnificent gown made for me. It contained thick garnet cloth with gold and silver accents, polished brass armor pieces, silver House Orodum studs, and was accessorized with gold and emerald rings and a necklace. Father insisted I wear my tiara as well. By his reasoning, if these warriors were fighting for the hand of a princess, I should absolutely look the part.

Today the Household would join me as I left the Orodum estate. Every servant, craftsman, warrior, and member of House Orodum was already outside and ready to go as I stepped out the door. There was excitement and anticipation in their eyes. Their Lady was leaving today to begin the process that would find her husband and their Lord. They had served me since I was a child, and they would all be a part of the journey that found my life's partner.

Faren stepped forward and bowed, "Princess, House Orodum is ready to accompany you to the Testament Bout Grounds. We await your command."

He helped me up onto my rhoarno, and I smiled out at the hundreds of dwarves who served under my patronage. "I want to thank you all for taking this next week to accompany me. I understand that it will slow many of you down in accomplishing your duties. You will not hear a single complaint from me. You have all helped to take care of me and raise me since the founding of House Orodum. It makes me happy that you would take the time to support me in this. Thank you all for your love and support! Now! Let's go show our support to the participants!"

The dwarves of House Orodum cheered and followed behind the warriors as I steered my rhoarno forward. The city streets were packed with dwarves. Merchant stalls lined every inch of the streets, and each one sent someone to our procession to offer a gift, which would be taken and carried by a House member. Cheers went up as we wound our way to the arena, and the bridge that connected the arena to the rest of the city was cleared so that we could make our way across without delay or obstruction.

I dismounted from my rhoarno several yards from the entrance doors and entered alongside Faren and Bilfern. The rest of my House entered and quickly filed through the large, open lobby to find their place in the stands.

Faren smiled at me, "Wish me luck."

I returned the smile and shook my head, "You don't need luck. You'll win. I believe in you."

Bilfern snickered and looked at us both, "I'm surprised anyone is willing to participate knowing Faren was going to enter."

We smirked back at Bilfern, and I quipped, "No one knew he was going to enter. He's putting his name in as a late entry. Such is the privilege of being my champion."

Bilfern laughed and clapped Faren on the shoulder, "You sly dog! The spectacle should be amazing! If she won't wish you luck, I will. Luck to you, Faren. I can't imagine anyone being more worthy to wed my sister."

If it wouldn't have shown favor, I would have kissed Faren's cheek. Instead, I simply bowed my head to him, and we parted ways. Bilfern and I made our way up to the viewing platform reserved for the most honored guests. This space was typically reserved for the individual whose honor the Testament Bout was being held in. This time, however, it would have my family, King Marshal, and the other Fated. When we stepped through the doors and onto the platform, all heads turned to gaze at us, and everyone stood.

Trianna stood and made her way over to me, giving me a tight hug. "Merida, you look beautiful."

I hugged her in return and smiled wide. "It's wonderful to see you. I hope you saved me a seat."

That got a laugh from everyone as Trianna followed me to my chair. King Marshal bowed to me. "You look absolutely stunning, Princess."

I dipped into a curtsy. "Thank you, Your Grace. I'm surprised you would come so far just to watch a Testament Bout."

Marshal laughed. "This is no ordinary Testament Bout. This will decide who the consort of the woman who will be my kingdom's greatest ally, and my good friend, will be. How could I not oversee such an event?"

"He speaks for all of us," Serena smiled and stood to rest a hand on my shoulder. "Only you could inspire so many with the possibility of marriage, Merida. How could your friends not come to stand beside you while it happens?"

"I can't help but notice we're not all here," Allen almost purred. "Where is Faren? The dress you're wearing is lovely, but you almost seem naked without him by your side."

Marylen slapped the back of Allen's head with a derisive hiss. "Do not be so crude, Allen. Apologies, Princess. I am slowly working on his manners. However, his observation, while crude in nature, is not without merit. You do seem to be lacking a bodyguard at the moment."

I chuckled and nodded to Marylen in thanks for her timely chastisement. "Faren is here." I turned and looked down into the arena where all of the participants were gathered. "He's entering the arena now."

"What?!" the collective Fated shouted and moved to the edge of the platform to look out onto the arena.

"I knew it!" Allen laughed. "I knew he wanted you!"

Marylen snatched Allen by the ear and drug him back to his seat. "If you cannot learn to be considerate of your friends and their personal relationships, then I will need to teach you. Now remain silent until the Princess allows you to speak again."

Everyone laughed at Allen as Marylen disciplined him.

Trianna just offered me a soft smile. "I'm glad he's there fighting for you. I didn't believe for a single moment that the two of you weren't meant to be together."

I smiled back and responded confidently, "He'll win."

"He has no equal as far as I know," Trenton said from his chair. He was sitting between Father and Ninta.

"It shows a great deal of faith in him, Merida," Father stood and approached me. He pulled me into a warm hug. "I think you found the perfect solution for your problem. No one can argue with the results of a Testament Bout. And I have no doubt you will get the man you're hoping for."

"I expect a warm welcome to the family when he wins," I winked and hugged him back.

"Of course, my dear, of course," Father chuckled and took his seat once more.

"Princess?" the Testament Bout Master called. "Are you ready to begin?"

I turned and nodded. "No sense in making anyone wait any longer."

"Very good, Princess," he bowed his head, then turned to signal to the dwarves around the arena, who blew into horns that caught the attention of the crowd. He waited for everyone to settle down before stepping to the ledge. "People of Cragmorrar! Today is the first day in the grand Testament Bout, which will decide who among these brave warriors will become Princess Merida Orodum's husband."

The crowd roared in excitement.

"The changes to the Testament Bout are as follows," the Testament Bout Master continued. "Multiple bouts will be fought at the same time, with a judge watching each match to assure that both combatants fight with honor. Any match thought to have been fought with anything less than each warrior's best effort will be considered suspect, and each participant will be disqualified. Next, if any third parties are discovered to have influenced a bout, the warriors for that bout will be disqualified, and the third party, regardless of rank or station, will be severely punished. Finally, because our Princess does not wish for anyone to receive permanent harm or death in the proceedings, all weapons used will be blunted until the final round, and any attempt at causing permanent injury or death will cause the offender to be disqualified."

The words hung in the air for several moments while everyone processed them. The Testament Bout Master looked to me, "Princess? Would you like to address the crowd?"

I smiled and nodded. "Certainly."

He turned back to the crowd and raised his hands. "Now, I bid you all to stand as Princess Orodum addresses you all!"

The crowd roared once again as I stepped up to the side of the Testament Bout Master and waved to everyone in attendance.

It took some time for the cheers to die down before I could say anything. "First, I want to thank all of the warriors who are willing to participate in this Testament Bout. Your bravery for entering the arena with such odds speaks to your opinion of me, and I am both honored and flattered. Just by entering the arena, you have shown me that I am loved by my people in a way I've never considered before. And to those in attendance, and those who have come from outside of Cragmorrar, it does my heart good to see the city so lively again."

"The creation of the Surface Caste and the retaking of the Holds has spread our people out over the expanse of the Under Roads and Falladrin," I smiled wide. "This feels like seeing all of my family coming home again. Thank you all for coming to this event, and good luck to all of you brave enough to step foot inside the arena!"

The roar of the crowd was deafening. I waved at everyone for a few more moments before returning to my seat. The Testament Bout Master instructed those not scheduled for the first bouts to exit the arena, and then the battles commenced.

Regardless of my wishes for the warriors to try and battle in as safe a manner as possible, the bouts were displays of sheer aggression. The warriors fought fiercely, digging deep into their skills and their determination to offer their best effort in every match. Bones were broken, blood was spilled, and the ferocity and skill of the dwarves were put on display for all to see. Each series of bouts lasted only a few minutes, with combatants resting until the final match in their group was finished. Then squires and physicians would rush onto the field to aid the warriors out of the arena. A large group of field hands would then quickly clean each of the combat areas of blood or broken equipment pieces so that the next group was allowed onto the Testament Bout floor.

So it went for the next six days. Warriors rose and fell. Underdogs rose among the ranks while some favorites surprisingly fell. Commoners were making a name for themselves, and nobles raised the prestige of their families. There was excitement in the air as people placed bets on who the winner would be in individual bets or who would win overall. The fights continued for ten hours every day for six days until only a handful of warriors remained on the final day.

True to my expectations, Faren was among the finalists. Each night he'd come home, I had Trianna work her healing magic on him to soothe any wounds he suffered or fatigue he might have been feeling. Compared to the others in the final round, he was still in just as good a shape as he had been on the very first day. That isn't to say that other families hadn't hired mages to help their fighters as well, but none of them were looking as fit as Faren was as they all stepped out onto the field for the morning ceremony.

The Testament Bout Master stepped forward and looked over the final four competitors. "People of Cragmorrar, I am proud to present to you these final four warriors. At the end of the day, one of these four men will have won the hand of our beloved Princess Merida Orodum!"

The crowd cheered with palpable excitement.

"Today's battle will adhere to the standard format of two combatants in the arena at a time," he continued. "There will be two matches, each match between two of these fine warriors. Then we will allow the warriors to rest for an hour before the match to decide the winner. Warriors, are you ready?"

All four nodded their readiness.

"Then I invite Faren Orodum and Mersh Brodens to remain in the arena and for—"

The Testament Bout Master's words were cut off in a gasp as a magical portal opened in the middle of the arena. Faren and the four other warriors went into a defensive stance, but the other Fated and I cursed in fear as a ridiculously tall human stepped through. The man had ungainly long arms with fingers that ended in long, talon-like nails. His body was stretched flesh over open wounds, covered by feather pauldrons and a long, black robe. His face was contorted and seemed to be pulled back across the left side of his head.

Varrimus. It was Varrimus! How had he managed to get revived? We all collectively looked at Allen.

"How is he here?!?" we shouted at him.

Allen could only shrug in panic. "I have no idea! My cousins are safe in the Tower, and my Father keeps in regular contact! None of my other relatives have gone missing!"

Varrimus was an ancient Vintari Magister and high priest of Dumah that Allen's uncle had sealed away with his blood magic. To be free, it would mean that someone from Allen's family had to have had their blood used in a ritual to release the seal. There he stood, surveying the arena. Then he looked up and stared directly at me.

"Ah," his voice rumbled through the arena with bass enough to cause me to turn my head as it ached, "there you are. The dwarf who would claim the souls of the gods, who would dare to step into the Dimvolmn and claim it as her own whilst spitting in the face of her betters. I will show you the fate of those who would tread in the path of a god."

The threat was made, but Varrimus' arrogance failed to let him realize that he was surrounded and that four of the strongest dwarf warriors in Thoros were within striking distance. Faren and the others charged the cursed magister, enlightening Varrimus to the precarious situation in which he found himself.

As the warriors began to attack Varrimus, I stood and moved to leave the stands so I could join them in battle. The Testament Bout Master put his hand out to block me, seeming to understand my intentions. "Princess, you can't. I understand what you mean to do, but look at the crowd. They wish to leap into the arena and aid in the battle as well. But this is a Testament Bout. None but the participants may enter the arena no matter what happens. Unless the four warriors fall, we can do nothing unless we dishonor their effort and the will of the ancestors."

I glared at him in fury and defiance, as well as frustrated understanding. I turned back to the arena and clutched the railing, "If they die, I will kill him..."

"You will not get the chance, Princess," the Testament Bout Master said with a sure tone. "You will have to try and get to him before the thousands of dwarves ahead of you do. They will cut him down in vengeance for the valiant warriors already fighting him and to protect you."

I looked back out on the scene unfolding before me and prayed quietly for Faren's safety. I knew I could use my abilities to kill or at least incapacitate Varrimus, but everyone would know I interfered. So I watched, waited, and prayed.

The prowess of the warriors was impressive. Even without magic, they were keeping Varrimus on his heels with coordinated strikes and deft maneuvers that the ancient mage couldn't predict. Each time Varrimus was ready to cast a spell, a shield would slam into him, a sword would cut into him, a mace would swipe his arms out of sync, a hammer would fly into his twisted face. Faren seemed to take charge, commanding and coordinating the others to dash in and out to keep the monstrosity off balance and guessing.

Varrimus was no fool, however. He certainly wasn't harmless without his magic. His lithe, wiry form was far more powerful than it would lead you to believe. Every so often he would retaliate, swiping out with a powerful clawed hand and sending the offending dwarf cascading away from him, disrupting the flow of the quartet's attacks. Varrimus was taking damage, but the dwarves were suffering more. Regardless of his appearance as a withered human, Varrimus was much more durable than he seemed.

One dwarf charged in to strike at Varrimus' back when the creature wheeled on him and snatched him up by the neck; his elongated fingers completely twisting around the dwarf's neck. He raised the dwarf up, the opponent kicking and clutching at the mage's powerful hand as Varrimus scowled at him. With an almost dismissive flick of his wrist, Varrimus snapped the dwarf's neck before releasing him and letting his lifeless body drop unceremoniously to the ground in a heap.

Varrimus' disapproving growl could be heard from the platform I watched from. He turned and looked up at me. "Pathetic. Will you not come down and face me yourself? How many of your people will you allow to die before you summon your courage to test your power against me?"

I wanted to kill him then and there. I wanted to show him the power of a titan, to teach him fear beyond comprehension before ending his wicked life. The fury on my face had to be apparent, but I straightened myself and put on an imperious air as I responded with all eyes on me, "You are a diseased worm. You do not warrant my intervention. You have entered the Testament Bout Arena, and the warriors you face now are more than enough to end your miserable existence. You will not conquer them. And as you lay bleeding in the sands with them standing over you, you will understand the power of our people and how far below us you are. If you think you are my equal, prove your power in the arena. Defeat these warriors. Only then will I deign to come down and face you."

Varrimus macabre features contorted into a sickening grin as he laughed, "You think these vermin are a threat to me? Very well, Princess. I will slaughter your warriors, and then I will flay you alive. Enjoy the show, for as soon as they are dead, your end will be close behind them."

I was betting on Varrimus' pride to get the best of him. His arrogance had made him sloppy in the game, and it played out to my advantage now as well. Varrimus turned to face the three remaining dwarves as Faren gave the order to surround him.

"Mersh!" Faren shouted as the dwarves spread out. "Look for openings. Spine and ribs. Keep him protecting his center! Serrimo! Watch the arms! Disrupt the somatic gestures!"

The two others acknowledged the orders. Varrimus was cunning, however, and was capable of weaving the somatic movements of his spells into melee strikes. His vitals were much higher than the warriors were used to attacking; similar in height to an ogre's, though more compact.

Another minute or so passed as the trio jumped in and out of the former magister's range, striking and hindering him to the best of their ability until Varrimus found his footing for a moment and jabbed his arm out in a blinding snap, pointing his clawed fingers forward like a spear to impale Serrimo Hermis. The skewered dwarf defiantly slashed his axe across the inside of Varrimus' elbow, rending the muscle from bone and causing the limb to go limp. Varrimus roared in pain and whipped himself to the side, flinging Serrimo's corpse like a missile so that it hit Mersh square in the chest, knocking him out cold from the force of the impact.

Varrimus turned to face Faren and snarled, "Now, little warrior, you are alone. I shall toy with you first; torture you in front of your princess, make you beg for mercy until the whim to kill you finally comes to me. Then, I shall take that cow of a— ARHG!!!"

The sound of pain Varrimus let out confused everyone but me. I understood what had happened because only I could sense it. Faren had willed the very stone beneath his feet to jump up into a spike to skewer the beast's foot.

"You have made your final two mistakes, wretch," Faren snarled. "While the others were alive, I was limited to fighting according to the limits of my peers. Your first mistake was leaving me for last. Now that you are my only opponent, I can use my abilities to their fullest. Your second mistake was insulting the woman I love. Before you die, I will reach into that gaping hole you call a mouth and rip out your tongue and let you drown in your own blood. Now ready yourself, creature, for I am your end and I do not fear you."

The arena cheered in response to Faren's defiance. Varrimus, now with time to maneuver, worked his magic to cast a spell of caustic green magic at the remaining warrior. Faren quickly shifted in the blue spectrum of the Dimvolmn using his dimvyum well dial, allowing the spell to pass through him harmlessly.

"What blasphemy is this?" Varrimus spat as Faren's spectral form charged forward. He summoned an arcane shield to protect himself, but Faren's spectral sword passed through it and materialized back into the physical realm just in time to bite into his gut, quickly puncturing the monster's innards and spilling its black blood in a fierce spurt.

"I am Faren Orodum!" Faren roared as he raised his shield to deflect a swipe of Varrimus' claws. He stepped in quickly and slashed at the magister's robes to bite at his ankles.

"Bodyguard to Princess Merida Orodum!" He phased into the red spectrum and repositioned himself to Varrimus' flank as the monstrosity summoned a circle of flame around himself in an attempt to get Faren away. Faren reemerged from the Dimvolmn and rammed the edge of his shield into the back of Varrimus' knees, causing the giant to topple forward.

"Gifted grace by the Titans!" Faren roared as he summoned a pillar of stone to quickly crash into Varrimus' head, sending him falling backwards as quickly as he had fallen forward.

Varrimus had tried to rise using his good arm, but Faren was already swinging his sword, twisting his body to add all the power in his form to the strike to lop the limb off through the bicep. The magister roared in pain as his body flopped back to the ground. With one arm gone and the other useless, he was now prone and nearly helpless. He tried to collect himself and roll to get his feet beneath him but Faren was too fast, kicking him hard in the face to force him back onto his back.

Faren planted an armored foot on the ancient magister's neck and glared down at him. "And as my Princess said before, you are nothing but a diseased worm, unworthy of her intervention. You have witnessed the power granted to the dwarves through her ingenuity. You have faced her champion and been found wanting. And now, as I promised…" He slammed his fist into Varrimus' mouth and took hold of his tongue, ripping it out with a bloody spray. "You will die, drowning in your own blood."

Varrimus panicked and twisted beneath Faren's boot as he struggled to save his life somehow. Faren's hold on him was too strong, however, and he would not be budged. The flailing became more and more desperate, and just as the death throws came to a climax, another portal opened and Faren was forced to jump back as a massive blade swung out from it in an attempt to cleave Faren's head from his body.

Faren brought his shield up just as Seven stepped out from the portal, a horribly wicked grin on his face. He looked around and found Faren before him, and the sight caused him to laugh, "You? The magister fell to you? It is good, then, that I allowed him to fall. You have done the work for me…" He looked around until he noticed me in the stands. "Ah! There she is. You should punish your bodyguard, Princess. For he has unknowingly granted me the power of a magister!"

As everyone tried to register what the Fated scourgespawn meant, Seven threw himself down and bit out Varrimus' throat. The magister arched his back as he tried to fight or delay the inevitable, but the blood loss and injuries took their toll, and his life left him. Seven stood and laughed as Varrimus' soul leapt to the closest scourgespawn in the area… Seven itself…

Seven roared in a way that seemed offensive to the ears of all. Varrimus' soul and power fought Seven's will for dominance over his body, and Seven dropped to his knees. There was a moment of silence, and Faren charged in, ready to end the threat before it could manifest itself. The attempt was too late. Seven waved his hand and sent a burst of concussive force, sending Faren toppling away from him. It seemed like he was still struggling with the power and will of Varrimus as he stood shakily to his feet. It looked as if he wanted to do more but resigned himself to a mocking grin in my direction before leaping back through the portal.

Everyone stared at the remains of the area as the portal closed. We waited with baited breath to see what would happen next. After several agonizing moments, Faren stirred and slowly stood to his feet. There was a collective inhalation of breath before everyone screamed in victory and joy.

I didn't wait for any announcement or ceremony. I rushed through the door of the platform and down the stairs and path that would lead me to the arena. I willed the doors open and rushed through, sprinting across the arena, jumping at Faren and wrapping my arms around his neck and kissing him deeply. He crushed me in his embrace, the black blood of Varrimus staining my gown, but I didn't care. The crowd's cheers grew to a fevered pitch in celebration, but I didn't care. There couldn't be any doubt now. Faren was worthy in the eyes of the ancestors and every dwarf that witnessed the battle, or those that would be told about it afterwards.

I smiled up at him, relief washing through me at his safety, "I love you so much…"

"I love you too," he rested his forehead against mine, his eyes locked on my gaze. "I will never let anyone hurt you."

"I would have stopped him if—" I tried to explain.

He shook his head in understanding. "I know. The rules of the Testament Bout. You don't have to apologize. We trained to fight like this. So we were ready together."

I nodded as my eyes began to well with tears. I sniffled to keep from crying and took his hand. Turning, I raised his hand into the air. "People of Cragmorrar! I present to you Faren Orodum, my betrothed as willed by the ancestors and proven in combat against the greatest warriors of dwarves and monsters!"

The arena shook with the cheers of the crowd.

Faren and I moved together to check on Mersh who had been knocked out. We moved Serrimo's body respectfully and helped Mersh to his feet. Dwarves from the stands rushed forward, to carry the body of the fallen warriors respectfully back into the waiting area that warriors used to prepare for their bouts. The next few hours were a surreal mixture of celebration and mourning as the people knew who I would wed while weighing that knowledge against the loss of fine warriors in the defense of Cragmorrar against a sudden, powerful threat.

Over the next few days a funeral was prepared for the fallen dwarves who would be interred in the arena with statues raised in their honor. As that was being taken care of, I had to try and figure out how Varrimus had been freed, how he and Seven had known to appear in the arena, and how they managed to do so when there would be so few warriors in the arena. The questions would plague me for some time, but they would also force us to begin an investigation. Trianna, Allen, Marylen, and I would begin creating wards around the city to prevent such magic being used to enter unwarranted again.

For all of the questions and work the intrusion had caused, Faren's triumph was celebrated. He was hailed as a hero among the dwarves and his battle was put to song and story. Now when we walked the streets we could do so hand-in-hand and be met with glad tidings and cheers. There was no need to hide our affection. It was a somber relief considering the cost.

There were many questions that needed answering. However, Faren's display of the dimvyum well system during his fight against Varrimus brought a unanimous vote for its implementation in Cragmorrar and the Holds. Because of the dimvyum well system's crucial role in the battle, Bilfern was chosen to be the Lord of Yivreon in the hopes that he would spearhead new dimvyum technologies to further protect our people from such magical incursions. In the end, Varrimus only served to strengthen the resolve of the dwarves and push my agenda forward. However, the expression Seven gave me before he left made my blood run cold whenever I thought about it.

It seemed to me that he had manipulated the events, hoping Varrimus would be killed… hoping that he could swoop in and claim the old magister's power. I wondered with dread in my heart if we hadn't done his dirty work for him. Only time would tell.

CHAPTER 30:

CONSOLIDATION AND INVESTIGATION

With everything that had happened, the next two months were spent in a rush. The first thing that needed to happen was for the betrothal between Faren and me to be formally recognized by Father. Papers needed to be drawn up and agreements made between my family and Faren's. However, this particular detail was rather pointless since Faren's family was already a part of mine by right of me taking them in when I became an Exemplar. Essentially, nothing would really change. Normally, the lesser family would offer a dowry and services to the higher-ranked family, but with Rita's business already giving me a substantial percentage from her earnings, this was essentially hand-waived.

Father insisted that we have a formal dinner to welcome them all into the family. He even had formal outfits made for Kara, Rita, and Faren as a welcoming gift for them to wear to the dinner. Kara was, of course, ecstatic that Faren had won my hand and wore the outfit proudly to the dinner. It wasn't the first time we'd all been in the same room for dinner, but it was the first time Faren, Rita, and Kara were allowed to sit with us. Everything went wonderfully as the families finally got the opportunity to truly engage in fellowship. We shared stories, jokes, memories, and hopes for the future.

Serena, Trianna, and Aelfric all returned to their respective domains. Allen, however, asked for my assistance in checking on his family. He understood that I couldn't exactly go too far, so he agreed to cross the ocean and head to Fetral while I agreed to go to Farthering to check on his uncle, aunt, and cousin. This was the option I wanted anyway. It would allow me to get back just in time for my birthday.

Because we would be heading in that direction, we prepared Bilfern to move to Yivreon. Over the past few weeks, we had been checking with nobles from Cragmorrar and the other Holds to see which would be the best to bring with him. Bilfern also had the idea to pick families from the Surface Caste to help with trade and manufacturing. By the time we were ready to leave, Bilfern had a retinue of warriors, nobles, and craftsmen enough to make up a small noble house and a small community of traders. These dwarves, along with the ones already operating in Yivreon because of the port, would make for a formidable start for the fledgling Hold.

The trip went quickly and smoothly. A decent portion of the road built out from Cragmorrar was finished down to the foot of the mountain. I spent the majority of the trip concentrating on creating more road every moment we were traveling. While I understood that I was actively moving stone and manipulating the geography so that the stone would appear above the ground and form into the road, leveling it out and molding it so that any rainwater would drain deep into the ground, the others simply saw the road appearing before us several yards ahead. I may not have seemed like I was working diligently, but the focus it required to search the area for proper stone, move it to where it was needed, while simultaneously making sure the soil filled in around it so that sinkholes wouldn't occur took quite the toll on me mentally. Especially when I was concentrating for nearly twelve hours a day for nearly a month.

We stopped in Cliffside, bringing the load along with us. There was an entire night of congratulatory celebration with the dwarves in Cliffside. They wanted to celebrate Faren's victory over Varrimus and our engagement. Earl Edward joined in the festivities and ensured that he would have shipments from Cliffside leave through Yivreon for the foreseeable future to bolster the Hold's revenue as a favor to me. Coralstine might be closer, but he had a suspicion that we would be able to turn Yivreon into a more efficient port.

Orlimar was, unfortunately, too far out of our way to visit, but Trianna and Aelfric visited up at the main road where a small town was slowly establishing itself as something of a trading town between Cliffside and Orlimar. I was surprised to see that the road from Orlimar was already built up to this point. Apparently, the Orlimar dwarves had been quite industrious and understood the value of a dedicated stone road that led to the city.

We continued on till we came to Yivreon. The path to Yivreon was narrow and didn't make for the most convenient for trading caravans. So, while I created the road, I also molded the mountain path to be wider and more inviting. We held a small ceremony, dedicating the city and the Hold that would be created beneath it to the dwarven kingdom and naming Bilfern the official lord of the Hold. One of the larger buildings had been set aside for him until the Hold could be properly excavated and his permanent estate could be created. I remained there for a week, helping Bilfern establish a council he could rely on for advice while he got used to ruling the Hold.

The largest loss was Darina. She had decided to go with Bilfern and work to make Yivreon into the city it had the potential to be. This would diminish House Orodum's overall arcane research and craftsmanship, but it would be a net boon to dwarves as a whole. Luckily, scholars and craftsmen interested in the dimvyum technology we had spearheaded had learned well from Darina and there was a large number of them I could rely on for new innovations.

After a week, Faren and I left Yivreon, wishing Bilfern luck and bidding him to write as often as possible. If he needed any advice, I would be happy to give it. We turned north and made our way to Farthering.

It wasn't difficult to find the Lemlal house. After all, Matthew had not been shy about giving me directions in the few letters we'd traded since I agreed to start a correspondence. When we arrived, a servant in the front yard seemed startled and rushed into the house to announce that we were coming.

Faren dismounted from his rhoarno then helped me down from mine. I didn't need the help, but he'd started doing it as a public show of affection. The warriors that were escorting us brought their mounts to the side of the road and began setting up camp.

"He's going to fawn all over you, Merida," Faren chuckled. "Try to be patient with him."

I huffed and looked up at Faren. "When am I ever not nice? People fawn over me every day, and I've never been rude about it."

"This is true…" Faren seemed amused, "but those are your people. This is a fan. And he's never met you before."

"Fair enough," I conceded as I removed my riding gloves. I folded the gloves and tucked them into my belt. "But I'm sure it won't be as bad as you might be—"

"Come on, Linda! Come on! We can't keep her waiting a moment longer!" a man's voice shouted excitedly from the house.

I looked at where the commotion was coming from and saw a man and woman somewhere in their fifties leaving the house surrounded by an uncoordinated handful of maids. I recognized the woman immediately as Linda Lemlal, the mother of the main character from Age of Dragons 2. If she were following the man, that would have to make him Matthew, her husband. Typically, he would be dead from illness by now if Allen hadn't intervened in that regard. The group scurried quickly across the front yard and stopped just at the fence, making an amusing show of trying to gather into a proper greeting formation.

Matthew and Linda stepped forward, and the group of maids followed along in a gaggle. Matthew seemed like he was about to burst with excitement while Linda looked like she was pleased but understood she was about to be embarrassed.

They stopped only a few feet away. Matthew dipped into a low bow as Linda and the maids curtsied. "Princess Merida Orodum! I am Matthew Lemlal, and this is my wife Linda Lemlal. It is the greatest honor of my life to be able to meet you in person. What brings you to our home?"

I did an excellent job of keeping my composure and not laughing at the exuberant display. I lowered myself into a curtsy. "Sir Matthew! It's wonderful to finally meet you. Your ideas and theories that you've shared in our correspondence have been truly fascinating to go over. They've made for excellent evening reading as my betrothed can attest to. I've been doing a great many comparisons to known magical theories with them."

"You flatter me, Princess," Matthew beamed. He was trying to sound humble but it was more like a child meeting their hero for the first time—

more awe than simply auspicious.

"Indeed she does," Linda said calmly. "Don't let it go to her head, dear."

I chuckled and patted the air. "I'm actually here to check on you as a favor to Allen." I arched my brows as I looked around, growing slowly concerned. "May I ask where your son Carter is? Isn't he supposed to be here?"

Matthew and Linda shared a look, and Linda answered, "He left a few months ago to check on our relatives in Fetral. We were going to go, but Matthew's health isn't the best, and travel doesn't really suit him. So Carter volunteered. Why do you ask?"

I turned and looked back at Faren and gave him a concerned expression. His face mirrored mine, and he gave me a nod. Turning back, I motioned to the house. "I think we should speak somewhere more private."

The pair looked curious, and Matthew cleared his throat. "Ah. Yes, of course, Princess. If you'll please follow us, we can speak in the study." He turned and waved his hands at the maids. "Go get food and drink for our guests. Quickly!"

The maids seemed to panic for a moment before they ran back inside to complete the command as Matthew and Linda led us into their home. We were brought into one of the warmest decorated rooms I'd ever seen. The wood was stained a beautiful cherry, the leather furniture a deep brown, and the lamps gave off a soothing orange-red glow. The books that lined the walls gave the room a wonderfully tangy, savory scent that only aged parchment and leather could give off.

Linda sat on a sofa while Matthew insisted I take the largest chair, which had some clear loving wear on it. It was obviously his personal chair. This was a clear sign of deference, and I couldn't help but be flattered by it. I understood the significance of the man of the house offering up his seat to another. Faren sat on a loveseat while Matthew joined Linda on the sofa.

"Now," Matthew offered, "may I ask what you needed to speak to us about, Princess? It clearly concerns our family."

I nodded. "Your mind is as quick as ever, Matthew. I'm sure you've heard by now that my betrothed defeated a powerful sorcerer recently in order to win my hand, yes?"

Matthew seemed understandably confused but nodded all the same, "Word has reached us of the tale, Princess, yes. Why do you mention this? And what does it have to do with our family?"

"Everything," Faren said, his tone dead serious.

"The sorcerer Faren defeated was the fallen Vintari Magister, Varrimus," I said.

"What?!?" Matthew shouted. He shook his head fiercely. "No. I don't know how you know that name, but that's impossible. You could not have met Varrimus, let alone defeated him. He is not a normal creature, and he has been sealed away—"

"Inside a Scourge Sentinels prison in the Vinmark Mountains," I finished for him. "Sealed away by a blood magic spell of your own design, and only able to be broken by using the blood of someone from your family line."

Matthew sputtered as I issued the information, "H-how do you know all of that?"

"Did your nephew not explain what he, Faren, and I are?" I asked. "We call ourselves Fated; individuals born with great knowledge of Thoros' past and future. It's how we have all been able to grow in stature and power, and how we were able to plan for and defeat the Scourge. We've all known about you and your past since the day we were born."

"But... how?" Linda asked, clearly amazed and skeptical at the same time.

"We don't know," Faren answered honestly. "We just were. We were able to find each other using that knowledge. So we've been working together to try and make the world better."

"We do know, however, who and what Varrimus was," I affirmed. "We all knew who he was when he appeared. We all looked to Allen, wondering how he could have been there since we knew the conditions that were required for him to be freed."

"...and you actually defeated him?" Matthew asked with awe.

I shook my head, "I didn't. Faren did. But before he could finish Varrimus off, another fated—one who was born as a scourgespawn—appeared and bit the magister's throat out and absorbed his soul. He didn't transform into Varrimus before making his escape."

"He didn't…" Matthew mused. He shook his head, "No, that cannot be. Varrimus is akin to an archdemon. If he's killed, he takes the closest scourgespawn and reforms himself."

"Well, he couldn't reform himself," I assured him. "There seemed to be some sort of conflict within the scourgespawn, but in the end, it seemed he won the contest of wills."

"If this is true, then he may now have access to all of Varrimus' power," Matthew shuddered.

"That is what we're afraid of," I sighed and lowered my head. "In order to determine how Varrimus was freed, Allen and I agreed to check on his family. I can't afford to take the time to go to Fetral, nor have I ever spoken or corresponded with any of them. So Allen has gone to check on your family there while I agreed to check on you here in Farthering. Right now, the only person unaccounted for is Carter…"

"Oh no…" Linda gasped and covered her mouth. "You don't think something has happened to him, do you?"

I could only shrug as Faren leaned forward to answer, "We can't be sure just yet. We expected to find him here, but if he left to check on your family in Fetral, he may be there or anywhere in between while traveling. When we speak with Allen again, we'll see if Carter made it safely to Fetral and send word to you about what we discover."

"As Faren said," I agreed. "We still need to find out the method, or who the scourgespawn used to awaken Varrimus. What is certain, though, is that the magister is dead. He is no threat to Thoros anymore, but Seven, the scourgespawn who absorbed his soul, will no doubt prove to be an even greater threat."

Matthew shook his head in distress. "I cannot imagine a greater threat to the world. However, if my seal was broken, it means I failed in my attempt to keep him locked away. That also means that I have a duty to help however I can. Is there anything you can think of that I can do?"

I took several moments to consider his question. "If I'm being honest, I don't think you're in any more danger at this point. Seven already freed Varrimus, so he has no more use for your family. If you want to help, I would appreciate it if you could research two things for me."

"Name them, Princess," Matthew bowed his head. "I will devote myself to their study."

"I need help researching the elven Pantheon," I admitted. "Specifically Trith'Emel, the Hungering Hound. I know who he is specifically, and I know of some of his abilities. However, there are gaps in my knowledge: his weaknesses, his failings, his limits. Anything you can find, regardless of how minuscule in nature it may be, would be invaluable."

"Of course, Princess," Matthew nodded, his eyes darting around his library as if already considering which tomes to begin with. "And what might the other be?"

"Soul capturing or destroying," I stated seriously. "I know there is at least one method that the elves used to capture a living soul so that they were able to communicate with it. With this knowledge, defeating Seven and Trith'Emel might be made easier."

"I understand, Princess," Matthew crossed his arms and nodded. "I will send you regular reports as I discover more. I will also endeavor to send you anything I find that might be useful in general."

I bowed my head in thanks. "I will be grateful for any information you can provide."

The maids came soon after with food and drinks. We talked at length about possible solutions and ideas that Matthew already had. I also went in-depth about my titan abilities to sate Malcom's curiosity. We stayed the night at Matthew's request and Linda's insistence. It was comfortable enough, and they were fine hosts, though Matthew did continually pry about my magical nature, capabilities, and potential.

We left the next day, taking the northern road home that would lead us past Demirren and Coralstine. I continued to conjure the stone road the entire time. King Marshal hosted us in Demirren and had a laugh at how he wouldn't be receiving much in the way of payments for Yivreon as he realized I was supplementing the road construction with my abilities. Still, he didn't seem to mind since it meant that the roads would be finished far sooner than he expected, which meant that travel would become faster and safer for his people.

Serena and Alford were happy to receive us. Serena, in particular, was excited to hear that we had begun settling into Yivreon and to hear our plans for it. I could tell that she was chalking that up as a success for her aspirations, but I wasn't going to bother telling her that she had no way to extort me for support. Still, I could appreciate her effort. She had some good ideas, in any case. I would consider her proposal when it eventually came.

It was a little over two months since I'd left Cragmorrar by the time we returned. Winter was creeping in, and I was rather surprised that the city was still bustling just as much as it had been during the tournament. Faren and I couldn't discern the reason why, but I suspected it was because I had said it made me happy to see the city so busy again. I couldn't have been more wrong.

CHAPTER 31:

CONVICTION

Orzamar was teeming with excitement as we arrived. Unlike the typical warm welcome I received whenever I returned, this energy was different. The people were already celebrating, dancing, toasting drinks, and merry-making. Faren and I shared curious looks, and I called to a nearby dwarf as we made our way up the pass that would lead to the gates of the city.

"Sir! Sir!" I called to the dwarf, who seemed well into his cups at this point.

He turned and looked amazed at who was calling him. He hurried over and bowed, "Princess Orodum! It is an honor to speak with you! How can this humble craftsman serve you?"

I waved my arm to motion to the rest of the cheering dwarves. "What is going on? What has everyone in such high spirits?"

He looked up at me in surprise. "Has word not reached you yet, Princess?"

I arched my brows. "Word of what?"

"Your brother's child has been born, Princess," the dwarf answered. "A baby—"

"STOP!" I shouted. "Don't tell me! Faren! Take my rhoarno to the House and meet me at the palace!" I shouted as I dismounted and handed the reins quickly over to Faren.

Faren laughed and took the reins to my rhoarno. "Of course, my love. I'll be there shortly."

I nodded and sunk into the stone, molding it so that it opened up beneath me, and then commanded it to push me along quickly through the mountain. I'd been practicing moving through the stone for some time now, and I finally had a reason beyond experimentation to use it. It took only moments for me to emerge at the palace entrance, startling the guards as I popped out of the very street.

"P-princess?" one of the guards started.

"Apologies for the strange arrival, but I'd just heard about the baby," I explained. I quickly added, "Don't say what it is! Just please allow me entrance!"

"Oh! Of course, Princess!" the other guard nodded as the pair opened the door quickly.

"Thank you!" I shouted as I scooped up my dress so I could run without tripping over it. I rushed through the palace, taking the halls quickly in practiced steps. At this point, most of the older guards knew to simply open the doors and laugh, as they had seen me do the same thing since I was a child. The newer guards no doubt questioned the veterans, but none dared stop me.

I burst into Trenton's chambers, finding him and Ninta sitting with Father near the fire. I was all smiles and energy and completely ignored everyone except Ninta and the swaddled child she was holding.

Ninta laughed and simply offered the baby up to me as I approached. "Well, I see you've heard the news."

I carefully took the babe into my arms and tucked it close to my bosom, taking in the sight of the child as I ran a finger over its cheek. "Only just now! And what is your name, little one?"

Trenton chuckled and stood, moving over to hug me gently and accept a kiss on the cheek in return. "His name is Durnan."

I gasped and looked down at the baby. "Durnan Nordrucan. Did you know that the ancestor who shares your name was a Scourge Sentinel? He served valiantly in the Western Approach and brought great honor to our House. I have no doubt that you'll prove to be his equal at the very least."

"Don't put such high hopes on the lad just yet," Father hummed, but smiled and shook his head. "We don't know his mind just yet."

"He is a Nordrucan," I squeaked at Durnan as I rubbed my nose to his. "He is destined to do great things for his family and his people. Oh!" I chirped as Durnan reached up and grabbed my nose. The tender touch of the baby's grip brought a laugh from me. "You see there? He's already grasping for greatness."

"You realize you just called yourself great, yes Sister?" Trenton huffed.

"She doesn't lie," Faren replied as he entered the room, quickly closing the distance between the door and the rest of us.

"Faren," Father hailed him, "how was the journey, lad?"

Faren bowed to everyone. "It went well, Majesty. Young Bilfern seemed well on his way to getting settled as the lord of Yivreon. And we found the information the Princess was looking for after the assault on the Testament Bout."

"She is your betrothed, Faren," Father smiled and chuckled softly. "I think you can call her by her name now."

Faren bowed his head. "Of course, Majesty. Forgive me. I'm still used to the formalities."

"You're family now, Faren," Trenton said as he clapped Faren's back. "I daresay Merida has considered you family since you were brought into service. Now we all consider you such. You're welcome to speak frankly with us."

As the others were speaking, I was thinking over the implications of

Durnan's birth. He represented the future of our family, the future of our people. He was the first of the next generation of Nordrucans, and I couldn't help but think that he might not live to see his potential fulfilled if the current threats I knew of remained at large. A shadow grew inside me and my chest tightened as I understood what had to be done.

"Faren," I said, my tone somber.

"Yes, my love?" he replied, his tone reflecting that he understood something was wrong just by hearing how I spoke.

"Ready the warriors immediately," I said as I turned toward him, Durnan clutched close and my expression deadly. "Full deployment. Every warrior. Every rhoarno. We're mobilizing."

"At once," Faren nodded and turned on his heel, marching quickly out of the room.

Trenton, Father, and Ninta looked around in confusion.

"Merida, what's wrong?" Father asked as he stood.

"I'm sorry, but I need to put an end to something." I kissed Durnan's cheek and handed him carefully back to Ninta.

"What is it?" Trenton asked, stepping forward and grabbing my shoulder. "Tell me, Merida. What has you in such a mood?"

I looked up at Trenton. "There are two enemies we need to put down as soon as possible. I know for certain where one is and I intend to attack his fortress."

"You're certain he's dangerous enough to warrant your entire House?" Trenton asked.

"And then some," I nodded firmly. "He threatens all of Thoros and every living being, Durnan included."

"Then you will wait a month," Trenton's tone brooked no negotiation. "House Nordrucan's forces will join you. I will help you kill this enemy."

"You need to stay with your new family," I argued.

"No," Trenton glared at me. "I need to protect my family. We need to protect our people. This is our duty as Nordrucans. If this enemy is strong enough to threaten even you, then all of Cragmorrar should be ready to go to war."

"He is a powerful mage," I tried to explain. "On par with my own abilities or even stronger. I can't guarantee I'll succeed. But I think I can."

"All the more reason for you to have reinforcements," Trenton said. "Call your Fated friends and see what aid they can send as well."

"I can't," I sighed, realizing that truth in the moment. "Except for Trianna and Aelfric, I'm not confident they won't send a warning to the enemy just to gain favor and be allowed to live."

"Then call who you can," Father insisted. "We must do our best to guarantee your success. If this mage is as powerful as you believe, then we should send word to King Marshal and request the aid of Templars. They can help against this mage."

I didn't like the idea of waiting, but Father and Trenton made good points. If I were going to attack Serevas, it wouldn't hurt to have a larger force at the ready. However, that large of an army would send alarms ringing throughout the Dragonspire Mountains and ensure that Serevas knew an attack was coming. He likely considered one would be coming eventually anyway. He'd remained in Frosthold since I'd suggested it, but getting any information from that place was difficult, even for the spy network I'd established.

I took a deep, calming breath. "Don't call the men from Nordrucan Hold. Prepare the royal army. Prepare as many banners as there are soldiers. I'll send letters today for allies and meet with you this evening. I think I may have a plan."

I left the family with a determined urgency. By the time I reached House Orodum, Jennia was waiting for me near the entrance. Faren had contacted the network and informed them that they would likely be needed.

Jennia made it her responsibility to answer the call.

Jennia bowed low. "Princess Orodum, I was told you had need of us."

I nodded and motioned for her to follow. "Accompany me inside. I need our fastest messengers to deliver letters, and I need our best scouts to get every ounce of information they can manage to get from Frosthold."

"Are we finally moving against the elf?" she asked with an eager tone.

"Indeed," I responded as we wove our way through the halls of the estate. "When is the next shipment of goods to be delivered to them?"

"I believe the next shipment is supposed to leave in a week's time, Princess," she replied as she went over the schedule in her head.

"Have some of our people who understand masonry go with the expedition with the premise that we will be looking to improve the foundations of the keep as part of our agreement," I instructed.

"And what will they be looking for as they inspect the foundations?" Jennia smirked.

We entered the study where I usually did my paperwork, and I moved to my desk, gathering parchment and my inkwell. I didn't pause as I began to pen my letters. "Defenses; both mundane and magical. I also want to know if they can discern where Serevas is staying within the Keep. In general, I would prefer to get him alone and not involve the elves he has with him."

"As you wish, Princess," Jennia waited patiently as I wrote my letters. "I will ensure they are exacting in their detail. Would you like us to prepare demolitions?"

I shook my head. "No. If nothing else, bring building supplies and shore up the weaker spots in the foundations so that they will believe we're preparing to do the work."

"Very well, Princess," Jennia chuckled. She rather enjoyed seeing my mind put to more devious use. She found the juxtaposition of my friendly, sociable demeanor with my cunning and devious side that allowed for the changes I was making in dwarven society and keeping our people safe.

I sent letters and specific instructions to King Marshal, Trianna, and Aelfric. I had Jennia take them and ensure their delivery, with directions to tell our allies to follow the instructions inside the letters exactly. I didn't want to risk raising any concern on Serevas's part. Over the next month, King Marshal, escorted by a group of Templars clad in royal armor, traveled to Coralstine to visit Clifford, Alford, and Serena. The three of them, along with the Templars, were then secreted into the Under Roads and guided to Cragmorrar. Meanwhile, Trianna and Aelfric announced they would be leaving for Cragmorrar to congratulate Trenton and the royal family on the birth of King Triston's first grandchild. They brought a small party of elves with them, as well as presents for the royal family.

We waited a few days after everyone had arrived to meet for discussions on the true reason for their visit. We gathered in the throne room where a table had been set up for food and drinks. At the head of the table was Father. To his left was Trenton, and I was to his right. Next to me was Faren, then Trianna and Aelfric. On Trenton's side of the table sat King Marshal, Cailain, Alford, and Serena.

Father cleared his throat to gain everyone's attention through the small talk that was being made. "I want to thank you all for your timely arrival. I have heard tales of my daughter's friends and allies, and it does my heart good to see you all respond to her call for aid. King Marshal, my old friend, I am especially pleased to see the respect you have shown my daughter in answering her request. It speaks highly of your opinion of her."

Marshal bowed his head. "King Triston, your daughter has proven to be a steadfast and trustworthy ally. She has aided my people several times, and I hold no one in higher regard than her. With everything she has done for relations between our people, the least I could do is answer her call for aid. Would that she had only asked for more. I feel like this is nowhere near enough to compensate her for her efforts."

Father smiled at me, his expression one of admiration and approval. "She has done wonders for both our people, which is why I should point out that I am here as a representative of our people. Merida will be leading this meeting while my son Trenton represents my army. I pray you all heed her words and consider her request carefully."

I smiled at everyone. "I would like to thank you all as well. I know the letters I sent you were rather demanding and particular. I also know they were secretive. I appreciate the trust you showed in me by following the instructions. I want to assure you, here and now, that those instructions were crucial to ensuring our chances of success."

"But success in what endeavor?" Serena leaned forward and asked.

"It's time we dealt with Serevas," I stated grimly.

"You want us to kill Serevas?" Trianna gasped. "Merida, you must know how fractured our people are on that issue."

I nodded apologetically. "I understand. However, he is only growing in power. The only thing slowing his growth is that we've denied him access to Franeth, and we've collected every Eluvian within a wide distance. But these steps alone won't stop him, and we Fated understand the threat he poses."

"Perhaps you would like to enlighten those of us who aren't Fated as to the threat he represents?" Marshal suggested.

Trianna raised a hand to signal that she would explain. "Serevas is better known as Trith'Emel; the Hungering Hound. He was originally believed to be a myth, part of the elven pantheon, in a sense. In our lore, he is said to have tricked our gods and the forgotten ones by locking them in their respective realms. In truth, he betrayed our leaders who had enslaved our people and posed as gods. He then tore the world apart, separating the physical world and the Dimvolmn, and placed the shroud between them."

"He now wishes to correct this action and reunite the spiritual and physical worlds together again," Trianna continued. "Doing this would kill nearly everyone in Thoros. He will strive to save as many elves as possible, but he will not care who else dies to see this goal to fruition."

"And you want to stop him before he can achieve his goal," Clifford said.

"I do," I replied, nodding and adjusting my posture to seem more confident. "I already have people in place doing reconnaissance in the keep, and I believe if we arrive as a delegation seeking to dissuade him from his goal, we can catch him off guard."

"You believe he'll allow us into his keep fully armed and armored?" Serena asked doubtfully.

"I believe he will think we are a delegation with normal traveling armaments and understand them to be the standard equipment nobility carries for their protection," I countered. "The large number of dwarves will be understandable since it's the Prince and Princess of Cragmorrar, as well as dwarven craftsmen coming to the keep as I promised. The contingent of human knights to protect the king would be expected as well. The same can be said for the elves accompanying Trianna and Aelfric."

"So we look like we're arriving with a normal amount of protection, ask to speak with Serevas about preserving Thoros as it is now…" Aelfric summarized. "Then you expect us to simply attack him when we meet with him?"

"It sounds simple, but I think he would suspect something like that," I nodded, understanding the slightly doubtful tone Aelfric used. "However, I believe we can lure him into a false sense of security by dragging the talks out over a number of days. When we think he's complacent and has his guard down, we strike. We attack him while our forces secure the keep."

"Do you mean to kill the elves with him as well?" Trianna asked, surprised at the aggressive plan.

"Not if we can help it," I shook my head, my face showing hesitancy. "I would prefer we only have to kill Serevas. If we can keep the elves secured while the attack is happening, it would be best."

"And if they fight back?" Aelfric pressed, wanting a clear answer.

"I will not allow my people to attack without being able to defend themselves," I answered firmly. "We'll do our best to keep any fighting or casualties to a minimum. But the question becomes, what do we do with them afterwards? They've been indoctrinated to believe in Serevas' vision. They will not want to return with you back to Orlimar and may attempt to rally more elves into attempting to achieve his goals by some other means."

"Are you suggesting that we should execute them for their beliefs?" Trianna's eyes went wide. "When all they are guilty of is believing in Serevas' vision for the world?"

"I'm not suggesting anything, Trianna," I sighed. "I'm saying that we have to recognize that they're also a threat. They're elves, though. I would suggest their fate be up to you and Aelfric. That is, if King Marshal agrees with that decision."

"I believe that is probably the best solution," Marshal agreed. "We see Orlimar as a vassal state of Falladrin, and thus see Aelfric and Trianna as its rightful rulers. They should decide what will be done with their people."

"We appreciate that, Highness," Trianna bowed her head, then turned to look at Aelfric. "If I'm being honest, we hadn't considered this. When the time comes, we may not be in the correct mindset to make the best decision. We will take them into custody and decide on their fate at a later date."

"As is your prerogative, Lady Trianna," Marshal smiled.

"There is also the option to put them before a tribunal of those whom they threatened with their actions," Serena suggested. "They may be your people, but their actions threatened all of us. You will be seen by your people as fair for allowing them to be taken into custody, and seen as a stalwart leader for allowing them to be tried by those they threatened. Your people will not see you responsible for the decision of a tribunal, so you escape blame in that regard as well."

"That's a rather inspired idea," I had to admit.

"We'll consider it," Aelfric sighed, not liking the conversation one bit. I could empathize. It wouldn't be an easy decision, no matter what.

"I have a question," Serena looked at me from the side. "What happens if, after a few days of talks, we convince Serevas to give up on his goal... and we believe him? What then?"

"Do we risk believing his sincerity when the fate of all of Thoros is at stake?" Marshal asked.

"If we can't risk it, then we are all simply agreeing to go there and assassinate him," Alford bemoaned.

"For all we know, Serevas is essentially immortal," Trenton thumped a fist on the table. "Even if he feigned sincerity, he could simply wait until alliances fracture, or manipulate events over the long term so that he can fulfill his goal. Do we really want to take the risk that he will not once again take up his desire to destroy our world? Do we want to leave the generations to come at his whim and mercy?"

I looked at Trenton and wondered if I should tell him that Faren and I, now touched or blessed by the titan, were also essentially immortal. My expression must have given something away because he seemed to grow curious. I thought quickly before responding, "I didn't think you were the type to think generations ahead, Brother. That's rather encouraging."

"Then you should know better," Trenton scolded me. "The goal is to kill this bastard once we get there. We can pretend for a few days, but the moment his guard is down, we should strike hard and without mercy or remorse."

"We have all answered Merida's call for aid," Serena interjected. "She answered ours when we asked for her help in Orlimar. She answered Trianna and Aelfric's when she noticed they were in danger. She recently aided Allen in checking on his family. She has put her life and time on the line whenever we have needed her. And we all understand the threat Serevas represents. If Merida believes now is the time to strike and she's asking us to help her, we would be hypocrites of the highest order if we refused."

Trianna and Aelfric looked at each other as Clifford and Alford both voiced their agreement with Serena. I knew the position I was putting the elves in, and I didn't want to, but this needed to finally be done. I looked at Trianna with an expression that sought her answer.

Trianna sighed and reached across the table to place her fingers on my hand. "Serena speaks the truth, Merida. You kept me safe when I was brought to Cragmorrar, you helped me unite the clans, and you've been like a sister to me ever since we met. You've helped us in so many ways that it would be wrong of us not to help you."

Aelfric stood and nodded. "Understand that aiding you was never in question. The fallout is what concerns us. But we should not have let you think there was any hesitation in giving you our support. Whenever you're ready to march, we're with you."

"Just… one more question, if I may?" Serena's tone was suspicious.

"What's that, Serena?" I asked, guarding myself for what she might be curious about.

"I can't help but notice Allen isn't here…" she paused before bluntly posing her question. "Why is that?"

"Truthfully? I don't trust Marylen with this issue," I answered flatly. "By that extension, and for that reason, I didn't trust bringing Allen with us. I believe Marylen could sway him to aid Serevas if she were inclined to see the world he would want to bring about. She doesn't have a child to care for at the moment, so her loyalty is too much of a risk to bring the college mages into this. That, and representatives from the College wouldn't fit into the delegation narrative we want to sell."

Serena seemed to weigh every word for its worth, her consideration of the explanation clear. Eventually, she nodded and sighed, "I can't fault you for your reasoning. I understand."

"Are there any other questions?" I looked around the table. With no other questions forthcoming, I nodded, "Then I suggest we spend the next few days going over our delegation proposals that we'll use during our talks, and also form a plan of attack when the time comes."

CHAPTER 32:

DISILLUSIONMENT

We left about a week after agreeing to assassinate Serevas. We spent a few days practicing discussion points on how we could convince Serevas to put his cause aside. The practice was futile, of course. No matter what we believed, we were determined to take Serevas down. We were on the road with a large contingent of dwarves, soldiers, and craftsmen, as well as the Templars, and a smaller elven force of mages and warriors. With us were a large number of carts of masonry and carpentry supplies, all to push the narrative of repairing Frosthold's foundations.

The trip through the mountains was easy enough since my scouts and other dwarven caravans bringing supplies to Frosthold had mapped the smoothest course. I also used my titan abilities to mold the path to be smooth and true for us. Still, the trip took a few weeks. During the days, we mostly sang marching songs and talked casually while enjoying the scenery. When evening came, we continued our meeting practice. Each time we practiced, we got more and more into the details and came up with more ideas to better convince Serevas. Trianna and Aelfric seemed to fall more and more into the belief that we might be able to genuinely convince him to stop. I wanted to break them of that illusion, but it occurred to me that their sincere hope in the possibility would make them more convincing.

We arrived close to Frosthold just before sunset. I had no doubt that our campfires were easily seen from the keep. Our numbers were so large that the light from the camps lit the mountainside as it reflected off the snow. That evening, we gathered together one last time.

"We should have stopped earlier, further away from the keep so as not to alert them," Serena contemplated as we sat near a fire to keep ourselves warm.

"They'll likely have known we were coming for some time," Marshal countered. "Their scouts have probably been reporting our position for the last day or so."

I was bundled up in thick clothes and a thicker blanket to stave off the biting cold. "Your Grace is correct. And they're scouting around the camp as we speak."

"Is that your stone sense kicking in?" Aelfric asked.

I laughed and shook my head. "That's not what stone sense is. No. My titan senses are honed around the mountains. I can feel the vibrations of everything going on for some distance now. These vibrations have been staying ahead of us, and now more have joined them from Frosthold's direction. We're being watched, but I doubt they'll attack."

"What makes you so sure?" Faren asked as he looked around with some concern.

"They're keeping their distance," I replied. "They're too far away for any weapon to reach. I'd wager that they're counting our numbers and seeing if we're preparing for an attack."

"Well," Trianna said with a smile, "we don't have to worry about that, do we? Only the camp guards and a few of our personal guards are even armed or armored. They shouldn't see much of a threat."

"Don't be too sure," Marshal cautioned. "They see an army on their doorstep. Armored or not, an army is still an army. And an unsolicited army rarely implies good intentions. They would be fools to not be prepared for us to attack."

Faren hummed in agreement. "Your Grace is correct again. If I were in charge of Frosthold's defenses right now, I would be preparing to turn that bridge into a killing field. We may be many, but that bridge turns our numbers into a disadvantage. We'll be packed in tight if we try to storm the place."

"Then it's a good thing we don't plan on storming the keep, isn't it?" Serena chided. "In any case, if they're keeping their distance, we shouldn't pay them any mind. Let them believe we don't know they're here. They can report our numbers and nothing more. If some, or all of them, go missing, the rest will know we're not here with peaceful intentions."

"Well considered, sister," Trenton chimed in. "I think you're right. Best to be seen as peaceful as we can despite our numbers."

"To that end, we should consider how we will approach the keep tomorrow," Serena said as she looked at us.

"I thought we'd send a rider ahead to let them know who we are and why we're here," Faren answered in a way that suggested the answer should be obvious.

"A single rider to represent all of our people?" Trianna asked. "Why not send one for each?"

"It only takes one person to relay a message," Faren countered. "And if the one doesn't come back, then we've only lost one person, not three."

"As for my opinion," Marshal interrupted as he warmed his hands near the fire, "I believe Trianna, Aelfric, Princess Merida, and I should ride up. We can speak with whoever meets us and sue for entry."

Serena's expression seemed to sour when she wasn't counted among those Marshal suggested but quickly composed herself. "Without any protection? It wouldn't do to let our leaders go up alone."

"I can keep us safe," I assured Serena. "Besides, I doubt that they would be foolish enough to attack us. If they did, all of our people would go to war with them."

"She's right," Faren agreed. "As much as I don't like the idea of letting her go without me, if, somehow, the dwarves didn't simply rush in and kill everyone, we could lay siege to the place and starve them out. Or we could simply wait until the armies of Falladrin and Orlimar arrived and take the keep then."

"That's why I enjoy dwarves so much," Marshal laughed and smiled at us. "They have a practical sense of things."

"And we're raised from birth to put our people above ourselves," I added with no small amount of pride.

"Practical and honorable," Alford smiled. He leaned over and rested his hand on Serena's shoulder. "We can wait with our forces until you all return. But it might be better to ask that at least some of your guards be allowed entry as well, at least during the talks."

"Of course," Marshal and I answered in unison. That brought a laugh from everyone to see us both answer as one, both of us assuming we were the one in charge.

The rest of the evening was spent talking idly, singing, and reminiscing on times past. By the time we retired for the evening, everyone was in high spirits.

Faren was escorting me back to my tent when Serena stopped us. "Merida? Can we speak?"

Faren and I stopped to regard her. I looked at Faren and nodded, signaling that he could go ahead. I looked back at Serena and adjusted the blanket I still had around me to rest more comfortably around my shoulders. "What is it, Serena? I was hoping to get out of this cold."

"I apologize," Serena said as she gave an apologetic bow of her head. "However, I was wondering if you'd given any thought to our last conversation. Have you considered helping me?"

I gave a slightly annoyed huff and stood a bit straighter. "I have considered your request. Frankly, I think you and Anna are likely equally capable in your ability to lead. You lean more toward improving infrastructure while she leans more toward diplomacy and alliance building. I would wager Alford is the more capable leader between the two brothers. Clifford is kind but not as decisive as Alford can be when push comes to shove."

Serena brightened up after hearing my conclusion. "So you'll help me in my bid for the throne."

I looked up at Serena with a stern expression. "Don't push me into a decision, Serena. We are friends, but a move like this requires subtle maneuvering and decisive timing. When I make a move to endorse your efforts, you'll know. This is a matter you shouldn't rush and rather have faith in me that I will aid you."

Her expression sobered as she looked down at me. Understanding slowly came to her, and she nodded. "Of course… You're right, Merida. I've done my part, and I should trust you to do yours. I apologize for trying to push the issue."

I offered as graceful a curtsy as I could beneath the blanket. "It's fine, Serena. I agreed to help you, and I will. The first step will happen soon enough once this is all over with."

Serena's smile returned to her. "Thank you, Merida. Now I leave you to your tent and your warmth. Till tomorrow."

"Till tomorrow, then," I replied and turned to make my way to my tent.

The next day, King Marshal, Trianna, Aelfric, and I gathered together after breakfast. Marshal was dressed in a splendid blue and white outfit with a thick coat. Trianna wore a green and black dress with a willowy shawl that seemed to stop the cold somehow. Aelfric wore a matching suit to Trianna's but with a long leather coat lined with thick cloth. I was dressed in a gambeson gown of my favorite garnet with polished brass buttons and a thick fur coat with a hood that covered my head. Our mounts were bridled in fine regalia. None of us carried a weapon on us.

"Are we prepared?" King Marshal asked as we moved into a simple formation with Marshal and myself in the center, and Trianna and Aelfric flanking us on either side.

"Ready as we'll ever be," I said chipperly.

"Let's hope for the best," Trianna smiled. "When you're ready, King

Marshal, we can depart."

Marshal bowed his head and turned his horse to start toward the keep, with the rest of us following. It took us several minutes to approach the start of the bridge, where a few dozen armed elves were waiting for us with weapons at the ready. We pulled our mounts to a stop a few yards from the group of elves.

One of the elves stepped forward and, with an authoritative voice, asked, "What brings an army to Frosthold?"

Marshal looked at me, and I simply nodded to suggest he could respond first. He looked back at the elf. "We are no army. I am King Marshal of Falladrin. With me is Princess Merida Orodum of Cragmorrar, as well as Lady Trianna and Lord Aelfric of Orlimar. We have come to speak with Serevas."

"You say you are no army, yet you number in the thousands," the elf countered. "Forgive me, Your Grace, but would that not constitute an army if it were outside one of your cities?"

It was my turn to explain things. "The dwarves are my fault. My people consider me precious to them and insisted that I be escorted by a part of our army to keep me safe. I tried to convince them that this wasn't necessary, but the Assembly would hear none of it, especially since my elder brother is also travelling with us. So, I've come with this delegation while bringing the craftsmen and supplies to repair Frosthold's foundation, as I promised Serevas I would. The army is here by decree of the Assembly. I apologize if they concerned you."

The elf considered my explanation for some time. "We have been waiting for the supplies, Princess. We're pleased that you've delivered them. I hope you can forgive our readiness and concern."

I bowed my head. "There's nothing to forgive. I can understand how concerning the sight of us would be. My friends and I would like to speak with Serevas while the repairs are underway. We're hoping that we can take some time to discuss everyone's position on his desires and possibly work with him to come to a peaceful solution."

"I will not stop you and these others from entering, Princess," the elf replied. "Lord Serevas has insisted that the leaders of the approaching force be allowed in to parlay. When he finds out that it's you, he'll no doubt be more relaxed."

"May we ask that our personal guards be allowed in as well?" Trianna asked. "There are a few dozen for each of us. They can set up a camp in the courtyard so no elves are put out for the duration."

"Of course, my Lady," the elf responded. "I'll see that room is made for them. The rest of the gathered forces will need to remain out here until it's time for you to leave. I hope you understand we don't have the room for that many people."

"Certainly," Marshal was quick to agree. "As the Princess has explained, they were sent by the Cragmorrar Assembly. Princess Merida has her own personal guard. The army will do as commanded and wait for our return."

"And if you don't mind, I'll have my brother come lead the wagons with the materials and craftsmen come in as well so the repairs can get started," I said with a bright smile.

"That will be fine, Princess," the elf said. "Why don't you all head into the keep, and I'll have one of my men send for the others?"

"Thank you, my friend," Marshal bowed his head and stirred his horse forward. We followed behind him.

The bridge that led to Frosthold proper was long and spanned a vast gulf between mountain peaks. We could see elves watching us from the parapets as we made our way across. The massive wooden doors groaned open as we got close and revealed a beautifully green and blooming courtyard. Grass carpeted the ground, and flowers and herbs spread around the area and climbed the walls. The scent of the herbs and flowers tickled our senses and helped to immediately bring a smile to our faces. I couldn't help but notice how much warmer it was in the keep than it had been on the bridge and road.

Serevas stood in the middle of the courtyard, draped with a heavy fur cloak and surrounded by a few dozen retainers and guards. He looked at the small procession with doubt until he noticed me. His expression changed to one of hesitant relief.

"Princess Orodum," he said as he lowered himself into a sweeping bow, "if I had known it was you, I wouldn't have had you stay the night in the cold. You should have announced yourself."

I bowed my head to him. "Apologies. I thought one of my people had told you I would be coming with supplies for the foundation repairs the next time we came this way."

He let out a huff of amusement. "They did. They failed to mention that there would be so many of you, however. And they made no mention of other royalty accompanying you."

We dismounted, and I approached Serevas, lowering myself into a curtsy. "I apologize for that. It was out of my hands. As I told your man at the bridge, the Assembly insisted I be escorted by a portion of the army so that no harm came to me on the road."

"You are a precious jewel to your people, Princess," he smiled and clasped his hands behind his back. "You have treated them fairly and have done much for them. I can understand their desire to keep you safe. Now, may I ask what the king of Falladrin, and the Lord and Lady of Orlimar are doing here with you?"

"We have come to speak to you about how we might live together in peace," Marshal replied as he approached. "We know of your desire to return the world to the way it was in ancient times, but we would like to be given the chance to dissuade you of this idea."

"Is that so?" Serevas asked, almost seeming intrigued by the idea. "I suppose that if you know what my goal is, then you also know who and what I am. If we are to have such a discussion, it could take some time."

"We assumed it would take several days for us to all have our say," Trianna stepped forward and smiled. "How are you, Serevas? I trust Frosthold has been treating you well?"

"Frosthold is sufficient for my needs for now," Serevas replied. "Princess

Orodum has been kind enough to keep us supplied with food, and now that she's brought people to repair certain areas of the keep, I suppose it will only grow more useful. But let's not keep you all out in the cold. Please, come this way. We'll go inside where it's warm and where you can more comfortably explain your proposal."

Serevas led us into Frosthold proper. The main hall soared above us, with large chandeliers lighting the area up with the help of dozens of sconces and candelabras. Long rugs covered the stone floor, and at the end of the hall sat a large table at the top of a few stairs. In Age of Dragons Inquest, the table would be replaced with a throne from which the main character would judge criminals and enemies alike. The table was a surprise.

We were led to the left through a series of small hallways into a room that held a large table made from the center of a tree, with bark still clinging to its sides. Serevas moved around to the head of the table and motioned for us to choose our seats. We all chose a chair and sat down.

Once everyone seemed comfortable, Serevas looked at Marshal. "King Marshal? Would you like to begin?"

Marshal cleared his throat and nodded. "First, understand that we came here in the hope that we could take our time to explain things. We wish to go into detail and make offers for you to consider. This conversation we have now will not be long enough to cover the issues we would like to go into."

"Understandable," Serevas nodded. "You believe that after many long discussions, I might change my mind. I doubt it, but I will not deny your request. I am, if nothing else, willing to consider what you have to say."

"You have our thanks," Marshal responded. "As for this conversation, know that we wish to join Princess Merida in providing your people with supplies until you can properly get on your feet. This is a harsh land you've claimed."

"I did not so much as claim it as it was suggested to me by Princess Merida," Serevas chuckled. "And I use the phrase 'suggested' lightly."

"I did not wish to fight you," I said calmly.

"And I do not hold your threat against you, Princess," Serevas responded. "You were there to rescue and protect your friends. Your mission was admirable, and your explanation was sound. Frosthold has been a boon to my people. We have found its remote location rather comforting."

"We would prefer that you rejoin us in Orlimar," Aelfric said. "We don't want to see our people divided. We hope that we can convince you that this world that you created is worthy of continuing to exist."

"And that your descendants are worth nurturing and guiding with your wisdom and experience," Trianna added.

"We are your legacy," I chimed in. "Our people— humans, elves, and dwarves—have all adapted to this world over tens of thousands of years. We've lost so much knowledge, and we've learned how to interact with the world in different ways than before your decision. You may regret your actions, but those actions created a whole new world full of new kinds of people and creatures."

"Do you think I haven't considered that?" Serevas asked with a sigh. "I take no pleasure in my decision. In fact, I lament the need to do what I must. However, I am still sure of my decision. The Dimvolmn needs to be rejoined to the physical world."

"And that is why we're here," Marshal said staunchly. "We believe there are ways to live in this world together. I will not lie and say I understand the entirety of the details, but I grasp the grand scheme of it all. We appreciate the chance to speak to you about these possibilities."

Serevas sat back and looked at each of us. "I can see that you are all fervent in your desire to discuss these details. And I am not apathetic to your point of view. I can also see that you've all prepared your own points and offers. So I'll agree to listen to your petitions over the next few days. I don't believe you will change my mind, but I will keep an open mind when listening to you. Is that agreeable?"

"I don't think we could ask for more," Marshal answered.

"And if my mind is not changed, do we still have an agreement to work together in order to defeat the scourgespawn?" Serevas looked at me.

I smiled and nodded, "As I said before, we will need to work together. I have no intentions on being the one to break our alliance."

"Then we are agreed, and we can speak honestly with one another," Serevas smiled. He stood and clasped his hands behind his back. "I will have someone prepare rooms for you. Until then, I invite you all to enjoy the whole of the keep. I will summon you when it is time for lunch; then we can begin our first talks. I trust this is acceptable?"

We all stood, and Marshal nodded, "Thank you. That is agreeable. We were told our personal guards could enter the keep. May I ask that my sons and daughter-in-law be allowed in as well? This will be a fine example of diplomacy for them to learn from, and one of the last that I will be able to attend in such a fashion."

We all stared at Marshal in surprise. He had basically announced that he was ready to retire from running his kingdom in practice and become king in name, and allow his heir to begin running affairs as regent in his stead. This brought a stunned silence to the room.

Serevas broke the silence with a simple bow of his head, "Of course, Your Majesty. It will no doubt be a fine learning experience for them. Now, let us adjourn until after lunch."

We all left the room and were shown to private quarters. Over the next few hours, the supplies and craftsmen arrived with Trenton, as well as the personal guards and Serena, Alford, and Clifford. I worked with the dwarves to start the repairs on the keep's foundations while the others mostly relaxed. We spent that morning situating ourselves and falling into our roles. Serena hovered around Marshal, taking his counsel and discussing matters of Falladrin with him, while Alford and Clifford seemed more bored with the situation than anything else. Trianna and Aelfric met with the elves to catch up with them.

We met with Serevas, and King Marshal took the day to discuss his position while we added in our opinions and clarifications on his behalf from our perspective. Alford and Clifford had been staring daggers at Servas the entire time and I could tell they weren't helping Marshal's case seem as convincing as it could be. Those talks took us well into the night, and we had supper at the meeting table. When Serevas declared the talks over for the evening, he asked that I stay behind to talk for a few minutes.

When the others had left, I looked at Serevas, "What would you like to discuss?"

"I do not pretend to not see the animosity in those young men's eyes," Serevas stated bluntly.

I arched my brows. "Young men? You mean Alford and Clifford?"

"King Marshal's sons, yes," Serevas confirmed. "They seemed like they were appraising me, as if they were estimating their chances with me in a fight."

"They're young men," I chuckled dismissively. "And they are aware of the threat you represent not only to their kingdom but to the world. They haven't had many chances to prove themselves, and they don't seem to be the type to want to prove themselves in diplomacy."

"Such is the ego of young men," Serevas mused. "But tell me truly, Princess; am I in danger? Have these others come in the hopes of stopping me one way or another? By hook or by crook, as it were?"

I replied with a sigh. "I can honestly say that at no point in our travels did anyone mention attacking you. Not to me, at least. In any case, we're not carrying weapons around with us, so I doubt they'll be much of a threat to you or anyone else."

"Nevertheless," Serevas replied, "it makes me feel uneasy that they would watch me in such a way. None of the others watch me in this way."

"Would it help if I told King Marshal that their behavior has offended us both and that I do not wish for them to be a part of these talks from here out?" I asked him plainly.

"You would ask such a thing for me?"

"Of course," I replied with a smile. "Serevas, we may be at odds but I have given you my word that I will work to maintain our truce at least until

Seven has been dealt with. This task falls within that promise. I want you to know that I am here in good faith."

Serevas smiled. The expression almost made me waver in my conviction. He sighed and pinched his nose. "You are a fine example of what is best in people, Princess. Would that all of Thoros were like you, I would seriously reconsider my approach."

I bowed my head. "You flatter me."

"Not at all," he smiled. Then his smile sobered once again. "But I must ask; for all your talk of maintaining our truce, what will happen if any of them do try to attack me? I doubt you can remain neutral in such a situation."

"I will defend my friends," I answered honestly.

"So you will side with them," Serevas grimaced.

"I said I will defend them," I repeated. "I will do my best to keep them from harm."

"You won't attack me? Surely they will see that as some sort of betrayal."

"I am a woman of my word," I looked at him sternly. "I will not be the one to break our truce."

"That is… reassuring," Serevas said after a few moments of consideration. "That is all, then. I simply wanted to see where you stood on the matter."

I stood and curtsied to Serevas. "I will let King Marshal know that his sons are no longer welcome to the meetings. I will tell him that I am the one offended by their behavior and that their presence threatens to disrupt our talks."

"I am in your debt, Princess," Serevas smiled once again.

We continued our meetings over the next few days. Alford and Clifford were not welcome into the room, so they stood outside guarding it along with a few elves and dwarves. Trianna and Aelfric took turns going over their opinions. Then it was my turn. At the end of each day, we would eat together and take time to relax. The repairs to the foundations went smoothly, and I would walk with Serevas to inspect them. Each night, Serevas would speak with me for a few minutes to reassure himself that I would not attack him. This was our routine for nearly a week until the final day of our talks.

Everyone sat around the table as we had finished our summarizations. Serevas had been silent for some time as he considered everything that had been discussed over the week. Trianna and Aelfric seemed nervous with anxious anticipation. Serena seemed doubtful and was on the edge of her seat. Marshal sat passively as he had no real expectation of this coming to a positive end. Trenton was taciturn and watched Serevas with animosity, though anyone would be forgiven for assuming that was his normal expression for anyone he was at odds with. I watched Serevas curiously. Each night we discussed my dedication to our truce, he would question the points made that day. It made me wonder if he might genuinely be reconsidering his desire.

A loud sound coming from the door broke the silence. We all looked to the door as shouts of panic and pain, and alarms began to ring out. It seemed like the whole of the keep was suddenly reacting to some kind of attack.

"What is this? Is this your doing?" Serevas asked Marshal.

"My doing?" Marshal snapped. "We've been in this room for a week. How could this be my doing?"

"There is an army outside my walls! Have you finally decided to attack?" Serevas turned his anger to me.

"Don't be ridiculous! We should be out there helping the others with whatever's going on, not sitting here hurling accusations," I shouted back. I stood quickly and turned to go to the door.

"Stop!" Serevas shouted. A flare of light erupted from his eyes, and I was frozen in place. I couldn't move and began to panic as I felt my body stiffen and then… nothing.

I felt the stone all around me. I could… hear through it. Through the vibrations. I could hear Marshal and the others shouting in protest and shock. I could hear Trenton's furious roar Serevas had turned me to stone but made the mistake of thinking I was dealt with. I let my senses flow through the stone to where I knew our weapons were. I pulled them down into the stone and through the keep's stone foundation and floor so they jumped up before the others. Marshal and Trenton engaged Serevas immediately. Serena and Aelfric began firing arrows to keep Serevas off guard while Trianna began to cast spells at the ancient elf.

I stepped out of the stone prison he'd made of me and picked up my staff. I glared at Serevas as he defended against Marshal's barrage of attacks. "You attacked me without provocation! We are not the ones who started this!"

Serevas ducked a swing from Marshal's sword and quickly brought a magical barrier up to deflect arrows fired by Serena and Aelfric. "If not you, then who?"

"You should have asked me before you tried turning me to stone," I growled. "I am the stone! I could have told you that there are monsters attacking the keep! But now I see that you never trusted me. You never trusted us! This was always going to be how things ended, no matter how we tried to work with you!"

Serevas shouted in pain as Marshal scored a glancing hit on his side and Trenton followed up with a powerful fist to the elf's jaw. The others were doing an excellent job of stopping him from casting any potent spells. "This world is wrong! And I will end it one way or the other!"

"And while you fight us, your people are dying to those monsters," Trianna shouted.

"My people?" Serevas scoffed. "A means to an end only. My people would not willingly and ignorantly mark themselves as slaves! I will rend this world asunder, and you will all regret standing in my—"

I willed the stone to open beneath one of Serevas' feet and closed around it once it had sunk in. I charged in, drawing my greatsword then joined Marshal and Trenton in attacking our enemy.

"You talk too much," I spat. "And you rely too much on magic when facing a foe your people could not defeat alone. And as you said, you are alone because those outside aren't your people!"

Spells clashed as Serevas expertly wove some into his movements. Trianna and I did what we could to counter them, but his power was great. Lightning, fire, ice, and other elements and effects flashed and dashed through the room. The battle in the room was furious, but the sounds outside were beginning to sound desperate. We heard Alford shouting for Clifford, and the cry took Marshal's attention from the battle for a moment. That moment gave Serevas all the time he needed to release a burst of arcane energy that sent everyone flying back.

Serena slammed into the stone wall. Marshal cried out as his arm snapped against the table. Trianna was knocked unconscious as her head clapped against the floor. Trenton slammed into the large window behind the table, and the only thing that saved him from falling to his death was getting caught on the wondow's ironwork. Aelfric pushed himself up from the floor as I did the same. He moved over to check on Trianna as I prepared to attack once again.

"You're finished," Serevas said with a tone of finality. "Your strongest allies are out of this fight, Princess. Now what will you do?"

I looked from Serevas back to my friends. When I looked back at Serevas, my eyes were glowing a furious dimvyum blue. "Now? Now I'll stop holding back. I wasn't going to endanger them. But now more of my friends on the other side of that door are in danger. So now I'll end this."

"You think you can defeat me alone?" Serevas quipped.

"I could have killed you from the moment we met," I snarled. "You are arrogant and have carried your arrogance with you since you were considered a god. But you have forgotten how powerful your ancient foes are. Now, I will remind you."

"You are no—" Serevas' voice was cut off as a hand of stone reached up from the floor and grabbed him by the neck. He worked a spell to shatter the stone, but two more arms, one from the wall and another from the ceiling, reached out to grab his wrists. A third hand lept from a wall and grabbed him by the throat.

"No what?" I asked as I closed the distance between us. I stopped just in front of him and stared up at him, fury evident on my features. "I am no titan? When my people lived symbiotically with the titans, you thought of us as ugly, lump, mindless drones that did their bidding. You didn't understand that we were all one and the same. You thought that after you separated the Dimvolmn from the rest of the world, and that connection was severed, that we became harmless? That the titans would no longer be a threat?"

One of the stone hands snapped Serevas' left arm. He let out a strained hiss of air in pain.

"You didn't think the titans would always watch over their children?"

Now his right arm was snapped, and tears ran down his face.

"You thought they were like you? That they would look at their children and see how they were no longer the people they used to be and scorn them like you did?" I reached up and rested my hand on his cheek as my anger grew. "Look me in the eyes and see what else is inside me."

Serevas looked down at me, and through his tears, I could see his realization. His revulsion was palpable.

"You see it, don't you?" I smirked. "One of the souls of the Gospinia. Jeron's soul, specifically. Given to me by Mythriel herself when she learned that I was going to oppose you. I have her soul within me. Soon, she and I will be the only remnants of your wretched pantheon. Just imagine it. A titan holds the soul of someone you would truly consider one of your people. And you never noticed because for all your talk of alliances and reassurances, you always looked down on me. On all of us."

Serevas snorted defiantly as his skin began to go pale from the lack of air.

I lowered my hand and wrapped my fingers around the pendant that hung from a rope around his neck. I snatched the makeshift necklace from his neck. "I think I'll keep this after you're gone. Something to remember your arrogance by. Now, I'll release your soul to enter the Dimvolmn. That should please you, yes? Knowing that your soul is trapped in a prison of souls of your own making for all eternity. A fitting end, I think."

I turned and moved to check on Marshal as the stone hands ripped Serevas apart. His limbs were torn from his body while he opened his mouth to scream, but the hand around his neck denied him the air to make a sound. When he finally died, I left him hanging there by the neck.

"King Marshal? Are you alright?" I asked as I helped him into a chair.

"Don't bother with me," Marshal waved me off. "Check outside. Help my sons."

I nodded and moved to the door as Aelfric helped Trianna and Serena recover. Trenton moved over to help Marshal with his arm. When I opened the doors, I gasped. The sight that greeted me was horrifying. Faren and Alford turned to us, covered in blood and gore. Clifford's body, which had been resting against the door, slumped into the doorway. Only a few of the guards remained alive, and among them were the fleshwroughts from Aronthok.

"Oh, no…" I whispered as I dropped to my knees to cradle Clifford's body close.

"My love, are you alright?" Faren asked as he moved to check on me.

"My wife? My father?" Alford asked.

"They're injured but they'll recover," I responded to Alford.

Alford rushed into the room to check on his family as Faren knelt beside me. He placed his forehead to the side of my head. "Tell me you're alright. I tried getting to you but there were so many of these things."

I turned my head and kissed his cheek. "I'm fine. But poor Clifford…"

I could hear Marshal beginning to weep. Alford had, no doubt, given him the news. The next few hours were spent recovering from the battle. We gathered the dead and built a pyre for them. Clifford was preserved and wrapped to be brought back to Falladrin. The remaining elves that were loyal to Serevas were chained and brought to the camp. We left Frosthold and stayed in camp that night. It was a somber, bitter evening for everyone, most of all for King Marshal. We didn't eat together that evening. Those who had been in Frosthold simply took the evening to recover. Trianna made her rounds to use her healing magic on everyone she could.

As I sat by the fire, Faren by my side, one of my guards poked his head into the tent. "Princess? Lady Thirston would like an audience."

"We said we didn't want to be disturbed," Faren barked at the guard.

"No," I said quickly. "It's alright. Show her in."

"As you command, Princess," the guard replied.

"You said you didn't want to talk to anyone," Faren looked at me.

"I know what she wants to talk about," I sighed. "Might as well get it out of the way."

Serena slipped into the tent and offered a curtsy of greeting. "Thank you for seeing me. I know none of us is really in the mood to talk. But I had some questions."

"If you're wondering about if I will still back your claim to the throne, I doubt that there's much need for that anymore," I said as I looked up at her.

"No. You're right about that," Serena agreed. "However, I got a look at those monsters and they're from Aronthok. Didn't you say you went to Aronthok?"

"I did. And I reclaimed it for the dwarves," I replied.

"Then you would have encountered the fleshwroughts," Serena said. "Strange that they should end up here when we were going to fight Serevas, don't you think?"

"Strange?" I asked. "No, I don't think so. I brought them with us, after all. They were an excellent excuse to start a fight."

"How? How did you bring them with us? I certainly never saw them,"

Serena said.

"I brought them through the stone," I smirked. "Just like I did with our weapons."

"They killed Clifford..." Serena moaned.

"Yes," I nodded and looked at her seriously. "And a few guards, just so it didn't look suspicious."

It took Serena a few moments to register what I had said. She stared at me in disbelief. "What did you say?"

"You heard me," I replied, the truth hanging between us. "The fleshwroughts weren't for Serevas. They were for Clifford. You wanted to be Queen, but you wanted me to back you because I owed you the favor after handing me Yivreon."

"But you don't owe me anything," Serena protested. "You bought Yivreon with your own money. If you were going to back me at this point, it would be because you believe I would run the country better than Anna."

I nodded. "You're right. And I have come to believe that. However, nothing you did or said would have changed Marshal's mind. Clifford is a true-born son, and the eldest. Regardless of his inability to rule, he would have been crowned king. Now, he's no longer an obstacle to your aspirations. You're welcome."

"By the Creator, Merida... you murdered Clifford just so I could become Queen?"

I laughed and shook my head. "Not at all. I removed Clifford so that you could become Queen, and you would understand that I only released about fifty fleshwroughts... out of hundreds."

The threat was implicit. It filled the air between us. I had let loose only a fraction of the fleshwroughts I had control of. I made sure that they were able to get to Clifford and some of the guards by sensing their movements in the stone while Alford was kept safe by Faren using his abilities. With Clifford's death, Serena and Alford's rise was assured. But because I was the one who ensured their rise, Serena would now owe me a favor. She would also understand that if she didn't work with me when I wanted her to, more fleshwroughts could always be let loose.

Serena stood there frozen with the horrible truth. She tried to remain composed, but her eyes were filled with barely contained fear. She took a breath to compose herself. "I understand… Thank you, Merida. I hope our friendship can continue to flourish as we work together to bring our kingdoms closer together."

"So do I," I smiled and bowed my head. "Was there anything else you wanted to speak about?"

"No," Serena shook her head. "I'll leave you to rest."

I smiled, and Serena took her leave. The journey back was quiet and filled with hurt. We all felt horrible for King Marshal. I especially felt remorse for what I had to do. In the end, Marshal brought Clifford back to Demirren and burned him there. Trianna and Aelfric went back to Orlimar to tell them the news of Serevas' death. Faren and I went home to Cragmorrar, ready to report to Father that the threat was ended. Little did we know that an announcement had been made in our absence.

CHAPTER 33:

UNWORTHY OF QUEENSHIP

A royal decree welcomed us back to Cragmorrar. As soon as we arrived, a large force of the city guard insisted we follow them to the palace. It was a strange request but not outside the realm of Father's power. I commanded the army forces that had joined us in our travels to return to their garrisons while my personal guard and Faren accompanied me to the palace. I noticed a different air about the city as we passed through. Where normally dwarves would be cheering my arrival, there were now quick peeks and excited whispers. I wasn't sure what was going on, but it was certainly new and not altogether unwelcome. Something unexpected was always more interesting than the same old thing happening.

When we arrived at the palace, the guards at the entrance allowed us quick entry and directed us to where Father was. Faren and I rushed through the palace only to find Trenton waiting outside of Father's chambers.

"Trenton?" I asked in surprise. "You're still here?"

Trenton approached to give me a hug. "I am, Sister. After Father made his announcement, we couldn't leave. We'll be needed here soon enough. I trust that you were successful in your effort to kill Serevas?"

I nodded, grim-faced. "We were. Prince Clifford died in the effort, however."

"I'm sorry to hear that," Trenton responded before moving directly to business. "Father is waiting for you. He wished to tell you of his decision himself."

"Should I be concerned?" I asked, canting my head curiously.

"That's not for me to say," Trenton dodged the question. "But it will put things in perspective for you."

"That's... disconcerting," I replied as I looked toward the door to Father's chambers.

"Then relieve yourself of discontent and speak with Father," Trenton patted my shoulder. "Go on, Merida." He nudged me gently as he used to do when I was still nervous about speaking with noble guests.

Ironically, that's exactly how I was feeling just now. I moved to the door and stepped through, closing it behind me. I found Father sitting at his desk.

Father turned and smiled at me. He stood and made his way to me, waving away my etiquette as I curtsied before him. "Now, now. Let's have none of that, my dear. Come. Give your father a hug."

I rose from my curtsy and wrapped my arms around him. "I've missed you, Father."

"And I you, Merida," Father replied as he hugged me close. He stepped back, took my hand, and led me to a sofa. He guided me to sit. "I'm pleased to see you home safe. I was worried about you."

"We lost several guards, and Prince Clifford fell in battle, but we were successful," I said with regret in my voice.

"Prince Clifford?" Father gasped. "Oh... poor Marshal. Clifford was a fine lad and looked to be a good and fine heir. He was such a gentle soul. Do you remember the night you first met him?"

I smiled sadly and let out a soft laugh before I nodded. "I do. He insisted on dancing with me the first night. It was such an awkward attempt. I don't think he'd considered our height difference at all. Still, he was a gentleman even then."

And I killed him. I wanted to say it. I wanted to scream it. I wanted to shout it, confess it. I wanted to tell Father what I had done and why. I wanted him to listen and understand. Would he understand?

"Do you know how I became King?" Father asked as he read my face.

I flinched, wanting to say no, but my expression told him I knew the truth—That he'd convinced his older brother to fight a murderer in a Testament Bout and had provided the poison that the murderer used on his blade.

Father sighed. "What I did, I did because I knew I was the best person to rule Cragmorrar. My brother was headstrong and hot-blooded. His patience was thin, and he was easily persuaded to do things a person with any wit wouldn't do. It was a sacrifice I made for the good of our people; one I do not regret now, but I did at the time. Soon, you will need to learn to make such sacrifices. You've made similar choices yourself while retaking the Holds and at Orlimar…"

Franklin and Petra's faces flashed before me at the mention of Orlimar.

I paled and looked at Father. "What do you mean I will need to learn to make such sacrifices?"

Father inhaled deeply. "I have come to the end of my reign, Merida. My memory is not what it used to be, and I am growing old. I have asked the Assembly to call the leaders of the Holds so that they might all decide on a new ruler. Usually, this would only be done after I had died, but I don't believe there is another choice beyond you, Daughter. Still, traditions must be upheld. But I'm telling you now so that you can prepare yourself. You, Merida, will soon be named Queen of Cragmorrar."

I stared at Father in shock and disbelief. It took me some time to find words, but they were words of protest about how he had plenty of time to rule yet. He assured me that this would be the best thing for Cragmorrar. It was too soon for any of this. I hadn't dealt with Seven yet, and had only just now finished handling Serevas. If I were Queen, it would severely hamper my ability to travel and hunt for ways to keep the people of Cragmorrar safe. But the wheels had been set in motion, and there was nothing I could do. There would only be a month or two before everyone who would decide on the matter would arrive.

Later that evening, after I'd returned home from Father's chambers, Faren and I sat by the fire. There was correspondence laid out in a pile between us, ranging from requests for meetings, funding, endorsements, House eligibility, and any number of other things from nearly every noble House or Family in Cragmorrar. This was the price I paid for my travels. Whenever I returned home, I would have months of backlogged mail to get through.

"Isn't that what you were working towards the entire time?" Faren asked as he finished penning a reply for me to a rather dubious business proposal in the most polite manner possible.

"You know that's not why I've done all of this," I sighed as I looked over a letter asking for a meeting from House Irono. I still considered them to be family and wondered what it was that they needed. I would certainly meet with them. "Everything I've done has been for the good of our people, not for political power or personal gain."

"The personal gain hasn't hurt, though," Faren smirked.

"Be that as it may," I said dismissively, "I was never trying to become Queen. I'd honestly just wanted to do what was best for everyone while I remained a good advisor to Trenton."

"Who already stepped aside publicly in your favor back when you were eleven," Faren reminded me.

"I know," I grumbled. "I could strangle him for that. Being Queen will limit me more than it will help. If I can't freely travel, how am I going to handle Seven?"

"You might not need to," Faren suggested. "He hasn't made himself known for years until the Testament Bout, and even then it was an attack that we'd quickly put down."

"I'm still uneasy that he killed Varrimus in that way," I mused. "If he has Varrimus' soul within him, he may have grown exponentially stronger."

"Something to plan for and use your influence as Queen, then," Faren replied as he opened another sealed letter.

Before I could respond, a knock came from the door to the study. Kara popped her head in and smiled at us. "Princess, Varren is here as you requested."

"Thank you, Kara," I smiled back. She was all smiles these days whenever she looked at me and Faren now, knowing that we were to be wed. "Please, show him in."

Kara disappeared from the doorway, and Varren sauntered in. He stopped near the table where all the letters were piled and whistled. "Got to say, Braids, you're pretty popular."

I smiled. 'Braids' was Varren's nickname for me since I'd never cut my hair but kept it styled in thick braids. He was the only person who ever called me anything other than 'Princess' or 'Exemplar,' apart from Faren or my family, who would just call me by my name.

"You're more than welcome to answer them all for me," I snickered.

"Me?" Varren asked. "Nah! You wouldn't want me to do that. I'd have too much fun seeing what I could get all the nobles to do just to get an audience for you. Then again… seeing Lady Triesse try to juggle mugs of ale while balancing on a ball would be a sight."

Faren and I both chuckled at the thought.

"What brings you here, Varren?" I asked.

Varren reached into his coat and produced a rolled-up map. "This." He moved the letters to the side and unrolled the map onto the table. "The Sourge Sentinel commanders were reluctant to give out these locations but we managed to convince them that you could get to the tombs where no one else could."

I gasped and stood up from my chair to look at the map. "They gave us the location of the final two tombs?"

Varren nodded and tapped two red X's. One was in the Independent Marshes, while another was in Fransway. "Here and here. They said that they have garrisons in the spots to try and look for scourgespawn activity, but since they can't actually get to the tombs themselves, tunneling scourgespawn aren't likely to be spotted."

I rolled my eyes. The Sentinels were excellent warriors, but sometimes they could be a bit short-sighted. "Will they allow us to handle the old gods?"

Varren seemed to hesitate before answering. "They would prefer that you not disturb the old gods. Something about them keeping vigil and not kicking the hornet's nest."

"You've got to be kidding me," Faren growled as he stood to join us. "Merida could kill the old gods while they slept the moment she got close enough to them. Why wouldn't they want her to do that?"

"You know, I asked myself the same thing," Varren leaned on the table. "I honestly couldn't think of a valid reason the Sentinels wouldn't want the old gods dead."

"I can think of one," I huffed in irritation. "But I don't want to believe it."

"Care to enlighten us?" Faren asked as he and Varren stared at me.

"Scourge Sentinels use scourgespawn blood, mixed with dimvyum and a drop of archdemon blood, to create new Scourge Sentinels," I explained.

"You think they want to keep the old gods alive just so they can keep their order going?" Varren asked.

"That doesn't seem to align with their purpose," Faren remarked.

"That's not their purpose," I replied as I considered the thought. "But without fresh archdemon blood, the Sentinels are on a clock. They can only make as many new Scourge Sentinels as their supplies last. But that shouldn't be an issue since they've gotten more blood from the archdemon we killed in Orlimar. So I'm thinking that their leaders, who have to be more concerned with maintaining the order, don't want to risk losing two new sources of archdemon blood in case the scourgespawn become a larger threat again."

"But without the archdemons, the scourgespawn aren't really that much of a threat," Faren pointed out. "They can only reproduce by creating Broodmothers, and while they can make thousands of scourgespawn over their lifetime, it's never enough that they'll be a genuine threat to anyone without leadership."

"He's got a point, Braids," Varren nodded in agreement. "You think the Sentinels want us to leave the old gods alone so that they can just keep making new Sentinels? Do you think they'd sacrifice thousands of innocent lives two more times just to keep their order alive for a while longer?"

"Sentinels will do whatever is necessary to achieve their goals," I said. "I want them to know that I will be traveling to the tombs with the intention of slaying the old gods and stopping the Scourges once and for all. I recommend they work with me. Otherwise, I'll need to show them that it's not the old gods that need to be feared these days."

That seemed to send a shiver down Varren's spine. Still, he bowed his head. "I'll send word to the Sentinels of your intentions. When I get a reply, I'll be sure to let you know."

"Thank you, Varren," I smiled.

"It's my pleasure," he bowed and took his leave.

Faren looked at me. "Do you really want to fight the Sentinels over this?"

I shook my head. "Of course not. But I'm not willing to leave the old gods alive while Seven can still use them to gain power. They have to be taken off the board."

"I don't disagree," Faren sighed and crossed his arms. "You know I'll stand with you no matter what you decide. I just hope we don't have to make an enemy of the Sentinels."

"So do I," I agreed.

It took a few weeks for all of the leaders of the Holds to arrive. Bilfern had even arrived as the newest Lord now that he governed Yivreon. The city was full of commotion with the news that the Assembly would be voting on the next ruler. As far as I was aware, there weren't any other contenders for the crown for once, making it possibly a first in dwarven history. Candidates couldn't cast a vote for themselves, but their proxies could. Candidates were allowed proxies in cases like this to represent them in the Assembly if they were a Caller. In my case, Rita was my appointed proxy.

The day of the Assembly arrived and I was summoned to the Assembly Chamber. Since I was expecting the summons, I was already prepared in one of my finest gowns. The gown was made of thick garnet cloth with polished brass Orodum studs. I wore my customary armored pieces to accentuate the outfit, emerald jewelry, and the ring Franklin had given me when he had proposed. The people were cheering for me as I made my way to the Assembly building, shouting their hopes and joy as I passed.

We stepped into the Assembly's waiting chamber, the stone doors closing behind us. The cheers from the people were muffled now but were still very audible. I approached the familiar sight of Steward Brandon with a smile.

The Steward bowed his head. "Princess Orodum, it's good to see you again. I suppose this will be the last time I can call you that."

I gave him a curtsy in response. "If I'm being honest, Brandon, I hope it's not. But I will do whatever duty the Assembly believes I am needed for."

Brandon stepped forward and gave me a hug. We were old friends by now, and he'd been the steward since I was born. He'd watched me grow from a little girl with powerful aspirations into a woman with humble hopes. "You've always been so dutiful, Princess. Our people are lucky to have you. And if I may say, I think you'll make for a marvelous Queen."

I gave him a resigned smile. "I don't suppose this is where you tell me the vote has already happened so I don't need to be here, is it?"

He laughed, remembering what happened the first time I'd arrived for a vote when I'd been working to create the Surface Caste. "No, Princess. I'm afraid not. You'll have to endure the process this time. Are you ready for me to announce you?"

I stared at the old man, fondly remembering how he'd helped me learn the ins and outs of the Assembly in ways Trenton never really could. I gave him a nod and he patted my cheek.

"You'll make us all proud," he said before moving to the chamber doors. The guards opened the doors, and Brandon stepped into the chamber, raising his voice for all to hear, "Now entering the Assembly Chamber, please all rise for our first candidate; Princess Merida Orodum, Exemplar of dwarves, daughter of King Triston Nordrucan, Hero of Orlimar, and slayer of the Archdemon!"

The Callers and Lords of the Holds thumped the hilt of their weapons or slapped their hands on the banisters before me as I made my way down the Assembly steps, escorted by Faren. I smiled at Father, Trenton, and Bilfern, who all sat together. I turned and nodded to Beltia, Woryek, Gniess, and Rita who were each nearby. I lowered myself into a deep curtsy, "I thank the Assembly for your welcome and have answered your summons as a candidate to take the mantle of Cragmorrar. I am prepared to answer any questions you may have of me."

The chamber went silent for a few moments before Father spoke, "The Assembly thanks you for your cooperation, Daughter. I am proud to see you standing there. I will ask the first question. What more do you believe you can do for our people that you have not already done?"

This was a rather loaded question. It essentially asked me to tell the Assembly if I was planning on continuing to blur the lines of influence between industrious commoners and nobles. I had to consider how best to answer. I bowed my head to Father, "I thank you for the opportunity to put forth my hopes for the future. In my lifetime, with the help of the Assembly and our nobles, we have created the Surface Caste. This single step has brought untold commerce and opportunity to our people."

"With the creation of the Surface Caste, we had to address key issues that had lingered for generations," I continued. "We have addressed surface time and its acceptability within limits, so long as that exposure was to the benefit of us all. We have also addressed the issue of the casteless; giving them the opportunity to work for the betterment of our people and regain an honorable reputation in the process, thus nearly wiping out the stigma of generational dishonor."

I looked around the chamber, then motioned to Faren, "Standing beside me is my betrothed. Faren Orodum was born casteless but has risen to the greatest of heights as a warrior of our people. You all now trust him to not only keep your Princess safe but see him as worthy of taking my hand in marriage. He is living proof of the potential greatness of all our people. It is my hope that we can continue to find ways to give our people more opportunities to reach their potential for the good of us all."

"I also hope that we can continue to expand our control and repairs of the Under Roads, rediscovering and repopulating lost Holds so that we can take back our legacy that was lost to the scourgespawn," I concluded.

There were a good many heads nodding in approval.

"What do our traditions mean to you?" Beltia stood and asked.

This question coming from Beltia held a great deal of importance. She was an Exemplar, and just like me, she embodied everything a dwarf should aspire to be. My answer to this question could sway votes one way or another.

"I appreciate the opportunity to voice my opinion on this matter," I bowed my head to Beltia. "Our traditions are what define us as a people. Past, present, and future, our traditions keep the foundation of our society intact. We have survived and persevered because of our traditions. However, I think we have found that some of our traditions can be changed to bolster the health of our society as a whole. We are richer, stronger, and more like-minded than ever with the creation of the Surface Caste and the limitations placed on who is designated as casteless. We have also found some of our traditions are so integral to our society that we would have been lost without them."

I motioned to Beltia, then to myself. "The naming of Exemplars, for example, gives dwarves benchmarks of greatness to strive for. Commoners can become etched into our history through this tradition, just as Pargon Beltia has been. Great Kings and Queens, such as my Father, have come from noble lines sired by Exemplars. I believe that these traditions are good and healthy, and that they promote the very best in us. And I believe as time goes on we will see which traditions will help us push forward stronger, and which ones may need to be altered to achieve the same goal."

Again there were more nods and mutterings of approval. A few decades ago, and this wouldn't have been the case. But the Callers were all richer now thanks to the changes of certain traditions, so they were willing to keep an open mind about it.

Silence followed for some time before Steward Brandon called out, "It seems there are no more questions. Is there anyone here who would like to voice any reason why the Assembly shouldn't vote to name the Princess as Queen?"

The chamber went silent. Just as Brandon was about to call an end to this part of the meeting, a familiar voice rang out.

"Aye!" Bilfern called out and stood from his seat. "I have reasons that I should share with the Assembly."

This drew a commotion of shock and wild curiosity from the Callers. None of them could think of a reason not to vote for me. However, Bilfern, my young brother and my ward for most of his life, was closer to me than almost anyone. The Callers were no doubt wondering if he had some scurrilous rumor to make public to diminish my reputation before the vote. I could see the morbid excitement in the eyes of some. I made sure to take note of the ones I noticed.

I turned to look at Bilfern in shock and disbelief. "Bilfern?" I asked in confusion.

Bilfern seemed to ignore me as he addressed the Assembly. "Lords and Ladies of the Assembly, I would like to give reasons why Princess Orodum should not be named Queen. First, we should look at the Surface Caste. Princess Orodum likes to point out that it has brought wealth and industry to the dwarves, and in this, she is correct. But the Surface Caste has become a considerable force in our society now, making up a sizable portion of our society. While we enjoy the wealth it brings to us, we also understand that it puts power and influence in the hands of the common folk."

"After that," he said, gripping the bannister tight, "she conspired with you all to hide the fact that she was taking the royal army, as well as many of your warriors, and a large portion of the Fallen Legion to retake Nordrucan Hold. This wasn't even enough. She continued to sacrifice dwarven lives to the scourgespawn to retake more Holds. These Holds took portions of Cragmorrar's population and spread it out over the width of the Under Roads and forced the Fallen Legion to continually patrol these large swaths of territory."

"Next!" he continued, still avoiding my horrified expression. "She dragged our people into a war no one truly believed would happen. For three years, she left us to prepare Orlimar, using our materials with no thought of compensation, and sacrificed dwarven lives, including the lives of her best friend and her betrothed, to stop a Scourge and an Archdemon; a duty that rests on the shoulders of the Scourge Sentinels."

"After that, she continued to leave our people for months at a time," he shouted. "Each time she returned with little to show. Once she returned injured in a way we can still only imagine after fighting off scourgespawn that she encountered. And just recently, she returned from the assassination of a mage that might have threatened us in the future. I hear tell that Prince Clifford of Falladrin fell in that battle after she invited him and his father to join her."

Bilfern looked at the Assembly, who seemed to be considering him carefully. "I ask you now: Are these the actions of a Queen?"

No one dared speak. No one dared to signal whether they agreed or not. I stood there speechless, horrified that Bilfern would speak about me in such a way. I had basically raised him since he was born. I had worked so hard to ensure that he wouldn't turn into the person who would betray me. But as I stood there in the middle of the Assembly Chamber, I felt my heart dropping.

"No," he said and finally met my gaze. He smiled, warmly and confidently. The smile threw me off, and I stood there confused. "These are not the actions of a Queen. These are the actions of an Empress!"

The title, shouted with all his might, now garnered shouts and debates from the Callers.

"The creation of the Surface Caste is one of the greatest achievements in all of our history!" Bilfern shouted. "It has brought more wealth, industry, and influence to our people than ever before! The Holds have allowed our people the chance to spread over parts of our lost dominion— parts that we have not held since our empire fell! With these two things alone, Princess Orodum has reclaimed more of our heritage than any other dwarf before her!"

He stepped down from his seat and entered the center of the chamber to stand beside me. "She spearheaded the forces at Orlimar and slew the Archdemon where even Falladrin's greatest champions failed. She has brought our golems back to us and has brought us closer to the titans of old. She has fought alongside our warriors and sacrificed as much, or more, than any of them in the pursuit of bringing peace and prosperity to our people. She is the friend of legends and ally to all. We cannot name her Queen because the title is unworthy of her! She has expanded our people beyond a simple kingdom!"

He turned and stared at me, a wide smile on his face. "I call upon the Callers of the Assembly to show their allegiance here and now! Bend the knee and all hail Empress Orodum!" With that, he moved to kneel before me.

Faren was the first to follow suit, followed closely by Steward Brandon, Trenton, and Rita. Slowly, every Lord and every Caller bent the knee, shouting in unison, "All hail Empress Orodum!"

The shouts continued for a full minute until Father stood from his seat and walked to me. The cries died down, but no one stood. They watched in silence as Father took my hand and smiled at me. "I could not have imagined a child of mine would do so much. I could not have imagined any dwarf could have done so much. I wish your mother could be here to see this. She wouldn't be able to hide her excitement for you."

He turned, keeping my hand in his, and addressed the Callers. "Today, you have all made history. You have decided in one voice that the dwarves of old have begun to reassert themselves once more. That the kingdom we have been limited to is once again a burgeoning empire! And you have chosen your Empress. I see no dissenting votes, so I declare that with unanimous consent, Princess Merida Orodum shall be crowned Empress Merida Orodum, first of her name, hope of her people, protector of the realm, Exemplar to dwarves, hero of Orlimar, and slayer of the Archdemon!"

The Assembly Chamber shook with the cheers of Callers who stood and continued their cheers of "Hail Empress Orodum!"

Bilfern stood and smiled up at me. "Admit it, Sister. I had you going there for a good bit."

I could only huff and laugh softly. "I nearly cried. Never do something like that again. I thought you were truly angry with me."

Bilfern laughed and bowed his head. "As you command, Empress."

"Hush," I said quickly. "I've not been crowned yet."

"That won't matter to the people," Trenton said as he approached and picked me up in a hug. "Also, I should let you know that this was my idea."

I looked up at Trenton in surprise. "What? Why would you suggest something so extreme?"

"I told you years ago, Merida," Trenton explained. "You are the person who should lead our people. When you retook the Holds, I saw our empire emerging once again. Then you began to add to your accolades, outshining yourself each time more than the last. An empire is what you've begun to build. It's only right that you're given a title commensurate with it."

I was blindsided by an excited hug. Rita smiled at me. "I knew it! I knew you would achieve amazing things, Merida! How could we all not support you?"

I laughed at Rita. "I suppose I should thank you, then. But I hardly believe I'm qualified to be an Empress."

"If you aren't, I don't know who is," she smiled.

"Wait..." I paused and turned to look at Faren. "Did you know about this?"

Faren made a mockingly shocked face. "Me? My dear, how could you ask me that? I'm just a lowly warrior. I've no mind for politics or secret keeping."

I smirked at him. "That's the last secret you keep from me."

"I'm sure it won't be," he chuckled as he hugged me tight.

"Princess?" Steward Brandon called softly.

I turned and faced the Steward. "Yes?"

"We have to make our announcement," he said. "It has been decided that King Triston will address the crowd first, then you will be allowed some remarks. The Assembly will then decide on when your coronation will be."

"Very well," I replied and looked to Father. "Are you ready?"

He nodded. "Come, my dear. Let's see this through together."

We left the Assembly with everyone in tow. Guards surrounded us, and the Callers filed in behind as we left the building. Our destination was the balcony that was above the exit to the Noble District. The last time I was there with Father, I was announcing the successful reclamation of Nordrucan Hold. Below us was a sea of dwarves, staring up in anticipation.

Steward Brandon waved to the crowd, "People of Cragmorrar. The Assembly has come to its conclusion. As is his right, King Nordrucan has decided to announce his successor."

The crowd cheered for Father as he moved forward so that he could be seen, "My people! It is with great pleasure that I present to you the decision of the Callers! It is with a mix of emotions that I must tell you that there will not be a new King or Queen of Cragmorrar."

This elicited a wave of confusion from the crowd.

"Instead, the Assembly has come to a different conclusion altogether," he continued. "Cragmorrar is no longer considered a kingdom by the Assembly. It has, instead, been acknowledged as returning to its former state as the capital of a dwarven empire! And it is with great pleasure that I present to you your first dwarven Empress, to be crowned on a date yet to be decided by the Assembly, Princess Merida Orodum! All hail your future Empress!"

The city shook with the crowd's elation as I stepped forward to smile and wave down at the crowd. Cheers and shouts of 'All Hail the Empress' and 'Long Live Empress Orodum' were chanted more times than I could count.

As happy as they were, all I could see was a snare. This elevation, this position, would keep me in Cragmorrar from now on. I would rarely ever get to leave. I wouldn't be able to do more than rule. I would be bound to the city from then on. If I wanted to achieve my goals, I would need to convince the Assembly to at least give me enough time to put an end to the old gods. If I could at least do that, then I could mostly ensure that Seven wouldn't be as much of a threat as he could be. I could diminish his ability to threaten my people.

Still, I hadn't realized until this moment that becoming Queen, or Empress, would essentially end my ability to adventure in the world of Thoros. The moment I was crowned, I would be expected to stay in Cragmorrar as much as possible, and whenever I did not need to leave... which would essentially be always. Unless some foreign power requested my presence for diplomatic talks or to attend some ceremony, I would likely never leave the city again. The thought saddened me. Was this what I had worked so hard for? Was my reward for all my efforts a leash that extended to the gates of this city? Was I willing to accept the will of the Assembly, the wishes of the people, and become Empress? Did I even truly have a choice?

While all of Cragmorrar celebrated, I stood there waving, with doubt and uncertainty weighing me down.

CHAPTER 34:

A GREAT DECEPTION

The moment we arrived home from the announcement of the Callers choosing me to become Empress, Faren and I set to work planning our next move.

"Let them know that I don't care one way or another," I shouted, pulling the maps of Fransway and the Independent Marshes to the table. "If the Sentinels don't want to help, I'll rip the continent apart until I find those tombs! They can have all the blood they want from those monsters, but one way or another, I'm going to kill them!"

Faren was doing damage control. Whenever I got angry enough, the stone would stir and shake, and he would use his abilities to put things back the way they were. It was rare that my temper rose to this level, but I'm not perfect. I did try to keep the anger contained, but that never worked out in the long run. I learned that in my first life.

"I don't think you need to go quite that far, Love," Faren said as he moved to the table to look at the maps. "The Independent Marshes are closer than Fransway if we want to start the search there."

"In the Raisend Mountains, yes?" I asked as I checked the map that Varren had brought us to the large maps we had of the areas.

"Indeed, My Love," Faren nodded and pointed to the general area. "From what I can tell, there are likely dozens of cave systems that could possibly lead down to the tomb. But if what the Sentinels claim is true, the ground around the tombs is too loose to properly tunnel or dig through safely."

"Then how do they know where the tombs are, I wonder," I moved to look at where Faren was pointing. "I have to wonder how they would know where they are if they couldn't safely get to them to find out."

"You think they're lying?" Faren asked and looked at me.

"They're either there because they could get there and see them…" I paused as I considered my next words carefully, "Or they're lying and are trying to keep us from them. My theory is that they were able to get close enough to sense it, but didn't have the tools or the skill to get to them. Dwarves have found such places at least once that I can remember: below Hardrin Hold."

"So what do you propose?" Faren asked. "That we go to these two areas and just start searching?"

"The moment we start getting close, I can begin reaching out with my stone sense," I explained. "If you sense for enemies and keep a lookout, I'll find the tomb."

"What do we do about Seven?" Faren took in a deep breath. "We know he's been trying to prod at the edge of your senses. Eventually, they'll notice the protection is gone, and they'll push in like they try to whenever you leave."

"That's what we have the Fallen Legion for," I responded. "We'll put them on high alert. And we'll also have them talk often and loudly about how I've found the next old god's tomb in the Cariok Wilds. Seven won't be able to resist that amount of power."

"Sending the scourgespawn down to the Cariok Wilds will put the elves of Orlimar in danger," Faren responded with concern. "We'll need to warn them."

"I agree," I sighed and sat down in a chair. "I don't think they'll be too much of a bother since they'll be tunneling deep beneath the surface. But I have faith in Trianna and Aelfric to handle any raiding bands as long as they're aware of the danger."

"And what happens if they grow too frustrated and head back to our home?" Faren continued to give me things to consider.

"Again, that's what the Fallen Legion is for," I said with more conviction. "By the time Seven believes we tricked him, or that the information was simply wrong, I think we'll be on our way home as well. The Cariok Wilds are vast, and we won't exactly be specific."

"You think it will be that quick? I doubt it," Faren crossed his arms.

"No, of course it won't be," I chuckled. "We'll be traveling from here to the Raisend Mountains, then to Fransway. The trip will take months. But we'll have roads and paths to travel. Seven will need to weave through the Under Roads, caverns, and even tunnel his way through the underground world of the Wilds. It will take him more time just to get to the Wilds than it will for us to get to the mountains in the Independent Marshes."

Faren moved around the table and pulled a chair up next to mine, taking a seat. "That's a fair point. How many men do you want to take?"

"We'll send the House guard and whatever retinue the Assembly deems sufficient south to Orlimar and put on a show of searching the Under Roads," I replied. "That will make the deception more convincing."

"It will also put their lives at risk."

I looked at Faren and nodded. "Yes. It will. But our people have been fighting the scourgespawn for a thousand years. We know what it means to die fighting them. Every death in battle against the scourgespawn means our people are kept safe. This time, it means that everyone, not just dwarves, will be kept safe. And the harder they fight them, the more convincing they will be. The safer we will be."

Faren nodded slowly. "You didn't answer my question. How many men do you want to take with us?"

"None," I replied quietly.

"The Assembly won't allow it," Faren reminded me.

I chuckled. "This is the last time I'll be able to leave Cragmorrar on any kind of personal task. And it's the only chance we'll ever get to be truly alone before I'm shackled to the throne."

Faren leaned over and took my hand in his. "Shackled is a bit much."

"Shackled," I insisted firmly. "I won't be able to do what we've been doing anymore. No more adventures. No more visits to see our friends just so we can visit them. No more meetings at the College to see how the curriculum is coming along. No more… anything. Just sitting and ruling."

"I'm sure there will be more than that," Faren patted my hand. "After all, your family found some time for levity. And besides, it's not all that different from what you've been doing all your life, is it? Since you were one year old, you've been planning for this exact thing: hunting down the remaining old gods and saving Thoros from future Scourges."

"But not ruling," I sighed and leaned over to hug him close. "I hoped Trenton would rule and that I'd be his chief councilor. I hoped to make the lives of dwarves better and be remembered that way. I didn't want to be a Queen, let alone an empress. I only ever wanted to do good."

"Well, you know what they say…" Faren said as he embraced me. "No good deed goes unpunished."

"I could kill you right now and not even your mother would say a word," I laughed and kissed his cheek. "But truly, I want this to be our adventure. I want us to be able to look back on a time when we were alone together. No guards, no nobles, no politics, no praise, no sycophants… Just us."

"As much as I would like that, I don't see how you'll convince the Assembly," Faren smiled sadly at me.

"We don't need to convince the Assembly," I grinned. "We just have to convince the soldiers."

"Just tell me what we need to do."

I spoke with the Assembly the next day to propose my idea. I never mentioned how I was going to leave the soldiers behind. The Assembly did not like the idea of their future Empress going to hunt down the remaining old gods, but they could appreciate the need for the mission in the long term. No more old gods meant no more Scourges and fewer scourgespawn. Possibly the complete eradication of the scourgespawn.

There was also the issue of my coronation. Father insisted that he would not postpone the transfer of power. He understood where he would be soon enough mentally and did not want to stain his legacy with that in people's minds. The Assembly gave me six months to return, whether I was successful or not. The business of running Cragmorrar and its Holds would not wait for me. I understood that part was not meant as an insult but as an unassailable reality. Life wouldn't stop just because I was gone.

As per my suggestions, dwarven forces were sent south with an explanation to Trianna and Aelfric. As we had guessed, they insisted on sending a force to guard me but couldn't afford to send any more forces from Cragmorrar. I suggested that half of the House Orodum forces that were to head south to Orlimar could come with me. They were loyal and would be sure to keep me safe. The Assembly agreed to my suggestion since they didn't think we'd encounter much trouble on the road with a decently sized retinue of guards. Once the Assembly agreed on some of the finer details, we coordinated with the Fallen Legion on when they could start spreading the rumors of my departure.

We left a week later when I was certain the probes at the edge of my influence had stopped. We took the Under Roads to Coralstine. My House guards waited in the Under Roads while Faren and I snuck onto a boat heading to Fetral. I didn't alert Serena to my arrival because I knew she would tell someone, and I wanted us to be alone.

Upon our arrival in Fetral, we bought food to go along with the supplies we already had. We took a few days to wander the city and enjoy seeing it in person to compare its looks and size to what the game was able to show. It was true that we were on a clock, but we could spare a few days. In fact, I knew how we could make up for some time. On our last night in Fetral, Faren and I went to Dredgeworks and entered The Skullduggery, a tavern with a rowdy clientele. Inside the tavern were dock workers, sailors, thieves, and more. I admit to being less than comfortable immediately. It probably didn't help that we were two very clean dwarves dressed in decent fashion. Still, I think Faren's scowl was enough to turn heads away from us.

I made my way to the bar. There was a drunk man sleeping on a stool, and I looked at Faren. "Could you ask him to sleep it off somewhere else?"

"Of course, my dear," Faren said as he hauled the man off the stool and threw him into a corner on the floor.

That got a laugh from the rest of the people in the Tavern.

I climbed up onto the stool, and Faren took the one next to me.

"That's one way to make some room, eh?" a woman's voice called from my side. She was dark-skinned, voluptuous, and lithe. She wore a white tunic, a blue headband wrapped over the top of her head, tall leather boots, and selective pieces of armor along her arms and legs.

"My betrothed likes to spoil me," I grinned up at her.

"So I see," she said as she leaned her back against the bar. "So what's all this, then? You two dwarf nobles come down to experience the seedy side of the city? Get a thrill once in your life?"

Faren barked out a laugh. "You have no idea what you're talking about. We've seen more than you can imagine."

"Oh, I'm sure you have," the woman teased.

"Forgive him. My betrothed takes great pride in his accomplishments," I chuckled. "We didn't come for the thrill. We came for something else."

"Is that so?" She leaned in and whispered into my ear, "So intriguing. What brings you to The Skullduggery, then?"

I turned and leaned in to rest my lips beside her ear and whispered back, "You do."

The woman stood up with a sly smile. "You intrigue me more and more, darling. Keep talking."

I turned so I could face her. "You're the captain of the Banshee's Wail, Trisha. And we need to hire a ship to take us to the Raisend Mountains, then Fransway, and then to Falladrin."

Trisha let out a long whistle. "That's weeks of sailing at the least, little lady."

I nodded in agreement. "That's true. And you'll be waiting for us while we look for things. That will probably take a few more weeks."

Trisha laughed. "You're asking quite a bit for someone I've only just met. Do you know how much that will cost you?"

I looked over my shoulder at Faren, who just smirked, then looked back at Trisha, "How much?"

"Going rate is a silver per mile," Trisha said, then took a draft from her mug. "But you're coming here because you don't want someone discreet. So that'll be at least triple the price. One gold a mile, and a gold for every day we have to sit there waiting for you. A good guess would be two hundred fifty gold, rounding up for my excellent service."

"Not going to lie," Faren laughed. "I thought it'd be a lot more expensive."

"Ugh!" Trisha groaned. "Here I thought I was going to get rid of… wait? What do you mean?"

I snatched Trisha's hand quickly and shook it. "Deal!"

"Wait!" she protested as she tried to pull her hand from my grasp. "Bloody hells, woman! You've got a grip like iron! But no! What did you mean by you thought it would be more expensive?"

"Eh," I smirked, "you'll get your price! When can we set sail?"

Trisha groaned and sighed. "We can set sail in the morning whenever you like. Best to come at noon, though. Give the lads some time to sober up."

"Tomorrow at noon, then," I smiled. I reached into my gambeson, fished out a small coin purse, and tossed it to Trisha. "This is going to be a grand adventure!"

CHAPTER 35:

WHERE I AM BLIND

Faren and I made our way to the docks in Dredgeworks. The area was teeming with activity as we worked our way through the streets. It'd been a long time since we'd been through such a crowded and bustling street. Cragmorrar was always busy, but the population of the dwarves was spread fairly thin over the surface and the Holds. We didn't get to see the streets this busy very often. Christmas did bring most everyone back, and so did the Assembly when it was time to choose the next ruler.

Unlike Cragmorrar, however, no less than six people tried picking my pockets. Thanks to my ability to track people using the vibrations in the stone, I was aware of everyone around me. No one got into my pockets, but the stone did leave them with a broken foot. I admit that it was nice to be treated the same as everyone. Here in Fetral, I was just another rich mark; someone to scam or steal from. Faren was ever alert and aggressive as always, but I was loving every moment of it. I hadn't been treated like everyone else since I was reborn into Thoros. It was refreshing.

We weaved our way through the docks to find Trisha's ship, the Banshee's Wail. The schooner was impressive and kept in good condition. We arrived just after noon. Trisha's crew was busy getting the ship ready to sail. I stopped to admire the vessel. I had been a sailor during my early twenties in my first life and had the pleasure of serving for two months on the USCG Eagle. The Eagle was a substantially larger vessel and faster than the Banshee's Wail, but the schooner was still a beautiful ship. It was likely faster and more nimble than the Eagle as well.

We walked up to the sailor on guard duty. I smiled up at him and gave him a crisp salute. "Request permission to come aboard."

The sailor looked down at me as if I had lost my mind. "What?"

"We're requesting permission to come aboard your vessel," I replied.

"Why? Who are you?" he asked.

I looked at Faren then back at the sailor. "We're the ones who hired your ship."

"Oh," the sailor said as if that fact didn't matter. "Why didn't you say so?"

"She just did," Faren stepped forward. "Give her the permission she very professionally requested."

"Fine, fine," the sailor huffed and waved us off. "Go ahead and get on board."

I couldn't help but deflate a bit with disappointment. The situation had sparked a very old, very specific piece of my training from my first life. I had hoped that the sailor would salute back, and give me a clear-sounding response. But it was all for naught. I sighed and turned to walk up the gangplank when I heard Faren behind me tell the sailor that he ought to work on that so long as we were on board.

Trisha greeted us as we stepped onto the deck of the ship. "Ah! There's my two favorite dwarves! Right on time, too! Have any trouble getting here?"

I put on a happy face and smiled at Trisha. "Just a few pickpockets, but they left empty-handed."

"Good for you!" Trisha laughed. "Always good to have a little adventure each day. We've got a cabin all set up for you."

"Are we ready to set sail?" I asked eagerly.

"That we are!" she exclaimed. "Ready when you are."

"Let's head out, then!" I said excitedly. I looked back at Faren. "Do you know what we should do?"

"I am not going to the front and shouting that I'm king of the world," Faren shook his head.

"First, it's called the bow of the ship," I huffed. "Second, we're not going to be moving that fast any time soon. We'd need a good strong wind for that."

Faren arched his brows. "And third?"

I walked over to him and kissed his cheek. "Third… you most certainly are. Well, I am. But we both have to be there."

Trisha laughed at us. "Well, you two relax. We'll take care of the sailing. I'll have one of my men show you where your cabin is."

We were shown to the cabin and given free reign of the ship while we were on board. I did manage to get Faren to reenact the scene from Titanic with me. I'm certain most of the sailors who watched us thought we were crazy, but I didn't care. We were on our own for once in our lives and I was going to have fun. I didn't have to worry about seeming like a proper noble, or a respectable Princess, or an honored Exemplar. And even with his protests, I think Faren enjoyed the reenactment.

Over the next few days, Trisha sailed us east as I'd requested, keeping the coast within sight of the ship. Faren and I relaxed as much as we could while swapping stories with Trisha. We kept our stories vague. We'd been a part of the retaking of the Holds, we fought at Orlimar, witnessed the magister that interrupted the Testament Bout for the Princess's hand in marriage. Trisha appreciated the stories and commended us on our luck for escaping the battles alive. All the while, I was sensing for anything in the ground that might be large enough, or conspicuous enough, to hold an old god. We had nearly reached the Coralstine Ocean when I finally found something.

I told Trisha we needed to search in the area. She weighed anchor and had one of her men drop a rowboat into the water for us. Faren rowed us to shore and we pulled the boat up so that the tide wouldn't take it away.

"How deep is it?" Faren asked as he tied the rope to a large rock.

"It's actually above us," I said as I grabbed a pack of food we'd brought with us.

"Above us?" Faren asked. "You mean it's actually up in the mountains?"

I nodded and pointed to one of the mountain peaks. "Right there. I'm sensing a large void with strange echoes coming from it."

"So we'll be climbing, then," Faren sighed.

"Oh, yes, we dwarves simply don't have experience climbing rocks," I said sarcastically.

Faren grunted and grinned. "You're going to talk your way into a situation you can't talk yourself out of one day, you know."

I stuck my tongue out and moved the pack over my shoulder. "Let me know when that situation arises, will you?"

"I certainly will," he chuckled.

I could use my ability to move us through the stone quickly to get to the area we were headed to, but I wanted the memory of climbing the mountain with Faren. We took things slow, and took breaks often so we didn't tire out. The climb would have taken us about an hour if we had been going seriously, but we came to a stop after four hours.

"We're here," I said as we crested the last ledge.

"No cave or other entrance," Faren commented as he looked around. "Can you still feel the echoes?"

I nodded as I looked at the mountain face. "I can. But I can't… make sense of the echo."

Faren looked at me curiously. "What do you mean?"

"I can't see into the void the way I normally can when I sense echoes in the stone," I said. "It's like… trying to find a picture in static."

"Maybe it has something to do with the power surrounding the old god?" Faren suggested.

"I guess we'll find out, won't we?" I smiled. "Ready for an adventure?"

"Not sure this qualifies, exactly, but sure," Faren said.

I shook my head, rolled my eyes, then turned and willed the stone to open before us.

We walked for several minutes before the cavern opened up ahead of us suddenly. The sight that greeted us was glorious and horrifying. The old god was sleeping in the form of an ancient dragon. Its form was awe-inspiring. I almost couldn't take my eyes off of it until movement from the side of the chamber caught my attention. I turned to see what it was, and my stomach dropped. The Crafter was standing there with a small horde of scourgespawn.

"Princess Orodum," it greeted me with a bow. "I would like to thank you for helping us find this great treasure."

"Crafter…" I responded cautiously. "Why are you here?"

"I have come to transform the old god into an archdemon," it responded mournfully.

"You said before that you did not wish to see another Scourge," Faren barked. "Why would you want to turn the old god into an archdemon?"

"The last time you saw Seven, he had killed Varrimus and contained his soul," the Crafter explained. "This granted him all the power that Varrimus wielded, including influence over scourgespawn. He is as much of an archdemon as this creature will become. However, his willpower is far stronger… I have my mind to a degree still… but I am under his compulsion. I have no choice but to obey his desires to corrupt the old god."

"I thought he wanted to take the old god's soul for his own," I said, thinking about how I could get the upper hand. "Why would he allow you to corrupt it when he could simply kill it and take its soul now?"

"Because he is in the Karaoke Wilds searching for its resting place," the Crafter replied. "However, when we noticed your sphere of influence moving, he commanded me to follow it. We did. When you began to head east, we followed as well. However, we began to hear the song from the old god. It called to us. It spurred us forward. We had only just arrived when you appeared through the stone."

"Why didn't I sense you moving?" I asked myself more than the Crafter.

"The water," Faren gasped. "You must have been so focused on sensing for large caverns that the feedback from the waves allowed them to blend in like background noise."

"I cannot attest to what your friend says," the Crafter sighed. "However, I don't believe it matters. Seven's will compels us to wake and infect the old god. We must wake it. Please, for your own sake, do not attempt to stop us or we will be forced to attack you."

"I was still relatively new wielding the titan's powers when we first met," I warned him. "I have long since mastered these abilities. It won't be a fight. I can't allow you to wake this creature."

"Then it seems we are at an impasse," the Crafter sighed. "I regret that things must come to this, Princess. Know that I do not wish to engage you."

The other scourgespawn behind the Crafter surged forward.

Faren had long since readied his sword and shield, and he moved in front of me. "Merida! Stay behind me!"

I willed the stone ground in front of us to jump into hundreds of spikes, skewering most of the charging scourgespawn. I was preparing to do more when a ball of fire shot by and exploded in a flash behind me. The Crafter wasn't going to give me the chance to focus. I summoned my battle magic effects, shifting partially into the Dimvolmn and enhancing myself and Faren with magic.

"Can you hold them?" I shouted to Faren.

"Don't worry about me," he roared as a scourgespawn managed to slip past the spiked ground, and his blade split the creature from its collarbone to its groin. "Focus on the Crafter!"

I nodded and commanded the stone to strike at it from multiple angles. Dozens of stone spikes sped towards the Crafter. However, as the spikes came close to striking it, they shattered against some unknown force.

"You are nothing, if not predictable, Princess," the Crafter said as he weaved a spell. "When I last witnessed your display of power, I understood how you strike at me. I have taken precautions." He finished his spell and fire erupted from the ground, burning the surface in a large area.

Faren and I both instinctively pushed the flaming stone away from us. I summoned a large blizzard centered on the Crafter, then a lightning storm as well. The combined effects hindered and harried the dawkspawn, and forced the Crafter to relocate. I had been foolish and left my sword at home. I hadn't thought we would engage in combat where I couldn't use my stone abilities. Faren wielded the stone against the base scourgespawn, using it to block their approach, impale them, or parry attacks so that he could get in a killing blow. I hadn't noticed how adept he'd become at it until I took a moment to watch him.

The crackling of magic that wasn't my own snapped me back into focus, and I dove to the side just as a black missile of smoking energy splashed on the stone where I had been. I had taken my eyes off the Crafter long enough to allow it to get another spell off. I reached out with my hand and sent a blinding arc of lightning out that struck the Crafter and several scourgespawn around it.

I sprinted parallel to the Crafter, dodging magical missiles of all sorts before I slipped down into the stone, disappearing from his view. I reached out with the stone and brought one of the fallen scourgespawn's greatswords to my hand. A moment later, I erupted from the ground in front of the Crafter and swung the blade up in a wide arc. The blade bit into the Crafter's ribs and it jumped away, roaring in pain. A handful of base scourgespawn lunged at me, but I quickly cut two of them down with my sword while the stone impaled the others.

Stone spikes sprang toward the Crafter and shattered, one after the other. The Crafter grimaced, "I told you, Princess. I have prepared for HUH!"

The Crafter shouted as the ground opened up beneath him just enough to cause him to fall to his knees. I dashed forward and swung the sword, barely missing the Crafter's neck and leaving a gash on its forehead as it turned away just in time. The Crafter shoved its hands in the air and a pillar of flame burst up from them. I barely managed to shield myself with a wall of stone to keep from catching fire.

Just as the pillar of flame dissipated, I brought the stone wall down and dropped my sword. I lunged forward and snatched the Crafter's wrists. I snarled down at him, "Fry, you filth!"

I screamed and summoned as much mana as I could pour into a constant series of chain lightning spells, all focused solely on the Crafter. We screamed together; me in a furious rage, it in excruciating pain. As our screams died down, the Crafter was a twitching, charred husk on the floor. I was breathing heavily, but I grabbed the sword I had dropped. I didn't think the Crafter could recover from the damage I had done, but I wasn't going to take the chance. I swung the sword with all of my might and took the Crafter's head off. I turned, ready to confront the rest of the scourgespawn, but found that Faren was handling the last few. I aided him with a quick summoning of stone spikes.

Faren collected himself before looking at me, "Is it over?"

I nodded as I continued to catch my breath. I'd never used that much magic in a single burst, and the drain was substantial.

Faren jogged over to me and took me in his arms, "Are you alright? Are you hurt?"

I allowed myself to rest against him and shook my head, "I'm fine. I just used a lot of magic. He… The stone couldn't get close to him."

"I saw," Faren assured me. "But it didn't help him."

"Still," I said with concern, "if he managed it, Seven may have as well. Especially if he became strong enough to control the Crafter…"

"Then let's take steps to ensure he can't grow any stronger," Faren nodded to the, thankfully, still sleeping form of the old god.

I stepped back from Faren and looked at the old god. I nearly had the stone skewer the creature then and there before I caught myself. I poured my senses into the stone and found that, while I couldn't sense into the cavern, I could sense out of it. I took a great deal of time as I spread my senses and influence as far out as I could. I mapped the land further out then we would be able to see from the mountain peak. From the surface down to the Under Roads, and deeper still. I took the time to mark every living creature that was moving and found each scourgespawn still underground. Once I was certain that I had found them all, I killed them all. Each of them was sliced to ribbons, then crushed to a pulp. Even the dead scourgespawn and the Crafter within the cavern were torn into pieces in a spray of blood and gore.

Faren jumped, startled. "What the hell was that?"

"When an archdemon dies, its soul transfers to a scourgespawn if it's close enough and reforms itself," I explained. "I made sure there isn't a live scourgespawn for as far as I could manage."

"Smart…" Faren said. "Could have warned me first."

I chuckled and pecked Faren's cheek. "I'm sorry, love."

He hummed and looked at the old god. "Let's get this over with, shall we?"

I looked at the creature and sighed. "It's a shame to have to destroy such an amazing creature. Still, if we don't, it will be responsible for the death of who knows how many people."

I stared at the creature for a few more moments, basking in its majesty before letting out a remorseful sigh. The stone jumped forward from a hundred different angles, skewering and slicing into the old god in a flurry of relentless attacks. The creature barely had time to wake and croak out a scream before it was already dead. The whole thing took only a few moments before it was over.

Faren looked at me regretfully. "Shame, really… If only there was a way to save them."

"I still wouldn't," I said as I shook my head. I turned and started back for the mountainside. "Serevas imprisoned them and tore the world asunder to keep them in check. They were worse than he was, and he wanted to destroy the world to get back to the way it was. What do you think they would do if given the chance?"

"You mean apart from starting a scourge?" Faren asked rhetorically.

I hummed in acknowledgment. As the stone moved aside to let us pass, we stepped back out into the sunlight. I leaned against Faren, and he hugged me to his side.

"You ever wish that this was what we could have been doing this entire time?" I asked as I looked up at him. "Not the whole… scourgespawn, old god-slaying thing… More like the traveling and adventuring in the wide world thing."

Faren hummed and shrugged. "It might have been interesting. But I think you've done so much good that it's worth missing out on a lifetime of this."

"That's a fancy way of saying 'yes,'" I snickered.

Faren laughed and looked down at me. "Come on. Let's get back to the ship."

"No," I grinned up at him. "Let's enjoy some time alone together. They'll wait a couple of days, remember?"

Faren smiled down at me. "As you wish, my dear."

CHAPTER 36:

THE PRINCESS CALLS

We returned to the ships a few days later. We'd take the extra days on land to explore the mountains and simply enjoy being alone together for what might be the only time in our lives. Honestly, I didn't even want to go back to the ship. If it wasn't to achieve my goal, I would have tried to convince Faren to run away from everything with me. But I couldn't bring myself to shirk the responsibility I had. The crew welcomed us back, and Trisha guided the ship to face west so that we could begin our journey towards Fransway.

I began to have strange dreams the first few evenings of the journey to Fransway. "Dreams" wasn't the correct term, though. I was in the Dimvolmn but always seemed to be in the same spot regardless of where we were in the world at the time. Each time, I felt like there were presences around me—others whom I couldn't see or hear. It felt like they were trying to communicate with me, but I couldn't quite connect with them. During my waking hours, I could still feel them. It was like I could almost see someone in the corner of my eye, but when I turned to look, there was nothing there. This went on for nearly a week.

Talking with Faren didn't help much. He didn't have the faintest clue how to help me and suggested that it might just be the fact that my earth senses were being interfered with over the water; that somehow the signals I was getting back were making me sense things that weren't there. It was pure speculation, of course, but there was nothing else he could do. I doubted his theory, but I appreciated his desire to help.

Progress was made the night before we docked in Fransway. I stood in the middle of an ancient stone chamber with a large circular pool resting in the middle. The pool's water was a black void that threatened to swallow me into infinity with its stillness. Thin, ancient trees twisted and wove themselves into a canopy over the chamber. This place was ancient, beyond the realms of my knowledge. It vaguely resembled the Well of Mourning from Inquest, but it gave off a sense of age well beyond that location.

As I walked around the pool to inspect it, I heard footsteps approaching. I turned and saw an elven woman with starlight in her hair and brilliance in her eyes. I canted my head to the side as I considered her. She was ethereal beyond measure but rooted in a hard reality that was completely alien to my mind.

Before I could address her, another set of footsteps echoed from the blur of the chamber's surroundings. Serevas stepped into the chamber. I began to move into a defensive stance but paused as he smiled gently at me and shook his head.

"You do not need to be afraid, Princess," he said softly. His tone was honest and sincere. "We are no longer enemies, you and I. I am as much a part of you as she is." He nodded to the other elf. "And as much as he is."

I turned to see who Serevas was referring to, and another male elf stood on the other side of the pool. His face was gaunt and tired, with long hair that shimmered like oil on water. He stared at me with a gaze that seemed to penetrate my very soul.

"Who are you?" I asked curiously. As strange as he appeared, he seemed like he cared deeply for me and was my best of friends.

"I was called Dalon'Tara," he replied, bowing his head slightly. "How did I come to this place?"

"The same way we all did," Serevas answered. "Our dwarven friend slew us and claimed our souls in the process."

"What?" I asked in shock. "I never claimed anyone's soul!"

Dalon'Tara smiled in understanding. "I see. So we will dwindle and merge with her spirit, then."

"In time, yes," Serevas smiled. "But we will never truly die now. Our host is a titan, and even as we slept for these many years, they still sleep as well."

Dalon'Tara walked around the pool and stooped next to the female. "Jeron? Why don't you speak to us?"

"She's too far gone," Serevas said. "Her spirit whispers to the Princess now. I'm rather surprised she could manage to manifest herself at this point. Perhaps this is the last time we will be able to see her even in this way…"

Dalon'Tara looked at me, "How is it you, a dwarf, can be called a titan?"

"Sense it for yourself," Serevas answered as I had to consider the question. "She may not even know it yet. But the titan she encountered didn't simply bless her; it infused itself into her. Where once there was a titan, there is now a wide gulf beneath the Under Roads. Where once there was a dwarf, there now stands a titan."

I looked at Serevas in wonder, "What are you saying? Are you telling me the titan is dead now?"

"Only as much as I am," Serevas replied. "Or as much as my peers are. Our power, our energy, is a part of you now. You have access to our knowledge and wisdom just as you have access to the titan's. You may not have realized it, but your connection to the world isn't growing; your connection to the titan's spirit is. I should have considered that before I attacked. But you, Princess Merida, are the titan now. In time, you will be as much a part of this world as the very stone itself."

I stared at my hands as if there was some answer in them, "I… am the titan? Then I haven't been increasing my power all this time? I've simply been growing into it?"

Serevas nodded, "Precisely so. You are a babe learning to crawl. When you grow into your full capabilities, your power over the world of Thoros will be all-encompassing."

I stared at Serevas silently as the information settled, "Then… once you dwindle into my spirit, does that mean—"

"That you will command his power?" Dalon'Tara interrupted. "In a sense. You will be capable of anything he was capable of, but you are far more capable than you should be even with your nightly practice in the Dimvolmn. If I were to guess, you are slowly adding Jeron's power to your own. In the end, once we have all melded into your spirit, your power will multiply with every spirit you take into yourself."

Serevas chuckled, "It would seem you will be a pantheon unto yourself."

I looked between the elves apologetically, "This isn't what I wanted."

"Your want had nothing to do with this," Dalon'Tara said. "There were only two possible ways our deaths would affect you. Either you absorbed our spirits, or we would be reborn into the world and fight you for the right to conquer it. You were lucky, we were not."

"I'm sorry that this is what happened to you," I said quietly.

"Do not be," Dalon'Tara shook his head. "We brought this fate upon ourselves. Our hubris caused Trith'Emel to trick us and seal us away."

"And my temper and arrogance caused my death," Serevas sighed. "If our power is to be used, I can think of no one better to wield it. You, at least, genuinely care for this world and will protect it. If this is to be our fate, then it is a good one."

"I concur," Dalon'Tara said. He approached me and placed a hand on my shoulder. "We waged war on the titans for thousands of years. We balked against their desire to mold the world because it meant our cities and creations would be destroyed in the process. But even in our immortality, we could not see that the only thing that remains is our world. We were too attached to temporary power, our temporary stations… when we should have been more concerned with the world we left behind. Trith'Emel says you will have a care for this world, so I am happy to leave my power to you."

I smiled up at Dalon'Tara. "I will put that power to good use."

Serevas smiled at me. "Of that we have no doubt."

"May I ask a question?" I said.

"Considering our positions, you should not need to ask permission," Serevas replied.

I nodded. "Very well, then. Pristaren is the only one of you left. You sealed him away. Will you give me the knowledge to find him?"

"All of our knowledge is yours," Serevas replied. "You do not have to ask for it. You need only consider it, like you do with anything, and it will come to you. But I will actively offer the information while I can."

"I've considered this, but have no answer for it," I said. "How is it I can now see you and speak with you?"

"Anything we say will be conjecture," Dalon'Tara replied. "However, I would wager that it has to do with your absorbing my soul. Mine is the power of life and death. In life, I could raise others from death, stave death off with but my will, speak with the spirits of the dead, and weave the threads of life."

"So I can speak with you because I'm tapping into your powers over the dead?" I asked.

"That would be my guess," he nodded. "You can speak with us because it is among the most basic aspects of my powers that you have tapped into. You may have had subconscious questions and have been trying to find the answers by calling to our spirits. This could be your way of getting the answers you seek."

"That's as good an answer as any, I suppose," I mumbled as I thought things through. The Gospinia, who were trapped in their draconic forms by Serevas, became the 'old gods.' Each of them was incredibly powerful in their own right. If I was a titan, that meant I was already vastly more powerful than nearly anything or anyone in Thoros. If Dalon'Tara was correct, and my powers multiplied every time I absorbed one of their spirits… I might become something beyond the titans or the Evnuris. I already had the souls of three Gospinia within me, and I was actively hunting a fourth. Dalon'Tara specifically said my powers would 'multiply,' not simply have their power added to mine. If, as merely a titan, I would eventually gain influence over the entire world, what would my powers be like when multiplied four times over?

"I wouldn't concern myself over the details, Princess," Serevas said reassuringly. "You will grow in power, only far more quickly than you believed you would. Our voices will always be here for you, to help you when you ask, and guide you when you need it. So long as you can learn from our mistakes, you will escort your people and the rest of Thoros into a golden age."

"Will I be speaking to you every night until you're all fully integrated into my spirit?" I asked.

"I don't think that's for us to say," Dalon'Tara replied. "You called us here. I don't suppose you'll see us unless you desire it."

I nodded to myself. "I see. Then I suppose I will have to take advantage of that window of time to learn all I can. For now, I think I'll wait until I find Pristaren, then meet with you all once again. Thank you for speaking with me and answering my questions."

The pair who were able to respond bowed their heads, while Jeron sat silently, staring into the pool.

I woke up a moment later and stretched the sleep from my bones. Faren was already awake and had left the cabin. I dressed myself and took some time to properly braid my hair before I walked out onto the ship's deck. Faren was sitting against the ship's railing, talking with Trisha.

I gave them a wave as I approached. "Good morning."

"More like good afternoon," Trisha laughed.

Faren smiled. "We docked hours ago, Love. Most of the crew has already disembarked."

"And you've just been waiting on me?" I asked. I felt bad for wasting their time.

"It's fine," Faren shook his head. "If you needed the sleep, you needed the sleep. We've just been chatting while we were waiting for you to wake up."

"Well, I'm glad you haven't been bored," I smiled and looked at Trisha. "It seems like this will be where we part ways. It seems our next target is in Manniford, somewhere near Tri Varieux. It will take us at least a few weeks to get there, and who knows how long to find what we're looking for."

Trisha looked rather disappointed. "Well, that's some shite news. I was hoping we'd be able to take you back to wherever you were wanting to go."

"So was I," I sighed. "But I doubt you want to wait around for a month or more waiting on us."

"Yeah," Trisha nodded, "that's true enough. Sitting and waiting doesn't pay my crew. I suppose we should settle accounts and go our separate ways."

"What if we let the Princess pay her to wait?" Faren asked me with a sly smile.

"Huh? What do you mean?" I asked.

Faren waved a dismissive hand at me, then looked at Trisha. "Don't tell your crew, but we're on business for Princess Orodum. Heard of her?"

Trisha chuckled. "Who hasn't? She's been making waves for years now. You saying you work for her directly?"

Faren nodded. "I've been one of her servants for years now. My Lady here is doing some research on the Princess' behalf."

Trisha looked me over. "A researcher, huh? You're built like a fighter."

"All dwarves are fighters," I responded. "We have to learn to be able to fight the scourgespawn."

"Fair enough," Trisha replied. "Still, I didn't think you nobles liked to do much beyond tell the others what to do."

"The Princess is inspiring everyone to go above and beyond," Faren interrupted. "But she's sent us to look for two items. We found one; now we're looking for the other. She gave us a decent amount of gold, but I'd be willing to say that she'd be happy to pay the Captain for her time if she waited for us."

"You think so?" Trisha asked. "Do you know how much we could make in a month?"

"Considering you were amazed by the amount we offered you to begin with, I'd say it's less than we've already paid you," I smirked. "But he's right. If we can get what we're looking for, she'd probably pay you well beyond what you could ever hope for."

"You know, I could sell this information to some mercenaries and have them kidnap you and hold you for ransom," Trisha grinned.

Faren shrugged. "Only if you hired mercenaries you didn't mind seeing dead."

"I'll tell you what," I said chipperly, "I'll pen a letter to the Princess. I'll explain our situation and how well you've worked out for us. You deliver it to our contacts in Coralstine and then come back here and wait for us. If she reacts the way she typically does, you'll probably have a bigger payday than you could possibly imagine."

Trisha hummed in contemplation. "It could be useful to garner favor with the Princess of the dwarves… And if she'll pay equally as well as you did, it would make for a nice quiet month for my crew. Alright, then. You write your letter, I'll deliver it, and then wait for you here at the docks. But I had better get the payment you're hinting at, or we'll have words."

I grinned wide at Trisha. "Let me go write that letter, then we'll be on our way."

I returned to the cabin and began writing a letter to my warriors in the Under Roads beneath Coralstine. I instructed them to have some gold brought to Coralstine and to look for something special. I also let them know how much longer I should be before I return to them. As I wrote the letter, Faren packed our things. By the time I had finished the letter and sealed it,

Faren was ready to go.

    Trisha took the rest of her payment since we were finished with this leg of our journey. She accepted the letter and assured us that she would leave the next day to deliver it. I emphasized that she was to hand it only to a dwarf and let them know Princess Orodum's men would need to see it. I knew that my warriors would see my handwriting and understand my desire. We left the Banshee's Wail as the afternoon dragged on. Instead of heading out right away, we rented a room at a local inn. The next day, we set out for the next tomb of the old god.

CHAPTER 37:

THE TRUTH OF VAR KORAN

Our journey to the Tri Varieux was in the northern part of Fransway and would take us some time to get to. Faren had bought some horses for us in the port town Trisha had left us in. We grabbed some extra food supplies and left the next day. Fransway was a beautiful country with rolling hills, colorful vegetation, and wide open areas. Its roads were better maintained than Falladrin's had been before the dwarves and I had a say in the matter. Surprisingly, we met regular patrols of armed men, typically led by a Chevalier. This was rather surprising, but they had been seen doing the same thing in Inquest. Patrols could be found encountering enemy forces, so I chalked this up to Fransway having enough of a standing army to have men regularly patrolling the roads to keep bandit activity down. With this small difference, it was understandable why Franswayian nobility looked down on Falladrin. I made a note to myself to discuss this with Serena.

The journey, while time-consuming, was refreshing. We enjoyed every moment being alone together. Faren would look for signs of game, and a few times we stopped our traveling so that he could hunt. With a little magic, the meat and pelts were preserved until we reached a small town where we would trade some of it for things like ale or salt. Or we'd make a gift of it to the local inn so that we could enjoy a room for the night. This life, while harder and more physically demanding than my life in Cragmorrar, was somewhat similar to what we had been used to before coming to Thoros. We missed it terribly, and when we finally got a taste of it again, we savored it.

We took days to fish streams, explore hiking trails, and even participated in a small summer festival we stumbled upon. It was a wonderful time, and over far too soon.

The mountains of Tri Varieux loomed before us, and I could sense the void area where the old god would be sleeping. However, something didn't make sense. I focused in on the sensations the stone was feeding back to me.

"I found it," I told Faren. "It's deep underground. Something doesn't make sense, though… There are well-crafted tunnels leading into and out of the area."

Faren looked at me quizzically. "Are you sure?"

I nodded. "I'm positive. If I didn't know any better, I'd say they were dwarven tunnels. There are people in them. They're not really moving, but I can tell they're alive."

"Perhaps they're guarding the place," Faren guessed. "Should we go greet them or head straight to the old god?"

I considered the question carefully. If we went straight to the old god, we might alarm those around it and have to deal with an aggressive force that we didn't need to battle. If we arrived somewhere close to some of those on the paths that led to the old god, we might be able to avoid a needless confrontation. The problem was that while I was sensing dwarves in the paths, there was something off about them. I could kill the old god from here, but if there were any scourgespawn in a large enough area, the old god's soul might seek them out and be reborn. Unfortunately, the lore wasn't exactly clear about untainted old god souls…

I took a deep breath to collect myself. "Let's go meet the people on the path. We have a better chance to avoid confrontation that way."

"As you wish," Faren nodded in agreement.

I took a few moments to find the smallest collection of beings in the closest tunnel to us. As I began to create a path into the ground for us, Faren took our horses off to the side and created a fenced area for them out of stone, making sure to give them plenty of room to run and graze. He gathered up our supplies and brought a large box over to me.

I looked at the box and sighed. "I was hoping I wouldn't need this…"

"If it's dwarves, then you'll need to use it," Faren insisted.

I groaned and nodded as I took the box. Inside was one of my armored gambeson gowns. I changed out of my traveling clothes and into the gown. As much as I didn't want to wear any noble clothes this entire time, Faren was right. If I were going to interact with dwarves, I needed to look the part of the dwarven Princess… or the dwarven Empress. Unfortunately for Faren, it meant that he was burdened with carrying all of our supplies. I knew he wouldn't complain, but I didn't envy him.

Once I was dressed and Faren had helped me with my hair, we began to make our way down. I sealed the path behind us as we went, giving us a small pocket of air to walk through so as not to overly disturb the local geography. I took the time to assess the world as far as my senses could reach. I found Var Koran, the other remaining dwarven city in the world, far north of our location. I mapped out the Under Roads and noted that every path that led to the void where the old god was sleeping connected to the Under Roads and directly back to Var Koran. This was as intriguing as it was concerning. I remembered the fan theories about the dwarves of Var Koran and I didn't particularly want them to be true.

The stone opened up into one of the carved paths, and we stepped out several yards away from what I ascertained to be a gatehouse or checkpoint of some kind. Our arrival did not go unnoticed. The strained cries of deepstalkers heralded our arrival and what looked to be dwarven sentries appeared from the side of the small housing area.

The dwarves all wore long hoods that mostly hid their features. One brandished an ax and growled, "Who are you? There was no word sent ahead that a tithing group was on its way!"

Faren stepped ahead of me. "Fool! Lower your weapon. This is Princess Merida Orodum of Cragmorrar!"

The other dwarves looked at each other in confusion but the one who'd spoken first replied, "What kind of idiot do you take me for? There's no chance that Cragmorrar's fairy tale Princess would be here. She isn't even visiting Var Koran, let alone the tithing tunnels."

I stepped forward, all smiles and courtesy. I chuckled softly, "Why do you call Princess Orodum a 'fairy tale Princess'?"

"If you heard half the things I have about her, then you'd call it one big fairy tale as well," the dwarf replied. "But that doesn't answer my question. Who are you and how did you get here?"

I smiled, "As my betrothed has said; I am Princess Merida Orodum of Cragmorrar. If you require proof…" I allowed my eyes to glow with dimvyum light and willed the stone to form into a contingent of dwarven soldiers behind me, and behind the other dwarves. "I will show you just how real the fairy tales are. Now, perhaps you would be willing to give me your name? It is a common courtesy even in Var Koran, I should imagine."

The dwarves all gasped and turned, each of them ready to panic as they were surrounded by living stone replicas of dwarven warriors. There were whispers of witchcraft and devilry.

The speaker had to collect himself before looking at me again, "My name is Charon. I'm the Captain of this checkpoint."

"Do you not bow before nobility or royalty in Var Koran?" Faren snapped.

The dwarves scowled at him, but one by one, they each bowed to me.

"Forgive us, Princess," Charon said the title with hesitancy, "but we weren't told you had arrived in Var Koran or were coming through a tithing tunnel. We didn't know to expect you."

I bowed my head by way of apology, "I'm pleased to meet you, Captain. You haven't heard of our arrival because we have not been to Var Koran yet. We have arrived here first."

"But… how?" Charon asked. "None of our scouts have reported your movements."

I smirked and looked to the tunnel wall and willed it to open ahead of me for a good distance, "By way of a fairy tale, Captain." I looked back at

Charon as the stone closed up once again. "As you may have heard, I have been blessed by the titans with the ability to mold stone to my will. And, yes, I am also a mage, though I doubt you wish to see me demonstrate those powers as well. My betrothed and I were traveling north along the surface and decided to come down here because it is close to our goal."

Charon seemed like he was trying to keep his composure as he considered his options. "What is it that you want here, Princess?"

"This path, along with several others, leads to the location of an old god," I said with as much surety and authority as I could muster. "Take me to it. I'm especially concerned now that I've heard you call this a 'tithing tunnel' twice."

Charon cleared his throat. "Forgive me, Princess, but I don't have the authority to take you beyond the checkpoint without permission from the Assembly."

"I think you've misunderstood the Princess," Faren growled dangerously. "She didn't make a request. She gave you a command."

Charon seemed more willing to confront Faren. His voice grew irritated. "I'm under no obligation to obey the commands of anyone from Cragmorrar, Princess, King, or otherwise. Var Koran is its own kingdom and we do not—ugh!"

Charon's words were cut off as the stone leapt up, wrapped around his throat, and lifted him several feet into the air. The other dwarves around him began to panic as they watched their Captain accosted by the very stone itself.

"My betrothed spoke correctly," I said, gaining the attention of the others. My eyes glowed fiercely as I took a step forward only to have the other dwarves step back. "I gave a command. And even if you do not recognize my authority as a Princess, you will recognize my authority over the very stone we all venerate. Take me to where this path leads. Now! Or I will drag you there myself!"

I lowered the Captain back to the floor and glared at him. "Do you understand me?"

Charon nodded quickly. I allowed the stone to release him and he dropped to his knees, coughing and gasping for air. It took him a while before he was able to stand. When he had composed himself he turned and motioned for us to follow.

As Faren and I began to follow Charon, I looked at his men as we passed. "No one leaves here to tell anyone about my arrival. If you try to, I'll know."

The display I'd put on with my arrival, the stone dwarven warriors, and snatching their Captain up into the air must have gotten my point across. All they did was nod fearfully and bow their heads while muttering, "Yes, Princess."

Charon led us down the last few hundred yards to where the passage opened up into a yawning cavern. It was just as large as the one we'd been to before but had been carved into with dwarven designs. The old god, however, was not in its draconic form. To my horror, it had somehow been transformed back into its original elven state and was suspended above a deep pit by a series of chains. Its body was marred by scars covering every inch of its exposed flesh. It still seemed to sleep. Either that, or it was simply unconscious and too weak to free itself from its shackles. It could be a combination of both since its body seemed emaciated, with its skin drawn tight against bones.

I looked at Charon in horror and disgust. "What have you been doing to it?"

Charon's expression was confused. "What do you mean? We've been using it to keep the scourgespawn at bay."

"By the Stone…" Faren whispered. "You found an old god, and instead of killing it to stop a future Scourge, you kept it alive?"

"Its blood has kept our people free of the scourgespawn and the Scourge," Charon insisted.

That's when it dawned on me. I glared fiercely at Charon. "Remove your hood."

"What?" Charon asked. "Why?"

Faren wasn't having any of Charon's attempts at delaying the inevitable. He marched forward and tugged Charon's hood down. What greeted us was nearly as bad as the sight of the old god. Charon's face was covered in black veins and sallow skin. His eyes were almost completely glazed over with a milky white color, with sickly yellow irises.

"What have you people done to yourselves?" Faren gasped.

"They drank his blood," I shook my head in disbelief. "There was always the theory… but I had hoped I was wrong. I didn't want to be wrong in this way, though. Tell me the truth of it, Captain."

Charon stared at us in anger. "Of course we did! We had no other choice! We were nearly wiped out by the scourgespawn when we found the creature. We had heard of how the Scourge Sentinels took in the Scourge and convinced one of them to share some of the secrets with us. We used similar methods on this creature, and it has allowed us to control scourge-infected creatures and given us an advantage over the scourgespawn."

"And it has poisoned you all as well, hasn't it?" I asked. "It has put your lives on a clock just like what happens with the Sentinels."

"It's true," Charon spat. "But so what? Better a shorter life than no life at all."

"How old?" I asked quickly. "How old do the dwarves of Var Koran have to be before they're given the blood?"

"When they come of age," Charon answered. "It's a rite of passage."

"No wonder the diplomats of Var Koran are so young," Faren hummed. "They haven't taken the blood yet so that they can keep up appearances…"

Charon nodded. "It's true that we keep a small amount of the population untainted so they can interact with Cragmorrar and other foreigners. But everyone else must receive the blood to continue protecting our realm."

"My realm," I corrected him instantly.

"Var Koran isn't your realm, Princess," Charon proclaimed defiantly.

"It most certainly is," I stated with authority. "Var Koran may have enjoyed some autonomy since the empire fell, and it has regularly ignored our traditions and authority. All the while, Cragmorrar allowed it because, as far as we all know, ours are the only dwarven people left in all the world. This allowance has confused you and your people into believing that you were separate from us; your own nation. But I have been elected to become Empress of the newly blossoming dwarven empire. That empire spans all dwarven holds, forgotten or not, that belonged to the dwarves. This includes Var Koran. Once I have done what I must here, I will enlighten your people to this new reality."

"Empress?" Charon spat in shock. "Then it's true that you have begun retaking the Holds?"

I nodded grimly. "And establishing new ones. All without having to taint our blood."

Charon tried to protest, but I waved his words away as I stepped toward the restrained man. I could hear the voices of the elven souls within me. They were saddened and enraged at the sight of their brethren being held in such a manner. I couldn't blame them. I would have the same reaction if I had seen someone I cared for in such a condition. I reached out and traced my fingertips over the scars along his thigh. This was cruel.

Suddenly, an urge came to me, pushed to the forefront of my mind as if spurred on by some unseen force. I reached up and took Pristaren's hand in mine, then pulled. Not physically, but with my will. I could see Pristaren's tortured soul slough forward, then twist in on our physical connection. As his soul wound its way into me, his body writhed and twisted against its restraints, screaming for several moments before finally going limp. I could feel a surge of power wash through me. This method of absorption was faster and far more efficient. I was already tapping into Pristaren's power. And I had to guess that what I had just done was thanks to Dalon'Tara's abilities.

Charon began to protest as doors around the cavern began to open and dwarves from the other passages rushed in. Threats and questions were shouted at us from every angle.

I summoned my power and enhanced my voice into a painful thunder as I shouted, "Be silent!"

The booming shout cowed the dwarves, and they backed up defensively.

I looked around at them sternly. "My name is Princess Merida Orodum. I have slain this wretched creature and claimed its power as my own. Your disgusting practice of tainting dwarven blood has come to an end."

Before any of them could protest I called magical fire to leap from my hands and summoned a swirling blizzard well above our heads. The stone floor raised itself up beneath me and turned into a dais I could look down on them from.

"You have this one chance to bow and swear your fealty to me, or I will send your tainted souls back to the stone," I announced authoritatively.

There was a hesitance among the dwarves, but Charon was the first to kneel. "Kneel, brothers! She is the one we have heard of. Cragmorrar has declared that she will be an Empress, and she has intentions of retaking Var Koran. Let us welcome her."

Most of the dwarves saw the wisdom in Charon's words and began to kneel. However, a few were stubborn and refused to show any sign of contrition. I looked at them and sighed. "Look upon your fellow dwarves. See the fate of those who will not heed my will."

Without a moment's pause, the stone reached up and engulfed every dwarf that remained standing. Their muffled cries of fear were quickly silenced as the stone contracted in on itself, crushing the dwarves like ants. The stone coffins then slipped back into the ground, bringing the bodies of the dwarves with them and leaving no trace that they had ever been there. The dwarves who had bent the knee watched the sight and then looked at me in horror.

I changed my expression to a regretful one and allowed my magical displays to disappear. I lowered the dais back down to floor level and spoke gently. "Know that I did not come here to kill anyone other than the old god. I have been burdened with the responsibility of rebuilding our empire. It has been nearly a decade since our people in Cragmorrar and the Holds have had to fight the scourgespawn. I will bring that same peace to Var Koran. Will you warriors help me make our homes a place where your children will not have to taint themselves in order to survive?"

"How do we know you're speaking the truth?" one of the dwarves asked.

I smiled. "None of you are dead. I told you to bow, and you did. I punished only those who did not. I keep my word. Cragmorrar is experiencing a golden age of peace and prosperity thanks to my creation of the Surface Caste and staunch defense against the scourgespawn. Our people live happier, more prosperous lives. That is all I want for our people. I want us to live in peace and prosperity. Will you help me?"

"We don't have much of a choice," Charon said as he looked up at me.

"You do have a choice," Faren countered. "But choosing to go against your future Empress would be construed as treason. Treason carries a heavy price."

"Empress!" one dwarf called. "Can you guarantee that we will not have to taint our children in the future?"

"You won't have the option any longer now that I've killed the old god," I replied. "But I can guarantee that you will not have any reason to, either. If you will escort me to Var Koran, I will explain things to the populace. If you can help to convince them to work with me, I will kill everything in the Under Roads from here to the ocean, ensuring that no scourgespawn will threaten you for enough time that I can help you secure the Under Roads all the way to Cragmorrar."

"Then I will help you, Empress!" one cried. Others agreed quickly. Within a few moments, all of the dwarves had pledged to aid me in my efforts.

I bowed my head. "You all have my thanks. Rise and heed my command. I want you all to go down your respective passages that you help to guard. Gather every dwarf along the way and meet me in the Under Roads.

There, we will explain things to the rest of your men. And from there, we will make our way to Var Koran and speak with the people and the Assembly. With your help, we will begin ushering Var Koran back into the Empire!"

The dwarves cheered and quickly began to disperse back into their passages.

I looked at Charon and smiled. "Well, Captain, shall we start gathering your men?"

Charon sighed and nodded. "It seems like we should."

Charon led us back down the passage. We gathered every dwarf at each checkpoint along the way, explaining just enough to get them to come along. Charon continued to lead the way, followed by Faren and myself, then the rank-and-file guards. It took a few hours to walk the path before we finally reached the Under Roads. It was some time more before the rest of the dwarves from the other passages joined us. I took some time to speak to the larger collection of dwarves. They also had their doubts, but less so than when the Captains had rushed in to challenge us in the old god's tomb. Apparently, their Captains had taken some time to tell them about what was happening already, which helped to smooth the waters a bit.

Charon was joined by the rest of the Captains, while the rest of the warriors fell in behind us. As we marched into Var Koran, Faren and I were surrounded by a few hundred hopeful guards. There was a large commotion that spread throughout the city as we arrived. Curiosity overwhelmed most of the dwarves as we passed by and they began to join the procession. When we reached the Var Koran Assembly building, the whole of the Callers were outside waiting for us. Word had been spreading and it was no secret that Princess Orodum had arrived in the city guarded by the warriors from the tithing paths. Typically, the Callers met in Karosh Hold, but today was not a day for the Assembly, so their members were in Var Koran proper.

The captains leading us stopped as one of the members of the Assembly called out, "Who enters Var Koran with our warriors in tow?"

Charon stepped forward, "My Lord, this is Princess Merida Orodum of Cragmorrar, and her betrothed, Lord Faren Orodum."

The Caller looked past Charon to match my gaze. "Princess Orodum, to what do we owe this visit? Why was word not sent ahead so that we could welcome you properly?"

I stepped forward and lowered myself into a deep curtsey. "My Lord Caller, it was not my intention to visit Var Koran. My business in Fransway brought me here by way of coincidence. However, I think it is good that it did. It would seem we have much to discuss."

"So it would seem," the Caller replied. "Please, join us in our chambers. We will speak with you."

The Callers all turned and filed into the building. Faren and I went after them, flanked by Charon and a few of the other captains. The remaining captains organized their men so that they could guard the building from the curious crowd that had amassed while we passed through the city.

These chambers were similar to Cragmorrar's, though smaller and less decorated. I took to the center of the room with Faren and the captains at my side. It took a few minutes for all of the Callers to find their seats.

When everyone was settled, the lead Caller stood and addressed the others. "Lords and Ladies of the Assembly. We have gathered to listen to our esteemed guest, Princess Merida Orodum of Cragmorrar. Some of you have met her before. We have all heard of her exploits, which include the creation of the Surface Caste, the retaking of lost Holds, and the defeating of an archedemon. With that in mind, I ask that we listen carefully to what she has to say, out of respect for the work she has done for her people, and for the respect and admiration we have for her father, King Triston Nordrucan. With this said, Princess, I ask that you please begin."

I bowed my head politely. "Thank you. And I would like to thank the Assembly for gathering so quickly and efficiently to speak with me. It is humbling to see such courtesy from my people, whom I have not yet had time to visit properly."

"We appreciate your thanks, Princess," another Caller said. "However, we are not your people. We are Var Koran dwarves. We are not of Cragmorrar."

"You are my people, regardless," I replied, still smiling. "We are all dwarves. The blood of the titans runs through us all. And we were all part of the great dwarven empire before the Scourges killed most of our people and destroyed or occupied most of the Under Roads. You may not see things that way, but I do. We are kin, all of us. And we should live and prosper together as such."

"You may say that," another Caller called out, "but where has Cragmorrar been all this time while we fight and die against the scourgespawn?"

There was a loud clamor of agreement.

"I cannot speak to the actions or inaction of my predecessors," I replied, keeping my tone calm and gentle. "Nor would I hold the actions of those who came before this Assembly against you. Our people have all done things others would find deplorable to survive in times of great danger. I have recently discovered that your people have been tainting themselves with the blood of the old god in order to stave off the scourgespawn. Before you grow defensive, let me say that while I do not agree with this practice, I can understand that you did what you needed to do in order to survive. I cannot hold this action against you."

A murmur of conflicting responses moved through the Assembly.

"That being said," I continued, steeling myself for the blowback I was certain I was about to receive, "that practice is no longer an option. I have killed the old god."

The Assembly erupted in shock, with many of the Callers hurling insults and derision my way.

I had expected such a reaction and used my magic to enhance my voice, "Sit and be silent! You will listen to what I have to say!"

This cowed the whole of the Assembly. Eyes went wide and fear crept into many faces at the small display of power.

"As I said," I continued, my voice now containing the authoritative tone of a parent scolding their child, "I understand the practice, but I do not condone it. However, I have also taken steps to ensure that you no longer have to practice it. With the death of the old god you were using, there are no other old gods left in the world. I have killed the rest. The scourgespawn can no longer start a Scourge. And I have been keeping the scourgespawn at bay for years. No doubt you have noticed fewer and fewer scourgespawn over the years?"

Another series of murmurs before the lead Caller spoke, "What you say is true. There have been fewer scourgespawn sightings since your victory at Orlimar."

"This is because the scourgespawn leaders have kept the majority of the horde in the south," I explained. "I am constantly pushing them back while our Fallen Legion secures the Under Roads."

"Don't you mean the Legion is pushing them back, Princess?" a Caller asked.

I shook my head. "I mean precisely what I say. I… am constantly pushing them back. Some of you may have heard rumors about my ability to mold the stone to my will. I am here to tell you that those rumors vastly underrepresent the truth. I met with one of the last titans, and it blessed me with its soul and its powers. Not only can I mold the stone with my will, I can sense everything in contact with the stone. At the moment, I can sense everything from here nearly to the sea. And my influence grows daily."

There was a mixed response to this admission: some in awe, some simply didn't believe it to be possible.

"I do not mean to call your claim into question, Princess," the lead Caller began, "but perhaps you could prove this to us?"

I smiled. "Of course." The stone formed a dais beneath me and lifted me into the air slowly, while stone warriors appeared beside every Caller, seeming to step out of the very walls. "I can tell you where every dwarf in Var Koran is just by feeling their vibrations through the stone. I can see them using this method as well. If I wish, I can tell where everything is touching the stone and the earth around it within my area of influence."

I allowed the stone to lower me back down to the floor of the assembly, and the stone warriors to meld back into the walls they came from.

"Is that satisfactory enough?" I asked with a smile. An awe-filled silence was my only response. When I thought I wasn't going to be interrupted, I carried on. "As I said, visiting Var Koran was not something I had intended to do. I did so only after realizing the Under Roads and passages led from the city to the old god's prison. Instead of killing the old god and leaving, I made myself known to Captain Charon. He was kind enough to escort me to the old god, though he was under duress. To his credit, he did his duty as a checkpoint Captain to the best of his abilities in the face of my powers."

I looked at Charon and smiled. "He is a credit to Var Koran. He understood the situation and did what he needed to do to keep the peace."

Charon bowed his head in thanks, realizing that I was already covering for him when the Assembly would begin to ask questions later.

"Now, I would like to address news that has no doubt reached the Assembly, but it seems that you have not shared it with your people quite yet," I said firmly. "The Assembly in Cragmorrar, which is made up of Callers not only of nobles of Cragmorrar but also representatives of the retaken Holds, has voted to name me Empress of the new dwarven empire. I understand that relations between our cities have been strained since the fall, but this visit represents an opportunity to begin healing that relationship. When I am crowned Empress, the whole of the dwarven empire will become my domain. This will include the city and Holds of Var Koran."

A clamor began to rise again, but a quick flash of dimvyum blue light from my eyes quieted everyone down.

"I would like to respect most of Var Koran's traditions and methods, with the understanding that many of them have come about in response to the way you have had to survive against the scourgespawn," I said with a tone that held no judgment. "However, I do not want you all to live with the illusion that things will not change. You adapted to survive against the dawkspawn; you will have to adapt once more as the empire joins together again. I would prefer this transition to be peaceful, with discussions on how things will be done over time. I understand that immediate change will only bring resentment, so I ask that, as representatives of your people, you work with me to make this transition as peaceful and amiable as possible."

"And what if we prefer to remain outside of the empire?" a Caller asked. "What if we wish to be our own independent nation?"

I looked at the Caller as if to educate her. "You don't understand. We dwarves are not simply individuals. We are unique to humans, elves, and the atoshi. We are diminished versions of our ancient selves, but we are all still connected through the stone, through the titans. We are extensions of each other. We are the one people in this world that are connected through our minds. It is why traditions and shared goals resonate so deeply within us."

"When the titan gave itself to me, I was able to see through this connection," I continued. "I could see and sense through the minds of other dwarves. Even now, I can reestablish that link with any dwarf. I hope to be able to find a way to teach this method of connecting to our people someday. But I am not giving you the choice to be independent because we are all unified by that connection, and we are at our strongest when we work in tandem. I am declaring my intent, not asking for your permission. I am offering you the peaceful path towards reconnecting and expanding our empire. I do not wish to have to force you."

"Then you are not here to ask us if we want to join," the lead Caller said. "You're telling us we will join or be made to join by force."

"If that is how you wish to see it," I nodded. "I prefer to see it as me extending my hand to bring you into the safety of the growing empire. If you reject my offer, you must consider that I do not have to force you to do anything. I merely have to remove the support you get from Cragmorrar by way of supplies and military assistance. You may not need our military assistance as much anymore, but without trade from Cragmorrar, Var Koran will fall in due time to starvation or revolt. I reward my people who work with me towards our mutual goals. And I punish those who do not work with me by allowing them to languish. You must choose what is best for the people of Var Koran: agreeing to join the Empire now so that you can begin to prosper, or allowing the people who take your place after a revolt caused by starvation to agree to join the Empire instead."

As the Assembly considered my words, I quickly added, "This choice is going to be forced upon you in due time. Better it come now, from me here personally, then from a diplomat sent here on my behalf. If nothing else, you have the opportunity to address any issue you might have with me directly, instead of waiting for intermediaries to carry word back and forth."

"With all due respect, Princess," the lead Caller said, "our concerns cannot be addressed in a single day."

I nodded in agreement, "This is true. But today you can agree on whether or not you wish to join the Empire now... or if your replacements should make that decision later. For the other concerns, I will say this: I will stay here for one month. Each day we can gather here in the Assembly, and I will address all of your concerns. Because I will be the Empress, any agreement we make will stand, and I will inform the Callers of Cragmorrar of the policies I have decided on. In this way, you can be sure to understand the terms under which Var Koran will be welcomed into the Empire because you all had a hand in making them."

In the end, the Assembly voted unanimously to become part of the new dwarven empire. True to my word, Faren and I remained in Var Koran for the next month to discuss which practices would be accepted and which would not. The caste system in Var Koran, which was a little more fluid than in Cragmorrar, was left mostly intact. I had insisted that moving into noble status be reserved for rare exceptional events, and that the nobles take on extra responsibilities as they had in Cragmorrar. We also discussed the recognition of Exemplars from Cragmorrar and Var Koran (which meant they also had to acknowledge me as an Exemplar). These topics, along with many others, were gone over in exacting detail.

By the time we were ready to leave, the people in Var Koran were excited for my inauguration. The Assembly saw me as a woman willing to listen to reason, and accepting of fair terms and policies. I believe I surprised them with the number of things I was willing to agree to. It was true that many of their practices stayed in place, but some were ended with minor begrudging acceptance. I had the Assembly list all of the changes as proposals that one of their number would offer me on the day of my coronation, as if it were something they offered as part of Var Koran's supplication. This way, it would look to Cragmorrar as if Var Koran had already planned on accepting my rule, and were simply requesting certain considerations about their culture with solutions that would appeal to me.

Faren and I left with hope for the future. Our horses had been sent for and taken care of during our stay, so we rode them back to meet Trisha. It was time we started heading home.

CHAPTER 38:

REWARDING LOYALTY

"You're late," Trisha crossed her arms as she pushed herself out of her chair.

Faren and I boarded the ship only a few minutes earlier. One of the crew had let us on, grumbling about how bored he'd been. We took a few minutes to put our things in our cabin before going to Trisha's quarters. Trisha had apparently instructed the crew to send us directly to her when we arrived. When we entered her quarters, she seemed rather annoyed. Understandable, since we estimated we would have been back a week or two before.

"Apologies," I said as I bowed my head. "We ran into some unexpected difficulties that held us up."

"Difficulties?" Trisha asked. "Those must have been some extreme difficulties."

Faren pulled a chair out for me and held it for me while I took a seat. "Monumental difficulties. We had a run-in with some Var Koran dwarves that ended up creating a whole set of issues we had to deal with."

"Family squabble?" Trisha pried. "I forget, are you lot related or not? I suppose not considering how far away you are from each other."

I thanked Faren for the chair and then shook my head. "No relation beyond some very distant, centuries-old blood ties that would be hard to prove even if they still existed. It was more of a series of…" I paused to think about how best to phrase how things had gone, "territorial and policy disputes. They didn't appreciate what I had to do and disagreed on the level of authority which I claimed to have. We sorted things out in due time though."

"Two weeks?" Trisha scoffed. "Is that what you call 'due time'?"

"Admittedly, dwarven politics are slow and meticulous, but they get solid results in the end," I smiled. "I trust you delivered the letter?"

Trisha nodded. "I did. They seemed rather confused, but thanked me all the same. They also assured me that they will bring it to the Princess's attention immediately."

My smile widened. "Excellent! I have no doubt that she will be as grateful for your patience as we are."

"I bloody-well hope so!" Trisha groaned. "Do you know how much grumbling I've had to hear from this lot because of all this downtime? They don't do well sitting in one place."

Faren chuckled and smirked at me, "I suppose the Princess will just have to see about compensating them somehow."

I shot Faren a smirk, "And I think someone else will have to take a more active role in another reenactment…"

"You wouldn't dare," Faren snarled playfully.

"Oh, I dare!" I grinned.

Trisha laughed, knowing exactly what to expect after having seen our display the first time, "So we're ready to set sail, then?"

"Aye, Captain!" I smiled with excitement.

We left port soon after. The crew's mood was much better once we were in open water. Sailors don't exactly do well just lazing about in port, but I was grateful they had waited for us. I had to think of what I could do to thank them later. Maybe I'd have some barrels of dwarven stout sent with them after we disembarked. One for each man! I was certain the men would love that, and Trisha would have mixed feelings after she sobered up. Faren ended up performing the Titanic reenactment with me, and this time he was Leo.

The trip went smoothly. No bad weather. No pirates. I was slightly disappointed at the lack of pirates, but I suppose I was on a boat that had its own notorious reputation, so that would explain that. Still, it would have been fun to engage in a little naval combat. Faren was happy that nothing happened, but I bemoaned the fact that our only chance to fight some pirates had come and gone. The trip back to Coralstine only took about a week, with some poor wind causing the crossing to take more time than it normally would have. When Coralstine was on the horizon, Faren and I began to pack up our things.

I met with Trisha and insisted that we dock as late as possible. When she asked the reason for the request, I simply said that we wanted to enjoy as much time on the water as possible. The truth, of course, being that I didn't want to take the chance of being spotted by anyone who would recognize me. So we waited a few hours for the sun to begin setting. And as the ship began to dock, Faren and I donned cloaks and our things.

"I don't see anyone here to welcome us with a reward," Trisha sniped.

I smiled up at her, "I'd wager they're holding it in the Under Roads until I arrive. I'll return first thing tomorrow morning with whatever the Princess has sent."

Trisha arched a brow. "I'm not exactly a fan of delayed payment… especially after such a delay."

Faren patted Trisha's shoulder. "Don't worry, Captain. The Princess never fails to disappoint when repaying a debt. I'd wager you'll get what was promised, and more!"

Trisha sighed and nodded. "I'm not one to doubt someone with her reputation, but this is business we're talking about. If you two don't come back tomorrow morning, what recourse do I have?"

"No matter what happens," I said with a bright smile, "I promise you we'll return with what was promised. One way or another."

Trisha nodded in resignation. "Alright. But I'd better see the two of you before noon."

I laughed and smiled mischievously. "Oh, you will!"

Faren and I disembarked the ship sometime later once it had gotten dark enough. We headed straight back to the Under Roads entrance and slipped through the milling dwarves until we arrived at the estate where my personal guard had been staying since I'd left. They welcomed us home, and a few of my servants helped us with our things. Once I had bathed and taken my meal, I met with the guards to discuss what, if anything, had happened that I needed to be made aware of. Apart from the Assembly announcing my upcoming coronation, not much had really occurred. I asked about any scourgespawn issues and was surprised when I was told that no scourgespawn had been seen in all the time we'd been gone.

That evening was one of the loneliest I'd experienced since I'd been reborn into Thoros. I had spent every day and night with Faren for the past few months, and when I finally went to bed, I felt like a part of me was missing. I lay in bed, staring up at the ceiling and wondering how much longer I would have to wait before we could be married. I respected and understood the need for us to stay separate until our wedding, but that didn't mean I was happy being without him. I would need to speak to Father and the Assembly about moving that particular timeline up.

The next morning, Faren and I dressed properly once more. I was dressed in a brilliant garnet and gold gown, with plate armor accents, jewelry, and thin mithril chains with jeweled charms woven into my braids. Faren wore his plate armor, polished and pristine as always. My personal guard went ahead of us to the surface to announce our arrival. They led us through the streets of people who quickly gathered to watch us pass. I smiled and waved at onlookers who cheered and waved back. We made our way to the docks slowly but surely.

One of the guards ran ahead as Trisha and the crew moved to the railing to watch our arrival. "Announcing the arrival of Princess Merida Orodum! She requests permission to come aboard!"

"Requests permission...?" Trisha asked and looked at her crew.

"Granted, I suppose."

The guards led Faren and me up the gangplank and kept us surrounded until separating and revealing us to the crew. The look on their faces was priceless. Most of them seemed confused, while the others thought it was hilarious.

Trisha's eyes went wide as she gawked at us, "You?!? You're Princess Orodum???"

I bowed my head, "And a good day to you, Captain. I'm here to thank you for your help and for your patience. First, I believe there was a matter of your payment."

Faren motioned for some of the guards to come forward. A pair of dwarves stepped forward with a large chest and set it in front of Trisha. One of them opened the chest to reveal that it was filled with gold coins and assorted jewels. The entire crew gasped and stared at the contents.

"I trust that will suffice as far as our agreement goes?" I smiled up at Trisha.

"Too right it does," Trisha shouted as she stared at the chest.

One of the guards cleared his throat, "You are addressing the Princess. Show some respect."

"Oh!" Trisha gasped. "Right!" She waved at the crew to get them to act properly. She led them in a very uncoordinated bow, "Yes, Princess. You are quite generous."

I bit the inside of my lips to try and not grin. But the change in the crew's demeanor was too funny. A snicker escaped me, and I burst out into a loud laugh. I clutched my stomach and continued to laugh as I looked up at them all, "I apologize, but it's so funny to see how you're all acting now. It's fine if you're not so stiff and formal."

The crew all seemed to visibly relax. Trisha smiled and crossed her arms, "Well, Princess, you sure pulled the wool over our eyes."

I chuckled and regained my composure, "I'm quite sure I have no idea what you're talking about. Faren wasn't lying when he said he'd been in my service since he was a child. In fact, he's been in my service since I was a year old. And I was doing work on my behalf."

Trisha nodded and smirked, "Yet you failed to mention that you were the Princess."

I shrugged puckishly, "You seemed happy enough to do the Princess a favor. Why complicate things and make you second-guess yourself, or act differently around me? Also, I couldn't afford to let the Assembly know I was out in the world without my bodyguards. So I'd appreciate it if you all kept that little tidbit to yourselves, at least until my coronation."

Trisha grinned, "Oh, I don't know about that, Princess. A story like that? That'd be a lot to keep under wraps."

I laughed and smiled, "I thought you might say that. Which is why I also got you this."

Another guard stepped out of the formation with a large, wide box. He opened the box and revealed a large, wide-brimmed hat with a long, plumed feather.

"Wow… it's… a hat," Trisha said hesitantly. She looked at me as if she was confused. "Thank you?"

I turned and walked to the port side of the ship and motioned for Trisha to follow me, "I just assumed an admiral should have a big hat. Isn't that the tradition?"

Trisha looked at me confused, "That is the tradition. However, I should point out that I'm a Captain, not an Admiral."

I hummed and smiled up at Trisha, "I think we can rectify that. If you'd agree to dedicate one of your ships to make a monthly run from Coralstine to Fetral and La Beutieu so that the surface caste dwarves can have a reliable northern port to ship through, I think we can change that."

"How do you propose to change that?" Trisha asked. "And what do you mean by 'one of my ships'? I only have the one."

I grinned up at her then looked out over the other ships docked around us. At this point, Trisha began to notice that the crew of several ships were standing on their respective decks. I took a deep breath and shouted, "Sailors! Salute your Admiral!"

Eleven ships full of sailors snapped to attention and saluted in unison. Trisha was awestruck as she turned and looked at me, "What… what is this?"

I grinned up at her, "This is your fleet. So long as you agree to my terms, you can take whatever jobs you like."

Trisha looked down at me in surprise, "You must be joking…"

I shook my head, "You're a fine captain, Trisha. You make some questionable decisions at times, but I think when you have a fleet of ships to concern yourself with, as well as a dedicated customer base, you'll think things over more carefully."

"You're really willing to take that sort of risk?" Trisha chuckled.

"Most of my greatest accomplishments have come with some of my most dangerous risks," I replied with a nod. "But you've proven to be a reliable Captain. So I want you to be a reliable Admiral. Would you be willing to look at the contract?"

Trisha smirked and placed the hat elegantly on her head, "Let's see it."

We took the next hour to go over the contract I had instructed my people to draw up. In it, Trisha would be required to dedicate a ship each month to transporting Surface Caste goods from Coralstine to Fetral and La Beutieu, and return with goods that would be sent from representatives from those ports. She would be restricted from smuggling any kind of illegal goods, including slaves. She also would be restricted from engaging in piracy, raiding, or reaving of any kind. Beyond those conditions, she was free to operate the fleet in any way she saw fit. However, while the fleet was under her command, it was under the umbrella of Rita's business. And since Rita's new family was under House Orodum, it meant that the fleet was mine. I would get a cut of the fleet's revenue, and it was my purse that paid the sailors and maintained the ships. Essentially, Trisha agreed to be the admiral of the fledgling fleet of the growing dwarven empire.

By the end of the day, we'd ironed all the details out, and I was happy to leave with a contract that I could bring home to offer the Assembly. I would start with a small fleet to move our goods. Over time, the ships would be moved to Yivreon and manned by dwarves. We'd become a reliable naval power to help with Falladrin's defense. This would make us even more indispensable to Falladrin, and thus give us even more bargaining power in diplomatic situations. With dwarves in charge of the roads, the water, and the majority of trade, the dwarves would essentially control Falladrin through every measurable aspect beyond religion, and legal noble authority.

However, with the announcement of my 'arrival' in Coralstine, I was obligated to pay Serena and Alford a visit. We stayed there for a week, catching up with our friends and discussing a few matters of importance concerning the expansion of Coralstine's docks, some minor trade issues, and Surface Caste taxes with regards to imported goods. The visit was short, however, as Alford and Serena were preparing to move to Demirren so they could be prepared to take over for King Marshal. They were also preparing to allow Anna to arrive and become an interim governor of the Earling until one of their children could take over. It was a raw deal for Anna, and I doubted she would remain content with it. I wondered how Serena would deal with that particular issue.

We left for home after that week. It was a sad journey for me because I didn't know when I would ever get to leave Cragmorrar again. Still, while I wasn't exactly looking forward to that eventuality, I was pleased to be returning with the loyalty of Var Koran and a contract that gave the dwarves a small fleet of ships. The fledgling dwarven empire was bigger and had a longer reach than when I had left, two of Thoros' greatest threats had been dealt with forever, and I had essentially doubled my eventual power. All in all, the trip, while a fleeting few months of freedom, was worth it in the end even if it meant I wouldn't be free for the rest of my life.

CHAPTER 39:

THE PANTHEON REUNITED

Our return to Cragmorrar was met with joy and anticipation. The mood of the city was one of excited curiosity. The citizens were happy to have us home and were wondering if we'd been successful in achieving the goal we'd set out to accomplish. We spent the first two days after our arrival secluded in House Orodum. Faren familiarized himself with new recruits and how training had been coming along. I went over the finances, Assembly proposals, and set up meetings with people who had asked for them upon my return. It took me two days because of all the meeting requests. Essentially every noble House and many of the top Surface Caste families had requested meetings. So had a number of Warrior Caste and Artisan Caste families. It took me a great deal of consideration and schedule balancing to get everything set up.

On the third day after our return, I went to the palace to visit Father. However, since Father was sitting in with the Assembly, it became an opportunity to announce my success. As I waited for the Assembly to call for me, Trenton arrived in the waiting chamber.

"Merida!" Trenton exclaimed. He approached me and hugged me close. "It's good to see you again. I trust your travels were successful?"

I returned the hug happily. "They were. Far more than I expected. You should sit in on the explanation. I think you'll approve."

"Of that I have no doubt," Trenton chuckled. "If things went better than you expected then I'll have to listen in. I assume you've been getting a deluge of requests to meet with you?"

I nodded and sighed. "Basically anyone and everyone you can think of."

"You need to delay those meetings," Trenton insisted. "They're just trying to gain some minor prestige by being able to say they met with you recently after you've been crowned. Either that, or they're trying to get some kind of agreement from you that they can call in after you become Empress. Make them wait. Make the meeting something they should thank you for. Once you have that title, no one will be able to hold any kind of sway over you—promise, contract, or otherwise."

I stared at Trenton for a moment, considering what he'd said carefully. It was true that the majority of those who'd requested a meeting would likely try to do something for me, hoping I would owe them something later or be grateful and show them favor. I may be loved by my people, but that didn't stop their ambition. The nobles would always vie for power, and merchants would always try to make more money. They would use almost any method to put their families at an advantage over others. That was something I would need to work on after I took the throne.

Our society needed to emphasize excelling at what we were good at to lift each other up, not excelling at the cost of others.

I gave Trenton a firm nod. "I think that's wise advice. Thank you, Trenton."

Trenton smirked smugly. "And here you were wanting to be my advisor. It seems I'm better suited for that role than you are."

I crossed my arms and glared at him in irritation. "Don't you even start. This is all your fault, you know."

Trenton laughed. "Only you, Sister, would complain about becoming the Empress."

"I'll have you know I'd give it all up if I could just to enjoy traveling like I had been," I sighed.

"I know you would," Trenton nodded. "But, sadly, that was never your fate. You're simply too good at rallying the people. I know you don't want to hear it, but you brought this on yourself."

Just as I was about to respond, a guard from the Assembly Chamber called out for me.

"Looks like it's time," Trenton smiled. "After you, Sister."

Trenton followed me into the chamber as the guard announced us. I took my place at the center of the chamber while Trenton moved to stand beside Father.

Father was the one to address me. "Daughter, it does us all good to see you home and safe once more. I hope you were successful in your ventures."

I lowered myself into a curtsey before Father. "I'm happy to be home. I am also very happy to say that I was more successful than I had hoped."

"Please," Father motioned towards me. "Tell us how things went."

I stood proudly and addressed the Assembly, "First, I would like to say that I was successful in my original goal, which was to find and kill the last two remaining old gods. The threat of the Scourges is forever a thing of the past. In time, with great diligence, even the scourgespawn will disappear from our world."

There was a cheer of approval. Several of the Callers even cried with relief.

"Also," I continued, "while killing one of the old gods, I battled one of the scourgespawn's most powerful leaders and killed it. Apart from the Alphas, we have only one great enemy left."

The Callers' approval only grew with that news.

I rested my hands behind my back. "While hunting the last old god, we went to Var Koran. I am pleased to say that their Assembly has agreed with this body. They have accepted me as their Empress and to fully rejoin the Empire. Our people will have to look at our traditions and how we approach them going forward, but this will only serve to expand our territory and bring us together. We will be one Empire once again!"

The cheers were replaced with murmured approval. Var Koran was always going to be a difficult hurdle to overcome, and many Callers had voiced concerns that we might have to force them to join us. This was welcome news.

"Understand that the dwarves of Var Koran had to take drastic measures to survive this long," I said quickly. "We should not hold this against them. And during my time there, I came to realize that a few of their methods may be worth adopting, and I will consider them over time. In the end, whatever helps to unite the Empire will only make us stronger."

The Callers were curious but nodded in agreement. I'm sure they were wondering what methods I was considering.

"Finally, I began creating a small navy for us," I smiled. "I've bought twelve ships, all with active crews, and contracted an Admiral to oversee them for us. For now, the fleet will take jobs according to the Admiral's desire while also shipping goods from Coralstine to Fetral and La Beutieu. In time, I will have the ships focus on shipping from Yivreon as well. Eventually, as more ships are added, our ability to ship goods will only grow, and our ability to project our power over the water will make us indispensable to our allies of Falladrin, Orlimar, and those overseas."

The Chamber buzzed with approval. They could see that their future Empress was already making moves to grow and secure the Empire. The reaction was overwhelmingly positive and I could hear the occasional suggestion that they move the timeline of my coronation up.

"I believe I speak for the whole of the Assembly when I say we could not have asked for a greater return," Father said as he clapped. "You have defeated our enemies, secured our alliance with Var Koran, and extended our military might in only the span of a few months. The Assembly has made the right decision to name you Empress. However, that point must be addressed. We need to decide on the date of your coronation."

"I have no doubt that the Assembly has considered a great many dates for my coronation," I replied. "However, I refuse to take the throne before I am married. I will have Faren standing beside me as my husband when I first wear the crown. To that end, there can be no greater first service for my husband than to escort me to my throne. In that respect, I propose we hold my wedding and my coronation on the same day. I will be married first, then Faren will walk me to the coronation. Would this please the Assembly?"

This suggestion seemed to excite the Assembly. A wedding and a coronation on the same day? They could see the potential in it. The day would raise spirits all over the Empire and would essentially become a holiday; the day the Empire officially returned, and the day the Empress was wed to a hero of the Empire. This idea quickly gained approval.

"I will turn twenty-five in three months," I added. "If the Assembly approves, I would like to schedule everything for that day. What better gift can my people offer me than a husband and an Empire?"

That got everyone's attention, and the excitement in the Chamber was electrifying. They could truly turn the day into one that the people would celebrate. My birthday was already celebrated throughout dwarven society, so adding my wedding and coronation to it would turn it into a celebration on a completely different level. I left the Chamber with the Assembly's approval while they began planning the events to come.

Faren was waiting for me in the large hall outside of the Assembly Chamber. His expression lightened when he saw me, but I could tell he had news for me. I approached him with a smile, "Something's got you bothered. What is it?"

Faren motioned toward the entrance, "You have a guest back at the House."

"A guest?" I asked. "That's rather vague of you. Who is it?"

He shook his head as if to suggest he shouldn't say where ears might hear him, "She said she needs to speak with you and that she has gifts for you."

I arched my brows and shrugged, "Very well. Take me home, then."

As we walked home, flanked by my guards, Faren was unusually quiet. Normally we would talk about the meeting with the Assembly. He would even interact with the public as they called to us. But not this time. Even as I greeted those who called out to me, received gifts that citizens offered, and accepted people's encouragement for my upcoming coronation, Faren just kept to himself. I didn't let it show as we made our way through the Noble District, but his attitude had me on edge. When we arrived back at the estate, the guards had already begun to heavily patrol the grounds. I had to wonder who the guest could be to get Faren to react like this.

We entered the House, and Faren led me to the study. He opened the door and whispered, "She seems too excited."

Faren shut the door behind me, and from behind one of the bookshelves, I heard, "Dimvyum?"

"Samy?" I called.

"Soon, my boy. Soon," an aged, raspy female voice responded. "Come. Let us say hello to our guest."

I knew that voice. I hadn't heard it in years, though. Sure enough, Franeth stepped out from behind the bookshelf with Samy in tow.

I put on a smile and bowed my head. "Franeth. It's been some time since we've seen each other. To what do I owe the honor of your visit?"

Franeth chuckled. "As polite as always, Princess. Or should I call you Empress? So the rumors say."

I could only shrug in acceptance before moving to the chair in front of the fireplace. "My people have made their decision. I can only bow to their will. Would you care to sit?"

Franeth's eyes narrowed in amusement as she took a seat. "So dutiful, as always. Samy, boy, come here and sit with us."

"Dimvyum," Samy smiled and sat down on a cushioned footstool.

"Faren said you want to speak with me," I began politely. "He also suggested you had some gifts for me."

Franeth nodded and grinned. "Correct on both accounts, my dear. You see, I have felt what has occurred in the past few months. The remainder of my kin are no more, and now that we are together, I understand why. I can sense their power in you. I can feel it beginning to swell up inside of you."

I felt a twinge of guilt at the reality of her words. She was the last remaining Gospinia in the world, but she wasn't a threat. She actively fought against the Scourge. I took a deep breath and nodded. "It's true. I took the time to hunt the remaining old gods and slew them before they could become a threat."

"And you absorbed their souls in the process," Franeth finished my admission for me.

I nodded again, "I did. And I've even spoken with them in my dreams somehow. Only once. They said it was my subconscious calling them together to get a better hold on their power."

"Then it is true," Franeth smiled. This time the smile didn't seem cunning or predatory, but sad… and perhaps with a hint of resignation. "You house them all. And Jeron's presence is now but a shadow. I assume this is because her power is slowly fusing with your own?"

"It is," I confirmed. "But the process seems to be speeding up. I believe this is the result of Dalon'Tara's influence. Their essences are fusing with me faster. I can notice it in the steady elevation of my powers. My influence is expanding further and faster than it has before. My magic is more substantial, where even my most basic of spells contain more raw power in them than the most powerful spells did only a few years ago. I'm also beginning to show new abilities based on the premier domains that each of the Gospinia were known for."

Franeth silently considered what I had said. Her smile seemed to contain a warmth reserved for someone who was finally understanding something in its purest, most emphatic sense. She gave me a gentle look, "That's good to know. And it makes me happy to hear. Truly."

I folded my hands in my lap and sighed, "Well, I'm glad it makes you feel better, at least. I'm still not sure what to make of it all."

"I don't think you have anything to be concerned over, my dear," Franeth chuckled. "You are special, and are becoming a being of power cultivated over millennia. What's more, you are a good person. Your heart is in the right place. You will make a fine leader; not just for your people, but for the rest of the world as well. And that settles the debate I've been having with myself since we last met."

"A debate?" I asked. "That sounds rather ominous. May I ask what the debate was and what conclusion you came to?"

Franeth hummed to herself, "I had to ask myself if I was doing the best I could for the world. After so long, what had I really managed to accomplish? I couldn't stop the Scourges. I couldn't rally the people. I became feared because of my magic, turned into a myth with sinister connotations. Was I really doing what I needed to do to guard the world? I couldn't even bring myself to hunt and kill my kin to stop the scourgespawn from claiming them."

She shook her head, "The conclusion I came to was that I was being selfish. I was safeguarding myself and the secrets of my people who were lost long ago. I accepted the fact that I wasn't working for the benefit of the world, but for the memory of a world that could no longer be… should no longer be… In short, Princess, I have concluded that I am no longer needed. At least, not in the form I currently hold."

Her answer surprised me, and I couldn't help but wonder, "What do you mean by 'not in the form you currently hold'?"

"Within you are the souls of nearly all of the Gospinia," Franeth explained. "Before you sit the remaining members. I believe we should join the others, and give you our strength as well."

My eyes widened in shock as I realized what Franeth was proposing. "But that would mean the two of you would have to die. I can't be responsible for your deaths, especially not Samy! He's innocent. How could I accept his sacrifice just to gain more power?"

Franeth laughed. "Oh, my dear girl. Samy does not have to die. His soul and Kaneya's have been bound for only a few decades. I admit, I had no idea how to pull them apart at first, but while I was having my debate, I searched the world for the magic that would allow me to separate the two. I am only here because I am confident in my ability to do just that."

"But what about you?" I asked. "You'll die."

"I have transferred my soul many times, child," Franeth nodded. "This will be the final time. You have nothing to fear. I will fuse into you just as the others are already doing. But yes, in this process, I will die. And the world will be better for it because you will use my power better than I have."

I looked at Samy. "But what will happen to Samy once he's separated from Kaneya?"

"Dimvyum?" Samy asked as we looked at him.

Franeth reached out and stroked Samy's hair. "I imagine, with his mind free, he will begin to mature and develop as he should have. Something I'd wager his father and friends would love to see."

I looked between the two and smiled at Samy. "That would be wonderful, indeed. Samy deserves that sort of freedom."

"I think so too," Franeth agreed. "Now, are you ready, Princess?"

I looked at her in surprise. "You want to do it now?"

Franeth grinned. "No time like the present, Princess. And delaying things won't help. I'll separate Kaneya from Samy first and take her soul into myself. Then, if you please, I'd like to send Samy out before you finish the work."

I nodded softly. "I think that would be best."

Franeth nodded in agreement, then shifted in her seat to take Samy's hand. "Well, my lad. Are you ready to finally be free?"

"Dimvyum?" Samy asked.

Franeth chuckled, "Just so." She closed her eyes, and a soft, violet haze began to encompass Samy. After several moments, a bright blue shade began to appear. The haze mixed and churned together but began to slowly sort itself, with each color congealing on opposite sides of the dwarf. The colors separated with a muted pop. The blue fused back into Samy while the violet seeped into Franeth.

After several moments, Samy looked around, "Dim… vyum?"

His tone was surprising. While it was still high-pitched and innocent, it held a genuine spark of confusion and slight maturity; like a child who was learning the truth of responsibility.

"Samy?" I asked with anticipation.

He looked at me and smiled, "Dimvyum."

He was responding properly! Or at least, as properly as he could considering his mind had only just been freed a few moments ago. Still, it was a promising first step.

I smiled and stood from my seat, "Come, Samy." I escorted him to the door of the study and instructed Faren to bring him to the dining room so he could have some cake. By the time I closed the door and turned around, Franeth was standing and waiting for me.

"Are you ready, Princess?" Franeth asked gently.

"I think I should be the one asking you that," I replied as I approached her. I looked up at the old woman, "After all, you're the one who's giving up their life for this."

Franeth scoffed, "Nonsense. I have lived my life. It is you who is giving up your life to serve your people. I'm simply happy to lend you my strength for the times to come."

I held my hands out to her, "I suppose you've made up your mind, so there's no point in asking if you're sure. I can take care of this next part. So, whenever you're ready, just take my hands."

Franeth smiled. For once, it was a genuine, grateful smile. There was no arrogance or pride, no slyness or predation. She was simply… happy.

Content. Resigned. She reached up and placed her hands in mine, "Thank you for this, Merida. I can never truly repay you."

I tugged at her with my will gently. That's all it took. She was ready and willing, and her soul slipped away from her as easily as if she had handed me a silk cloth. As her soul was absorbed into me, Franeth's body began to slump to the floor. I caught it quickly and helped ease it into the chair she'd been sitting in.

There was an ache. And a sudden weariness set in. It was like a heavy blanket being pulled over me. I swayed and managed to get to my chair only just in time as darkness overtook me. In one moment, I was trying to settle into my chair. In the next moment, I was standing before the pool in the old ruins once again. Jeron was still kneeling beside the pool, but she was a shade, barely visible at all. Serevas and Dalon'Tara were standing on either side of the pool. Serevas was beginning to fade as well.

Another elf that looked suspiciously similar to Dalon'Tara approached the pool. His hair was shorter, and his eyes were more vibrant than Dalon'Tara's. This had to be Pristaren.

Two other elves, both females, appeared soon after. One had white, braided hair that reached down to her ankles, and yellow eyes that were sly and full of mischief. The other had shoulder-length hair the color of a wheat field, and sharp, green eyes that looked like they could see everything happening in the area. Mythriel and Kaneya.

I smiled brightly, "Franeth!"

She smiled and bowed her head, "Please, Merida, call me Mythriel. I am myself again."

I nodded, "As you wish. But I don't know how this happened. The only time I've met with the Gospinia before was when I was sleeping. Did taking the two of you into me cause me that much fatigue?"

Kaneya laughed, "She really doesn't know anything, does she?"

"And how could she?" Serevas asked. "It's not as if she's ever truly experienced a gathering like we have. She's only ever called on us once before.

Perhaps you would like to explain things?"

Kaneya snorted, "If I must…" She glared at me. "Whenever you call on us like this, it is something we used to call 'Pantheon'. I assume you did it by accident this time, and probably the first time as well. In our height of power, any of us could use this ability to call a meeting with the rest of those of us who were connected to each other. While our minds and bodies could still operate normally, our spirits would join together like this and speak. When our spirits returned to our bodies, we would have all of the memories of the meeting as if we'd been there ourselves."

I thought over the explanation, "But if all of you are within me, what happens when this ends?"

"We sleep," Dalon'Tara responded. "And diminish. As we sleep, our powers are added to yours."

"It seems to work regardless of whatever world the person is from as well," Mythriel surmised. "Most of the Gospinia were originally part of the original world and were brought into you after Trith'Emel broke the world in two. Once you are connected with someone on this level, you seem capable of calling them into the Pantheon at will… or, at least, whenever you sleep for now."

"You'll master the ability in due time," Serevas smiled. "Of that, I have no doubt."

"Why didn't any of you tell me this the first time?" I asked, looking at Serevas and Dalon'Tara.

"You did not ask what it was," Dalon'Tara responded. "You asked how it happened. With that question, I assumed you knew what it was and simply didn't know how you accomplished it."

"I'm not partial to semantics," I replied.

"Then do not leave room for interpretation," Dalon'Tara shrugged.

"Or ask more specific questions," Pristaren added.

I shook my head. That was just going to be a pointless, roundabout conversation. I decided that it would be best not to pursue it.

"Will I be able to call you all even after you've dwindled?" I pushed the conversation along.

The others looked at Jeron.

"It would seem not," Mythriel responded. "Once we have been completely absorbed into you, it's likely that you won't be able to call us together anymore."

"And it would seem the process is growing faster, just as you thought," Serevas added. "Much faster. If the rate had stayed the same, I should still be solid for a year or so before I began to dwindle."

"And, as you guessed, it is probably thanks to my influence," Dalon'Tara added. "The more of me you absorb, the faster we will all dwindle away."

"So the effect is exponential," I crossed my arms. "That means that I probably only have a few months left to speak with you all."

"Weeks, I'd say," Pristaren replied. "You may not be able to notice, but Dalon'Tara is already beginning to fade."

"It seems like this won't be worth much in the end," I sighed.

"I wouldn't be so sure," Mythriel smiled. "I'm sure that you'll find a use for it in time. I would practice calling us while you still can. The practice will do you good. Practice in your sleep and even during the day when you're doing other things. I think you'll find that the results are surprising."

I smiled, "I'll do that, then."

Over the next few weeks, as I went about my day, I would use Pantheon to call to the Gospinia. The first time I tried it, I was walking to the Assembly Chamber with Faren. I was disappointed at first because I didn't think it had worked. I didn't feel any different at all. In fact, I was in the middle of the Assembly meeting when the effect registered. Suddenly I had full recollection of a meeting between myself and the Gospinia. We discussed how I had used Pantheon on the way to the Assembly and how my conscious self was still doing exactly that. While we met, I was also walking with Faren, meeting with Callers, and listening to proposals.

It seemed that Pantheon allowed my spirit, or my subconscious, to meet and experience things while my conscious mind continued on normally. Once Pantheon's effect had ended, I would instantly gain the memories and knowledge of what happened during the discussion. It was an excellent way of gaining knowledge from the Gospinia while I could, and I took full advantage of it. At first, the meetings were short, but the more I used it, the more time I could get in. By the end of the first week, Pantheon lasted an entire day.

I prioritized learning from those who would diminish fastest. That meant Serevas, then Dalon'Tara, then Pristaren, and finally Mythriel and Kaneya. By the time Mythriel and Kaneya dwindled to the point of unresponsiveness, I had learned a great deal about the original history of the elves, how they would manipulate and control the spirits, their methods of enchanting and weaponsmithing, and even how they came to master their more unique abilities considered their domains for which they were known by their descendants. It was a treasure trove of priceless knowledge that I would have to share with Trianna and Aelfric's people. I was certain they would be eternally grateful.

By the time invitations to other kingdoms' leaders and nobility were sent out for my coronation, I had fully integrated the souls of the Gospinia into myself. This integration had some side effects. For instance, just as I could see the stone's movement where others only ever saw it sitting still, I could see the shroud and the spirits and the world beyond it. This was something I could channel with focus. I could see it or not at my preference. The Gospinia's magical power had combined into my own, and with all seven of them fused with me now, I could see how all of the Gospinia could kill Titans. It genuinely surprised me how potent my magic was and how deep my power reserves were. I was almost scared of the magical potential I had now. I felt almost invincible!

One other use I found for Pantheon was that I could continuously train and research magic in the Dimvolmn while I was going about my day. I was no longer restricted to waiting to fall asleep to train my magic. It had only meant to be an experiment after I wondered if it would work, but when the experiment was a success, I began dedicating nearly every moment afterwards towards this new form of constant practice. One interesting thing I discovered was that I wasn't pulling from my magical reserves when doing this. My spirit seemed to either have its own magical reserves or was pulling directly from the magic of the Dimvolmn itself. In the months between the Gospinia fading away and my birthday, I was able to get in nearly a full year's worth of magical practice. This had such extreme potential!

When I tried explaining how I felt to Faren after all of these new discoveries, he was kind enough to warn me that feeling invincible could make me overconfident. Overconfidence could lead to ruin. Still… It was an amazing feeling. It seemed like all that was left for me was our wedding and my coronation.

CHAPTER 40:

DAY OF RECKONING

The day finally came. It would be a historic day for the dwarves. We were declaring the reestablishment of our lost Empire. Dwarves crowded the city's taverns and inns. Every dwarven house was packed to capacity with family members several times removed returning from their ventures on the surface and in foreign lands to be in Cragmorrar on the day. No one wanted to have to admit that they weren't in Cragmorrar on the day their Exemplar, their Empress, was crowned. The week prior to my birthday was essentially one big celebration. Vendors sold memorabilia, groups danced in the streets, and alehouses shook with sing-alongs. I hadn't seen a celebration like this since the Surface Caste was instituted.

Along with the festivities came dignitaries and leaders from every corner of Thoros. Obviously, King Marshal, Alford, and Serena had come. Allen and Marylen, as well as most of the head mages, came to represent the Lemlalian College. Trianna and Aelfric, along with several Elders, arrived from Orlimar. The Empress of Fransway, Empress Kiria Trebue, arrived with a massive retinue of guards, Franswanian nobles, and retainers. Marlowe Dumar, the Viscount of Fetral, also arrived with several nobles in tow. Much to everyone's surprise, the atoshi sent a delegation as well. However, as surprising as the atoshi delegation had been when it arrived, the most surprising guests by far was a sizable group of Vintari Magisters, along with Vintari dignitaries, as well as their servants and, rather brazenly, their slaves.

I met with each of the visitors in turn, taking time to not only greet them but begin minor talks on how our relationship could be improved. Empress

Trebue merely wished to congratulate me and offer her assistance in matters I may need help seeing my way through. Her experience would no doubt be invaluable, by which she meant that she would leverage it in talks further down the line.

Viscount Dumar, who surprised me by being a much more energetic and humorous man than I had expected, was excited to begin negotiating trade talks now that word had reached him of our growing merchant fleet. He found the whole idea of a dwarven fleet rather peculiar and spectacular, and he commended my willingness to expand dwarven sensibilities.

The atoshi were a genuine treat. They first began by offering their thanks to me as they understood that I was the reason that Vintari was running low on dimvyum. Because dwarves now had a firm anti-slavery stance, we did not trade with any foreign power that dealt in slaves. While Vintari had been managing to get dimvyum from Var Koran, that supply had gone dry the day I left. Now the atoshi were managing to gain ground against the Vintari Empire since the Magisters had to more carefully manage their remaining stockpile of dimvyum. The atoshi also offered their hand in friendship and suggested an alliance against Vintari so long as the Magisters continued their aggressive policies against Ven Parlol.

The Vintari Magisters were all in sour but diplomatic moods. They expressed excitement at the rising of the dwarven empire once again. They also expressed disappointment in the anti-slavery policies since it put their empire at odds with their longtime allies. I explained that it was true that the dwarves and the Vintari Empire had long been allies, but our society was changing and evolving for the better. The policy was meant to signal what we hoped the world would be like in time. I stood firm that we could not deal with Vintari in matters of trade until they released their slaves and altered their stance on the issue, but I also suggested that they meet with Trianna ad Aelfric, since many of their slaves were elves and that they would be happy to discuss compensating the empire for each elven slave released to them. The discussions were curt but respectful. In the end, I welcomed them to stay longer after my coronation to discuss things in further detail since I would have more power to negotiate once I was crowned. This seemed to satisfy them for the moment.

I slipped out of bed with a stretch, and Kara seemed to know I had woken without me calling for her. She slipped into my chambers quickly, all smiles and energy.

"Good morning, Empress!" she cheered as she helped me from my nightclothes.

"I'm not Empress yet," I chuckled. "I'm still the Princess."

Kara shook her head and let out a puff as if I were talking nonsense. "You were the Empress the moment they decided to name you such. Today is just for the ceremony."

I smiled at her. "Well, don't tell any of the Callers that until I'm crowned. They need to believe they're still important until the end of the day."

Kara laughed and hugged me close. "Oh, I'm so proud of you, my dear. You deserve nothing less."

"Well, that's rather cruel to say," I said with mock sadness. "I'll never be allowed off that throne from now on, you know."

"You're the Empress," Kara countered with a smirk. "You may do as you please."

I laughed. "You're a bad influence, you know."

"Good!" Kara smiled. "At least someone in your life can be."

We shared a laugh together. I knew she was as proud of me as Mother would have been, and in all respects, she had become as much my mother in spirit. I loved her dearly, and the way she doted on me like a mother tending to her child made me feel loved in return.

"So, we need to get you your breakfast," Kara began, "then the other ladies will assist me in getting you into your gown. The palace guards, as well as House Orodum's guards, are ready to escort you to the dais for the ceremony."

"What about Trianna?" I asked.

"I'm here," Trianna poked her head into the door, smiling. She slipped inside and moved over to hug me. "Sorry, I just finished breakfast. I know how we get if we eat together, and we don't need to chat the morning away."

I hugged her tight. "I'm nervous."

"I don't blame you," she laughed. "Married and crowned on the same day in front of a few hundred thousand people. It's a bit much."

"I'm more nervous about afterwards," I admitted.

Trianna looked at me for a moment trying to figure out my meaning. "Are… you talking about tonight? Do you not know what to—"

"Lady Trianna!" Kara gasped.

I laughed and shook my head. "Stone preserve me, no! Not that! I meant about ruling as the Empress. I'm worried about living up to everyone's expectations."

Trianna smiled. "You've already exceeded everyone's expectations. So you have no need to worry about meeting them. You'll do wonderfully. And your friends will always be there to support you."

Kara brought in breakfast for me. I tried to eat quickly, not wanting to waste anyone's time since I knew we were on a tight schedule. However, as I sat down for my meal, Serena and Rita came in to visit with me before the ceremony. We probably took a bit too much time catching up and talking, but Kara assured me that we were still able to keep on schedule.

After I finished eating, Kara, Trianna, and the others helped me into my gown. The gown was a fierce garnet with dimvyum Orodum signet studs. It was accented with polished gold-plated armor pieces crafted by Beltia and inlaid with dimvyum sigil enchantments that glowed whenever the light hit them. My hair was woven into intricate braids, with mithril and gold thread woven into it. Emerald and sapphire jewels were also threaded into my braids so that they accentuated both my hair and eyes. The design was meant to give me an air of elegance and dwarven sturdiness.

In addition to my gown and jewelry, I wore the mithril collar that Kroff

Tegran had gifted me on the day that Franklin and I had visited his family's shop. It had been far too big for me at the time, but now it fit perfectly. I had promised the old man that I would wear it one day, and that he would be among the first to see me wearing it. I intended to keep that promise. As such, I had made sure that Kroff was allowed a seat in the Noble District to watch the wedding. He had been more than kind to me that day and I wanted to repay the kindness.

I also decided to wear the ring Franklin had given me as part of his proposal. I had discussed wearing it with Faren, and he thought it was a noble idea to keep Franklin's memory alive.

Finally, I wore the ring Mother had worn when she was still alive. She had insisted to Father that he give it to me when I came of age. So I decided to wear it in her memory. It was the very least I could do for her.

When I stepped out of my chambers, all of my servants were gathered in the halls. They had lined up all the way through the estate to the front doors. Everyone was smiling with excitement. I took time to speak with each of them, thanking them for their service and accepting small pieces of jewelry that could be set into my hair. Apparently, they had all decided that they would get a single piece of jewelry to decorate my braids with, and Kara had assured them that she would fix my hair in such a way that this could be done. I couldn't deny them this gesture. It did pain me somewhat that they had all spent money on me, but it made me smile to think that they went to the trouble.

By the time I had gotten to the front door, my braids were heavy with jewelry. I made a mental note to give them all a bonus as a way to compensate them for the jewelry. They would know why they got the extra money, but I knew they'd know me well enough to understand that I couldn't let them spend so much on me.

I stopped at the front door and looked at the servants gathered in the main hall. I smiled brightly at them. "I want to thank you all for this wonderful gesture. Ever since I was a child and House Orodum was established, you have cared for me. You've taken great pains to make House Orodum the envy of Cragmorrar and have watched me grow. Each of you has guided me in some way and left an impact on my life during these trying years."

"You've supported me in my efforts and looked after me in my weakest and darkest moments. It was your support that helped me become the woman I am today, and I can never truly repay all the kindness that you've shown me. As we transition from the Orodum Estate to the Palace, I want you all to know that I consider you a part of my family. Thank you all so much for taking on the daily burdens of my life so that I could succeed in my efforts."

I dipped into a deep curtsy, the last one I would ever give. I always gave them to express genuine pleasure in meeting someone. It was a sign of respect and mutual admiration. And this final curtsy was given to the men and women who worked in the background. While I knew all of their names, history would forget them. But it was thanks to their hard work and their willingness to do the mundane tasks of everyday life that allowed me to focus on the important details and to perform the necessary steps. Without them, none of what I had accomplished would have been possible.

Smiles, tears, and grateful expressions were my answer.

I took a few moments to take in those gathered before me before I had to leave. I rose from my genuflection and bowed my head. I turned, and the doors opened for me. Outside were hundreds of warriors; many from the palace and the full guard of House Orodum. As soon as they caught sight of me, they knelt in fealty.

"Princess Orodum," the Commander of the palace guard said from his prostration, "we are here to escort you to the dais. We serve at your command."

I looked at the warriors and sighed softly. "No sense in making the people wait, Commander. Please, escort us to the dais."

The Commander stood and turned to the rest. "On your feet, warriors! Fall in and prepare to escort your future Empress!"

The warriors stood and moved into formation. The palace guard moved in front, while I came next, then Trianna and Serena, then Rita and Kara. Behind them came the whole of House Orodum's household. The warriors of House Orodum fell in last, keeping a rear guard against a foe that wouldn't dare attack. Still, appearances and ceremonies were important. The people would want fanfare and a show.

We made our way through the Noble District. Entire noble families lined the main thoroughfare and cheered as we walked by. There were cries of 'Good luck, Princess!' and 'Long live Empress Orodum!' as well as a dozen other well wishes were shouted as we passed. The nobility rarely showed such excitement. Though, to be fair, the transfer of power from one dwarven leader to another had never come with such ceremony, and never with so many visiting dignitaries. This was history in the making, and they all wanted to be seen as part of it or were genuinely enthusiastic and excited to see me. I waved as I passed by, occasionally calling out to certain nobles to make sure that each family was recognized at some level.

As we came within sight of the dais, I could see the important members of the Dwarven kingdom gathered there, as well as the foreign visitors. However, before I made eye contact with any of them, I looked around for Mister Kroff. I knew about where he should be seated. When I finally spotted him, I called a halt to the formation. The Commander relayed my order, and all of the warriors stopped in unison.

The Commander turned and looked at me. "Princess? Is there something wrong?"

I shook my head. "Just wait here for a few moments, please. I need to speak to someone."

"As you command, Princess," he replied.

I turned and approached Kroff, nodding and smiling to a few nobles as I closed the distance. I stopped in front of Kroff and smiled as he bowed before me.

"It's wonderful to see you again, Mister Kroff," I said with a friendly smile. "Thank you for accepting my invitation."

Kroff looked at me gratefully. "I could never refuse such an invitation, My Exemplar. My Princess."

I canted my head to the side slightly, offering him a grateful expression.

"It's a pleasure knowing you were willing to be here. I wanted to ask you what you thought of the collar. It's my first time wearing it."

Kroff smiled at me, wearing his family's collar. "As always, Princess, you are a beautiful sight to behold. You do the heirloom more justice than anyone ever could. I could not imagine anyone more worthy to wear it."

"I promised you that you would be among the first to see me wear it," I chuckled. "I hope you don't mind that I didn't invite your son."

The old man laughed. "I think it's appropriate. He wasn't there the day you first visited, so I'm happy to have this moment to myself as well."

I smiled wide. "I hope he's been the one to man the store more often now and given you the rest you deserve."

"He has indeed, Princess," Kroff replied. "Since then, he's hoped for a repeat visit."

My expression sobered, and I raised my hand up to look at the ring Kroff had made from my favorite materials that Franklin had commissioned from him. "Yes, well… I do admire the quality of your family's work. It's why I commission you so often. But going back in there…"

Kroff nodded lightly and stepped in to place a hand on my shoulder. "I understand completely, Princess. That was a day you remember sharing with Lord Irono. Returning would invite heartache. Never apologize for avoiding what brings you pain. Focus on the joy life brings you, Princess. And my family will be there to create the items you use to remember your memories by."

"Thank you so much, my old friend," I said as I hugged him close. "Now, if you'll excuse me, I need to keep moving."

Kroff returned the hug and nodded. "Go, Princess. Become the Empress you were always meant to be."

I turned from the old man, happy that I had finally been able to fulfill my promise to him. As I returned to the formation, I smiled. "Continue on, Commander."

The Commander called for the formation to continue forward, and we soon reached the stairs that led to the dais. Serena, Trianna, Rita, and Kara each went ahead of me, taking their places among the family gathered on the dais.

I could see Father moving to the top of the stairs. "I present to you all, my daughter, Princess Merida Orodum, Exemplar among dwarves!"

I smiled, hating the announcement. I was happy to be climbing the stairs to my wedding, but hurt knowing that as soon as I was wed, I would be crowned. I finished the ascent to the dais and took Father's arm when he offered it. Cheers echoed throughout the city as I appeared on the dais, in full view of those below.

It was at this point that I saw Faren for the first time today. A new set of armor had been fashioned for him. The armor was thick and styled to exude the presence of command. It also carried dimvyum-engraved enchantments, sported House Orodum's symbol, and was accented with House Orodum's colors. His beard had been carefully brushed and braided, his hair was pulled back into a ponytail, and his expression was warm and relieved to see me. I wanted to run over to him right then.

Father walked me to a point across the dais from Faren. "Today I entrust my daughter to the protection of another. She leaves my arms and is embraced by her beloved. Her safety, her prosperity, and her happiness are now the concern of Faren Orodum. On behalf of House Nordrucan, I ask the prospective bridegroom if he will accept this most sacred of responsibilities."

Faren smiled. "I am Faren Orodum. I will take this woman under my care. I am proud to say I have guarded her all of her life. My every day has been dedicated to her safety. It is my honor and my privilege to now see to her prosperity and happiness as well. She will be chief among my concerns, my first priority when I wake, and my only concern when I rest."

"The Stone and all of Cragmorrar have heard the promise of dedication from the bridegroom," Father replied. He looked out to the sea of dwarves below us. "See now, I freely offer my daughter's hand to this man. From this day until his last day, you shall all hold him accountable should he fail in his promise."

Father looked at me and smiled, pride, joy, and sorrow all mixed in his expression. Pride in me. Joy in the fact that I could now be with the man I loved. Sorrow in the fact that Faren would now be the primary man in my life. I suppose he knew he hadn't been the primary man in my life since I'd become an Exemplar, but this was different. I had always been his daughter, and I had always been his and his alone. But today, he was giving up that connection of parental protection and entrusting it to someone else.

He whispered quietly to me, "I am so happy for you, Merida. You're not my little girl anymore. You've grown into a beautiful and capable woman. I wish you all the happiness in the world."

I leaned in and pecked his cheek. "Thank you, Father."

"I only wish your mother could have seen this day," he said with some sadness.

"She's watching," I assured him.

He nodded, then escorted me over to Faren, who took my hand in his.

"I declare now that Princess Merida Orodum and Faren Orodum be forever known as husband and wife!" Father announced.

Cragmorrar shook with cheers. The sound was ear-splitting but not in a bad way. The joy and happiness were palpable. Faren and I shared our first public kiss there on the dais, and the crowd cheered even louder. There was nothing to compare to that moment of happiness… until fear and confusion replaced it.

Out of the corner of my eye, I saw a commotion among the foreign dignitaries. The Vintari Magisters' leapt to their feet and cast a number of spells. The guards were on them almost immediately, but the damage had been done. Within moments, hundreds of black and violet portals began to open all over the city. The crowds were shunted one way or another as the portals forced themselves into existence. Then came the screams of fear and pain as scourgespawn swarmed through the portals alongside mages dressed in Vintari-styled robes. This would have been a massacre, but my people were already well prepared.

Once the initial panic had subsided, the whole of Cragmorrar's citizenry faded into red ghostly specters as guards around the city activated the Dimvyum Well Defense Systems in their area. The scourgespawn and mages, who had been easily slaughtering the unarmed citizens, now flailed at the specters of the citizens who were being safely evacuated by the guards who had shifted dimensions with them.

The Vintari delegates had been quickly subdued, and the guests in the Noble District had been protected by the palace guard. But there was still the issue of the thousands of scourgespawn and mages pouring through the portals. In the center of the city, a large portal opened up, and I could see Seven step through, surrounded by dozens of Vintari Magisters. He was laughing at the initial carnage.

I looked at Faren. "Take command of the guards! Stop the scourgespawn and the mages!"

"What about you?" he asked.

"I'll handle Seven," I replied. "Hurry! Our people are in danger!"

Faren nodded and activated his gauntlets, sending messages through each shifted dimension as he ran off. The guards would be quickly organized and put to the task of defending the city.

I stepped off the dais and willed the stone beneath me so that I could be brought down to street level. I was ready to unleash the full might of my power on these invaders. As I marched toward the center district, the stone leapt up around me, turning any scourgespawn that dared to come close into a red mist. Vintari spells were countered easily enough thanks to Jeron's knowledge of crafting, which included spellcraft. Whenever I spied a mage preparing a spell, a simple glance in their direction allowed me to see and alter the spell's component energies to cause it to erupt in the caster's face, melt the caster's hand, or drain the life from the caster. The damage was only ever enough to put the caster out of the fight and never enough to kill them. I made sure of that.

I stopped in the area I had initially cleared and moved to the dwarves who had been slain. I knelt beside one and ran my hand over the open wounds, drawing out the corruption, then infusing the wounds with healing magic. My connection to all dwarves allowed me to find the body's soul in the ether and bring it back to its body. The dwarf, a young woman, opened her eyes in shock.

She looked up at me as a torrent of stone and arcane winds surrounded the area, keeping it safe from enemies. Her voice was frightened and full of panic. "Princess? What happened?"

I smiled in a way to comfort her, "Don't you worry. You're safe. I need you to get up now. We need to help the others, then get you into the safety of the Dimvyum Well System. Can you stand?"

She nodded, confusion still clouding her mind. "Yes, Princess. Thank you!"

It took a few minutes to get the rest of the slain back on their feet. All the while, I was actively countering spells and controlling the stone to keep the enemy at bay. Once I had gotten the dwarves to one of the Dimvyum Well panels and into the red dimension, I released the arcane storm. The sight before me was filled with scourgespawn swarming the streets. I could see pockets of Cragmorrar guards shifting in and out of the dimensions to perform quick attacks on the scourgespawn.

I growled. These creatures were nothing. They weren't even ants. They didn't realize where they were or what they were attacking. The whole of the world, from here to Fransway, was under my influence. I was the very ground they walked upon, and I was the currents of magic within the Dimvolmn. I marched forward, and the scourgespawn in my path erupted in bursts of blood and gore as I summoned magical energy inside of them and let it explode. I activated Pantheon and used my second self to claim the magic in the Dimvolmn for as far as my influence reached. This denied the mages access to their magic. The stone wrapped around their limbs and crushed them, leaving them as lumps of screaming flesh. A quick death would be too good for them.

As I sewed chaos in the physical world, my soul self worked its power within the Dimvolmn. Not only was it claiming the magic within it for me, but it was able to target any spellcasters who were calling upon magic. The weakest of these poor souls were pulled into the Dimvolmn against their will, where Purpose led an army of spirits to attack them. Summoning spells were met with nothing to answer the caster's call. Thanks to my absorption of Serevas, I understood how the shroud truly worked and how to manipulate it. This meant that the Dimvolmn and the physical world were always at my command. Wherever my influence reached, I controlled the flow of magic, energy, and the very stone beneath my feet.

I alone cleared the street I was on toward the center of the city. I allowed the guards to clear out the rest of the streets so that my focus could be solely on the anomaly emanating from the city's center. That had to be Seven. There was something strange about his location. The Dimvolmn and the shroud were churning around him in a maelstrom. Nothing about it was natural. It was as if his mere presence was causing the carefully placed balance of the shroud to recoil as if in disgust.

It took me several minutes to reach the center. When I arrived, the Magisters that had accompanied Seven were all writhing in pain on the ground, their magic having turned against them, and the ground having pummeled their bones to dust. Seven was just standing there, waiting. He wore his twisted grin that seemed almost manic. When he saw me, he began to laugh.

"Well, if it isn't Princess Orodum," he laughed and offered a mock bow. "I did not receive an invitation to the wedding or coronation, so I assumed it was lost. I decided to come anyway. I hope you don't mind."

"You've allied with Vintari and attacked my people and my home," I said in a commanding voice. "I told you what would happen if the scourgespawn ever attacked the dwarves again. I gave you the chance to live out the rest of your lives in peace."

"You offered me the chance to simply die in obscurity," Seven spat. "How magnanimous of you! I'm willing to bet that you are also here to offer me one last chance to go and live in some dark hole, peaceful and left alone until I die."

"No," I said dangerously. "You threw that chance away, then somehow allied yourself with Vintari to attack my people. I will show you no mercy."

Seven threw his head back and laughed. "Somehow allied myself with Vintari? Princess, you basically introduced our people to each other! The moment you stopped the trade of dimvyum to slaveholders, the Vintari Empire began looking for anyone else that could safely mine the stuff. We've been allies for years now! The only thing that gave me command over the Empire was absorbing Varrimus' soul. I gained so much power and so much knowledge… You would scarcely believe it! And you only have yourself to blame."

"You're right," I conceded. "I am to blame for you being left alive. If I had allowed some of my friends to die, I could have killed you before you took Varrimus' soul, stopped you from allying with Vintari, and prevented this attack on my people. All of this is my fault. But I am here to correct that mistake here and now. You won't leave here alive."

"Funny," Seven hissed. "I was going to say the same thing about you!" He raised his hands, and black energy pulsed toward me in a wave.

My mind raced. He shouldn't have access to magic. I was controlling the Dimvolmn and the shroud with Pantheon. I had to assume that whatever effect was causing the anomalous whirling of the shroud around him was allowing him to bypass my hold on magic. I raised an arcane barrier to stop the black energy, but Seven pushed his way through the clashing energies, brandishing a wickedly barbed sword.

As the sword raced toward me, the stone leapt from the ground and slammed into Seven's side, then crushed him into the street. The stone began to bring him down in order to crush him into the earth below, but he disappeared. It was thanks to Kaneya's influence that I was able to track him. His anomalous signature appeared behind me. I conjured a greatsword from the stone and turned, bringing it around to parry a thrust of Seven's sword away from me. I lowered myself so that Seven's follow-through backfist went over my head. I used my momentum to swing my makeshift sword up in a quick arc, but Seven disappeared once more. My sword threatened to carry me with its momentum, but I released it, allowing it to fly into the air. When Seven's signature reappeared in my senses, I had the sword separate into a thousand shards and sent them flying in his direction.

Seven laughed as black energy appeared in front of him, deflecting the shards away. "You've come a long way with your magic and stone manipulation, Princess! But I've caught up! Varrimus' power, along with some artifacts that I've collected from Vintari, have allowed me to be able to counter your power."

My eyes went wide with surprise for a moment, but I wasn't an average person in their mid-twenties. I had the memories, experience, and power of beings millennia old. I smirked. "You don't seem to understand how wrong you are. Don't you understand yet? I'm only holding back. I've been jabbing at you so far, seeing how powerful I need to strike to put you down without endangering the world and the people around us."

Stone spikes jutted from the ground one after the other to keep Seven moving and focused on avoidance.

"Varrimus? Power from artifacts?" I snorted dismissively. "You're playing with parlor tricks while I'm wielding true magic."

Seven charged in, slashing and thrusting purposefully and expertly with his sword while weaving dark energy in between his attacks. "You speak as if this fight is so one-sided, but I'm still here! If it was as you said, then I should have been long gone by now! Got you!"

He stepped forward, thrusting his sword into my gut. Or at least he would have if I hadn't purposefully left myself open. The sword did go through my guts, but I had shifted my physical self into the shroud, turning me insubstantial. With Seven off balance, I stepped forward and shifted back into the physical world to slam a stone-covered fist into his side. This blow doubled him over, and I was able to land a quick uppercut to his chin to send him stumbling backwards. Before he could recover, I moved in to deliver several more blows to his abdomen. He defensively raised a protective burst of black energy.

I jumped back and considered the energy. What could it be? It felt like magic, but it was darker, like it was the antithesis of magic. Still, this wasn't antimagic. I could use antimagic, and this wasn't a form it could take. I reached out with my senses and nearly vomited. The energy was corruption. It was Scourge manifested as magic! He'd learned to conjure the corruption itself; he had made the aura of the infection that coursed through every scourgespawn into a weapon.

"You're wielding the corruption?!?" I gasped.

Seven's grin widened. "Ah! You've figured that much out, have you? Yes, Princess. Thanks to Varrimus' memories, I was able to figure out how to wield the corruption that created scourgespawn. Its power warps the shroud around me, and I can gather the energy from the Dimvolmn and corrupt it! This isn't magic you can control! This isn't magic you can negate! It's the purest expression of the Scourge! And you will die screaming from it!"

"You're so hellbent on making everyone else suffer because of your poor luck when you were reincarnated," I yelled. "So determined to make sure that everyone experiences your own hell that you're willing to kill and corrupt the entire world! But I won't let you!"

Seven laughed. "You can't even stop me, let alone kill me! There's nothing you can do but die!" He charged forward and released magical geysers of corruption to keep me on the defensive till he could close the distance. He swung wildly, forcing me to dodge quickly.

I slipped into the stone and emerged behind him, only to have to raise a stone-covered arm to block a strike that came around unexpectedly. The shower of rocks and dust that erupted from blocking the strike obscured my vision just long enough that Seven was able to get past my guard. He appeared in an instant, his face wild with anticipation and glee just before he bit down onto my shoulder. If I were anyone else, his teeth would have pierced my skin and ripped out a chunk of my flesh. Even if I survived, I would have been corrupted by the Scourge. But he was biting me, and not someone else.

Seven's teeth shattered as he bit down. While he thought he was biting into a thick gown, what he didn't know was that there was another aspect to my outfit. I was wearing many things that were gifted to me over the course of my life. Sewn into the shoulder and neck of my gown was the mithril shoulder guards that Faren had given to me for my birthday some years ago. I had made sure to have it placed into the gown so that I could have something he had given me as part of my ensemble.

As Seven reeled back from his teeth being shattered, stone spikes pierced his body by the dozens and exploded. Pieces of his body flew in every direction in a burst of blood and blackness.

I looked around to assess the rest of the situation, ready to begin exerting my power to end the scourgespawn invasion in only a few moments. Before I could begin, though, Seven's voice began to chuckle maniacally behind me. I turned around to find a humanoid figure of broiling corruption standing there. Yellow, manic eyes peered at me and a similar mouth smiled far wider than he should have been able to.

"That's it, Princess?" Seven asked with venomous amusement. "Knowing what you know of me, knowing what I possess, and your solution was simply to destroy my body? Pathetic! I expected more of you!"

I stared at Seven and sifted through what I'd learned. Pristaren's vast secret knowledge led me to a conclusion: "You're not just corrupted anymore… you are the corruption. You've merged your soul with the corruption of the Dimvolmn when the Magisters first forced their way into it!"

"You understand now!" Seven laughed wickedly. "You cannot stop me because I'm no longer a person to be stopped. I am like the old gods themselves; a soul that can inhabit any corrupted vessel! But unlike the old gods, I can also exist outside of a vessel. I wield the power of the Dimvolmn itself, corrupted into perfection!"

A pulse of black energy erupted from him and warped the world around us in a way indescribable to mortal minds. It shook reality with the weight of the Dimvolmn and forced me several steps back.

"Now, Princess, will you die quietly?" Seven chuckled. "Now that you know how outmatched you are, will you fight and die violently? Or will you be a good girl and die quickly?"

I steeled myself and stood as tall as I could. "Stop calling me that!"

"Hm?" Seven asked as he began to walk toward me. "And why should I?"

"Because I am an Empress!" I roared. I expanded my influence over the physical world and out into the Dimvolmn. "I am the very world around you!

I am the Master of the Dimvolmn, the one who can pull back the shroud. And you are nothing but an infection! You might be able to channel the Dimvolmn through your corruption, but I understand the root of your corruption. I was there when it first manifested, and I was the one who admonished your arrogance when you broke into where you don't belong! If you want to act like you understand power, then I will show you power!"

As my senses fused with my influence, I summoned all of my power. "It's true that I had hoped to end this fight without destroying my home. So instead, I'll bring this fight to a place I can destroy!"

I locked onto the corrupted energy of Seven and dragged him with me. The writhing bodies of the Magisters disappeared. The dead scourgespawn, and the sound of battle vanished. All the damage done to the city was repaired in the blink of an eye. This was a pristine and empty Cragmorrar, void of any other living souls.

Seven stopped and looked around. The transition wasn't subtle. In fact, the stillness and silence was jarring.

"What just happened?" Seven asked. "Where are we?"

I smirked. "What do you mean? Don't you recognize Cragmorrar?"

"You know damn well this isn't Cragmorrar!" Seven growled.

"Oh, but it is," I assured him. "Your ignorance is astounding for someone who claims to 'wield the power of the Dimvolmn itself.' The Dimvolmn isn't just a single dimension where spirits were bound and souls go when their bodies dream. It's uncountable dimensions layered one on top of another, flowing through one another, as multitudinous and various as there are dreams in the minds of mortals. Can you imagine it? And Serevas separated it all and sealed it away behind the shroud. To spite the other Gospinia, to torture them, he made what had once been a part of the world only accessible to the unconscious minds... and limited that access to a random puzzle combination of daily events and concerning thoughts!"

"And this?" I opened my arms to encompass our surroundings as I closed my eyes. "This is just one of those dimensions that is now under my control. I come here occasionally in my dreams, and more often with my newfound abilities. I have destroyed this world countless times over. And each time I've destroyed it, I've remade it anew. And now, you're here. And I can show you my full power."

Seven tried to speak, but this was my realm. I didn't allow his voice to make a sound. The world itself opened up, like it was peeling back to reveal its innermost secrets. The void of space swirled around us, and the air became palpable, thickening more and more every moment as I drew power from several dimensions of the Dimvolmn at once. My Titan essence raised itself into the ever-expanding world of my personal domain, as tall and vast as the open sky.

When I opened my eyes, they glowed with dimvyum fire. My physical mouth moved, but my Titan essence spoke, "You think drawing from a well grants you access to the ocean? You are nothing but a bucket, pulling from and poisoning the energy of the Dimvolmn. I AM the Dimvolmn! And you will draw from my power no longer! You are an infection, and I will now cleanse you. I hope, if you are reincarnated once again, that you will choose to live a happy and peaceful life…"

My power surrounded the energy essence of Seven. I felt him struggling, clawing with every ounce of his being. He wanted to strike and curse and scream in defiance of his fate. It was pointless. He was a grain of sand trying to defy a hurricane. I felt him with my power and first ripped his soul and Varrimus' apart. He hadn't absorbed the ancient Magister's soul; he'd merely contained it and used it. I claimed Varrimus' soul for myself, then ripped away the corrupted energy that anchored Seven's soul to the world. The corruption was seared away by the cleansing power at my command.

I held on to Seven's soul for several moments, considering whether or not to destroy it then and there. Even in my anger, I understood why he was the way he was. But I had to have hope that he could have a better life than the one fate had given him this time. Hopefully, he could have a life without hate or bitter resentment toward the world. Hopefully… he could be happy…

I released his soul, and it faded away. Where it went, I didn't know. Even Dalon'Tara's knowledge of death didn't pierce the shroud of the afterlife. Would he simply fade away? Would he reincarnate again? I couldn't know… But I could hope.

I shifted back into the physical world, containing my power once again. While we had spent a few minutes in the alternate dimension of the Dimvolmn, we'd only been gone in the blink of an eye in the physical world. I doubt anyone would have noticed we'd even disappeared. I could feel the combat going on in the rest of the city and shook my head.

"Enough," I whispered. The stone throughout the city rose in anger and entombed every scourgespawn, crushing them into pulp in the darkness of the stone. Magisters were crippled in an instant, left to scream helplessly on the floor.

As the silence of the battle ending abruptly filled the city, I reached out and connected my consciousness to the minds of every dwarf in the city. "My people. This is Empress Orodum. I am speaking to you through the natural link we all share with each other through the Titans. I have ended the attack on our city. The Vintari Empire conspired with the scourgespawn to kill me and slaughter you all so that they could gain control of our dimvyum. It was my insistence that we stop selling dimvyum to them that provoked this attack. I am ultimately responsible for the horrors that have happened today."

"However," I continued softly, "I will make amends. This day, I will demonstrate some of my powers for you. I do not ask that you forgive me for this attack. It is what I owe you all for causing such a travesty. However, I will not let this attack go unanswered. So, after today, I promise you, Vintari will pay for this betrayal."

I let the whole of the dwarven populace see through my eyes as I willed the stone to bring the bodies of every dead dwarf before me. I could feel the sadness, the anger, the fear in all of my people as they watched the stone set the bodies of the slain before me. However, I also felt one thing among all of those other emotions: Orodum. I chose the name because it meant 'hope'. And hope was the one emotion that I felt from each and every dwarf I was connected with.

All of the dead were recently deceased, so they were still within the limits of my newfound power. I willed mana to seep into their bodies; I directed it to burn away any corruption and repair the wounds each dwarf had suffered. Then, one by one, I returned their souls to their bodies. I felt the shock, the joy, the disbelief, and the devotion from every dwarf as each of the dead woke in turn and joined in the vision. As the last of the fallen had been brought back to life, I shifted the vision of the collective to those dwarves who now stood before me so that every dwarf could see me through their eyes.

I looked at them, stern and commanding. "This will be my coronation. I stand before you all after defending our city. I am your Empress. I am your Titan. I am your Protector and your Mother. I consider you all my children. And like any mother, whenever anyone, or anything, threatens my children, I will destroy that threat. I swear to you that from this day until my last day, I will always keep you safe."

I released the connection and stood before the group of dwarves whom I'd just brought back to life. I smiled gently at them. They were commoners and were staring at me in awe.

"Would you kindly escort me back to the Noble District? I would like to apologize to all of you personally," I said. Before they could answer, I began to walk back to the entrance of the Noble District. The dwarves all walked behind me in silence, none speaking after the miracle they had been party to.

When we reached the Noble District, Faren was standing there with the palace guards and House Orodum soldiers. The rest of the foreign dignitaries and nobles were there as well. All of them were staring at me in awe.

Faren moved forward and wrapped his arms around me, hugging me tight. "You shouldn't have faced him without me! What would I have done if I had lost you?"

I smiled up at Faren and placed a hand on his cheek. "You will never lose me again. I will always be by your side. But you did your job and helped to keep our people safe. Thank you for that."

Faren inhaled with a sound of both happiness and worry. "From now on, if you go into battle, I will go with you. No exceptions."

I laughed softly and nodded. "As you wish. For now, though, would you see these citizens somewhere comfortable? I want to take some time to apologize to them personally for what they suffered through today."

"Empress, please," one of the dwarves who had followed me said. "You don't owe us an apology. You've done more for us already by bringing us back and healing us. Please, let us thank you somehow."

I turned and smiled at the man. "Please, allow me to do this. My husband will find you some seats to watch the coronation, then I will offer you some compensation."

The man looked like he wanted to protest but Faren quickly cut him off. "Come along, you lot. We had some seats freed up just as all of this nonsense started."

I wanted to laugh at Faren's joke. He was referring to the Vintari diplomats who'd been subdued as they opened the portals for the others. He had a subtle sense of gallows humor that I loved. As the dwarves followed Faren to their seats, I moved back to the dais.

The citizens of Cragmorrar had begun to fill the streets once more. They were talking and pointing at me. I could only imagine what they were saying. It took a few minutes to get everyone situated once more. Faren joined me at the dais once again and took my hand in his. This view of the Empress and her consort brought a round of cheers from the onlookers. We turned and waved down at them until Father and Steward Brandon joined us.

Father received cheers from the crowd. He'd been an extremely popular king who had helped to bring the city back to prominence even before I was born. His policies and diplomacy brought more prosperity than the last four kings combined. He was well-loved by the citizens, and their reaction to seeing him proved that.

Steward Brandon raised his hands to call for everyone's attention. "People of Cragmorrar! An attack has occurred on our city. The Vintari Empire has attempted to kill our citizens and our leaders. But see now that Cragmorrar stands unscathed! The dimvyum Well Defense System kept the majority of our citizens safe and allowed our defenders to safely oppose our attackers. The system, devised and provided by Princess Merida Orodum, is one of many advances made by our Princess that has brought security and prosperity to our people in her short lifetime thus far."

"The Assembly has spoken," he continued. "It has declared Princess Merida Orodum to become our next leader, that she will take on the crown and be named Empress of the renewed dwarven Empire! What say you, people of Cragmorrar?"

The crowd cheered wildly in response.

Once the cheering had mostly settled down, the Steward continued, "The Assembly and the People have spoken. Princess Merida Orodum shall be given leadership over all dwarves. I ask now that King Nordrucan speak his peace and offer the crown to his successor."

There was a great round of applause for Father as he stepped forward. The applause came from everyone: dwarven commoners and nobles, as well as the Empress of Trebue, King Marshal, and the rest of the human and elven dignitaries. Father had done much for the relationship between our people and theirs, and they were happy to see him able to retire with a sterling reputation.

"My people!" Father called out. "It is with great pleasure that I address you today. It is always a father's hope that his children will succeed him and carry on his legacy of good works. It is also the hope of a father that his children not only meet the standards he sets for them, but surpass them and overshadow his accomplishments. To watch such a thing occur is a bittersweet victory. I can say now with all confidence that each of my children has done just that."

He turned and motioned to Trenton, who stood off to my side. "My eldest is a far better commander than I could have ever hoped to be. He rules Nordrucan Hold, where I plan to retire, and he has helped to raise my daughter into the inspiring figure she is today."

The crowd cheered for Trenton. Perhaps not as loudly as they did for Father and myself, but there was no doubt he was well-respected and loved.

"My daughter," Father tried to continue but had to wait for the cheer that rose up when he mentioned me, "has become an Exemplar, a hero, a mage, and a worker of miracles. She is a living legend that shall never be forgotten so long as dwarves draw breath."

The roar of the crowd was deafening, and it took a minute or so before it died down enough to allow Father to continue.

"And my youngest son," he motioned to Bilfern, who stood proudly next to Trenton. "He has created such wonders as the Dimvyum Defense System, which has kept you all safe today. I only hope that I can live long enough to see a few more of the wonders that his clever mind will produce in the years to come."

Bilfern received a louder cheer than Trenton, likely because the Dimvyum Well System had been pivotal in reducing injuries and casualties during the attack.

Father took a moment to look down on all of the people gathered below. "I look at you all now and cannot claim to have been the primary reason why you are all prospering so well. My policies and rule were bolstered by someone who was more forward-thinking and more in tune with the hearts of my people than I could ever hope to be. So…" He removed the crown from his head and looked at me. "I bid you, Princess Merida Orodum, to kneel."

I smiled sadly. I never wanted to see the day when Father would not be King. I also never wanted to see the day when I was crowned as ruler. But those two things paled in comparison to the love and pride I saw in Father's eyes. The expression hurt my heart because I didn't think I could ever truly live up to the image of me he had in his head. I took a moment, faster than the blink of an eye, to see myself through his eyes. He wasn't seeing me as I was. He didn't see a grown woman, firm with muscle, standing tall, recently wed and scathed from battle. He was seeing a little girl filled with anxiousness and fear. He was seeing pig-tailed braids and a smile that longed for his approval. He was holding on to that image even as the reality of the situation threatened to shatter it.

I did as he commanded and knelt down to one knee.

"Princess Merida Orodum," Father called out, "I charge you with rulership over our people. You are commanded and expected to always put their health, prosperity, traditions, and future in mind. Your burden is now that of their safety, the preservation of our way of life, and to work towards always ensuring that they thrive." He placed the crown on my head and called out, "Rise now, Empress Orodum."

As I stood, I took another look through Father's eyes as he was finally seeing me as I was. I stood before him, a proud, grown, mature dwarf that radiated with joy in the pride he had in me. "It is with great honor that I present to you your new Empress! Raise your voices and your cups in celebration! I present to you, Empress Merida Orodum, crowned in this thirty-fifth year of the ninth era! All bow and hail Empress Orodum!"

Father was the first to bow, and then all others followed. I thought I was ready to be crowned, regardless of the apprehension I felt about becoming the Empress. However, the sight of hundreds of thousands of dwarves, elves, humans, and atoshi bowing in my presence brought a tightness to my chest. I was nervous and anxious at the feelings that swam through my head. After everything I had experienced in this life, I hadn't thought anything was able to leave me speechless.

This did.

I took several moments to process through my feelings before I lowered myself to guide Father up to his feet. I smiled and failed to hold back a few tears as I embraced him. It was a small, private moment between Father and Daughter, one no others would share in. I held onto him as long as I thought I was able to get away with before releasing him.

He gave me a confident nod and whispered, "Speak to them, Merida."

I almost wanted to refuse, but I knew the turmoil that would cause. I took a deep breath to give myself some confidence and turned to face the citizens, and spoke with a magically enhanced voice, "Rise, my people. Hear what I have to say."

Everyone stood and looked at me. This was something I was accustomed to. Ever since I was little, all eyes were on me. Everyone would watch me to see what I was doing and listen to what I was saying. This time was different. All eyes were locked on me. There was a palpable sense of anticipation, awe, and expectancy. This moment was monumental; a point in history that would be recorded and memorized by scholars and laymen for time immemorial. How did you plan what to say for something like that?

"After the attack, I linked with every dwarf to speak with you directly," I began. I kept my tone firm yet compassionate. "I told you that today's attack was the result of my decisions. I stand by that statement. I also told you that I think of you all as my children, and that I will protect you. I stand by that statement as well. My coronation was one born of battle and christened in the defeat of a powerful enemy. And while you all understand my love and dedication to you, our allies may not."

I turned and motioned for the other Fated, as well as King Marshal and Empress Trebue, to join me.

"Many of you will recognize Lady Trianna from her time spent in Cragmorrar," I continued. "Here now is her husband, Lord Aelfric. They lead the elves of the Cariok Wilds."

Trianna and Aelfric both smiled and waved at the gathered dwarves.

"Here is Allen Lemlal, Headmaster of the Lemlalian College and representative of Falladrin's mages," I said and motioned to Allen.

Allen offered a sweeping bow.

"My dear friends Serena and Alford Thirston, heirs to the Kingdom of Falladrin, and King Marshal of Falladrin," I smiled.

Alford and Marshal bowed while Serena curtsied.

"Empress Trebue of Fransway, who I hope to become close with over time," I said confidently.

Empress Trebue bowed her head.

"We also have dignitaries from the Independent Marshes and Ven Parlol," I explained. "It is my hope that in time we can establish good relations with each of these great powers and that we can continue to foster closer relationships with our current allies."

"However," my tone grew more stern, "we have also had war declared upon us today by the Vintari Empire. I stand before you, my people, and our allies to say that no declaration of war against the Dwarven Empire will be met with anything less than quick and decisive action. Our Empire does not believe in half measures or equal responses. If we are attacked, we will strike back with overwhelming force that the world will look upon with fear."

I approached the balcony of the dais and placed my hands upon it. Faren came up behind me, as did the rest of the others to symbolically back up what I would say next: "I will suffer no threat to my people or my allies. My first act as Empress will be to acknowledge Vintari's declaration of war and lead our people to Vintari's destruction!!"

The roar of approval felt like nothing compared to the expressions of shock coming from the Fated and the others.

"Vintari will be an example to all who would dare think to attack the Dwarven Empire or its allies," I pressed on. "What remains of it will have to claw its way back into relevancy, but it will do so with our assistance. Their leaders will fade into memory, and we must hope that their descendants will learn from their mistakes and become a better nation."

I turned and looked at the others. "It is my hope that representatives from our allies will stand beside me in this effort to offer shelter and aid to the freed slaves of Vintari. This way, we can show the world a better way to move forward."

I took Faren's hand and gently encouraged him to stand beside me. "My consort, Lord Faren Orodum, will lead our forces into battle. His General will be Lord Woryek Irono. In a week's time, we will leave to begin this campaign. I hope you will all support us in every way you can! I don't believe this will be a long or difficult campaign."

The dwarves roared with ferocity. The Vintari Empire had made a mistake attacking Cragmorrar. Dwarves held friendship and hatred in equal regard, and their stubbornness to hold a grudge was unrivaled. Dwarves could go generations holding onto the smallest of grudges, so an attack on our capital city aimed at assassinating their Empress would have called for nothing less than war. So war is what I gave them. Anything less and I doubt they would have had faith in me to make any hard decisions in the future.

I held up a hand gently, bringing the fervor back down to a simmer with that simple motion. "However, that concern is for tomorrow. Today, I ask that you all celebrate with me. Celebrate the day of my birth, the day of my coronation, and most importantly, the day of my wedding. I wish to see joy and revelry on this most glorious of days!"

The simmering anger boiled over into joyous cheers, and it seemed like the merrymaking began immediately. I turned and looked at the others standing around me. "It's a tradition on my birthday that I walk the city and celebrate with my people. You're all more than welcome to join me. If you please, we will begin talks about the Vintari campaign tomorrow."

Empress Trebue looked down at me cautiously. "While I agree such an attack cannot go unanswered, are you certain your people can handle a war so soon?"

King Marshal laughed. "If Empress Orodum commanded her people to tear the sun from the sky, we'd already be living in darkness. I can assure you, Empress Trebue, that the dwarves are more than ready for war."

"Very well, then," Empress Trebue conceded. "Then let us enjoy the festivities."

The rest of the day was spent walking through the city. We sang and danced with my people. We ate at their tables, accepted and gave gifts, and enjoyed the fellowship of my fellow dwarves. The group of dwarves whom I had resurrected were given five hundred gold each and were offered a stipend for life from my coffers. They all declined the stipend. That evening there was a feast with representatives from every noble House, where they each offered their fealty to me and my bloodline.

After the feast, all the Fated gathered in my new palace chambers for a more personal celebration.

"You really shouldn't have faced him alone, though!" Trianna protested. "Do you know how worried we were?"

"Speak for yourself!" Allen laughed. "We all watched the same thing! She was a monster! Seven never stood a chance!"

"He surprised me a few times," I admitted. "He even got past my guard twice."

"I think we're all just happy you're alright," Aelfric smiled.

"I think we're all grateful she's on our side," Serena chuckled. "I still can't believe Vintari worked with the scourgespawn to attack Cragmorrar when all they had to do was stop their practice of slavery. It's ridiculously irrational."

"The practice is too ingrained into their way of life," Faren countered. "It shows off their status, it's integral in their economics, and makes up the majority of their labor force. Telling them they can't have it any longer if they want dimvyum was basically telling them they couldn't be Vintari anymore."

"And now they can't," I said as I nodded to myself. "I was hopeful when they sent their delegates to witness the ceremonies, but I should have been more cautious."

"I don't think you should beat yourself up over it," Trianna replied. "They've been good allies up until they couldn't get dimvyum. Everyone thought that they'd come to negotiate."

"And so they should have," Aelfric tapped the arm of his chair. "The attack had to have been Seven's decision. I'd very much like to know how Seven managed to gain so much influence without anyone outside of Vintari finding out."

"I'll learn that detail when I visit the prisoners tomorrow," I smiled.

"You're actually going to interrogate them yourself?" Serena asked, shocked at the prospect.

"They're all mages," I explained. "They currently have no access to their magic. The person stopping them from accessing it is the one person they'll see as a superior. Even the Magisters will have to admit that I'm a more powerful mage than they are if I can choose whether or not they can perform even a simple cantrip. They'll bargain for the return of their magic while offering me any information I desire."

"And if they don't?" Allen asked.

"I'll make them beg for death," I almost purred.

"I am… so irrationally turned on right now…" Allen mumbled.

"I'm just being the shortstack dommy mommy you think of me as," I chuckled.

Everyone got a good laugh out of that. Allen looked at me in surprise, blushing and trying to contain his embarrassment. He tried to sputter an apology or think of some kind of excuse to make up for what he thought I perceived as an insult.

"Oh, please," Faren rolled his eyes. "Did you honestly think we hadn't heard?"

"I just hope you don't call me that around anyone else," I snickered. "It'd rather soil my reputation if a nickname like that took hold."

Allen stammered, "I'm sorry! We were all basically still kids when I first said it!"

"And kept saying it," Serena smirked.

"Constantly," Trianna chimed in.

"Over and over again," Aelfric nodded sagely. "Sometimes even drooling."

"Alright," Allen sighed. "I think I can find a corner to go die in now… Thank you."

Everyone laughed.

I stood and raised my cup. "Really, though, I'm thankful that I have all of you as friends. You've all helped me learn and grow so much over the years. Faren gave me confidence. Trianna gave me friendship. Serena gave me rivalry. Aelfric gave me amazing food. And Allen gave me quite the ego boost whenever I needed one. I am who I am today because of you all. Thank you. Here's to our friendship."

"To our friendship!" everyone joined in on the toast.

CHAPTER 41:

IN ALL THE YEARS TO COME

The war against Vintari was the first full mobilization of dwarven forces in centuries. Cragmorrar, Var Koran, and every Hold provided warriors for the battle. The war was stationed out of Var Koran. From there, I had influence over the world beyond Vintari. While Faren and Woryek worked with their officers to plan out their strategies, I locked down all the magic in Vintari. While we could have attacked after a few days, I waited for two weeks; enough time for the Magisters to panic, scramble, and vainly attempt to regain their magic. Every so often, I would give their magic back to them for a few precious moments at a time. I wanted to give them hope, something to let them believe that whatever phenomena was occurring might be temporary.

On the day of our attack, the magic was locked down completely. I opened several portals through which our warriors marched. Each portal opened up at a point just on the edge of Vintari's border. Hundreds of thousands of dwarves, including every member of the Fallen Legion and the majority of warriors from every warrior family and noble House from Cragmorrar, Var Koran, and Hold, were battle-hardened warriors who had been fighting scourgespawn all their lives. Now they were ready to turn their experience and fury on Vintari.

Unlike most other countries, the dwarves had standing armies. We were constantly engaged in combat, so we didn't have the luxury of raising troops in times of need. Only the dwarves and atoshi had standing armies, while allies like Fransway had a large retinue of guards and Chevaliers; they weren't an army. Vintari, however, did have a small force that was dedicated to harassing Ven Parlol and the atoshi. Those would be the soldiers to look out for, but we had the numbers and the experience. I wasn't overly concerned.

I joined Faren's battalion, stepping through the portal last after everyone else had gone through. Faren had insisted on this because it would keep me safe. As soon as Faren ensured the area was secured, he gave me the signal that we were ready to begin. I reached out and connected to every magical item in Vintari, sending reverberations through them so that my voice could be heard. With as many enchanted items that Vintari had, my voice rang out through every home and street.

"People of Vintari," I began. "My name is Empress Merida Orodum of the Dwarven Empire. Your country has declared war on me and my people. Every Magister you sent has been stripped of their magic. I am here to tell you that I am the one who did this. My power over the Dimvolmn is absolute. So long as you are within my influence, it is I who chooses whether or not you may cast even the simplest of cantrips."

"To the Magisters," I continued, my tone unwavering and authoritative, "your entire country is surrounded. Nearly every dwarven warrior is prepared to march into your country and kill everyone in their way. However, I am not without mercy. If, within the next thirty minutes, a representative of the Magisterium comes before me and surrenders, I will guarantee that some of you will live."

I moved on to the next part of my address. "To the citizens of Vintari; I do not wish to harm anyone I do not have to. However, anyone caught with slaves, or having killed their slaves, will be executed on site. Release your slaves this instant, and you will be spared. Give them food and money, and send them on their way to Vintari's borders. My warriors will soon meet them as we make our way into your country, and they will be cared for."

Finally, I connected myself to every dwarf in Vintari. "To my people who reside here; your families have a long history of trade in Vintari. However, the Magisters have attempted to assassinate me, allied with the scourgespawn, and attempted to slaughter our people all in the hope to gain access to the dimvyum we mine in Cragmorrar. They knew precisely where to appear in the city. This tells me that one, or more, of you helped them in this attack in the hopes of profiting from my death, and the death of hundreds of thousands of your people. Know this: I will find every traitor among you. There will be no mercy shown to any who aided in that attack. If any of you know someone responsible, you will be rewarded for detaining them for me."

In the end, no one came to barter for peace. The dwarven forces marched into Vintari. They were joined by Orleasian Chevaliers, elven archers and scouts, as well as Falladrin soldiers. The atoshi had asked to join the campaign, but I had refused, citing that I didn't want this to appear as if we were taking a side in their conflict with Vintari. They did, however, place a few Dreadnaughts along Vintari's shoreline just as a show of force.

Every dwarven battalion met with thousands of freed slaves fleeing Vintari. They were met with care and open arms. The elven forces took most of the slaves to camps where they were tended to. Any harm or illness was dealt with, with wounds or trauma treated carefully. Most of the slaves were brought back with us and introduced into their respective societies. Over time, they would begin to live happy and productive lives.

The Magisters and the Magisterium were quickly rounded up. They had tried to hide, but my stone sense made them easy to find. They were carefully questioned, but since none of them had decided to surrender in the time I had given them, they were all put to death. In the end, we discovered that Seven had used Varrimus' knowledge and memories to hunt down ancient artifacts, which proved to the Magisters that he was one of the ancients. He used that influence to gain power over the Magisterium and convince the whole of Vintari to consider Cragmorrar an enemy. Once I had the dimvyum legislation passed that forbade dimvyum being sold to anyone who trafficked in slaves, it was easy for Seven to foment more and more aggression against us. It wasn't difficult for him to find others who were willing to support an attack on the city directly.

Thousands of Magisters were killed over the next few weeks. The small fighting force Vintari had mostly surrendered in the face of overwhelming odds. Any mages in the fighting forces were immediately killed, while the others were taken prisoner. There was a lesson to be taught in this confrontation, and that lesson was that magic would no longer be used to subjugate others. The mages in Vintari that fought against us would learn that lesson.

The Magisters who had been questioned gave us the names of the Vintari dwarves who had betrayed our people so that they could gain dominion over Cragmorrar and control over the dimvyum supply. They gave this information in the hopes of having their lives spared. They weren't, but they received much more lenient executions.

As far as the dwarves who had betrayed our people were concerned, they were to be made examples of. I met with each of the named conspirators personally and sifted through their memories. Anyone who was aware of the conspiracy and did not protest or make some attempt at stopping things was brought before the linked minds of our people. I showed them the memories. I showed how they worked against their people, their King, and their Empress. And while I was content to put them to a swift death, I let the collective thoughts of the people decide what to do with them. The people were far less forgiving than I was. Their families were stripped of all wealth and privileges. Every person who actively participated in the coup was executed. Those who knew but weren't active participants and did nothing to try and stop things were banished to the surface, with their names spread throughout the kingdoms of all of our allies so that even finding work would be difficult. Their families, however, were granted Servant Class or Merchant Class status depending on their level of knowledge.

Vintari was reformed into the nation of Forialst. It changed from a magocracy to a satellite state, watched over by a revolving number of nations including Fransway, Falladrin, the Independent Marshes, and the Dwarven Empire. Each nation would watch the new nation for five years at a time for fifty years to ensure that no further issues would occur. However, each overseeing nation would also be responsible for assisting Forialst economically and militarily during their years of oversight should they need it. However, each request for aid was looked over by representatives from all presiding nations and considered for its legitimacy based on Forialst's current economics and resources.

At the end of fifty years, Forialst was its own independent nation with a wealth of allies its ancestors hadn't known in millennia. The nation had a stricter stance on magic than Falladrin did at the time, with mages needing to register and attend the newest location of the Lemlalian college. Mages were also required to enter government service or serve in the college as professors and researchers. One major difference was that mages were no longer allowed to hold any political office, regardless of how small the post's influence. It also became an elective democracy, similar to the old Dwarven system I was born into. I was honored to have been asked to attend the coronation of Forialst's first king.

Alford was crowned only a year after the war with Vintari. He had earned some recognition in the campaign by spearheading the relief efforts. He and Serena brought food, water, and mages well-versed in healing magic. His forces were held back to guard the slaves and worked to ensure the Vintari citizens were kept safe during the days we were still looking for their mages and Magisters. Not long after Alford's coronation, his father, King Marshal, died due to an illness. Faren and I attended the funeral, deeply saddened by his loss. Marshal had done us both the favor of training us in our youth and worked closely with me to teach me human politics and how to navigate the ins and outs of the human noble intricate family ties. We owed him a great deal.

I would like to say that the war against Vintari was the only conflict that we had to deal with. While the Atoshi had appreciated our efforts with Vintari and stopping the aggression, they insisted on trying to spread the Atosh, their rigid religion focused on service to the state, where it wasn't wanted. We tried to explain to them that their definition of order wasn't the same as ours. We also tried to explain to them that our mages were not falling to temptation and becoming possessed by demons at the rates they believed. In fact, those instances had fallen to almost zero with the implementation of the Lemlalian colleges and the freedom given to them in places of minor authority with the protection of towns and villages under their charge.

Ven Parlol would not hear us. Eventually, after all the diplomacy had failed, the atoshi attacked Vitren in an attempt to make it the first mainland nation brought into the Atosh. This choice was made because Vitren had a small settlement there called Kim-saar, where emissaries would regularly work with the Vitreni. This attack was a surprise to them. While Vitren wasn't a part of the Dwarven Empire's allied nations, we answered their call for aid. Faren led the dwarven army to Vitren alongside forces from Falladrin, Orleasian, and the Independent Marshes. The joint forces were welcomed into Kritova and allowed to march through to Vitren. When the joint forces arrived, they immediately began pushing back the atoshi line. The fighting was fierce, with our people pitted against the giant atoshi for the very first time. However, this was not simply a land battle. Over the years, the dwarven fleet had grown exponentially. Our navy, along with the navies of Falladrin and Fransway, engaged the atoshi dreadnaughts. While they had blackpowder cannons, we had mages who could use their magic.

Faren insisted that I not take part in the battles this time around, wanting our warriors to gain the experience of actual combat. I honored his request, but that doesn't mean I stayed out of the conflict altogether. After so long, my influence over the Stone and the Dimvolmn had become worldwide. I didn't even have to leave Cragmorrar to use my influence over the Dimvolmn to deny the Varikoss, the atoshi mages, access to their magic. I also raised the seafloor up in large pillars to prevent the dreadnoughts from escaping and stop reinforcements from coming in.

The atoshi were soundly defeated after only a few weeks. Ven Parlol was forced to keep to themselves for years afterwards. There were calls from the Melindrian Church for a new Holy March on Ven Parlol. Pressure was put on the Franswaynian Emperor to sanction the March, but Serena and Alford's eldest son, King Bertryn of Falladrin, and I managed to talk the church down. It wouldn't do to attack them and provoke them even further.

The conflict did manage to bring Vitren and Kritova into the fold of the allied nations. While the dynamics of certain freelance organizations like the Kritovan Ravens and the fact that Vitren did not support the Saint Mellinaan Church were small issues, they were eventually figured out. I admit that it was nice to have another group of people who didn't worship Saint Mellina within the allied nations. It allowed me to push back against the church, which would regularly insist that a church be allowed in dwarven Holds and cities.

While I was responsible for pushing my people forward in many ways, I was also responsible for upholding our traditions. This meant that our caste system, which remained firmly in place, became much more flexible. However, it also meant that we kept true to our origins and to our creators. We were connected more than any other people in the world. We were connected through the Titans. We were the Stone. And any threat to that connection was met with refusal and scorn. Dwarves did not take well to threats to their tradition. While individuals were not banned from worshiping Saint Mellina if they wished to, the church itself was not allowed a presence within the Empire.

The second war against the Atoshi came nearly a century later. This time, they didn't have a foothold to start with and instead attacked Forialst. There was no way of talking the Saint Mellinaan Church out of an Exalted March this time. The whole of the faith was ready to burn Ven Parlol to the ground, but I offered to handle the situation myself. While Faren didn't want me to engage the Atoshi personally, I was resigned to put this issue to bed permanently. However, to put his mind at ease, I agreed not to leave Cragmorrar. By that time, I had managed to erase my blind spot as far as water was concerned.

I scryed the location of the ships and the ongoing battles. Every Atoshi soldier was dragged beneath the earth. Every ship was sunk. And then I turned Ven Parlol into a tomb. Every Atoshi above a certain age, and every member of the Atosh on that island, was crushed beneath the surface of their home. As an act of mercy, I had the dwarven fleet sail to Ven Parlol and rescue the children who had been too young to be indoctrinated into the Atosh. The children were brought to Vitren, where they were welcomed and cared for.

Not everything was worry and war, however. Faren and I had our first child two years after we were wed, a boy who we named Franklin. A year after that, we had our second; a girl we named Trianna. Three years later, we had a set of twins, a boy and a girl that we named Triston and Kara. The children were everything a parent could hope for. They worked diligently to be shining examples of the Empress. They became ambassadors, smiths, warriors, and enchanters. Kara and Triston focused especially diligently on dimvyum technology development under Bilfern's tutelage.

While everyone around us was aging, Faren and I were not. Serena was the first of the Fated to pass away, mourned by Alford, her children, and grandchildren. Next was Allen, who died a celebrated mage and father. Regretfully, his only child died in a magical experiment. Then went Aelfric, loved by his people and the rest of the world for having brought such amazing new food to Thoros. Trianna was the last to go, and her passing broke my heart. Her children, her grandchildren, all of her people, Faren and I, our children, and our grandchildren all mourned her passing. She was my best friend, and it hurt to lose her.

With the realization that Faren and I weren't aging, we stopped having children. This was among the best decisions we made for ourselves. We loved our children deeply, and our grandchildren as well, but the pain of the loss of our friends, and the hurt we knew would come when we outlived our descendants, convinced us to have no others. We watched as our children grew old, how our grandchildren had children, and their children had children. It was a mixture of joy and sorrow. However, our descendants continued to make us proud regardless.

The dimvyum technology was something nearly all of our grandchildren gravitated towards and became the primary export of our people, even over dimvyum itself. As a matter of fact, the world experienced a radical change as dimvyum technologies advanced. Communications, defenses, and weapons technologies made leaps and bounds thanks to them. By the time our great-grandchildren arrived, things were looking much more advanced than the world I'd been born into. The funny thing, however, is that magic still kept things relatively similar in most other ways. The mother of all necessity was mostly taken care of by magic, so dimvyum technology handled things that magic couldn't easily replace since war and communication couldn't be handled primarily by magic.

Apart from the few wars mentioned, Thoros enjoyed centuries of relative peace. I helped to reclaim every inch of the former Dwarven Empire and expanded it nearly three times over. I would have expanded it more, but dwarves couldn't populate it fast enough. I didn't want to spread our numbers too thin. Still, the Empire was thriving and boasted the largest economy in the world. It also made itself indispensable to every other nation in terms of trade and military power. Through my diplomacy and the hard work and diligent effort of my people, we became the foremost nation of Thoros.

I kept my tradition of walking the streets of Cragmorrar on my birthday, giving gifts to the people and celebrating our Empire's anniversary as well. I also honored the memory of the Battle of Orlimar by visiting the memorial mausoleum each year. These two traditions were two of the most important ones I wanted to keep up, even if the rest of my people didn't.

"But that's not something I had to worry about," Merida said with pride as she looked out on the dwarves gathered in the mausoleum, knowing full well that the city, the Under Roads that led to it, and the mountain path that led to the city's gates were packed full of dwarves. Her image was being relayed through dimvyum mirrors to everyone in attendance across the entirety of the Dwarven Empire. "I went to sleep one evening in the four hundred fifty-eighth year of my reign and did not wake. However, I did not die, either. I still sleep to this day. My descendants and my people honor me with their love, their hope, and their devotion every year by visiting me."

Merida turned and motioned to Faren, who stood next to the glass encasement where his wife slept soundly. "I am guarded each and every day by my husband. He stands watch, devoted and without doubt that I will one day wake and take up my crown once more. This was the tale of my life, with all of its secrets and details laid bare. I was a stranger born into this world, born a dwarf, born a mage. I used my knowledge of the world to do right by my people. I spent every day working for the betterment of all dwarves. I am the very world itself. I am the Dimvolmn. I am a mage, a champion, a hero, an Exemplar, a Titan. I am the Mother of Dwarves. I am Empress Merida Orodum."

Faren looked at Merida and smiled sadly. This was his and Merida's great-grandchild thirty times over. This was the millennia anniversary of the Dwarven Empire, and the five hundredth second year that the Empress had been sleeping. It was surprising to see how much the speaker favored her ancestor.

Looking out over the crowd, Faren gathered himself and smiled proudly. "Hello, my children. I call you my children not just because I am the husband to the Mother of Dwarves, but also because you are all descendants of us. By now our children's children's children and so forth have multiplied and married into every family of dwarves over the millennia. You are all our children. And it does my heart good to see those of you who visit our Empress throughout the year."

He took a deep breath and let his gaze wander over the eyes of those in the mausoleum. "But I am never more proud than when I see you all gather here each and every year to honor the telling of her life's tale. Knowing that you all make the journey from so far away each year without fail humbles me."

Faren turned and looked at the sleeping Empress, smiling her youthful, vibrant, infectious smile even in her sleep. "What's more, I know that wherever her mind is, she feels our love for her. I know it because we can all still feel her influence. With every decision we make, we feel her guiding us through our shared link, which she reawakened in us. We know she is still with us because even as she sleeps, she still calls out to us. We've heard her call to her people; we've heard her call out names."

He turned and smiled at the crowd once more. "Each year we gather in the mausoleum where she rests with her fallen friends and comrades. Each year we hear about her life from birth to her great sleep. And each year we renew our hope that she will one day wake. Be it a thousand years, ten thousand years, or even a million years, we know she will wake one day. And on that day, we will rejoice. We will show her that we were not idle in her absence. And we will show her how much she still means to us. Thank you all for coming once again this year."

With that, Faren and Merida stepped to the side so that the crowd could, over the course of the next few days, walk by the sleeping Empress. Each dwarf would leave a coin, and the total would be spent on medical and social programs.

As Faren stood by, he looked at his sleeping wife. He watched her chest slowly rise and fall. He looked at her beautiful smile. He relived their memories together and ached desperately to hear her voice again, to see her eyes gaze up at him once more. He watched her and prayed silently to himself, "Please, my love. I don't know why you're sleeping. I don't know where your mind is. I don't know what you're doing. But please… come back to me. Come back to us. We need you…"

As if she had heard him, the Empress spoke in her sleep, "Aelfric? Is that really you?"

Faren let out a soft chuckle. What could possibly be going on in her dreams?